ANTIPHONY

Books in the Sartorias-Deles Timeline

Historical Arc

"Lily and Crown"
Inda
The Fox
King's ShieldTreason's Shore
Time of Daughters (two volumes)
Banner of the Damned

Modern Arc

The Young Allies as Children Series
The CJ Notebooks
Senrid
Spy Princess
Sartor
Fleeing Peace
A Stranger to Command
Crown Duel
The Trouble with Kings

The Rise of the Alliance Series
A Sword Named Truth
The Blood Mage Texts
The Hunters and the Hunted
Nightside of the Sun
Sasharia En Garde
The Wicked Skill
The Norsunder War Series
Ship Without Sails
Marend of Marloven Hess
Seek to Hold the Wind
All Things Betray
A Chain of Braided Silver
Let the Torrent Dance Thee Down

ANTIPHONY

SHERWOOD SMITH

BOOK VIEW CAFE

Published by Book View Café
304 S. Jones Blvd., Suite #2906
Las Vegas, NV 89107
www.bookviewcafe.com

ISBN: 978-1-63632-172-1

Author's Note

My grateful thanks to my readers at Patreon, whose comments, corrections, and encouragement mean so much to me.

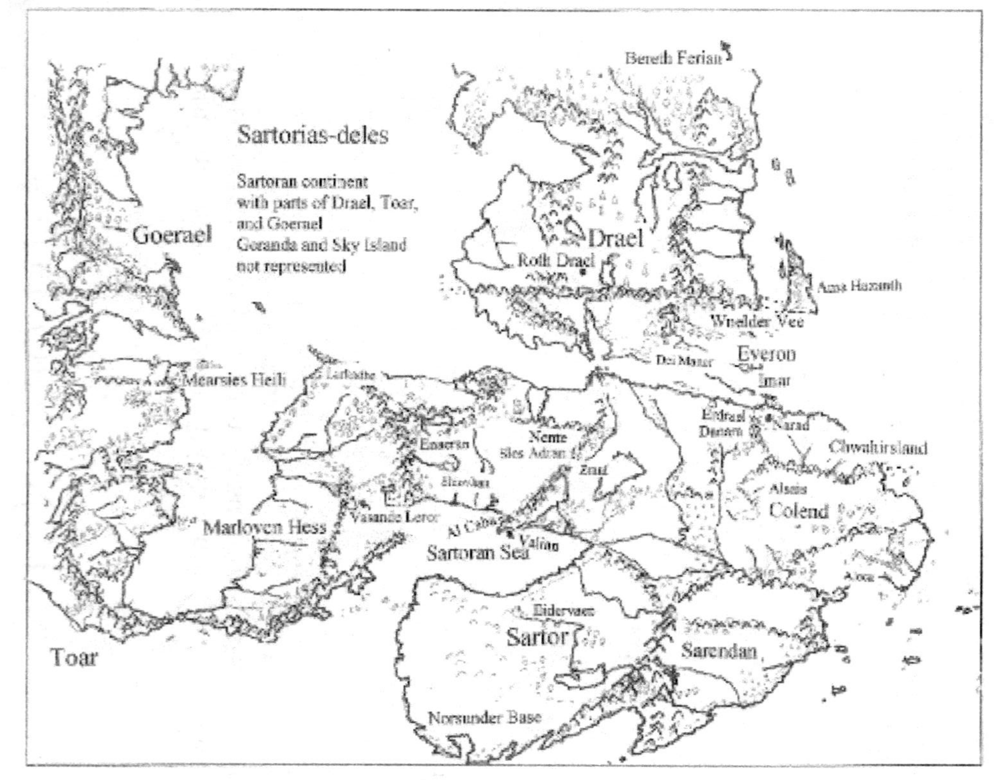

Sartorias-deles
Sartoran continent
with parts of Drael, Toar,
and Goerael
Goranda and Sky Island
not represented
Goerael
Drael
Bereth Ferian
Roth Drael
Amas Hazanth
Wnelder Vee
Everon
Imar
Mearsies Heili
Larheitte
Dei Mattar
Eidrael Darran
Sarad
Chwahirsland
Ennersin
Neme
Sles Adran
Znal
Alsais
Colend
Elsorvan
Vasande Leror
Marloven Hess
Al Caba
Valian
Sartoran Sea
Eidervaen
Sartor
Sarendan
Toar
Norsunder Base

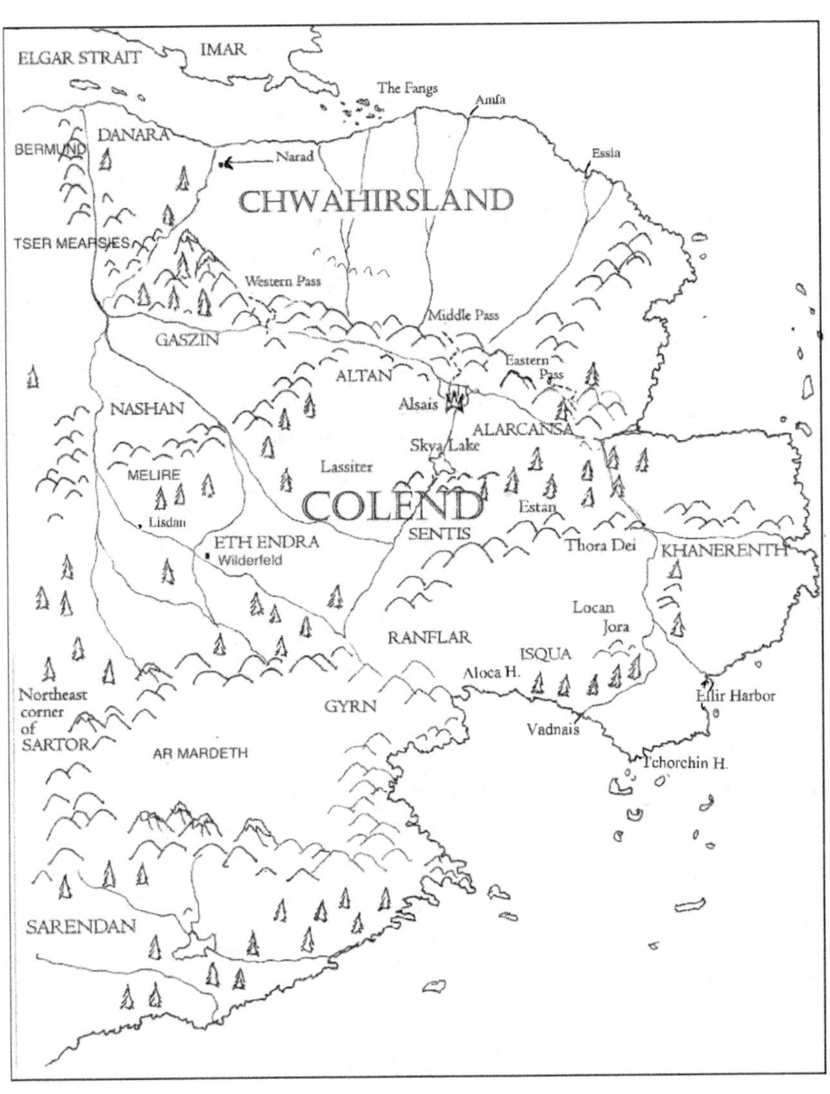

ELGAR STRAIT
IMAR
BERMUND
DANARA
The Fangs
Amfa
Narad
Essla
TSER MEARSIES
CHWAHIRSLAND
Western Pass
Middle Pass
GASZIN
Eastern Pass
ALTAN
NASHAN
Alsais
ALARCANSA
Skya Lake
MELIRE
Lassiter
COLEND
Estan
Lisdan
ETH ENDRA
SENTIS
Thora Dei
KHANERENTH
Wilderfeld
Locan
Jora
RANFLAR
ISQUA
Aloca H.
Northeast
corner
of
SARTOR
GYRN
Ellir Harbor
Vadnais
AR MARDETH
Tchorchin H.
SARENDAN

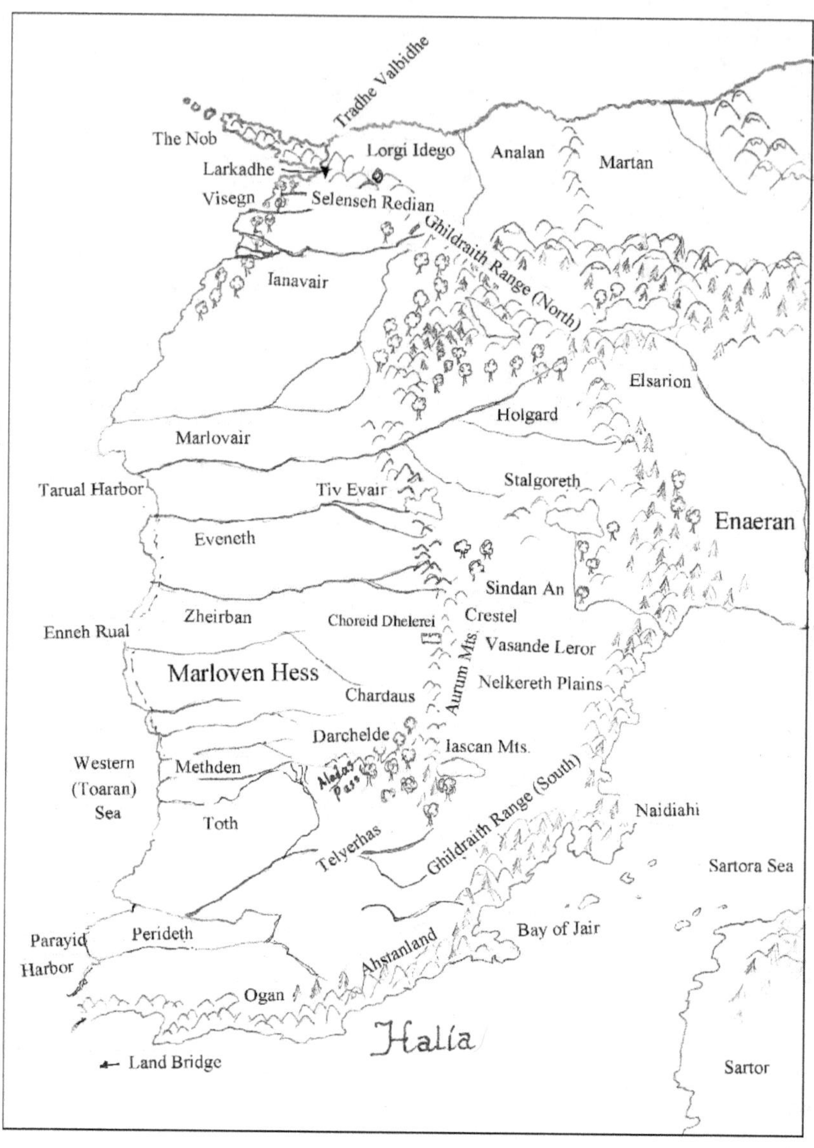

Tradhe Valbidhe
The Nob
Larkadhe
Visegn
Selenseh Redian
Lorgi Idego
Analan
Martan
Ianavair
Ghildraith Range (North)
Elsarion
Holgard
Marlovair
Stalgoreth
Tarual Harbor
Tiv Evair
Enaeran
Eveneth
Sindan An
Zheirban
Choreid Dhelerei
Crestel
Vasande Leror
Enneh Rual
Aurum Mts.
Marloven Hess
Nelkereth Plains
Chardaus
Darchelde
Iascan Mts.
Western
(Toaran)
Sea
Methden
Aldar Pass
Ghildraith Range (South)
Naidiahi
Toth
Sartora Sea
Telyerhas
Parayid
Harbor
Perideth
Bay of Jair
Ahstanland
Ogan
Halia
Land Bridge
Sartor

DRAMATIS PERSONAE

NOTE: Name most frequently used comes first, so sometimes first name, sometimes last, sometimes nickname.

LIGHT MAGIC MAGES AIDING THE ALLIANCE

Erai-Yanya Vithyavadnais: One of a long line of mages dwelling in the ruined city of Roth Drael. Trained partly by the northern Mage School at Bereth Ferian, and partly by Tsauderei, she works independently, her specialty magical wards. She has one son, ARTHUR (see BERETH FERIAN). Erai-Yanya's student mage is the Marloven exile Hibern Askan. After the Norsunder War, student far outstripped teacher, but they still work together.

Evend: [deceased] One-time colleague of Tsauderei, King of Bereth Ferian (a courtesy title only) and head of the mage school there, he surrendered his life to bind rift magic from being used in Sartorias-deles by Norsunder. His place as titular king was taken by ARTHUR.

Igkai: Hermit mage living on the peninsula on the Sartoran Sea. An oddball all his life, he is a friend to birds and animals — and tolerates humans who do well by animals.

Lilith the Guardian: She was a lower-ranking mage and what might be called an officer of rites and rituals in Ancient Sartor, which was as close to a government as they got. She had one daughter, Erdrael, who was killed along with most of the rest of the population when Norsunder tried to wrest control of the world, for reasons explored in a volume to come. Her name is a modern adaptation, and she found herself trying to combat Norsunder on this and other worlds around the sun Erhal; she came out of hiding beyond time whenever she found evidence that Detlev had been in the world, acting for Norsunder's Host of Lords. After the war, once she understood Detlev's intent, she became his defender before the Norss of Songre Silde. Ready to retire, she has chosen HIBERN to take over her guardianship.

Mondros "Rosey": Big, bluff, and bearded, he began life as an exiled son of the disgraced Glenereth family, warlords of Ralanor Veleth. He studied magic, aided by Gwasan Sonscarna, Princess of the Chwahir, whom he married and with whom he had a son, REL (see SARTOR) before she was assassinated by the mad king Wan-Edhe. When Mondros made it his life's goal to defeat Wan-Edhe, he stashed Rel with a trusted friend, where Rel grew up a part of the family, until the urge to travel caused him to take to the road. Father and son reunited, and Mondros relishes his role as grandfather.

Murial of Mearsies Heili: Recluse mage, living hidden in the western wilds of Mearsies Heili. Born a princess, she supported the transfer of the throne to her niece CLAIR (see MEARSIES HEILI) on the death of her sister. Protecting the kingdom from a distance, she has seen to it that Clair got magical training.

Oalthoreh: [deceased] Head of the northern mage school in Bereth Ferian

Randon Amdrelya: Originally from Vandary, Randon is an accomplished mage who did the Child Spell when around thirteen, to avoid limiting expectations of his culture. Travels around looking for kids to rescue.

Tsauderei: [deceased] Oldest of the senior mages, independent of the two leading mage schools, who once lived in a historic mage retreat located in the mountains bordering Sarendan and Sartor in the Valley of Delfina. Worked until the end, aiding Mondros against Wan-Edhe of the Chwahir. Having lived more than a century, once the war was safely one, he was ready to die, taken by Detlev to a Selenseh Redian.

FROM OFF-WORLD

Caris-Merian Rhoderan of Geth-deles: "Rhoderan" is a name adopted by her father, the disinherited and disgraced Harold Dei, who tried to take the throne of Everon a couple of times before he was booted off-world. He had three children, the middle one being Caris-Merian. She came to Sartorias-deles's northern mage school to study magic right before the invasion. An accomplished singer and a scholar when she was not seeking revenge for her brother's death. She came close, giving David, one of Detlev's boys, a nearly mortal wound, after which she saw that revenge benefitted no one. After the war, she returned to Geth to reclaim her life, refusing the crown of Wnelder Vee, which Tahra of Everon tried to foist on her.

Les (Leskander) Rhoderan of Geth-deles: [deceased] elder brother to Caris-Merian, and a problematical figure in his home archipelago. He discovered vagabond magic, and tried to weaponize it and build an empire for the underaged and poor. Very charismatic.

Mildred of Geth-deles: a martial artist, now living most of the time in Sartorias-deles, at Tsauderei's old cottage as she studies magic, and practices martial arts with MV, one of Detlev's boys.

The Young Allies and Others, Listed by Kingdom

Ama Hazanth

Crow (Prince Marseth Ghandorjien): Before the war, crown prince, keeper of the Fire Ruby (which wards storms from the island). After the war, became king. He built solid friendships with Laban of Wnelder Vee and MV, to name a few.

Bereth Ferian

Arthur (Yrtur) Vithyavadnais: He adopted the nickname Arthur after his rescue by young worldgate-crossing friends. Son of mage Erai-Yanya, he early showed great ability in learning and magic, but he was unhappy living in isolation. He was adopted as heir by Evend, the former head mage of the Bereth Ferian Mage School, and presiding King of the loose federation headquartered at Bereth Ferian. After Evend's death, Arthur shared this courtesy title with Liere Fer Eider in her persona as Sartora, the Girl Who Saved the World until she rejected it. Now Arthur is establishing an archive of ancient Venn collective wisdom, plus translations of the ancient Sartoran works that came to light at the war's end. He is largely aided by Roy, one of Detlev's boys.

Evend: (see Light Mages)

Liere Fer Eider: Also known as the Girl Who Saved the World, she was the first of her generation to be born with *Dena Yeresbeth*. At ten years old she left her small town to escape being captured by Siamis, who had extended an enchantment over the world, which Liere later broke. The enchantment is generally known as The Lost Year, as most lived in a dream world while it lasted. She was lauded by all, and given the courtesy title of Queen in Bereth Ferian, a title with no powers or responsibilities whatsoever—but which still chafed her unbearably. Liere was the poster child for Imposter Syndrome until she went to Geth-deles for five years to study magic; on her return she aided Andri Elsarion, king of Enaeran, in regaining his kingdom. During the Norsunder War, Liere and Andri married, and she became queen of Enaeran. Eight years later, Macael Elsarion of Sles Adran invaded, killed Andri, and threatened to kill Liere and Andri's son MALCOLIN unless she gave him an heir, which she did, while also completing dyr studies at Curtas's House.

CHWAHIRSLAN (AKA LAND OF THE CHWAHIR)

Dassler Anjit, Company Scribe, Crimson Army of Chwahirsland: One of the "Sunrise Generation" —so named after Jilo removed enough of Wan-Edhe's toxic magic for awareness to return. A leader of the resistance to Wan-Edhe; became Jilo's Household Chief Director.

Dirk Sonscarna: Son of the problematical Kessler (see below). Has Dena Yeresbeth and considerable martial arts as well as magical knowledge. At the war's end, assassinated Wan-Edhe, the hated Chwahir tyrant who intended to live forever. On realizing that his father had raised him specifically for this purpose, he reacted badly, until Detlev sent him off-world to recover.

Crimson General Furo: Chwahir general on Jilo's side. Worked a silent truce of sorts with Shontande Lirendi, without Norsunder realizing. Disabled by Efael in torture-for-entertainment captivity, rescued by MV's raid, and now Military Chief Director, which is administrator for army and navy.

Duin, Fassler: (Duin his chosen name) Imry Llyenthur's chief aide-de-camp. Born in Chwahirsland; at war's end, Imry Llyenthur got Jilo to take Duin on. Duin subsequently earned his way to the chief of scribe communications for the Chwahir.

Gwasan Sonscarna: [deceased] Princess and mage, married a disinherited swordsman from Ralanor Veleth who later became the mage Mondros (SEE Mages). Their son is Rel the Traveler (SEE Sartor)

Kirech, Gold Army General: Utterly loyal to Chwahirsland, which for most of his life was embodied in Wan-Edhe. So loyal that to call his work into question—his loyalty—was a blow worse than mere sword wounds.

Jilo: Son of a lowly one-syllable sergeant, heir to elderly *Prince Kwenz Sonscarna,* he found himself acting king of Chwahirsland, after Norsunder's removal of the previous king, who had ruled for more than a century. What that means is, he was slowly poisoning himself in trying to remove the toxic accretion of dark magic enchantments over Chwahirsland, and especially its capital. After the war, provisionally accepted the idea of kingship as he worked to transform Chwahirsland.

Prince Kessler Sonscarna: [deceased] (SEE also Ex-Norsundrians) The single living descendant of the ruling Sonscarnas, who were systematically killed off by Wan-Edhe, blood relations notwithstanding. Prince Kessler escaped at a young age, made his way to a martial arts group where he mastered military arts. He allied with a Norsundrian mage, Dejain, and began to assemble followers for his plan to remove all the hereditary rulers of the world and replace them with his followers, chosen solely on merit. When defeated, he was forced into Norsunder by Dejain, who betrayed him. He learned magic, his secret goal to take Norsunder-Beyond for himself, so that he could once again implement his plan to reorder the world according to merit. Killed by Efael, leaves a son, DIRK.

Gold Admiral Opun: current naval commander, after several purges of his predecessors for mad reasons, or no reason at all. Like Furo, a two-syllable Chwahir, meaning not the lowest background, but low enough—no Nanijo, or warlord background—that Wan-Edhe did not think it necessary to hold his entire family hostage, or slaughter them outright in case any of them thought of conspiracy.

Wan-Edhe (born Shnit Sonscarna), King of the Chwahir: [deceased] Descendant of the ruling Sonscarna family, has ruled for close to a century. A powerful dark magic mage, he has managed to create a powerful citadel in the heart of his kingdom, where time itself is distorted in his effort to ensure that he will live, and rule, forever. He killed off his family and descendants, including his brilliant heir, Princess Gwasan; only his grandson Kessler escaped, but years of abuse told on Kessler's emotional landscape. Known as The Hate to most of Chwahirsland, at the end of the Norsunder War he was killed by Dirk Sonscarna after Jilo confronted him and tried to get him to reconsider his rule.

COLEND

"Bee" (Aural) Keperi: Chief scribe to Shontande Lirendi. Being blind, he does all his work by memorization.

King Carlael Lirendi: [deceased] Regarded generally as Mad King Carlael before he was assassinated by Efael of Norsunder. He was as beautiful as he was strange. He mostly existed in a world of dreams imposed by magic, from which he emerged now and then, very alert and very aware. There was a regency council made up of the chief nobles who oversaw the kingdom when he was unable to respond to the world around him, and they ruled until very recently, refusing to relinquish power, though Carlael's son Shontande had come of age.

Prince Shontande Lirendi: Son of Carlael, King of Colend, and new king. Visited Sartor as a ruse to retake power from the loathed regency council that would not relinquish it. Was crowned king mere weeks before the war started. During the war, he ran a resistance dressed as a woman, his guise a teacher at a girls' school.

Karhin Keperi: [deceased] She was a teenage scribe student in a small town in the west of Colend, who volunteered to function as the center of the young allies' communication network. An indefatigable letter writer, she first met Puddlenose of the Mearsieans, and gradually got drawn into the Alliance; she was murdered by one of Detlev's boys, and she is still missed.

Lisbet Keperi: Younger sister of Thad and Karhin; restaurant owner after the war.

Thad Keperi: Red-haired brother of Karhin, also a scribe student, but much less passionate about the scribe life. Very social, and friend to all the Alliance; was Shontande's ambassador to Sartor, and then chief agent of trade during and after the war.

ENAERAN

Adon Marsael: [deceased] Distantly related to the royal Elsarion family, tried to take throne. Allied with Norsunder in order to keep the throne. Killed by angry dock workers at the end of the Norsunder War, after extremely repressive rule.

Andri Malcolin Elsarion: [deceased] Inherited his throne at end of the war, after years of civil war. Nearly ten years later, assassinated by his distant cousin Trevor Macael Elsarion. Had one son by Liere Fer Eider, Trevor Andiran Elsarion, now known simply as Malcolin.

Gared Inmael: [deceased] Close friend and adoptive brother of Andri Elsarion: it was Gared's father, the Elsarion Master of Horse, who took in Andri when he was disinherited. The boys grew up together, and Gared was unswervingly loyal to Andri.

Malcolin, born Trevor Andiran Elsarion: Son of Andri and Liere, eight years old when Macael took the kingdom. Sent by magic to Senrid in Marloven Hess, where he joined the academy.

Marten (Martande) Eldias: Lifelong friend to Andri Elsarion, from a very high-ranking family in Sles Adran in particular. Was Andri's ambassador to Sartor, recalled on Andri's death, and agreed to serve as Macael's "voice of conscience" for a year, before being sent to Colend as ambassador.

Baras Parael Otobris: [deceased] Andri's Commander of the King's Guard,

Trevor Macael Elsarion: Third cousin to Andri, from what had been the main branch of the family. Holds the rank of duchas in Elsarion, a very old province. At the end of the Norsunder War he married Chantala Shagal, heir to Sles Adran, and was crowned king when Chantala took over after her uncle's death. Assassinated Andri and combined his kingdom with Sles Adran under its former name: **Enaeran-Adrani.** Has a son by Liere, Iliosi Mathias Fer Eider Elsarion. ("Yossi")

EVERON

King Berthold and Queen Mersedes Carinna Delieth: [deceased] Former king and queen, survivors of rough earlier years. Mersedes, daughter of a con man, became one of the

Knights of Dei, dedicated to protecting the kingdom. They were both killed (at different times) by Henerek of Norsunder, who had come from Everon, and had been booted out of the elite Knights of Dei for countless petty and then not-so-petty crimes.

Prince Glenn Delieth: [deceased] Heir to the throne of Everon, and convinced that a strong army solves all questions, especially the threat of Norsunder attacking; he died in a duel with David, one of Detlev's boys, after forcing the fight on him.

Hatahra Delieth (Tahra), Queen of Everon: Younger sister of Glenn, passionate about numbers, and in her unrelenting hatred of Detlev and his boys. Between Birth Spell and adoption had seven children, **Jessan and "Carl"** (Berthold Jessan, and Mersedes Carinna), and four younger children: Madelon, FJ (Franklan Jessan), twins Sedron and Glenn, and the youngest, Gwenlin, or Wenwen. Tahra loathed physical proximity, but maintained a lifelong love for her distant cousin **Merewen "Merry" Dei**, the tapestry weaver.

Jenel Sandrial: Now head of the palace domestic staff. Her family has served the Delieths for generations. Many of her descendants also serve, such as Ansa, Carl Delieth's maid.

Roderic Dei: [deceased] Commander of the Knights of Dei, once defenders and protectors of the realm. The Knights were decimated in the war Henerek brought, and Kessler Sonscarna finished. Roderic Dei survived to serve as regent for Tahra Delieth until she reached the age of majority. He longed to retire, but Tahra prevailed on him to stay in command of the Knights until he died, several years after the war ended.

Roderic Dei was married to Seiran, Duchas of Valenn, the most powerful of Everon's nobles; the Deis and the Valenn family are all intermarried with the Delieths, and Seiran could have made a claim to the throne, but did not. They had five children, the eldest being Carinna ("Carl") who gave up her lifelong nickname when Tahra began calling her eldest daughter,

Princess Mersedes Carinna, Carl. Both brothers died in the war. **Theanra and Merewen ("Merry")**: Successful in their chosen pursuits, especially Merry, who is chief of a world-wide respected tapestry making concern. Merry was Tahra's beloved, and so, for the peace of the kingdom, lived in the palace to try to be Tahra's emotional support.

IMAR

Fer Eider family: Liere's mother, Elenzeh, father [deceased] Lesim; Milnat, one of Liere's four brothers, owns a pastry shop. Has two sons and a daughter: Lesim, Milnat, and Marga.

Marga Fer Eider: Cousin to Lyren-Sartora, niece to Liere Fer Eider: sirei-atanrial. Spent most of previous book as a tree.

Tolia: baker. Also friend of Eras, harbor-worker, Marga's male best friend. Both regarded Marga as their beloveds.

KHANERENTH

Jehan Merindar Zhavalieshin: Adopted into the ruling family on his marriage to Sasharia. Became king not long before the war began. Attended the Marlovan academy as a teen and spent many years afterward at sea, fighting pirates and dodging his father's forces until the former king, Math, was restored. Now king on Math's retirement.

Sasha (Sasharia) Zhavalieshin: Daughter of former king Math, married Jehan Merindar, who adopted into her family. She and Jehan became co-rulers when her father retired from the throne, not long before the war began. Sasha studied some magic before she and her mother, Sun, lived for a number of years on Earth as fugitives.

MARLOVEN HESS

Baudan, Anderle: One of Senrid's inner circle of desk jockeys.

Crystal Ingrid Montredaun-An: [deceased] Daughter and heir to Senrid, the king. Five years old. Her chief passion was dogs.

Daltan: Cobbler, middle aged. She was a resistance leader during the war.

Forthan, Retren: [deceased] A young man from a farm background, Ret Forthan was the best of the leaders to come out of the military academy. He became Harskiald, a resurrected title that means trusted commander in chief of Marloven Hess's standing army; before then, commanders in chief were appointed per mission. Struck his banner at Aladas Pass before the defeat of Marloven Hess. Married to Fenis Senelac (see her entry for their children)

Hibern Askan: Light magic student, tutored by Erai-Yanya of Roth Drael, who learned in the northern mage school. Hibern was disinherited by her family; during the war she was imprisoned in Norsunder-Beyond by Ilerian, before the world was closed off. Too bad, so sad, Ilerian — Hibern was the wrong person to leave loose in the Beyond. She figured out the time-bindings and lattice understructure, and gutted the place. After the war, Lilith made Hibern her heir as Guardian.

Indevan-Harvalder Montredaun-An, previous king of Marloven Hess: [deceased] Second son of Kethadrend, and raised to be a scholar. Indevan was, like his elder brother Kendred, skilled in martial arts, but he was never competitive. His leadership was entirely through a likable, easy-going nature and intelligence. He traveled to the neighboring lands, where he conducted himself so well, and so knowledgeably, that he did a great deal to lessen the negative Marloven reputation. Married the King of Telyerhas's daughter, Lesra. Had one son, SENRID, [see below] before he was killed by his younger brother Tdanerend, who was appalled at his ideas about limiting royal power and disbanding the army in favor of a militia defense.

Kendred Montredaun-An, Prince of Marloven Hess:

[deceased] Eldest son of Kethadrend, and grandson of the grim Senrid who caused the various treaties to be made limiting Marloven Hess. Trained in martial arts at a very young age, sent to the academy too young. He had too much of his grandfather's angry drive, and when his father failed in various forays against those treaties, Kendred tried to rally the young Marloven heirs around him to take the throne. He ended up escaping over the border at the gallop with a company hot on his heels. Had two sons, Imry and David, both of whom he sold to Detlev after unsuccessful plots. Changed his name, became a pirate, before joining Norsunder, dead by age thirty.

Keriam, Janec: [deceased] Career military man, Commander of the Marloven military academy, also titular head of the Palace Guard. Acted as guardian and foster-father to Senrid, protecting him from the regent as much as possible. Headed the academy well into very old age. Offered the surrender in the war, and lived long enough to see Norsunder defeated.

Marec, Evred: Academy instructor, now academy Headmaster.

Mordan Nauldra: Formerly the royal desk jockey for the Jarl of Methden. Interim military commander for Methden, then returned to the royal city to live with his beloved.

Savarend Montredavan-An, "Fox": Ancestor of Senrid's, pulled out of time eight centuries previous by Detlev in the guise of Ramis of the *Knife* as a reserve against Norsunder's inevitable war. Led naval defense during the recent war, and recently retired at last, in his eighties, to his castle in the family lands at Darchelde, restored by Senrid. Helping to set up a new navy.

Senelac, Fenis: Wife to Retren Forthan and head of horse training for the military academy, equal rank to the Master of Horse in the city guard. She also was a chief figure in the resistance, communicating with her brother Janred. Has four children, three boys and a girl, Mardran "Hatch" [more below], Evred "Yip", Senrid "Stinker", and Maddar "Fuzzy."

Senelac, Janred, "Jan": Cavalry Captain in the army, now chief of Senrid's coverts. Youngest of elder generation of Senelacs, brother Jardan, eldest, is a cavalry captain (skirmishers) who defended the northern border of Marloven Hess in the war.

Senelac, Mardran "Hatch": Eldest son of Retren Forthan and Fenis Senelac. Served in the war as a runner. At the academy, along with Blackeye Ventdor, led the seniors; the pair hunted down and caught the first Norsundrian commander, which led to a ritual trial and execution. Senrid reacted by giving the pair scutwork for two years, after which Hatch was appointed Garrison Commander at Methden.

Senrid Montredaun-An: Young king of Marloven Hess, a mage studying both dark and light magic. First friend to Liere Fer Eider, and second to make his unity in *Dena Yeresbeth*. The Marloven army is one of the most formidable in the world.

Stad, Indevan (Van): Second in command, Marloven army, at the start of the Norsunder War, promoted to commander in chief on the death of Retren Forthan.

Tdanerend Montredaun-An, Prince of Marloven Hess: [deceased] Third son of Kethadrend, raised to be "shield arm" to his brother Indevan. Tdanerend was short-tempered as well as short-sighted and uncoordinated. He tried to learn magic, but where that as well as everything else came easy to Indevan, he had trouble learning, and eventually surrounded himself by toadies and traditionalists uneasy at the changes Indevan contemplated. He married Caras, the second princess of Telyerhas, and there, too, he was unfortunate: she was ambitious, despised him as much as he came to despise her after she tried to scorn the Marlovens into setting up a court. He killed her first, before he took out Indevan and Lesra. His daughter, NDAND, was Senrid's chief companion. Tdanerend tried control spells on her meant for Senrid, which motivated Senrid to master magic at a young age so he could fix his cousin. Tdanerend went over to

Norsunder before losing the kingdom, and then his life. NDAND left the kingdom to become a musician.

MEARSIES HEILI

Aurora of Mearsies Heili: Clair's daughter, already showing signs of being a wanderer, like her Uncle Puddlenose. Prefers ship life.

Clair of Mearsies Heili: Queen of Mearsies Heili, a small agrarian polity on the northeast corner of the continent Toar. Niece of the hermit-mage *Murial* and cousin to the wanderer known only as *Puddlenose*, she has adopted a group of girls, most of them runaways. Her right-hand and designated 'heir' was *CJ*.

CJ (Cherenneh Jenet): Found by Clair, who traveled through the worldgate, CJ is from Earth, adopted into Clair's gang of runaways and rejects. She learns magic fitfully, and is generally regarded as the leader of Clair's gang of girls.

CJ's Gang of Girls: Falinneh and Dhana currently wear human form but are not actually human; Seshe has a mysterious past, suspected of being a runaway princess (which is actually correct); Irenne thought the world was a stage and she was the heroine of the play, which got her killed by accident by one of Detlev's boys, but she is still very much a presence among the girls; Diana, killed by Efael during the war, was a martial artist and forester, also very much missed; Sherry and Gwen (a scrappy street kid from Australia) are followers. They are a very tight found family.

Mearsieanne: [deceased] Once Queen of Mearsies Heili, on her return to the present time she stepped in and in the nicest way possible, shouldered aside Clair, her great-granddaughter, in order to show her how ruling ought to be done. After the invasion, she bound Mearsies Heili in a protective lattice-ward that was tied to herself, then she walked into a Selenseh Redian and surrendered her life, binding the enchantment onto her. The key is Clair.

Murial: *(see Light Mages)*

Puddlenose of Mearsies Heili: Bereft of family at a very young age, thus no one knows what his actual name was. He was abducted and used by The King of the Chwahir in his complicated plots. He was rescued several times by Rosey (Mondros, see LIGHT MAGES). He wanders the world, determined to have fun. His chief companion is a worldgate wanderer from Earth named Christoph but sometimes he's joined by Rel (see SARTOR). Gradually he traveled on land less and on the sea more, until he was made second in command by Captain Heraford of the *Tzasilia*, former privateer. During the Norsunder war, Puddlenose was promoted to captain of the *Lheit*, Christoph to be his first mate until Captain Heraford retires.

REMALNA

Bran (Branaric) Astiar, Count of Tlanth: brother to Meliara, wife NEE

Meliara Astiar, Queen of Remalna: Children Alaraec, Elestra, and Oria (born during the war, and submerged while in utero in a magical pool in the goldenwoods, which may have influenced her development of Dena Yeresbeth)

Nadav Savona: Vidanric's oldest friend and chief aid, son Nadav

Vidanric Renselaeus, King of Remalna: Trained at the Marloven academy, led the civil war against Galdran Merindar. Children: Alaraec, Elestra, and Oria.

RALANOR VELETH

Flian Elandersi, Queen of Ralanor Veleth: Was a princess from Lygiera, distant cousin to Garian Herlester of Drath.

Jaim Szinzar: Brother to the king, and nominal leader of the army, though Jason commands in action.

Jaimas Szinzar: Younger child of king and queen

Jason Szinzar, King of Ralanor Veleth: [deceased] Military background, inherited the throne and the care of his siblings at a young age. His chief rival is PRINCE GARIAN HERLESTER OF DRATH

Jewel Szinzar: Married to the King of Lygiera, MAXL ELANDERSI, has several children

Liara Viana Szinzar: Eldest child of king and queen

Markham Glenereth: Disinherited, technically denied the Glenereth name, though the king intended that to be temporary. Liege to the king, a martial artist of superlative skill.

Lexan Glenereth: Son of Markham Glenereth; runs for help to Sartor, becomes a guerilla fighter under his father; later runs to Sartor for help, is rescued by Detlev's boys. Studied at Curtas's House, then went home to help.

SARENDAN

Darian Irad: [deceased] After his defeat in a vicious civil war, Darian Irad stepped down from the throne and ended up as a military consultant on the sister-world Geth-deles. On his nephew Peitar's assassination, Darian Irad insisted that he was a regent for Peitar's son Darian and not a king: he had gone to Geth, where he married and had a family.

Darian Selenna: Son of Peitar Selenna and present king, though he rules according to Peitar's design, which is evolving into a parliamentary monarchy. Has Dena Yeresbeth.

Derek Diamagan: [deceased] Charismatic leader of the revolution, a commoner who wished to overthrow all the nobles, and institute common rule. He was a far better speech maker than he was an organizer; his revolution was a disaster. Close friend of Peitar Selenna until his assassination by Siamis, at that time nominally of Norsunder.

Lilah Selenna, Princess of Sarendan: [deceased] Younger Sister to Peitar. She, with friends *Bren* (artist), *Innon* (a noble-born accountant at heart) and *Deon* were deeply involved in the revolution.

Peitar Selenna, King of Sarendan: [deceased] Reluctant king who would rather study magic, he came to the throne after an especially vicious civil war. Nephew to the former king, Darian Irad, he was one of the leaders of the revolution, but advocated non-violent means. His accession was a compromise between the commoners, who adored him, and the nobles, who recognized that at least he is nominally one of their own; on his assassination, he was, at his own order, replaced by his uncle. His writings on the evils of single-rule government spread through the Sartoran continent and beyond, finding fertile ground after the war and generating a shift toward popular rule in several forms.

SARTOR

Atan, (Queen Yustnesveas Landis V): New young queen of Sartor, after the oldest kingdom in the world was removed from time by nearly a century. She was found as an infant on the border by Tsauderei the mage and raised by him before the enchantment was broken. She began her queenship as a mage student with little training in statecraft but well-read in history. Married Rel at the end of the war, and now they are co-equal rulers. They have three children, Kailan-Dei ("Kay"), Mondros Tsauderei ("Froggie"), and Meridanaria Diantas Gwasan ("Gwasan").

Gehlei: Former guard in the days before Sartor was enchanted for a century, escaped with the infant Atan. Raised Atan to age fifteen along with Tsauderei the mage. Served until recently as royal steward, now retired.

Hinder and Sinder: Morvende (cave dwellers), friends of Atan; Hinder chose self-imposed exile with a band of other morvende in order to aid the counterattack.

Julian Landis: Born Julian Dei, she is Atan's cousin who wore the Child Spell for a considerable time. She relinquished it on Atan's promise that she would not be considered an heir nor a princess. She is a wanderer by nature, and was happiest when staying with Dtheldevor of Wnelder Vee's gang. Inherited Dtheldevor's island and ship after the war. The ship, the *Berdrer*, is largely captained by Gwen of the Mearsieans.

Mistress Veltos Jhaer: [deceased] Former chief of the prestigious Sartoran mage guild, until the enchantment the foremost mage school in the world. Now a century behind. She was further burdened by guilt for having lost the kingdom to enchantment and left the guild woefully behind as they struggled to recover their old prestige. Assassinated by Efael of Norsunder, she was replaced for a time by Tsauderei the mage.

Old Helas: One of Rel's city guards, left from before Sartor's 100-year enchantment. Along with BEAK, a young guard.

Rel: Known as Rel the shepherd's son, and more widely as Rel the Traveler, he was happily raised by a guardian in Tser Mearsies until wanderlust caused him to leave home. Met Puddlenose of the Mearsieans, and consequently became tangled in some of the Mearsieans' adventures. Friends with Atan, and one of the Rescuers. He was the only outsider ever invited to join the Knights of Dei in Everon; in the previous volume he discovered his parentage (SEE Mondros the mage), which he is still trying to process. He is very proud of being the son of Princess Gwasan Sonscarna of Chwahirsland, and of Mondros Glenereth, formerly of Ralanor Veleth. At the end of the war, married Atan, adopted into the Landis family, and is now King of Sartor.

SLES ADRAN

Bartal na Shagal, King of Sles Adran: [deceased] Allied with Adon Marsael of Enaeran, and Norsunder; killed by his Norsundrian commander in chief toward the end of the war. After which TREVOR MACAEL ELSARION took over as king.

Chantala Shagal: [deceased] Niece and heir to Bartal, daughter of Chantal, Bartal's sister. Cared for by her elderly nanny MARIANA, who was Chantal's devoted nanny. Married Trevor Macael Elsarion at the end of the war, and was nominally co-ruler with him. Died at Enaeran, triggering Macael's plot to reunite both kingdoms.

Haries: Last name of the pair of artists who shelter Chantala na Shagal during the war.

Kinarde, Arandos: [deceased] Sarendan-born Norsundrian, placed as watchdog and then commander over Bartal by Norsunder. Assassinated, along with his minions, by an action backed by Macael, soon-to-be king.

Navor Mandracar: [deceased] Army commander and close friend of the king.

Master Orthal: Runs an art school along the river. Other artists in training: LEMETH, LISI.

TELYERHAS

Havlan Casarod, King: Family the most direct descendant of the Cassadas, who were regarded as visionaries (or mad). Son of a queen known for her lack of skill at ruling but her genius for music, he had two sisters, LESRA and CARAS, who married Marloven princes and ended up dead. A scholar, he has a consort who is also a scholar but he handles a lot of minor ruling issues. Has a son and a daughter.

VASANDE LEROR, NOW SINDAN-AN

Kyale Marlonen: Adoptive sister to Leander, relished being a princess, and was jealous of Leander's attention. Discovered her family in northern Goerael, and has become a stage magician and player.

Leander Tlennen-Hess: Like Senrid, a young king, though of a tiny polity that historically belonged to the Marlovens, then broke away four centuries previous. Leander prefers scholarship, and before the second year of the war began, formally ceded Vasande Leror back to Senrid.

Llhei: [deceased] Sarendan-trained nanny (sister to Lizana, nurse to the royal children of *Sarendan*), governess to Kyale, remained after evil Queen Mara Jinia defeated.

Alaxandar: Captain of royal guard, quit under evil queen Mara Jinia, protected Leander. Became a ranger after the war.

LAND OF THE VENN

Erenlara Sofar: Barely into her teens, princess of the Venn until her brother's death in the invasion. Has Dena Yeresbeth, and embarked on a self-appointed training regimen that would daunt the toughest of the tough.

Kerendal Sofar: [deceased] Was king of the Venn until the invasion. He committed suicide rather than submit to a blood-binding forcing him to act according to Norsunder's will. Met Rel the Traveler [see SARTOR] the one time he was able to escape Venn and his duties, as a young boy.

WNELDER VEE

Dtheldevor: [deceased] Daughter of a privateer (some say pirate) who was killed when Dtheldevor was small, but not before she was taught martial arts. She became the champion for the young prince Murgeh Troiad, sailing against pirates infesting the shores, and helping to fight off an enterprising Norsundrian.

She established a hideout called Dthel Rendm on one of the hundreds of islands off Wnelder Vee's coast. She did the Child Spell decades ago; in lived time she is in her late seventies. She accepted kids on the Wander on her ship and her island, but her most loyal shipmates were Sarmonwilda, born a dawnsinger; Sharly, a centaur from the northern reaches; and Sidres, another centaur; Gloriel and Peridot Warren (twins, from Earth, born with mundane names); and Joey and Ellen Warren. All died with Dtheldevor in the war except Gloriel, who became a mer, and now lives near the island.

Dtheldevor left her island to Julian Dei Landis of Sartor.

Troy, King Murgeh Troiad: [deceased] was regarded as king in Wnelder Vee. Though kingship was little more than a title — the guilds do what little governing is required in small, very rural Wnelder Vee — he resisted even that much, preferring to wander the world and master music, and kept the Child Spell in order to avoid royal duties. Was considerably skilled as a bard.

Laban Dei: Raised by Detlev. Always felt a sense of responsibility toward Everon, Imar, and Wnelder Vee. Became king of the latter despite Tahra Delieth's strenuous efforts. Aided by Silvanas, one of Detlev's boys, ostensibly a horse trainer, but also a superlative scout and defense chief.

NORSUNDER

Aldon: [deceased] Military leader with a thirst for warfare, the bloodier the better. Wants to command the invasion in order to foster eternal war, his goal to take over Marloven Hess, where he was born, to make it an empire again. Killed by Siamis.

Alsaes: [deceased] First came to notice as Kessler Sonscarna's companion in Kessler's plan to take over the world. Given a mortal wound, surrendered self in exchange for bloodknife spell to preserve his life. Extremely vain. Dyes hair blond to hide Chwahir origins.

Benin: [deceased] Ambitious mage, his specialty the soul-bound (people caught at the point of death, their wills bound to the command of whoever holds the soul-bound magic). Benin tends to not wait until potential soul-bound are dead in order to experiment.

Bergan: [deceased] One of Imry Llyenthur's staff, along with COLLERON, and Duin [see below] These are all typical flunk-ies though Bergan sells info to whoever will buy it, most of all to Aldon and Efael, the latter of whom tortured him to death in order to elicit a confession that he was secretly conspiring with Imry Llyenthur—the only one Bergan wasn't conspiring with.

Bostian: [deceased] Ambitious Norsundrian military captain, obsessed with making himself king of Sartor.

Connanre of the Host of Lords: [deceased] A charismatic musi-cian. It's still unknown if he was turned or born without a vestige of conscience. He was the one who precipitated the Fall of Old Sartor by turning one of the rituals into a bloodbath, it is said to win the attention of Yeres. He is the Host's master spy.

Dejain: [deceased] Mage specializing in dark magic, one of a succession of Norsunder Base commanders, who tended to be summarily replaced by violence. Now deceased.

Duin, Fassler: (Duin his chosen name) Imry Llyenthur's chief aide-de-camp. Born in Chwahirsland. Began life as a cull under the Bi name. At the end of the war, went to Chwahirsland.

Efael: [deceased] Considered himself one of the Host of Lords, the authors of Norsunder. Had a penchant for cruelty. He was the Host of Lords' chief assassin, bloodhound, interrogator, and errand boy; he and his sister Yeres considered Detlev their rival for a seat among the Host of Lords, until the war, when Efael was forced to share command with Imry Llyenthur, after which he spent a great deal of his time plotting against Llyenthur. And Aldon, another rival commander.

Elzhier: One of Connanre of the Host's best spies. She joined Norsunder as a young, angry teen. After the war, was ready to sew chaos in revenge for the defeat, but met Marga, resulting in becoming a tree at the now-destroyed Norsunder Base

Henerek: [deceased] Ambitious low-ranking young Norsunder military captain, originated in Everon. Wanted to be one of the Knights of Dei, but was cashiered due to excess cruelty, drunkenness, and inability to follow orders. Led a brutal war in Everon, now deceased.

Host of Lords: [deceased] Authors of Norsunder, existing beyond time, readying for a second try at taking the world. Or worlds.

Ilerian of the Host of Lords: [deceased] Wore the shape of a beautiful and promising morvende, though morvende did not come out of their caves until a couple thousand years after the Fall of Old Sartor. The story put around is that his turning was Detlev's first act on emerging from Norsunder-Beyond. Ilerian is not the architect of Norsunder; he founded Norsunder-Beyond using the life of the architect, Sfenaraec. Destroyed by Detlev with a circle of Dena Yeresbeth youth at the end of the war.

Imry Llyenthur: Shared field command of invasion with Efael of the Host. A mage and a martial artist, he has Dena Yeresbeth. He's essentially a strategist, while he deals with an unwanted talent for healing. Now at large.

Svirle Treloar of the Host of Lords: [deceased] He was heir to Yssel, and still uses that title, though Yssel is long gone. His underlings address him as "Lord Svir", the word 'lord' being

                    SHERWOOD SMITH

an ancient title. He was the organizer of the Fall of Old Sartor, recruiting and forming plans. He is the ultimate in assumed privilege: nothing he does could be wrong because he deserves the world. It was he who lured Ilerian to the world, then discovered that he could not control that entity, so he exerted himself to function as go-between between Ilerian and everyone else — until Ilerian turned on him at the very end of the war. He lived just long enough to see the Beyond destroyed, his pet project.

Theronezhe of the Host of Lords: [deceased] Their military chief.

Yeres: [deceased] She and Efael, her brother, were born off-world, and so thoroughly and spectacularly corrupted that they caught the attention of Svirle of Yssel, one of the authors of Norsunder. Yeres was a powerful mage. She and Efael gladly executed the errands that the Host of Lords, steeped in evil, consider too distasteful but her true desire was to live forever young and win the worship of all men. Killed by Imry Llyenthur.

EX-NORSUNDRIANS

Detlev Reverael ne Hindraeldrei: Chief visible mage and sometime military leader, answerable to Norsunder's Host of Lords. Born four thousand years ago, has lived in and outside time ever since. Like his nephew Siamis, has Dena Yeresbeth. Left Norsunder in 4753: much speculation on both sides as to why.

Kessler Sonscarna: [deceased] Renegade Chwahir prince with considerable military abilities, forced into Norsunder as a result of treachery by the mage Dejain. Hates Norsunder. (See *Chwahirsland* below)

Siamis Reverael: Nephew to Detlev. Formidable mage, and like Detlev, has Dena Yeresbeth. Left Norsunder previous to Detlev after furnishing the means to free the Venn from an eight-century-year-old binding of their magic. Adopted Yanli, the last descendant of someone Siamis was close to on his first visit to Sartorias-deles. He has reason to believe that the woman, Isa Cassadas, was pregnant with his child before he was forced to return to Norsunder. They were both teenagers.

Sveneric Reverael Hindraeldrei: Detlev's son, trained with the boys. Lives currently most often with Adam and David (see below) at Curtas's House.

DETLEV'S BOYS

Adam: Artist, formidable talents in Dena Yeresbeth, artist until his hands were ruined by Efael. Still likes to draw, but he is the chief instructor at Curtas's House.

Alaki (Ferret): Acutely observant, aware of overlapping worlds, once a spy, now a scout and investigator.

Curtas: [deceased] Strongly responsive to line and harmony, especially in building. He designed both Detlev's house and the future dyranarya school. He died rescuing Shontande Lirendi during the war, and is still deeply missed by Shontande as well as all the boys, who agreed that the new dyranarya academy would be named for him.

David: Captain of the group, best in most areas; began the dyranarya school with Adam at Curtas's House on the disirad plateau

Erol: Chwahir-born, plucked off a battlefield. Excellent at stealth, became an aide to Jilo of the Chwahir, and gradually took over as chief of security.

Edde (Noser): [deceased] Taken from another world, at best a mascot

Laban: Volatile and longing for what he cannot have, a Dei descendant; king of Wnelder Vee after war

Leefan: Quiet, strong martial artist, cousin to Rolfin. A scout and a ranger, appreciates the free life, though he and Rolfin turn up most often in Ralanor Veleth.

MV (Mal Venn): Martial artist, studying magic, excellent sailor. Lives with Mildred of Geth at Tsauderei's cottage in Delfina Valley.

Rolfin: Cousin to Leefan, superlative martial artist

Roy: Strong Dena Yeresbeth, mage and scholar, lives with Arthur of Bereth Ferian

Silvanas: Martial artist and horse master, aided Laban Dei in Wnelder Vee.

FOR MORE INFORMATION...

Visit the Sartorias-deles wiki here: https://reqfd.net/s-d/

PART
ONE

1

The justice of my effort to illuminate the maneuverings of someone who expects to pass unremarked into the silt of history can be left to future generations. My purpose began simply, to break that silence. But how can one truly comprehend another's motivations, much less follow their every action?

Impossible. Perhaps all I've achieved is to expose the arrogance of my youthful goal. I know not, except to say here it is, the last chronicle.

As always, where, when, and with whom to begin? Especially with someone whose concern extended to an entire world?

Why not begin with the last day of the year 4768.

A bitter winter had swept across the Sartoran continent weeks ago; of late the topic of most concern was the sudden acquisition of Enaeran by its neighbor Sles Adran.

In the north?

The transfer from the southernmost continent to the far north left Sveneric dizzy for a breath or two, as his senses adjusted to the different air. The season in Twelve Towers, the capital of the Land of the Venn, was mid-summer, but the Land of the Venn, just east of the sea of storms, seemed more like winter to anyone else.

The transfer Destination lay on the outer perimeter of the royal palace. The city's stone towers surrounded him, with almost no west-facing windows. The wind howled around the spires, keen as the edge of a new-forged sword. You could feel the weight of history here. Sveneric forced his inner heat to ignite as his tearing eyes watched the bright-colored pennants snap and stream like live things.

A wide stone-flagged terrace opened to an antechamber. Two Household Arm guards scanned him briefly. He stood still under those appraising gazes, expecting the moment he passed a signal would go by a faster route to report: young man alone, unarmed.

You had to be tough to live up this far north. He'd liked reading Venn's history, but in childhood had never thought to see it—until he met the new ruler of the Venn, Erenlara Loryard-Araeth Sophar, during the war.

A woman in layers of livery, mostly blue, glided silently between two pillars and gave him a formal greeting. "With whom have I the honor of speaking?" the woman asked, her palms together, fingers pointing downward.

He told her, and, "Sven-rik," she said, the middle vowel completely absent, as it was in Marloven and related tongues — audible reminder that they had all come from these people, ages ago.

She waited for the rest (there was always a rest in the Land of the Venn, even from the meanest vagrant, if that person came to the capital Twelve Towers), and he added, "of Sartor. I came to give your queen New Year's greetings."

He was led to a high-ceilinged room painted deepening shades of blue, so that the top emulated a twilight sky. All the moldings and decoration drew the eye to symmetrical, elaborately interlocked forms that pleased the eye. Outside the chamber—completely out of sight—Sveneric sensed one of the brown-garbed knights taking up a watchful stance.

He'd barely had time to take in the room when he heard the sound of running feet and Erenlara herself appeared at the great doorway. "Eren!"

"Sveneric," Erenlara cried in delight. Though she'd seen him now and again over the past few years, he had not visited the Land of the Venn since they were sixteen or so. And this year they would both turn twenty-five.

She wore white with gold and blue embroidery, a garment of complicated panels and folds. Sveneric glanced from her slim form to a face of perfect symmetry, and noted with dismay a fresh scar near her hairline—like her people, who seldom saw the sun, she was light of skin and hair.

And she moved with one shoulder held rigid and stiff. Her hands gloved in soft cotton.

It hurt him to see this evidence that she was still driving herself to impossible standards. He had once assumed it was lingering grief for her brilliant, beloved older brother, whose reign had been so short. He knew she had assiduously carried out his plans for dismantling the weight of power on a single individual, which had been so disastrous for the Venn over the centuries. He considered ways to approach asking, and began with, "Traveling the worldgate still?" the implied *why* in the air.

They had begun their friendship at age twelve, speaking frankly to one another about everything, from debating earnestly on how Sartoran and Venn history diverged from the southern granting of defense rights in castle-building, to speculating whether or not a bird could hover in the air if there was no wind. But when they reached their mid-teens, and he found his feelings for her intensifying from friendship to headier realms, she had begun to seem more elusive, not less.

His question sounded idle. It was not.

"I was a catalyst," she said, touching the healing cut on her scalp with a gloved finger. "Very nearly a catalyst for catastrophe. I did save the situation." She looked down at her gloves; he could smell the medicine from where he sat. "But I should not have come so close to disaster in the first place. Ah, there is yet so much to learn."

"Why?" he burst out. "The war is over, Norsunder gone. Your ships patrol for peace, and your trade is welcome in every harbor. Why spend yourself so far from home, in others' causes?"

She faced him directly, and his senses, by now focused all on her, registered the prickle of suppressed intensity. "Why," she asked in a soft voice that did not carry, "did you give yourself over to the enemy during the war?"

That one took him completely by surprise. "Who told you that?"

"My surmise was then correct?"

His astonishment must be showing; he saw a hint of smile at the corners of her schooled mouth. She was never rude, but he read in that smile: Am I really the only one who hides motivations?

What she said was, "We are the same age, Sveneric. There is very little that would astonish me, these days."

And her voice in memory echoed, the context being self-sacrifice, *I would do that — willingly! — for the Venn.*

"I apologize for being insufferable," he said straitly, as she began to walk again. They crossed a hall with a stream thundering down from an upper level over boulders, and all along it trees and ferns and the most delicate flowers grew in profusion, lit from a great row of clerestory windows set toward the south.

"Not that. Never that," she said when they had passed the thunderous falls. "You do not wish to answer my question?"

"Only because it was a *stupid* idea. And dangerous, not just to me but others, for I was playing at being grown up without understanding the conflicts of the adults around me."

"Ayah," she breathed, wincing in sympathy, though her gaze was ahead, and not on him.

"And not only did it not accomplish what I was after — which was Imry's ear regarding his hidden talent—but I managed to set off several near-disasters."

"Detlev was angry with you?"

"No. Yes. Not because of my action, you might say, but because I did not consider the consequences thoroughly. The disasters did not happen, though I deserve no credit for that."

Two huge golden doors swung open. Sveneric gazed in awed silence upon a throne room the likes of which he had never seen.

"A fine example of barbaric splendor?" she asked, her smile wry again. "I noticed that in the south the mode is now simplicity."

Is that a shaft at Detlev? Sveneric laughed inwardly at himself. He'd never been able to predict how she would react; the last time he had come here she had said, *My eyes are fixed beyond the stars. Oh, how silly that sounds out loud, how pompous. I am so ignorant, and there is so much to learn.*

He'd pondered those words ever since. He hadn't asked because he was not certain he could bear the answer.

He looked around the throne hall. It was huge, of course, carvings and art and fantastic mosaics a mighty riot of upward- and outward-moving color in the great tree covering one wall. Crystal, highly polished silver and gold, and various faceted jewels were set into the whole so that the colors worn by the person on the throne, and the movements made by that person, would be reflected in brief and no doubt occasionally startling flashes of light throughout the vast room.

He tried one last time. "That was a fine deflection, throwing us back to my blunder during the war. But I answered your question. Mine to you remains, why? I'll narrow, it, why drive yourself so hard when there is peace, and you have done well, and we're still young?"

She turned to face him, there in the chamber of her ancestors, her pupils so large that her eyes seemed dark, except for the reflection of the light overhead. "Because," she said, "time is running out."

"For?"

But she turned to describe the decorations, and the New Year's ritual to come, which would see yet more Eyes of the Crown sworn to service—these chosen by the people, and Sveneric accepted that that rare window of confidence had closed.

My earliest of these records illustrated an example of oblique interference, in the matter of the transfer of what came to be known as the Lirendi Diamond, when Colend first became a kingdom. Now, centuries later, we go to Shontande Lirendi, king of Colend, who had always had difficulty making friends. However, once someone crossed that invisible barrier, his friend Thad Keperi had discovered, Shontande never ceased looking out for those he cherished. He certainly had not been taught that loyalty; his early life had been one of enforced isolation. That loyalty seemed to be innate, in contrast to the wariness that his life experience had taught him.

After nine years as Colendi Ambassador to Sartor, Thad Keperi had been recalled to Alsais, in time for New Year's Week oaths and new appointments. He probably ought to have arranged for magic transfer, but he loathed the transfer reaction, and besides, he'd wanted to stop at his birth home on the border to see his family before continuing northeast to the capital. A series of hard storms had lengthened his travel time. At least he wasn't late—by a single day. Tomorrow would be New Year's Day Firstday, Oath Day in most southern continent countries.

It was, strictly speaking, unpardonably rude to appear at the last moment like this, but Shontande Lirendi had been

Thad's friend since their boyhood. The ambassadorial post had begun as a momentary fix that had spanned the war plus the years since. Thad was ready to come home.

As the sled he'd hired bumped gently up the river, he avidly, even hungrily, studied the familiar buildings at the southern end of the city on the Ala-Skya Canal. That was the less decorative end of town, given over for shipping and business. But in Alsais, nothing was ever unsightly. Warehouses and dockside establishments alike boasted fresh paint and diamond-glassed windows and climbing vines slumbering in winter. All war damage had been rigorously eradicated, except in memory. As he slid past familiar buildings, his eyes picking out the most minute changes, he could not help the chill of memory: how he'd wept as he fled — on Shon's orders — the noise of the Adrani invasion beyond the horizon. He'd been so certain he would never again see those he loved.

Thad climbed out of the sled on the Crown Skya Canal and made his way along the footpath to the servants' entrance to the royal palace, sure that his younger brother Bee would sense him; that uncanny ability he'd possessed since babyhood turned out to be Dena Yeresbeth. Bee was the only one in the family to be born with it.

Bee approached at a swift, smooth walk, his stick flicking to each side almost as an afterthought; he'd learned at a young age how to navigate a world full of obstructions.

"Bee," Thad exclaimed, and stopped so that Bee could find him.

There was no smile, for Bee had not learned facial expressions, but Thad heard Bee's genuine pleasure in his voice, "Thad! You've returned."

"I'm here," Thad said, taking Bee by the shoulders first, so as not to startle him, then hugging him. "Our mothers sounded well. They said you write every week, so you probably know all their news. Our sister's restaurant flourishes, and one of our nieces appears to have an eye for art."

Bee said, "Thank you. How are you dressed?"

"My old scribe-student winter robe," Thad said, a little surprised. "I thought it would get me in, especially today, when everyone is surely busy setting up for Oath Day tomorrow."

"Did anyone stop you?"

"Three times. They asked my name, and then let me go."

"Ah, good."

Thad eyed his brother, who was taller than Thad remembered, his face bonier, framed by darker hair than when young. The protective urge toward a little brother ought to have ended at the outbreak of war ten years ago, when Shon sent Thad away for his own safety while keeping Bee for the resistance, but old habits are hard to break. "You're looking well. But, is there trouble?"

"Merely watchfulness," Bee replied, underscoring to Thad that he was definitely back in Colend, where people did not like to say "no" even between siblings. "The heralds ought to be stopping everyone, no matter what livery they wear. I don't think it's likely to change in our lifetimes."

Thad caught himself nodding in agreement. Time to resume old habits. "It's a bit the same in Sartor. Though nothing bad has happened since the war ended. I ought perhaps to add that Norsunder is gone, it's not forgotten."

"So very true," Bee agreed. "That makes the celebrations the better."

"Ah-ye!" Thad looked around. "There's an army of young runners here, hanging colored lanterns. Those surely are not for Oath Day?

"You are very much behind the times! The Lastnight masquerade has become famous," Bee said, laughing a little.

"And you must oversee at least a part of it? Of course you must. I'm keeping you from all this extra work," Thad exclaimed. "I ought to have thought of that. What can I do to help?"

"It's all progressing as it should," Bee replied. "Court is no doubt putting on their finery, and my part is finished until the event. Come. I ordered dinner as soon as I heard you." He tapped his head. "We'll eat in my rooms."

A kitchen runner appeared with a high-piled tray. He set this down and scudded out as Bee said, "Help yourself." And, as Thad began to load his plate, Bee went on, "It is so very good to have you back! When last I heard your voice, it was when Shon sent you back to Sartor, and he thought it was to relative safety. Then those long two years of war with no messages going anywhere, and we did not know if you even lived. And when the war ended, the secret messages from Rel that Sartor was starving, living in tents and broken buildings ... we had no idea it was that bad. We'd never believed anything the

Norsundrians said about Sartor or Rel."

"It was terrible for Sartor," Thad said. "Since you know the general history, I will spare you the specifics. For me, it was not so terrible. Most of the war I spent in Shendoral, a woodland quite magical and strange. Norsunder dared not approach. I began as a messenger, my one skill. Desperately needed. As for Eidervaen, once Norsunder was defeated, while not every building was destroyed — for one thing, each commander, worse than the last, wanted a palace, so at least their head-quarters survived — a good part of the city was rubble. But one thing about archives and archives of drawings and pictures, there was sure to be at least one image of every cartouche and pilaster. Just as I can see around me here, there was a determination to rebuild exactly as everything had been, in order to eradicate Norsunder's presence as much as possible."

Bee laughed under his breath. "The thinking here was so very much the same. Thad, of course I know what you did for Sartor after the war, but I want to hear it in your voice. There are many in court who believe we saved Sartor. That was *your* doing."

Under Bee's encouragement, Thad explained his insider's view of the deal that he and Rel had worked out with Shon. The result was, supplies, mostly foodstuffs, were an outright gift from Colend, though on the surface it was presented as a trade deal. Same the next year, until Sartor, by the third year, began to establish itself again. The benefit for Colend began to accrue by the fourth year, excellent tariff-free trade going both ways.

"… pretty much arranged itself," Thad finished up. "All I had to do was be a mouthpiece. There was no real work, certainly no wit on my part. I'd known Rel since the alliance days, and I knew he was good for his promises. Though I didn't know Atan at all, I came to see she's very much like Rel in that way. Shon believed me, because he's Shon. That was the extent of it."

"He's missed you," Bee said.

"He has you here with him."

"Yes, but my post is to listen, as well as to be his personal scribe. He is so very visual. He catches himself constantly, even now, on such questions as, *But his left hand, was it tense?* And *Where was her gaze?* While I can explain the shades of voice, those questions about what hands are doing? Or eyes? Ah-ye, those I cannot answer."

"But how is he otherwise?" Thad asked. Alone either with

or without Shon, they could talk in the familiar, using the elusive king's nickname, but before the staff, they employed the forms of court informal, and of course in public, when necessary they'd observe full court formal mode, complete to referring to themselves in the third person, and Shon only by honorific.

"How is he?" Bee repeated the question, then hesitated. Little could ever be read from his face, but Thad had learned to sift his brother's silences.

At last Bee said, "On the surface all is as expected. Colend thrives. He is a very well-liked king, in court and in city. But the little birds chirp more as each year passes, expressing concern that there is no heir. And that causes, ahhh, the ambitious to maneuver."

"Talian Ariath," Thad guessed. "She was raised to regard herself as the future queen."

"Indeed. But she is not the only one with ambitions. "

"And Shon?"

"I believe you would do best to evaluate for yourself," Bee said.

The carillon rang the Hour of the Lily.

As the last chord died away, a small palace page appeared, breathless. She made the peace to both, then said, "His majesty sends his regards and apologies and his message is…" Here she straightened up, her skinny ribs expanding beneath her livery, and her piping treble dropped a note or so in her attempt to replicate the king's voice as well as his tone, 'They were holding up both walls. Now I must go straight out to ring the city.'"

"Thank you, Page Niha. No return message," Bee said, and the girl began to run off in a hissing of slippers.

"Soft step, Niha," Bee cautioned mildly.

The little girl slowed a little, conscientiously practicing the heel-toe glide that she would master by age twelve, if she wished to become inner palace staff.

"And that answers that question," Thad said. "If holding up the walls still means the courtiers were lined up each with demands to be settled before they make their oaths tomorrow."

"It does."

"Do you know why he summoned me this year?"

Bee spread his hands in apologetic ignorance, which—Thad reflected—might or might not be true. And so the dance of loyalties begins. If Bee had been requested not to say anything, Thad would gain nothing by pressing.

"Whatever it is," Thad said easily, "I'm sure to find it interesting."

"Indeed. I ought to make my own last round of inspection."

"Go ahead. I'll reacquaint myself with the palace." Thad knew that Bee would home straight for him, just like the bee he'd been nicknamed for. As a small boy, he'd navigated by humming everywhere he went, and listening to how the sound changed in different spaces, before he learned to navigate by Dena Yeresbeth.

Bee glided away, his stick arcing in half-circles, and Thad ventured out. He paused under an aromatic cedar, his breath clouding as he watched a swarm of royal servants flowing noiselessly out to light the colored lanterns in the ballroom and adjacent antechambers. Gradually a welcoming effulgence brightened Alsais in spite of the cold, the brilliant hues reflected in the canal ice.

Presently Bee found him.

Thad said, "Ringing the city. What does that mean?"

"He progressed in royal sleigh along the main canals, stopping now and then to sample offerings from vendors, and hand out gold pieces until shortly before the Hour of the Harp. This is while the courtiers are busy dressing in their masquerade costumes. At the ring of Harp, it all reverses. The courtiers will be coming back in to gather for an hour, while Shon retires to dress for the masquerade. I'm to say, please join him. He's had his wardrobe staff send along some choices for you to look over."

"Lead on," Thad said, and as they passed a cluster of hanging lanterns, cold and dark, "I note that lavender seems to be back in fashion?"

Though Bee's idea of lavender was still the taste of blueberries in thickened cream, a description their sister Karhin had given him when he was small and struggling with the concept of colors, he had gradually learned what colors signified when discussed by others.

"The embargo on lavender only lasted a few years after the war," Bee said. "The Adrani ambassador never seemed to notice, and as there was no more trouble from Sles Adran, and apparently lavender is a well-liked color—it certainly tastes good—it did not persist."

"I wonder what they make of Adrani lavender now?" Thad asked.

"Ah," Bee said. "You refer to the recent assassination of the Enaeraneth king by his cousin, the Adrani king?"

"Exactly."

"It certainly was a topic of discussion this past couple of weeks, but as the trouble went west, rather than east toward us, courtly interest has subsided. The Adrani ambassador now insists on being recognized as the Enaeran-Adrani ambassador, and he no longer wears lavender, but blue, I am told. So lavender is no longer to be associated with the Adranis. Is there much talk in Sartor, or did it happen after you left?"

"A few days before. All that I heard was speculation about what Sartora will do."

"She never liked that name," Bee said. "I remember little about her, but I do remember that."

"It was a name for a legend, not a person," Thad returned. "And much of the world that does not know her as Liere still thinks of her as the legend."

They reached Bee's rooms, and the subject of Sartora and Enaeran's troubles was forgotten.

2

The court had an hour to gather and admire one another's costumes, trying to guess one another's identities — or pretending to — until the chimes of the Hour of the Crown, when Shontande Lirendi reappeared in his own splendid costume to commence the festivities.

Thad entered the ballroom from a side door, catching his first sight of Shon across the room, an elegant figure in shades of gold from ochre to the palest cream, his mask a feathered crest. A fanciful figure rather than a figure from history: no indirect message, then. Why was everyone so alert?

Ah! Of course.

As Thad had dressed, Bee explained that in the lean years directly after the war, costumes tended to be remade from items hidden in attics or larders. The masquerade had been a lot freer then, people still rejoicing over regained freedom and the defeat of the enemy. But now court was back to the age-old social and political maneuvering.

Shontande made his way into the brilliantly decorated ballroom, with round mirrors behind every sconce, and luminous lanterns glowing in rich color against the ceiling. The courtiers revolved around Shon in a loose circle as he greeted each person. The fluttering fans and the tighter parabolas revealed anticipation: it was not Shon himself so much as the prospect of whom he would choose for the opening promenade. If his partner was young and female, what would it mean?

Thad murmured in an undervoice to Bee, "Oldest and highest rank?"

Bee's only response was a laugh so soft it was barely audible.

Young and handsome and clever, Shontande Lirendi was certainly not averse to dalliance with equally young and handsome and clever persons, but that was dalliance. The vital question, Thad began to perceive, especially among women, was when—if!—he would choose a queen. Marriage was generally considered a monarch's duty, whatever it might mean personally. His father had never married, but then King Carlael Lirendi had been … odd.

As Thad had expected, Shon went to the eldest and highest in rank, signaling in the kindest way that there was no one favored for that lily crown.

After the promenade ended, the atmosphere loosened as the guests turned their attention to dance, to the music, to the artfully displayed refreshments — and to each other.

Somewhat freer now, Shon made his way to Thad's side. "Shall we talk a little later?"

"Whenever you wish."

"Enjoy yourself." Shon's smile below the exquisite mask flashed, then faded to his invincible king smile as he moved on. Thad reflected that Bee, in his soft-colored scribe robe, was effectively invisible, a status he handled with graceful unself-consciousness. He was there to handle any necessary errands, for Shon was king first whenever he was in public.

It was so good to be home! Some of the music was the same as Thad had become used to in Sartor, and many of the dances, but there was something essentially Colendi in how people moved, and the way they used hands and fans to express that which could not, or need not, or ought not be said. He waited long enough to determine which dances had altered and which hadn't, then went out to dance with anyone who held out a hand.

As the night sky wheeled the stars toward morning, there were those whose ambitions caused them to seek the king to flatter or beguile their way into ending the evening in the king's own Chamber of Cranes, for there was always hope of advancing in power through the heart. But though his costume was always easily spotted among the fabulous silks and jewels and tassels of the guests, somehow no one ever quite saw when Shontande vanished, along with Bee and Thad.

By that advanced hour, Thad found himself hungry again,

especially when he smelled warm pastry fresh from the oven. He and Bee and Shontande settled on cushions around a low table, and Thad's eye caught on a round shape that hit him behind the ribs with its familiarity: that almond-cake had been the first pastry Nalisse had made, back when she kept slipping into the kitchens to experiment between courier duties.

He bit into it ... and his eyes flashed wide. "This is Nalisse's," he gasped. "It is! She made it. Where is she?" Tired as he was, Thad actually glanced around, as if practical, wren-like Nalisse might suddenly pop up from behind a screen.

"She did not make it, but it was made by her staff. She still refuses to sell the secret to that flavor."

Thad knew very well what it was. Nalisse used honey from bees that favored a rare flower from the great lake region, not far from where she had been born. "Where is she?" he asked, not even trying to hide his anxiety, and as he asked, he became conscious of the fact that this was something he could have asked Bee. But the habit of the older brother still persisted, as to be expected after nine years! It had not occurred to him to refer to his broken relationship, though by now, Bee surely had love affairs of his own. He might even be married! Thad had not thought to ask—and Bee was so very reticent.

"Nalisse went home for the festival week," Shontande said. "Her first time being able to do that, I ought to add."

Thad had been enjoying the layers of flavor, but at those words, his appetite dried up before the wave of regret that suffused him. "I never said farewell," he murmured. "When you sent me south. I knew it was for my own safety, because I was the only one out of all of you who had never so much as touched a sword." Nalisse, though not a herald, had received self-defense training from a young age, as all couriers did.

"I still regret sending you," Shontande admitted. "I really thought that Sartor would somehow escape the war, by withdrawing from the world again, or some other arcane magic. I ought to have known better."

"Ah-ye, you have apologized enough! No one was to know it was far worse in Sartor." Thad, taking to the courier life late, had not received martial arts training, but he had learned how to spot less-traveled paths, and how to hide himself and his mount. "I told you then, and I tell you now, I survived just fine. My regret was my parting with Nalisse. I thought it right not to force her to a choice, whether to go with me or to stay. I knew she had disliked Sartor when we were there that summer. And if she chose to stay, I couldn't bear the thought of kissing her good-bye. I really feared that none of us would see each other again."

"As did we all," Shontande said reassuringly. "Look, Thad. This much I can tell you, though I believe you could guess the half of it in the taste of the pastry before you —"

"She got her wish, and trained in pastry-making."

"Not just that. She became a master in only five years, the youngest in I forget how many decades. She ran a restaurant — a very successful one — and when Chilre retired last year, I was able to bring her to the palace. She is now the head pastry chef."

And now Thad was fairly certain he understood the silence from Nalisse of the past few years, since the reestablishment of the scribe desk. On his part, cowardice. He'd told himself that if she didn't write first, it meant she had gone on with her life, leaving him behind. But now he suspected she had been too busy, and perhaps even thought the same of him.

Five years lost, though each of them had achieved success in their outward lives. Thad turned to Shon. "Do you think she will want to see me again?"

"You know I cannot speak for her. But I expect she might feel much as you do now."

In saying so little, Shon managed to say a lot. Thad's heart surged with hope.

The chimes sounded the notes of the Hour of Repose then: an hour before dawn, and the change of the day. Shon said, "I have been spending the dawn hour somewhere else each year."

"Somewhere else?"

Thad's mind went not unexpectedly to lovers, so he was taken by surprise when Shon said, "Have you kept up with news out of Chwahirsland?"

Shon was watching obliquely, and his heart expanded at the sudden, bright smile Thad flashed his way, though a trace of the earlier regret lingered in his glance. His heart would not be completely whole, it seemed, until he and Nalisse reached an understanding. But Shontande was certain that would not take long.

"Rel used to bring private news of Jilo," Thad admitted. "He was so worried in the year or two after the war. But he kept repeating that Detlev had sent Erol to shadow him."

Shon's face tightened slightly at the mention of Detlev, but otherwise he did not react.

"And when Mondros turned up at the palace to see his grandchildren, he always gave a thorough, if incomprehensible, magic report. It sounded as if Chwahirsland was slowly emerging from the swamp of ruin and rot that Wan-Edhe had condemned it to."

"It is," Shon said. "And has a very long way to go. For so many reasons. But Jilo gave me leave to visit when I wish. I extended the same to him. It's mostly an expression of good will, for we are both so busy that there is scant time for chat. Oh, those long evenings while we hid in the girls' school, talking over history and what we would do *if*. We had no idea how precious those conversations would become in memory. Or at least, so it is with me." Shon's smile was whimsical, a little sad.

But then his expression changed. "Come, Thad. I think you will like what is about to happen as much as I do. But we first must change our clothes."

Puzzled—intrigued—Thad tried to blink away the burn of tiredness from his eyelids.

To his unexpressed astonishment, the change of clothes meant laying aside the fine fabrics of the masquerade costumes to pull over their winter underthings shapeless robes of plain gray wool, over which Shon wore a ragged hooded cloak to hide his gold-touched auburn hair. Thad was given a sagging, much-pilled knitted hat of a disagreeable dark gray shade, which he pulled down low over his brows to hide his own red hair. When they were ready, Shon touched Thad, and they stepped painlessly into a different world of sights and smells. How had Shon bypassed the horrible shoved-through-a-wall transfer reaction?

Thad forgot magic and glanced around with intense interest. He was actually here, in the mysterious, sinister Land of the Chwahir! The city walls were made of thick, dark stone, massive and high, though as far as he knew, no one had ever dared to attack them. Like Senrid's Marlovens—until the recent war—all enemies had emerged from within.

Once they reached the main street, Thad was surprised to find it crowding up with people. Granted, they all wore dark colors, as expected of Chwahir, and they all walked with lowered gazes, though not in silence; in every direction there was a normal buzz of talk, and even a laugh here and there, though some of these were followed by hushes. But the hisses for silence were not threatening. There was too much of an atmosphere of anticipation for that.

As the two walked past an open door from which golden light spilled, Thad glanced inside in time to see a circle of people of all ages raising shallow bowls high, in unison. He didn't see what they did with them until two houses later, through an unshuttered window, where eight people stood in a circle. This group was just bringing their bowls down, and they sipped with a deliberation that suggested ritual to Thad.

"What am I seeing?" he murmured to Shon.

"Rice noodles," Shon whispered back. "Families and twis are sharing rice noodles. A very old custom, of course forbidden by Wan-Edhe."

"Is this what we came to see?" Thad asked. He liked the idea of Chwahir getting to share anything besides punishment and death, or orders to attack, but did they have to come all the way here in this bitter, icy cold — far colder than Alsais — before dawn to see it?

Shon uttered the softest of laughs, and then he stopped. "Watch. Listen."

They had paused behind a growing crowd. Thad looked around. They were at the edge of a great parade ground. Shon murmured in an undervoice, well below the whispers of those around them, "This was once the great square, now restored to the people. Wan-Edhe had reserved it for army parade maneuvers and punishments."

On three sides, houses and shops, light glowing in all the windows. On the fourth side, another massive wall, the south curtain wall of the royal castle.

"Look up at the tower," Shon said. "It was important for the Chwahir to learn that they could raise their gazes and not be put to death for it. So it begins at the highest tower, there on the east side."

"It? What's it?"

"You shall see."

As if in answer, a high, beautifully clear soprano uttered a long, wordless note, rather like a singer warming up. The sound flowed from the unseen singer on the tower. A woman's voice, Thad recognized. Singing. In public. Once forbidden.

Then, startling him, the people behind them, and in front of them, began joining in, one by one, then in twos and threes and fives and eights: deeper voices humming, or uttering a low *thrum, thrum, thrum* on a steady beat.

"The first year, when they were all still starving — including Jilo — and he was fresh from an assassination attempt, he invited one of the assassin's twi to begin the hum, as a way of signaling change. Few dared to join," Shon whispered. "The next year was slightly better. And the next. But the fifth year, when Jilo said they could begin replanting, everything began to change…"

Beneath the chant, voices soughed on a sigh, as lanterns were released, floating slowly up toward the sky. These were not the beautifully crafted lanterns of Colend, suspended on thin chains so they seemed to float above as they cast their multi-hued luminance. These were simple paper lanterns, but in such numbers that they made an awe-inspiring spectacle as they rose, each with its candle. The scintillant glow illuminated what Thad had missed: the long banners at the castle corners.

These were not the old black and white circle of Chwahirsland (also in later years forbidden by Wan-Edhe) but the even older eight-sided circle of heart-shaped linden leaves. Thad could not quite make out the color, only the shapes, and the long streamers that rippled in the slight breeze.

The voices around them were joined by higher voices now. The deep *thrum, thrum, thrum* swelled and deepened until the sound seemed to vibrate under Thad's feet. No, it resonated through his skull and bones. He closed his eyes, swaying a little as he surrendered to the wonder. Then the sound changed as female voices uttered stylized animal sounds on single notes, *Sssssa, sssssa*, and *chicka-hee, chika-hee*, and *korroo, korrow*.

Thad drew in a slow breath as his nerves chilled. "Are we witnessing the Great Hum?"

"Yes." Etched against the glow of a distant window, Shon's profile was barely visible in the hood as his smile flickered. "Just wait."

More and more voices added themselves, blending with the chord established by the deep hummers. Somewhere, a beautiful voice began a simple melody, a minor key threnody that caused the hairs on the back of Thad's neck to prickle at the strangeness, the beauty — and the intensifying emotion all around him.

The singers added more sounds of animals, and sounds of the trees rustling in the new forests, and the wind combing through long rice leaves. The melodic repetitions soared above the audible symbols of everyday life, and Thad began to perceive that the Chwahir did have music, an immensely complicated music they made with voices and bodies, in celebration of the blessing of work, which was the Chwahir form of melende. Honor.

He had barely begun to assimilate this when whispers serried through the singers, though the song did not falter. It was very much like a wind rising over the sounds of the sea and the land: "Here he comes."

"Who?" Thad asked — and then shut his mouth as a single figure shambled through the crowd, which parted, heads bowing low to right and left. Lanterns held high revealed the bony, unprepossessing face of Jilo, now a young man a few years Thad's junior.

Jilo crossed the square. Many joined behind him, crowding close together. Others parted to the sides. The hummers softened their voices, though they still hummed, but the air of expectancy heightened, until Jilo drew abreast of what looked like an ordinary shop selling baskets and other items of straw, wicker, and hemp.

"Fear not the waves and the wind," he said, loud enough to be heard.

A woman gave a sob, as someone used a brush and swiftly reproduced Jilo's words on both sides of the door frame.

> *"Lift your eyes and ride the clouds singing.*
> *And know the world is endless..."*

"What's going on?" Thad whispered.

"See how he goes down an alley of poorer shops," Shon said.

> *"I have wandered the world.*
> *What sights have I not seen?*
> *I have sung all the world's songs.*
> *And shared my bread with a king and a*
> *beggar..."*

"He does this every year," Shon murmured, his gaze following Jilo as they, in the midst of the crowd, were drawn after that slightly stooped, shuffling figure. "He never remembers what he said. He thinks he's merely throwing out random lines from reading he did as a small boy. But every line becomes a guerdon for these ordinary shops, a distinction in a way that hallows the old people and the women and the disabled veterans — the people Wan-Edhe considered trash. Worthless."

*"At the height of the cloud-crowned mountain
Where shivering I dreamed of the birth of stars
And laughed to see the eagles play…"*

"Eagle! It is an eagle year," voices all around exclaimed, and the hum dissolved into a shout of joy. Hands rose high, and Thad saw the gleam of tears standing in Shon's eyes.

But when they transferred back, and Thad had recovered, Shon was himself again, his smile quirked with self-mockery.

Thad said, "What is the significance of an eagle year?"

"Long ago, the Chwahir counted years in groups of eight, within a ruler's life. Their counting of years had nothing to do with Ancient Sartor and the Fall. Of course Wan-Edhe forbade counting in his last mad years as he rejected the idea that his reign might come to an end. He'd intended to live forever." Shon gestured Rue. "I'd thought nine years ago that Jilo and his Chwahir would be grateful to be led back to civilization by us Colendi. And both kingdoms would benefit, but we would be the leaders, bringing enlightenment to them."

"I see nothing amiss with that," Thad said, his hands in query mode. "Is not the intention the benefit of both peoples?"

"Ah, but what I did not expect was for them to embark of a far greater discovery — of themselves. It's still very much a beginning, and there are still so many problems besetting Jilo. Even so, I believe it is well to remember that in the very distant past, perhaps far older even than Ancient Sartor, the Chwahir were known as the dragon-keepers."

"I remember that. In the stories my sister and I read during our scribe training, some of them had wings," Thad said. "We were taught that this was mainly legend."

"Perhaps, perhaps. But each year, when I see Jilo give the Chwahir back the name of their year, which in turn is bringing back perception of long-ago greatness and forgotten custom, it occurs to me that we are seeing, not the renascence of dragon-keepers, but the gradual awakening of a great dragon itself: Chwahirsland."

3

In Colend's royal palace, Thad went off to sleep, and Shontande to prepare for the Oath Day ritual. At the same early hour in the royal palace in Ferdrian, capital of Everon, Princess Gwenlin Mersedes Delieth, youngest of Hatahra's seven children and known as Wenwen since the next-oldest child had looked into her bassinet and tried to say her name, ran through the spotlessly clean, shabby halls, looking for her oldest sister.

Some of the palace staff greeted her, and some ducked their heads in the short bows due to the queen's children. She called new year's greetings over her shoulder but kept running, until she heard familiar voices outside the old archive that once was the King's Library, and as memory receded and new habit altered life-patterns in the old palace, it became the Study.

The royal children all came to hate the Study, which was where Queen Hatahra Delieth summoned them when they were in trouble. The two voices Wenwen heard, both female, one low and one high, belonged to her mother and to Mersedes Carinna, her oldest sister who—like she—had been named for their grandmother, familiar only through legend. While Wenwen also had a name of her own, her sister had both the queen's old names to bear, her given one *and* her nickname Carl, carried at the end when Grandmother Mersedes Carinna died saving Everon from the Norsundrian Henerek.

Quite a burden, Wenwen had always thought. Which was why she preferred to keep her nickname, babyish as it might sound. Everyone was used to it. And it didn't sound princessy, which she hoped would keep Tahra-Mama from forcing her into some dull role for Everon's service as poor Carl had been.

Wenwen paused outside the Study, fighting to slow her breathing. She wiped her sleeve across her face, discovered she was still wearing her winter coat, and hastily shucked it, flinging it inside one of the big old carved and gilded bureaus that lined the hallway, where the servants stashed stuff.

Then she looked down at herself, decided her tunic and trousers would do, for after all, no one expected to see the younger sibs at the excruciatingly dull Oath Day ceremonial. She slunk back to the door and opened it.

Two narrow Delieth faces turned her way: her mother's tired, lined one, and Carl's sober, sweet one.

Carl's expression lifted from somber to happy as she jumped up. "Wenwen!"

Wenwen suffered a hug, then went obediently to kiss her mother's flat cheek. Tahra-Mama's eyes searched hers with the anxious quickness familiar to Wenwen from babyhood.

"You're back," Carl exclaimed. "It's been a hard winter. I confess I've been worried."

"I said I'd be back by New Year's Week, and here I am. I even paid for a transfer token! I've been snug in harbor, working," Wenwen said, not mentioning that the 'harbor' was not in Everon, but Onder Vaes, tiny harbor to the pirate island Dthel Rendm.

Tahra-Mama frowned, but at least she said nothing. She had stopped overtly criticizing the actions of her children when Jessan had renounced his half of the throne — and Wenwen had announced that she would do the Child Spell when she reached fifteen. Tahra-Mama hadn't said anything when Glenn and Sedron took off on their world tour, or when FJ had decided at fifteen that he, too, wouldn't age past puberty. Like Wenwen, he had the sense to avoid mention of Dtheldevor's island, which had joined so many other names and places under embargo.

There was one name no one ever spoke in Tahra-Mama's presence: Detlev. But the avoidance — the obsessive hatred — extended to anyone, and anything, that had any connection with Detlev in Tahra-Mama's mind. The list now included Welder Vee, because after the war, Laban Dei had taken the throne, despite Tahra-Mama's strenuous efforts. The embargo now even included Lyren Sartora Fer Eider, because she had left Ferdrian to live with Laban. The Detlev subject was so very forbidden at home, Wenwen had realized when she first stayed away for any length of time, that it was ever-present.

"Have you returned to commence serious study of any sort?" Tahra asked. Her tone was careful, but Wenwen could feel the accusation behind it.

"Promised to return to harbor. I'll be back here in spring," Wenwen said. "I like to keep my promises and finish any job I start." She hated being defensive—apologizing for just being herself—but that was part of life in Ferdrian's royal palace.

It was also why the sibs were so seldom home.

"Very well," Tahra said, her tone dry.

Annoyance burned through Wenwen. Still expecting her to get into harness on some joyless task that most likely had to do with numbers, huh?

She backed to the door. "I'll go change!" She left before she'd get mad and say something that would just hurt Carl, and stopped only to retrieve her coat.

The children's wing was silent. Wenwen slowed as she passed the old schoolroom, its furnishings and floor scuffed and dinged from games that seven fertile imaginations came up with during their tenancy, broken by the war years, which they'd spent in Mearsies Heili.

How weird it looked, that old room. So huge in memory, not large at all when she stood in the doorway and glanced in. Being the youngest, she remembered her sibs as big, along with the schoolroom.

Her own room was untouched, the frilly blue furnishings that she'd picked out when she turned six kept clean and tidy. She crossed the blue carpet to her wardrobe and selected a gown, thinking about how next year she would turn fifteen. She had become unsure about the Child Spell. Really, the only reason to do it would be to avoid being guilted and scolded into some dull princess job. And to keep visiting at Dtheldevor's Island, at which adults were not welcome, unless Julian Landis of Sartor approved of them.

Wenwen passed through the cleaning frame; there was no time for the extravagance of a bath. Then she put on the gown, knowing it would keep Tahra-Mama from complaining, which would make Carl happy. She was lacing it up when the bells rang for breakfast.

Apparently none of the other sibs were at home. Not

surprising. But it meant that unless there was company at the table, Wenwen would probably end up getting all the Comments and Looks from Tahra-Mama.

She trod downstairs, feeling very ill-used, and noted with relief that Aunt Merry was at the table, plus some visiting nobles, adults all, there for Oath Day. Boring. Boring, but safe, for they would keep Tahra-Mama's attention away from her.

Wenwen stayed quiet as the adults discussed some new play. It wasn't until the plates were nearly empty that Aunt Merry turned her kindly eyes Wenwen's way, and said, "It is so good to see you home, Wenwen! You've been so quiet. Traveling? Tired?"

Wenwen had her topic all ready. Avoiding her mother's gaze, she said in her chirpiest tone, "Oh, only tired of winter. And thinking about my trip to Loriseh. I used my leave-time from the ship to travel to Aroth to meet the local dawn-singers. Hear them sing. You know, they do vary their songs from region to region." She knew her mother would approve of that. As long as Wenwen didn't say *when* she'd gone.

Aunt Merry looked interested. "So I have heard. And there are times I wish I'd traveled more, just so I could experience these differences for myself. Maybe someday."

"Lots of guild-work?" Wenwen asked. So long as nobody pestered her to sew again, she didn't mind asking after Aunt Merry's tapestry-making house.

"Enough for either a hundred years, or a hundred more busy needles," Aunt Merry said with a soft laugh. Her kindness showed in the contours of her face; Wenwen had often thought that she ought to have been Carl's mother, for the two were in so many ways alike.

Carl said, "Bringing me to my own question: how goes progress on the new Raising of the Lake?"

Aunt Merry sat back, spreading her hands. "Slow. I won't let it be more than slow, for this is really going to be our best yet."

Wenwen knew that the question had been put to draw attention away from her, not because Carl needed to know the status of the latest tapestry. She probably knew the status down to the latest stitch. Carl loved the tapestries that Aunt Merry designed and made. These were apparently gaining world notice.

Wenwen had little interest in tapestries, but she had to

admit that this unfinished one really was amazing. It depicted the very end of the Norsunder War when the mysterious Marga Fer Eider had summarily banished the entire Host of Lords from Norsunder with one gesture, healing overnight the blasted land that ordinarily would have taken centuries to right itself. Wenwen had never seen so many shades of gray and silver—silver-white, silver-blue, silver-gray, blue-white, gray-blue—swirling in a chaotic yet somehow harmonic pattern that hinted at the tremendous power Marga had at her command. Water in sky, land, air—it was a tapestry no one would ever forget, and so others had ordered their own versions. Each was slightly different.

Wenwen was grateful as always for Carl's kindness and understanding. She was even more impatient to get Carl alone, and poked at the hot berry dish that had just been set before her, wondering how she would manage it. If Carl liked her surprise, she'd only have a week to prepare.

Then the bell clanged and Tahra-Mama put down her utensils mid-bite and stood. That meant everyone was done, too. Tahra-Mama marched away toward the throne room, Carl at her heels. Poor thing would have to sit through the tedium as Tahra-Mama grilled every holder of rank on their ledgers, and then made them swear to never deal with Wnelder Vee and its "traitors." And then it all would be done again on Debt Day, if Tahra-Mama had found two duckets' worth of errors in last year's ledgers.

Wenwen tried to occupy herself, hovering around the edges of the throne room until at last the courtiers streamed out, looking tense and tired. Was Carl with Tahra-Mama?

No! Tahra-Mama had kept Cousin Carinna Dei, new Commander of the Knights of Dei, behind. Tall, thin, distant-Cousin Carinna, who was as nice as Merry, bent her sober profile toward Tahra-Mama as Carl exited, thumbing her eyebrows above her eyes.

Her hands dropped when she reached the door and saw Wenwen. Who grabbed her sister's thin, cold fingers, and dragged her, faintly protesting, out into the hall.

"Was it tedious beyond all bearing? Did Tahra-Mama rant at anyone over half a pinch of salt unaccounted for in the ledgers?" Wenwen asked as she hurried Carl down a servants' hall and to the children's wing, where Tahra-Mama seldom went. Especially the playroom, whose messiness had never failed to make Tahra-Mama look away as if it was physically painful to see things out of place.

Carl winced, sitting down on a small toy horse in her fragile, expensive gown. She really had pretty dresses. As pretty as Lyren Sartora's, though always in sober hues like the blue-gray of rainclouds, or dark green, or burgundy so dark it was almost black, the decorations rich but modest. She always moved with care, so she never got them dirty or torn.

"Well?" Wenwen prompted.

"Please don't talk like that." Carl didn't sound angry, or irritated, she sounded hurt, as if Wenwen had called *her* a ranter. "She knows you all don't want to be around her. She knows, and tries to understand, and can't, and so she feels horrible."

"Does she know Jessan went to Detlev's school? Does she know that you want to meet Laban?" Wenwen asked in a hard voice.

"Of course not."

"Then she's still trying to control everyone's life, and if we were all home, we'd have to stand in the Study while she ranted about enemies and honor and how we must never, ever, ever brush against the wickedness of anything Detlev has ever touched, seen, breathed, or heard of. You *know* that's ranting."

"But you're not all home, so what's the point of brangling?" Carl asked, now looking not only weary but dispirited.

"Not brangling, ranting. I'm sorry I ranted!" Wenwen jumped up, angry with herself. Her whole purpose in seeking Carl was to cheer her! Though she was impatient of physical affection, she knew that Carl was by nature a tactile being, and so she hugged her sister, feeling those frail bones, her thinness, and again guilt wrung her. In not liking touch, Wenwen knew she was like her mother; she had never faulted Tahra-Mama for her lack of affection, but her earliest memories were of caresses and warmth from Carl. Was it then, when she was a baby, she had come to love her oldest sister so much?

"Your problem," Wenwen said, hugging her again, "is that you are too good for anyone, including us brats. But I know something that will make you happy, and that's what I meant to say. Laban is coming to Dthel Rendm on First-Day of the new year." She let go of her sister, and stepped back. "Eight days from today. Well, seven, starting tomorrow."

Carl's eyes widened. "Are you certain?"

Wenwen grinned at her. "It's a fact. And it's also outside the land-border of Wnelder Vee, so any spy spells Tahra-Mama set up won't work. You have all of New Year's Week to think of some excuse to get away for a candle or two. I copied out the Destination at Dtheldevor's island. You just need to get transfer tokens for going and coming. If you want, I can see to that."

Carl's thin lips pressed into a white line. "We have plenty of tokens, though I do have to account for them. If only —"

"No 'if only.'" Annoyance sharpened Wenwen's voice. "This is something you *wanted*. For *ages*. And any *other* ruler would want to know the neighboring ruler, for defense if nothing else. That's what Mad says. *And* Jessan. They made me promise to hang around the island until I could find a way to let you meet him, *since you wanted to so much*."

Carl's eyes gathered light — tears, Wenwen saw. Not at the prospect of meeting Laban, but at this sign that her siblings made efforts for her own benefit.

"You're *good*, Carl," Wenwen whispered fiercely. She couldn't help it, because anger and grief and guilt and love ran a pirate attack inside her, making her innards squirm. "You're more a Mama than — well, I won't say it since you don't want to hear it. We *all* feel bad that you're stuck here, being the heir, and can't get away even for a tip-glass without being hauled to the torture chamber." Wenwen stabbed a finger in the direction of the Study.

"I feel sorry for our mother," Carl said. "I wish one of you would grow up enough to see how tragic her life has been —"

"Jessan is almost twenty, same as you."

Carl sighed. "And he does see it. But he has to keep his distance, because of his loyalties to Detlev and his vision. Oh, Wenwen, I wish —"

"Don't wish. Do. Go meet Laban, and talk policy until you both drop," Wenwen said, forcing a grin. "He's expecting you. I told him you'd come, and everything about you. Here is the Destination pattern."

Wenwen thrust a grubby, crumpled paper into her sister's unresisting hand and ran off, buoyant with the feeling of duty done; if Carl couldn't see her, she couldn't argue with Wenwen, protesting that duty or some wretched thing like that would prevent her from doing this one thing for herself.

Carl watched after her, feeling more oppressed than before, then tucked the paper into her inner pocket, and went back out, knowing that their mother would be looking for her to go over the day's decisions over dinner.

Carl did her best to listen, but inwardly she argued with herself just as fiercely as Wenwen had feared she would. She knew how much Tahra-Mama would hate her going. Exactly as much as Carl hated lying, but only a lie would gain her enough time to get away. The only excuse that would work would be doing something with the Dei cousins. Cousin Carinna, commander of the Knights, would not approve of lies, of course. But most of the younger cousins felt the way the sibs did—those who were still at home, and not off sailing, or wandering the world, now that it was safe from Norsunder.

Carl argued with herself until it was time to retire. And there, alone in her room, she gritted her teeth and forced herself to acknowledge the real reason she was reluctant to go.

She made herself stand in front of her mirror, two lit branches of candles at either side shedding their merciless glow on the homely face that stared back so mutely.

These sessions at the mirror reinforced truth over fancy.

Truth. Narrow, grayish eyes of an indeterminate shade too uninteresting to further descry; sallow skin; dull dark brown hair expertly dressed to induce a semblance of sheen and to soften the contours of a narrow face. Mouth just a mouth, compressed to look even thinner, nose plain. Scrawny body gowned with grace and expertise—but never enough to mask the scrawniness—and plain hands with twig-skinny fingers. The only standout feature were two round ears, jutting at an angle that she loathed. Why couldn't she at least have nice ears, like Lyren's pretty shell-curve, lying flat to her head?

She knew she ought to be grateful she had two good eyes, functioning ears, and a body that worked without pain, and she was! She counted up the things she was grateful for every time her spirits sank, and yet, she could not prevent herself from wondering who would take an interest in such a person, were she not heir to Everon and (Tahra-Mama insisted) Imar? No one, of course. Certainly not Laban, bright-eyed, quick, handsome Laban, he of the dashing, mysterious, and sinister past, now king of Wnelder Vee. She'd glimpsed him in memory-images, caught from Lyren long ago, and from her brother Jessan in dreams, before both had learned how sensitive she was, and had shielded themselves better.

Of course she'd never met him. She'd planned to, once, but

somehow—she suspected interference from well-meaning elder Dei relations, back when Grandfather Roderic was alive—the plan had fallen through, and there'd been no opportunity since.

Another cause for gratitude: at least her mother had not found out. Carl worked very hard to maintain peace with her mother, but Tahra-Mama's obsessive hatred was so great that Carl could not have borne the months-long lectures and resentment and distrust if her mother found out that she had even thought about meeting Laban. That had to be why the older relatives had closed ranks, just to protect her.

The only person who used to be able to get Tahra-Mama to ease off a little, even smile, had been Lyren. How Carl missed those days! She knew her sibs did as well, for when Lyren had lived among them the atmosphere over this somber, war-shadowed palace had scintillated with talk and laughter, and with art and music. Lyren knew just what to say and how to say it; her background connection with Detlev and his people had been tolerated because it was inadvertent, not chosen, and because she and Tahra could revile happily against Detlev with one another, though Lyren's hatred of Detlev had mostly seemed like a game. There was never any force in it.

Then, during the war, Lyren met the grown-up Laban. To Lyren he'd been a long-lost brother, to the others a figure of romance. After Tahra found out Lyren was visiting Laban, Lyren had had to leave, but Carl knew the real reason.

Though Lyren had never said it, and the siblings did not know it, it was Carl's own fault.

She glared at her image in the mirror, and said, "You are ugly. And you have an ugly heart." Even her thin mouth looked awkward when she talked, her lips too thin.

She turned away, angrily reveling in the shame of memory.

The girl's name was Amarithe, and she was the same age as Carl. Honor Amarithe had inherited her parents' holding, as neither had survived the war. She came to court for the first time that year, when they both were fourteen, gabby and braggy, tossing her golden curls after every other sentence. As soon as Amarithe laid eyes on Lyren, she began copying her manners, her voice, and her clothes. How Carl had scorned Amarithe, who was short and squat with a turned-up snout for a nose and ears that stuck out even worse than Carl's, for the way she minced along in what she thought was Lyren's walk, holding her pinkies out when she gestured, and modulating her voice in what sounded to Carl like a parody of Lyren's style of speech.

Just as Carl had been doing.

Lyren always seemed to accept people as they were, and never, ever had she prefaced a remark about walking, or sitting, or handling a fan, with annihilatingly poisonous advice beginning with "Girls like you ought better to..."

Carl had come to realize that she had imposed her own standard of beauty, and what might be tolerated in the unbeautiful, not just on herself, but on the rest of the world. And Lyren had seen her scorning Amarithe for trying to make herself, and think herself, pretty.

Nothing had been said. But Carl had seen the shock in her eyes, and when a couple months later she was somehow caught visiting Laban, and she and Tahra-Mama agreed that Carl was old enough not to need a governess following which Lyren went away, Carl had known it was her own meanness that had made it happen.

She'd subsequently trained the Lyren gestures back out of her habits of movement, so that she could cultivate quietness and even invisibility, as best suited a homely girl. And whenever Amarithe came to court, Carl made extra time to sit with her, and smile at all Amarithe's bragging. But there remained that scar in her heart, the knowledge that she was a mean creature. Surely a mean creature did not deserve to meet Laban.

Only ... only ... Wenwen had gone to such effort, and there was that about policy talk, which Jessan said Carl needed, as she was only permitted to hear Tahra-Mama's side of things...

Did she dare?

4

Wenwen had never met Dtheldevor, the legendary and long-lived pirate girl who had died along with most of her gang during the war. In fact, few of the children who came to Dthel Rendm had ever met her, but they'd found that, living in her home and using her things as they did, she remained a kind of laughing, freedom-loving presence. There were few rules governing the rowdies drawn to Dtheldevor's Island, but there were customs, all meant to perpetuate the kind of life her pirate gang had lived — or, that was what they all believed, anyway.

"You know Laban is coming for a visit. Do you think Dtheldevor would be proud to have her hideout seen like this?" Julian Landis asked that morning. "Here's a hint," she said, arms crossed. "She hated mess."

Those who had sailed aboard Dtheldevor's ship all knew that neatness was a tradition on the ship, if not necessarily in the underground cavern that had formed Dtheldevor's land-base. Teens and younger children alike worked at rolling and stashing the old maps and charts, polishing and racking practice weapons, sweeping the cavern floors, and neatening the haphazard sleeping arrangements and belongings and keepsake clutter that otherwise never quite found a place.

While that was going on, not far to the west, in Wnelder Vee's capital Fortnyal Roth, Lyren Sartora Fer Eider found Laban frowning at the map showing the entire southern half of the continent of Drael, the Elgar Strait at the bottom. "Uh oh," Lyren said. "Trouble?"

Laban's eyes ranged over the mountainous country midlands, to the west of Wnelder Vee. "Rumor so far. Renegade Fhlerians. Aldon's plants, Ferret thinks."

Ferret? Lyren grimaced. Ferret, best of the covert scouts among Detlev's boys, never spread rumors. But if he was claiming rumors, that meant he was investigating himself. So whatever trouble might be out there was at least far off in time as well as distance.

"Why do you ask?" Laban asked, glancing her way — and noting that instead of dressing up in something courtly and flattering to her figure, she'd put on riding clothes. "Going somewhere?"

Habit shifted his glance away from her body to her face as she said, "The *Berdrer* is warping in, whatever that means."

"Being towed into a narrow harbor, or against the tide," Laban said automatically. "*Berdrer*?" He snapped his fingers, recollecting the surprising news that one of Dtheldevor's old crew, now a mer, was coming home. And he'd wanted very much to meet a mer, his thought going to continental perimeter watch. "Right. Dtheldevor's ship. They're here?"

"CJ says they are warping in this moment, and we ought to come now."

"CJ?" Laban repeated. "I thought she was in Mearsies Heili."

"Sailing with Gwen." Lyren plunged a hand into a pocket and pulled out her golden notecase. "CJ writes to anyone who will write back."

Laban's eyes strayed toward the map again, revealing the trend of his thoughts, then he said, "They can wait the turn of a glass. I thought this visit was about the mer. An almost-mer," he corrected himself. "Or is it mer? A land human turning mer and coming back is so rare I don't even know if there's a term for them. Remind me. I remember it's one of Dtheldevor's crew, but not much more."

Lyren had expected something like this. She knew from having traded personal histories, in detail, with Laban, that he'd only met Dtheldevor twice, both times briefly. "*Berdrer* was Dtheldevor's ship. Now captained by Gwen of the Mearsieans, who spent five years training with Puddlenose. Julian made her captain after there were too many fights over who'd get a year as skipper, which was how they started out."

"Got that. But where does CJ come in?"

"She's been sailing with Gwen this past few days, after they found Gloriel Warren. Who is the mer. According to CJ, Gloriel was trying to find her way home, once she was released from whoever it was undersea who made her a mer. I don't know more. Maybe she can explain. But she wants to come home, and the *Berdrer* led her to the right island, which I guess she couldn't recognize from underwater."

"Not among the hundreds of tiny islands, no surprise there," Laban said. "Got it. What's the transfer Destination?"

"Wait," Lyren said.

"I thought we had to get going?"

"Real quick, there's a chance that Carl Delieth might be there. Wenwen returned home last week specifically to invite her face to face, without Tahra hearing."

Laban whistled. "Tahra actually let her out?"

"I very much doubt it. If Carl turns up, it will be on the sneak. She's coming to see the island, somewhat, but she's really coming to meet you."

"Oh, that's right, the whole forbidden fruit mystery. That's me. Interestingly evil kumquat." Laban's expressive eyebrows slanted. "All right, I'll be a not-evil kumquat, but I don't want it to interfere with talking to the mer about … wait. Maybe Carl could convince Tahra how much damage her punitive tariff on wool and woolens is doing here, and how much the Imarans are starting to maneuver behind her back. All right, let's make time for both."

Lyren dipped her chin slightly. "No quarrel with any of that, just, oh, be careful with Carl. She knows better than anyone what Tahra is like. She regrets it. And she's sensitive."

"Got it," Laban said again, and they transferred.

The island lay under the same low, snow-laden clouds as Fortnyal Roth. The weather held off as the *Berdrer*, a long, narrow, rake-masted pirate ship, was drawn in by cable. Across the cold gray-green voices high voices rose in song. Children's voices, singing a complicated melody with tremendous gusto. As the ship rocked its way gently to the dock, blocks clattering, the words gradually emerged:

"Yo Ho!
Oh No!

I loooo-v-e thee so!
"Thy teeth are as green as green can be,
So do me a favor and abandon me!
Yo ho…"

Laban and Lyren had recovered from transfer reaction by then. He slanted a questioning glance at her, then answered his own question when they spotted the long black hair of a familiar slender figure: of course it was CJ conducting a choir singing one of her Mearsiean gang's favorite parodies.

Teens and children gathered along the dock, some laughing and cheering until the song ended a verse later, and then Gwen joined CJ on the foredeck, bawling orders.

The ship was made fast, a ramp extended to the dock, and islanders swarmed back and forth, some coming to circle Lyren, who was generally recognized. She greeted many by name and then paused as CJ ran down the ramp, followed by Gwen, a sun-browned young woman not much taller than she'd been as a girl, but a lot more solid. Her hair, still clipped short below her ears, had gone yellow-white in the sun.

Lyren greeted both, said, "That was a wonderful concert. But where is Gloriel?"

CJ leaped up on a piling to peer down into the water. She pointed triumphantly, "There she is! She can't come out of the water anymore. But I wrote to Julian to have a boat ready, so you can talk to her."

Laban turned to Lyren. She successfully interpreted his glance as a request to keep the horde back, as he greeted his way past curious islanders and descended to the floating dock, where a boat had been tied up.

While all this was going on, the mer who had been Gloriel Warren gazed up at the familiar inlet from this unfamiliar angle at water level, sorrow and joy crowding her heart to bursting. She knew, of course, who had lived and who had died: the first thing she'd seen when the mers changed her were the bodies of her sisters and brother floating, horribly burned, on the water. But they and Deon of Sarendan were beyond pain, and anyway, her strange new face didn't seem capable of tears, and so she had gone to each one and Disappeared them.

Dtheldevor had not been there among them, giving Gloriel hope that she had somehow survived. It was not until seasons and seasons had passed that she made her way to Jaro Harbor, at the eastern end of Drael, above The Fangs. She had surfaced among the ships and boats—and immediately recognized *Berdrer*, there for a supply run. And on board, Gwen of the Mearsieans in Dtheldevor's old place abaft the wheel.

"Where's Dtheldevor?" Gloriel cried, her voice reedy.

Gwen exchanged wide-eyed looks with her crew, who just looked back. She was the skipper, and the elder, now full-grown.

"Be right back."

Gwen still carried her magic paper from the war years. She immediately contacted CJ, only home for three days from her trip to Enaeran. But she was always up for something interesting, and meeting Gloriel again sounded interesting. Gwen was a doer, not a talker. It was CJ who always knew what to say.

CJ went right to the rail, leaned down, and cried, "Welcome back!"

"Where's Dtheldevor?" Gloriel called again, as loud as she could.

CJ considered what to say, then decided that after ten years, ripping the bandage off was probably best. "She didn't make it. But the island is still there. Julian is now in charge. That was by Dtheldevor's wishes, because she didn't know you made it."

Gloriel sank down, then surfaced again. It was as she'd always feared; if Dtheldevor had lived, she never would have stopped searching, if she thought any of the others were alive.

The island was still there? Then home was still there. Of a sort.

She peered up at CJ, still leaning over the rail, her black hair blowing in the cold wind. "Happened?" she called.

"Hey, we'll boom down a boat, so you won't have to yell."

Ignoring the bitter wind, CJ climbed down to a dinghy lowered to the water, and they exchanged stories. Gloriel learned that the war was indeed over, but Dtheldevor had not seen its end, and Sharly and Sedres had gone back to the north to the centaur lands.

"But Dtheldevor's Island is still there," CJ had said earnestly, crouched shivering in the boat as Gloriel floated before it. "Gwen is taking it back home. Can you follow us?"

Gloriel wanted nothing more, though she wasn't quite sure why, now that she knew that Dtheldevor had not survived. But follow she did, still trying to navigate mentally between two vastly different worlds. Whenever she thought of a question, she'd wave, and the ship would brail up, and CJ would descend in the boat to talk to her. Then they'd set sail again.

And here they were, and it hurt so much, but felt good, a little, to see the familiar shore of Dthel Rendm, and now here was Laban the poopsie. Only grown.

Laban had dropped his mind-shield, listening on the mental plane as he stared down into Gloriel's face. He had never known her, but even if he had he doubted he would have recognized her with that extra eyelid, the gills in her neck, and her nose changed to two slits. Her skin had turned to a shiny grayish white, not unlike dolphins, and her hair had thickened, trailing like seaweed. She could control it with a flex. It floated all around her, obscuring her body, but he made out the powerful fish tail slowly fanning beneath the surface, keeping her afloat.

"Welcome back," he said.

Gloriel did not like to talk — air whistled in her gills and her nose. Some of the Changed forgot how to talk. She had worked hard to remember how in case she found Dtheldevor again. "Not the same," she said.

"No. Few things are. But it's made everyone here happy to see you back. Are you here to stay, or to visit?"

Gloriel had been changing her mind back and forth as she swam after the *Berdrer* the relatively short distance between Jaro in Imar and the island here. Her gaze moved past Laban to Gwen and CJ, then to Julian Landis, up on the dock, who waved when she caught Gloriel's glance.

All people Gloriel remembered. She didn't really know them, except for the Mearsiean girls, who had visited a lot. "Dunno," she said.

Laban put his hands on his knees as he knelt there. "That's fine," he said. "There's no reason you have to answer me now. Or ever. It's just that if you decided to stay, and wanted to try being a sea scout, Crow of Ama Hazanth — he's king now, finally — and I want to work up a way to watch for pirates and the like."

"Ships…" Gloriel began, but her gills whistled, and her skin was drying. She ducked underwater to draw in a sweet draft of brine. When she came up, she saw that CJ had joined Laban, her eyes bright blue.

"…told us that all ships look pretty much alike from

below," CJ was saying to Laban. "They'd have to surface, which not every mer likes to do. Any more than, oh, you want to dive to the bottom of a lake, except for a quick look around if you're curious."

"I get that," Laban began.

CJ heard the unsaid but, and added, "My point is, she's alone. Most people who fall into the sea, if they don't drown before mers find them, forget their land life by the time they work off the magic to change them. There's lots I don't get about how, or anything much about mer life. Gloriel can't talk long. But I had an idea. Since she does remember the old life, I thought of contacting Falinneh. You know, she's a shape-changer. If she wants to try to change to a mer, maybe we could, I dunno, find company for Gloriel?"

"Yeah," said Gloriel, relieved that someone else got all that out.

And that, Laban was thinking, was why his great idea hadn't been implemented centuries ago: the two forms of life really were vitally different.

He agreed with everything. Since Falinneh wasn't here among these others, it was clear that no one was in a hurry to try the great experiment. And none of them were thinking of sea perimeters. He made his way up onto the dock as the first snowflakes began to float down, and CJ disappeared back into the ship, for she didn't know what to say to Lyren about Liere, back in Enaeran, sitting on that throne next to Andri's killer, and looking so miserable.

Wenwen anxiously watched the interview with Gloriel from the mass of teens, her gaze training up toward the Destination square every few heartbeats. Laban climbed back up to the dock, greeting anyone who came forward. Wenwen suspected he was ready to go as he made his way toward the Destination square. Then, alone and completely unnoticed as the snow began to fall faster, there she was.

Wenwen ran straight to Lyren. "She's here! Carl's here!"

"I see," Lyren said, her eyes narrowing as she considered Carl, who stared without moving, fingers stiff at her sides. "Don't worry. Let's see if we can separate them off. Or Carl will never get the courage to say anything."

This was exactly what Wenwen had been thinking.

Wenwen bolted toward her eldest sister, who for some reason had decided to dress like one of the servants, her hair plainly pulled back into a braid, her clothes a sturdy brown woolen tunic, and brown riding trousers. She looked quite strikingly like Jessan; Wenwen was amazed that her sister even had such boring clothes.

How to get them together? She glanced in despair toward Lyren, who was talking to Julian.

"Hot chocolate in the galley," Julian called.

A stampede headed down the tunnel.

That cut three-quarters of them out, right away. Then Lyren approached with Laban, and Wenwen sighed with relief, trusting that Lyren would fix everything, as usual. She bolted after the others to get chocolate before it was gone.

Carl greeted Lyren, but her wide gaze reached beyond to Laban, who was even more handsome than those brief memory images she had gained long ago. And his expression was kind as Lyren introduced them.

She had almost not come, until Jessan appeared in her dream the third night of tossing and turning and struggling against herself. "I don't deserve to meet him," she cried out in her dream.

"Deserve," Jessan repeated, his dream-voice vast as the sea with his irritation. "Laban is not some ancient wise one, he's just another person like you, me, and the youngest Sandrial kitchen helper. Wenwen went to a lot of trouble to arrange a meeting you said you wanted. But when you talk about deserving, you are beginning to sound like Tahra-Mama."

That had decided Carl, and she'd slept for the first time since Wenwen put forth her invitation.

Now she followed as Lyren, long familiar with Dthel Rendm, led Carl around, pointing out the sights, and then, once they'd shed curious hangers on, left Laban and Carl in the shelter of the old hollow tree in the midst of the grove on the island's lee. In summer the grove was shady, in winter secluded.

The air inside the tree was still, the snow falling outside, but frigid, but Carl scarcely noticed as Laban actually addressed her, asking after Jessan and the rest of the family. He was kind when he asked how Tahra was doing.

"I'd hoped that one day we might establish communication," Laban then said. "Trade could only benefit both kingdoms."

"Yes," Carl whispered. "And I know what my mother did

to prevent your succeeding. I—I'm here to apologize in person, I guess. And to hope that ... some day ... we might be able to communicate freely. For the benefit of the kingdoms."

"You do not wish to contrive anything at the present time?"

"I can't bear to sneak behind my mother's back. There's—well, there's too much of that as it is, and the knowledge of it is a burden." Carl spoke quickly.

"I honor you for your forbearance," Laban said, bowing.

"Oh, don't," Carl exclaimed, and gave a weird, gasping laugh. "My motives are nothing but cowardice, and weakness—"

"And a desire to make everyone around you happy, no matter how unreasonable their demands," Lyren cut in to say, reappearing again.

Laban smiled. "But I won't press. Or say more in that regard. No one feels comfortable being complimented by a stranger." The implication, unspoken, hung in the air: *especially someone who hears so little of it at home.*

Carl wrenched her tightly gripped fingers back and forth, watched by Laban in pity, and Lyren in grief: things had clearly gotten worse since she left.

Lyren regretted leaving, though it had seemed necessary at the time. She was trying to think of something to say to keep Carl longer, but Carl was far too anxious, too overwhelmed. "Thank you," she said. "For meeting me. For ... for a shared hope. That someday my mother will see a way to relent. About the trade, I mean." She flushed, aware she was making no sense, and used her token to transfer back.

Lyren sighed. "And that is Carl."

"It's bad. Worse than I expected," Laban muttered. "Can't Jessan do anything in that family? He's been up there with Adam and David for years."

"Not always there. He also helps Darian Selenna a lot. In any case, Carl once admitted to me before I left that it was with the idea of bringing the dyr to Tahra that he went in the first place, but no matter how wise a dyranarya is, if the person utterly rejects the idea of needing guidance, there's an end to it."

Laban winced. "Yeah. I know. I forgot about that aspect. She'd never cooperate."

Right before they reached the Destination square, Wenwen

scampered up, and it struck both Laban and Lyren how much she looked like Carl, and Tahra, yet her expression would never have fit on either of their faces. Not that grin of triumph and hope. "How did it go? Will you write to her?"

"She doesn't like going behind your mother's back," Lyren said gently. "But still, you did a good thing, Wenwen. Please let me know if it gets worse. I'll try to come again."

"You're a good sister," Laban said. "I suspect her life is very lonely. I'm glad you and your siblings are watching out for her."

He smiled, and the two continued to the Destination square and transferred, leaving a very guilty Wenwen watching the tiles where they had been standing, and fiercely making resolutions in order to assuage that guilt.

5

Tahra had looked forward all autumn to going into the woods to hear the dawnsingers' music only sung at year's end, when the night was longest, and the sun was about to begin its slow journey southward again. But she had been so furious with herself for driving her children away — not just away, but apparently into useless playing as if they were five again — instead of preparing to do their part in bringing Everon back to peace and plenty, that she had forced herself to stay home and work.

There was always work. Too much work. But her vision of the Delieth family working together to see to the kingdom's needs had never come to pass, and she knew that much as she wanted to blame Detlev for that, too, it was her own doing. None of her children except Jessan had been tainted by Detlev. At least she had managed that much to their benefit.

She was so alone. Oh, Clair kept writing to her, offering a visit and inviting her to Mearsies Heili, but Tahra would never go there again, now that there was peace. She could not forgive Clair for permitting that villain in her home, when it would have been the easiest way to get rid of him. She hadn't even needed to dirty her own hands. Just forbid him the kingdom, so that the Host could take their own back again. But Clair had not done it. She had not only let that villain come and go freely, but when it turned out that Siamis had been lying all along — was not Detlev's enemy at all — it was all pretense, Clair had not only accepted him, but spent days in his company.

Could her former allies not see the truth? That if Detlev and his get lied about something so important, that they would keep lying? Instead Clair shadowed that Siamis so continually that Tahra wouldn't be surprised, now that Clair had finally done her duty and released that cursed Child Spell, to find her married to that soft-spoken, ever smiling Siamis.

Disgusting.

And so Tahra maintained a polite distance, claiming that work kept her from socializing. Which was true. There was always too much work. But she could trust no one else to do it correctly. Except Carl, she reminded herself. Out of seven, Tahra at least had one who thought correctly, and was not afraid of work.

New Year's Week passed, and Tahra had only memory of former Raisings of the Sun to fall back on. Another weary year began, and another weary tread into duty — though why was Carl so absent-minded? She kept staring into space. Tahra didn't trust that tiny smile, as if she'd hidden her dessert for later, as she used to do when she was small.

At first, all Carl could think of was her incandescent happiness.

Not since the day before Jessan left for Detlev's faraway academy on their birthday, had Carl been so utterly happy as she was the first week of the new year. It was a rich happiness, a joy all the more intense for having to keep it strictly to herself.

She'd intended have fun during her brief escape to Dtheldevor's island. She'd planned to talk to adventuring children, and to see the things they brought back from their travels, but she scarcely carried away any clear images of the place from her short tour. Her mind, and her heart, bloomed with the memory of Laban.

His reality had transcended all those brief, stolen memory-images with a sweeping intensity for which she had been totally unprepared, leaving her breathless with longing. This giddy feeling, as if her entire body had filled with stingless bees made of light, had to be love. She was nearly twenty, and she was in love. Actually, she knew she had been in love since she was small, though she would never tell anyone that. Of course they'd scoff, saying it was simply a crush. Crushes were practice for real love, the way scrawling your letters on paper lined by a teacher was practice for writing.

But this feeling was the same, just … bigger. Real. Complex in all the senses. She'd kept her hands at her sides because of the yearning to touch his hair, to discover if it was as soft as it looked. To get close enough to see how long his eyelashes were. To sniff his scent. Of course he'd smell good. How could anyone that handsome, with a voice a rich and smooth as a cream dessert, not smell good? She wanted to know how he smelled after a bath, and after he'd been riding, and when he was warm under the covers.

She wanted to taste him. His lips, that little hollow in his throat. Behind his ear. His eyelids. And go from there. And why not? She was almost twenty — a month away — and she had had her courses for five years. This was *normal!* Mad had been kissing girls for at least two years, and she was younger than Carl!

Except Tahra-Mama would not see it as normal at all.

Carl tried to govern herself strictly, only letting herself think of him at night when she was alone. But memories would obtrude during the day. Like when the word "trade" came up. She'd hear it in his voice, not Tahra-Mama's, and there he would be again, vivid against that low gray sky, moving with such easy grace, his head bent slightly as he listened to her bleating like a sheep instead of talking like a grown person ought to talk. But he'd listened, and spoke, as if she had responded like a grown woman, responsible, heir to a crown.

He was *kind.*

A week of cherishing those secret memories turned into two, broken by her mother's sharp voice, and the growing question in her eyes. Carl *had* to pay attention when they were in the Study!

At least mealtimes were easier with the sibs there. But that did not last. As Firstmonth measured itself out in storms and work and care, bleak and cold and snow-silent outside, care-worn patience inside, Tahra-Mama's long looks became more steady. Her comments about two people left to carry the burden that would be so much easier if everyone did their share, got less general. One moment they'd be sitting at the table, and Carl would relish having them all together, then quick as a cat flicked its tail there'd be looks, and tightened shoulders, and utensils dropped with a clatter. One by one they'd slip away, leaving Carl alone with Tahra-Mama, who remained where she was until the bell, then down fork and march to work. Same every. Single. Day.

The sibs lingered through the month, the twins exercising

the horses in the stables, Madelon Elise surrounded by books and scrolls, writing constant notes to Aurora in Mearsies Heili, and FJ running about with a group of boys from the city who also loved long, complicated games that took days to act out and required half the capital as their domain. Wenwen lurked around the most, sometimes asking, "Can I get you anything, Carl? Some hot apple tart with cream? Some chocolate?"

"I'm not hungry," Carl would say. "Thank you. Your company is all I need." Which wasn't true. What she truly needed was Wenwen to want to help with the endless tasks Tahra-Mama felt necessary — a good ruler was ever vigilant, for tiny mistakes overlooked soon turned into peculation and corruption. But if Carl even so much as glanced toward her desk, Wenwen would slink away.

The best times happened after dinner, when Tahra-Mama closed herself in with the day's reports from every holding brought by the scribe on duty at the desk, and Carl was free, the sibs closed around her, and it was almost like the good times in childhood.

Wenwen saw the tension gradually growing, and bitterly resented how their mother soured everything. Still, how could they all be so selfish? FJ was staying out, playing longer and longer. The twins got chased back by Cousin Carinna, who said right in front of Tahra-Mama, "We'd welcome you in Knights training, boys."

Tahra-Mama looked up in hope, until the twins sidled away. Oh, maybe someday, but not now, not with it so boring, having to inspect roads — which the Road Guild was supposed to be doing — and making sure traffic flowed correctly, and Cousin Carinna's long, sober horse face in the command center, relaying constant orders from Tahra-Mama about vigilance along the borders lest Laban's criminals pollute Everon. The patrols had to write reports every night over what exactly they had seen, which Cousin Carinna read before Tahra-Mama saw them, in order to compare overlapping fields of vision, to make certain no one was letting anyone from Wnelder Vee by.

Both twins felt that the Knights had gotten boring since old Grandpa Roderic died and Cousin Carinna was appointed commander by Tahra-Mama, who expected reports every day. It was just like lessons at home, a dreary atmosphere of drudgery and scolding.

Wenwen didn't blame them for wanting to escape by

riding just to ride. But that didn't fix things for Carl. And this winter seemed extra dreary. Felt like it was going to last forever.

She woke one morning thinking, of course! Her idea had been such a success before, why not fix up something similar, to surprise Carl? She scampered into Mad's room and yanked her awake, gabbling ideas as fast as she could.

Mad rubbed her eyes, then sighed. "Yes, I've noticed that it's getting harder to cheer Carl up. But Wenwen, you can't send her away again. It's a miracle Carl's excuse didn't get discovered. 'Visiting relations.'"

"She couldn't bring herself to lie, and both Lyren and Laban are relations. If ten generations away."

"Exactly. All it would take is Tahra-Mama asking which relations, and then going to question them about Carl. *Is she happy? What did she talk about? You can tell me, I'm her mother, and if everyone is honest there is no need for secrets.*" Mad mimicked Tahra-Mama's voice. "You know she would, especially if it reached her ears Carl had gone twice."

"How about a … a surprise of some kind? Maybe not her going anywhere, but them coming here?"

Mad rolled her eyes. "What do you think would happen if Lyren turned up here? Laban turning up is unthinkable. The Knights have orders to *kill* him, Wenwen, if he gets caught in the border ward. You and the boys go to Dthel Rendm, and see Lyren or Laban and think it's fun to get round Tahra-Mama. This is dead serious, because Tahra-Mama makes it dead serious. What would happen to any of the Knights if Tahra-Mama found out they'd seen Laban and didn't do it? And it's not just them. You put the servants at risk. No one gets past them unnoticed, which makes them complicit."

"How about a … a thing, then? A letter, or something?"

Mad was going to scoff, but then tipped her head. "Letter writing has the same problems. But a little keepsake? Actually, that might work. Something pretty. Carl loves pretty things. One of my best memories of Carl is when Lyren gave her some ribbons a million years ago. Carl was always wearing them, and even petting them, until they got ragged. But I'll wager you anything she's got them tucked up in a little box somewhere. I remember how she loved looking at them and feeling the silk. Tahra-Mama pays no attention to decorations. All she likes is dawnsinger music."

"Can you write to Lyren, so she can send me a transfer token?"

Mad scowled. "I will this once, but it's time for you to get your own notecase. I know you didn't want one because Tahra-Mama would pester you to report on what you are doing and where you're going, but Wenwen, you're practically fifteen. Surely you can keep it from her. She doesn't know that Aurora and I still use our beige papers that Siamis gave us during the war. We'll keep using them till the magic wears out."

Wenwen agreed, promised, and a day later she was in Fortnyal Roth, her idea cascading out. Lyren (who transferred back from Sarendan, where she was visiting) and Laban both listened, and then looked at each other.

"It's true," Lyren said. "She values beauty so deeply. I think that's what brought us together, because we both feel the same way about a world filled with beauty."

Laban tossed down his pen over his half-written letter. "I'm all for it, if it won't get her into any trouble. Pick something you know she'll like, and send it with Wenwen here. I'll replace it," he added. "If it's yours."

Wenwen shook her head. "It's got to be from you. Even if Lyren picked it out, she was so happy after that visit at New Year's. Much happier than Lyren's visits. You're a hero to her."

Laban grimaced at that. The idea made him uncomfortable, but on the other hand, what harm in it? Poor Carl, so thin and anxious, why not give her something to hold onto in that barren life? "Tell you what. I'll write a small note, which she can then burn. It'll give meaning to the thing. Go pick the right thing, Lyren."

She flitted off, and soon returned with a little carved statue in hand.

"Oh, I remember that," Laban exclaimed. "I bought that from an Everoneth, actually, before we broke camp."

"Exactly," Lyren said. "It's something you picked, even if it was meant as an excuse to give him money. But you picked it."

Wenwen nodded vigorously. "If it came from someone in the resistance, that will matter to Carl."

Laban recollected Carl's still little figure standing so stiffly, thin fingers pressed to her heart as if to hold in a world of emotion too strong to bear. She'd been very tightly shielded, poor little soul. "What should I write? I don't know Carl. What do 'heroes' write?"

"We should ask Rel," Wenwen declared, but Lyren raised a hand. "Something that makes it clear that Carl matters. Not as a princess or heir to Everon or a possible conduit or to Tahra, but in herself."

6

arl worked hard to bridge the growing gulf between Tahra-Mama and the sibs, and she sometimes succeeded, though never with Lyren's ease and grace. There were so many conversational dangers! So many times, though the sibs obviously tried to look ahead for possible shoals, the talk would rush too quickly, a spring stream, only to suddenly falter into covert glances or stuttered words, then sudden silence and the dreaded Look from Tahra-Mama, her mouth pressed in a white line. After that, the tedium of stilted, painfully careful conversations, on subjects that interested no one. Carl knew—and she feared that Tahra-Mama probably suspected—that the real conversation went on mind-to-mind between those who could.

Wenwen hoarded the gift at the bottom of her trunk containing her summer clothes, trying to figure out when would be best to give it to Carl. Or should she leave it in Carl's room, to be a real surprise?

Half the decision was made for her when, a week before month's end, Mad got into a fight with Tahra over what exactly happened at the Dei manor in Imar when Norsunder's Host of Lords was defeated.

Tahra, so scrupulous about facts, was certain that her memory was always correct: Marga, that mysterious figure, had defeated the Host with a wave of her hand. She still wondered why Marga hadn't troubled herself much earlier, but hadn't asked Erai-Yanya, whose interest was so clearly in the magic end of things. Was there uncertainty? But Erai-Yanya had been very definite about Marga suddenly appearing, raising her arms, and a magic-laden rain sweeping away all the Host's terrible wards.

Mad cut in, "You keep saying that, and it isn't true."

"My memory is particularly clear, and I know Erai-Yanya to be truthful."

"But *you* weren't there! And Erai-Yanya got it from Hibern, who was only there at the very end! She says herself she didn't see everything!"

"You were not there, either. And before you interject her name, neither was Aurora."

"But CJ and the others *were* there, the *entire time*. And I heard them talk about it, when I was in Mearsies Heili last. That's one degree away, Mama, whereas you are at least two degrees away, if not more, which is how you heard a garbled version. Detlev was *absolutely* there. He killed that horrible Efael, who was trying to kill CJ."

Tahra sneered. "Then the great Detlev was in two places at once? Because Hibern insists that he and his criminals were hiding in a lake somewhere, supposedly fighting the Host by magic. I think CJ was so distraught she imagined things. You know how she exaggerates when she wants to make a good story. Or, more likely, Detlev did something to her mind. As he did to Carlael Lirendi, King of Colend, and who knows how many others?"

Mad slammed her fists down at either side of her plate. "I will write to CJ and ask her to come here and tell you."

"Don't bother. Whether she writes or speaks, the lies will still be the same."

"Oh-h-h-h, you're impossible!" Mad jumped up and ran out.

Tahra-Mama kept eating, though Carl, and Wenwen on the other side of the table noticed a tremble in her fingers. Since she was still eating, they had to remain, and so the interminable meal stretched endlessly until the hour bell clanged, and as always Tahra-Mama stood immediately, which released them.

Wenwen hurried back to her room, leaving poor Carl to try to placate Tahra-Mama. She was best at it, Wenwen reasoned. When she passed Mad's room, she saw her older sister inside flinging things into her carryall.

"You're leaving?"

"If I stay it'll only get worse. She won't even listen to the truth. That's when I have to get out."

"But if you leave, the boys will surely go."

"I wouldn't stop them even if I could. There's been enough controlling going on." Mad's voice shook.

She was gone by the time Wenwen woke up, and the boys vanished by midday, even though the weather was terrible. One look at Carl's face at dinner, and Wenwen knew it was time for the gift.

After dinner, when Carl went off with Tahra-Mama, Wenwen dug out the statue and the note, slipped into Carl's dark room to leave it there, and then lurked near the door to her room to wait, as on the other side of the palace, Carl's head throbbed. If only their mother didn't get so angry. Her anger was so cold and yet smoldering, so unending. It seemed to burn away every other emotion from everyone around her.

Carl's head hurt so much that when the evening bell finally donged, releasing her, she retreated to the relative safety of her room without lighting a candle or lamp. She threw off her gown and climbed straight into bed.

She rose after a night of broken, restless sleep. She lit a candle, for the dawn was bleak indeed, and as she went to get a fresh robe, an anomaly caught on the periphery of her vision. She turned toward her desk in the far room, and stared.

A carving of a bird just taking flight sat in the middle of her desk. It was simple but beautiful, the warm golds and reds in the wood grain sweeping back along the bird's wings. Her breath caught.

Reverently picking it up, she examined it with wonder, then turned it over and over, admiring it from every angle and loving the smooth grain under her fingers. She sniffed it, breathing deeply of the resiny wood smell. The bird, the wood's colors, reminded her of warm autumn days.

The delight was so surprising it was some time before she considered where it might have come from. Wenwen? Perhaps even her mother? No, neither of them had shown a taste for this kind of thing.

Then her gaze returned to the desk, and this time she saw the square of folded paper that had been under the statue's base.

She picked up the paper, and immediately her heartbeat accelerated. The paper was heavy, smooth, expensive — somehow masculine.

She opened it.

Inside, in a strong, bold, flourishing hand:

*This year began well because we met as
friends. L.D.*

Only the initials, but it had to be from Laban Dei. Running her fingers over the words — where his own hand had brushed as he penned them — her entire body glowed with joy.

And fear.

How did he get it to her? Tahra's magical wards prevented his crossing the border by magic transfer, and any spell he might perform would set off an alarm. And he knew it. Someone had slipped into the palace to put this on her desk, risking Tahra-Mama's wrath if discovered. Wenwen, of course.

She went to Wenwen's room, but paused when she heard light snoring. Wenwen was not an early riser even at the best of times.

Carl retreated to her room again. Her fingers shook as she set the statue on a side table in her bedroom, which her mother almost never entered. The note she slid into the heavy velvet of her bodice, to be worn all day next to her heart.

Consciousness of the note's proximity made her step light as she proceeded downstairs, and eased her through breakfast, though Tahra-Mama's mouth was the white line, for the boys were gone as well as Mad. The note made it easier to face the prospect of court. Bad weather or good, Tahra-Mama sat on the throne on court days, and if no one came, she worked. They worked.

Despite the weather, a petitioner was already waiting, a representative of the cloth merchants. The man was very angry. He had no Dena Yeresbeth, and his angry thoughts bombarded Carl, despite his humble attitude and strictly modulated voice.

"Your majesty," he said, bowing, and a bow to Carl. "Princess. I am here not as representative of just the Ferdrian weavers, but I have been asked to speak for those whose livelihood was once delivery, and for our treaty-bound cotton merchants in the south. We need wool. Everon does not produce enough wool to enable us to do the business we've done in the past. You know that our cotton-wool is justly famed all up and down the continent. There is no smoother, softer weave, for we've secrets that have belonged to our weavers for centuries. But the weavers cannot earn their bread if they cannot get wool—"

"Have you," Tahra cut in, "obtained samples from other lands? I have here the receipt for the crown funds given your guild for an exploratory trip."

The man ran his hand through his graying hair. "We found good wool in one place, but we could not meet their price, for they already have a sharp demand. Another place had plenty of wool, but it was inferior in quality. We did find good wool, and plentiful, but it turned out to be imported from Sarendan, at the far end of the Sartoran continent! We can't afford the cost of shipping, or the time it would take, to order wool from Sarendan!"

"Find out the cost," Tahra said. "The crown will cover the difference."

Carl watched the man fight to keep his face under control. His thoughts hammered at her: his realization that he ought to express gratitude, that a mistake here would be a disaster for everyone who trusted him ... the grief he felt for betraying his cousins in Wnelder Vee whose wool he desperately wanted, who desperately needed his business—and only two days' easy cart ride from the border!

Carl's palms began to dampen, and she pressed them together.

And again, as uncanny as always, Tahra's narrowed gaze went from his face to Carl's hands, and then back to the guild speaker.

"You would not," she said softly, "dare to come before me and flout my orders against dealing with the Norsundrian shit-eater who has claimed the throne to the north?"

The man blinked at the vile language; the shock of her mother's thick rage smacked Carl right in the heart.

"But he is not a Norsundrian—" the man began helplessly. "During the war, they fought—"

"This war." Tahra's voice sharpened. "The last, they killed half our people. More. Have you forgotten? I have not, I assure you. Every single day I remember my dead mother, my brother. My father. I will *never* dishonor their memory by dealing with the murdering soulsuckers who ended their lives."

"But—"

"So he *says* he's an ally. How convenient. One day, when it seemed they could get more, they suddenly became allies. And one of these days they will revert back. You'll see," Tahra stated, her voice strident now. "In the meantime, no, I do not have pity for the people of Wnelder Vee. If they are stupid enough to remain living under that stinking soul-rotted liar and murderer, they are welcome to him. But we will not defile ourselves by dealing with them."

The man was silent, looking down.

"Find out the difference. I will pay it. Find your wool, do business. But never again do I want to hear any reference to the betrayers of our sacred dead. For that," Tahra finished on a low note, "is treason."

The man's face blanched. He bowed, awkward, his neck and shoulders tight, and withdrew.

Carl forced herself to breathe, and then to wipe her sweaty palms down her gown.

Tahra said, "We have four more appointments, but I doubt they will be met, not with this weather. All three can as easily be resolved by scribe desk. Now, here's what we will do about the copper question..."

Carl stood by in silence while her mother dealt with the remaining crown affairs. It was a day that would ordinarily have weighed like boulders on her spirit, for she disagreed with the basis for Tahra-Mama's decisions: all these torturous and expensive side-routes were the result of the embargo against Wnelder Vee. The only ones who benefitted were wagoneers. But this time Carl did not feel the cost of suppressing her instincts, good sense, and emotions. The letter was a powerful anodyne, enabling Carl to nod serenely as her mother hectored her yet again about the necessity to wall off the villain and the weak idiots who permitted him to rule them.

Carl thought of her bird, symbol of friendship. Of freedom. Secondmonth passed.

Every day on waking, Carl turned her head so that her bird would be the first thing she saw on opening her eyes. Before going back north to Dthel Rendm, Wenwen had admitted to bringing it, which added to its preciousness. Carl loved the idea that her sister and Lyren and especially Laban would care enough to find this way of making Carl's life better.

Carl was sorry to see her youngest sister go, but Tahra-Mama's sharper and sharper hints about selfishness and ignorance and lack of education befitting a princess, and above all, duty, duty, duty, had driven Wenwen into retreat.

However, Wenwen had listened to Mad and surrendered

some of her hoarded earnings so that Mad could get her a golden notecase, rather than risk using palace funds set aside for the royal children — which always had to be accounted for to Tahra-Mama, right down to each ducket, which might get you a very small baked apple on the street.

Wenwen assuaged her guilt in abandoning Carl by writing to her often, though Carl, from habit, said very little about herself. She repeated local news and asked about what Wenwen was doing.

At least at first.

Thirdmonth arrived. Carl was again alone with her mother; even Aunt Merry was gone, having traveled to another land to study some arcane aspect of tapestry-making there.

For a short time the weather warmed, bringing a succession of bright days in a world of melting ice, but then the sky closed over again, bringing sleet alternating with rain. There was no walking out. Carl's spirits dropped dangerously low, except when she could be alone in her room, but those times were rare, for the emphasis on duty seemed to increase. Wearing duty: no decision-making, only the necessity to listen to her mother go through reports line by line, explaining what Carl should think and why, then she was required to recopy ledgers so that she would really, truly understand the power of exact numbers. Then she must stand at her mother's side and listen.

Her notes in response to Wenwen got shorter, until she ceased to mention herself at all, as the days dragged drearily to the 30th of Thirdmonth. By the 31st, Wenwen was worried. Should she go back? Except what could she really *do?*

Another present seemed the obvious answer, since the first one had worked so well. And here Carl's and Jessan's birthdays were coming on the 32nd. She hunted for her pen to write to Lyren, then remembered that Lyren was still in Sarendan. She paced from the oak tree to the overlook as she thought it all out. She did not know Laban's sigil, but she was sure Julian did. She didn't dare use Tahra-Mama's scribe (whose only purpose was to receive and sort reports and letters, and then send answers after Tahra-Mama had written them) to receive the gift, but she could send it to the scribe desk in the city. She knew that the scribe guild kept people's letters private, no matter who asked. Even rulers.

Yes! That was the way to do it. And if Laban was willing to

send something, the person to send it to would be Ansa Sandrial, Carl's maid. Ansa was fervently loyal to Carl. If Laban was willing at all, he'd surely pay the expense of transfer, and all Ansa would have to do was get the message, and the gift, and put them in Carl's room.

She wrote a note to Julian. Then she paced some more, an endless hour or two until she felt the weird little tap that meant a letter. It was short, no more than *I'll see to it, LD*, and his sigil, but that was all she needed.

She went off to join the game forming in the lower cavern, brimming with the satisfaction of a job well done.

The 32nd dawned bleak and miserable, the night having brought a brief blizzard and the morning a hard frost. Carl woke to Jessan's contact; he was far away, working with his dyra-companions in jails, trying to fix lives one at a time. Carl hid all her emotions from him with the expertise of years of practice.

She rose a little later than usual, for today she and Jessan turned twenty. Twenty! It seemed impossible, but then ten had seemed like such a huge number.

Oh, if only the twenties would bring …

She dared not form any other thought than "change." She dressed swiftly, thoroughly tired of her winter things. If winter was going to drag on forever, as it showed every sign of doing, then she might as well throw out everything in her trunk and order new. Except she couldn't do that, because all those clothes had plenty of wear left, and how would she account for the expense, when the palace was as straitened as the kingdom?

Already weary, she walked to her study to look over the day's work—then halted at the sweet scent perfuming her room. She stared, stunned, at the armful of white roses lying on her desk, the thorns expertly removed.

Roses. A gesture of breathtaking extravagance, for they had to have come from very, very far away.

The scent of summer was stronger than that of the usual wet stone, a scent as beautiful as the exquisite blossoms. Carl gathered them to her breast and buried her face gratefully in the soft petals, joy suffusing her—until the crackle of paper struck her heart with warning.

She looked up.

Tahra-Mama stood there, having picked up the waiting square of paper that had lain under the roses. "What's this?"

"Mama—" Carl began, reaching for it.

Tahra jerked it away. "I have no secrets from you, and you had better have none from me. Secrets mean guilt. Is one of your siblings grudging me again? Surely this isn't from Merry—"

Her fingers had unfolded the paper, and she paused, looking down. Then her eyes widened, and she flung the paper into the fireplace as if it had burned her. Then she spat on her hands, rubbing them on her over-robe, then spitting and rubbing again, desperately.

Carl stood mute, her arms still full of roses.

Tahra's eyes lifted, pupils wide and black with fury. Her gaze struck Carl like a sword to the heart.

"You knew. You *knew*."

She moved too quickly for Carl, who had never known physical violence, though she'd lived her entire life bolstering her spirit against the poison of violent emotion.

Tahra backhanded her across the face, hard enough to snap her head around. Carl staggered back, the roses scattering. The side of her head thunked on the corner of her desk, then her forehead struck the decorative molding on the seat of her chair. White lightning blinded her, and she fell gratefully into the dark.

7

Consciousness returned within a breath or two. Carl moaned, longing to slip back in the darkness, but instinct forced her eyes open. She sat up dizzily, and recoiled against the desk's leg when the buzzy weird sound resolved into her mother's harsh breathing. Carl squinted against the dizziness, and Tahra-Mama's jerky movements also resolved into intent as she kicked every rose and leaf and petal into the fireplace.

"Traitor," Tahra's voice thinned with rage. "*You*. Of all of them, lazy and selfish, not a *one* working for the good of Everon. I never expected *you* to be a sneaking, lying, vile, shit-souled traitor."

Grief, desolation, and finally anger broke free, at last. "Traitor only to your crazy hatred. I'm a traitor to crazy actions formed solely by hatred," Carl cried. "I'm a traitor to the crazy, hateful poison I'd thought only belonged to the likes of Norsunder. Which you, Mama, you *alone* are recreating all over again with all your *hate, hate, hate*."

Tahra whirled around to stare at her, her face blanched.

Carl stood up, the room spinning nauseatingly. Her lips felt like they belonged to someone else, as if they didn't fit right, and her knees had been replaced by water. Warmth trickled down one ear, from her nose, and the side of her mouth. Her vision blurred as the world swerved, checked, swerved, checked.

Tahra-Mama's face had gone impossibly pale.

"Want a knife?" Carl cried, lurching dizzily to the desk,

where she scrabbled for the slim opener she'd always used to break seals. "To finish the *traitor*? Do it. Do it, Mother, for it will end the pain my life has become." She couldn't grasp the golden opener — her fingers didn't work either — so she flung her hands wide, noticing with increasingly detached consciousness that somehow they were covered with blood.

"Carl," Tahra whispered. "I am so sorry —"

She stepped forward, and Carl flinched back, stumbling against her desk.

Tahra recoiled as if she'd been slapped. One step, two, and then she whirled round, her robe flaring, and stalked out.

Still dizzy, Carl made her way to the fire, and saw that nothing was left of the note that had come with the roses. Nothing left of the roses, either.

She turned away, sick with pain and remorse and the aftereffects of her rage. How would they live together now? Carl looked ahead into a torturous future of Tahra's recriminations, and for a long breath she envisioned picking up that letter opener and plunging it into herself to end this anguish in her heart.

But that would hurt Jessan. And the sibs. If she was dead, there would be no buffer between Tahra and the family. The country.

She roused herself, opened her window, scooped up a handful of fresh snow from the windowsill and pressed it against her aching face. The cold added to her aches, but the bleeding stopped, and then the aches numbed.

She was still there when Ansa Sandrial found her, and burst into tears. "The princess was so sure you'd be happy, and I was so careful…"

Carl didn't hear the rest of the maid's apology, though the observant part of her mind noted the solving of the little mystery: the maid was part of the gift conspiracy. Somehow that made it even nicer. Which princess? Oh, it had to be Wenwen.

Carl ceased to think at all as gentle but insistent fingers guided her back to her warm bed. She didn't mean to sleep. There was so much to do. She closed her eyes against the vertigo, and consciousness gave way to sleep.

Her dreams were strange, blown through by white snow. But they were not bad dreams. Much as she hated winter, there was no threat in this dreamland snowscape; instead, a message of comfort blanketed her spirit and eased her heart. She sensed a familiar presence: Jessan: *Sleep, Carl. Sleep and heal. I'm on my way.*

She slept.

When she woke, it was to Ansa and her cousin standing by her bedside. Carl's face, her head, everything ached, but a vague sense of emergency forced her to open her eyes and struggle to sit up. "Am I needed?" Her voice seemed to come from someone else — except it was too loud, as if one ear had become an echo cavern.

"Yes, Princess," Ansa whispered, her light blue eyes puffy from weeping.

Alarm tingled more insistently. Carl sat up and swung her feet down. The room lurched, then steadied. She drew in a shaky breath. Jessan? Was he here? Not yet, or she'd know.

"A hot bath awaits," the cousin said with quiet firmness.

The Sandrials had always served the Delieths, gaining moral ascendance when it came to the virtues of everyday living: they told her to take a bath so Carl rose obediently, and gratefully slipped into the blissfully hot water, which was scented with summer herbs. Listerblossom appeared on a side tray as she soaked. Its warmth suffused her with healing energy, and she felt measurably better when she climbed out and dressed. Except her face still hurt.

She avoided her mirror, for she did not want to see the damage. She walked out of her bedroom to find more servants — Jenel Sandrial herself, the head steward, plus the master herald, and even the cook's assistant — waiting. "What is amiss?" she asked.

They exchanged glances.

"Princess Carl," the master herald said, slowly, his eyes lowered. "Your mother the queen has disappeared."

The cook's assistant said in a quick, nervous voice, "I was talking to Tam of the stable, and coming back, when I saw her walk out into the storm. Saw it myself. No coat, no hat."

"Wait. Please. Let me search." Carl sank down onto one of the hallway benches, and put her throbbing head into her hands. "If she's not shielded I can find her."

She sent her mind out, seeking her mother's mental signature. It was always a dull red, imperfectly shutting away a furnace of anger and longing for "justice." Everyone had come to hate the word almost as much as "duty."

The storm was not empty. Surprised, Carl encountered a

myriad of swirling, dancing motes of comforting shades of pale blue and green and violet and gold. "Geres." She was not aware of speaking out loud.

There, in the center of the greatest group, she found her mother. Her mental signature was diminishing rapidly — not in intensity, but in distance. She looked up at the cook's assistant. "Where was she going?"

"Toward the woods."

Of course no one would dare stop her. Carl considered what she had sensed. Tahra-Mama had always had good relations with the dawnsingers in the local woodland. She had no doubt appeared among them, soaked through, and they had conferred with their more magical cousins north of Wnelder Vee.

Oh, let that be so. Perhaps there, for a time, human cares would no longer plague her. She might find the peace and healing that Carl had not been able to give her, in spite of all her striving.

Carl looked up, but did not see the waiting faces. The compassionate gesture, the patience of these beings who must have watched over Mersedes Carinna's unhappy daughter all these years, unlocked Carl's grief at last, and she buried her face again in her hands. "She's alive, and I believe that she is safe." She surrendered to the tears she'd hitherto never permitted herself to shed.

By nightfall, Jessan had used farsense to find the rest of the sibs one by one. Mad arranged for magic transfer through the Mearsieans. In Ferdrian's royal palace, as Carl slept off the terrible headache, the siblings gathered in the old playroom.

Wenwen crossed her arms, saying tearfully, "Don't blame me. Carl was so happy when I arranged for her bird statue, and it was her *birthday*..." She choked on a sob.

Jessan lounged against the battered old desk, strangely familiar and unfamiliar to Wenwen. His long, narrow face, dark gray eyes, dark hair — those were all familiar. The strength in his lean body, that wasn't. He'd always been thin, like Carl, stringy and gawky; now the way he moved, with controlled strength, reminded Wenwen a little of Laban. So odd, how he and Carl were exactly the same age, but he looked older than twenty, and she looked younger.

He said, "Come, there's no value in blaming one another."

"Why not?" Mad turned on him, her arms also folded. "It's the truth. Not any one of us, but all of us. We all left Carl alone with Tahra-Mama, and we knew it was horrible, but we all explained it away to ourselves, and made it worse."

"I wish they'd tell us what happened," Sedron mumbled.

"I saw all those bruises on her face when I looked in her room. Did Tahra-Mama take a stick to her? Push her down the stairs?" Glenn chimed in, as always adding to Sed's comment.

Jessan said, "Doesn't matter now."

"But it does," Mad stated. "I have to know."

"Why?" Wenwen spoke now. "Will it erase what happened?"

Jessan sent her a brief glance, but she felt his approval.

"Of course not," Mad said, prowling the room. "Don't be dense. I want to know because I want to feel it the way she did, so I can share it, and maybe lessen her pain. If not, at least maybe I can expiate my own guilt."

"Mad, that's a good thought," Jessan said. "But Carl's not going to talk about whatever happened with Tahra-Mama. Try to understand how Carl thinks, something we've all helped shape. To talk about it is to relive it, not relieve it. And to see you suffer would increase her own pain, not ease it. Her whole life has been one of protection. Of us, of Tahra-Mama. That doesn't change overnight. Let it be."

Mad sighed. "All right. But from now on, every time I look at her poor face it's going to be a blow to my spirit. And I know the servants are talking."

Wenwen shuddered. She'd caught from Ansa Sandrial a horrific memory of Carl's blood-smeared face and hands, her eyes so expressive of perplexity and anguish.

"The servants have always talked." FJ shrugged. "They know more about us than we do. Can't be helped. And why should it? That's part of the bargain. If they spend their lives taking care of us, then they've the right to comment on the play, because it affects them, too. It's like we're on stage, there for them to laugh over when we act like twits."

That was the way Wenwen felt, but she was surprised to hear it from her brother. Had his travels made him see how birth-titles had all the solidity of water, too?

"Anyway," Glenn added, "if the others get too cruel, the

Sandrials will muzzle them before Carl finds out."

Jessan said, "You all knew that if there was a problem, you ought to find me."

"Where?" Mad asked in a goading voice, hands on her hips.

Jessan answered in a calm voice, as if the question had been a real one, underscoring how much he meant it. "The scribe desk works at Curtas's House. And if you need me fast, through any of the mages. They all know how to transfer someone, or a message, to Detlev's place, and he can always find us. I do try to monitor, but Carl shuts me out from the worst of it, which is why I depend on the rest of you."

"We did try," FJ put in. "You *know* we stayed for *weeks*."

"But Tahra-Mama kept going on about selfishness —"

" — and duty."

"Worse than ever." Sedron kicked a table leg over and over.

"Couldn't bear it," Glenn added.

"Did Tahra-Mama go back to interrogating you about what you were thinking and reading?" Jessan asked.

"Nope." Sed kicked the table leg so violently Mad, sitting cross-legged on the table, jumped. "Ooop. Sorry."

"That was all aimed at *me*," Mad said. "She knows the boys don't read unless they have to. You know what it's like. The only news outside of Everon that she would have let anyone talk about would have been Detlev's death — his or one of the others of his gang."

"We found out about Liere's husband being killed by accident," Wenwen added. "*You* know how stifling life here has been. You ran away from it! And FJ is right. It didn't really seem that we were helping, and you could see how it fretted Carl."

Mad added, rolling her eyes, "Every time —*every single time*—I saw Tahra-Mama she gave me the old guilt about a proper education in being useful, dutiful, and just. And I could bear that if in the next breath there wasn't a rant about treachery and evil. It upset Carl to no end. So I took off again."

"After a big ol' fight," FJ added with a grin.

"About the end of the war, of all things!" Mad rolled her eyes again.

Jessan said, "I'm going to stay to help as long as she needs me—and in case Tahra-Mama comes back. She will never lay a hand on Carl again. If she tries, I'll take Carl away."

"Good," Glenn said.

"But she won't stay," Mad muttered. "She goes on about duty as much as Tahra-Mama."

Jessan gave a nod. "I'm going to try to work on that, too. The rest of you, please try to urge Carl to have fun, listen to music, read, watch plays. To bring her out from under the shadow of strain she could not escape."

Rain drummed against the window. Wenwen looked around at her sibs. She sensed that they were all in agreement, and that felt right and good. She smiled. "Well, then, if we all stay and help, it should fix things, shouldn't it?"

Jessan surprised her by not smiling. Instead, he looked out the window into the rainy garden. "Not everything," he said.

8

arl woke to discover that her siblings had all come home again. Or, had come *back*, as Mad said. It hadn't been *home* since she first got to go to Mearsies Heili, which is where she wished she lived. But everyone was used to her grumbling, and paid little heed. She was here. Carl rejoiced when she sensed them all around her.

She dressed and winced her way to the breakfast table, her face hurting at every step. At first she braced for the storm of questions she did not know how to answer, but none came. As she sat down, finding Jessan in his old place, only taller than she remembered, she understood that Jessan would keep them from interrogating her.

Breakfast was the most cheerful in memory. Everyone was aware of that empty chair at the head of the table, but of the seven of them, only Carl struggled against the secret relief she felt.

Jessan saw that as well as the more overt relief from the others. There was at least nothing mean in the others, no cruel glee, which was his own unspoken concern. But they all continued to be good at heart, whatever else they were doing with their lives.

When the court bell rang, from sheer habit most of them jerked or jumped, then noticed no one else slamming down utensils and surging to their feet the way Tahra-Mama had. Carl did set her cup down, but she only said, "If someone comes to court, I think I had better be there. I'll merely say that Tahra-Mama has made a journey, and court is suspended for a time."

No one had anything to say to that. It was her business, as far as the younger sibs were concerned. Jessan said, "Would you like my company?"

Carl was going to exclaim *yes, very much*, except that his presence, with Tahra-Mama absent, might raise the kinds of questions she knew not how to answer.

And he saw it. "If you want me, I'll be in my room. I have some letters to write," he said, and that saved Carl having to say anything at all.

Three guild assistants turned up, avid with curiosity, and spurious excuses from their chiefs. One was the Wagoneers Guild Chief's assistant. Carl knew that gossip was already rife, but she was firm about the queen having departed on a trip. She could be firm because it was true. Tahra-Mama did go on a journey. Nothing else needed to be said.

All three assistants tried within the boundaries of court protocol to press, but they each found the skinny, mousy little princess unexpectedly firm. Not unlike her mother, in fact, though her voice was soft and calm and not stridently nasal. Still, the vision of pressuring her into some changes in case the gossip was true dwindled with each repetition of, "The queen is journeying." And vanished when, after the third repetition, she asked, "Shall I interrupt her with an emergency query from you?"

No, no, no, absolutely not! They retired in good order, and no one else turned up out of the nasty weather.

Carl left the icy throne room, pulling her outer robe more closely about her. She went straight to the Study from habit, then faltered outside the door. She was afraid to go in there, and yet no one else had more lawful reason.

She heard Jessan's voice behind her. "You can't be scared," he said.

"Not scared. I know it's correct for me to go in, but is it right?"

"It's both," he said. "Who else will see to any crown business that turns up?"

"But if I try to tend it. Or worse, make the wrong decision..."

"Wrong?" he asked as he entered first. "Or one she wouldn't like?"

Jessan going in first seemed to remove the incipient guilt, though when she looked at the desk with its perfectly lined up pens, the exactly squared piles of reports, and the rows of ledgers, a sense of oppression chilled her, and she stood uncertainly in the center of the room.

Jessan shut the door so they were alone. He pushed aside one of those precisely squared piles with an ease that caused Carl to catch her breath. "It's just paper," Jessan said.

"I know, but she hates anyone touching anything. You know how she is about mess. What she calls mess."

Jessan said, "But she is not here. And it's just paper."

Carl's gaze lifted to his face. It seemed somehow he was testing her. Or rather evaluating her. For what purpose? He'd never had any interest in ruling, and she would be very surprised if he'd suddenly began. He said, before she could speak, "You know the law as well as I do. Since Tahra-Mama isn't dead and didn't abdicate, it requires a wait of a year and a day before a new coronation."

"Which means there is a lot to do and I don't have the authority to do it," she said, her gaze ranging over those reports.

"That's not true. The authority is inherent: someone has to be queen, or king, until such time as another sort of government evolves."

"What other kind is there?" Carl asked. "History seems to be firm about the fact that some strong person always comes forward, and either kills or converts other contenders, and others follow. We have to hope the strongest is a good person." He acknowledged with a slight smile, and she rushed on, "I always thought Tahra-Mama would live forever, or at least till someone gave her grandchildren, and the throne and its decisions would bypass me."

"Assuming you are now queen. What would be your first move?"

"Oh, but she—"

"*Your* first move," Jessan asked.

Carl's breath hissed out as her eyes closed. Through her still-aching mouth she said, "I would rid the borders of those terrible wards. Or, find someone to do it. I know the basic magic, but Tahra-Mama has added to the wards so many times, I can feel that the magic is in an impossible tangle."

Jessan smiled. "That's a start."

She eyed him. "You know something."

He pinched his fingers between his brows, his narrow

forehead so much like hers furrowed. "It really is more difficult to try for detachment and emotional equilibrium when it's one's own family. But I'm going to feel my way." He dropped his hand. "Tahra-Mama is not coming back. She really did try to kill herself by walking out without a coat, and the dawn-singers stopped her. You know how much she loves them, and they respect her."

"Yes, yes."

"I asked Sveneric's help in tracing her, then Adam's, because we both reached … anomalies. Adam says that she's in the Fereledria, where she will remain. You know that there, time's measure is … strange. Adam says what that means is, if she heals enough to leave, it might be in generations. If she comes back at all. Her first step toward healing was to let every-thing go."

"Including us?" Carl tried to swallow past the boulder in her throat.

"They let her know we're all safe. And that we want her to heal."

Carl let out a shuddering sigh.

Jessan said, "A good part of her anguish was knowing how much she had estranged us all, and it was only getting worse as we grew and began to question and form our own opinions. I think her sense of self got bound up in the necessity to be right all the time, or what was her joyless labor for?"

"Yes," Carl whispered. "I see that."

"It doesn't make her right."

"I know."

"Good. You have the time to figure out how to go on, without being afraid of another attack, physical or emotional. I didn't know that your emotional damage was this severe," he added, his mouth long with pain. "The problem is, you're every bit as good as I am at shielding, and you hid it from me."

"Or you would have come back, and I couldn't bear it, the way she would accuse you of the 'taint' of Detlev every time you disagreed."

"Because of my friendship with Sveneric and Darian. I'd still have to come. But I would have listened better." His voice, though light, was not easy, and Carl intuited that he, too, hid things he thought might hurt her. But what could possibly hurt him when he'd gone to the life he wanted?

"Ah, we are here. And I must make it all work, for that's

my sense of responsibility. What shall we tell the sibs, and when?" she asked. "My instinct is to wait a bit. FJ won't be able to resist telling his friends in the city, and once he tells one, all Ferdrian will be in on the secret by nightfall. And we cannot tell the others but leave him out."

"Agreed," Jessan said. "What is the next step, then?"

Carl said, "I think I need time to truly believe that Tahra-Mama is not going to fly out at me in anger. Especially if I begin doing things the way I've longed to. I think I expect her to come at me partly from habit, but perhaps from guilt?"

"Of all of us, you've the least reason to be guilty," he said.

Carl shrugged. "From your perspective, perhaps. But I was the one she trusted most, as much as she could trust anyone but herself. Because I don't think it was seeing me bleeding all over that sent her into that storm, much as I wish to. Because that thought lets me see myself wholly as victim." And, unasked, she offered her memory of that morning.

They had shared thoughts and memories as children. The habit was still there, still easy, the more because each had learned mental boundaries, then control, once they understood that they were separate people. He saw only the incident, and though he intuited more, he merely said, "Ah. You said crazy."

"Yes. Knowing she hated how people used to call her crazy when she was small. I heard her telling Erai-Yanya, once. And Aunt Merry told me it was true. Grandpa and Grandma Dei also told me. No one else knew what to do with her insistence on counting steps, and keeping right turns the same number as left turns, and strictly regulating herself by the bells. Grandpa Dei said it was her way of establishing order, when so much had been so terrible during Henerek the Norsundrian's attacks when they were young. I knew it but I said the word anyway, over and over, not just once, and I think it acted on her like a last betrayal every bit as much as finding Laban Dei's initials on whatever he wrote for my birthday roses."

Jessan gave a slow nod. Then he said, "Nothing will ever *excuse* it. But there is an aspect that might help *explain* it. This is important, because I know that you are a lot like Tahra-Mama in being quick to lay blame. Though always on yourself."

"Go ahead."

"You lost control of your temper exactly once. Until now, you have always been on the receiving end of Tahra-Mama's tempests. You endured more angry rants, but you could not respond. And anger begets anger, even if it's not at the same target. Anger is poison, and it is contagious. You've endured it all your life, and did your best not to give in to it. Finally, you did. It does not make you evil. It does reveal you are human, with all the human frailties we are all subject to. But now you know what anger does. And if you become queen, you've *got* to remember what happened, because you and I and Wenwen in particular are a lot like Tahra-Mama in our single-mindedness when something matters."

Carl listened closely, her eyes wide and unblinking with the intensity of her focus. Finally, she whispered, "I see. Yes. I see. Have they taught you how to get rid of it, up on your mountain?"

"Same way anyone can, either let it go, or do something that helps you shed it. Some work. Others laugh. Some fight. Or build. The important part here is to learn to stop turning it on yourself as the safest target. It's no better than turning it on others. Especially if you have authority."

"Yes," she said again.

He waved a hand at the desk. "Here's another suggestion, and only a suggestion. Go ahead and read the reports, with an eye to how to proceed. You don't have to decide a thing right away. Right now you have the time. The weather is on your side, and the fact that no one outside of the dawnsingers and the Geres know that Tahra-Mama is not coming back any time soon. If ever."

Carl jerked her chin down in a nod, and moved to the chair. Her mother's chair, now her chair. Sitting down felt momentous, the first decision on her new road.

She swept her gaze over the neat piles, her fingers reaching automatically to tidy the one Jessan had pushed aside, then she looked up at him. "You said you'll stay?"

"For a time. As needed. Don't worry about my other tasks. I have a lifetime for those."

"What do you want to do? Do you want a part of governing, now that you know she's not coming back? You sound so assured. I think your training has made you much wiser than me."

"But these are things we study. If I were to try to tackle that stack of reports, I'd make a terrible mess." He raised both palms, pushing them toward the desk. "I think what I'm going to do is go through the city. Just listening. Talking now and then. Get a sense of things."

"Oh, that would be such a help! I always knew that no one was telling her what they truly thought, but only what they wanted her to hear. As I did."

"So did we all," Jessan said. "It was self-defense. But if you are to begin a new way, my suggestion is to enable real communication, though that will inevitably lead to arguments. I can help you with finding ways toward handling arguments that don't lead to relying on force."

"Oh, thank you."

"It's what I ought to do. When do you want to tell the sibs?"

"Not immediately. Let me read everything here, and think. But no later than tonight," she said. "Any longer, and it might create bad feelings. I don't want to start that way when they rallied so loyally. I might even be able to prevail on FJ to keep what happened to himself for a time, if I think of the right approach. One that isn't an accusation, or a demand for duty, trust, or loyalty. Those words, each so vital and so good, have..."

"Become tarnished. By the poison of anger. It helps me, at least, to think of anger as a thing, not as the person expressing it. Nobody wants to wake up angry, or at least so I believe. It happens over time."

"I believe that's true of Tahra-Mama," she said. "That's the way I will think of it."

"And that ought to do it," Hibern said, wringing out her hands. Actual sparks seemed to stream off, gone in an instant.

Carl had read only one stack before realizing she could not concentrate on those columns of numbers, so she wrote to Erai-Yanya—who had tutored Carl in the fundamentals of magic during the war—to ask if she knew how to get rid of those border wards, after explaining in a couple of short sentences what had happened. Not half an hour later, there was Hibern, wearing a senior mage robe over plain riding clothes, her long dark hair streaming over it.

"Oh, yes," was all she said. "I know exactly what to do." And did it.

Carl was not certain if it was the aches on the side of her

face or the magic that Hibern had done that made the air buzz and scintillate so weirdly. Or maybe it was the disappearance of those border wards around the palace and the more distant ones following the river that marked the border with Wnelder Vee.

"People can come and go freely now," Hibern said, her black eyes friendly but discerning. Yet she asked no awkward questions. "If you have any more magical needs, I'll be glad to help you."

"Ah, how much do such things cost?"

Hibern flashed a rare grin. "To you, nothing. I realize many thought your mother difficult, and you'd know best how successful she was as a ruler. But I met her when we were both girls, and I know she did her best. She did not have an easy time of it. I feel that I owe her this much."

Wenwen burst through the door, then stumbled to a stop. "I heard voices here in the Study, and I thought..." Her gaze flicked between Hibern and Carl, and her mouth worked like a fish out of water.

Hibern chuckled under her breath. "Wenwen, am I right? How time does race along. Last time I saw you, you were trying to walk from a chair to a cushion, and having a tough time of it. Carl, when you have a chance, Erai-Yanya would always welcome you in Roth Drael. Same with Arthur up at the archive." She vanished.

Wenwen gasped. "I didn't know what to say. I thought Tahra-Mama was back, and I thought I'd ..."

"Protect me. Thank you for the thought. Listen, will you tell the others we need to talk over dinner? Just us seven."

Wenwen seemed to swell at this important request. "On my way!"

Carl looked around the Study. She did not need to keep checking each total before entering it into a ledger. Numbers told all kinds of truths—she believed that much—but not all truths. She could trust Cousin Carinna to account for the Knights' expenditures. She could trust many, and if someone turned out to be untrustworthy, surely they would know whom she'd been trained by, and how fast she would be able to track down embezzlement. But really, wouldn't they all be better off spending their time on other things than counting bags of flour consumed at breakfast, lunch, and dinner, and who requisitioned a new pair of socks instead of darning the toes yet again?

Anyway, those wards were now gone. Detlev, or any of his people, could walk over the border with an army, and no one would know until they turned up in the city. The shabby city, impoverished due to stringent controls on trade that kept them back in the postwar years. Who would even want to take it over?

She swept up the daily reports and chucked them into the fire. The flames, usually sedately burning off the magic bound to the firesticks, surged at this new fuel, and smoke curled up from the withering pages, until all that was left was ash.

She turned away. However much resistance she faced, she was not going to continue the same rule. From her earliest memories she'd been drilled on awareness that there were consequences to every action. Much of her interior life had been taken up with imaginary conversations based on *what-if*, and *then*. Most of those had arisen out of frustration, imagining approaching her mother with "What if we did it this way instead?" The *then* was her mother invariably retorting with the usual rants. But the what-if-then habit was so deeply engrained that by dinner time, she had planned what to say, and responses to likely questions.

The siblings were more prompt than they had been for years. Carl had always seen their tardiness as reluctance, but she understood now that it had also been silent resistance, even though it never failed to bring reproof. Tahra-Mama had believed that a life ruled by the bells was a life well ordered.

Carl waited until the food had been served, and FJ said happily, "First time I got in here before the bell."

The twins laughed at that, Sed muttering, "Because you *like* beans," and Carl bit down on a comment until everyone was well into the meal, which was always cornbread and bean soup on Secondday.

As if thinking in parallel, Sed said, "I hate bean soup. Carl, is it going to get me thrown in prison if I want something else on Secondday? And if I want it later?"

Carl blinked, having not foreseen that. "I guess. But you ought to talk to Cook first. Meals need planning and cook time."

Sed looked mutinous, and Jessan said mildly, "Mother made it easy on the kitchen with her exact routine. Nothing went to waste."

Glenn muttered to his twin, "We'll look like walking turds

if we order dinner at breakfast, and breakfast at midnight."

Carl said, "I know you like bread, and muffins. Shall I talk to the kitchen about having muffins in the basket for any time you get hungry? Otherwise, shall we consult with Cook about having meals at different times?"

Sed brightened at that, and continued making a dinner entirely of cornbread.

When the meal was nearly finished, Carl said, "I have news about Tahra-Mama. We do." She nodded at Jessan. "He checked for me..." And she went on to tell them what he'd discovered.

At the end, everyone gazed at each other. The emotions in the room rioted, a whirlwind of rejoicing, triumph, relief, some anger, and a bit of regret. Then the storm of questions.

"Hold on," Jessan lifted his voice, when Carl couldn't get herself heard over the yammer.

Carl looked around at them. "What I would like to do is have everything prepared before we let the heralds pass the news, because the noise you just made, nobody hearing anything, and everyone talking at once, is probably what will happen in Everon when the word gets out. That means, I'm asking you to say nothing to anyone until I'm ready."

"How long?" FJ asked. "People keep coming at me."

"Soon is a good answer," Jessan said. "Or, pass them on to Carl or me."

Glenn had been scowling at his spoon. He looked up at Carl, his round face earnest. "Tahra-Mama always wanted us to join the Knights. But I hated it, because it meant writing those stupid reports, counting every tree I passed, and looking for friends of cousins on the Wnelder Vee side to shoot at."

"I'll have to speak to Cousin Carinna first. But I feel sure in promising there will be no more shooting," Carl said. "And no more writing those reports. Grandpa Dei trusted the Knights to be responsible, just as his forebears did. Tahra-Mama seemed to think those reports would be a help to Cousin Carinna in taking command of the Knights —"

"Which she didn't want to do," Mad interrupted.

" —which she didn't want, but she did her duty. Anyway, if she doesn't object, she can return to the weekly briefing that I remember Grandpa making."

Sed slammed his glass down, his grin wide. "I'm joining, then!"

"And me," Glenn added, to no one's surprise.

Carl smiled within. Tahra-Mama had always wanted one of the two to inherit command of the Knights. It was far too early to predict that would happen, but this was a step toward something she would have favored.

"I can stay, and do some scribe work for you," Mad offered. "I love scribe work, but not copying reports of numbers."

"Have you had any scribe training?" Carl asked.

Mad's gaze slid away. "Yes. Here and there. Well, mostly with Aurora, who got started on it keeping the log for Puddlenose aboard his ship. But that's because there were no lists of numbers or calculations. I know how to do that. Numbers were our earliest thing. You all know that. I hate it."

"Me too."

"And me."

"Me too!" Wenwen looked around. "What's there for me to do?"

Carl said, "You're fourteen. You don't have to declare your entire future right now. But I could use help with..." Her gaze moved around the room, then she had it. "Helping to make our home a little nicer? One thing I know well is the treasury numbers, and until I can cancel those horrible expensive tariffs and the like, importing wool from far away and so forth, we're still going to have to be frugal."

Wenwen's eyes gleamed with moisture as she whispered, "You could have a kitten. Tahra-Mama won't be here to be bothered. A dog, even!"

Carl's throat hurt, but she smiled. "It's true. I can have a cat. Two!"

9

Carl's bruises began to throb a little after dinner, so she decided to lie down and make a mental list of all the things she needed to plan before releasing the news.

Queen. She had never believed it was possible. Tahra-Mama was such a forceful presence, Carl had assumed she would always be there. Crown Princess simply meant assistant. Her own opinions had never been sought, or rather, had been sought but never considered unless she had repeated what she'd been told.

But now, suddenly, without really being trained how, she could make her own decisions. Of course her chief fear was that they would be the wrong ones. She could feel the tug toward Tahra-Mama's way of doing things, because it would be so much easier. Everybody was used to it, even if they didn't like it.

While trying to decide which of many, many items ought to be number one, she fell asleep.

The next day, before breakfast, she stopped in to talk to Cook and Jenel Sandrial, to be told that five of the seven had already been in, with all kinds of demands.

"I'm sorry," Carl said immediately. "I did tell them we'd decide together, and then consult you."

Cook humphed, his jowl jiggling. "No need to apologize, Princess. You have to stop that now," he added. "Some will take advantage, and I know who."

Jenel Sandrial halted Cook with a glance, and turned to Carl. "Take your time, Princess Carl. The other princes and princesses are used to rules. I offered a few suggestions, and they accepted those. It will be fine." She saw no utility in reporting FJ's exuberant demand that from now on he could eat what he wanted, when he wanted. Jenel Sandrial, head of a huge family, knew a teen testing limits when she saw it, and FJ had conceded with a shrug when she was firm.

"Thank you," Carl said.

The two bowed instead of nodding, though she was not yet the queen. This startled Carl. Was this how the transition happened, when two well respected servants firmly put you in the place they saw you fitting, to make an orderly world?

She bit back an apology, another habit she must break. It had been so much easier to apologize rather than endure angry rants for small infractions. But Carl knew small infractions had genuinely irritated Tahra-Mama. Cook was right, though. A queen who apologized constantly was inviting attempts at intimidation from those inclined. She had to pretend to be firm even if she did not feel it.

Oh, life was so, so splintered! She had not considered until then that she liked order, too, things progressing in a routine. It was just that her idea of order and her mother's differed.

She went to the Study to begin that list, this time writing it down, and what she would say to whom. But when it came to the details of change, she fought the impulse to reach for those ledgers. There were so many questions, for example about this wool situation. For Tahra-Mama, it was simple: get good wool anywhere in the world at whatever cost, in order to destroy Wnelder Vee. Carl did not want to destroy Wnelder Vee. But that left a big hole where possible trade might fit.

She gave in. She was running her finger down the commodities ledgers, looking for the yearly wool tallies, when she sensed a change in the atmosphere. Someone sought her. Instinctively she ran her hand down her robe to smooth it, as the other hand checked her hair, which she'd braided up as usual. Why would she even...

She whirled around a heartbeat or two before a light tap at the door. "Enter," she called—knowing, fearing, hoping it was...

Laban opened the door, large as life. No, taller. His bright blue gaze filled the room, sharpening all her senses as he stood framed in the doorway. "Ah, I should probably confess I sneaked in," he admitted, flashing a rueful smile. "Wasn't sure what kind of reception I'd meet. Though I felt the wards lift."

"Enter. Please." Her heart tried to crowd into her throat.

Laban entered about three steps, then winced. "Oh, I hope that does not hurt as badly as it looks. Though from the account that reached me last night, it sounded like you were next to dead."

"Mad and Wenwen writing to everyone?" she guessed unerringly. "They were supposed to keep it to themselves—but I see I did not express that right. I asked them not to say anything to anyone here in Everon."

"I suspect they were scrupulous about that," Laban said.

"Come. Sit down. If you like," she said quickly, finding her manners, before she realized that there was only Tahra-Mama's straight-backed, hard chair, and her own stool to choose from.

"I won't stay long," Laban promised, unmoving as he took in the hope in her countenance. He was going to have to step carefully here; it would be far too easy to crowd her. Maybe even with her compliance. "I had to see for myself that those roses hadn't gotten you killed. I feel terrible about that."

"Not your fault," Carl said, and then in a soft voice, "What did you write? I did not get to see it."

Another wince, this one entirely internal. "Just the usual cheerful birthday greeting. I promise, no secret plans for world domination!" He assumed a jocular tone.

And saw a corresponding flash of humor in her expressive gray eyes. But then she sobered, "Not anyone's fault, really. Except anger. I think … I think anger gave Tahra-Mama a sense of order."

Laban sensed her evaluating him. For? Didn't matter what for. Step easy, step easy. Keep things general. "One of my brethren was a little like that."

"You mean one of Detlev's boys?" she said, surprised she could say the words out loud and the walls did not crumble.

"Yes. Ferret. He had to know, and catalogue, absolutely everything around him, for self-defense as well as to make sense of the world. Later, well, he remained that observant, but learned to leave the anger out." A another of those rueful smiles. "Not everyone can do that. Or has the chance to do that."

Though Tahra-Mama had never ceased to vilify this man, even in the crudest language, Carl liked the fact that he didn't say anything bad about Tahra-Mama. And he could have. She would have understood.

He said, "I'll take myself off now. I had to see for myself that I hadn't managed to get you killed, or nearly."

"I'm fine," she said quickly. "It probably looks worse than it is. It feels terrible, but in the way that I know will fade after a week or so."

"Excellent. I'll go, but first, if there is anything I can do to aid you in any way, you know where I am. Or write me a note. It might be quicker than a long gallop over the border." Another of those flashing smiles, causing a long dimple to appear in his cheek.

Her face burned again, this time with emotions that she kept firmly shielded. Her crush was hers. Absurd it might be, but she was going to enjoy it, because he was even more handsome up close, and his gaze was smiling, and kind.

"… ah," he stopped himself. "It might help if you have my sigil?" He approached the desk, dipped one of the waiting pens, and scrawled quickly across the top of a blank sheet of paper.

"Thank you," she said, and swallowed. This new thought was not mere crush, but crown business. "About Wnelder Vee's woolens…"

"Oh, please tell me that means you are thinking of reopening trade? Though I probably should not say anything, at least until you have had a chance to look through your records and decide how to proceed."

"I know those," she said. "I think. Deciding how to proceed…" She studied him with those wide gray eyes. "You had to figure out how to proceed, didn't you, right after the war? And you were no older than I am. Younger?"

"All true. One thing at a time, was how I did it. But I'd had the advantage of watching from afar for some time. Actually, don't you have the same advantage? Even if what you saw was not what you agreed with, you could think out alternate paths?"

"Yes," she said. *It's the guilt I have to struggle against.* But she couldn't say it. Yet. Instead, "I'm just beginning to comprehend how much my mother kept in her head. But I'll learn my own way. I have all the component parts, except Wnelder Vee's. I've got a blank page there."

"Ah! I can send some of my own reports over, though it might take a while to stuff them all into a golden notecase. Those are really only meant for notes."

"I'm going to instruct the royal scribe desk here to follow a different set of guidelines," she said. "Beginning with accepting communication from Wnelder Vee. I planned to do that today, in fact."

"That sounds very promising. I've an army of sheep-herders who will cry real tears if we can get trade going again."

"I'll be looking for those reports," she said.

He smiled back, exited politely, and she knew when he transferred. His absence was like the sun vanishing behind a cloud.

Carl was still on Hibern's mind all through the rest of the previous day. The next morning, as Carl and Laban talked, Hibern decided to consult Rel and Atan.

She had not been back to Sartor since directly after the war, when she and Erai-Yanya were invited to confer with the chiefs of both the southern and northern guilds. Invited, heh. Before that, every time she turned up, they looked as if they wanted to shove her right back out the back door, and then check to make sure she hadn't stolen anything. But on this recent visit their attitude was very nearly pleading, or as close as those tradition-bound Sartorans could get and still keep their dignity.

She'd meant to visit with Atan and Rel after that, but during those post-war years when so much was going on, it was always easier to write a note. Quicker, too, when she'd been involved in that massive project to ward Ilerian's type of entity from all the worlds circling the sun Erhal.

She transferred to the Mage Guild's Destination, and walked out, by habit expecting to be ignored, but the attendant blinked, then her eyes widened. Hibern had to smother a laugh as the teen bowed deeply. Actual recognition—or notoriety? "May I be of service?"

"Just taking in the improvements." Hibern said that to test her status.

The mage student bowed, and made no move to dismiss her, or even to shepherd her away.

Hibern walked to the middle of the polished-stone floor and did a quick mental sweep to assess the Sartoran Mage Guild's progress in overcoming the devastation of the war. She meant to appreciate the work they had done as well as see if there was anything more needed. After all, whatever had happened in the past, they were all on the same side, dedicated to the good of the world. And they had pretty much conceded that they had not only been completely wrong to distrust her, but also wrong in condemning Marloven Hess because of a somewhat anomalous history.

She swept her awareness through the complexities of the interlocked lattices, ancient and modern, appreciating the sustained hard work of the mages, who were bound to the arduous form of magic that had slowly and painfully evolved over the millennia since the Fall—

And almost passed a tiny flaw. How to express it in sensory terms? A seemingly random shadow against the immensity of the protections, no more than the size of a leaf, but where no shadow ought to be. She dove deeper, and deeper still, into the matrices at the fundament, going back almost five thousand years, as unaware, she stood there in the center of the floor, her gaze blank.

Oh, why not just fix it? That would take less time than explaining it...

The duty student, seeing her standing there, tittered softly, wondering if the great independent mage was lost. Or so astonished she did not know what to do next. Should she ask?

A couple of others, entering from the door across the way, saw the mage in the deep blue, edged with the silver of the senior, who stood as if a stone spell had dropped on her. But no stone spell would cause the air around the enchanted person to scintillate with wildly fluctuating magic. More mages appeared. Some perceived colors, some a wind of glittering motes. Others saw only that a few of her long dark locks lifted, as if in a breeze, and her robe slowly billowed.

This was mighty magic, and she wasn't speaking a word, or making any gesture.

Up in the seniors' wing, the chief mage in charge of wards dropped a very old scroll and looked around in alarm, startling the other two mages, who had been reading in customary silence. They sat bolt upright. One uttered a faint squeak. Then all three scrambled for their magic journals, to try to identify the spell work they all sensed even before all kinds of warning tracers alerted them. The chief was the first to gasp, "It's focused on the Tower of Knowledge!"

They were still scrambling for the oldest books on defense

when a nearly subliminal rumble ended with an abyssal *crump* more felt than heard. Magic rang out in a shockwave. Then those who were able to sensed the resettling of the fundamental lattices.

The three looked at one another. Who? Where? What? Why?

"The white tower..." conceded the oldest. "But it's not an attack."

"No."

"It's ..."

They, and a number of others, descended in a semi-dignified haste to the marble hall of the entrance, and halted. They stared at Hibern, who stood where she had stopped, surrounded by students and instructors and mages of every degree. A couple of scribes who worked with the mages had joined them, and a herald connected to the Mage Guild.

In silence the crowd made way for the three chiefs.

Then Hibern blinked, and stirred, aware that the light slanting down through the arched window had shifted. An hour had passed. Ah, and here were the seniors. "One of the enemy left a nasty surprise between the ancient layer and the first of the new magic wards," she said to them. "I take it you did not find it."

The mages looked at one another. "After the war, Ganrithe was certain something was amiss," one mage said slowly. "But none of us could find anything. You know Norsunder tried to destroy the Tower."

"I know. I was here," Hibern said. "With Liere Fer Eider. We were unable to do anything to prevent that attack, but we did see that it was unsuccessful. I think this happened much later. It has Svir's signature, which I learned to know well."

Whispers — *Svir! Norsunder!* — quickly hushed.

Hibern grinned. "I think he put in a trap for one of his own people. From what I can learn, he never expected to be defeated. Anyhow, it's gone, no sign of it." She smiled around. "Ah, I was going to visit Atan and Rel. Does anyone know if she's free? Never mind. I ought to ask at the palace for that, right."

She walked out, not even seeing the profound bows made by the three senior mages, which everyone else hastily copied.

By the time Hibern had been passed from page to steward, word obviously raced ahead. Hibern was personally conducted to Star Chamber, Sartor's ancient throne room.

She blinked in amazement. She and Liere had not been able to get into the palace during their attempt to defend Eidervaen early in the war. The palace had been infested with enemies. Though she'd been friends with Rel, and to a lesser extent Atan, since they were all teens, she had never entered this chamber, from which the Landis monarchs had been governing Sartor for millennia.

Rel and Atan both looked up as she came down the shallow steps of the outer circle. "Hibern," Atan said, holding out a hand in welcome, and Hibern descended the rest of the way, still looking around.

"This is not at all what I expected," she said, peering up at the vaulted ceiling, with its many keyhole windows fitted with crystal to refract light. Below these, tiny snaplights glimmered at various heights, slowly moving, like a star field at night.

The throne itself was no grand chair with a high back or a canopy, as were most thrones Hibern had seen. This throne was a great tree carved from golden marble, real gold inlaid in wood-grain patterns. Cleverly shaped slivers of mirror had also been worked in, so that the seat in the center could be seen from all angles.

"How did that possibly survive the war?" Hibern burst out.

"It didn't," Rel said, with a hint of humor.

"It comes apart," Atan said briskly. "The stewards take it all apart for cleaning and restoration each year. They had it dismantled and hidden by the end of the day we got word Bostian was marching out of Norsunder Base. The problem has been certain of the magic protections. Various Norsundrian mages of course used this room for target practice and then traps. We cleared it all out. Or thought we had, years ago. But that might not be true."

Hibern suspected then that messages had been flying back and forth from the Guild to Atan. Giving a mental shrug, she said, "Let me see." Again she used her senses for a quick scan, and then again more slowly. Nothing obvious, and yet...

She reached farther, caught another shadow, this time very low. Ah. There. Hidden quite literally in the fundamental understructure of the stone palace, as well as in its lower levels of magic. "Very malicious," she said. "Quite deliberately set up to begin altering emotions toward..." She stopped there. "Gone."

Both Rel and Hibern breathed out. Rel said, "And that was no doubt behind the headaches of these past few years."

"Never severe," Atan murmured. "But always when there was conflict." She turned her steady gaze to Hibern in appeal. "I'd like to request you not mention it outside of this room. I don't want certain parties to use that as an excuse to call into question all my judgments."

"Only the ones they don't like." Rel's voice was a low rumble.

Hibern was no beginner in what she thought of as the sleight-of-hand of kingship. She was largely sympathetic, as from her own experience as a young mage student, she had witnessed Senrid trying to hold onto that mystique as sheer self-protection when he was a short, skinny fifteen-year-old boy who had never trained in the Marloven academy, which shaped all their military commanders. And the person she held closest to her heart was another yoked to a throne.

"I'm silent," Hibern said. "Wouldn't say anything anyway. I learned long ago it does no good whatever to get involved in any way with governing matters. That rule covers actual thrones, I guess."

"Is there anything we can do for you in return?" Rel asked. "Did you come to visit, or what?"

"Yes and no. Yesterday I lifted the border wards between Wnelder Vee and Everon."

"Ah. We heard a little about that," Atan said. "Poor Tahra!"

Rel shook his head slowly. "If Mondros is right, she's better off now than she has been since she was a girl, wanting to run away to the woods to live in dawnsinger treehouses."

"Here's another instance of that same rule: I cannot get involved with governing matters," Hibern said. "But it would ease my mind if I knew that friends were keeping an ear cocked for poor little Carl. You ought to have seen her face. Whatever happened with Tahra must have hurt a lot."

"You can be sure of that," Atan said crisply.

Rel smiled. "I was already thinking of going to visit old friends among the Knights."

"Thank you." Hibern turned to him. "I feel much better."

They chatted about other recent events, touching on Chwahirsland, which she knew Rel and Mondros had a care for, then she vanished.

"Huh," Atan said, as the two left Star Chamber and started

toward their wing. "I believe we have a likely candidate for slipping into the hole Tsauderei left in the world, after all."

They switched to the version of Ancient Sartoran that the mage world had taught—which sounded quite different from that spoken at Curtas's House and the archive at Bereth Ferian.

"You think Hibern will replace Tsauderei?" Rel asked.

"She's so like him. World's foremost mage, though he'd strenuously rejected any semblance of a title. But he had cared very deeply about world events. Like her. And when necessary, he slipped into leadership roles. I think she could teach the high magics if asked. Then she'd no doubt slip out again, just as he did, valuing her independence foremost."

"It's possible," Rel said; he was not sure that anyone would fill Tsauderei's place. His mind lingered on the fact that Hibern, unlike most of the rest of the world of mages, thought about the Chwahir.

10

Carinna Dei, Commander of the Knights of Dei, stepped out of a spring rain, ducked under the low lintel, and entered her family's old, cramped house in the city. It was a comfortable round room with the porcelain stove in the center, and sleeping spaces built into the loft overhead.

Her mother, Duchas Seiran of Valenn, foremost noble of Everon, had given her the house when Carinna was appointed Commander in place of her much-mourned father, but Carinna still thought of the house as the family's, not hers. She still slept in the same narrow bed in the loft that she'd used as a child. With whom would she share it? Canold Farher, First Knight and her beloved, had died early in the war.

Carinna sat on one of the benches around the stove and held out her cold hands to the heat emanating off the stove. Noises in the kitchen alcove preceded a cheery voice, "Carl!"

Carinna looked up as her cousin Sweetpea (born Hatahra Dei) entered, hefting a tray filled with steaming dishes. Among themselves, Carinna was still Carl, a nickname she'd been proud of as a child. But when Aunt Tahra had declared that one of her twins was to be nicknamed Carl (also with the same birth name as Carinna) her parents had quietly taken her aside and told her she would have to let the new little princess have the name, for there could not be two Carls.

Behind Sweetpea came Carinna's elder sister Merry, bearing the tray of hot pear cider. "How was Knights' practice?" Merry asked. "Problems?"

Sweetpea forestalled Carinna's answer by saying, "The

twins."

Sweetpea was exactly Carinna's age, raised with her through the bad years and the good. Sweetpea had no real interest in the Knights except as a family concern; her passion was reserved for food. Though her family tree included nobility as well as royalty, she wanted to run a restaurant filled with happy people, like a perpetual festival, with herself as host. She was currently overseeing the Knights' mess hall, constantly experimenting with recipes and trying them on the ever-voracious appetites of the Knights and their trainees.

Carinna shut her eyes, rolling the hot soup around her tongue. "Ah, what is *in* this? It's so delicious," she added on a sigh of pleasure.

"Gold wine," Sweetpea said, grinning all over her narrow face so like Carinna's own. "I ought to say that I know Sed and Glenn are good at heart. It's just that I also know it's going to cause trouble if they keep insisting they can bypass the squire year and go straight to riding. I hate to see the inevitable friction."

Carinna allowed herself a private smile. "Oh, I think the problem is going to resolve itself."

Sweetpea sat on the bench and picked up her spoon; she'd kept her own dinner back so she could eat with the other two. "Oh?"

Merry canted her head. "Silvanas," she predicted.

Sweetpea whistled appreciatively. After Laban's much-admired friend Silvanas turned up as a volunteer a month ago, Sweetpea had been making any excuse she could to come to the practice field to watch morning exercises with the Knights, and lately, no excuse at all.

Carinna said, "The twins are beginning to see that they have habits to unlearn before they can hope to emulate Silvanas's skill."

Sweetpea wiggled her brows, a pair of fuzzy dark lines like Carinna's own, and muttered, "I do wonder what other skills he has."

Merry choked on a sip of pear cider, and sputtered, half-laughing.

The three of them had been close as teenagers, the only girls their age interested in boys. So many of the various Deis and Delieths were inclined toward their own gender, or none at all. Like Carinna's and Merry's middle sister Theanra, who led a busy, cheerful single life painting pottery, auntie to everybody.

Carinna said to Sweetpea, "Alas for your entertainment, it seems that King Laban established a fabulous training run just inside the Wnelder border, back in the bad old days. They've invited us to train there."

Carinna considered adding what Silvanas had told her privately about troubling hints of renegades in the mountains, but decided against that, lest it reach Princess Carl, who had enough to contend with. Carinna did not want Carl frightened by vague rumors. If anything concrete turned up, of course she would report it. Until then, there was enough to do to begin raising the Knights' training to what she acknowledged freely as Silvanas's superior skill level.

Sweetpea sighed. "That's disappointing! Ah, just as well. I really need to get my spring orders in..." She went on to describe, in detail, her complaints about suppliers who charged swingeing prices, as Merry thoughtfully studied Carinna's sober profile.

Carinna had always been a quiet, dutiful person even when they were small. Except for that all-too-brief, giddy time when she was a teen, falling in love with Carnold the moment the two were old enough for their long friendship to ripen toward adulthood. They had entered Knights' training together, and Carinna had watched with pride as Carnold earned his way to the position of First Knight. He and Carinna planned to marry at twenty-five, thus not only making the pair happy, but solving the problem of tradition dictating commanders of the Knights come from the Dei family. Of course he would have adopted into the Deis. The Farhers had encouraged that, wanting the connection—and Grandpa Roderic had declared that at that time he would be able to retire at last.

But then the war came. Carnold died protecting others in retreat from Norsundrians sport-shooting fleeing refugees, leaving Carinna only memories, and his sword. Merry often worried about her silent sister; Sweetpea was more like Merry herself, regarding men as delightful distractions, but their hearts remained free. Carinna seemed to be born with that Delieth fixation on one beloved, however that might be defined.

The conversation stayed general as they finished their meal. By then Carinna had mostly dried from the rain. All three dunked their dishes, so the kitchen was clean in no time, then Sweetpea stuck her head out, pronounced the sky clear, and took off for her own place.

Alone with Carinna at last, Merry said, "You seemed hesitant, there, about this new training field across the border."

Carinna lifted a shoulder.

Merry said, "Silvanas the buck is very pretty to watch. Especially on horseback. But I'll hate him forever if he's giving you any trouble."

Carinna's eyes widened. "Oh, not at all, not at all. I don't think it's in his nature to be a troublemaker. He's been very respectful. Almost painfully so. His first day, he went to the back with the beginners, and I kept having to invite him to the front so that the others could use his perfect form as a guide. He never assumes."

"But? I still sense a but coming."

"Nothing, really. At least, not from his intention," Carinna said slowly, then, with her gaze on her callused hands, she said quickly, "You know I never wanted to command the Knights. But Father begged me before he died, and then Tahra begged me. And I've tried my best."

"I know that. I think everyone knows that."

"But the fact remains, I didn't see until Silvanas came that we've slowly dwindled into, well, a band of inspectors. We put in so much time with the daily reports. Carrying those notepads around all the time, and having to keep count of things, and where we encountered them. We kept losing training time to these other matters... No, I'm beginning to whine about Tahra's orders. We both know what she was like. What she wanted and why. She never understood the Knights, really, or even liked them."

"She didn't like men. And a good part of them are men."

"All true. So, here comes Silvanas, who Carl asked me to include, and he's what the Knights ought to be." Carinna lifted her head, giving Merry a pained smile. "And though I never wanted to command, and often wished something would come along and free me, I look ahead, and see that it's inevitable he will take over. In deed, even if I command in name. And ... I'm ambivalent! Isn't that just ridiculous?"

"It's human nature."

"Ah, what does that really mean? I suspect it's because I don't know who I am without the Knights."

"Can't you just be another Knight, the way you were with Father?"

"First Knight, you mean? But that was really a family appointment. I wasn't the best, the way Carnold was. I think, if Silvanas inspires improvement to his skill level, my inadequacies will be even more obvious."

"I'm sorry, Carl. You deserve better."

"Ah, it's probably a good problem to have. In fact, no one outside of me would actually see it as a problem. Rightly, they'll see it as improvement. You ought to see Sed and Glenn. They've gone from distractable lazies to hard workers. Their enthusiasm carries to all the other recruits. If they will just settle into their squire service, all will be well. As for me, of course I'll be fine. Nobody likes to come face to face with their own mediocrity. I'll survive." Carinna smiled firmly, and Merry knew that the subject had ended.

But she still spoke. "You know best how to assess your skills, but *you* are never mediocre, my dear sister. Never." Merry finished her pear cider, rinsed her cup, then picked up a lamp to light her way back to the palace for the night.

Carinna blew out the rest of the lamps and made her way to the loft to sleep, and to the northeast, Silvanas sat over his dinner with Laban.

"…and Carinna Dei said that if she gets permission, she'll take the trainees up to our old rat-hole."

"Did she agree, or was she obliged to agree?" Laban asked.

Silvanas's palm rose. "No crowding, I promise! I've been very careful not to crowd her. Easy enough. She has my full sympathy. It's clear that Tahra kept them pencil-pushing rather than training. Morale has been low in spite of all her efforts."

Laban sat back, thinking rapidly. He had not expected Carl to write to him two days after that apology visit, requesting an explanation of several points in the reports. Then another, a week after that, after which he offered to send Silvanas over if they needed more Knights. Carl had accepted with genuine enthusiasm. Since then, she seemed to expect a weekly visit.

Silvanas eyed him. "What are you thinking?"

"That I don't know where this new path is leading. Three months ago, I was laying plans for a lifetime of avoiding Tahra's vindictive monomania. Now, suddenly, that's gone. It's not only gone, but her daughter is also coming to me for advice."

Silvanas laughed. "She's after *you*."

Laban winced and waved a hand.

"No?"

"Oh, I admit she's crushing hard, though she works hard to hide it. But it's merely a teenage crush, the lure of the forbidden. And total lack of experience. How could she have any, with Tahra counting her every breath? It should die off, now that it's no longer forbidden. And I am very careful to be as general as possible with my advice, and to ask about her brothers and sisters. No personal talk."

Silvanas's large, deer-dark eyes regarded him askance. "First, she's not a teen. She's of age. Second, that family is known for its obsessions."

"As I said, I'm careful. And she really does seem to want my advice. She listens carefully, and next time we see one another, it's always apparent that she's done due diligence in checking on what I said. She's learning faster than I did after the war, and she's got a bigger concern, with far more complex problems, than I'd had."

"Such as Imar."

"Such as Imar. She's beginning to understand that Tahra was getting Everon into deep debt there, promising the Knights would defend the harbors, just so she could call herself queen and thereby choke off trade to me. What's more, I think Carl just might extricate Everon without rousing the city-states. That's not the mind of a teen."

Silvanas grunted. "Glad you're aware. I just don't want to see another tragedy there."

"You just don't want girl trouble, even one degree away," Laban retorted.

"Which is why I look around to see if Lyren is back before I let myself be seen," Silvanas said.

"I told you, just talk to her forehead. She really can't help whatever it is that makes you want to fling your clothes to the winds if only she'll kiss you. I am very sure she's not the least aware of it."

"She'd be intolerable if she was," Silvanas said ruefully.

"No, she'd be irresistible. Because, unlike so many who have that innate charm, or whatever it is, she's not mainly in love with herself. She actually cares about other people. Even boneheads like you."

Silvanas laughed, though he did not disagree. Someday,

maybe, he might settle down. Right now, he cherished his freedom without the shadow of Norsunder on the horizon, his main goal to find a way to get the Knights of Dei shaped up, in case another shadow formed. But he had a weakness: a single warm smile from a pretty girl or boy lit his candle. And Lyren was more like a wildfire.

11

Lyren Sartora Fer Eider was in her fifth month of acting as one of Darian Selenna's roamers. It was the end of an exhausting but ultimately satisfying day, a day on which she'd actually made a difference. That didn't happen every day, alas. She sat in the audience, pressed between an old woman who smelled like peach tarts, and a skinny teenage boy of eighteen or so who didn't seem to know where to put his hands, as everyone howled with laughter at the antics on stage. She smiled and clapped with the rest, but internally reviewed the triumphant moments after she'd resolved a three-way dispute. *How* good that felt! *Nothing* better!

Anyway, after two stalemates elsewhere, a true resolution was more satisfying to relive than trying to figure out which local figure was being lampooned. Then she felt a contact on the mental plane, and there Liere was in her mind, far earlier than usual.

: *You all right?* Lyren asked. It was far too soon for Liere's child to be born—the child of the icy, sinister Macael Elsarion. Lyren still did not know all the details of that, beyond the bare facts of a heartrending choice: either Liere gave him an heir, or he'd kill her eight-year-old son. Liere had shared no details beyond that, and Lyren was just as glad.

Liere responded immediately: *I'm fine. But tomorrow is my mother's birthday, and I really don't want to go. I'm not ready to explain my situation to my family yet.*

No surprise there! Liere the hostage, having a baby for her jailor. The imprisonment mostly metaphorical, making it all even stranger. Lyren actually shivered, and the old woman murmured, "Do you need my wrap, child? I don't need it. I never get cold."

"Thank you, I'm fine," Lyren said, and to Liere: *I can't believe I forgot her birthday was coming. I haven't been keeping track of the date, and spring has barely arrived here. I'll go for both of us. How's that?*

No answer, just Liere's warmth and gratitude.

Lyren gave up on trying to follow the play. She stayed long enough to enjoy the climactic dances, then slipped out during the bows at the end. Back at the local guildhall guest room, she shut her eyes and reached for Darian: *My grandmother's birthday tomorrow. I'll go spend a couple of days.*

Darian, typically, made no attempt to talk her out of it, though he'd have to find another roamer for this area in Sarendan's eastern reaches. He thanked her for all she'd done, and invited her back whenever she wanted to come. Within a few moments a soft clinking sound inside her golden notecase indicated that Darian had sent her a transfer token, so she wouldn't have to buy one the next day. Also typical.

Why not leave now? With long practice, she quickly calculated time difference. Ah. Right around closing time.

Once she recovered from the wrenching jolt of the transfer, she walked down Baker Street in Belann, Imar, and breathed deeply of the delicious aroma of fresh-baked pastry as she entered the family shop.

She surprised her relations in the middle of wiping down the display shelves and the counter. "Hello," she caroled. "I'm here to help celebrate Grandma Elen's birthday."

Her aunt blinked, using her wrist to push a lock of hair out of her eyes, as her cousin Milny gave her an absent smile. As if she were an afterthought. Always welcome, of course, but—

Her uncle Milnat said, "Marga is back."

They gazed at Lyren with the round eyes of wonder. Marga! Lyren was intensely curious to meet this cousin who'd had all of Norsunder's Host hunting her. Re-meet. They'd last seen one another when Lyren was a toddler, and Marga a few years older. "I hope that means I'm still welcome?"

Grandma Elenzeh burst through the back door, flour swirling in the air after her. "Of course you are, darling granddaughter, of course you are!"

Everyone began talking at once, and Lyren found herself

drawn into the family fold once again. She soon sat down to a pre-dinner snack of newly scalded coffee and hot bread smeared with honey whipped together with butter.

Marga came smiling from the storeroom from where she'd been setting up for the morrow. "Cousin Lyren! This is a happy surprise!"

Lyren smiled back at this cousin who was rumored to have spent the last few years as a tree. She looked so ordinary: blue eyes; dark, curly hair like Lyren's own, worn short about her ears. She was taller than Lyren, with a round face and a snub nose, and she wore the long over-tunic and trousers gathered at the ankle that were common in these parts. Nothing about her outward appearance suggested that she had become a part of the world's innate magic.

Everyone took turns in giving Lyren family news: Marga said she had been immersed in learning. *Did* trees learn? They must. When it was Lyren's turn, she took her cue from this comfortable mundanity and said that she had been helping some friends.

So the big news was from Cousin Milny's twin brother Lesim, who had gone to South End after the war to take over the old Fer Eider family shop, Uncle Lesim having not survived the fighting. Lyren had of course known that from her various earlier visits, but what she hadn't known was that Cousin Lesim was getting married at Midsummer.

Grandma Elen clasped her hands, uttering in a voice low and whispery with matriarchal greed, "Great-grandchildren!"

Lyren hoped that would make up for the grandchild to be born in autumn whom she might never meet—keeping that thought strictly to herself. Especially as Grandma Elen looked a little lost as she commented that she had not seen Liere, or her delightful little boy, for a long time, and was she still mourning Andri? "So very friendly, Andri was. Not like my idea of a king at all," Grandma Elen said, her voice trembling. "I still don't believe he's gone. Liere only sent a message, so we don't quite know what happened there—some sort of trouble—but she said in the note that she is safe."

"Who would have thought there'd be more trouble? Wasn't the war enough? But someone always seems to have to mind other peoples' affairs," Lyren's aunt murmured as she brought another plate of pickled cucumber to the table. Enaeran and its problems might as well be on another world as far as they impacted Belann.

But Grandma Elen still looked unhappy. Lyren took her hands, putting as much cheer into her voice as possible. "Liere is getting over losing Andri, really. You'll see her soon enough, I promise. Remember, she was a queen, and queens have responsibilities."

"Oh, that's true, yes, I ought to think of those people in Enaeran," Grandma Elen said, and blinked away the incipient tears.

"Her little boy — did you know he wants to be called Malcolin now? He's busy at a school, having the time of his life," Lyren said, smiling. "You'll be seeing Liere again soon. We all will!"

Grandma Elen rallied a little. "We've never really understood one another," she murmured. "But I did so enjoy my visits to Shiovhan. The people there treated *me* like a queen. So friendly."

Marga said, "Wherever Auntie Liere goes, she makes friends. I think she gets that from you, even if you don't always understand each other."

Grandma Elen pinked with pleasure, and the rest of the meal passed pleasantly, as did the talk after, during which they planned a picnic in Grandma Elen's honor the next day, once the shop was closed. "If the weather stays nice," Grandma Elen added.

"Oh, it will surely be a perfect day," Marga predicted. "Now, let's see, what can we make for punch?"

Plans made, they all went to bed early — or most did. Lyren found she was expected to squeeze up with Marga in the attic, but Marga murmured, "Take the bed. I've a few errands to run. I'll be back before anyone wakens!" Before Lyren could speak, she flickered, and was gone.

Lyren found Marga just like she was when they were little, happy and good-natured. And most definitely odd. Lyren shook her head as stretched out on the mattress set under the window.

The next morning, Grandma Elen was full of smiles to have two granddaughters there, but her occasional caresses and long, tender glances focused mostly on Marga. Lyren noted it, for a moment thrown back in memory to the desperate time when Detlev and his gang as well as the leaders of Norsunder were all out hunting Marga. Lyren had been, what, thirteen?

She stood not twenty paces down the street below this window, enduring the worst struggle of her life, as for that brief time, she had been the only person in the world who had discovered Marga's identity. For that short, painful time she'd actually toyed with not telling anyone — a struggle she'd never revealed to anyone. For that struggle had arisen out of nothing but jealousy, the most worthless of emotions.

But she'd done the right thing, and Marga had gone on to do great things at the war's end, and yet … here they were, bunking in the attic of this bakery. How odd life was at times!

Grandma Elen's unspoken favoritism was understandable. During Lyren's mid-teens, while she was Carl Delieth's governess, she'd observed that favorites often were caused by similar or complementary natures. Clair of the Mearsieans called it affinities, and had gone into a long explanation about how there were blood families — your near relatives — and soul families, and sometimes the two blended, making those people favorites of one another. Lyren wasn't sure about what a soul family even meant, but one thing for sure: Marga had plenty of this mysterious characteristic. And Grandma Elen tried valiantly to hide her favoritism.

By now Lyren had become used to helping at the shop, in a limited sense. They didn't trust her to measure, knead, layer, or shape, but she was permitted to do simple icing, and of course she could sell at the front counter. After lunch, the Fer Eiders took advantage of Lyren's and Marga's presence to leave them to run the shop while they did errands, beginning with a visit to the miller's, while Grandma Elen went up the street to the poulterer for more eggs.

Lyren tended the counter as Marga worked in the back, humming softly to herself. Lyren found the sound comforting, even compelling, though it would be difficult to say why. It wasn't that Marga had a particularly musical voice.

Lyren was soon distracted by a customer coming in, who asked for a basket of butter rolls. "Like the ones sold yesterday. In fact, if you have any stale ones, I'll take them."

"No stale items for sale," Lyren said, for this was so. What they didn't eat was donated to the guilds' home for seniors.

"If these are as good as yesterday's," the woman said fervently, "I'll buy twice as many next time, stale or not."

"Having a party?" Lyren asked, just to make conversation, as she used the scoop to fill the basket.

"No." The woman bustled out.

Three more customers came in, one needing a nutcake, but the other two wanted butter rolls. The man bought a dozen. The girl wanted three, for which she paid with a handful of the smallest denomination of coin, carefully counted out. Then she hugged the rolls to her aproned chest in a way that was usually reserved for cherished pets.

The shop emptied, and Lyren ducked into the prep room. "Has the recipe for butter rolls changed?" she asked, as Marga paused in rolling out dough in a snake form, then, with a twist of her wrist, rolled her snake into the familiar coil shape. Lyren eyed the white dough. Butter rolls? Marga added this last roll to a line then hefted the filled tray. A slant of sun in the high window swept over it, and Lyren blinked as glittery motes on that last roll seemed to sink into the dough.

"No…" Marga opened the oven and slid the tray in. Then she snapped her hands and wrung them.

Lyren blinked. Was that motes of light coming off Marga's hands? "Are you using some kind of magic?"

"Magic?" Marga repeated. "I didn't mean to. But it might be … getting in, a bit. Ah, it won't do any harm."

There certainly wasn't any feel of anything sinister. Lyren shrugged, and when the bell on the door ding-a-linged, returned to the front. Where a very old woman stood, a single coin on her hand. "A butter roll, please," she said.

She wrapped her roll carefully in a clean handkerchief, and moved slowly out—where she was almost run down by a grubby blond urchin of twelve or thirteen, followed by a short, buck-toothed friend.

"Butter rolls, one each," Blondie declared.

"Seems to be a run on them," Lyren commented. "I've only got one left, but more just went into the oven."

"Shall we share it?" Blondie said to Buckteeth.

"Yes. Then we'll come back."

The boys bought the roll, split it in half, and devoured their share right there. Blondie closed his eyes, his head tipped back. Buckteeth grinned, rocking back and forth from heel to toe.

"Do they taste extra good?" Lyren asked.

Buckteeth looked at her. "You mean you can't tell?"

"Tell what?"

"How it feels! They're so good, it's like summer inside." He pawed his scrawny chest.

Blondie put a grubby coin on the counter. "That's for one, when they're done. Save it for us!"

They ran out, laughing.

Lyren returned to the back. "There's definitely something going on with your rolls, Marga."

"I'm just wishing happiness into them," Marga said, wiping her damp forehead on her upper arm. "It's good to work with my hands again. For a few days I wasn't sure I remembered how to talk. Or walk. But now it's all back."

"I want to ask about that, but right now, did you make the rolls yesterday?"

"Yes. Ma and Da don't trust me with the layered pastries. It's been too long."

"I saw golden sparks in that last one," Lyren commented. "For less than a heartbeat. And when you wrung your hands."

Marga sighed. "I didn't think anyone would notice. My thought was, people might enjoy eating them as much as I'm enjoying making them."

"A small boy told me he feels like summer." Lyren smiled. "It's a nice thing you're doing."

"Maybe it is, but if they are noticing, I guess it's not fair to the others on Baker Street. I'll make some other things, and leave the rest of the butter rolls to Milny or Mother to put up."

Nothing more was said, though the butter rolls sold out as fast as the family could make them. Then Lyren's aunt and uncle closed the shop early, and they went down to the point that overlooked the harbor to have their picnic.

The day was perfect, which was just as well, as it transpired that their walk through town revealed that Marga was back, and old friends—and their relations—turned up to welcome her, and pelt her with questions. Where had she been? Nobody had seen her since the end of the war, and that was so brief! Was it true she was learning magic? Could she make this old rag into a new dress? Could she make Brother's ears not stick out?

Marga responded cheerfully, answering questions with questions, which the growing circle responded to as fast and loud as they could, jostling the others. Marga backed up, laughing, but looked around a little helplessly.

Lyren saw that many arriving now lugged covered baskets, and several toted musical instruments. She got an idea.

Stepping in front of Marga, she smiled around, meeting

each gaze as she lifted her voice. "Let's make this a festival day in honor of Grandmother Elenzeh, and every elder here. After we eat, Marga and I will dance with every one of you!" She gave her robe a little swish from side to side as she executed a neat little braid-step, raising some laughter as people began to turn away and settle down on the grass.

As Marga dropped down beside Lyren, she said, low-voiced, "That was well done."

"I might not know how to put magic in food, but I do know a little about parties," Lyren said.

"You do magic," Marga said, smiling.

"I do not. I don't know any magic! Not really — I kept stalling out on memorizing the fundamentals."

Marga was silent as Milny passed around plates, then she said, "Those, what did you call them? Motes. That is how your mind perceives magic. You don't seem to see your own."

"I don't do magic. I wish I did!"

"You do it," Marga corrected. "But it's part of your nature. It's very mild, and very subtle. But the potential is there. As for those fundamentals, mmm, learning those is very like filling a lake from cupfuls carried from a pool, when you are a river."

Lyren snorted.

Marga went on, "And there are, mmm, ahhh, different ways to learn how to, mmm, shape your river into canals? Eh, I think I'd better drop that. Our language, it doesn't have the words for so very much."

"Four, almost five, thousand years after the Fall, when magic nearly disappeared, of course language will evolve in another direction. Siamis told Mac and me that when we were little, and we — well, I, was yawning over language lessons."

"Even so," Marga said. "What were you doing before you came back to Belann?"

Surprised, Lyren said, "I was a roamer for a friend."

"Tell me more," Marga murmured, as around them, people chattered, ate, drank, and the occasional speculative glance was cast in their direction.

Marga seemed unaware, or maybe she was uninterested, but Lyren was always aware. She said, "My friend is the king of Sarendan. His father, Peitar, established a type of kingship in which a lot of decision-making lies in the hands of guilds and town councils and gatherings of elders and the like. But there are people who go about observing, and who have the king's permission to act for him in resolving disputes. They also observe for the king, for instance if they witness unfair practices of any kind."

"Can the disputants you mentioned not go to the king?"

"Of course they can. This type of intervention is most effective far from the capital. For example, yesterday I was in Jalkenna, which is about as far from the capital as you can get."

"I see," Marga began, and was going to say something further, but Milny elbowed her in the side. "They're going to start the music. Better eat now, or you might not get any."

Marga laughed, and she and Lyren ate their spiced eggs, crunched through some pickled carrots and cucumbers, and washed it down with citrus and mango punch, the mango newly arrived in Belann from the islands.

They were soon dancing, and didn't stop until very late, when the musicians had traded instruments around for the last time.

Everyone was tired as they packed up the empty containers and trooped back up to Baker Street. Bakers are all early risers; the windows up and down the street were mostly dark by the time they got things readied for the following day.

Lyren and Marga climbed up the ladder to the attic, where they sat cross-legged on the bed. Marga said, "I noticed whom you chose to dance with. That was a part of your magic."

Lyren lifted a shoulder. "It's easy to pick out the people who've had their sense of worth eroded by teasing, or bickering, or others' expectations. It makes me feel good to make them feel good. If your context here is magic, that's not magic."

"I won't argue with you," Marga said, leaning back on her elbows. "Did you get training to be a roamer?"

"No. That's kind of the point of it, that ordinary people can serve. Of course, if there are complaints against them, Darian asks them to do something else."

"But no complaints about you?"

"No, but again, there is no magic involved. I've been traveling and attending gatherings all my life. Grand balls, and picnics like today's. You get a sense of how people in groups behave. It's always been a kind of game for me to pick out the person who is breaking the harmony, or who is about to. And try to dissuade them, and then find out how they are hearing their disputant's words. Sometimes it's merely a matter of miscommunication. I have a much better time, and so does everyone else if I can restore harmony. So often it comes down to paying attention. Everyone likes it when someone listens. If they get a sense their words matter."

Lyren paused, and grimaced. "It sounds a bit like I'm bragging, doesn't it? I'm wrong. Often. Especially if I underestimate motives. Then there are those who are just going to walk their path no matter what. People like our Grandfather Lesim, I don't know if listening to him would ever have helped."

"Oh, I think Grandma Elen listened and listened until her world got to be this small," Marga said, shaping a circle with fingers and thumbs curved in, touching. "I think back, that's the first thing I learned to do, try to make her circle … bigger. She was so much happier."

Lyren's lips parted. Liere had been unable to help her mother. She'd said so herself. Though she'd tried, through dreams, until she learned that could be seen as manipulation. But Marga had managed as a child.

"You," Marga said, breaking Lyren's thoughts, "used your own magic to cheer Grandma Elen last night, when she was worrying about Auntie Liere. But it might not help to think of it as doing magic, if your, mmm, context for that is spell books and gestures. Which is reasonable. As you say, that's how magic has come back into use over hundreds and hundreds of years."

Lyren stretched out on her side, her elbow on the rumpled blanket, her head propped on her hand. "How do you see magic, Cousin World-Shaker?"

"I try very hard not to shake things." Marga chuckled, an infectious sound. "And I am still learning. Very much still learning." Her expression sobered as her gaze wandered to one side, and fixed there for a breath or two.

Not on the wall, Lyren saw that immediately. Her unblinking stare was too distant for that. The family? No. They were below, and Lyren could sense them all dropping contentedly to sleep. The street? No, farther. That direction was south. The strait? It was merely water. Oh, with ships on it, except Marga didn't seem to notice the movements of naval fleets. She apparently hadn't known about Darian Selenna's experiment in kingship.

What was south of the strait? The entire Sartoran continent.

Or, a little less general, Chwahirsland.

Marga broke into Lyren's thoughts again. "In spite of all the flirting, to the rest of Belann, the Fer Eider girls are oddballs who can't seem to settle to proper work. Half don't believe Auntie Liere is really a queen. Let's give Grandma Elen some attention, shall we, before we go off to our next pursuit?"

"I am free, and I know she wants to attend Cousin Lesim's wedding," Lyren said. "I'll ride up to South End with her. See to all the travel fuss, and give her lots of attention."

Marga's answer was a brilliant smile. "*You* are magic. Don't ever think you are not."

12

Traveling with Grandma Elen was a very leisurely process, with frequent stops to visit old acquaintances, or just to take in the wildflowers. Lyren had no other demands, so she set her mind to enjoy the journey, and enjoy it she did. They hired an open cart from a well-known line of post houses while the weather was fine, and though the summer sun got hotter each day, there was always a breeze off the ocean by afternoon.

Grandma Elen regaled Lyren with anecdotes about the family. Lyren could see her Dei forebears in some of the stories, not always pleasant. But almost always ambitious.

The summer berries had ripened and been picked by the time Lyren brought Grandma Elen safely back to Belann, happy and full of details about how Lesim had been successful with the shop, how popular he and his bride were, and how lovely the wedding.

Lyren took her leave with fond hugs all around. She'd already discovered that Sveneric had replaced her in Sarendan, so she decided to return to Wnelder Vee and catch up with things there. Sveneric was so very much better at just about everything. She knew that he would immediately defer if she returned to Sarendan, no doubt to Sarendan's disappointment.

Six months away ought to have cured Lyren's former flirt — or what she'd thought was a flirt, though Knight Ferold had had different ideas — of his obnoxious expectations. She could ride the border again, enjoying the woodland in full leaf. Also, she missed living with two very attractive men like Laban and Silvanas. She liked looking at them, liked listening to them, liked fencing with them, and dancing with them—and she liked the fact that none of the three of them had the least desire to pursue any closer relationship.

Laban was so very much like a brother. Vana, more like a cousin. Despite his piratical good looks and swashbuckling abilities on horseback and with sword, he had no interest in art, or grace, or wit; she liked looking at him, but she was not attracted to a mind that lived mainly for outdoor action. The three of them had lived in companionable proximity as the seasons had stretched into years, though in the past year or two Silvanas was absent more than he was around.

Lyren arranged for transfer so that she would not go near Everon, where she was forbidden, and on a warm, summery day that smelled of honeysuckle, she walked into the palace, to find the two finishing breakfast.

"Lyren, you're back!" Silvanas said.

Laban asked, "How was roaming for Darian Selenna?"

"Interesting. Ooh, it's warmer inland than at Belann!" She shook back the filmy gauze of her sleeves—it was too warm here even for those—and wound her hair up to a loose bun on top of her head. Spotting a pen, she nipped it up and thrust it through the knot of her hair, which got it off her neck. And there she was with loose curls dangling about her face, her light robe clinging to her figure. Her rounded, utterly charming figure.

As she reached for a single berry muffin on a plate otherwise left with only crumbs, and delicately broke it in pieces, Vana blinked and pushed back his chair. "Going to run those horses before the rain hits." He walked out.

"That storm is hours away," Lyren commented.

"Vana's only here for the morning. Then back to the Knights."

"Oh?" Lyren propped her elbows on the table. "Are you playing some kind of game with them along the border? Isn't that a bit dangerous?"

"Dangerous?" Laban repeated, gaze on her hairline.

"Tahra's orders haven't changed, have they?"

"Tahra—" Laban blinked, glad of the distraction. "Lyren, I take it you haven't been writing to Carl?"

"Carl? I told you two years ago I had to stop. *Three* years ago. Tahra kept demanding to see her notecase if anything arrived during the day. I had to remember to calculate the hours, and only write after Tahra's usual retiring hour, but Carl had begun to fret about what to say if Tahra interrogated her on whether or not she'd heard from me. So I relied on Wenwen to convey my greetings to her, whenever I saw her at the island. That's really why I went to the island!"

Laban whistled. "I forget who knows whom and who talks to whom. That's right, Jessan has been here since it happened, and Darian would keep mum..." At Lyren's confusion, he explained everything that had happened.

Lyren sat back, the muffin forgotten. "Tahra? Gone! For good! Or as near ... oh, I'm so glad it's the Geres, at least. Poor Tahra! But ... why didn't Carl write to me?"

"I don't know, maybe because she's been insanely busy trying to learn how to run a kingdom, without any vestige of real training?" he retorted.

"So she's completely on her own?"

"Yes. No. Jessan is there, as I said. And the younger siblings, though they are more moral support than useful. Jessan doesn't involve himself with matters of state, external or internal, but he's been Carl's go-between with the guilds and the nobles in a communication sense. As for other help, I've been making weekly visits since she invited me that first week."

Lyren had been gazing into the middle distance, ruefully acknowledging how very much she had been shunted to the side. At one time she would have sworn Carl would tell her first. Strange, how one's own sense of importance outweighs one's actual importance. But then she had never wanted to be tangled up as buffer between Tahra and her children. Tahra and the rest of the world...

Then she comprehended his statement, and pinned him with a narrow gaze. "Every week? How is that going?"

"Fine."

"I'm sure it's fine at your end. You're a hero to her. You're being kind to her, I hope? Sarcasm annihilates her."

"And I'm too brick-headed to see that?" he retorted — heard himself, and had the grace to flush. "Not with her. I saw that at once. I keep things general. Talk over guild or border matters, then leave. Nothing personal, and certainly no sarcasm. Keeping things strictly general is why I didn't know she wasn't writing to you every night."

"I think I'm much overdue for a visit to Carl."

"Excellent idea," he said. "Do that. I'll send along some papers from the Wood Guild that she asked about. That'll free me up for an overdue scouting trip I really need to make."

The palace at Ferdrian still looked shabby, except there were differences after all. The entry was filled with potted blossoms, which gave off glorious scents. Lyren spotted at least three cats, one calmly grooming her paws, one walking along a window sill, and a huge, plump tabby that approached, tail high, as if someone had appointed it a door guard.

Lyren stooped to run her fingers behind its ears and cheeks as she assessed the atmosphere. Specifically the total absence of the tension that Lyren had accepted as a condition of life in Ferdrian's royal palace.

Lyren thought back to the intense, earnest teenage Tahra she'd first met when she was two, and grief squeezed her heart. This, Detlev, is your fault, she thought as she walked from the Destination alcove, and was approached by a young steward. I don't care how wonderful your long-range plans were. The cost in individual lives is terrible, but you're too isolated by your thousands of years to ever see it.

This comprehensive and virtuous judgment lasted until the steward took Lyren to the Study, which was more or less the same, only in place of those daunting shelves of ledgers, a grouping of colorful plants brightened the room. But the desk was piled high with stacks of papers, just as neatly aligned as in Tahra's day.

Carl leaped up from behind the desk, her delight a beacon on the mental plane. "Lyren! I'm so glad to see you!"

"I've wanted to see you for ages. But I was down in Sarendan, and apparently Jessan didn't know I was there, or he was being typically discreet. Same with Ian and Sveneric. So I didn't find out what happened until this morning." Lyren enfolded Carl's reedy body in an embrace. Carl had grown taller, and the baby curves to her cheeks had flattened, making her face look even more narrow, but her gaze held the same sweet, wistful honesty of old. "I'm sorry it happened, Carl. But it does sound like Tahra gained some peace."

"That's what I believe," Carl said. "Makes our horrible parting bearable."

Her gaze shifted, and Lyren sensed she did not want to say more. "I like that gown," Lyren commented, standing back and surveying with approval the gray-blue velvet that Carl wore. It was severe in cut, almost bare of decoration except for the tiny gold buttons from neck to hem, and the dainty edge of lace at wrists and underskirt. The close fit made the most of a very slight figure, giving Carl a more mature look. "It's austere, but elegant."

Carl smiled, face mottling with pleasure. Her thin hair, threaded simply with tiny pearls, also looked elegant. To another girl that wouldn't matter, but Lyren knew how much Carl craved beautiful things around her, and how romantic she was — or had been, and had her years with her mother squashed that out of her?

She studied Carl with renewed compassion, until she realized the intelligent, candid eyes were assessing her. A jolt. Carl really wasn't a child any more. She was a young woman. A queen in all but name, and that would happen soon.

"I'm sorry about Liere and King Andri," Carl said. "We heard about the assassination very late. It was a relation?"

"A cousin, from the deposed branch." A vivid mental image of Macael Elsarion flashed through Lyren's mind: tall, powerful build, utterly unreadable, with the spectacular Dei coloring. "I don't know anything more about what happened than that, other than the fact that the Adrani king regards his invasion as a reuniting of the two halves of his kingdom."

"How is Liere?" Carl asked.

"She had to remain in Enaeran a year, to prevent civil war."

Carl pressed her thin, frail fingers to her throat. "That's horrible. And no one to be with her?"

"She doesn't want anyone. But it's only a very few months to go, and she will be free. Carl, I'm sorry I never came back," Lyren added in a quick voice.

"I'm sorry my mother drove you away." Carl's honest gaze was steady. "And you were justified." She blushed, then she squared her shoulders. "Something to eat or drink?"

"I breakfasted not long ago. But if you haven't eaten, I'll join you. You're much too thin."

Carl looked pained. "So Jessan says. And the others. They mean well, but they do hover. Come! It's nearly noon, and they are all out in the garden. They would very much like to see you."

Lyren realized then that she had indeed been hovering — just like a governess. She'd fallen right back into the old habit, and Carl tolerated it with an adult's generosity. Lyren was so seldom awkward anymore that she felt an inner quake, as if the world had shifted.

In an attempt to even the balance, she swept round in a circle, holding out the gauzy panels of her over-robe, saying, "I had to dress soberly while I was in Sarendan. Well? Am I out of fashion?"

"You are the fashion," Carl said. "Or, you were when you lived here. And that is a beautiful robe."

Carl walked out, and Lyren fell in step beside her. "I bought this robe in Imar, when I went to a family wedding. And I wore it here to see you as there's no use in putting on pretty things in Fortnyal Roth."

"Does Laban not like the social rounds, then?" Carl asked, turning a quick look to Lyren.

"No. Well, sometimes. He mostly stays aloof from it, busy with all his projects. The kingdom is so desperately poor."

"Is living with him fun?" Carl's voice, her manner, her gaze, niffed of suppressed intensity, bringing Tahra to mind. Carl had always been interested in Laban, which Lyren had assumed was because the forbidden was always interesting. But if he'd been visiting for weeks, keeping talk to business, surely that interest had faded? Or — horrible thought — was Carl like Tahra in single-minded passions?

Oh, no, was Lyren seeing a tragedy in the making? "Oh, he's fun enough," she said, and then, recollecting that Carl could not bear angry voices, "He's careless. We share the same temper, thunder one day, sunshine the next."

"So much easier than bitter rain," Carl whispered.

"We do a lot of riding, and arguing about all manner of subjects, including his various plans for the country. Wnelder Vee was so very poor!"

"Argue?" Carl tipped her head. "He likes to argue?"

"At times. His moods change faster than the weather, and he can bite your head off with sarcasm one moment, and then laugh over it all as a very good joke the next. Like me, I am afraid — don't think I'm criticizing." Lyren took in the unblinking force of Carl's focus, and added easily, "You have to remember how he grew up. Rough and hard-hitting would about sum up Detlev's poopsies, you know, and a great deal of that remains."

Carl's gaze lowered to the shabbily carpeted hall.

Lyren said, "Anyone who is annihilated by anger would not be comfortable around any of them, except maybe Adam. He too can get sarcastic, but it's so very subtle, never angry, that most don't even see it when he's being ironic. Laban—you don't miss his moods. You can feel 'em across the palace. But that's what makes it fun," she added. "Oh! And that reminds me. He sent along some papers. Wood Guild, he said, asking if I'd save him a trip." Lyren slipped the folded sheaf from her inner pocket and handed it over.

Carl's lips moved soundlessly as she took it: Lyren saw the words *save him a trip* as she watched Carl brush her fingers over Laban's handwriting, and her emotions twisted again.

She hadn't lied, but she knew she'd chosen the words and tone that would describe Laban in the way Carl would find least attractive. To protect her. She had to protect her. Carl was too sensitive to end up anything but hurt unless this apparent crush burned itself out, the sooner the better. Her first love ought to be someone kind and gentle. Lyren thought of her own experience with a first crush, which had lasted about an hour. A very intense hour, beginning with David's awareness and indifference, and her own internal scolding as she rooted it out.

She shuddered. Physical attraction was all very fine in the songs, but unless it was shared, it was humiliating, unless a person was the kind who could embark carelessly on a dalliance, and go away from it with heart untouched.

That was *not* Carl.

They found Mad, Wenwen, Jessan, and FJ gathered in the back garden, a picnic spread invitingly on a blanket: the twins, Mad stated proudly, had joined the Knights, and were busy serving their squire year. The younger sibs jumped up to greet Lyren with pleasure and surprise, and Lyren greeted each in turn, noticing as she did that Carl's favorite foods from childhood formed the main portion of the picnic menu.

Chatter resolved quickly into one of their old word games, the guesses and hints whizzing back and forth, punctuated by laughter. Lyren could do this kind of thing without thinking about it. Her real attention was saved for evaluation.

Whom to talk to? Lyren considered then dismissed Jessan. He'd always been close-mouthed, and that would only have increased during these past years he spent with Detlev's gang, Sveneric in particular. But Madelon, now—the social one, the writer. Madelon might be a better choice, or even Wenwen, fifteen now, loyal to Carl. Nothing much got past her observant gaze.

Lyren let the others lead the talk and games. Her moment came after Carl and Jessan went back in to deal with some local matter, and FJ promptly vanished on an errand of his own. The three walked in the garden as Mad gabbled happily about scribe studies, and how much you learned about customs in various countries, merely in how people folded and addressed their letters.

When she paused for breath, Lyren said, "I was concerned to see how thin and worn Carl looks."

Mad's cheeks flushed, and Lyren realized the sibs felt guilty about that. "Well, we didn't know —"

Lyren waved a hand. "This is not finger-pointing. I know quite well how dutiful Carl is. She needs watching out for, and I'm so glad to see all of you here doing it, is all I'm saying. She's so good, so quiet, I think we all assume that she's stronger than she is."

Wenwen walked backwards, her eyes gleaming with a blurring of tears. "Oh, oh, oh," she whispered. "What else can we do? I've been scared to try anything, after the horrible mess on her birthday."

"Quite understandable. Want a suggestion?"

"Yes," Mad said as Wenwen nodded vigorously. "Please. You were the only one who made our lives worthwhile, back in the old days. And you made Carl happy. What can we do?"

"She needs a social life," Lyren said. "She needs to meet young men. *Scholarly* young men. Kind ones. Gentle ones. Talk to the Knights, to anyone you deem appropriate. Unlike the rest of you, she never had a chance to get some experience with flirting. Talking, even, on subjects besides monthly tax reports. Dancing. All the things she ought to have been doing these past five or six years."

Both sisters murmured agreement; they'd all had to get away from the palace in order to do something as simple as have friends. Extra people made noise and mess, that they'd learned when they were small, and noise and mess were disorderly. Tahra-Mama had not meant to be stern, but they all could see how noise and mess genuinely disturbed her.

"Carl has a lot of Tahra-Mama's intensity. It would be devastating if she were to decide the time was right to fall in love, and for lack of anyone else, she picked the wrong person.

I'm afraid ..."

"Of what?" Mad asked, her fingers writhing in her skirt.

"That she could become, oh, as single-minded in what she thinks might be romance as Tahra was in her hatreds."

Wenwen drew in a deep breath. "I'm not sure about romance things. At all."

Lyren laughed. "Wenwen, I felt the same at your age."

"And boys are just loud, to me," Mad said. "I don't pay any attention to them, so I don't know what would be right or wrong, or how to pick one for Carl. I think you ought to talk to Jessan. He knows her best."

"He does. And he's the most protective. And the most close-mouthed. Also, you're her sisters, and this subject is somehow easier between us, especially sisters who care as much as you two do, than with a brother."

"Oh." Wenwen looked blank, and Mad smiled, gratified.

"That's very true," Mad said, frowning at a line of inoffensive queensblossom. "We'll see what we can do."

13

Seshe looked around the underground chamber that had been her room, aware that this, now, was farewell. The Junky, hideout for Clair's gang, had been the center of her life for so long: a safe cocoon. But butterflies have to break free and fly, or shrivel to dust.

It was not easy to leave so many memories behind! A kind of sweet sorrow panged deeply in her heart. She relished it because she never wanted to forget all that the girls had experienced together. But now Irenneh and Diana were gone, Gwen sailing the seas. Falinneh would never change, nor Dhana, and though Sherry had grown, she was exactly the same as she had always been, like a shaft of summer light on a gloomy winter's day. She and CJ no longer needed Seshe, and Seshe needed to be needed.

Clair no longer needed her, either.

She slung her cloth satchel over her shoulder and walked slowly up the tunnel to look about the forest once more. Summer sunlight winked between the tossing leaves. So very beautiful. And she would be back; she might never live in the Junky again, but she could visit.

She raised her hand to transfer to the White Palace, but halted when a high, clear soprano rang through the trees. She recognized CJ's voice immediately. CJ had always had a surprisingly good voice, though she preferred to sing silly songs, but growth had brought that voice to its full promise.

The song resolved into another silly one, punctuated by the thud of footsteps, and Clair and CJ appeared from between the trees, finishing a run. CJ stopped mid-song, and flopped onto a grassy spot. "Whew! I had to sing us through that last bit," she said to Seshe from upside down.

"Where did you run to?"

"We did Diana's entire run," Clair said, her cheeks ruddy. "I needed to clear my head, and CJ came along to see if she could do it."

"And to get hungry enough to do justice to that hazelnut cake Janil made for tonight," CJ said. "With extra cream frosting."

"Were you looking for me?" Clair asked.

"I'm going back," Seshe said, watching as the smile left CJ's face.

She flipped over and sat up. "Do you need any of us?"

Seshe said, "I was just getting some things." She indicated the satchel.

"I thought you'd stay longer," CJ said, and then quickly added, "Well, next time!"

Seshe said, "You can always come visit." And suppressed a bubble of laughter at the changes in CJ's expression — horror, confusion, regret. Seshe easily followed the progression of those thoughts: the horror was leftover habit, the confusion was CJ catching that and remembering that Wan-Edhe's toxic shadow was receding, and finally, regret at the implication that Seshe had said "visit." As if she had another home.

Which she had.

Though CJ was still unable to hide her thoughts, she had begun to mitigate the old instant reactions. "It seems weird to want to visit, but actually, it's interesting to see the changes happening. Even if they're slow," she said.

"Slow is good," Clair said.

CJ threw her hands up. "Not arguing!"

Seshe said, "I told Aurora that Mad can have my room in the Junky." She held up her satchel. "I got the last of my things out that I know no one would want. If not Mad, any strays who turn up and need a home."

CJ's smile twisted. "I do like the thought that the Junky would keep on being a retreat for kids who need it."

"Oh, I think that's going to happen," Clair said.

CJ and Seshe waited, but Clair said nothing more, which meant she was not yet ready to talk about the plans that they all sensed she had been making while recovering from the war.

They had seen a part of those plans, as she studied diligently, occasionally consulting Roy, Arthur, and Adam when he could get free of his duties in Sartor.

The three ate a meal together, Clair talking readily about the memoir written by an herbalist five thousand years ago. Seshe had requested this translation, which Clair had been sending to her a few pages at a time.

When they'd finished off their toasted bread-and-cheese, Seshe took her leave.

It was very late at night in Chwahirsland. As soon as Seshe recovered, she stepped out of the Destination to the balcony overlooking her herb garden in what had once been Wan-Edhe's private execution courtyard. The smell of stone and herbs and fresh air off the mountains to the west filled her lungs, dissipating the transfer reaction.

The landing guards bowed. She forced herself to acknowledge them with a little nod as she met their eyes. Bowing! She had risked her life to escape that kind of hierarchy, and the poison it generated, yet here she was, back in a hierarchical society. A much more hierarchical society, its layers going back so far that the early records were mostly legend, recorded on aged scraps that were copies of even older scraps.

But oh, the differences!

She cut inside, glancing down the now clean hall, the stone floor once again polished to a gleam, and as she passed Jilo's suite, she glanced in. Two maids were in the process of snapping out fresh sheets before making up the bed. Seshe saw to it that Jilo slept on sun-dried sheets in a clean bed, which she knew he appreciated, though until she began reorganizing the castle, he'd slept on a wretched, narrow bed whose covers were so old and grimy and dust-covered that she had not known their original color.

Quiet as she tried to be, Chwahir women were still far too wary out of sheer self-defense, and the two household staff dropped the sheet and bowed.

"Looks very fine," Seshe said, having discovered that stating the obvious both acknowledged their work—that is, acknowledged their dignity—and reassured them that all was well.

As soon as she finished the word *fine*, Seshe walked on in hopes they would not bow three times, even nine times, in frantic worry because they did not know what else to do with praise. Especially praise from the Outlander, as she was mostly known.

It wasn't overt intolerance. Seshe knew what that looked like. It was a reaction from people who had not laid eyes on anyone but Chwahir for generations; the only ones who did not react to her as if she had been invisible had been the few on Jilo's staff who had spent time outside Chwahirsland.

She opened the door to the balcony that bridged a corridor down below, then entered the residence wing, where lights glowed all along that floor. Those tall keyhole windows were another small triumph, besides the herb garden: it had been her first suggestion to Jilo, to knock out the windows that Wan-Edhe had had filled with stone.

Her second had been that garden, which was filled with leafy lister and hardy loethe, aromatic peppermint, and mullein. Not everything grew well in the garden. She'd had Jilo import spices such as turmeric, which had failed to thrive. But she grew enough other medicinal plants to combine with beeswax and olive oil in order to make pain balms, which she gave to the garrison medic to hand out as needed.

She entered the study, with its two windows that transformed it utterly. That and the fine table edged with carvings of linden leaves in patterns of eight. Usually she paused to enjoy the elegant, quietly pleasing effect of this room, but a glance at furrowed brows, and the tension in Jilo's hands as he thrust his fingers though the silky black strands of his hair, meant trouble.

But when he saw her, his face transformed. "You're back," he said—as he always did. As if he was surprised that she would return. She knew he felt that way, though she always returned.

"I'm back. I was going to ask if you'd dined." If he'd remembered to eat, in other words. He'd begged her to remind him of such things, but it was her own intuition that prompted her to frame her questions so that they did not sound like nagging reminders when she spoke before others. Even before those he trusted.

Acknowledging that, she turned a smile to the other men in the room, beginning with Military Director Chief Furo first, as he was the eldest. "Would you be interested in a meal, Military Director Chief?" She never stared at his horrendous scars, testament to what he'd suffered while serving as Efael's torture toy before Jilo, with a group of Detlev's people and the Colendi king, among others, had rescued him on a desperate raid.

"I drank soup before reporting, but I salute the kindness of the offer," Furo said with grave dignity.

Seshe turned to Dassler Anjit, a tall, thin man whose age was impossible to guess. "Household Director Chief Anjit?" she asked.

Anjit reddened; one of the Sunrise Generation — the Chwahir who had served as flunkeys around Wan-Edhe as the evil king's magic sucked out their life forces, before Anjit was promoted to the once-despised Crimson Army — he had once put his considerable skills to work avoiding further promotion. Under Wan-Edhe, it was one of the few ways of hiding in sight. But that avoidance ended with Furo's rescue, and Jilo's accession. If that's what you could call Jilo's slow drift throneward.

Never forward, Anjit turned to see what Jilo had to say as Seshe smiled warmly at Duin, the third man, who was, if possible, even more self-effacing than Anjit.

Chwahir born, Duin had joined Norsunder a few years before the war began, a step up from being an utterly despised Bi, twi-less and unpromotable, until he left Wan-Edhe's Chwahirsland entirely. One of Imry Llyenthur's last acts before vanishing entirely had been to dump Duin back in Chwahirsland, saying, "Jilo said he'd take you on." And transferred away, the last time Duin ever saw him.

Jilo and he had looked at once another, then Jilo had produced a knife from his sleeve — and to Duin's utter surprise, pressed it into Duin's hand. "Do it," he'd said. "If you're going to kill me, do it now. Save me a mountain of work that I have no idea how to resolve. I'd rather just die now than have to worry about whether or not the knife is coming at my back."

"I'm comms," Duin had bleated finally, flinging the knife away. "Not enforcement. You want dispatches organized, in and out, that I know how to do."

And he'd proved it, gaining steady promotions over the nine years since the war ended. Nine years, but in his dreams, he was still waiting for someone to shove him before an execution squad, yodeling, *It was all a joke, ha ha!* While awake, Duin never ceased to appreciate Jilo's trust. Or little signs that someone else saw him as a human being. For instance, this outlander who smiled and respectfully used his title as she said, "What about you, Communications Director Duin?"

Duin still didn't know how to answer such fraught questions, and Seshe saw it, so she turned to the fourth man, one of Detlev's boys. Erol was tall, slight, and so nondescript that among the Chwahir he was invisible—until you saw him move. If you saw him. As expert in covert action as he was in martial skills, he had come to be Jilo's most trusted individual (besides Seshe); so far, Erol had refused a title, but he was well known to be the unofficial chief of Jilo's personal guard. Which might have been sinister, if it wasn't also known that Erol and his carefully chosen coverts were not allowed to kill anyone. Not even would-be assassins.

Seshe looked her question, and Erol made a slight pass with one hand. This threw the question back to Jilo, who couldn't remember when he'd eaten last. He stared down at his stomach as if it would tell him if he was hungry or not. Since he didn't feel hungry, he got to what mattered. "The border fortress," he murmured. "It seems the shells have taken it. And they are ready to fight all comers unless I give them the Dragon-spring concession."

"Which is the very best variety of steep," Anjit said to Seshe, in case the outlander did not know. "Far better than the Sartoran summer steep. Everyone who can bear high mountain living wants that concession. Dragonspring grows best on high slopes, where roots can reach hot springs."

Seshe shrugged off the commodity, her concern for the people involved. "Shells" was the long-standing Chwahir nickname for the women who had had to live as men, most of them in the army. In his later more mad years, Wan-Edhe had "solved" the famine problem by declaring that all excess female babies were to be smothered at birth. Naturally, no one wanted to obey that. and so the Chwahir had resorted to various subterfuges to get around it. The most common had been to meet army quotas with girls living as boys.

"I thought you dealt with the shells five or six years ago," Seshe said, remembering the midsummer celebrations that attended to gradual opening of more land, and the assigning of plots to those who wished to farm it. There had been other programs as well, especially attending the transformation of flax into linen, once one of Chwahirsland's proudest products.

"Those were the ones who wanted to return to livng as

women," Jilo pointed out. "And who also wanted to get out of the army."

Anjit said, "Many shells know no other life. Or had to endure very painful magic to alter them into men."

"Or a semblance of men." Jilo lifted a shoulder, uncomfortable with a subject that had caused so much silent suffering. "Endured half the magic. Or none at all, but were raised from the start as boys. Which is why I don't know how many there are still hiding in the lower ranks, much less how many slipped up there to the fortress to join the rest. May never know it, until the last of them get too old." He sighed. "Counting them does nothing for me now."

"Except that you did make provision for them," Erol observed. "The problem being, these ones who deserted and turned up at the fortress either don't want or don't believe your provision."

"Or cannot see themselves returning to civilian life as women," Furo said.

"Are you requiring them to?" Seshe asked. "Does it matter what they live as?"

"Not to me," Jilo said. "I regret to say that many, perhaps most, communities do not feel the same."

And there it was, the tight interweave of Chwahir social relationships. Family, twi, kin, community. Mostly a good thing, but sometimes restrictive. Exclusive, rather than inclusive.

Anjit nodded soberly. "Especially in the army. While everyone was keeping his head down during the reign of The Hate, many of these shells thought they had passed notice. But since the war ended, it turns out that wasn't always true."

Seshe knew from the manner in which Anjit looked away that these people's lives had probably become worse than ever. There had been all kinds of problems as the army had trouble adjusting to the new rules; only fear, and inertia, Jilo sometimes said, had kept them from rising against him.

That, and the fact that the rest of the kingdom, including their families, almost universally welcomed each improvement with ceremony and celebration. Concession meant the crown provided not only the land, but a living for two to five years, depending on the industry, and if a family made a success of their concern, ownership would be duly registered, gaining them the precious tally with the eight-leaf crown imprimatur.

Jilo laced his fingers together and pressed them over his eyes. "They want the concession partly because of the potential wealth and prestige, but I think it's also because they would be living high on mountain slopes, away from others. Their only contact would be in trade. If I give Lanit's shells the concession under these circumstances, what does that say to the rest of the Chwahir, who have been obedient to all the changes?"

"But you're not thinking of sending someone against them?" Seshe asked.

Furo made a warding sign, murmuring, "That fortress is full of evil."

"Evil was certainly done there," Jilo said. "In any case, I can't stomach the thought of taking action against people so very betrayed by their own ruler, and their own people, though innocent. But I've got to find some solution; I promised that this year, we could plant for steep. Marga had said we could terrace for it this year, and I've already granted the ground-level varieties. Lowlands. All that's left is high mountain Dragon-spring, the rarest and the best."

Steep had been limited to the army under Wan-Edhe, and of course the finest was reserved to the king and his upper command. Because of the severe drought, worsening every decade, Dragonspring had all but vanished entirely. But, as with other specialties of the Chwahir culture, there had been carefully tended and hidden plants, in hopes that Wan-Edhe would one day die.

Jilo spoke, eyes still covered, "This is a stalemate. Senrid once told me about authority of position, as opposed to authority of tradition. The army, under me, holds authority of tradition. But the two shells that the others are following hold authority of position—I placed Crimson Patrol Captain Lanit up there myself, to watch in case renegade Norsundrians turned up from either the Erdrael Danara side or our side."

He dropped his hands. "The way I see it now, I either have to go up there in force, or grant what they want. I can't do either." He paused as Seshe's hand touched his shoulder, her fingertips pressing slightly. He blinked as he looked around, then perceived Furo's wan complexion, his tight mouth. Jilo slid his fingers over hers, gripping, as he said, "But it's late. Let's all get some rest. Maybe an idea will occur in our dreams."

Anjit helped Furo to his feet. Duin followed them out, halting at the door when Jilo said, "Duin, keep an eye on the incoming messages, would you? Bring me anything from them, no matter how late."

Duin saluted, and went out.

Erol remained, looking a question.

Jilo said, "What would Detlev do?"

"I can ask," Erol offered.

Jilo looked tired. "That was partly a joke, in expectation of you telling me he'd wave his hands and we'd restore Chwahirs-land to what it was five hundred years ago. Or all those people up there would suddenly wake up with a miraculous change of heart. If any outsider understands the background, he might, but I'm reluctant to invite an outsider, even him. Bad precedent. Let's list what we know. What we need."

Seshe said, "I'd offer to go talk to them, as no one expects anything of me. But I imagine I'd be the worst one to send."

Jilo sighed. "In the sense that they'd see you not just as an outsider, but a privileged one. They have learned to think like men, but a lot of them resent men. Mondros won't be any help here. He's insisted firmly that his area is only questions of magic. And Rel told me five years ago that he hadn't been aware of the extent of the shell situation."

Jilo and Erol then separately began to make a last list so they could compare their ideas. Though they'd already done that at least twice. Seshe exited soundlessly, and, spotting a runner in the hall, gave orders for hot coffee and fresh corn cakes to be delivered to the two. The coffee Chwahirs now drank, thanks to the Chwahir pirate patrols, was fresh from the islands, the best quality.

Seshe smiled at this unspoken sign of something going well, and picked up a lamp and a basket to go down to her herb garden to do some night work; though the hour was late here, it was not in Mearsies Heili, where she had been. She would not be tired for some time yet. Might as well be useful.

A couple of guards, seeing her approach the garden with her satchel, basket, and trowel, brought out some lanterns from the garrison unasked. She thanked them gravely, and let her mind range as she stooped over the rows of healthy plants. Where there was a hole, she carefully selected a seed from the jar she'd put in her satchel. These seeds she had hoarded over the years: ginger root of a specific kind.

Once it had been understood that her garden was entirely for the welfare of the castle staff, she had begun to be visible.

The world sometimes overlooks the enduring effect of generosity. Seshe's generosity was like a spring, or a gentle rain. Never confrontive, but there, and noticed, when needed. The garrison was used to keeping injuries to themselves, or at most furtively repairing each other within the secret twis; at first, when Seshe handed off the produce from her garden to the garrison medic, it went unused because no one dared report illnesses or wounds. Wan-Edhe's method of dealing was to make weakness disappear, and a warrior who couldn't fight was weak.

But one, then two, then twelve ventured to the lazarette, where those fresh-smelling herbs had been put to use in salves and medicines. And so, as Seshe went about planting, and harvesting blossoms and leaves and roots, the lanterns were moved with her, nothing ever heard except her soft, "Thank you."

14

It is believed by many among the Chwahir that the greatest era of the Sonscarna dynasty was its first half, culminating in the reign of Queen Lammog. The downward slide began when her brother assassinated her in 4302, culminating four hundred years later in the madness of Shnit Sonscarna, who claimed the honorific Wan-Edhe—the king of all kings—but who in all records save the official archive is referred to simply as The Hate.

That fortress in the mountains overlooking the high pass that serves as border between Chwahirsland and Erdrael Danara could be said to exist as a physical metaphor for that downward slide.

It began as a protective fortress shared by Chwahir and Danarans, built thick-walled not for military reasons (what army would be mad enough to attack fighting uphill all the way?) but purely to stand against the winters, which at that altitude began early and ended late.

Once the brief spring arrived, there followed a mellow summer during which many types of vegetation thrived. The fortress was largely self-sufficient, and so for a century or two, those who lived there watched over the pass, pulling mired wagons free, saving travelers from sudden snowstorms, and patrolling to discourage banditry.

Early on in the Four Centuries of Tyrants, the Chwahir border was closed, and the Danarans turned from allies to targets in the first of many expansion attempts. The fortress became a staging point for westward pushes, then as a prison for recalcitrant Sonscarna princes, and finally as Wan-Edhe's retreat. He had windows bricked up, destroyed the gardens in favor of a dungeon wing, and laid wards and time-distortions over the fortress so thick and heavy that even light had difficulty getting in.

The lour that resulted appealed to Efael, who made it his retreat during the war; he not only needed the time-distortion, and the ready and waiting dungeon, but he also delighted in forcing Wan-Edhe to submit to his whims.

After the war, Jilo used what he had learned in clearing Narad's royal castle of Wan-Edhe's lethal webwork of spells to destroy the similar webwork over that fortress. Otherwise he'd left it to itself, having no good memories of the place, except to order a general sweep once a year to make certain no Norsundrian renegades turned up to infest the place once again.

This spring, the sweep had been led by Crimson Army Patrol Captain Lanit. The newly promoted patrol captain led a patrol up to the fortress, looked around speculatively as the patrol searched for hiding Norsundrians, then came back up at the beginning of summer, leading a sizable contingent of deserters from all five armies. All shells — that is, warriors born female who were forced to join the army as men.

The same soft summer night that Jilo and Erol tried once again to cudgel their brains for a solution to the shells' desperate demand for the Dragonspring concession, the shells themselves, having received no answer from the royal castle, gathered in the fortress's central court to escape the summer heat in the upper chambers and to discuss what to do next.

That central court was built around one of the many vents veining the mountaintop, heating aquifers to steam. This particular vent was quite large, and in better days, the long winters had been made bearable as the castle denizens gathered in the chamber below, which was warm, fed by boiling water at one end, meeting a diverted stream in a central pool.

Wan-Edhe had covered it over, of course; disliking being wet himself, he saw no reason why anyone else ought to waste time down there that they ought to spend patrolling endlessly to keep him safe. So when that expanse of tiled stone began to vibrate, making little pebbles jump and clatter, the shells broke off their discussion—which wasn't going anywhere anyway—and turned their horrified gazes to the center of the court, where the pebbles jumped higher.

"He wouldn't attack us by magic. Would he?" Lanit asked the circle of astonished faces.

No one could answer that; "he" meant Jilo, the specific pronoun used reserved for men at the top of a given hierarchy.

"He didn't know we'd desert, much less rebel with demands," someone observed sourly.

"You're here," another pointed out.

"Quiet," Lanit snapped, wishing it was daylight; now all the dust as well as bits of gravel jumped, the whole a blur in the light of the sinking moon.

The low rumble got gradually louder, and everyone scrambled back as the tile cracked, then exploded upward in a thousand shards. Ruddy light glowed in the hole blasted through the courtyard tile before a shape shot through, into the air.

Glowing wings of fire snapped out, and everything stilled for a heartbeat as the shells stared at a magnificent firebird. It stared back, its affable eye bright as a star, then the shards of tile began to fall. "It'll cut us to shreds," someone yelled.

But as the amazed rebels began to scramble about, seeking cover, the bits of tile exploded in puffs of sand, which floated away harmlessly in the soft night breeze. The firebird folded its wings, its blazing glory gradually dulling to ember-red, thence to a lighter, dimmer orange as it elongated, the wings blurring to the shape of arms.

Before their astonished eyes the fire died out altogether, leaving them staring at a slim, barefoot person in a long worker's tunic and loose trousers, feet bare, hair short, dark, and curly. Almost like a Chwahir, except the person's skin color was something between sand and brown pottery, and the eyes in a round, button-nosed face that could be Chwahir-ish were bright blue.

"Hello. My name is Marga," she said, borrowing their language from the mental realm.

Though Chwahir legends were full of fire dragons and creatures of light, no one had ever seen such a sight. They stood frozen in a ring, some gripping weapons.

Marga gazed back, having sensed from far below a cluster of humans whose emotions radiated anger and grief and frustration, where she had expected no humans to be. "Why are you here?"

The question was simple, but could be perceived as cosmic

by those who had in early years listened to whispered tales of the great Chwahir past, full of magical beings. Firebirds definitely belonged to the legends.

Faces turned Lanit's way. Lanit perceived that, swallowed in a throat tight with tension, and said, "We have made a demand. Of the king who is not a king."

"The king who is not a king," Marga repeated. She knew Jilo slightly, of course. While she paid scarce attention to matters of borders and governing, she had liked what she saw of Jilo: he had heeded her from the beginning, and this poor land, so long a wound on the world, was recovering as well as Marga could have wished. No, even better, as the Chwahir, used to making much of very little, were excellent caretakers of land.

Lanit swallowed again. "Our oldest word for king" — Marga heard *wan* — "has been so poisoned by the one we know as The Hate…" Here she spat on the ground, and *ptooi!* most of the rest spat as well, clearly a ritual reaction, though fervently meant. "… and so, to say it is to poison one's lips and tongue. "Until *he* decrees another title, he is the king who is not a king. But we know him for a king," Lanit explained.

Marga sensed their roiling emotions settling, and said, "Tell me more!"

"We are warriors, but the army, in its troubles, turns on us, who were once a part —"

"But we are mere shells," someone else put in bitterly. "We could cry eight times eight before the Court of Rule, but our own commanders would give us no justice."

"Shells," Marga repeated. "The word I understand as part of little undersea creatures, or turtles."

"It comes from turtle, and once was a word for armor," Lanit said. "There are other slang meanings — soft-shells being us, hard-shells being men who saw themselves as women — but —"

"That's confusing. Get to the demands," hissed someone from the background.

Lanit had been floundering about, trying to figure out how to tell the history of the shells in a few words, and abandoned the notion. She said to this person with the strange name who had been a firebird, "After the war, Jilo, our king who is not a king, found work for the navy."

Marga heard the word *work* as an honorable, meaningful

thing, almost a sacred thing.

"Our navy patrols the strait and the southwest, as the Venn patrol the north, and in the east, we are told, Khanerenth and ships from Goerael patrol, for there are renegades from Norsunder hiding still, and there are always those who would turn pirate."

Marga listened patiently, thinking that she was unlikely to be able to help after all. These matters were government affairs.

"…what to do with our army. Many wished to leave…" Lanit was on surer ground here, explaining that as the land began to improve, those who had never wanted to be in the army in the first place were the easiest to demobilize.

At this point, a couple of Lanit's patrol broke in to describe how many in Furo's Crimson Army had gone over the mountains to Colend to work in the renovation. Left were those who wanted the army life — among whom not a few resented the loss of the old perquisites and prestige they'd enjoyed under Wan-Edhe. Sure, there were a lot of executions in those days, most of them summary, but if you looked sharp, kept your eyes on the ground and your mouth shut, it was an easy life. Especially after the war ended, when there was no expectation of being ordered to go die in some foreign land. Except the perquisites and prestige began to erode, along with their numbers.

"And so," Lanit said sharply, riding over the other voices, "debates within those left in the army became fierce. People — men — wanting to hold onto what they'd had, they turned on us shells, the lowest of the low. Though the king who is not a king had begun to promote many of us."

"Then word spread that this year, the leaf concessions would be granted," another stepped forward to say eagerly. "My family has kept the true Dragonspring leaf for generations, in hopes that The Hate would die at last, and we could go back to things as they were. Lanit here saw that the land around this fortress has the right climate, and excellent soil."

Marga said, "But cannot everyone who wants to plant good things do so?"

"Oh, you can," Lanit said bitterly. "But how do you live until the plants mature enough for trade, unless you are already part of a farm family? Most of us were turned away by our families, or cannot return even if they want us, for what can we contribute but knowledge of weapons?"

"But we want to learn, together. And form our own twis, and use our own customs. That's why we want the concession, which we heard that certain influential commanders at the top were going to demand for their families. But here, so far from anywhere, we could survive and raise our plants, and trade—"

At that, many voices broke out, fear no longer keeping them back. Marga did not try to listen to them individually. She withdrew to the mental plane, assimilating the fears and yearnings that were bolstered by sharp flickers of memory: a small child reaching along with other small children toward some treat in a bowl, to have that hand slapped away, and a scolding, *Not for you, until the boys are served first. But I am a boy, Ma says I am a boy, Da says I am a boy. You are only a shell boy, and shells must defer to real boys, just as flatfoots defer to leaders, and leaders to captains. I want to be a girl again! Hssht! Do you want to die? If you were a girl, you would not get any. Girls only serve. You are a boy! I am a boy...*

It hurts! It will hurt until your body gets accustomed. Listen, you are too young for it to matter now, but remember, when you get older, it will never rise. Understand? That kind of magic is so forbidden I don't know if it even exists. But you'll pass a cursory inspection, which is what matters...

...don't know the first thing about women. They have a different language, a different way of moving, and they want nothing to do with me. At least with the other flatfoots I am seen, even if I am always a wax-scraper...

The anguish reverberated through Marga, almost overwhelming her. Her impulse had been to rise among these unhappy people and solve what must be solved, but she understood she had been impossibly arrogant. This was a matter for those on the far-off mountain, except they were none of them Chwahir.

She opened her eyes and raised her hand.

"Quiet," Lanit ordered, for this young person half her age was a firebird, a being altogether outside of army chain of command.

Marga steadied herself, recollecting why she had been in the mountain at all. She understood that she had been gone not a matter of hours but weeks, for she sensed the sun on the other side of the world had shifted past the midsummer arc.

She said, "I learned many things as a tree."

Silence from the Chwahir.

"But there is more I must learn before I can speak with assurance. Your problems with your king who is not a king, that I cannot address. This much I can tell you: you cannot be here." She pointed down at the hole she had blasted through the floor.

All eyes turned toward it, perceiving only a wisp of steam glowing dimly in the fading light of the sinking moon.

"It is not now. And I am not completely certain that I am right, but enough to warn you that it would be better for humans not to be in this place at all. And so I must tell Jilo."

The Chwahir stared, still silent, puzzled, wary.

Marga found herself even deeper in a quagmire entirely of her own making. What was it Lyren had said, as they dunked and dried dishes? She had told Marga about some of her roamer tasks in Sarendan, and, ah, she had said, *I learned there are two parts to a successful resolution of a dispute. First, accord everyone their dignity, even if you find their argument absurd. It isn't absurd to them. It might even be vital. And second, find what each party sees as common ground. It might look very different from all sides. But if you can find what all can accept, without them being forced to defer to greater power, then you have a better chance of everyone going away with good intentions...*

What was common ground here, for a king who was not a king, and for people who had been forced to defer since birth, for no good reason, and for no reward? Marga remembered the talk of Dragonspring, which was a name for a specific plant. "May I see your Dragonspring?" she asked.

An exchange of glances, and Lanit pointed to someone. One of the shells vanished, and soon reappeared, elbowing past the circle while holding something precious in cupped hands. "Please don't bruise it. We really need to get it into the ground soon," this person whispered.

"Fear not," Marga promised. "It will take no harm of me."

She cradled the little plant on her palms, eyes closed as she sank her perception into its being, down to the roots. Some gasped softly as Marga's hands began to scintillate, the glow extending to the limp leaves of the plant. Before their eyes, the little plant straightened.

Oh, how grateful Marga was to her time as a tree! She opened her eyes and smiled. "I have strengthened it some, so that it will sustain itself until you can get it to the ground that will nourish it best. Not here," she added. "Do you know the mountains east of the middle pass?"

"I do," spoke someone from the back.

"There is where this plant grew in the long-ago days, its heart tells me. It will grow best there again. And there are no humans on those slopes. Yet. I just checked."

How, many wanted to ask, but the memory of that explosion, and the firebird hovering, and the glowing plant, was too fresh for that.

"I think this would be a proper middle ground, yes? If I speak to your king who is not a king, and you leave this mountain, and go with all haste to the east? I will mark the best ground for you."

Lanit studied Marga, wavering. Then said, "You are a creature of magic?"

"I would say that I am learning magic," Marga responded with caution, not wishing to make claims she might not be able to fulfill.

"Can you transform us, as you transformed yourself?"

"To firebirds?" Marga asked, about to explain that she could, but they would probably not flourish in the depths of the world.

"To ..." Lanit looked around, then down at her body in a revealing manner, and Marga's heart sorrowed.

She said, "I could restore each of you to what was altered so badly by magic."

"As girls," someone said softly.

"Yes. I could return you to that form, because your body will remember its components."

"But what about those who are not women here." A tap to a forehead. "Can you transform us the rest of the way into men?"

Marga considered that. "I ... think I can? I have not tried it."

"How much will it hurt?"

"Can we father children?"

"I had the beard spell. Will that interfere?"

Marga held up a hand as she considered. "This is too new, I think. But I can find out. I believe such magic was common to healers in the ancient days. That would give you time to discuss, and decide what is best for each, as you travel east. Yes?"

Lanit had been thinking rapidly. This Mar-Gah had not

actually done anything besides that first transformation. They would be taking a lot on faith.

The eldest among them stepped up, whispering, "What have we to lose? We will not win here. I told you before, young Jilo cannot give in, and our having received no answer proves it, does it not? You know well who would immediately make demands, using us as precedent. And then, if he says no, who will suffer from their disappointment?"

"Us," Lanit predicted. That, at least, was clear enough. "We had to try."

No one argued.

And so, to the rest of the circle, "Everyone, return to quarters. Pack. We will begin our march down the mountain at first light."

Lanit bowed.

The others bowed.

Marga smiled and bowed back, and then leaped into the air, transforming to a snowy-backed kestrel with a speckled chest, and with a strong flap of wings, sailed out over a cliff and vanished.

When she reached Narad, she discovered that most of the castle was dark, save the few on night patrol—and a lone figure in a square garden that breathed of healthy vegetation. Starlight shone palely on very long hair.

Marga landed, and transformed as she came face to face with Seshe. "I think I've seen you once before, have I not?" she asked.

"You are Marga," Seshe said. "I saw you in Imar, when you washed away the evil manor of the Norsundrians, and made that lake."

"Ah, ah," Marga said, clapping her hands lightly. "Yes, that was it."

The guards, alerted, approached, but Seshe smiled their way. "It's all right. She is an ally."

The guards bowed and retreated.

Seshe said, "I know what you've done for Chwahirsland. Is there a new thing? Ought I to waken Jilo? He just went off to sleep an hour or so ago."

"You can decide," Marga said. "I will tell you about the people I just met, and what I promised them."

Seshe listened in silence, as was her habit. At the end, she said, "East of the middle pass. And as for the magic, I hadn't thought of it, and ought to have. I can talk to Clair about transformation magic. If she doesn't know, Yanli might." Or Siamis, when he returns, she thought.

Marga thus relinquished the matter into the proper hands, twirled around, exulting in the clean air over the city that had been so noxious, and then she leaped into the air, transformed to her kestrel, and flew off, watched by the night guard, who added this amazing sight to the stories about Jilo: it seemed their king who was not a king was served by legends out of the past.

When Jilo woke, it was to a hot summer day and a pile of work that began with the vexing question of the shells and their desperate but impossible demand. However, when he came out of his room in search of breakfast, he found Seshe waiting for him, so broad a smile on her face that his heart lightened at the sight.

As he dug into the meal she had ordered for him, she repeated what Marga had promised. Jilo listened, then put his eating sticks down. "It is good to know about the eastern pass. And about the possibility of that transformation magic; the process now is so lengthy and painful and there are so few left who know how to do it. Wan-Edhe killed off most of them. I don't know any of it—all my study went into wards, as you know. I'm hopeless there."

"I'll write a note to Clair today."

"Thank you. I can pass orders about abandoning that fortress, which I never want to see again anyway, whatever the problem might be. But even if the shells are on their way, their demand is still untenable."

"Not if you wait," Seshe said. "I was thinking about it as I planted my ginger root. If you declare that since there is such interest in Dragonspring, and you have recently been told that the best land for it is east of the pass, the first to reach that land will get the concession, then that would take care of the problem, would it not?"

Jilo rubbed his eyes. "Oh, I see. I'd say nothing to anyone, so that it's clear I will not be pressured by any demands. But then I make the announcement when I know the shells are nearly there?"

"Yes."

"I wonder if they can get there without raising a dust over their motions. Ah, I'm not thinking. No one saw them desert and gather, though they are drawn from all five armies, much less noticed them going up that mountain. I think we can safely assume they will go covert to the middle pass." He smiled, and, daring, leaned over awkwardly to kiss Seshe — realizing too late that he'd just been eating.

She laughed silently, and kissed him back. "I like the taste of gut balls," she said, pointing to his half-eaten rye biscuit. "Let's see, what else can we accomplish today?"

15

Fortnyal Roth's palace was quiet. Lyren? Peacefully asleep. Ironically.

A few hours before dawn, Laban's eyes burned from hours of diligent work, and he was no closer to sleep. He prowled once around the quiet building, then gave up and braced for a long transfer. The sun was sinking as the kingdom of Yaldar ended its day.

The transfer nearly dropped him, but he steadied himself against the wall outside the tree-secluded pleasure house to which Siamis had thoughtfully introduced the boys years ago. Here the arts were all sensory, and the artists well-trained.

He walked inside. Music set an atmosphere of leisure as well as pleasure, a threesome on string, flute, and drum. Spiced wine and fresh apple-tarts scented the air, layered with subtle herbs that had been thrown on the fire.

The hall gave onto the great parlor, redecorated every year by someone with both taste and money. Around the room people clustered, customers and workers mixing freely. At Laban's appearance most of the former looked up. Laban saw that he was recognized; his gaze sorted them until he found the one he'd hoped was free. In this place, her name was Anelie.

She was tall, blond, ten years older than he, and moved with the dancer's grace that reminded him suddenly of Lyren. Or did Lyren remind him of her? He was too tired to tell. Too grubby, he realized belatedly, but in this place, the customer was always greeted with a smile. She disengaged from the people with whom she'd been talking and approached, her intelligent brown gaze assessing him with expertise. She linked her arm within his, and they walked upstairs to her chamber, which was always made fresh and ready every time she left it.

"Anelie," he began, as she pushed him, laughing a little, through her cleaning frame.

"Don't tell me. It's that silly, selfish girl again."

"Not selfish," Laban said as she guided him to a chair and began to knead his shoulders. "Ouch," she exclaimed. "Your muscles are like rocks."

He already knew that, or he wouldn't be here. "Not selfish," he repeated, because, though he knew Anelie was entertained by stories about people she'd never meet, those people were part of his life.

"Mmmm, someone who plays come hither to every passing someone else, but won't let them touch, is worse than selfish."

"If she were one of those," Laban said, "she'd be intolerable. And I would have booted her out ages ago. She's utterly unconscious of her effect."

Anelie kneaded for a while longer, as his eyes rolled in his head. "Don't stop," he managed to utter when she paused.

"I won't. But I can't help thinking: if she's remained unconscious all this time, then it's you at fault."

Laban sighed. "Neither of us wants the firestorm of a first timer. You know Vana. His affairs don't even last as long a visit here, boys or girls. He's terrified of the prospect of being her first time."

"Ah, he thinks she'll get serious? My, my, my. The horror!" She chuckled.

She had taught him, years ago, that giving pleasure could be as satisfying as the getting; that the give and take of physical congress, if not an act of love, could at least be an art. She had shown him, with skill and laughter, that the mind could disengage and free the body to the dance of desire, anticipation, and release.

Mindful of his partner's needs, he tried to lift his hands to her bodice laces, to find them slapped away. Her fingers paused in drawing the laces of his shirt, and pressed against his lips. "Don't talk," she said. "Don't think. You are far too tense."

She pushed him face down onto the bed, and her strong hands began working their way down his back, pressing, sometimes painfully, those knotted rocks until his muscles began to silken.

"Don't think," she said again. "But before you return, I want you to promise me, you're going to talk to that silly girl."

"That's the problem," he mumbled, face down into the mattress, euphoria and mounting desire nearly making him drool. "No longer a girl."

"If she's giving the world the hot eye without understanding what she's doing, she's still a girl." Anelie gave his butt a stinging smack. "Promise me!"

At that point he would have promised anything. "I will."

Neither Laban nor Silvanas was there when Lyren rose bright and early the next morning. No matter. She had to get ready, for she was hosting a music party out in the garden behind Ferdrian's royal palace. Mad had talked to the Dei cousins closest to her age, who had all promised to bring unattached young men. The rest of the guests would be the Dei cousins, and anyone else they thought might add to the fun — most known to Carl, so that her first party would be mainly comprised of familiar faces,

Lyren dashed through the cleaning frame, then frowned at her clothes. Here was her butterfly over-robe, light, pretty … and it tended to catch the eye. Remembering Carl's plain gray, Lyren grimaced, and settled on an older robe of fine linen in muted lavender. Usually she wore it under gauzy layers, but she wanted to make certain those boys' eyes went to Carl and stayed there.

She put on her plainest party sandals, braided her hair back and tied it with a lavender ribbon. That would do.

The party was a huge success. The Dei cousins had talked of this party so much that many friends asked to be included. The targeted potential suitors all accepted the invitation, some looking forward to diversion, others curious, and a few with ambitions of their own. Imagine! Ferdrian's royal palace having a party, like the ones they heard about in their grandparents' days!

The sun was bright and hot by the time everyone gathered, but it was pleasant beneath the chestnut trees and the two great oaks that had shaded the Delieth siblings' great-grandfather when he was young. Cook, delighted to use all his training at last, and given permission to hire new helpers, provided a splendid array of summer foods, and refreshing citrus punch, chilled all night in the cold room.

FJ led the younger guests in some outdoor games, and Mad was the first to call for dancing. When the heat defeated even the most indefatigable dancers, there was the fountain spray to cool them. The average age being seventeen to nineteen, no one minded clothes getting wet; after the first few self-conscious moments, dignity gradually flitted off with the birds startled out of afternoon somnolence.

Lyren moved about in the background, keeping her eye on the flow of food and drink, and watching Carl's every smile as Mad and her two closest cousins made sure that their chosen young men were part of the ever-changing circle around Carl. Not that any of said young men were reluctant. Oh, no. Who would forgo the chance to get acquainted with the soft-spoken princess who would be crowned queen next spring?

Carl had worn gray again, but it was an elegantly designed, simple robe in soft pearl gray that went well with her brown skin, and brought out the silver in her gray eyes. She looked her best, and Lyren cherished the dusky rose that came and went in her cheeks, and her occasional soft laugh. Although she never stirred from her seat, she seemed to be enjoying herself.

The party broke up as the sun began its westward descent, but as people began to disperse, Mad, FJ, and Wenwen assured everyone that there would be more parties.

Carl thanked her sisters, having successfully hidden how much she'd dreaded it. She hadn't any idea what to do at parties! But when Jessan asked if she wanted the sibs told to cancel any further efforts, she said, "No, no. I want to learn! It's just that I never had the chance."

Feeling guilty once more for his having left his gentle twin to that arid life, Jessan encouraged Mad and Wenwen to plan more. "Easy things," he cautioned. "Picnics. Games days. Riding parties up the river. No grand balls. I don't think she's ready for that yet."

When the girls clamored to Lyren—for they were all ready for a masquerade ball—she disappointed them by agreeing with Jessan. "It's all new for Carl. But that doesn't mean never. I happen to know all the latest dances in Sartor. Let's teach her those first, and then have an afternoon dance party for the cousins so she can practice with a partner, and then we'll see about a ball. You have that fine ballroom here. Seems a shame not to use it."

"That's what *I* say," Mad declared.

And so, over the next month, that's what happened. Carl discovered that parties were easy — and though she invariably stayed up late to make up for lost time, she found herself looking forward to the next one.

If only she had the courage to ask Laban to come to one, then everything would be perfect. He continued to visit her once a week, but he only stayed long enough to confer over crown business. At least she had him to herself during that time. He listened patiently, and when he spoke, it was always a suggestion, never a demand. She began to exult in how extensive his thinking was — how he foresaw things she still did not see yet. Though he'd been ruling for nearly ten years, and she for barely half a year, she strove to learn as much as she could as fast as she could. And so, though she attended each party, and practiced her party manners with conscientious care, whenever she was left alone, she shut her eyes, listened to the music, and thought about things Laban had said.

She never told anyone these thoughts. Jessan, she had discovered, had his own private life, one he did not speak about, nor did she ask. She took her cue from him. The boundaries that they had crossed so easily when they were small had become different paths.

She liked looking at many of the comely young men her sisters seemed eager to introduce to her, but to Carl, nothing in the world was more attractive than Laban sitting across from her, sleeves rolled to the elbows on a hot morning, discussing tariffs and trade, precedents and pitfalls. In these past weeks she found herself exerting her wits to prolong those talks. He never asked about the parties, though Carl had suggested to Lyren that she might invite him if he had time. She hoped to find him at each new party, but it never happened. And she couldn't quite bring herself to ask him herself. It would be so horrible if he said no. She didn't mind the occasional disagreement over state matters, because they always talked those out, and they were never … personal.

Mad said at breakfast later that month, "Let's plan a ball. I think we're ready!"

"A ball," Carl repeated. That would include couples dances, which she had been practicing with her sisters. But the thought of one of those smiling boys holding her close made her exclaim, "You can host it without me. I have so much work to do."

"There's no purpose in it without you there," Wenwen whined.

Carl looked surprised at this. "I scarcely ever see you at the parties. But when I do see you, you're having a wonderful time. What is it about me that would take away your fun?"

Wenwen's mouth opened, closed, and she cast a desperate glance Mad's way.

Madelon crossed her arms. "You don't have too much work to do when it's a lawn party, Carl. And you don't have to do anything but dress and come. Lyren's been teaching us how to organize parties, so we'll do all the work. You have to be there because we finally have a real court. Finally. I was even thinking of asking Aurora to come. But if you don't come it'll be … it'll be like Tahra-Mama all over again."

That random shot stung Carl, who reddened guiltily. "I didn't think of that. I'm sorry if I'm being selfish. Of course I'll come."

"Not selfish. Never that," Mad exclaimed with real regret. "But we're trying to give you a good life. Lyren says it's better for you than if you just work all the time. That might be all right now, because you're still learning, but if it gets to be habit, you *will* turn into Tahra-Mama."

Carl bit her underlip. "I don't want to sound stingy, but we do still have to be careful with money. And aren't balls expensive?"

Mad was on sure ground here. "We're not going to have ridiculous decorations, the way they talk about in the south. Lyren says, all a ball needs is plenty of dancing space, music, and refreshments. Cook says we never have used all of what we have here, which is why most of our produce goes to the guild homes for the old."

Carl's brow furrowed. "I would not want to short them, if they depend on us…"

"But they don't. FJ says that a lot of it gets sold off on the side, and the money goes into someone's pockets. Anyway, it's *our* kitchen garden. We're *supposed* to use it. And Lyren says the best decorations are garlands and flowers, which don't cost anything. The entire garden is a-bloom. We just need to get everyone to help make the garlands, and we can have a party to do that!"

Jessan, watching his sister covertly, remained silent, glad

to see Carl coming out of that habit of isolation. When she laughed and gave in—promising herself that this time, she had to gather her courage and ask Laban to attend—Jessan went away pleased, and when Lyren turned up later that morning, he told her what Carl had said. "As long as you don't load the planning onto her, in addition to everything else she's trying to learn, it seems she's beginning to be a little more sure of herself."

"Excellent," Lyren said. "I like planning parties. My goal is for Ferdrian to host a real masquerade, maybe for Harvest Festival. This would be for the entire court. I overheard Rel saying once that Ferdrian's court used to be the merriest one he'd ever been to in his traveling days. We need to convince the elder generation as well as the young that the bad days of war are truly over. I think that will do its bit to bolster Carl's rule."

Jessan's rare smile emerged, and they went about their separate business, Lyren to consult with Jenel Sandrial and Cook.

She scarcely saw Laban during this time, and Silvanas even more rarely. This was perfectly fine. She had not forgotten Carl's shy hint about inviting Laban, which she most emphatically did not want to do, because she knew if he came, Carl would spend all her time watching him. She would not avoid him. That didn't sit quite right. If she didn't see him, she couldn't pass on the invitation, could she?

But one very early morning they met at the breakfast table, each intending to be up and away without disturbing the other. Laban said, "It's just after sunup. I thought you'd be sleeping half the morning."

"Scavenger hunt in the garden," Lyren said. "I promised FJ I'd help him design it and get the clues laid out."

"Your revelries in Ferdrian seem to be a huge success."

"Oh?" Lyren could not remember having said anything about the court life.

"Carl mentioned at our last meeting over the cotton trade question that she's having fun. Keep it up," he said. "Especially now." He cast a rueful glance westward.

"Trouble?" she asked, glad at the shift in subject.

"Of a sort. I hope it's no worse than an annoyance. I'm going to have to do some scouting since Silvanas is riding with the Knights. And I don't want Carl worrying until I've figured out what it is and what to do about it. She's anxious about enough things."

"Understood," Lyren said. And if Laban had some urgent task beyond the border, then he wouldn't have time for a ball. Perfect.

Lyren left, relieved everything was settling out relatively easily, as Laban returned to his room, and glanced down at the small folded paper he had received that morning, written in a tiny, clear hand:

> *I have tried twice to mention this at our meetings, but I find it easier to bring it up in a note. I don't know if you have the time or inclination, and please don't feel obliged in any case. But if you have nothing to do the following Sixthday evening, we are hosting our first ball. You would be most welcome!*
>
> *You don't have to answer. Come or not as is best for you — whichever you choose, it will not impair our state dealings in the least.*
>
> *Carl*

16

The first dropped leaves of impending fall kicked up around the horses' feet. Laban checked saddles and equipment on the horses while Silvanas leaned against his favorite mare, yawning. At Laban's skeptical glance — they were supposed to be fresh for this exercise — Vana's grin flashed white in his sun-browned face.

Laban turned away, scanning the mossy-stoned courtyard of the inn he'd chosen as the rendezvous.

Vana yawned, then wiped his eyes.

The innkeeper emerged, his face anxious. "We can raise half a dozen folk off the haying, if you need them," he said. "All of 'em saw some fighting in the war. Though I don't understand why the Knights aren't here."

Laban forced himself to smile reassuringly. He did not want to insult the villagers, who he suspected hadn't touched their blades in ten years.

"It's all right. Your people have more important work right now, and we can handle them. And the Knights are riding to far more important demands than this one. We're just waiting for one more of us."

The innkeeper's wife appeared in the doorway, square and gray-haired. She cast one narrow-eyed glance at Laban and Silvanas. Recognizing the latter, she gave a nod of grim approval, then tapped her spouse on the arm. "We've spuds to peel, Hrad."

Her accent was local. His was not. With a last anxious glance backward, Hrad retreated inside.

Laban turned to the horses once more, to make what he

knew was an unnecessary check of their feet, when he sensed the tingle of transfer-magic. David appeared, having used Laban as a Destination. No transfer reaction, though Curtas's House down in Sartor's mountains was a very long way away. Laban renewed his vow to master the slide transfer as David cast a glance of appraisal at their surroundings, then said, "Sorry. Had to dust off my hat."

By which both Vana and Laban knew that he'd faced some sort of crisis at his mountain school, which he'd either straight-armed into resolution or else had left to Adam. If he'd solved it easily, he would have been more forthcoming.

Vana cocked an eyebrow. "Imry?"

David gave his head a shake. "He's behaving with exemplary manners."

"That's a bad sign." Laban tossed the reins of the gray to David.

"We'll see." David's face was bland, a sure warning for any who cared to heed it.

Laban suspected that if the problem wasn't Imry, then it likely lay in Marloven Hess. "You sure you want to do this? It seems you don't have a lot of excess time. And I can always yank MV in for backup."

David tipped his head sideways. "You could. But he's actually busy as well, these days."

Laban's brows slanted. "At what?"

"Oh, he'll yap when he's ready. It's not like he could hide it." David shook with silent laughter. "Let's ride." He mounted up, the black sword slung over his shoulder, and a long knife at his side. The rest of his weaponry was hidden beneath his loose-fitting common laborer's clothes.

The truth was, Laban could have pulled in Leef or Rolfin, Erol, even, if things were quiet in Chwahirsland, but he knew that David was always going to consider a problem in Everon to be his problem to help solve, if he could: residual guilt from his having killed Glenn Delieth, however accidental. No matter how hard everyone argued that Glenn had been an obnoxious shit, worsening by the day, David maintained that was irrelevant. He'd gone against orders and killed someone, with consequences they were still dealing with now. Death was not an accident one could back away from, however sorry one was.

"Ride it is."

Laban had only an old, blunt sword in a saddle-sheath. His role required a pacific demeanor. Vana wore his old stable yard gear, the clothes he liked best for horse-training; hidden on his person he probably carried more hardware than David, who disliked going about armed at least as much as MV preferred it. The only hint of prosperity was the gold ring in one ear.

They started up the winding road toward the Darfaed Pass, which was Everon's main route between the lakes to Daraen to the west. The horses were young, and fresh, beautifully battle-trained by Vana—so responsive Laban did not have to think about his reins, and his mind instead began the past-present-future mental assessment that was his habit.

Like the prospective ball the following night. Laban had been wavering for days. Go, or not? Laban knew that Carl had been striving to make her note sound neutral. Not just that, almost apologetic, inviting his regrets, but he'd seen the nerves in her tiny print. He could hear the rush of her soft voice, a quaver beneath as she tried so hard to smother her feelings. If he turned up, there would be more invitations. He didn't think it was arrogance to suspect where that path would lead—Carl was far too easy to read, in spite of her heroic attempt at hiding her emotions.

That path would be the easy one. But was it the right one? Yet turning her down would hurt her. Which would be like kicking a kitten. And yet he was aware that she was crowding him. Hard as she tried not to. And she was not to be faulted for her nature. He should have foreseen this possibility when he so carelessly agreed to Wenwen's suggestion to send a little gift…

He was so involved in trying to think out all possible consequences that he scarcely noticed that the other two spoke very little. Mostly they rode, alert in all senses; David was indeed tense about Liere's situation, or more specifically, he was tense about Senrid waiting in the background, his emotional fortress nigh impregnable…

Even Silvanas, whom everyone envied for his life of total freedom, had his concerns, mainly in the shape of Carinna Dei, Commander of the Knights of Dei, who had said to him the week previous, *We both know that you are qualified in every way to command the Knights, more qualified than I am, or can ever hope to be. I can see you'll be good for us—and our strength is going to be needed sooner than later, if I'm reading the signs from some of those Imaran private armies aright. I really don't care what my great-great grandfathers did. I don't want to fight a duel over command, and I know some of the veterans are pushing you to challenge me.* Silvanas respected her far too much to let that happen…

They camped above the well-traveled road, dusty in the summer sun, and started out when darkness began to lift.

"You gave me the general. How about the specifics?" David asked Laban, having noticed at last that Laban was restless. "Or are you second-guessing yourself?"

"No." Laban scowled. "Here's the summary. Since winter, especially the past few months, scouts said various hill villages reported the sudden appearance of strangers, adults all, mostly men, in twos and threes. Raffish strangers, who looked about with interest. Asked a lot of questions, then left, often with stolen goods. Never anything major, but most often steel implements."

"Questions about? No, let me guess. Daraen lies to the west of Everon. Not much for them to trade outside their ore."

"And there it is. Since last year, two wagon trains of ore have vanished. One, anything could have happened, including the wagoneers stealing it themselves. Two?"

"Stealing ore," David said. "That's a bad sign."

Silvanas glanced back. "The trail to their camp is up past that outcropping with the three lodge pines."

"Ride around and flank 'em?"

"No," Laban said reluctantly. "We need information, not surprise. I need to know if this is it, or if there's a larger force of them hiding up somewhere, and this gang is merely an outpost. I need to know who's leading. If I know the name—"

They thought they'd gotten all Efael's Black Knives, but turned out there were still two unaccounted for. "Right."

"—and yes, I'll be the bait. Vana's familiar with the area. Come in when I send, will you?"

"And you don't want the Knights in this?"

Laban glanced at Silvanas, who shook his head, saying, "Not ready. Tahra pretty much yanked their weapons and replaced them with tally sheets these past ten years—"

"Except for orders to shoot me on sight," Laban put in.

"—which might be why these renegades are sniffing around." Silvanas lifted a shoulder. "But with Tahra gone, the Knights are starting to shape up. Give them a couple years. They'll be back to what they were. Better."

That was fine for the future, but right now, that meant two

against how many? David shrugged. If it was impossible odds, Laban would think of something. "It's your stunt."

The turnoff to the new path had been obscured by bushes and rocks. They skirted this mess, the horsts picking their way, ears atwitch. They started single file upward, overshadowed by pine, hickory, and other old growth.

Presently David said, "Just niffed a brace of sentries not far ahead."

Laban sighed. "Time for me to blunder into them."

David smiled with sympathy. Nobody liked being the bait, except maybe MV in certain moods. "Are we coming in easy or hard?"

Laban lifted a shoulder. "I want them running away in fear, spreading the word that the Knights are too tough to mess with. But if any of 'em are Aldon's or Efael's grays, trash 'em. There's been rumors of murder sprees up in the mountains back there."

The other two obligingly turned their mounts aside, halting under a spreading oak, its leaves beginning to edge ruddy yellow on the sun side.

Laban rode alone uphill, the trail getting narrower, though there were signs of recent use. His 'disguise' was the two saddlebags full of wool samples. As he rode upward, a breeze began to rise, kicking up dust, which stung his eyes and went down his neck, for he'd clubbed his hair in order to look the part of the sober businessman — and to facilitate action when and if it were needed.

As he rode, he worried at his situation. He knew how certain kinds of moral or ethical compromise led by subtle degrees to the undoing of even the best intentions. He had set himself a standard when he took Wnelder Vee's empty throne, and he would stay to it, though it might very well require a lifetime of effort. He sometimes wished Tahra had been able to see the irony in how her own unrelenting hatred had set him up as some kind of mythical hero to Carl in a way he never could have accomplished on his own.

Morality was always going to mean conscious choices, he knew it and accepted it. It was not instinctive, and would never be; whether caused by his upbringing in Norsunder or by his having inherited the adaptable nature of the Deis, or a combination of both, it didn't really matter. He had sworn he would never raise a hand against Tahra, though he could have easily contrived her death, and now she was gone. He had sworn he would remain strictly general with Carl, rather than use the hero-worship she couldn't hide. But that had been before she reached out to him.

The clatter of rocks tumbling down a hillside brought his attention to the trail. His mount danced, her eyes rolling. Laban made soothing noises as from either side riders plunged down to block him from going in either direction.

Miming bewilderment, he looked around. "Here! What's going—?"

"I'll take that." One reached for his sword, pulling it; the other gripped his reins at the bridle.

"Who are you?" Laban stuttered. "Is there some trouble on the Pass?"

"Yes," the one with his sword said, grinning. It was an ugly grin, smug and anticipatory. "And you're in it."

"I protest," Laban whined.

The answer was a clout from behind. Laban forced himself not to use the momentum against the one in reach. He fell, knowing he was supposed to fall. A moment later a heavy body thumped atop him, pressing him face down into the dirt and rubble of the trail. His hands were wrenched behind his back, and bound there.

His cheek ground against a stone. Pain lanced up his arms, and through his eye. Fury and laughter swooped through him; why had he been so quick to volunteer to be the target? Next time Vana offered, he'd be prompt with his YES.

He was yanked to his feet, blindfolded, and force-marched up the hill. When he tripped over unseen roots and rocks, one or other of his captors jerked him more or less upright. It was not a pleasant trip. By the time they halted, his laughter was gone, replaced by anger.

"Well now," someone new said. "What've we got?"

Laban's captors blustered some brag about their capture as Laban scanned on the mental plane. The blindfold made it easier to concentrate. No one was shielded. He used their eyes to mark the path, including traps and hidden watchers along the way.

He shared these gleanings with David and Silvanas on the mental plane.

"Search him," the leader said, stepping forward, and radiating menace as he ripped the blindfold free.

Rough hands ran over Laban, finding no weapons, of course. The searcher whooped when encountering the money pouch Laban had prepared, then cursed at the scant handful of low coinage amid fresh-picked walnuts.

David's contact came: *Black Knife?*

: No. But I'm pretty sure I recognize the leader's voice. One of Aldon's grays, from the Fhleria campaign.

Like the two scouts, the leader was big, maybe forty, armed with sword, club, and a long blackweave whip. A fire fifteen, twenty paces away sported iron rods thrust in. Torture?

Laban's saddlebags thumped to the ground before the leader. Laban kept his gaze forward, sensing half a dozen more flanking him, three one side, three the other. Besides the two east-side sentinels.

"Samples. No money in the bags," the searcher called up. "Trained mount."

"Well, then, you forgot your toll fee." The leader bent over Laban, elbows out. "I'm afraid that means you're the fee."

Guffaws from the audience at this wit. Torture, it seemed, was the entertainment of choice.

Laban stepped back, casting about for some way to postpone the inevitable. Where was the other gray? Over there on the other side of the fire, along with a cluster of others. Good thing? This was definitely their leader. This was not a scouting expedition ahead of a bigger force hiding up somewhere.

Bad thing? He was to be the entertainment.

He glimpsed the blurred approach of a fist, and instinct was too fast for control. He ducked, one foot sweeping out to hook the man's ankle. The leader went down, and one of the men snickered.

Damn. Now the game plan would be to bypass the Terrify the Prisoner chat and proceed right to target practice.

The leader scrambled to his feet, snarling curses. The two scouts grabbed Laban's arms before he got three steps, and the next few moments were extremely painful.

Laban, doubled over from a blow to the gut, sent out a mental call: *Any time now, shitbirds.* He tried to whistle to the horse—it was too late for playacting anyway—but his lips had already begun to puff up from the first smack.

Shouts of surprise, quickly cut off, from down the hillside caused everyone's heads to turn.

Laban grinned, ignoring the pain that caused, and snapped

a kick to the leader's gut. When the man bent over, trying to remember how to breathe, Laban followed up with his heel to the jaw. Crack! Broken neck. One more of Aldon's killers dead before he hit the ground.

"The rest of the Knight trainees are coming along when they finish lunch," came David's loud, cheerful voice. "The real Knights are letting us get some practice—"

Horse hooves sounded behind. Laban cursed. Where? Ah. The scouts and the perimeter guards had spread to face this new threat. Vana unlimbered his sword and a long double-bladed knife. Plunging toward the biggest knot, he weighed in, grinning.

From beyond the hill the rest of the renegades came running. For a desperate few moments, it looked as if the two would be overwhelmed by sheer numbers as the renegades screamed invective and orders at one another.

"David!"

The blond head cut Laban's way, the horse sidled, responsive to knee-cues and ignoring the flashing swords. Laban turned his back, wrists straining to keep the ropes taut. Did David have his old precision? The familiar whistle of the black sword cutting air—a whoosh, a brief tug at his arms—and the ropes fell away.

David tossed down a knife, which Laban nearly dropped; his fingers tingled with a million angry beestings as he fumbled it.

Find the other gray ... Laban shook his head, fighting to clear it enough to do a mental scan. When he niffed that mind, it was just in time to see David whirl and strike his way through four or five of them. The ex-Norsundrian torturer's mental flame snuffed suddenly; David had, in one smooth motion, cut his throat.

"Think the Knights will let us join the patrols?" he called over his shoulder, ducking a blade and using his hilt to club an attacker across the back of the neck.

"Carinna Dei thinks you're just too slow," Vana called back.

Weren't they overdoing it a little?

No—a glance around showed that the gang was pretty well terrorized, and Vana was actually in pursuit of three of 'em. So, now, was David.

Two came Laban's way. He dropped the knife—his hands

wouldn't work anyway — and kicked out a knee, broke a couple ribs with another side-kick, and that was that.

When they were all on the run or down, groaning or unconscious, David looked around, hands on hips. "I thought there were more of 'em," he complained. "Get well soon, boys," he called, and as one staggered to his feet just behind him, knife raised, he whirled around and used his palm heel to flatten the fellow. "And hurry back! Next time, our first-year trainees are going to want some practice."

Laban retrieved the old sword from a groaning scout, mounted up, and they rode back downhill.

"Well, that was bracing," David said when they reached the road. He didn't wait for an answer; he raised his hands and transferred.

Laban had it now. David's mood definitely had to do with Senrid. Laban had respected Senrid since they were fifteen-year-old boys trying their best to knock one another's teeth out. He hoped that situation would resolve, but it was not even remotely his problem to worry about. He had enough to deal with, beginning with — he glanced at the sun — a decision to make about a ball he was expected to grace once the sun had set.

Only … what was that about MV?

Wincing at every step as his bruised muscles began to lock up, he left Vana to deal with the mounts, and transferred to Fortnyal Roth, where he stood in the middle of his room, imagining the hurt in Carl's eyes if he didn't turn up. She wouldn't say anything to anybody. Not even to him the next time they meet to consult. But the hurt would be there.

17

Laban's entire body ached. Why didn't they keep any lister-blossom on hand? He couldn't risk drinking a glass of wine to take the edge off the pain, for he needed all his wits for the evening ahead.

He didn't think he'd manage transfer reaction without puking, so he took clothes to change in and winced his way down to the bathhouse. He paid for a private alcove rather than use the big pool, from which he could hear cheerful voices. The fewer questions the better. Not that he had anything to hide from a collection of artisans and scribes, from the sounds. He just didn't want to make the effort to speak.

The bathhouse was very old, a rudimentary building that was built around the pool diverted from the river. He'd arranged for the building to be renovated, with a huge cistern on the roof for the hot water; he'd done the magic to heat the water himself during his first two years as king. He flung off his filthy clothes and stepped hissing into the bath. His stiffening muscles protested for a breathless moment, then began to ease to almost bearable. He leaned his head back against the rim and closed his eyes…

A hand on his shoulder and an insistent voice roused him.

"Eh?" Laban said, and realized he was immersed in barely lukewarm water.

Everything rushed back as the bath attendant said, 'You fell asleep. I called out to see if you wanted more hot water, and you didn't answer, so I came in. I was afraid you might slip down and drown."

Laban hauled himself out. The aches promptly returned, worse than before. He winced his way back to his end of the rambling building regarded as the royal palace. He chose a shirt cuffed with lace that reached almost to his knuckles, which he hoped would hide the rope-burned flesh around his wrists, and loose trousers. He cast a glance in the mirror as he laced up the shirt. Purplish stipple-marks, what MV used to call knuckle-dusting, marked his ribs. The way his gut felt, he'd expected to see bruises the size of a dinner plate.

The big bruises had been reserved for the back of his right shoulder, and the leg where he'd fallen. Definitely the hero, he thought as he winced and grunted his way into a paneled robe the color of his eyes, which he hoped would draw attention from the purple swelling on his jaw. He'd wear his hair loose, as it might help hide that jaw. A sash, some fineweave boots, and he was as ready as he'd ever be.

He transferred to Ferdrian's royal palace, using as Destination his now customary spot outside Carl's study. He'd survived the transfer, though for a few painful heartbeats he wished he hadn't. When the reaction eased, he looked around the dark hallway. Of course no one was there. The bright sounds of dance music beckoned, and he moved in that direction, trying to work some of the stiffness out.

When he reached the ballroom, it was evident at a glance that the festivities had been going on for some time. How long had he slept? Red-cheeked dancers pranced and twirled and leaped in the center of the room. A glimpse through the two sets of double doors on the far side revealed at least as many dancing out on the terrace, which was lit by what appeared to be every lamp in the palace. The effect, along with garlands of flowers, and tiny candles hung from the branches of the potted trees, transformed the drab terrace to unexpected charm.

Laban scanned the dancers, but did not see Carl. His plan was to catch her eye, bow, smile, and wave, in hopes she thought he'd been there longer, then leave. But he counted without that Delieth vigilance: she had been watching every door all evening, and so she appeared at his side while he was still searching the crowd. "You came," she said, her eyes wide and bright with the reflections of the chandeliers' flames. "Welcome."

So much for attempting to imply he'd been here all along. He smiled. "Late, I know. My apologies. I lost track of time."

Her welcoming smile bloomed all over her face, but by the end of his speech, which he meant to sound cheerful, her smile faded to a pensive question, and gaze fixed on his jaw as she whispered, "What happened to you?"

"Horse kicked me," he lied. Careless shrug. "My fault—I was daydreaming."

Her breath hissed in. He heard it, in spite of the music and chatter and clink of crystal glasses. Her hands clasped and wrung together as she fought against expressing words of concern. She was too scrupulous to utter them; she was morbidly afraid that she had not the right.

"It looks much worse than it feels," he lied some more, holding out his arm. "Dance? Though I'll confess I might not be the best dancer out there right now." He'd do his duty—he could endure one turn around the floor—then he'd be free.

To his surprise she shook her head, glanced around, and gestured to one of the curtained alcoves along the inner wall. He walked in, and ah, spotted a chair. She followed him. Before she let the curtain fall she caught the gaze of her maid, who had retreated out of earshot. Ansa understood immediately and took up her station outside the curtain after Carl closed it.

Laban eased himself onto the chair. The chair had a nice, plump cushion. He had never before been so grateful for so homely an object.

Carl drew her chair forward a bit, so that she could see his face in the light of the single lamp. She sat, toes and knees together, her hands tightly folded in her lap, and said barely above a whisper, "Thank you for coming. But I think you ought to go back."

"Not as bad as it looks," he said, touching his jaw.

"Please pardon me for contradicting, but to my eyes, you move as if everything hurts. I felt that kind of pain only once, but I remember what that was like."

Laban forced a smile. "I've been in worse shape and survived."

Emboldened by the fact that he hadn't annihilated her for her presumption, Carl rushed on, "It was something, a danger of some kind, on the border? Our border. Everon's border. Wasn't it? Cousin Carinna wouldn't tell me outright, but I knew that something disturbed her. Her latest report mentioned scouting beyond the foothills but she said she knew little about it."

"There's no problem now," he said.

Carl's gaze remained steady. "Because you dealt with it, nearly at the cost of your life?"

"It was never that bad," he began, and stopped, aghast because her eyes sparkled, gleamed—and the liquid gleam spilled down her cheeks in tears. "Carl, I'm sorry."

"You should be," she whispered.

He stared, stunned.

Her face reddened, and she gasped. "Oh! No! I don't mean it like that. I don't. *Truly* I don't. I do not mean to be ungrateful! I'm a little uneasy only because people will. *Not. Stop. Keeping* things from me, supposedly for my own good." She wiped her eyes on her pale blue sleeve, blotching the silk. "Oh, I'm truly appreciative that everyone cares. But if I am to learn to rule, I need to know these things. And be part of making the decisions. Not have them made for me."

"I apologize, Carl." He grimaced. "Again."

"It's not just you," she said. "I will have to talk to them all. Even Jessan, who of all people ought to know better." She smiled painfully. "I am so happy you came. It's the best thing to happen to me this year. That you came. Tonight. Even though I am very sure you would rather be lying down, sound asleep. But you came anyway." Her gaze shifted. "I won't trouble you again."

"The timing was not the best, otherwise we'd be out there sweating up a storm with the others," he said, smiling. "Me tripping over my own feet, most likely. It's been a while since I practiced." And when she didn't answer, he dropped the joking tone. "I can give you a full report. Do you want it now, or at our usual meeting Firstday morning?"

Carl had been remembering how terrible she'd felt for several days after Tahra-Mama had slapped her, and she'd fallen against her desk. Laban looked like he was much worse off. "I won't be here," she said, making a sudden decision, and striving to sound as if she'd planned it all along. After all, two could make plans that the other did not know about. "I will not be here," she said again, more firmly. "Jessan has encouraged me to travel around to see things for myself. Since harvest season is on us, I am doing that. I know I'll learn much more by seeing everything, and speaking to people face to face. But I will send you a note when I return. Is that all right?"

Laban—usually so articulate—gave a mute nod. He was

too tired, too full of aches and pains and unresolved knots that needed mental space for untangling, to notice anything besides her decisiveness.

"Transfer from here. It's all right," she said. "I'll feel better to see you safely gone."

He braced himself, and obeyed.

The other vigilant observer was Lyren. She noted Laban's appearance, and the oddly stiff way he walked. She sighed as Carl and Laban vanished into the alcove; when Carl reappeared alone, she sighed again, this time with relief. It was not a long conversation at all. State business that couldn't wait?

Maybe, but Carl continued to avoid all the couples dances. Lyren watched from the sidelines, wondering if Carl had grown to be more like Tahra than anyone suspected, in disliking being touched. A whoop and holler went up from the terrace, followed by laughter, then the sight of the younger guests, regardless of their good clothes, chasing after something.

What looked like a white mop on very short legs shot into the ballroom, dodged around couples, who staggered, laughing or exclaiming, then leaped into Carl's arms. Carl clutched the little dog, who covered her face with frantic licking.

"I'm sorry," Wenwen called, racing in. "Lace-lace must have got through the crack in the window. I know I shut them all in."

Maybe it was only the touch of prospective suitors, Lyren wondered; Tahra had disliked cats and dogs within doors, and barely tolerated them outside. It was their randomness, and the shed hairs, and of course the licking that had disturbed her, but Carl had always loved animals, and it was clear that she still did.

Whatever the truth of the matter, Carl was not paying any but polite attention to any of these boys. And some of them were very much worth paying attention to. Like that handsome one with the bright red hair, laughing in the far corner with a couple of friends. They were surrounded by admiring girls, fans fluttering.

Mad sidled up to Lyren. "Jessan says Laban was here. Was he?"

"For about ten heartbeats. But Carl saw him. I don't know

if it was a planned meeting or not. She went into that alcove, then came out alone."

Mad rubbed her hands. "That's good, isn't it?"

"I don't know," Lyren said. "Let's see if we can get her dancing."

Mad charged over to her sister, and yanked her into the sprightly dance that had just begun. Lyren watched, trying to assess Carl's mood. She seemed to be enjoying herself. She was certainly smiling at Mad's antics as she added extra twirls and mocking poses. But for the remainder of the evening, Carl either had to get something to drink, or to go outside in the cool air, whenever a couples dance was played.

Lyren transferred back to Fortnyal Roth very late. The next day, Laban didn't appear at all. The following day, he showed up at breakfast, a purple bruise on his jaw. When he winced into his seat, Lyren asked what had happened.

Silvanas sauntered in and said, "We had a little dust-up with some renegades. Laban volunteered to be the bait."

"Which I will never do again," Laban muttered, frowning at them from under his brow. "I'm not old! But I feel as if I turned a hundred yesterday. Why did it hurt so much less when we were boys?"

"It didn't," Silvanas said. "It's just that after an assignment, we seldom had much to do, so we sacked out and Curtas or Adam or Ferret dosed us with kinthus or listerblossom. You're up because you have to be."

Laban met this insight with a curse, cut short because it hurt to talk. "Listerblossom," he muttered.

"Ordered," Silvanas retorted. "Since you didn't."

Lyren expertly assessed Laban's expression, and decided against asking about Carl. In the mood he was in, she would very likely get her nose snapped off.

Later, she was glad she'd remained silent, for the next time she transferred to Ferdrian for a strategy session, it was to the news that Jessan and Carl had left not an hour previous for a harvest season tour of the kingdom.

Wenwen said, "Do we continue the parties?"

"Absolutely," Lyren said. "Let's get a regular court established. It'll be good for Carl to be away for a time. She'll have other things to think about than Laban, and new people to meet. We can use this time to really assess our candidates for suitor. We don't want to disinvite anyone, but we could start talking up the possibles. Have them over more often."

They put this plan into execution over the next few weeks, as Carl and Jessan made their way eastward, south along the coast, and then inland when they neared the Imaran border.

Carl surprised herself with how much she enjoyed travel as long as the weather was fine. Everything was so *interesting*. The scribe desk, with a trusted Dei cousin as chief scribe, kept her in daily contact with affairs at home.

Everything she learned, or saw, she kept wanting to share with Laban, to demonstrate how much she was gaining by the experience. She choked off the impulse to write to him, of course. If he wrote to her first, that would be different, but he didn't. She finally compromised by adding at the end of her reports to her scribe desk that if Laban wished to see any of these, Carl granted permission to share. After all, there was nothing *personal*. All kingdom matters. And yet, as soon as the idea that Laban might read her words took root in her mind, she found herself shaping her reports for his eyes.

I knew about cutting hay, but did not know that harvest season begins with the haying, which must be done before the first thunder. There's an entire song about it. Sung in round, over and over. The melody is simple enough, but when done in round, it becomes wonderfully complex, especially when high or low voices add a descant or countermelody.

The words make little sense:

> *King Barley wags his chin-ah, lei-li nei-li nettle-*
> *ye-oh-ya!*
> *Queen Oatie sheds her skin-ah, lei-lo, nei-low,*
> *nettle-YUP-oh-ya!*

It's the high-voiced YUPs that put the skip in the melody, and though I only heard the song the once as our carriage rolled past, it's been echoing cheerfully in my ears since…

18

Laban recovered fast after those first couple of days, and was soon restless for news of Everon. But he knew he ought not to interfere. Not his kingdom, he kept repeating to himself, until Firstday rolled around again, and he decided to shift to Ferdrian in case there might be a report for him. If not, he'd take the hint and back off. But if there was…

A stack of reports waited for him, the middle-aged Dei relation regarding him with an unreadable expression. Not disapproval, but not a welcome, either. Guardedness. What did they expect? He was not going to answer that.

He thanked her as if she'd spoken graciously, and transferred back with the papers, which he tore into. Ah, there was Carinna Dei's write-up of the border incident, from her perspective. Of course she knew no details, but she scrupulously repeated Silvanas's summary; he could hear it in Vana's words. There were local reports as well as Carl's accounts from her travels. These, Laban saved for last. By midnight he'd caught up with all the Everon reports.

He began to read Carl's the following morning over breakfast. He was in the midst of a description of the wonders of malting when the sound of snickering reached him. Silvanas appeared, grinning so smugly that Laban was immediately suspicious. "What have you done?"

"Nothing! Except put Ferret on the case. It was what David said about MV a few weeks back. Realized I hadn't seen anything of him at all. Nor Mildred. Nor Siamis, except really briefly."

Laban lifted a shoulder. "It's not like we live at Detlev's house."

"But none of them live there either. When one shows up with news, everyone tends to show up, and catch up. Not those three."

"Siamis is translating that ancient stuff," Laban said. "What's new about that?"

Silvanas lifted his voice. "Ferret!"

Lyren appeared then, Ferret right behind her. He was still nondescript—easily overlooked. No one glancing at that unprepossessing face would ever guess that he had one of the most calculating minds of all the boys.

Lyren said, "He was just telling me that he'd heard Liere had her baby. He didn't know that I knew."

Laban peered up at her. "You didn't say anything."

"That's because I haven't seen him. Liere still doesn't want anyone there. Hard to believe he even exists."

"Does he have a name?"

"Not yet. She's letting Macael Elsarion name him."

Laban grunted, shrugging the subject aside, and turned to Ferret. "What is MV up to, and why didn't we know?"

Ferret rocked back and forth, his lips pressed to hide laughter. "Because he didn't want anyone to know until he was ready. The news being their baby."

"A baby? Liere's new one?" Laban asked, looking from one to the other.

"No. That was a separate subject," Lyren said. "If Liere has given her baby to MV, my eyes would fall out from the shock. Though I'd love to see Macael Elsarion try to take it away from *him*."

"*Whose* baby?"

"MV and Mildred's baby," Ferret said.

Silvanas added, "And Siamis was up there in that valley for the past few weeks, giving them lessons in infant care."

"MV?" Laban exclaimed. "A baby? MV? Mal Venn, and a *human* baby?"

"They're at Detlev's house right now," Ferret said. "Them and the baby. Siamis has taken off again."

Lyren's hair blew back as one after another, the three vanished, and imploding air rushed around. She had no business following after, something that MV was likely to comment on. And she didn't really care all that much what

Detlev's gang got up to.

She sat down to eat the abandoned breakfast, mentally considering plans to discuss with Madelon, as in Detlev's house, the three appeared in the order they had transferred. They joined the others encircling Mildred and MV sitting side by side on a settee, and all except Detlev, smiling in the background, stared in fascination at a chubby baby sitting on Mildred's lap. This baby, dressed only in a diaper in the summery breeze coming through the open windows, looked like any other baby, save his blue-black hair stuck straight up like duck's down, as if the child had been caught completely by surprise.

Silvanas found this hilarious, and half-smothered a snicker. Laban saw that the baby had Mildred's cat eyes, his pupils vertical slits.

"That's right," MV said, giving the three newcomers a narrow glare. "Everyone gather around and stare. What a bunch of sh—"

Mildred shot him a look.

"—birdwits," MV finished awkwardly. "Damnation, why do I have to watch my language? It's not like he won't be cussing up a storm by the time he's ten, whatever I say." He glowered at Mildred. "We sure as sh—da—anything were."

"But he'll know what he's saying." She glowered back. "And so he'll know the consequences. Remember, I was raised in a prison, by a gang of thieves, cutthroats, and a warrior who wanted to be king. They thought it was funny to teach me the nastiest curses. My language was worse than a dockside matey's by the time I was two, and it marked me apart even more than my birth. And my eyes."

MV sighed in defeat.

"What's his name?" Laban asked.

"Stinkboy," MV said, grabbing the child and tossing him up in the air. The baby crowed with laughter. "He's got one talent, but he's got that one honed." He jerked a thumb at the diaper.

The baby laughed again, kicking his bare feet. Clearly he found his upside down status entertaining.

Mildred kneed MV in the thigh. "His name is Gunter."

"Named him for my cousin in Geranda," MV said. "For a king, he's actually pretty decent."

"Have you decided on a family name?" Roy asked.

"Considering both Mildred and I were disinherited before we could walk, question seems moot," MV said. "There's time to figure it out. Or not."

"Never thought you'd be the first of us to replicate," Laban commented.

"That's because you're a … birdwit," MV finished on another hissing sigh. "She wanted a family. I couldn't get her back without agreeing to it."

They all knew that Mildred and MV had been pretty tight—for a couple of people who liked cruising the harbors for sailor-girls in the mood for some fun—but about five years after the war ended, Mildred had vanished back to Geth, and MV had been grim and unspeaking, the rare times anyone saw him. Then, in the last year or two, they'd reappeared together.

It seemed that this baby had been part of their resolution.

MV said, "The geez once told me the Valley is a great place for brats. I could see that. Fuzznoggin here can hunker there till he's ready to come out. I'll see to it he can handle himself by then."

No one had any doubt of that.

Outside of David, Adam, and Laban to an extent, who had traded off care of Sveneric with Curtas, the rest of the group had little or no experience with babies, and so the conversation languished. They stared, unsure what to say, until the baby, who had been gumming MV's knuckles with drooly intensity, suddenly assumed a fixed expression, and then from his other end emitted a ripe fart, followed by a noise that made it apparent there was no smoke without fire.

"Ugh. I'm gone," Laban said, waving a hand.

"What did I tell ya?" MV said proudly. "Talent!"

Laban vanished on him turning to Mildred to say, "Whose turn is it…"

Silvanas appeared directly after. "Not sure that was worth the pain of two transfers. MV!" He exited in the direction of the stable, cackling and shaking his head.

Lyren was finishing the last of her steep. "Well? Is it true?"

"It's true," Laban said.

Lyren tipped her head. "You look bemused. Let me guess. MV is a terrible dad?"

"Judging by the way the baby laughed at being tossed in the air, they're two of a kind. Three," he amended, thinking of Mildred's martial saunter, and her roving eye. "I *am* bemused.

I was thinking about sudden changes. How fast time goes by when you aren't particularly aware of it."

She set her cup down and shrugged, absently graceful even in small movements. "A reminder that I probably ought to get busy. There's thunder in the air. Everyone can feel it. We're each writing to likely sources for inside games. Mad's writing to the Mearsieans, of course. I was trying to decide if I would write to Julian or go to the island."

Laban waved her off. "She'll know games, but they won't be court ones."

"Neither will the Mearsieans' suggestions. But Dtheldevor played laughter games, too. It wasn't all competition."

"True. But I'll wager Dtheldevor's idea of funny won't be Carl's."

"You're probably right. I was distracted by Wenwen's enthusiasm."

"She's fifteen. Her idea of a laughing game is still probably Dtheldevor's."

"I'll write to Atan," Lyren said, and whirled out, leaving a trace of magnolia and acanthus on the air.

Laban resumed reading Carl's travel accounts, which were largely her observations of the intricacies of harvest. As each successive page turned over, he gained the impression that at least some of these details were written with him in mind, though not directly addressed to him; he saw references to things they'd talked about over these past months. Pretty much as he'd predicted might be the case if he accepted that invitation to the ball. Even though he was scarcely present for the count of ten, and there had been no dancing. How to proceed? Stick to the study meetings, and keep the talk strictly on the affairs of their respective states?

He was still mulling this matter when he transferred to Ferdrian the following Firstday, as thunder rolled across the sky over the mountains to the north.

In Ferdrian, the storm was merely rain, though slanting down hard. He made his way to the scribe desk, to be told, "Princess Carl has returned. I am to pass the word that she is available in the study, should you wish to consult in person." Again, that rigidly neutral tone and gaze.

"Thank you," he said, and decamped.

When he knocked at Carl's study, she exclaimed, "You came!" It was the same tone of delight with which she'd greeted him that night at the summer ball. "And Cousin Hinari says that you took the reports I had her set aside for you," she added as she gestured him toward a chair. Her gesture was not fussy or flourishing, though he'd seen her do both. It was conscious, but neat. As though she thought out everything carefully.

"Took them, read them, and I have a mental list of questions about specifics. But first, do you want the much belated report on the incident at the Darfaed Pass?"

"Does it differ from Cousin Carinna's report?"

"Not in essentials," he said.

"Then it isn't necessary. Unless you have details that I ought to hear. I just hope that if there is a next time, I will be a part of the decision about what to do."

"And so you shall," he promised.

"Your questions?"

He offered them, Carl listening intently. Like her mother, she had the supporting figures immediately to mind, but her tone—her outlook—was worlds different. She resembled Tahra, and shared certain characteristics with her—like the way her fingers kept neatening the piles of papers on the already tidy desk—but her own style was beginning to emerge.

The time flew by before either of them noted, until Laban realized he'd reached the end of his list. Time to go! Keep things general, impersonal, safe—

Before he could speak, Carl rose, walked toward the door, then turned back, her hands clasped under her chin. He half-rose, the words of farewell ready on his lips, when she half-held out a hand, palm down, as if to stay him.

He stood there, knees bent, unsure whether to sit again or get himself away, when she gulped, and in a high, thin, but firm voice, "Will you marry me?"

Plunk! He dropped onto the chair.

She uttered a noise somewhere between a laugh and a sob. "Astonishment, but not horror. That's a start. Look, I thought it all out. While I traveled," she said quickly. "Jessan and I, we both have… I think he will never get a chance, and I am so sorry—no, I ought not to say anything. Forgive me. I really am trying not to keep things solely in my head, because that encourages people to keep things from me. Do you see?"

"Carl," he began, unsure what to say next.

"Do you see?" she repeated, softer. "Do I make sense? Oh, I didn't give you the reasons. I know I have nothing whatsoever to offer as a person. No, don't bother with politenesses. I know what I look like. What my bad habits and weaknesses are. But I can bring a kingdom to you, which probably never ought to have been separated from yours in the first place. And you are so good for Everon. I can see that—I've seen that since our first conversation. It would of course be *strictly* a treaty marriage. You are utterly free to have a thousand favorites if you want them."

"Only a thousand?" he couldn't help saying.

She paused, her brow puckered, and then it cleared, and she huffed a small laugh. "No more than two thousand. But they will have to share rooms," she retorted, then her smile faded. "But this is not a joke. Nor a whim. I've been thinking it over since I left Ferdrian. You even have the right background, being part of the Deis."

"Except my particular branch was booted out of Sartor. And my father was poison."

"But you aren't," Carl said. "Nor is your sister, Aunt Merry said. Or she'd surely be here demanding things and making trouble, though she doesn't know us or even speak the language. She formally rescinded any rights and went back to Geth to make a life for herself, the way someone who is trying to be a good person would do. You needn't answer now. In fact, I'd rather you don't. I will just ask you to think about it, will you? I haven't said anything to anyone. Nor will I, because I know they will all try to be helpful, and point out what I already know, that I am just twenty, that I have all the future, that I have nothing to offer someone like you, except a crown, and it's supposed to be terrible to marry for just a crown, but what if that person is excellent in every possible way? Which you are. Also. I am enough like my mother to know that my mind is not going to change any time soon. If at all."

"If so," he said slowly, gently, "is that not really unfair to you?"

Her arms crossed tightly against her thin frame. "I can take responsibility for my own feelings. That's what adults do, is it not?"

"That's what they are supposed to do, certainly," he said.

She looked away, glowering at the window. He realized she was fighting tears. "Carl, my apologies. I didn't mean—that is, it must have sounded worse—"

"No, no, it's such a *relief* to be able to speak right out! You know I couldn't, for ever so long." She gave another of those breathy laughs. "Here I am, proving my adulthood by blubbering. I really do stay in my head too much. Ignore the blub. I'm working on breaking that habit. I truly am relieved. Today I spoke my mind, and the world did not end. Will you go now, and think over what I said? You don't have to answer me next week, or next month, or even next year. Just ... consider it?"

"I will," he promised gently, and bowed to show his respect. Then he transferred away.

19

Laban's head rang.

He wandered around his rooms without seeing any-thing as rain poured outside the windows. Where had he made a misstep? Or was it a misstep? He knew what disturbed him: the hitherto unexamined assumption that the initiative would always belong to him. He was nearly ten years older, with more than ten years of experience—though he could hear Detlev's voice on the subject of emotional maturity, *Of course you believe yourself emotionally mature whatever age you are. Because that's as much experience as you have. It's only in retrospect that you perceive that what you thought was a pinnacle was merely another turn in the path upward.* No doubt others considered him backward.

But Carl Delieth, for all her timidity, was a Delieth, and whatever else you could say about them, once they knew what they wanted, they were like arrows to the mark. And she wanted him.

It was a generous offer. Miraculously so. Anyone in his position should be grateful to have perfect freedom along with his lifelong desire right there for the taking.

Silvanas walked in without knocking, wet from the rain, to say that the animals were in the barn. He began to give a report, for he was in the process of working with some of the Knights' cherished white horses, whose training had gone by the wayside ever since Roderic Dei's death. It was a matter of vital interest to them both, and yet Laban was looking through Vana as if he had disappeared and left his ghost yammering into the wind.

"Laban!"

"Huh?"

"You didn't hear a word I said. Lyren again?"

"No! Though I'm going to have to keep that promise to talk to her before I go north again. It'll be awkward. But at least it'll be over, and we generally understand one another. If Lyren was at the other end of this offer, we'd each go our way when we were in the mood, and—"

"What offer? What are you talking about?"

"Carl. Asked me to marry her."

"What!"

"Asked straight out. Charge at the gallop, lance leveled." He smacked his chest. "Knocked me right out of the saddle."

Silvanas whistled. "I kind of thought you'd be the one to bring up marriage. Or not. In five or ten years."

"You thought wrong. And so did I. Though I could put it off five years. Probably ought to. The Dei elders would probably hail that with glad cries."

"But Carl won't," Silvanas said shrewdly. "Every day of those five years you'll have jealous eyes hanging on you."

"Not jealous," Laban said. "Hurt. She's not the type to hate another for what they have. Still less to want to take it away. She judges herself as not good enough. Far worse. Shit." He whirled around, his first instinct to go for a long ride, but he was not going to take a horse out into a thunderstorm. Ah. There was always the salle. "I need to clear my head. Let's go get the staves."

"Oh, fine, you want to take it out on me." But as Silvanas spoke, he was already heading out the door.

To no one's surprise, no answer to Laban's dilemma occurred while they fought first with quarterstaff and then hand to hand. The hours of exercise left both of them wringing wet, after which a hot soak at the bathhouse while thunder rolled and boomed across the sky restored a semblance of good humor.

Laban knew that he could go to Adam and get a sympathetic hearing. He could go to Detlev, who tended to turn your mind inside out in order to examine each wriggling thought, no matter how tiny. Bracing—when it was over with—but Laban resisted. He felt quite strongly that if he was really to take his place as a king, he ought to be able to solve his own problems before he could hope to do that for a nation. Two nations.

Wnelder Vee very much wanted to reunite, he knew.

Three nations, if you counted Imar, only they would expect to be foremost as they had been centuries before. Not because of any intrinsic merit so much as the fact that Jaro Harbor was there at the southeastern tip, where wealth in coin and idea had flowed in and spread out. Ferdrian had always been a market town, and even in its greatest day earlier in the century, it hadn't been much more than a watered-down emulation of Colend's capital. If he was to woo the Imarans, he would first have to establish Ferdrian as a new Alsais ... if. An image of gray-eyed Carl rose before him.

Later, later. She had given him plenty of time.

The storm season was on them. Lyren had learned that one of the reasons for the fortress-like manor houses of Imar was the storm season in this corner of Drael; this was where the great current from the north hit the belt of the world as the current from the south and the air currents above collided, forcing the cold water westward down the strait, all through the south's winter.

Wave after wave of showers drove even the gleaners inside. Shutters were put up, summer bedding laid in trunks with sprigs of herbs, and quilts brought out to air for winter.

During a lull in the wave of storms, Lyren transferred to Ferdrian, where she found all the siblings together, except for Jessan, who had returned to Curtas's House.

"Lyren," Carl exclaimed, her eyes crinkled with pleasure. "I'm so glad you came! I wanted to thank you for everything you've done for us this summer. With all the tax things coming in are notes and letters from the holders and nobles, all saying that this has been the best season in memory. Like old times for the elders, and those our age are hoping there will be a winter season."

"But not now?"

"Not with harvest and tax matters, and the roads so uncertain," Carl said. "In our grandparents' day, harvest season was spent at home."

"Ah, so I take it our Harvest Masquerade has been ... postponed until New Year's, then?"

"Go ahead and just say cancelled," Madelon grumped.

"Jenel Sandrial said there's no tradition for a masquerade ball at harvest time, or any other kind of ball, and are we turning into a lot of Colendi wastrels." She rolled her eyes, giving unnecessary emphasis on the last two words, as if Lyren could have possibly missed her injured innocence: the masquerade had been entirely for Carl's benefit, but of course they couldn't tell the servants that.

Wenwen slumped, disconsolate. Lyren considered them, then the twins—and caught the tail end of an assessing glance from Carl before those expressive gray eyes shifted a bit too quickly. Carl was comparing herself again.

What to say? There was nothing graceful to say, especially as Carl began thanking her again, even more graciously than before. Something had to be going on, but Carl was not going to talk, that much was clear.

Lyren was pressed by all to stay for the midday meal. She did, mostly to see if Carl would change her mind and talk to her the way she had in Lyren's governess days. But at the end of the meal she thanked them all, and said she had to return to the Study to get to work. Alone.

Shut out. Regret seized Lyren, along with puzzlement: why was Carl not talking to her? She used to chatter about everything. Or maybe Lyren only thought she had, and she'd only chattered about what mattered least. It was a sobering, even humiliating thought, but one she couldn't dismiss before she considered everything.

Lyren transferred back to Fortnyal Roth.

What now? At least there was no danger of Laban becoming the center of Carl's focus if there were no more parties until New Year's Week. But did that mean he would continue to go to Ferdrian for those weekly crown business meetings? At least nothing dangerous had come of *those*.

She wasted some time going through her wardrobe, packing away some summer things and designating others for the head housekeeper, whose daughter sold used clothing at the other end of town. Out came last year's cold weather clothes, which she inspected, wondering where her mind had been when she put them away. She added more to the donation pile.

When that was done, time still lay still and heavy in the air around her. She went out to set her pile of clothes in the housekeeper's outer room, and caught sight of Laban prowling around, obviously still in one of his moods. She decided to be elsewhere. Everything seemed too close, too crowded when he was in a thunderstorm mood. Which she didn't resent. She was exactly the same way.

Time to make a visit … to whom? She wasn't going back to Belann until she could tell them about Liere, or preferably, Liere had done so. It was late for roamer season in Sarendan. She'd arrive in bad weather that was only going to worsen as winter drew nigh. Atan was out. Oh, she'd welcome Lyren, but since their children were born, Rel and Atan had definite public times and private times, and the private times centered around those three noise-makers. Lyren's visit would be comprised of nodding at boring anecdotes, and repeating *Oh, how clever*, every time one of the small ones shouted, "Lookit meeeee!"

But there were always the Mearsieans. Everybody was welcome, no matter what they were doing. And Clair was always a sympathetic listener. Not that Lyren needed sympathy. What she needed was insight. Had she done something wrong? She did not feel as if she had, but then why was she so unmoored?

When the transfer reaction wore off, Lyren entered the white palace, conscious that her calculation was correct. It was morning, but not too early. Noise emanated from the kitchen, and when she entered, to the welcome smells of hot muffins and coffee and the ubiquitous hot chocolate, CJ called a cheery welcome from the round table in the corner. Lyren headed her way, finding her both changed and unchanged.

CJ sat next to light-haired Christoph, Puddlenose's first mate. He was another who had changed little, except he was taller and broader through the chest. He sat between CJ and Ben, the brown-skinned, brown-haired shapechanger who was still a young teen, and across from Randon Amdrelya, the mage from the far north.

Ben and Randon apparently were conducting some sort of eating contest, refereed by Christoph, with plenty of insults.

"Yuk!" Ben exclaimed, before shoving a huge bite of elderberry-drenched pancake into his mouth. "Scum yourself!"

"Say it, don't spray it," Randon hooted, brushing himself off with dramatic vigor.

CJ got up and crossed to Lyren. She wore a blue gown, and was barefoot as usual. "Is this a friend-visit or is there trouble?"

"Friend-visit," Lyren said in an undervoice as the insult-salted contest roared noisily on. "I was thinking the same question: is there trouble? Why is Randon here? I know he's a mage."

"He sails with Puddlenose and Christoph a lot," CJ muttered behind her hand. "Ship is down at the coast, getting repairs. Some nogoodniks tried to turkey the Tornasio Islands. They didn't get far, but the *Lheit* took damage."

Christoph eyed Randon, his fork paused midway to his mouth. "Did he get that much on ya?" he asked Randon. "From one bite? If so, you gotta teach me that trick, Ben. Be a surefire hit with villains."

"I think I better experiment further," Ben said, cramming more pancake into his mouth.

When he turned purposefully toward Randon, the latter didn't even look up, just muttered softly and snapped his fingers. Magic flashed. A particularly warty specimen of toad hopped and flopped at Ben's plate.

CJ said to Randon, "My, you do have that spell fast. Use it often?"

"Only about twenty times a day," Christoph said. "Usually it's something more interesting than a toad."

"It helps that he's already a shapechanger," Randon said calmly, as the toad croaked in earnest at him.

"Wart ya think now?" Christoph asked, addressing the toad. "Hoppin' out with any new insults? Time flies, but you catch 'em — ulp!"

Randon was just as fast even when someone wasn't a shapechanger: Christoph's squawk choked off as he turned into a crab. He scuttled around his plate, then headed toward Randon.

"Don't even *think* about it," Randon warned. "I told you. No puns while I'm eating, or I'll croak ya —"

The toad gave tongue, and the crab danced about, clattering against the dishes.

Randon sighed. "All right. Fair's fair. Besides, I'm done." And he reversed the spells.

"It doesn't last long anyway," CJ said. "He can't make it permanent for Christoph, and Ben can fight it off."

"How does that even work?" Lyren asked, fascinated.

"I dunno. Randon said we're actually mostly water, so it's a matter of rearranging the gunk that isn't water, except that it wants to go right back to its customary shape. Which is why his shapechanging spells only last a minute or two. Want some breakfast?"

"Not with them," Lyren said. "Elderberry splatters would not enhance my rose robe. Is Clair here?"

"Sure. But she's upstairs." CJ's blue gaze shifted.

"Upstairs? In the library?" Lyren asked. "Or..."

"With him," CJ muttered, reddening to the ears.

"Him who?"

Though the gathering around the table was clearly having too much fun to pay attention to anyone else, CJ drew Lyren out onto the terrace, snaked looks in all directions, then whispered, "Siamis."

"What's wrong with Siamis?" Lyren asked.

"Sh-sh-sh," CJ hushed, eyes shut, hands patting the air. "I don't want anyone to think it bothers me. Because it doesn't. It's great! Clair is happy, and she ought to be happy..."

CJ had never been adept at shielding. While she blathered, Lyren caught from her a vivid image, so vivid it might have happened moments before, instead of a few days ago: Siamis entering the white palace, tall, fair-haired, and handsome. He looked around as he greeted them, and Clair said nothing, just opened her arms. Lyren experienced all of CJ's shock as Siamis walked straight into Clair's embrace as if he had arrived home.

Lyren blinked away the image as longing punched her behind the ribs with an invisible fist. *Everyone* seemed to be pairing off. Maybe she was just too superficial for such happiness ever to come her way.

Hating that thought — so very selfish, ugh — she said firmly, "CJ, it's fine. I don't think anybody would ever accuse you of not being loyal to Clair, whatever happened in her life." And when CJ gave her a doubtful look, Lyren added with a grin, "No one has ever accused you of being subtle, either. If you hated Siamis, or thought he was a danger to Clair, wouldn't you be defending her with sword and fire?"

"I would." CJ grinned back. "That's true. It's just that it took us by surprise. Well, most of us. Seshe saw it coming, when none of the rest of us did. Oh. Except Erenlara of the Venn."

"Erenlara?" Lyren remembered meeting her when they were both twelve, during the war. At first Eren had seemed another pretty blond princess, very well educated, but toward the end of her stay there had been an intensity to her, as if she had pulled a decorative ceramic shield up to hide the fierce burn of the sun. She had talked often with Atan and the other adults, as if she had reached twenty-two instead of twelve, and yet there had been nothing show-offy about her, for her manner had been very much that of a seeker.

Though Lyren had not heard that Erenlara was particularly close to the Mearsieans, somehow it didn't surprise her that she would observe what others might miss.

CJ went on unaware, "Sometimes a stranger sees things that people ignore every day. Anyway, Seshe thinks Siamis and Clair had some kind of understanding evèr since the war, but he waited until she caught up, sort of. You know, getting rid of the Child Spell. One thing for sure, she's really happy. It's just, argh! Everything is *different* now. I can't just barge into her room anymore, like I always did before."

"How is Aurora taking it?"

"Oh, I think she's another who knew all along. Seshe was one of her tutors. So was Siamis, actually. Anyway, she seems to see him as one of the family." Her wide, questioning gaze flicked to Lyren's face. "Did you come for a thing? Do you need Clair for something?"

Lyren hesitated, not wanting to disturb Clair's happiness. "Is Seshe still visiting in Chwahirsland?" she asked brightly, to get off the subject of her purpose in coming.

"Visiting, huh. She visits *here*. Sometimes. She's *moved* there. Who woulda thought years ago that when she said she didn't think ol' Pilo so bad, they'd end up mushing it up." CJ perched on the low terrace wall, her bare feet pulled up, her chin on her knees. Lyren had a sudden fanciful image of CJ, old and wizened in another fifty years, sitting in just the same way. "She wants us to come visit. Says it's not like the old Chwahirsland at all. Says, for one thing, the ring houses are back."

"Ring? Houses?"

"Houses built in rings around a central area. All the doors face in. She says they're three stories, with all the kids sleeping up in the third story, under the roofs. Everything in fours and eights, as usual. Except they do a lot of their ritual things in threes and nines, and their military junk in threes and nines and fives. Who knows why."

"My guess is, because there's also a leader. I'd like to see that," Lyren said. "I mean the ring houses. Everywhere?"

"No. Only certain places. Wan-Edhe had forbidden them. Of course. I forget his insanitic reason. Had them knocked down, but Seshe says that every ring house, and even every castle or cottage, that fell apart, the people kept track of every stone and brick. Can you imagine? Anyway, so I guess it all went back together again pretty fast. And they have trees there now. Lots and lots of trees. I don't remember seeing a single one. Oh, and the rice terraces from a billion years ago? Those came right back in a year or two. It was as if the ground remembered how to be a terrace..."

CJ rambled on like this for a little longer, Lyren reflecting that Chwahirsland had always been a shut door. Mostly ignored, as if history went around it. Except when it was cursed for its villainy.

"... and you know what Hibern said? She said that what she liked most is that Jilo brought censors back. As if she expected Jilo to turn around and start cackling and rubbing his hands and speechifying before his new skull throne about how he was going to conquer the world. When anyone could tell you if he was that type, he would have started on it by now. And Seshe would have dumped him hard."

CJ scowled out over the vast forestland below, the tops of the trees a riot of orange and yellow and red along with the different shades of green.

"I'm sure that's leftover scruples," Lyren said. "I mean, on Hibern's part."

"About?"

"Historically, mage kings have usually headed the list of tyrants," Lyren said. "Right above military leaders. And she's now the equivalent of senior mages. They think in terms of the world balance, Siamis used to tell Mac and me when he made us read history."

"Of course. Wan-Edhe sproings to the top of the list of reasons why kings should never be mages, or mages never should be kings," CJ said. "But there's Senrid, from the same kingdom Hibern comes from. And Atan. And Erenlara of the Venn. Though her kind of queenship is a lot like Darian Selenna's — with the power spread through a lot more people — only with a lot more ritual. And they used to have these blood-binding tattoos to keep them honest." CJ made a face. "They still do the tattoos, but it's ritual now, Eren said. Blood bindings are forbidden."

"As well. But you overlooked Clair," Lyren said with a grin.

"No, she's different. For one thing, being queen here is not like being a symbol, the way Eren is, for a powerful kingdom. Or an arbiter, like Darian Selenna is down there in Sarendan. Here, being queen is mostly like being a librarian."

"A librarian?"

"An archivist, or the like. You know, answering questions, maybe deciding something about the budget, but no hurling armies around, or swanning in front of fancy balls, and all that foofoo. Leander was another one, but he was king of an even tinier country, and anyway he dumped his throne onto Senrid. Can't think of others offhand."

"Seems to me we've come right around to Jilo again."

"I guess you could call him another mage king, though he insists he's not a king yet, and his magic is really, really formidable in one direction: wards."

"I don't know much about magic," Lyren observed, "but I believe that ward magic is about as powerful as you can get. Well, it sounds like Clair is busy, and so are the rest of you. I should get going."

CJ turned toward Lyren, and Lyren forestalled a question by saying. "Pass on to Clair that Liere's baby was born. It's a boy. Liere ought to be free very soon. Oh! And she might also find this interesting, MV has a baby, too."

"MV?" CJ's eyes widened, two blue marbles. "That poor kid! Oh, but of course it'll turn out to be just like dear old dad."

"Half him, and half Mildred, I should think," Lyren said, laughing.

"Oh! *Mildred's* the mom! Then there's hope for the kid," CJ declared. "MV. Wow! Who woulda thought!"

Lyren laughed and waved a hand, leaving CJ with the impression that she had come to share news. The Mearsieans were busy with other matters. It seemed selfish as well as fussy to unload her small problems onto them. She'd just keep doing what she thought was right. After all, she wasn't doing any harm, at least, even if she could claim no success.

She transferred back to Fortnyal Roth, which seemed quiet and closed in after that noisy, open space with the mellow fall weather.

20

The sun had gone down, and she found Laban alone in the dining room, which smelled of spiced pear cider. He had pushed aside a half-eaten dinner, but seemed to be making up for it with the cider, judging by the fumes.

"Help yourself," Laban said, glancing up from reading what looked like a ledger. "Warm you up."

Though she usually avoided wine or hard cider except for the occasional half-glass, she recklessly poured a full cup, and sat down to sip it. The bite was not unpleasant, and it did warm her inside.

She began brooding over the fact that even hapless Jilo, who more often than not tripped over his own feet, had managed to find someone. Though it probably was more like he'd been found. The point was, he *had* someone…

Laban said, "Did you go visit Liere?"

"No. She said not to come. I'm respecting that. I can tell it's hard enough on her, just from the brevity of her contacts."

"And yet she's still there."

"The baby's Name Day is coming up. Oh! Today, I think. Tomorrow? Anyway, I guess she'll leave right after."

Laban sat back, lifting his cup toward the lamp. He'd loosened the laces of his shirt, and his hair, usually so ordered, hung loose, a few strands lying against his cheek and down over his collar bones.

Lyren shut her eyes and turned her head: she was staring. She discovered she'd finished her cup. She poured another, as once again her gaze stole toward Laban, slouched sideways to the table in his wing chair, one foot propped on the other knee. The pear cider tasted good. And slid down her throat like water. And because the quality of the silence had changed, she decided to fill it. "I don't know how she can bear to leave the child, but she agreed to, to keep little Malcolin safe. And, I think, Andri's old circle as well."

She turned her gaze back to Laban. The blandness of his face—what she could see of his expression—at last registered. "You know something," she accused. "Why aren't you telling me? Something worse than Macael forcing her to choose between him and Malcolin's life?" Horror gripped her, easing when he waved a hand.

"Maybe not worse. Though by the way, when word gets out about that choice, there's going to be a firestorm in diplomatic circles, at least on the southern continent. As for what I know, is it worse? You tell me. Too much was missing, and Detlev's 'hands off' order bothered me. It was he who told me that your Trevor Macael Elsarion has one of those grand passions for Liere, the type you find in forty-verse poems and long, dull historical plays." He finished on a sardonic note.

Lyren clunked her elbows on the table, her cup clutched between her fingers. "But ..."

"Had it for years. Since the war. Probably since the first time he laid eyes on her." His tone had edged into sarcasm.

Lyren frowned. "That's not what Liere says."

"Would she recognize it?" Laban retorted, eyebrows aslant.

"No. Maybe," Lyren amended, considering the tone of some of Liere's recent contacts, brief as they were: mostly the contact was wordless love, an infinite sea that Lyren reflected back. So sustaining, not needing words. As a child, Lyren had pushed against that unconditional love, finding it confining. And Liere, pushed away enough times, had thought herself inadequate, and had gone away to learn.

They had resolved that. And Liere had promised they would talk again, face to face, once she left Enaeran. But what could she even do with the realization that the man keeping her hostage after killing her husband was in love with her—maybe had been all along?

Lyren shivered. "It might not be worse, in the sense that no one lost a life, but it's utterly disgusting. More disgusting. Oh, what does that even *mean*, grand passion? Sometimes I think it's merely a poetic excuse for a lot of bad behavior. Especially when it's obsessive. Case in point!"

"Not arguing," Laban said, swung to his feet, and began prowling around the room, his gaze on the floor, the new paneling, out the window into the blackness of a rainy night. "Because I don't believe in love at first sight. Lust, yes. Detlev seems to think it was the real thing, not just the itch for a hammock dance." His next thought he almost hid: *If you believe there is a real thing.*

"But Macael Elsarion married that poor, frail princess. She was like a ghost! What was her name? The heir to Sles Adran?" Lyren stopped when Laban made a face. She went on slowly, "It's just that he was so good to her, so kind. I saw that in Sartor the one time I met them. Liere was so sure he loved her, and she respected him for that. Profoundly respected him, just for that." She watched Laban's tense hands, his averted face. "So what you're saying is, that was a marriage of convenience. As rulers do. For dynastic reasons, or treaty reasons, not personal reasons. Personally, Macael married the ghost-princess but lusted after Liere? Who was married to Andri? Oh, yes, it's worse than disgusting."

"I wasn't aware that any of these marriages were ring vows," Laban retorted. "Anyway, I find it ... human. Sad. Disturbing. Rather than disgusting, with its whiff of moral superiority."

"I should think moral superiority in this situation is perfectly justified," she retorted. "When did Detlev see fit to pass on this gossip?"

Laban lifted a shoulder. "Last winter. When he said hands off."

Why hadn't Laban brought it up nearly a year ago? They'd certainly talked about how Macael Elsarion had killed Andri, but he was to remain unmolested. Then came the staggering news that Liere had to stay there as a hostage and give him a child. But Laban hadn't discussed this new wrinkle in the whole nasty affair. She realized then, though they did talk about most things, from history to hosting difficult social gatherings to personal tastes in scent, they had never talked about sex.

She hadn't thought about sex. She'd assumed that Laban didn't either, that he lived a free and easy life, exactly like hers, without the emotion-fraught pitfalls of the physical side of romance. Lyren began to contemplate, for the first time, that there just might have been a closed door where she'd assumed there was no door at all.

Lyren pinned him with a narrow gaze. "You brought this up now, after all this time, for a reason. What is it?"

"Carl asked me to marry her," Laban said.

"You told her no, of course."

He went on as if Lyren hadn't spoken. "After she enumerated the benefits for all three kingdoms. She had it all thought out. What's more, she was right on every single point relating to state reasons." Laban stared straight back, his eyes very blue in the lamplight. His mouth curled slightly at the corners in wry self-disparagement. "She insists she wants me, but she's too self-denying to count that as a benefit."

"You want to be king of Everon." Lyren uttered the words as an accusation, picturing Carl's thin, plain face ecstatic with shy, sentimental emotion. She tried to picture Laban skillfully enacting the part of romantic lover (as envisioned by a very young, sheltered, romantic girl) and her mouth soured. "That makes me want to puke."

Laban said, "I didn't intend to tell you because I knew you'd helpfully interfere for our own good. In fact, you already have been."

"Don't tell me you'd even consider it for a heartbeat? You'd risk a life of misery for Carl, which she does not deserve, merely for, what was it, dynastic and treaty gain? For *politics?*"

His derisive smile was a mirror to hers. "You don't think I can make her happy?"

"I think it's reprehensible that you could marry anyone — considering the fact that you don't believe in love, but Carl most especially does — for mere political gain. But that would be one of Detlev's first lessons in the Long View, wouldn't it?"

Laban had been pacing the room, which very definitely seemed far too small. At that, he halted, and swung around. "Don't fling Detlev in my teeth," he warned. "I had enough of that from Tahra and those she poisoned with her venom. That Chief Scribe still looks at me as though she expects to be knifed in the back."

"Hinari Dei? She looks at everyone like that. She's actually a Delieth through the great-grandfather. Married a Dei. She's like Tahra in some ways but with her, it's words, not numbers. Archives. I take back the question, but not the comment."

"Mere political gain," he repeated. "'Mere.'" His emotional energy was so intense the proportions of the room seemed diminished to the dimensions of a cage. "You don't know what you're talking about."

She set her empty cup down and folded her arms. "Horseshit."

"You keep telling me you've no sense of place, or of responsibility. No temporal bindings except family. I'm glad you have family. I wish I did, outside of a sister from another world, who I haven't exchanged a hundred words with. Even MV wants a family of his own, something I'm still trying to get used to. But all my life I dreamed of being precisely where I would be—if I agree, and I'm not at all sure of that—doing what's been desperately needed while Tahra mucked about and didn't even see how she made everything worse than the wars ever did."

Lyren struggled to see it from his view. "King of Everon. The old Everon—wasn't Wnelder Vee a regional name for the woodlands? And Commander of the Knights. They always want a Dei heading them, and you're the right family, if the wrong branch."

He made an impatient movement, pushing the subject aside. "Vana can do that. Carinna Dei even seems to want him. I envision my role more like seeing to it there is no necessity for military intervention. But I know how to command if needed."

Lyren blinked, trying to get her emotions to stop roiling so she could focus. Now she regretted that last cup of cider. Both cups. "I admit you'd be good. None better, if I can judge by the turnaround you've managed here. And yes, marriages are made for all kinds of reasons. And conditions. Especially royal marriages."

She abandoned politics with a twitch of her shoulder and an arched turn of the wrist; every movement was rounded, caroming the eye from wrist to opposite shoulder, then in and out in parabolic curve to her hip, as she aimed for what had always been most important to her: the personal. "But if you do say yes to her, and marry her, do you realize that from now you are going to have Carl's sensitive, intelligent, adoring face gazing ardently on you over the breakfast table every single day? No matter what she promises as to personal freedom, and hoola loola loo? She's a Delieth, and she has fixed on *you*. She will be exerting every nerve to gain a tenth of her ardency in return."

"She insists that it would be a treaty marriage."

"Do you really think it would be so tidy?"

He flushed with annoyance, but she dashed right on. "And though you think love is nothing more than poets' mawkish sentiment dressing up lust, I *know* Carl believes in love. And she wants more, whatever she says about the economic benefits of treaty marriages. Oh, what a stomach-turning mess! I can just see it, you running off to your pleasure house and leaving Carl yearning in an empty bed."

"Why do you keep coming back to sex? Because that's what it is, when you moan about love, you mean sex. What's it to you?"

Nausea clawed at the back of her throat. "How did *I* get into this discussion?" she cried. "The subject was Carl, and the fact that all that impassioned Delieth focus will be — is! — on you. So I don't have any experience with lust, or even love. Any successful experience in physical intimacy with another person. But ignorant as I am, I am still an observer of others in love. If you marry Carl and *that* happens to you with someone else, it will tear her apart, and maybe even you as you try to hide from those honest eyes of hers something you will feel with all the power of the sun and stars."

He had stopped pacing, and leaned an arm along the cold marble mantelpiece as he gazed down into her face. He was too close to her, having stepped for the very first time within her invisible personal boundary. She did not like it, but she refused to move. Why should she retreat? He was in the wrong.

"All my passion, as you put it, has been devoted to bringing all three kingdoms out of years of depression," he said steadily. "Decades, actually. As for the rest, it seems you expect disaster from the outset. As if I'm too ignorant to see any of the obvious pitfalls. Why?"

She drew breath to deny his words, then closed it again.

"What do you want, Lyren?" he asked.

She turned her head, and though he had not moved, she felt the impact of his desire just as strongly as if she'd walked out of a snow bank straight into the sun. She could blame the pear cider, except she knew that right now, in this moment, her pulse beat all through her body, a throbbing pulse as every nerve tingled with not-quite-heat. Cider did not cause that, though it might blur its suppression. All her senses clamored with urgency, pulling her toward him, though she knew if he touched her, she would explode into flame.

It was … delicious.

"What do you want, Lyren?" he asked again, and she watched his mouth, relishing the curve of his lips. What would they taste like? Feel like, pressed on her heated skin? "Not in the future. Right now. This moment."

This moment? The subject seemed far too fraught. Yet people came together all the time, for idle or ephemeral fun, without taking harm of it. She had begun to believe that she could only be with someone who loved her, because she never wanted to feel the humiliation she'd endured when her first crush had turned her down.

But what about when she felt nothing but pure, uncomplicated lust?

"You," she said.

He uttered a quick laugh. "Please don't tell me you've been harboring a secret—"

"*Ugh*, no," she exclaimed. Swallowed. "It's simple lust. Nothing more."

"And you can't take it to the professionals? Who make a livelihood out of 'simple.' There are those who specialize in first timers, for people who for whatever reason don't want their first time to be with someone they know." As her face squinched up, he said, "You've claimed they would all fall in love with you, but I can assure you their training—"

"That's not what I said. Or, maybe I've said silly things, but what I meant was, I'd do everything I could to make them fall in love with me, because I can't bear the idea of sex—the first time, anyway—with a stranger." Her voice shook.

"Fair enough," he said, and his eyes raked down her from lips to hips. She felt every increment, and licked her lips. Then uttered a low laugh as his forehead sheened. He grinned back, the same reckless grin he'd given Imry Llyenthur across a campfire when he knew he would lose, but he was going to fight anyway. "Right now we are both free agents. Nothing promised to anyone. But this can only happen once, whether or not I accept Carl's offer. Once is teaching. But for you and me, too much alike, twice would be an entanglement."

"Done," she said.

Later—much later—they sat at either end of a private alcove in the bathhouse, their knees touching companionably. Steam rose from the water, along with the clean scent of dried orange blossoms, which Lyren had thrown in. Sensitive to scent, she was always experimenting with aromatic herbs and flowers. He'd never thought of scented baths, but he suspected that they would become an occasional indulgence from now on.

Lyren smiled sleepily at Laban as curls whorled and stuck to her skin. "You're a good teacher."

"But?"

"As you say, it can never happen again."

He grimaced as if in acute nausea. "You're not going to claim you're falling in love."

She chuckled, a husky sound, then said, "No. I would never spoil that gift, freely given, and gratefully accepted. And maybe that's the problem."

"Problem?" His brows lifted.

Another chuckle, more rueful. "The experience thoroughly cauterized a ... call it an inflammation I hadn't realized was galling me. That's gone, but leaving me, oh, emotionally unmoored. And." She shook back the ribbons of her floating hair. "Please do not think I am reopening an argument, but I'm still afraid that the knife-edge you might choose to walk is killingly narrow. I want it to work, I do. But I can't bear to stay here to see if it ends in tragedy."

"You don't trust me after all." His wry tone did not quite hide a note of hurt, but he hid it by sinking down, and stretching out his feet below the water, one at each side of her.

"I trust your intentions," Lyren said swiftly. Her eyes stung with tears blurring the light-spangled water as she said in a rush, "You would be moving anyway — Ferdrian is central, and a better capital in all ways. So it's natural that our life here comes to an end. And I couldn't live in Everon if you two marry. I do love Carl, but she is always comparing herself to me and finding herself wanting. It bothered me years ago, and I couldn't live with it now."

He laughed, and though she admired the shape of his head, and the curve of muscle along shoulder and arm and over his chest, the fire was gone. His relationship to her remained what it had always been, close friendship. And while she knew she was not in love — whatever that meant — something had changed, enough that she needed to get away to consider it. And give him the freedom to do whatever he was going to do next.

21

"**. . .A**nd it was clear that merely changing the name back from the Hall of Judgment to the Hall of Justice was not enough. The Hate's poison had putrefied the stone. It took a year to burn the residue from his presence, down to clean rock, before we could reconstruct. But here it is."

Jilo held out a hand, palm up, in invitation.

Gold Army General Kirech, a grizzled, lantern-jawed, sallow man, walked into the chamber where too many of his peers had been slaughtered, and looked around.

It might be the same place, but it was not the same space, the same air. Gone was the iron tang of old blood, and the stench of fear mixed with mold. Clean air flowed from somewhere as Kirech looked around. Everything was lighter, not merely due to new windows high up. The stonework was indeed lighter, but what drew and kept his eye was the magnificent carving of linden leaves behind the throne. And it was a new throne, carved from wood; gone was the tarnished gold and the great height of the old one made largely of black iron, and gone was the upward line at either end of the top, the "horse-head" look, that was reputed to be left from the days when dragon symbols were everywhere. Though The Hate had never made any reference to dragons; he had considered himself above all such traditions. He was the center of the world, not some beast of ancient legend.

This throne sat on a dais so that its sitter could see and be seen, but otherwise was plain except for fine carving of linden leaves along the arms and around the base. From the ceiling hung banners with streamers below and to either side, one banner from each of the holdings of the ancient nanijo, or warlords, representing each region.

Kirech turned to Jilo. "Are you bringing back the nanijo?" In other words, removing army command structure.

"No. Nothing is changing, except for the addition of chiefs from the four departments to be established in each region. They will meet with the local commander and the elders' council chiefs."

Kirech gave a tiny nod; as a general, he had always prided himself on knowing nothing of civilian administration. Any shift from military to civilian had been a lowering of prestige during the Four Hundred Years. He turned a silent question to Jilo, who said, "I would like to appoint you to be First Censor."

Kirech knew that General Furo of Green Army had been given an important civilian post, but the man had been badly tormented by Norsunder, and was no longer able to sit a horse, much less ride at the front of battle. Civilians were a lower form of life, so Kirech had been raised to believe. But he also knew his history, taught him in secret by determined parents. Censors were from the times before the Tyrants — from the days of Great Chwahirsland, that much he knew.

Warily, he said, "What would that entail?"

"You would of course keep your army command," Jilo said. "No one else could be Gold Army General."

A good part of Kirech's wariness vanished.

Jilo saw this reaction, but gave no sign as he continued. "If there is need, you would put on your armor and be first among the generals once again. But there is not a need, and right now, as I return to governing in the manner of our great days, there is a need for a Chief Censor whom everyone recognizes for his probity and courage."

Certainly no one minded hearing that!

"You would appoint your two assistants, and oversee their assistants, for all complaints and accusations will be coming through you. You will have your own wing, and as many workers as you need, for your department of course exists separate from the four branches."

Kirech said, "I am still head of Gold Army?"

"You are. You know them best, so if you wish to recruit your two assistants from among your officers, who I know to be trained by you, feel free to do so. Naturally they will keep their commands as well, and be ready to don armor and ride should the Chwahir be threatened."

Kirech clasped his hands tightly behind his back. "Is this a command?"

"Not yet," Jilo admitted. "But after New Year's, I will sit in that throne. The departmental chiefs will attend court when it's called, and we will need the censors listening as much as we'll need scribes to record everything." Jilo lifted a hand, palm up — a gesture of appeal The Hate would never have made. "Take a week to consider. I know this is a change from a lifetime of habit, but we are returning to an older tradition. There is no reason we cannot have Chwahirsland's great days again."

Kirech agreed with that. And though some among his peers doubted this supposed greatness, his family had no doubts whatsoever. His mother had appended copies of Jilo's New Year's poems to either side of their entryway herself.

Jilo went on, "There will be robes to be made, and proper ritual to be learned. Everything done according to tradition."

Kirech saluted and departed, aware that "Take a week" had not been a suggestion, but an order. One he had accepted, as already his mind galloped along this new path: who among his upper command would do the work well?

Erol came out once Kirech was gone. "How did it go?"

"I think he's with us. He's honest. Not afraid to argue. But no tyrant in the making, and not a plotter. And he very much respects tradition."

Erol rubbed his jaw. "And if Gold Army takes the lead in accepting civ posts, the others will want to follow. Is that it?"

"Yes. And if we have no wars in my lifetime, he and his department will be effectively living their lives as civilians. Their armor and swords will rest on racks in the newly-restored ancestral alcove."

"What tradition would that be?" Erol looked around. "Still need a court ritual."

Jilo grinned. "Seshe and I have been looking into that. What Kirech doesn't know is that pretty much every ruler changed the order of things, so we can, too. But there's a basic progression—"

He paused as steps heard on the polished slate floor in the

doorway. One of his new pages started in, collided with Seshe coming from the other direction, and stumbled back, nearly falling over the masonry equipment left there by the sculptors in the process of putting relief work around the doors.

"We're going to also have to figure out a flow of movement through the castle, especially when the departments begin filling," Jilo muttered to Erol, as Seshe said to the nerve-wracked page, "No, go ahead. You can speak your message. Mine will wait."

The servant bowed, head low, knees bent. Erol muttered in Sartoran, "And you're going to have to resolve the bowing. They still seem to think they have to go head to the floor, unless you get specific."

Jilo pinched the skin between his brows. "You know I hate bowing."

Erol lifted a shoulder. "Take on the job, take on the pose."

Jilo knew that. Before he and Erol had argued about it, he'd talked endlessly with Senrid about how power works, not in the obvious sense, but between one person and the next, if neither is actively bashing the other over the head. He'd also talked to Clair of the Mearsieans about what she called her social contract—she who had governed her small polity without any force whatsoever.

The social contract with the Chwahir seemed simply defined: it was his job to see to it they could lead their lives safely and well. Just as the Chwahir had in ancient days. He had to get used to the idea that the semblance of power could actually be reassuring. So a bow was an acknowledgment that he was alert and working, ever working (in the sense of work as the Chwahir definition of honor) for that person. To acknowledge the bow acknowledged the person.

Erol, successfully following his train of thought, said, "Your response says *I see you*. That's the benign reaction. There are some who regard every change with suspicion. And unless you give them a form to follow, will be looking for Wan-Edhe's spies waiting to pounce. Wan-Edhe's louring presence is locked into bone and muscle. Don't know that you can change that. Only time, and generations without Wan-Edhe's poison, can."

Jilo didn't answer as the still-bobbing page crossed the wide expanse of the floor. He drew near and bobbed more. "Lord, there's the Colendi here."

"Bring King Shontande in," Jilo said, making another

mental note: honorifics for outsiders as well as protocol. And what were they to call him? The castle denizens seemed to have settled on ijo—lord—among themselves, because he kept hearing it.

Seshe joined him, holding out his golden notecase as Shontande Lirendi entered, graceful in shades of very pale pink, reminding Jilo of a heron soaring down to light among the frogs on the mudflats. Then he noted Shon's expression of pleasant but unreadable politesse, and knew it immediately for a façade. "What happened?" Jilo asked in Colend's Kifelian.

"Am I that maladroit?" Shontande asked, smiling ruefully.

"You're wearing your trouble shield." Jilo gestured toward his own face. "And it's early. When you come for a visit it's always later."

"So it is! Two things," Shontande said, looking around to see who was in earshot—and distracted himself. "What you have done in here. It's very fine."

Jilo's sudden grin lit his entire face. "Think so truly?"

Shontande appreciated the fact that someone among Jilo's Chwahir had an astonishingly good eye. The castle was still austere, but light and decorative motifs here and there had changed the prison look to a quiet elegance that was distinctively Chwahir. Would pointing it out sound condescending? A short answer might be prudent. "Truly." He remembered his errand, and focused. "First: Atan of Sartor wrote that Liere Fer Eider had a child recently. Did you know that?"

"I didn't know about the child," Jilo admitted. "Wasn't she a hostage?"

Seshe looked away, hiding her distraught expression, as Shontande went on, "I've never met her, but of course I've heard of her. Who hasn't! Apparently the rumors about her remaining as a hostage are true, but there's worse. The child was by the Adrani king, who assassinated the Enaeraneth king personally. She was given a choice between having this child with him, and leaving it with him, or losing her eight-year-old son. This report is third-hand, but I trust Atan, and she in turn trusts her eyes in the old capital of Enaeran."

Jilo had no interest in Sles Adran or Enaeran, but he knew that the Colendi still resented having been invaded by the Adrani under their old king, who had sided with Norsunder. "I thought the new king was an ally," Jilo said.

"So we thought. But if he can do that, what else will occur to him as expedient? There's little to stop the Adranis from coming back over our western border for a second try. Ah-ye, that is my problem. I thought you ought to know; no doubt someone will be relating more as it comes out. But I'm having my heralds increase vigilance along the river."

Jilo nodded soberly, as Seshe said softly, "Oh, poor Liere. It must be breaking her heart to have to leave that innocent little baby behind."

Shontande gestured Rue, and then glanced reflectively at Erol as he lowered his voice. "There is a second thing. I am very certain there is an unexceptionable reason … but, especially with this troubling news from the Adranis. That is, our herald scouts on their customary border rides are somewhat concerned to have noticed a contingent of your military crossing the middle pass, and then coming up along the old path on our side of the border, to the higher ranges. Are you contemplating construction of another fortress there, or…?"

Jilo grinned. "Not the least. That's the shells."

"Shells? Ah, yes, the quota-warriors forced to live as men. And so?"

"They actually deserted from the army," Jilo said. "But I expect their uniforms are pretty much all they have. They came over to your side of the border to escape notice from us so that they could get to those south slopes up there, to gain a steep concession."

"They're there to … plant steep?" Shontande repeated.

"They are. It's apparently the right soil and climate for a certain type of leaf. I'll be going up there to award the concession to them officially, but first, Clair of the Mearsieans, and I think Siamis, went up there to see if they could do something for them, magic-wise. In fact, wasn't that today?"

Seshe said, "It is. I came in to remind you."

"Would you like to go inspect with me?" Jilo asked Shontande. "I can set aside this other stuff."

Jilo sensed the relief that Shontande was endeavoring to hide; Shontande strove to hide his relief so that Jilo would not think that Shontande assumed their trust had been breached. A complex relationship indeed, but the Colendi were used to complication, which at its best diffused conflict.

Shontande had always been aware that this friendship between them and their two very different kingdoms had for centuries been impossible. Jilo had a clear conscience, and it showed. Shontande understood that to Jilo, Colend was the peaceful, sophisticated, wealthy neighbor whose king had held out the hand of friendship, even when the Chwahir had been ordered to invade, and Jilo had striven to demonstrate his gratitude in every way he could.

As for Shontande, he had also seen Colend as the peaceful, wealthy, sophisticated neighbor who could show the rough, crude Chwahir the pleasant path to civilization. And, considering what Chwahirsland had been like under Wan-Edhe's bloody grip, it was understandable. But it was not turning out that way. For example, on his previous visit, Jilo had left out a swatch of silk brought by one of his people. This silk was so deep and dark a red it had looked black, except when the light shimmered over it in ruby red glints.

One subject Shontande knew well was silk, and not only because most of his clothing and bedding and furniture coverings were made of it. Fine silk was a good part of Colend's trade. He knew all the grades. This piece was not only equivalent to the finest Colendi silk — single thread, heavy strand weight, closely woven — but the feel was so exquisite, the light so lustrous, he suspected it might even be a grade above Colend's best.

Jilo had told him three or four years ago that the silk-makers were able to work again, after generations, now that the mulberry woods were not just reestablished, but thriving. And when Shon had asked, "Are the rumors true, the Chwahir raised a breed of moths that emerge from the cocoon, leaving it intact?" Jilo had said, "Oh, that's ancient news."

Confirming Shontande's belief that sericulture in Colend really had come from the Chwahir and not the other way around, as his Colendi insisted; in Colend, either you killed the pupae by boiling them, which made the threads come out a single strand — and some countries would not accept that silk because it required the death of the creatures making it — or the silk-makers dealt with the shorter threads left as the moths fought free. The weavers used the short fibers expertly, of course, but it added much extra labor to the process of producing fine silk.

Shontande had had to give up his assumption that he would be gently shepherding his grateful Chwahir allies into civilization and plenty; when Jilo decided to trade Chwahir silk, it was going to change everything. And Shontande would keep his promise to aid them.

"I don't need to go, unless you would like me to be there," Shontande said. "Though I confess I would love to see the steep harvested one day, when they are established."

"That you shall! You'll probably be our chief customers. I'll need your advice on how we can present it best," Jilo said with another of those unshadowed smiles, his aura glowing gold.

Shontande took his leave, and Jilo turned to Erol. "It just occurred to me, why don't we ask Siamis about ancient Chwahir ritual, now that he's back from wherever he was?"

Erol said doubtfully, "Remember, he was only twelve when Norsunder took him."

"But he might know something. Or he saw something written in those ancient scrolls. We've got so little to go on."

Erol agreed. The few ancient records to survive made references that were clearly too well known to spell out for contemporaries, and those in charge of records must have thought that knowledge would pass down in classrooms forever, and only the details of decisions about long-lost affairs would be of interest.

"We can go ask," Jilo said, turning from Seshe to Erol, who murmured, "If you don't need me, I'll stay with the artisans."

Seshe, standing by silently, watched how unconscious was the trust between these two as Jilo effectively relinquished the royal castle—and the kingdom—to Erol so that they could complete the assignment of the Dragonspring concession as promised. She found Erol unfathomable, but that was true of most of Detlev's boys.

She'd asked Jilo once, when they were alone, and Jilo had laughed. "You mean you also noticed that Erol is better educated, far better at martial skills, and a better candidate for king than I am?"

"I don't think that," she said.

"He doesn't either, mostly because he has no family. No name. I've got great-uncle Shiam and my cousins. Not famous. Not wealthy. But they have a reputation for good work, and many's the invitation for twis for the young cousins. And Erol knows it."

Seshe nodded soberly.

Jilo went on, "I asked him. Since I've always got my back to him. In a sense. You know what I mean. He said, *Detlev plucked me off a battlefield. No telling who my family was. I'm Chwahir, is all I know. And I never thought that Chwahirsland would be anything but a sneer and a curse in others' mouths. That it's not is your doing. I like this work, protecting you. It's work that gives me a reason to live.* Those last words, his stutter started coming back, so I dropped it. I figure, trust has to start somewhere. And if you start, it can't be half-measures. Not with some people. He's one. Clair was the first. Then Senrid." His smile was lopsided. Wistful. "And you."

"And you," she said, and saw him blush.

His words were a sobering reminder of how vital it was for him to be trustworthy, and to be able to trust. She could understand that, having been utterly betrayed so early in life, and now she had found herself surrounded by all the same trappings—thrones, armies, wealth. But she was no longer a child, thrust into circumstances she had not asked for. She had chosen this road, and this man.

She would protect him any way she could.

22

E rol watched Jilo and Seshe vanish.

"Who is she?" he'd asked Detlev not long after the war ended, when Jilo brought Seshe into Narad not once, but twice. Jilo was still somewhere in his mid or late teens then, his growth stunted by the years he'd had labored in the center of that toxic time distortion. This interest in a Mearsiean girl his own age did not look like lust; Seshe was a lot like Curtas had been, genuinely kind, her manner more like that of a person handling a badly wounded dog who might growl and snap at first, until trust was earned.

Detlev said, "She doesn't talk about her origins."

"But you know?"

"Yes. Like you now, I wanted to know who Jilo was letting into his life. She will be good for him, if she stays."

It was an answer, probably the answer that mattered, but Erol had grown up with Ferret as his most frequent roommate, and so had absorbed Ferret's belief that knowledge was a vital weapon in your defense arsenal.

He hated using Dena Yeresbeth except to scan his surroundings. Anything beyond that tended to trigger vertigo, which brought on nausea. But by the time Seshe had been back long enough to plant that first garden, he had to know who she was and why so pretty and well-put-together a girl would follow a hapless fumbler like Jilo. It certainly couldn't be for his looks. Was she hankering after a crown?

The obvious time to try would be while she pottered in that garden. He was able to find a spot and sit cross-legged, eyes closed. She wasn't shielded, a good sign. But then he began to skim over the surface of her thoughts, her mind like most minds a jerky jumble of words mixed with sensory impressions and flickers of memory, visuals foremost.

Here came the nausea. He breathed slowly, sweating rivers as he held on. A few drops of rain splattered the windows; Seshe, down below, looked up into the gray sky as a raindrop or two impacted her face, and slam! There was a deep memory.

Erol dropped out, hands over his face as he fought to keep his long-ago breakfast from making an unwanted reappearance. When he'd calmed his jangling nerves, and made sure his own senses had refound their equilibrium, he reviewed everything Adam had tried to teach him about looking at others' memories. Ignore the distortion, ignore the mis-aligned sensories — if the person remembering hates the smell of onions, but you like onions, the emotional reaction and your own reaction fight one another, triggering vertigo — look, feel, listen, a fly on the wall, a tree, a rock.

The visual was close to the ground: a child's perspective. Cold, shivering, but the top layer of reaction was a wary delight at the sight of a very wet hen with her wings outstretched as a cluster of chicks huddled together under the wings, which partially covered them. All those feet were wet, but the chicks moved very little, and the hen stood fast, only her head jerking from side to side, as, from above, a woman spoke: *Always choose love, third highness.*

Do chickens love? The high little voice came from all around: self speaking. *Grand tutor says animals have no feelings.*

They have chicken feelings. Look at the chicks pressing together. Are they fighting each other to get closer to their mother's warm body? No, they are not. Will the mother care about them when they get their adult feathers? I don't know. But right now, what we see is her protecting them as they press together. Is that not one of the many forms of love?

And the memory was gone. What did it mean to Seshe? All Erol knew for certain was that rain prompted it. Seshe and the woman had been speaking in one of the Toaran languages, and the woman had addressed the child as a social superior.

Since that time Erol had listened when Seshe spoke, which was seldom, and watched when she acted and was not aware she was watched. He braced to do more scanning, but as always the ordinary jumble of another's thoughts and experiences defeated him. He still found her a mystery, but he had Detlev's judgment to go by. He could wait.

Unaware of Erol's unexpressed questions, Jilo and Seshe transferred to the slope that Marga had marked with a Destination. A little way down a goat trail they discovered a tent city, neatly laid out with military precision. A fine rain misted all around, the extreme edge of the storms centering around The Fangs at the eastern end of the Elgar Strait.

The first sight that caught Seshe's eyes was a blue-white head of hair waving down a square back: Clair. She sat on a camp stool near the entry to a large tent. Siamis could be made out within the interior of the tent. He was surrounded by Chwahir warriors in various fading shades of black, from rust to blue.

Clair had finished with her last healing. Her job had been easiest: the removal of bindings on female organs for those who wished to have their bodies restored. The spells were relatively easy, translating over from Sartor's ancient magic to the magic Clair was used to. It was the mental part of the magic that she'd found a challenge, but she'd followed the steps, and each successive case got easier. She watched her last one walk away, enjoying the sense of satisfaction that brimmed her heart.

She peered down at the scribbled notes she'd made; she'd remember what they meant if she transcribed them as soon as she returned to Mearsies Heili. Right now, the air was far too damp and her fingers too cold to write up her progress on each situation.

She looked around. They'd discovered on arrival that the greater segment of the shells had decided to remain as they were; because they were going to establish their own leaf farm on this mountain, where no one would bother them, they could live as they wished. That included avoiding not only traditional pronouns, but the disparaging army slang for their kind.

These shells—they claimed that noun proudly, for to them it symbolized strong backs bent to honorable work—had begun laying the foundations for the first building, to serve first as a long dormitory to get them all through the winter, and thereafter as village center.

Siamis, farther within the tent's interior, had the most complicated work, completing his group of shells' physical transformation to men. Some had half the magic done, some only a little. A few, he'd warned her by contact, had had painfully inept magic done on them, apparently in a desperate attempt to enable them to pass one of Wan-Edhe's inspections. All were different, their only similarities being that they had been born women, but now were men.

He, unlike her, had had the advantage of healer training. He was finding ways to combine the cumbersome magic that Clair had been trained in with mind-directed ancient Sartoran magic: the magic of today could not see inside bodies, so it had its limitations. Using the ancient magic, Siamis entered the mind of each patient, reaching down to see inside their bodies. It was very difficult, but he had been working at it for years.

She closed her eyes, listening as Siamis explained in slow, somewhat stilted Chwahir that he recommended the more complicated cases return to Mearsies Heili with them for recovery between magic sessions. Unlike Clair, who had learned the language, he had to translate via contact, as the Universal Language Spell was woefully behind in Chwahir.

Clair turned on her stool, aware of some change on her periphery. Jilo was here. And Seshe! Clair had never even in her own mind ranked the girls; she'd made CJ a princess because CJ had wanted to be a princess, and she had proved to be a natural leader, looking out for the others with loyal and indefatigable determination.

Each was precious in her own way. Each had strengths that had sustained Clair over the years, ever since her mother's last "Go away, make noise somewhere else," and Clair had returned to Janil holding her close and explaining that Mother had died in an accident. But in the last year or so, Seshe and she had come to understand one another even more than they had as girls.

Seshe and Jilo headed her way, their footsteps *slush slush slushing* in the tall autumn-yellow grasses as rain spangled blond hair and black. The shells, seeing Jilo bearing a carryall, whispered and parted respectfully; as usual, he didn't seem to notice, as Seshe came to stand next to Clair. "How's it going?"

"Siamis is trying to convince them to come back with us, so we can make them more comfortable. They don't want to go. They insist they are used to pain, and they need to remain to get their building up before the first snow."

Seshe nodded soberly. Clair wondered, as always, how Seshe was adjusting to being the one outlander in Narad, so close to Jilo. Seshe had said once, "It's my hope to get the women to accept me. I know the men never will." Which was as close to complaining as Seshe ever got.

"We need to ask Siamis about court rituals," Seshe murmured as the shells saluted crisply to Jilo and backed away several steps. "Chwahir, I should say. I know the Ancient Sartorans had a lot of rituals."

Clair had been so thoroughly through Siamis's memories that she said unerringly, "He won't know. He was barely aware of Chwahirsland as a boy. He lost interest as soon as he found out there were no flying people, much less dragons there. Has Jilo decided what to do about the 'king' matter?"

Seshe said, "I think he'll tolerate ijo. Which would make him Jilo-Ijo."

"Military lord."

"Exactly. Nanijo—warlord—is the oldest title. In Chwahir, there is no separating the military from lordship. Wanijo is the oldest term for king, but 'wan' was so thoroughly poisoned by Wan-Edhe that no one says it without spitting. Jilo is beginning to believe that simple is the least of all ills. The problem, really, is what to do about me."

"But they have a term for queen—their Queen Lammog was highly respected."

"Yes, but there has never been an outlander queen. Jilo admitted that he tried to convince them that I was royal, and even gave them my birth name when I was not present to ask him to desist. Was that ever a mistake!"

"What's wrong with Seshemerria?"

Seshe's eyes rounded. "*Five* syllables? Even Sonscarna is only three. Two is noble. One is common. They flatly refused to believe him, until he let them explain it to themselves as family name and personal name combined. I've told him I really don't care if they never acknowledge me. Truly."

"But it isn't a solution to live an invisible life, is it?"

Seshe looked away. "That's what Jilo says. He keeps bringing it up."

"You might have to tell him your story," Clair ventured, avoiding the words *trust him with your story*. But that was what she meant.

Seshe closed her eyes. "I made a promise to myself to leave that behind. I've never seen any reason to break that promise." She turned a pretend-frown on Clair. "As for names, would *you* like to resurrect Clevarlineh?"

"No." Clair grimaced. "I've long ago gotten over my hatred of my mother. I've felt nothing but pity for her for years. She held so firmly to her rage and her sense of injury that she wouldn't let the white palace reach her. That speaks of terrible pain, doesn't it? And I know that Wan-Edhe found ways to worsen it for all of them."

"As he did for all the people whose lives crossed his."

"Even so, all I hear in memory is her '*Cluh-VAR-R-R-lin-eh*,' that horrible howl on the *VAR*, before she told me off for my noisiness, my selfishness, my uselessness, and her head-aches. Clair is precious to me." It having been the shortening of her name by Jennet, Clair's first friend, a little Chwahir girl who could not get all four syllables out.

Seshe said, "Then you understand me. In retrospect, I should have made up something entirely new back then. Except I was never certain I'd like anything I chose over long term. Or I might forget—"

A new arrival by transfer appeared in the central area: Detlev.

The shells noted the newcomer, who was not armed and seemed no threat, so they ignored him, as Siamis said to the leader of the men's group, "No, I understand. If you cannot leave, you cannot leave. Then I will come back to you once a week to check on you, and we will proceed from there. Is that sufficient?"

The shells bowed deeply, and Siamis slipped away as they closed around Jilo, who pulled from the carryall a very official-looking scroll.

Detlev stopped a little way outside the tent, ignoring the fine rain. Siamis, Clair, and Seshe joined him.

"Shall I wait for Jilo?" Detlev asked.

Seshe said, "I … didn't know a message got sent to you?"

"Erol indicated you two had a question to ask," Detlev said. "I'm always glad to come, if I am at liberty."

Seshe knew he didn't mean to be intimidating, but she was intimidated. But he was here, and it seemed rude not to ask her question. "What do you know of the rituals of the ancient Chwahir?"

Detlev squinted up into the fine mist, then turned to Seshe. "Not much."

"Was there a lot about dragons, do you know?" Seshe asked. "Jilo took Wan-Edhe's dragon throne completely out.

Some of the more tradition-bound thought it wrong."

"I can answer that, at least. The adoption of dragon symbols was much later, in particular by the kings I think you now call the Tyrants, yes? The later Sonscarna kings, after Lammog's day. In my own youth, I was told the Chwahir still resented being left behind by the dragons who departed through the worldgate, taking a number of their fellow Chwahir. All I know is that theirs had been a caretaker relationship. Custodial. On the dragons' part. The humans were, oh, perhaps more symbiotic? That is an impression, gained when I was young and focused elsewhere. And so far, we've seen little reference to the Chwahir in the scrolls we're translating. The Chwahir were very reclusive."

They turned toward the medic tent to see Jilo take a small cedar box from his carryall. From it he removed a seal carved from luminous sea-green stone, dipped it in ink, and pressed the seal before all eyes to the paper now lying on the makeshift camp table.

The shells bowed again, Lanit bowing as she accepted the paper with both hands outstretched. She carefully rolled it into a scroll, and Jilo looked around at the scavenged wood the shells had collected on their long trek, and at the stones some were rolling toward those digging the foundation. He joined Seshe, his attention on Detlev.

"I'll tell you later," Seshe said. "Are they going to need supplies?"

"Yes." Jilo scratched his head. "Not sure what to send up."

Detlev said, "This is only a suggestion, but I believe Mondros would like to be asked to help with this sort of thing." He lifted a hand toward the workers busy with the foundation, mud-covered to the waist. "He might have some suggestions on supplies to send along."

Jilo reddened. "I thought he was in Sartor now. He was done with Chwahir mage defense."

"Mage defense, yes. I suspect he would like never to have to fight another mage war again. For anybody. But you know he took deep pleasure in his garden at his cottage, and in the arts of cookery. He'd surely know exactly what this community will need to get through the winter, and to plan for spring planting." He lifted a hand and vanished before Jilo could get his tongue untied to protest—thank—explain.

Siamis met Clair's gaze, each reading the other: time to go.

"Next week I'll return," Siamis said, clasped Clair's waiting hand, and they did the slide transfer to the white castle.

Clair yawned to pop her ears after being on the mountain heights, as Siamis slid his arm around her shoulders. She fitted herself against him, every nerve alive to his warmth, his strength, his scent as he asked, "How did it go?"

"As you said, the toughest part is getting the women's awareness of their bodies to mesh with my awareness, so that I can truly see the scar areas to be removed. But at least I had a relatively straightforward task. And the magic itself was easy enough, once I followed all the steps. What you are doing has to be so much harder."

"Small changes first. Sadly, they are used to pain, I could see that in each as he braced. But it will happen. It was common healer magic in my day, using Dena Yeresbeth to see their bodies from within."

"Common in that it was known, but not everyone could do it." She sensed how proud he was to be using his talents to benefit these men. And he was right. Slow and patient, and write everything down. "Write everything down," she murmured. "I'd better do that now. My notes are a scribble."

He agreed. By the time they'd finished patient records, they could smell lunch—which would be their dinner, after laboring all day in Chwahirsland while Mearsies Heili slept.

They talked intermittently until joined by Sherry and Falinneh, and the conversation became general. Clair relished every moment. How odd it was that Siamis had been back only a few days, and yet it felt so very much like they'd been together years. No. Time was the wrong metaphor. It was more like she had reshaped herself since the day—the moment—she had woken after five years of steady labor, knowing the last of Ilerian's poison was truly gone. Before then she'd thought herself cured, thought herself ready, but that had been the desperation of her wounded spirit wanting Siamis to come and prop her up. That had become habit during the war. Necessity. But not after. She had to heal without warping herself around him like twining ivy. Only then could she find herself again. Find purpose again, while her body finished reaching its natural state of being.

And so, when he walked into the white palace after nine years away, they met as whole adults and they fit exactly, body, mind, and soul: the unity of three.

23

Laban tried to keep himself too busy to think about Carl's proposal.

That was the idea, anyway. But he found himself thinking about not thinking about it, an exercise in frustration. Which forced him outside even in impossible weather, and when he faced the lengthening nights, he ended up back in Yaldar once. Twice. Three times, bringing ever briefer respite from the clamor in his head. Sex was great while it lasted, but when it was over, it was over, and there was his dilemma, still waiting.

Lyren holed up in her rooms. Liere had left Enaeran at last, but she was not yet ready to see Lyren: *I keep crying, Lyren. I don't want you to have to see it, or feel it. It's mere separation grief, nothing worse, in that I know Iliosi Mathias is well taken care of, and loved. Unless you want to come to Curtas's House?*

Lyren was more curious than not to see the place, especially as she had learned that Detlev was seldom there, and Siamis even less often. She was quite certain that if she saw either, they would nag her about finding something to study — some discipline — nag, nag, nag, with the familiarity of uncles who weren't even uncles.

But she knew that Jessan was there, and if she saw him, she suspected that she would not be able to hide what Laban had told her. Oh, Jessan might even know. Her real fear was that she would not be able to hide her conviction that Carl's disastrous proposal was a straight path to tragedy.

She busied herself writing letters, and reading. Balked of sharing her opinions with reclusive Liere, Atan poured out her considerable ire against Macael Elsarion to Lyren, along with pages of heartfelt advice. Lyren knew better than to pass on the advice, but she relished Atan's fulminations against Macael Elsarion, and wondered if it made her a bad person to look forward to some diplomatic doors being slammed in Macael Elsarion's ever-so-handsome face.

There came a night when Liere did not contact Lyren at all. Lyren knew Liere was safe on that mountain, surrounded by poopsie power, so nothing was happening to her. Maybe she got involved in one of her reading projects—so like her.

But the following day there came a contact, along with a Destination, Liere's contact scintillating with a deep joy that was wholly unfamiliar. Even at the height of Liere's passion for Andri, to Lyren's skeptical eye Liere had seemed frenetically obsessed. Not joyful. Though would she have recognized joy?

She left that question behind as she transferred, then looked around in wonder at a perfect house. It wasn't large—if one was used to palaces—but exquisitely proportioned, surrounded by a garden that was a riot of color even in the dying embers of autumn. Tall, aromatic cedars whispered in slow swells around the perimeter. She knew she was in the south, as the northern half of the world was heading into spring, but otherwise? Where could she possibly be?

She spotted a gently curving stone path and dashed up it as a door with paned glass opened, and out stepped Liere, wearing an old blue robe that Lyren recognized from ten years ago, her arms wide. They hugged, and Lyren let go, studying Liere searchingly. "You are far too thin."

"I know. My appetite goes away when things are fraught."

"Fraught!"

"I'm eating again. I'm always cold when I find myself like this."

"Where are we?"

"At Leander Tlennen-Hess's old house in Tannentaun."

"Vasande Leror? No, Sindan, isn't it, now? I never knew this house was so pretty! Why did they live in that hideous castle? *Now* I understand why Princess Kitty complained about it all the time, and I don't blame her a whit," Lyren exclaimed, turning in a slow circle as she took in the charming room with painted arabesques under the ceiling. Mirrored sconces, windows that looked out at bright splashes of color from dahlias, lilies, and mums, complemented furnishings in warm colors with accents of dark green. "I love this place. I want this place," Lyren exclaimed. "But why are we here?"

"Because Senrid and I needed a little time to ourselves."

"Senrid!" Lyren drew a breath of sheer pleasure. "No wonder you're smiling!" Though Lyren could sense lingering grief, she did not point it out. "Tell me everything!"

"There is not much to tell," Liere began, and when Lyren rolled her eyes in a way she hadn't since she was fourteen, Liere laughed. "It's a lot, but most of it is … clearing up misunderstanding. On my part."

"I don't like hearing you taking the blame, as usual, but oh, the result makes me so happy I won't argue."

"I did say most. A fair share is mine, but I've been working on that. Senrid and I understand each other now, and it's only going to get better," Liere said. "Now, tell me about you! I know you returned from Sarendan. How are things in Everon?"

"A muddle," Lyren said, and to the surprise of them both, her lip trembled. "And I've been wondering if it really is me to blame…"

Liere drew her to a low couch filled with comfortable cushions. "Senrid has gone back to Choreid Dhelerei, and I've nothing to do but read, and try not to miss my little Yossi."

Lyren fought for control. "Yossi? I thought his name was much longer, named for a poet."

"His nursemaids are already calling him Yossi when Macael is not by," Liere said. "They say it with such tenderness. I will never tell on them."

Lyren accepted that, trying to take an interest in a baby she doubted that she would ever meet. A brother she would never meet. A brother, though she was twenty-five. "Was I a mistake?" she asked, bitterness coming out from somewhere. "No, I know you will say I wasn't. But, that Child Spell. You were *twelve*. Who thought that was a good idea?"

"A question so vast I cannot pretend to answer it," Liere said. "So I will only stick to my own situation. First, the Child Spell comes to no one who has not lived in the world a certain number of years—possible puberty, you might say. So though I looked twelve, I was sixteen when I would have gotten pregnant with you; there are some who believe that through the worldgate, in addition to other distinctive worlds, there are parallels to ours, each differing in some way. In fact, Senrid and Jilo were in them for a time, during the war. Christoph maintains he came from one of these, a parallel to Earth."

"All right," Lyren said on an interrogative note.

"So, supposing in some other parallel of our world I did not do the Child Spell, but crushed hard on some young man and decided I needed a family, the way I did with you. I still believe that in both—all--versions of me, you and I would have been more like siblings. I still would have been backward emotionally. Backward for sixteen, which is rarely an age of discernment, except in very few."

"Clair," Lyren said. "And apparently Erenlara of the Venn. *Clair* looks up to her."

Liere gazed into the distance, then said, "Erenlara works very hard. Very," she added under her breath, eyes closed, then turned to regard Lyren. "But the subject was my callowness at sixteen. Though surely you know of adults who seem more like children when it comes to emotional clarity?"

"Tahra," Lyren said. "I think she froze emotionally when that horrible war happened, long before the Norsunder invasion."

"I agree. In short, I've been growing up while you grow up. I'm sorry I was not better—"

"Stop. I am *not* criticizing you. It was a general observation, probably a silly one. Sveneric would no doubt have a ready lecture about that. As for you and me, I suspect I would have been a brat no matter when in your life I was born. And I had a wealth of ready family. Detlev hurled uncles at me whether I wanted them or not. The Mearsiean girls were the best of aunties. Arthur. Rel. Atan. And even Tahra tried to be one, as much as she was able."

"She did."

"And when I found the Fer Eiders again, I'd finally learned to appreciate them."

"It is a generous view to take of my failings as a parent, and I'm grateful. And so, coming back to emotions, do you want to talk about your muddle?"

Lyren wanted nothing more. She was aware that Liere had just come out of an experience that would scar anyone, but—as usual—she didn't seem to want to talk about it. Well then, the next best thing would be to give her something else to think about?

"It's *very* muddled," Lyren warned, and launched into it.

She'd meant to glide over the surface to the most vexing

aspect, which was Laban's unaccountable refusal to (gently!) let Carl down. Oh, those regrettable Delieth fixations!

She kept backtracking to explain what she really thought, what he said, what everyone did. She talked until her mouth dried, and she kept talking as she trailed after Liere to the kitchen at the back to get some hot steep. She interrupted herself when she glanced through an arched doorway down a hall covered with painted vines and hanging wisteria, into a salon with different motifs painted under the ceiling. "Oh, how I love this house," she exclaimed. "It's exactly what I always thought a house ought to be like, charming in every direction."

"Go ahead and look around," Liere invited. "The rest is just as beautiful."

"Who made it? Not a Marloven—I'll eat those embroidered pillows if it was a Marloven."

"A Marloven queen, but she was born elsewhere," Liere said. "So the pillows are safe from your teeth."

Lyren laughed, and while her steep cooled from scalding to merely hot, she poked her way from room to room up to the lovely attic dormitory, longing for the first time to have something like this place to call home.

Then she returned, and picked up right where she had left off, alternately sipping and talking until she heard herself repeating *oh, but*s for the third time.

Finally she set down the beautiful gold-rimmed, celestial blue cup and clasped her hands. "Well? Am I completely wrong?"

"Right and wrong seem fairly useless in this matter," Liere said slowly. "Let's start with the dangers of proceeding on generalizations. It's easy to say, oh, those Delieths, they all obsess, as if matter and degree were as alike as a row of buns on a baking tray..." An image flashed into Liere's mind: a chance moment when Jessan Delieth's gaze rested on Sveneric, who was painting tiny dragonflies and dandelion puffs on the varnished wood of a clothes rack. The longing there had gone straight to Liere's heart, for there was little hope that that would go anywhere. Sveneric's own gaze followed girls.

At least Jessan was in the right place to get aid should he want it.

She shook that off, and forced her mind back. "You don't know the depth of Carl's feelings for Laban, because the two of you have been silent. And that brings me to another point, my second of three."

"Go on," Lyren said tightly. She'd asked, she'd better listen, though the urge to argue was nearly overwhelming.

"You and Carl used to talk about everything. I realize that friendships can wax and wane as time and lives progress. You know the story of my friendship with Devon. Once so vital, but we ended up wanting different things of the other."

"She wanted you to be Sartora while you wanted to be Liere."

"That's certainly a tidy way to put it. And I could argue, but I will let it go. Carl's feelings might have begun as a heroic crush when she was ten and longing to get free of the invisible cage she felt closing in around her, but you don't actually know how her emotions have evolved because she no longer confides in you."

"She could! We never had a falling out, if that's what you're after."

"I'm glad of that. But isn't it a bit more insidious to assume you understand her emotions, when you have not heard her thoughts, and you still exert all your considerable talents toward changing the circumstances around her to fit your idea of what she ought to do?"

"Insidious," Lyren repeated, her brows drawing down.

"I know you don't mean ill. But her silence might very well indicate that she feels an ill effect. She's not a child anymore. In a lot of ways, Carl skipped over the frivolous ignorance of childhood. It seems from this distance that she grew up very early, however we want to define 'grew up.'"

Lyren twisted her fingers together, and gritted her teeth against bursting out with self-defense. Liere wasn't accusing her. Or angry with her. But each word scored her spirit like reaching among roses and snagging one's hands on thorns. Finally, she said, "You think I was manipulating her. Or trying. Or manipulating the siblings. And Laban. Oh, ugh, I feel *sick*."

"I will say only this: why did you not go directly to Carl and offer to introduce her to other young men, in case she might like to venture into the social world? Or encourage her to talk about her feelings for Laban? She might have refused. It sounds like she is a private person. And she might have agreed happily to the first, so she could do some comparing. But you chose for her, indirectly, using the siblings' care for her."

Lyren's eyes stung. "Just when I begin to think I might not

be a frivolous, selfish…"

"Stop that. I know you meant well. And you might even be right. Carl might be galloping straight toward the Valley of Pain. But you can't make choices for her."

Lyren thumbed her temples, then looked up with a crooked smile. "You said three things. Go ahead. Stab." She knuckled herself on her breastbone.

Liere uttered a laugh, and then said, "The last observation I have to offer concerns Laban, and you are probably not going to want to hear this, either, because of your own jealousies."

"Jealousies! I am not jealous!"

"Call it what you will. I think the word is imprecise because being jealous can take so many forms. Carl is jealous, but it comes out solely in hurt: she does compare herself to others, especially when it comes to things she desires. And she always finds herself wanting. This might be part of the reason she didn't confront you about all these suitors."

"And I?"

"I think you like Laban's attention, though you are not in love with him. It's fine, it's human—but it needs to stop if it interferes with him endeavoring to live his best life. In plain words, the tragedy you foresee seems to be based on a conviction that Carl isn't good enough for him."

Lyren sighed. "I really don't think of it that way. It's just that beauty is important to him. As it is to me. Though I know people consider us both frivolous. When I first began living with him and Vana, the girls—and boys, for Vana likes both— the flirts they invited over were flirty and fun and above all, pretty. Carl is none of those things."

"And Laban eventually got tired of them, yes? Because here's the thing, Lyren. The fact that he didn't turn Carl down immediately indicates to me that he is considering it very seriously. Might even have made the decision, but has doubts about himself. If I'm right, I feel inclined to respect him for that."

Lyren said slowly, "You think he wants to become what Carl wants? Isn't that a bad thing, to try to change your nature?"

"I don't want to guess because I don't know him. I'm going off what you told me of his words. I think your instinct to get yourself away is a good and generous notion. Human emotions are messy things, and despite everyone's good will, you and

Laban seem to have a strong attraction for one another, even though neither of you wants it to go anywhere. Getting yourself out of their lives for a time seems the simplest way to let that attraction wither. And there is also," Liere said calmly, "the possibility that one day he might find Carl beautiful."

"Away it is, then. *The world is my home, and I am a drifter,* isn't that a song?" Lyren's eyes sheened, but she lifted her chin and tossed back her long, glossy hair. "I was just going through my wardrobe, and decided that all my winter things are unutterably practical and dreary. There was no social life in Wnelder Vee to speak of, as everyone was too poor. I might return to Bereth Ferian to get new things, unless Arthur has spent that vast fortune on books."

Liere smiled. "I think he's trying! You can always come to me. Senrid would probably let you have this house. He says he wants to keep it for a retreat."

Lyren looked around longingly. She adored the house, but the idea of living all alone in it made her shake her head.

"Or you could come to Choreid Dhelerei. It would be a chance for you and Malcolin to know one another better."

"I think you and Senrid need your time to make things better, as you said. Neither of you needs my moods dumped on you. Thank you for the—"

Noises from elsewhere caused both heads to turn, and Lyren saw that brilliant smile of joy light Liere's face again as she murmured, "Senrid's here."

Lyren knew that Senrid would welcome her. He always had. But her emotions could not be trusted right now; she needed to take them, and herself, away.

She did her best to be social and smiling, turned down an invitation to dinner, and transferred back.

To find the rambling excuse for a palace nearly empty— Laban was gone.

Not long after she'd left that morning, Laban came wearily downstairs in search of the strongest coffee possible, after the second of two restless nights. He had two more days before his regular meeting with Carl, and though she had said he could take as long as he needed—years, if necessary—he knew that question would always lie between them. Further, the longer he waited, he was absolutely certain the more she would be secretly hurt that he had not accepted what the world would see as the most generous offer ever made.

He scalded the beans on the iron plate dedicated to this purpose, then ground them, and even the smell of freshly scalded and ground coffee beans did nothing for him, so he abandoned the coffee where it was, and transferred to Curtas's House.

The moment he recovered, he looked around warily, ready to slam back to Fortnyal Roth if Imry Llyenthur stuck his unwanted nose into the Destination alcove. In that short time Adam, who was aware of everything, alerted David, who was down in the wood room learning how to carve combs.

He left the class, took his piece and his carving knife with him, and jogged up the stairs.

"David," Laban said.

"Eh?" And then he pointed with the knife. "My room."

"Imry's not around, is he?"

"Do you want him?"

"No!"

"As well. Not here."

Laban threw himself into David's chair, his splendid profile turned toward the window. David took the window seat, and began carving.

"It's about Everon," Laban said.

"Figured it might be. Trouble?"

"No. It's Carl. Asked me to marry her."

"When's the wedding?"

Laban flushed. "If you're going to get sarcastic with me, you can—"

"I'm not," David said, without any sarcasm. "Seems to me if you didn't refuse her outright, then you're considering it. Right? What's the problem, conditions you can't stomach?"

"Opposite," Laban said, surly. "Open offer. Be king. Combine the kingdoms. Watch over Imar."

"And?"

"Free. Treaty marriage."

David had managed to achieve a long, thin curl of wood. "What's the problem, then? Is it the idea of marriage? I remember you insisting you would never marry."

"Not a ring marriage. If it wasn't her, I could see a treaty marriage."

David lowered his hands and eyed Laban. "Why not her?"

"Because though she insists it would be purely a treaty

arrangement, it would be one-sided."

"That matters to you, what she thinks but won't say?" And when Laban's color rose, David observed tranquilly, "You care what she thinks. Isn't having scruples a good thing? Or are you still letting Imry mess with your head, and he isn't even around?"

"Shit. You're no help." Laban vanished.

David chuckled under his breath as he kept carving. Adam entered presently. "Anything I ought to know about?"

"Laban is fighting scruples. He wanted me to tell him he'll lose. But I evilly gave him permission to scrupe."

"Very evil."

24

Every day for that very long week, Carl Delieth awoke before dawn, dressed with care, and then began her labors, her heart full of hope that this would be the day that Laban might come. But there was no Laban, nor any message.

She dared not write him. Instead by night she tortured herself with imagining how repulsed he was at her bluntness, for she had seen how she had taken him completely by surprise. Obviously he harbored no vestige of her own secret yearnings.

By day she struggled to be sensible. People proposed to one another all the time. Including monarchs. They did it in all sorts of ways. And he might simply be considering all related matters, as she had asked him to, and he might come on his regular conference day.

She did not sleep at all the night before. She had so thoroughly convinced herself that he would not come at all, because of course he was disgusted by her bumptious, intrusive proposal, that she did not go to the Study right after breakfast. Instead she went back to her room, and comforted herself with her dogs leaping up, plumed tails wagging, at this unexpected reappearance—for they knew her schedule, and it was pouring rain outside, so they couldn't go play.

She flopped onto her bed, running her hands over backs and bellies, and relishing the slitted eyes of bliss her touch gave her pets. With them, everything was simple. She loved them. They loved her. Nobody was afraid to show it—if she paused, a muzzle under her hand would remind her to get back to those caresses.

Then came a knock at her outer door, and a page announced that the King of Wnelder Vee was in the Study.

She stared witlessly for a heartbeat, then her flash of intense joy was followed by cold terror: he'd come to tell her face to face that he couldn't stomach the thought. Or, he would talk about the gathering of taxes, and trade issues, and pretend that nothing had been said last week, and oh, how fervently she *wished* she had kept her mouth shut.

She dashed out of her room and began to walk fast, then consciously slowed herself down. A stern reminder of what she saw in the mirror made her stiffen her back to hear the worst with a semblance of dignity.

She paused outside the Study door, gulped in air to subdue the sick tension roiling in her stomach, and wrung her fingers to shed the tremble.

She walked in.

Laban sat in his usual chair, head a little tipped back, eyes closed. His profile, etched against the shelf of this year's ledgers, was so beautiful that her heart squeezed within her, then he opened his eyes and turned.

He took in the painful dread expressed in her entire countenance, and committed himself for a lifetime: "I am honored to accept your proposal."

There. It was done.

Her breath escaped as if she'd been hit, but then she could not prevent the rush of blood that she knew made bright red lamps of her horrible ears that stuck out like jug handles.

But he had said yes.

She dropped into her chair behind the desk in an undignified thump. Her legs had turned to water. "Thank you," she managed, then blushed even more painfully. They were supposed to be equals! In fact, hers was the greater kingdom. Jessan had tartly reminded her of that, when she'd been worrying too long at what Laban might think about Everon's harbor question, and about the guilds trying to push back against the road repair proposal.

Laban and Carl looked at one another, two very tired people intensely aware that they were embarking on a decision that was now catapulting them both into unknown territory.

He cleared his throat, reminding himself that though he was older, she was still queen of Everon and he must not begin by crowding her. "Had you thoughts about when?"

Grateful for this sensible question, spoken in his velvety voice that made shivers run through her, Carl steadied herself. She still didn't quite believe it. But she knew she would hug the memory to herself as soon as she was alone, reviewing it over and over until she could believe it was real.

Before then, on to the rest of her plan, so often ruminated! "You know the law: because Tahra-Mama is neither dead nor has formally abdicated, a year must pass from the day she left. Everyone in Everon expects a coronation. It will reassure the people that we are following the law, and everything will be done right."

"Agreed," he said. "Continuity is powerful."

"And so, we could do both, that day? Marriage first, and coronation for us both? That way there is no question of con-sorts. We'll be like they say my grandfather and grandmother were, in the days all the older people claim were so golden. Equals, I mean," she amended quickly. "We'll have all winter to figure out what each of us can do best. Does that sound sensible?"

"It does."

She blushed again, looked down at her hands, then up. "I've wanted to refurbish some of the palace. Beginning with moving from the children's wing. But you can have whatever chambers you like," she added quickly, in case he thought she was insinuating what she dared not even approach.

He sat back. "There's plenty of time for those decisions," he said easily.

She began to relax—and in relaxing, her mind flitted from the echo of his words *I am honored to accept your proposal* and outward to questions about what it would mean, until she couldn't think at all.

She filled the silence by talking about the road repair proposal, of all things, though nothing could be done until winter was over—a winter that had not yet begun. But she couldn't seem to stop talking; she heard herself nattering on without reaching a point. Bleating, that's what her voice sounded like to her own ears. Lovely in a lamb, and irritating in a human. She shut up abruptly.

And he, sensing her tension and having marked the dark smudges under her eyes, stood up. "Seems to me we've all winter to settle these questions. Do you agree? Right now, that's the only thought that sticks in my mind. I didn't sleep much at all last night. Kept imagining conversations. I know that Everon, and Wnelder Vee, are equally important to us both, and we'll want to start out as we mean to go on. But this morning, I'm just glad we're in agreement. The details can come, eh?"

She agreed fervently. He took his leave, and once he was gone, she wandered in a daze back to her room. Maybe an hour's nap would make her feel less like her head was about to float away from her body . . .

In Fortnyal Roth, Laban surprised Lyren in the breakfast chamber. She looked up from her crumb-laden dishes, her golden notecase and a note beside her plate; the note was from Liere, who had written to say that she and Senrid were now at his castle in Choreid Dhelerei, and that Lyren would be most welcome to come and stay while she decided what to do next.

It would be so wonderful to have you here, Liere wrote, and below it, in Senrid's neat handwriting: *Liere wants me to add my exhortation. You know you are welcome. Stay as long as you like.*

Lyren had been considering what to write back when Laban turned up. She glanced at his exhaustion-marked eyes and said, "I thought this was your meeting time."

"Done. I accepted Carl's proposal," he answered bluntly, leaning against the doorway, arms crossed.

"All right," she said, her head tipped in question.

His brows rose. "Aren't you about to let loose a rant about what a terrible idea it is?"

Lyren considered several flippant answers, remembered what Liere had said, and shrugged. "I try not to repeat myself. So boring. Anyway, you wouldn't do it if it wasn't something you wanted, so what would be the use in saying anything but 'congratulations, I wish the both of you well.' And if there's anything I can do, say the word.'"

He sighed. "How much of that do you mean?"

"What?"

"All of it. But especially that last. About anything you can do."

Her expressive brows drew down. "What do you mean," she began warily.

He knew where her mind was so ready to go. His was as well. But *that* was ended. "I hope you'll go tell those words to Carl," he said. "And make the same offer, because I think it more than likely she will ask you to organize the wedding, at the least. She's already got so much to do. And you're so good at those things."

He waited for an explosion, but none came. She tipped her head, and smiled. "That would actually be fun," she said, surprising him. "I've gotten really good at trying to make the most of little."

"Make the most of a lot," he said, and it was her turn for a surprise. "Lyren, that palace is shabby and it never was any kind of cohesive in design."

"No—it was Atan's friends who each thought up how to furbish a room," Lyren said. "From what I can tell it's sporting at least five different styles. Tahra wouldn't touch any of it. But I doubt Carl suddenly has a budget for the kind of renovation it really needs."

"No, but I do. I earned something in my years away from Sartorias-deles, and I saved it in case I ever returned here. Some I already sank into Wnelder Vee, right after the war. The rest I was holding in reserve against Tahra stepping up her determination to starve us out. Not needed anymore, obviously. Anyway, I don't want to go in there and start running her people. We'll negotiate those things in time, but before then, if Carl asks you to put together a wedding, I'm asking you to do something about the rest of the place. I'll wager you anything the Sandrials will unite behind you, if you approach it right."

"Oh, I have *no* doubt of that."

"Over to you." He shoved away from the door with a grunt. "I'm off to sleep for a month."

Until tomorrow, she translated. Good; that gave her a day to work out her next step, because she was very aware that during this conversation it had been difficult to keep her gaze on his face. She had always liked looking at him, but now she knew his body—just in time for him to, in effect, give it to someone else. The world was filled with other attractive men. Time to find one that would cauterize this idle desire to follow him to his room.

She tucked Liere's note into her pocket, carried her dishes to the kitchen to dunk, then prepared for the jolt of transfer.

When she left the Destination alcove, she told a waiting servant that she was there to see Princess Carl. Then she looked out at the quiet hall, closed up tight against the roaring rain outside. There was still a trace of last night's meal in the stuffy, still air, a reminder of the wretched venting in this place. Lyren glanced down the hall toward the old children's wing, and it occurred to her that Carl might have been as tired as Laban had obviously been.

She was mentally composing an encouraging message to be delivered to Carl when a little page pattered down the hall toward her, and said breathlessly, "Princess Carl invites you to join her."

Excellent.

Carl had indeed gone to her room, expecting to nap, but her mind would not slow its gallop. Laban Dei was actually going to marry her. He was going to live in this palace. He was going to unite with her in defending Everon, and improving it. And once the crown was on both their heads, *nobody* could interfere with that.

The page returned, with Lyren following, always prettier than Carl remembered, her gown a rustling froth of layers in pale and dark green, edged here and there with gold.

And there again was her deepest fear, that Lyren and Laban would make a match. They were so perfect for each other. But it had not happened. He had accepted Carl's proposal.

Carl fixed her with an unblinking gaze. "Lyren, it's so nice to see you back. I thought, well, no, that doesn't matter. You're here." Her brow puckered. "Did Laban tell you? That I proposed, and he accepted?"

Lyren smiled, dimpling. "He did. Congratulations!"

Carl drew in a shuddering breath. *Now* it was truly real. She had told Lyren, and Lyren was smiling. She wanted to ask what Laban had said, what he was doing, but she choked that off. That was personal, and she had offered him his personal freedom. He had accepted her proposal, without saying anything about personal things … and there it was, her first doubt. No, she must not doubt, must not doubt.

Lyren intuited some of that from the tensing of Carl's thin shoulders, and her shifting gaze, and said, "I came to ask if there's anything I can do. For you. Before I go off to stay with Liere and Senrid in Choreid Dhelerei for a time."

"You're going away?"

Lyren shrugged as indifferently as possible. "Oh, it seems time to move on. After all our fun this summer, Wnelder Vee is even more boring than it was before. Especially with winter coming on."

She watched Carl drink in every word. Liere had guessed

right about the jealousy. Poor Carl! It was definitely time for Lyren to take her poisonous self away.

But then Carl said, "Could you, perhaps, give me some advice? About how to plan a wedding? I want it to be fine, but I'm not really sure Mad is ready to organize something that Laban will—that will not be embarrassing. You know Tahra-Mama never did social things, ever. And I don't know how to put it together. I need Laban and me," she said consciously, "to be leaders. I want us to have a court. Like we were this summer. Does that make sense?"

"It does. And you know there's little I like better than planning such things. I'd be happy to do as much or as little as you want to make it a wedding to remember all your lives."

All our lives. Carl's lips moved on the words. Lyren was saying that she expected it to last, was that it?

"Oh, Lyren, do," Carl exclaimed. "*Please* do. Everything was so wonderful this summer. And I learned so much. I mean, I learned how to talk to people. About things that aren't related to road repair, and guild taxes, and arguing with Imar about tariffs on our ships at Jaro." At Lyren's encouraging smile, she began in a rush of words, "It's easier than I thought, once I realized there was always dogs. And cats. But mainly dogs. If you have nothing to talk about, you can always talk about dogs, and most people are like lamps just lit. And if they aren't, maybe they are not people I want to talk to very much. Unless they're afraid of dogs, which is different than hating them. Because dogs have such loving hearts, how could anyone not love them back?" She was talking the way she had in the old days—but just as Lyren was registering this achievement, Carl became aware that she was babbling, and shut her mouth.

"That's exactly the way I feel," Lyren said. "You can add in horses, if you happen to like riding. Same thing. I should think birds, too, if you make friends with birds."

Carl's shoulders relaxed. This was the real Lyren, not the Lyren she'd built up to fear in her mind, who wanted to keep Laban to herself. So grateful, and so very weary all of a sudden, she swallowed against her throat closing, and said softly, "Will you stay? I mean, you don't have to. I understand if you want to go to Liere, now that she's free. Just to get things organized?"

Lyren pushed back the lace at her wrists. "Nothing easier. Liere says I can come at any time. Is my governess room still empty?"

"I think there might be some old toys in it, but the twins won't mind if we move all that back to their rooms, especially since they've pretty much moved to the Knights' barracks."

"I'll pack my trunk when I return. But right now, would you like me to talk to Jenel Sandrial? Just a general conversation, perhaps? I'm thinking ahead to what might need to be ordered. But there is no rush. We're not even at New Year's Week yet, and it was your birthday, wasn't it, that things would be official?"

"Official," Carl repeated. The best way to put it. Lyren always knew how to word things. *Official* was so much better than *Your birthday was the day Tahra-Mama knocked you down over a gift of roses, and went out to kill herself in a snowstorm.* "Oh, yes. That is, I told Ansa, I haven't made an official announcement yet, but I suspect that once one Sandrial knows, they all know."

Lyren noted that Carl was indeed exhausted, and though the tension had begun to ease, she was still emotionally wrung out. "Once everyone sees how happy you are, they'll be firmly behind you," she promised.

"The sooner we start planning, the better," Carl said fervently.

"Excellent! If you want to lie down for a bit, I'll go consult with Jenel Sandrial, and when you're ready, you can tell us what you want."

Carl cast one glance at her bedroom beyond, and agreed.

Lyren left, closing the door softly behind her, mentally writing a note to Liere. Who would certainly understand. And approve! Lyren was going to make this the best wedding in Everon's history, her own apology to Carl.

She ran middle-aged Jenel Sandrial to ground in her office beyond the kitchen. The way the steward looked at Lyren made it clear that Ansa had indeed spread the word.

"Carl has asked me to plan the wedding," Lyren said. "I'm here to consult with you. Not only on the wedding, but on your thoughts about refurbishing the palace at the same time."

Jenel's brows rose. "Is Laban Dei bringing an unexpected treasure forward?"

"Actually, he told me he is ready to do that. You'll have a good-sized budget to work with."

This, Lyren knew, was exactly the right track. Jenel Sandrial's demeanor cleared, not just at the promise of money, but the implication that she would be part of the decision-making. Lyren remembered the frustrations of Tahra's day.

"Come," the steward said, gesturing toward the door. "I think that you ought to see this." She led Lyren to the royal wing, closed off for a year.

In silence they crossed the palace, until with a wooden expression she opened the door to the royal suite. There beyond the usual parlor, which was nearly bare, though well swept, lay two large chambers, their outer doors opening into the parlor. One room had clearly been Tahra's: there was a narrow bed, neatly made up. Everything else squared with military precision, a pair of slippers waiting on the floor beside the bed. Tahra would have found all those perfectly straight lines soothing, Lyren knew.

There was a connecting door on one wall, opening into another royal chamber. So, Lyren realized, the previous king and queen had had the semi-public separate doors, and then there was this private connecting door. Which would have suited a couple who were reputed to have adored one another, while each having strings of favorites.

Jenel Sandrial threw this door wide to reveal floor to ceiling shelves of ledgers, and nothing else.

"Each year's gets put here on New Year's Firstday," Jenel said. "What to do about these?"

Lyren gazed, appalled. She suspected she was looking at years of daily reports on what everyone did, bought, earned, ate, from the Knights of Dei to the servants to the family to the nobles, and the guilds and beyond.

"My own reaction is to burn it," Lyren said. "But I don't have that itch to keep royal records that most of the rulers I know seem to have. Archives?"

"Full," Jenel Sandrial said. "And the queen liked having these at hand."

Lyren put her hands on her hips. "I thought it was kind of early, but now I wonder if there is going to be enough time to get it all done."

Jenel Sandrial's brows rose, all the agreement she would express.

Lyren turned back to that appalling wodge. Well, she had always liked a challenge.

25

They settled on the first day of Fourthmonth for the coronation and wedding, the beginning of spring.

One of the vagaries of human nature that Lyren had discovered during her governess days was how a tightly-knit group of people, such as the Delieth royal siblings, could squabble passionately and yet at the first sign of intrusion from outside, unite instantly. For the siblings, that usually meant that no matter how angry they got with one another, nobody had tattled if Tahra-Mama demanded to know who was making noise and why.

In adult terms, Lyren decided she needed to be there when Laban Dei was introduced to Jenel Sandrial, steward of the royal palace, and descendant of stewards. The Sandrials were as lively as any family among themselves, but at the first hint of someone disturbing their Delieth charges, they locked arms and raised shields. For some past visitors who had been much disliked, that had meant damp sheets, cold meals, inexplicable holes in socks (discovered when the knit gave way), and no servant in sight when they wanted something. She didn't know what she could do if they took against Laban. And she had been avoiding Laban as much as possible — made easier because she strongly suspected he was avoiding her — but this meeting was so important.

Carl was there, of course. She said proudly, her chin up, "This is the future king of Everon, Laban Dei. Laban, Jenel Sandrial is the Palace Steward."

"I know," Laban said. "The Sandrials are mentioned often

in family records."

It was a promising beginning. No fulsome praise, but acknowledgment of their importance. Lyren exulted at the very slight easing in Jenel Sandrial's face.

Carl looked from one to the next, and then added more diffidently, "I realize I am no use in planning a wedding, even mine. I'm just in the way. So I'll leave you to it, shall I?" And she whisked herself out of the study—now merely a study— where they were all gathered.

Jenel Sandrial remained silent, as she was still in formal mode, which meant servants did not speak until asked a question. Lyren tried to think of something innocuous to say before the pause became awkward, when Laban observed, "In fact, I've been delving into family records as I try to learn how things were done. I'm sure you are aware, though I wasn't, that there used to be a Chief of Ceremonies, with a staff, for planning royal events?"

Jenel Sandrial ticked her chin down in the tiniest of nods, but her mouth relaxed as she said, "The last one was in my grandfather's day. But Princess Carl appointed Honor Lyren to serve."

"I know," Laban said. "And I'm grateful. I'm bringing it up because I've spoken to the treasury staff. You'll hear soon that Wnelder Vee's treasury has been added to crown funds, which will I believe extend to restoring that department in the next year or so. If you've a likely candidate in mind. And with that, I also will take myself out of the way." And with a slight smile Lyren's way, he was gone.

Jenel Sandrial did not say anything directly, but from that point on, Lyren noticed through little things that the Sandrials had decided in his favor. In fact, she thought wistfully on the last night of the year, as a blizzard howled around the eaves, life in Everon was about to become a whole lot better.

But she would not be there to enjoy it.

Everyone had their favorite signs of prediction, most of them from nature, from the thickness of animals' winter coats to the early hiving of bees, which had caused Ferdrian to shutter itself tight. Carl had sent notice—her last official edict as Princess Mersedes Carinna—to nobles and guilds that New Year's Firstday did not necessitate attendance unless there was an issue, as everyone would be expected to attend court on the first of Fourthmonth for the wedding and coronation.

There were few festivities over New Year's Week. The Knights' squires had liberty, and Jessan returned from Sartor, so Carl had all her siblings there to meet Laban, who—experienced as he was in groups—set a tone of hilarity in games of wit, and paper chases. Lyren observed Carl's glow, and how her eyes always followed Laban, and wondered how that relationship was going to work itself out.

But it was not her affair. She had to remind herself of that: she would not know. Carl was as affectionate as she had been in early days, and she was consciously learning to talk about matters rather than keeping them inside, but one subject she was silent on: Laban.

Firstmonth sped by, and the cold and gloom of Second-month was made colder and gloomier by thick fogs when it wasn't snowing or sleeting, but inside the palace voices rang down the halls, along with the constant sounds of chipping and scraping and hammering. The work was going well. Lyren had redesigned the royal suite entirely—Tahra's ledgers having been consigned to one of the storage warehouses now dedi-cated to this purpose—but once the workers started restoring those rooms, she never set foot there again. The finishing touches could be overseen by the two who would live there.

She lived for her nightly contacts with Liere. Sometimes these were quick. The words didn't matter. Even wordless was fine, as she was often so tired she was half-asleep. She was sustained by the limitless love, unconditional. No matter how tangled her emotions, how much she regretted her own actions and words, that love was there, and getting stronger.

Liere let Lyren know that her wedding would occur on the 33rd of Thirdmonth, when the Marloven jarls came to drop off academy candidates for the new season. That gave Lyren the perfect reason to move to Choreid Dhelerei during the first week of Thirdmonth.

One day there, seen everywhere, nodding and smiling with approval, the next she was gone.

"Where is Lyren?" Carl asked at dinner, which now as often as not included Laban. "She said something about riding out to see Aunt Theanra about the new dishes, but surely she'd be back by now."

"*That's* already done," Wenwen spoke up, glad to be the one in the know. "Delivery in two weeks. Such a pretty design. Everything is going to match, for the first time!" She grimaced at the jumble of plain dishware that Tahra had favored, with the occasional finer pieces left over from earlier days. "Lyren said everything is now ready, or nearly, and you can finish deciding the little things, but she wants to help Liere. It's her own mother getting married. Who would be better than Lyren to help?"

Who indeed? Everyone accepted that; Carl could not suppress a quick, anxious look Laban's way, but he was talking to FJ about Colend's yearly music festival, and didn't even seem to notice.

As for Lyren, she walked across the enormous stable yard from the outside Destination, and peered up at the familiar castle in Marloven Hess. A fast contact, and Liere arrived, breathless from running down three flights of stairs. Once she and Liere had hugged each other tightly, this time it was Liere who peered with concern into her daughter's face, and murmured, "You are much too thin."

"Am I? Well, I'll soon fix that, if that pastry store is still over on that street near the academy entrance."

Liere gave a soundless laugh. "If you like pastry, tell me what kinds. I believe pastry is not unknown to the castle kitchen. It's just that Senrid never much liked very sweet things. But I do. They make a delicious egg-custard cake here."

Lyren remembered the honeycakes and sweet tarts that the kitchen had made for Crystal Ingrid. A pulse of grief wrung through her, and she tried to imagine what Crystal Ingrid would be like now: Wenwen's age, probably horse mad, maybe over there in the academy, bashing swords around, and loving it. Or else out training dogs and horses. She had so loved dogs especially.

But that, she kept to herself. "Egg-custard sounds good," she said, making an effort to sound hearty. "However, I was thinking of that shop because there were always handsome young men coming in and out. I never realized before today how flattering that black and tan uniform is to men's bodies." She wiggled her eyebrows.

"I hadn't noticed either, until my return after so many years away," Liere admitted. "We are a pair of late-blooming roses, are we not?"

"Late blooms linger longer, isn't that the saying?" Lyren said. "I don't see any of the crazed building and scrubbing and clipping and painting that I left behind, and your wedding is a week before Carl's and Laban's. Don't tell me Marloven weddings are just vows and maybe an excuse for some more martial arts, and it's done?"

"I'm very much afraid you will be seeing a bit of martial arts," Liere said.

"If it's done by some of these fine fellows I see around, I'll not complain."

"The only martial arts you will see will be performed by me," Liere admitted.

"You?"

"Me and two swords, to be precise. I've been practicing since New Year's Week."

Lyren stared at her. "Do you fight someone for Senrid's hand, like in the barbarian days?"

Liere laughed, her eyes two slits of glinting gold in the morning light. "No, no. No fighting, though there will also be the traditional sword dance. The queen's sword toss hasn't often been done in recent centuries, I'm told. But Senrid says it's always proved to be popular. Dates back to the bad old empire days, when queens led the defense of the kingdom while the men were out conquering. He thinks the people here will enjoy it, but he actually wants word to trickle down to Perideth."

"That sounds like Marlovens." Lyren sighed, looking around. "Everything is so much bigger than Ferdrian. Castle bigger, walls higher. And stone everywhere. In Ferdrian they mostly cover the stone with plaster and paint, or get ivy or wisteria to grow over it. But here, the stone is right in your face."

"I don't mind it," Liere admitted. "I think it's the color. I find the mottled gray stone common in so many other places to be dreary, but I like this sand-colored stone. It looks peachy in the morning sun. When the sun is stronger," she amended as they glanced up at the brown walls, wet from a recent rain shower. "It even looks gold when the sun is setting."

Lyren heard the ring of affection in Liere's voice. This place had always been a haven for her, and now, it seemed had become a home.

Lyren liked Choreid Dhelerei. She was used to it. But it would never be home; she sighed inwardly at the ubiquitous aroma of cabbage and rye. At least that was from immediate cooking. The Marlovens didn't use glass except in the upper stories, some places. They put up shutters in winter, and took them down at the first thaw. Marlovens liked fresh air, even if it was cold enough to put a film of ice over your jug of water of a morning.

Liere took her upstairs to Senrid's study, where he dropped what he was doing to greet Lyren. She met his searching gaze with one of her own, thinking that he actually looked younger than he had last year about this time, when she'd come to offer a place to Malcolin.

He asked no intrusive questions. He never had. It was easy to fall into old habits, for this had also been one of Lyren's many havens.

At sunset Malcolin appeared from somewhere outside, covered with dirt. He ran off to bathe, then reappeared clean, damp, and looking startlingly like his father. Except he had a quick, lopsided grin that was his own. He looked curiously at Lyren; she saw that he had to reach back in memory for her, but then it was there. He chattered about his local friends and some involved game they were playing, half his words muffled by his dinner. Lyren realized that the gap in their ages seemed larger than the fifteen actual years, but time would change that.

He dashed off the moment he finished his food, and Lyren said, "Is there anything I can do to help?"

Senrid said, "What needs doing is pretty much done. Once the vows are over, we ride around the city, stopping at guild buildings. The guilds are responsible for those. Where we could use you is in entertaining the Fer Eiders when they come."

"Glad to." And to Liere, "I've been avoiding them because I didn't know what to say, and I knew Grandma would be asking."

"It's all right," Liere said. "I was there right after New Year's Week. Marga came for a visit, too, which I think helped to diffuse matters."

"Uncle Milny wanted to take a rolling pin to Macael Elsarion?" Lyren asked.

Liere's smile looked a little pained. "How did you guess? But I promised they will get to meet Yossi one day."

One of Senrid's runners appeared at the door. He got up, the fingers of one hand trailing over Liere's cheek in a light caress before he left. Lyren watched, and thought she'd maintained her social face, but Liere said, "Has it been difficult?"

"Yes," Lyren breathed. "I had to get away. But I did it."

Once again, all those pent-up emotions poured out, and Liere listened closely, as if she had nothing else to do in the world. She made none of the tiresome predictions people were apt to hand out and expect to be thanked for ("Oh, it'll be all right!"), which Lyren appreciated.

As for Liere, she sifted Lyren's range of expressions, and her words, and tone, and heard mostly resignation. The only anodyne was time.

Which passed faster than Lyren expected, beginning with the sudden reappearance of Senrid's cousin, Ndand Montredaun-An. She was, they discovered, a very odd woman. Short, square, and dark-haired, she did not resemble Senrid except in her jawline and her square palms and long fingers. She had brought with her a group of musicians, whom she expected Senrid to house. It fell to Lyren to host Ndand and her group during the days until Senrid was free, which mostly meant squiring them around a city that had no street signs, interpreting for them, and sitting quietly to listen to them rehearsing.

This actually turned out to be interesting as Ndand listened to locals singing their ballads and drumming, then brought back what she heard and began introducing Marloven motifs into her music. It was then that Lyren began to understand that this odd woman was extremely talented, and that a lot of her silences were not static, but an acute observance of the effect of her music on the Marloven runners and sentries and others passing by the open windows through which the rehearsals could be heard: when Ndand observed a halt, a cocked head, a sudden smile, or a changed gait so that footsteps matched the beat, she cemented the latest iteration into the piece.

"I always assumed music was written the way we write a letter, or a report. Once, and it's done," she said over dinner to Liere and Senrid a few days before the end of the month.

"Some rewrite reports many times before they copy it out," Senrid said. "Our seniors do, when they develop plans."

"Oh, well, military exercises," Lyren said, waving a hand.

"I think it's true for anything," Liere put in. "There can be a number of versions. I look forward to hearing this music."

"It's such an interesting blend of the galloping beat that so many of the ballads here have," Lyren said, "and melodies with

Sartoran triplets and the like."

Senrid glanced up, giving her a half-smile. "We're not unacquainted with triplets here, but they tend to show up in battlefield trumpet flourishes."

Lyren rolled her eyes, certain he was teasing her, but his words came back to her at the end of the week, when fanfare after fanfare peeled out in cascades of chords, brassy and thrilling, from the towers and the galleries high under the vaulted ceiling of the throne room. Then the rolling thunder of big drums rumbled under the blood-stirring triplets.

Lyren's bones resonated, her heartbeat thrummed, and sheer, compounded reaction made her laugh, though her voice was utterly lost. So much for her assumption that the tasteful, elegant combination of strings and flutes that she had helped select for Carl's wedding would transcend anything the Marlovens could possibly put forward. No one would call those trumpet fanfares elegant, nor the syncopated rhythm of those drums, but that music certainly reached down to grip you viscerally.

Senrid and Liere walked side by side from the great doors to the throne, both dressed in black and gold. Liere's only ornament was her hair, tied in a long four-strand braid with black ribbon. To keep it well out of her way, she'd told Lyren. Ah yes, the swords.

The two spoke their vows, which were akin to the vows heard in other lands: promising to cleave to one another in good times and bad, and to defend the kingdom to the death. Grandma Elen held Lyren's hand so tightly that Lyren's knuckles began to crepitate, but then it was done, and Grandma Elen let go to mop her eyes.

The power of resounding cheers crashed around Senrid Montredaun-An and Liere Fer Eider. Liere's face seemed lit from within, her eyes sparkling in the torchlight. Her happiness was very nearly palpable, and Lyren was thrown back in memory to Liere's first wedding, which she herself had arranged, in Mearsies Heili early in the war.

It had seemed right on the surface, though Lyren now could not recollect without wincing her secret desire to make a grand gesture. Manipulation, even though Atan had agreed; she'd seen how fervent Liere was about her romance earlier in summer, before the invasion, and she'd thought the wedding would be a welcome thing for all in the face of so much war and misery. Lyren distinctly remembered Liere's fixed grin, her repeated thanks, that night in Mearsies Heili. Oh, she had been thoroughly enamored of Andri. But Lyren now wondered if Liere had been having second thoughts...

She flinched again and looked away to banish the memory. Regret had to be acknowledged—but not today! There on Lyren's other side was Malcolin, slim and straight in his academy uniform, bouncing on his toes in his eagerness for what was to come next. The rest of the Fer Eiders stood on his other side, clearly enthralled.

The last gunvaer had been Senrid's mother, a gentle princess from Telyerhas with a literary bent. She had not been expected to do much beside produce an heir, which she had, in Senrid. She was murdered before she could do much else. Senrid barely remembered her, except in a tactile sense: her hugs, the fragrance she wore, the warmth of her arms and body. Her voice softly singing little ditties in her own language.

Commander Keriam had told Senrid once that his parents' wedding was a quiet one. But Senrid wanted the world to know whom he was marrying, and Liere had agreed: though she was foreign-born like his mother, she understood the Marloven culture. And now she proved it. As the cheers resounded around them, she took a pair of swords from David, who looked so strange to Lyren in Marloven black and tan instead of his usual loose laborer's tunic and trousers and bare feet.

David stepped back as Liere, with firm assurance, threw the swords high in the air. The gathered guests shouted anew as the glinting steel spun end over end. Before falling—to be snatched out of the air with either hand by Liere, who tucked the blades expertly under her armpits and offered the hilts to Senrid.

The company screamed their approbation so loud that they nearly drowned the drum rolls as Senrid clashed the swords overhead, causing a shower of sparks. Then he threw the swords down on the dais before the throne. He was joined by Hatch Senelac, Garrison Commander at Methden, representing Retren Forthan, revered army commander killed in the war. Indevan Stad, the current army commander mounted to the dais. And to make up the diamond, Senrid had asked David, who had backed off, saying that the sword dance was distinctively Marloven. So Senrid had turned to Hadand Keriam, old Commander Keriam's eldest niece and commander of the north shore defense during the war, who, despite being in her seventies, clashed her swords with as much vigor as the younger men, raising respectable sparks.

Then, in a total break with tradition, Liere stepped out, and danced the swords with Senrid, mirroring his movements.

Lyren watched her mother, amazed and impressed. You could feel the intensity of their bond as they danced around those crossed blades, never quite touching, but no more than a hand's breadth of air between them.

The dance came to a triumphant finish. Senrid's and Liere's hands gripped together as they started together down the dais steps and under the archway of glittering steel made by the drawn swords of Senrid's provincial governors and his military leaders, both foot and cavalry, the latter's blades sporting a slight, wicked curve.

Lyren turned to her half-brother, who tugged at his collar. "Whew," he said. "Now comes the easy part."

"A progress through the city is easy?"

He grinned. "I get to ride my new horse."

Well, of course. This made perfect sense if you were nine years old.

With a self-conscious smile, Malcolin held his hand up at the correct angle, and Lyren placed hers on top of it. They did not intertwine their fingers tightly as Senrid and Liere had; though she and her half-brother had established a comfortable relationship. He'd reached that age when any kind of public gesture of affection was acutely embarrassing, if not downright repellant.

So involved in his own little-boy perception of the world was he that Lyren knew he was not the least aware of the intense fire-snap of physical attraction between the two walking ahead.

Then, from the crowd, emerged Atan and Rel, both wearing purple and gold, Sartoran colors, and fell in behind Lyren and Malcolin. They had transferred in shortly before the ceremony, and Lyren had barely had time to greet them.

The Marlovens saluted, fists to hearts; for them the weight of centuries — millennia — of tradition carried not as much importance as the fact that Atan had commanded the last great battle of the Host War, and Rel had led it. And many were quite aware that Sartor had for centuries mistrusted the Marlovens, denying them magic, even, when they could. All that was over now.

David joined the Fer Eiders in following the Sartoran monarchs. By then the king and his queen had reached the archway between the throne room and the equally massive great hall of the Marloven castle. Everywhere you looked had been decorated with hundreds of white flowers. Though it was still early for gardens, that had not dissuaded Senrid's people; Lyren saw flowers made of silk, and wool, and other fabrics, some simple twists of painted paper, others brocade gathered onto golden wire. The effect was not aesthetic, but the beauty lay in being heartfelt.

More blossoms lined the courtyard, flung by children's hands, as Liere and Senrid mounted the fine plains-bred horses that had made Marloven Hess's cavalry famous — infamous — for generations.

As they began riding slowly along the narrow path between throngs of cheering Marlovens, two more horses were brought forward by self-conscious academy seniors. Malcolin grinned at the girl and boy holding the reins, and they grinned back, hastily straightening their faces when Lyren stepped up, having settled on wearing a plain linen robe of cream, with gold accents.

Despite a rather chilly day, with threatening rain, they still had to ride. Marlovens always rode. Even the old rode everywhere.

Senrid looked resplendent in the form-fitting high collared tunic-jacket, trousers, and cavalry boots of his ancestors. Not as tall as his cousins, he was, like them, built on the slender side — and like them was in formidably good condition. He was also, it was obvious to see, tremendously popular with his Marlovens.

They proceeded around the city, at each stop acknowledging little gifts and short speeches by guild chiefs and other well-respected figures, before the final stop in the great square before the city gates, to eat a symbolic amount from the dinner hosted by the Choreid Dhelerei Guild Council. For the wedding party still had the banquet in the great hall ahead of them.

As they closed the last distance before the great guildhall, Lyren thought back to the story she'd heard of Senrid's rise to kingship. Lyren and Mac had jealously regarded it as a great adventure, but it must have been fairly harrowing, for his uncle and his Norsundrian allies had thought they'd have an easy time taking Marloven Hess from a fifteen-year-old boy.

They had been dead wrong.

That was where Senrid's real genius lay, Lyren decided, observing the man she'd regarded in the light of an uncle ever since her early childhood—especially during the years Liere was gone off-world. It wasn't his military prowess, which anyone with intelligence and training could master. It was the fact that he'd managed to guide this fierce people into using their discipline and respect for martial ability into productive purpose, instead of destructive. Nearly bludgeoned into extinction during the war, they were beginning to value making and doing. Lyren foresaw nothing but joy ahead, for the two people she loved above all others. Joy, at long last.

So why did her eyes keep tearing up?

26

David waited until the hall emptied, then held out a hand to Fox Montredavan-An, who had been leaning on a stick. "You didn't want to walk with Senrid?" David asked.

Fox shot him an interrogative glance. "I notice you didn't."

"I'm family, not really Marloven. Thought it better to hang back."

"I would have, but I didn't want these damn knees of mine giving out halfway along," Fox muttered. "I'm glad I lived long enough to see that. I was beginning to believe the family name would die out with that boy. It won't now. If those two aren't hammock-dancing every chance they can get, I'll eat this stick." He whapped his walking stick against the flagstones. "Might as well get themselves some brats while they're at it."

They proceeded slowly out of the throne room, and across the drafty hall between it and the great hall, where banquets had been held even before the Marlovans took the castle from the Iascans nearly a millennia ago. Only the decorations had gone, a silent act of resistance utterly unnoticed by the Marlovans.

Detlev appeared at Fox's other side.

Fox grunted a greeting and waved off Detlev's extended hand. "I'm fine. I wondered when you'd turn up." Another grunt, and as the two helped Fox sit down at the head table, he said, "Good job, eh?"

Detlev smiled. "I take no credit for Senrid's achievements."

"You kept him alive," Fox retorted. "I've heard plenty of

stories this past year. You not only kept him out of Norsunder's sticky fingers, but you also fended off that shit who did for his father. Sounds to me a lot like Anderle Montrei-Vayir, who was another shit." He made to spit—recollected there was no convenient railing of a ship at hand, only a swept floor, and the eyes of reproachful kitchen runners hovering to pour hot spice-wine. He uttered a disgusted, "Tchah!"

Detlev said, "Not unalike, but where Anderle Montrei-Vayir was devoted to his brother, and to the idea of glory, Tdanerend was gnawed from within by envy. He made many enemies, but the worst was himself."

Fox muttered a curse, then took a hefty swallow of the hot wine. "Ah," he said appreciatively, smacking his lips. "One of the few pleasures left."

They were alone, just the three of them as guests filed in to other tables. Many recognized Fox, and David, but none approached without invitation.

Detlev murmured, "You have done all I asked. And it was well done. There's little I can give you, except a peaceful end when you are ready."

"Nope." Fox flattened his hand. "Few enough of those I killed got peaceful ends. I'll take whatever's coming. And my life is not all pain and woe. On the good days I can still get up to my tower, even if it takes me half a morning to get there. Spring is coming, I can smell it on the wind. And I'm very interested in how my navy is shaping up." He slewed around in his chair to face the both of them. "But the *Treason*. What's to become of it? Those boys and girls in Senrid's navy are excellent, but none know the magic in that drakanship."

"What would you see done?"

Fox's eyes nearly closed as his gnarled, scarred hands held the wide, shallow cup, its shape much like the cups of his young days. Some things had not changed. "Nothing wrong with the navy," he said again. "They're following Barend's regs. They're good, and getting better. But that ship. With all those added spells and whatnot. It should go to someone ... someone like Inda," he said finally. "He was barely in it, but somehow I always thought it ought to have been his."

"I can see to that," Detlev said.

"Done." Fox set the cup down. "I've nothing more to ask."

He looked up as Siamis approached, with Clair next to him. Fox's eyes shifted to Clair's white hair, then to her hands, but there were no talons there.

Jilo shambled up to Clair with Seshe at his side; after the introductions, the two couples went to sit at one of the waiting tables, whispers susurrating through the jarls and the army commanders present, *King of the Chwahir.*

In typical Marloven thinking, the Chwahir, though they had been the enemy during the war—dealing the last telling blow that led directly to the fall of Choreid Dhelerei—had fought hard and well. Forced to obey the orders of a terrible king. Marloven history was full of similar tales. What's more, except for very minor looting of small objects on their retreat, they had done none of the wanton destruction that had entertained bored Norsundrians. And at the war's end, the powerful Chwahir navy had held off the shore of Halia, refusing to attack.

They exchanged greetings, and joined Army Commander Indevan Stad, who sat with several academy mates, along with Vidanric Renselaeus and Meliara Astiar—who had resigned herself to the refighting of various battles as Vidanric and his old academy friends moved utensils around on the table.

The room was filling steadily now, voices brightening as the spice-wine had its effect. The tables had been set along the perimeter, leaving the central area free for dancing. Up in the gallery, Ndand's musicians began playing, at first softly, the music almost unnoticed as the room filled, but as more arrived and sat down, the music swelled, tapped, and beckoned, demanding listeners. A few young people, eager to get started, moved out to form dance circles: though elsewhere on the continent, different types of songs called for various dances, all Marlovens needed was a steady beat.

Everyone knew they had to wait for the wedding party to make their circle of the city before the food would arrive, so they drank, chatted, and danced, as at the guild hall, Senrid, Liere, and family sat in the seats of honor while the speeches were got through.

Under cover of these, Lyren, next to Liere, murmured, "I didn't understand until I saw you making your vows that I began my wicked career in manipulation with your first wedding. I'm sorry."

Liere slid a reassuring hand along Lyren's back. "Not wicked. What Ilerian did to Clair was wicked. As for that wedding, I take responsibility, too. I could have said no. In fact I ought to have said no. Andri would have been fine either way. He'd said at the outset he never expected to marry. But I let circumstances push against my better judgment. And I did my best; my reward is there."

They both looked at Malcolin, who was playing a foot-shove battle under the table with the guild chief's grand-daughter his same age.

Senrid didn't hear a word of the speeches, which at least were short; the sky was looking more threatening by the moment. He let his mind range wide. David was, as requested, tending to Fox, who had aged considerably in the past year. It seemed insulting to think of that fiery old warrior as frail, but there it was.

Ndand was content—he could sense her. She had refused to walk in the wedding as a family member. "My father was a disgrace. Everyone knows it, and if they see me, and ask who I am, they will only think of him. You know I'm here. That's what matters. I don't think I'll ever come back," she added. "Unless there is new music. There was no music in Father's day, remember?"

Senrid agreed. She was who she was—she'd been abrupt, but frank, since Ferret located her, and David brought her address. They'd exchanged occasional notes, always through a scribe desk, and when he'd said she'd be welcome back, she said only for an event, and she would bring her music.

So she had.

Now he understood its importance to her. She knew nothing of mind-shields; her thoughts were filled with melody. He suspected that during their childhood, her silences hadn't been empty, though she seldom spoke, and rarely listened to his blab. Her escape from her terrible father had been entirely in her head, taking all the noises around her and weaving them into harmony.

A thrump of drums interrupted him, and the bear of a guild council chief bellied up to hold out a hand to Liere. Senrid glanced at Lyren across Liere's empty seat, her smiling countenance exactly as blank as a courtier's. It was a slight shock to see again what a beautiful person she'd grown into. Not the tranquil moonlight and deep-water beauty that characterized Liere, but the brilliance of sunlit diamonds.

He said, "Better brace yourself. We're going to be expected to dance once before we can get to the banquet."

"Terrifying prospect," she returned in the same conspiratorial whisper. Her mental signature scintillated like sunlight on water. "But you don't scare me. I can outdance you Marlovens any time, any style."

"You think you're tough? I believe you'll partner with yon grain-wagon chief." A glance at the other end of the table, where a self-important fellow was heading their way, big feet tromping.

"Ah, but I see your partner." Lyren flicked a gaze under her long lashes at the jolly woman halfway up the table who'd at that moment stood up, proposing a toast. Her elbows knocked into both her table companions, a fact that she either didn't notice or good-naturedly figured no one would mind. Senrid knew her. As a guild chief? There were few better. As a dancing partner? He'd better be quick on his feet.

Lyren chuckled, and lifted her glass along with the others. Then she merely pretended to sip, and set the wine down untasted as their respective partners appeared. They joined the circle, men outside, women inside.

Senrid jettisoned the myriad other matters occupying his attention and concentrated on Lyren, a familiar dilemma, as she had been since the days when Liere had gone off to Geth and left behind her daughter to be raised by whoever could deal with her best. Senrid had stood as a kind of brother/father/uncle, along with Siamis. Lyren had made Marloven Hess a second home, and Crystal Ingrid a kind of cousin.

Those had been good days. Uncomplicated days. They had not lasted.

But nor had the desolation that followed.

Senrid was beyond happiness, for the emotion-spikes called happiness were ephemeral. The past had taught him this perspective: whatever happened tomorrow, next year, next century, each moment he and Liere had together from now on was a gift of grace. He'd do what he could for Liere's troubled daughter. But it would require care.

He finished out the dance with minimal elbow-knocks in the ribs as an octet from the coopers guild scraped their way through to the end. They weren't all that practiced, but Senrid led the clapping when they were done, indicating his obvious approval; that so many of his people had taken up music as a hobby was a good sign, even if it was relatively recent. The more traditional wedding-night entertainment of the war dance and death duels was not so very far back in the past.

Then, as though to prove him wrong, to finish the guild offerings, a boy and girl sang in their sweet young voices an old, exceedingly graphic ballad about Senrid's illustrious ancestor Sharend-Gunvaer, who led the final and successful attack against the notorious pirate fleet that had resurrected the name Brotherhood of Blood. The Marlovens paid attention to that one, from the old woman three seats down who'd managed the blade-making guild through four reigns, to the guild council chief's granddaughter, all joining enthusiastically on the refrain while the teens beat time on the table with their knives.

Keeping his amusement hidden, Senrid joined in marking the rhythm, and again led the clapping at the end.

Their part was done. The guild banquet would carry on as long as the wine lasted and the weather held off, but it was time for the wedding party to return to the castle before their noble and royal guests started gnawing the tables.

They mounted up and trotted back to royal stable, waving at those who lined the streets cheering and banging on drums. Senrid scanned their surroundings and above, not quite relaxed even in this triumphant moment. Especially in this moment. But there were no assassins lying in wait, and even the weather cooperated, the storm holding off.

They dismounted and passed into the banquet hall, where Senrid gave the sign to the head runner to serve out the food. Liere, walking with him, understood then the wisdom of the symbolic meal with the guilds — they'd each eaten no more than a muffin stuffed with cheese, but that would get them through the next hour or two as they began with Rel and Atan, moved to Senrid's relations from Telyerhas, and progressed from there to greet all the guests. Meanwhile, the runners streamed in with covered trays to serve the food.

There was no time for real conversation; when Senrid saw Vidanric Renselaeus of Remalna sitting with Stad, questions crowded his mind, to be abandoned — they needed half a night to catch up, and he had to keep moving. "I'll write to you," he murmured, then nodded at Meliara, who had, despite Vidanric's and her son's assurances to the contrary, persisted in her expectation of a décor featuring bloody swords and tapestries of fierce battles.

There were war banners hanging high, but not a drop of

blood on them; this castle, she thought privately, was not nearly as nice as Athanarel, but it certainly was a whole lot bigger. She was mostly impressed by Liere, whose welcoming smile felt real as she looked right into a person's eyes. She really was as beautiful as everyone said.

Leander and Hibern sat with Thad Keperi and the Mearsieans. These old friends understood that all Senrid and Liere had time for were their words of welcome before they moved on to greet other distinguished guests.

At last the newly married pair sat down, and were served. Someone, mercifully, had thought ahead and held their food back so it arrived hot, though everyone else was finishing up, and already the younger guests were moving out into the center to start up the dancing again.

While Senrid chatted with Fox and David, Liere checked on her children. Yossi was always a poignant ache in her heart. He was sound asleep over the mountains in Shiovhan. Lyren was talking to others at the head table, and Malcolin slipped bits under the table to either a cat or a dog. Had to be a dog—a cat would strut right across the tabletop. Liere smothered a laugh.

When his plate was empty, Malcolin made his way to the Senelacs, where he joined his friends. Liere ate with one hand, and slipped the other under the table to grip Senrid's, warm and strong. She tried to do justice to the food, though she was not really hungry, until a couple of women approached tentatively, and Senrid murmured, "Bride dance first, looks like. Only the married women."

Liere got up and made her way to the center, where she joined with women young and old in forming a circle.

Senrid looked around for Malcolin, who was now racing along the walls in some sort of game with a pack of urchins, the Senelacs' black heads prominent. He turned to Lyren, catching a tremulous smile, her eyes sheening with suspicious brightness. "Lyren, are you all right?"

Caught. But it was all right. This was Senrid, who never nagged. She sighed. "I hate, I hate, I hate being blinkered by my own emotions. I hate being so self-involved I think I see everyone's best course, and I don't even see the half of it."

Where did this come from?

"Who does?" Senrid replied. "You've got to remember that we all put considerable effort into maintaining private boundaries. And so what we might think is someone's best course isn't."

"What if you're sure you're right? No. What if you're afraid you're right?" The bright golden eyes lifted, their impact intense.

"People make their choices. As long as you didn't force them…" He shrugged. "You have to let them live with the results." He grinned. "Unless you want to take over from Detlev?"

"No!"

He laughed as someone called for the unmarried women to join in a second circle, and Lyren flitted away from the subject of Detlev. Liere had included Lyren in her lessons in Marloven dances, so mother and daughter passed one another in the circles, one going one way, the other the opposite. Senrid watched them both, wondering how to characterize their different styles of grace: Liere gliding smoothly without a wasted movement, and Lyren controlled to the fingertips, laughing and flirting.

Then the dance finished, and it was time for the king to lead the married men in stamping, twirling, and leaping in their circle, soon joined by the unmarried men. After that, everyone could join the circles, and for a time the crowd was so thick the circles were more of a jostle, but gradually most of the older folk dropped out, leaving the dancing — and the flirting — to the young.

By that time, Atan and Rel were ready to transfer back to Sartor, followed by a number of the other guests who had arrived by magic. Senrid thanked them all for their presence, and escorted Fox to the door himself, where a couple of Fox's attendants from Darchelde waited to aid him.

Senrid was now officially finished for the evening. He sat back to enjoy hot spice-wine and watched Liere assess the room, her gaze going to Malcolin, thence to Lyren, and outward, a commander surveying the field.

Then she sat down next to him, her hand sliding over his. "Enjoying yourself?" he asked.

"Yes. I'm trying to consciously imprint as many memories as I can. I don't want it to be a blur."

He said, "Not to cast a shadow over your pleasure —"

"Lyren," she said unerringly.

"She has never been predictable, I'll say that for her."

Unpredictable, but not capricious. "Watch," Liere said.

Senrid had been paying scant attention to the dancers; he searched among them, and found Lyren on the other side of the room, talking to a gawky young academy senior whose body was so weedy with sudden growth he looked like he'd been stretched on the rack. Senrid recognized him immediately, of course; an unprepossessing, earnest sort, more comfortable with numbers than with people, he was clearly a desk jockey in the making. Senrid smothered a laugh at the glazed look in the senior's eyes as Lyren drew him out into one of the couples' circles, the senior following as if he could not believe this was happening to him. Lyren smiled, and chatted each time they passed in the circle, until she won a laugh at last. When the dance was over, she strolled with him—a lot of the social leaders watching—until they stopped by the youngest daughter of a jarl, another timid one.

Liere and Senrid both watched as Lyren added her to her twosome, and then talked the two over into a corner, where she began demonstrating the neat steps to some foreign dance. Then the three danced it together, clapping on every fifth beat, which gradually drew the attention of the bolder boys vying to draw her eye. The circle grew larger, until there were enough of them to move into the center—and there they were, doing a foreign dance, the two shy ones included.

Liere sighed, her gaze on the dancers. "I never realized, but she's so deft at this life, the world of the social gathering. Royal courts to her are the same as guild parties."

One dance followed another. Lyren slipped in and out of knots and groups, and somehow she managed to find not just time to exchange chat but ways to draw in those who had been standing in elbow-stiff groups, looking on. She did it with such ease that one had to be watching to realize what she was doing, and how she edited herself out of the center and moved on.

Unaware of this scrutiny, Lyren was enjoying the challenge. This was exactly what she had been doing all summer in Everon. While she searched around, spotting those who clearly longed to join, but were too shy to do so, she found them likely partners. Once she was satisfied that everyone who wanted to be mixing was part of the whole, she realized she hadn't thought about Laban all day or night. It really was just lust—he had become a habit, so she told herself. She could replace him.

She *would* replace him.

Her wandering gaze lit on the wickedly handsome man around her own age, who had done the sword dance with Senrid. Lyren had been riveted by him—but when she finally found him again in the crush, he was smiling down at a tiny woman with short black curls and bright gray eyes. The secret smiles between the two made it clear what was going on there, and Lyren was one step into a hasty backtrack when they became aware of her.

So, why not introduce herself? "I'm Lyren," she said. "I'm trying to meet everyone."

Marend Ndarga and Hatch Senelac introduced themselves. They knew who she was by now, and Marend had just been talking about how impressed she was that the famed Sartora could handle the sword toss as if she'd been doing it all her life.

The three of them began discussing dances, the history of dances, the old duel-challenge dances, and before long, Hatch was showing off his gymnastic moves as Lyren and Marend looked on, commenting and laughing behind their hands.

Lyren then danced with Marend, challenging each other with their own showoff moves, until a small circle gathered around to clap and cheer them on. Then Hatch was drawn by old academy mates into one of the circles to do one of those old duel-dances—minus steel—and Lyren and Marend chatted about life in Methden. Lyren learned that the two were not just jarlan and garrison commander, they had recently begun to discuss marriage.

Lyren said everything that was right, while thinking that here were two people her own age who knew exactly where they fit in life, and with whom, as Senrid and Liere watched from afar.

Some hours later, they were at last alone in the king's suite. Yawning, Senrid looked around, wondering for the first time if this had also been Ivandred's suite, four centuries ago. He'd given orders for Ivandred's exquisite renderings to be hung on the walls. Liere loved them.

He removed his tunic, out of habit hanging it up neatly, then he carefully removed the age-yellowed shirt he'd worn beneath. Liere, seeing the unsteadily stitched embroidery again—owls and ships and racing animals—drew in a slow breath.

With careful hands Senrid laid aside Inda's shirt, then

pulled away from his skin the shirt he'd worn beneath so he wouldn't sweat up the ancient one, though Detlev had insisted the linen would survive. The plain cambric shirt was damp and wrinkled. He left the laces loose, and crossed the room to stand behind Liere, who sat on the edge of the bed, unraveling the black ribbon from her braid.

"Don't you want to leave that for now?" he asked.

"This four-strand braid is like a rope. I don't want to sleep on a rope—I'll make a flat braid," she said, her fingers working rapidly. "What should we do with Inda's wedding shirt?"

"I expect Detlev will be along to take it away. If not, I'll see that it's stored safely."

He stretched out beside her as she said, "I know you're worried about Lyren. I am as well. But matchmaking never works. And even if it did, I can't imagine who in the world would be right for Lyren."

"I'm thinking more about her having to return to Everon this week. Think that might lie behind her mood?"

"It might. But unless she says something, I won't interfere. The only thing I can think of, unless she asks for aid, is to keep on the watch for a situation that might divert her for a time."

"Best compromise," he said, and then, gaining permission from her smile, he began massaging her temples as she leaned against his chest. Both took these quiet moments to appreciate, no, to revel in the awareness that from this night forward, they were together, on the same path.

27

Clair had been chatting with Leander about Kyale's success as a player in the far north when Detlev came up to their table.

Hibern, who had been listening to Leander's anecdotes, glanced up. "Nothing magical," she said.

Clair blinked, reaching for the context as Siamis murmured, "No sign."

Detlev gave a short nod. "I'm going to take Fox back to Darchelde."

Clair whispered to Siamis, "No sign of what?"

"Who," Siamis breathed. "Imry Llyenthur. Detlev didn't think he'd turn up, but I thought the odds were even. I've scouted by mind, Hibern by magic."

Clair's brow furrowed. "Senrid never did anything to him that I've heard of. It was all one way. Would Imry Llyenthur really be so spiteful as to try to disrupt Senrid's wedding?"

"Not disrupt, but I was afraid he would turn up to confront Senrid face to face. Senrid was wise enough not to lay wards against him, which Imry would probably have found irresistible. If Imry wants to turn up some other day, Senrid can deal with it however he wants to, but we decided to be vigilant today."

Clair sighed. "What would be his motive? Is it leftover poison from the elder generation?"

At this mention of the past, Leander the archivist spoke up. "All the records insist that Kendred was thrashed constantly into being better and tougher than anyone else. Prince training, it was called. Torture might be a better term. The old king endured it, and so would his eldest son."

Siamis added, "Whether or not it's Imry's motive, his wretch of a father did turn around and pass on the torment to his younger brothers in the name of training them to be tough. Indevan shrugged it off. But Tdanerend's nature made him the perfect target. And he, in his turn, used that method on his daughter and Senrid."

That explained a lot about Senrid's horrible childhood; Clair's gaze flicked to the gallery, where she had spotted Senrid's cousin, not seen since Leander brought her to Mearsies Heili, infested with not only unnecessary protective wards in dark magic, but weird experimental spells meant for mind control. It had taken the two of them considerable effort to remove them all those years ago.

David had pointed Ndand out earlier, when they all were gathering to witness the vows. Ndand had not joined the wedding party. Clair watched as the musicians finished the last piece, and then began packing up their instruments.

"Will she come down to mingle now?" Clair asked. "I met her long ago. I'd like to say hello."

David turned his hand flat. "Doubt it."

Impulse brought Clair to her feet. She slipped through the departing guests, most of whom had left after Senrid and Liere finally withdrew. She waited at the back stairs as the tired musicians trooped by in a string, some talking to one another in Sartoran.

Ndand was last. Her indifferent gaze brushed over Clair, hitched at her white hair, and moved away again.

Clair said, "Your music was wonderful, Ndand."

Senrid's cousin bowed at that, then the fact that Clair had used her name caught up with her. "I know you," she said slowly. "Don't I? I remember that white hair."

Clair remembered Ndand's bluntness, which apparently had changed little. "I'm glad you found your music school. It's evident you did well there."

Ndand said, "It was a mistake to send me to Colend. But you were not to know how crowded it was in Alsais, everyone wanting to audition. Probably worse now. But Sartor was just coming back after a century away. They took me in, even though I knew nothing, probably because they were a century behind. But I learned the basics."

Ndand had obviously gotten rid of the Child Spell some time ago, for she was approaching middle age, unlike Senrid, who had halted aging for something like fifteen years. Her tone was flat—not impolite, but it was clear that she was tired, she barely remembered Clair, and judging by her Sartoran robe, she no longer identified as a Marloven.

"I'm so glad that you came," Clair murmured. "I've always wondered how you were doing."

"My music was my gift to Senrid. He was good to me when we were little," Ndand said, and then brushed by, hurrying under the torches after her musicians, who were heading for the Destination.

Clair turned back, and ducked inside as cold spats of rain hit her cheek and her ear. She slowed when she nearly ran down a knot of people in the middle of mutual farewells. "You'll come and dance at our wedding?" a young woman called, before walking off hand in hand with a very handsome young man.

The last person in that group was Lyren, who called back, "Just let me know when, and where Methden is, and I'll be there!"

Lyren turned away, her smile fading, then fixing when she spotted Clair. "I scarcely saw any of you," she admitted.

"You were having too much fun dancing," Clair said. "I would have joined in, but those steps looked tricky, and I've never been much of a dancer. Even CJ was intimidated."

"Because, like Dhana, she usually makes up dances as she is inspired," Lyren said. "I know, I remember!" Her smile was forced—Clair felt it—but there.

Clair studied her in concern. "I imagine you're tired. Shall I see you at Carl's wedding?"

Lyren's eyes widened, barely a flicker, then her expression shuttered. "I—I was considering just not going," she admitted.

"Too tired from this one?" Clair didn't believe that for a heartbeat, not after seeing Lyren dancing and chatting all night.

Lyren paused, her unblinking gaze meeting Clair's gaze, then she sank down onto an empty bench beside a table that still gleamed from having been wiped down, and breathed, "I hardly know."

Clair sat beside her. "I've been hearing through Aurora, who gets scroll-length letters from Madelon Delieth, that everywhere in Ferdrian you're praised for how well you've organized Carl's wedding. Surely you want to see the result of all your effort?"

Lyren rubbed her hands down her thighs, then said, "What else have you heard?"

"What ought I to have heard?" Clair asked, gently.

"I … I … I don't think I'm ready for this conversation." But when Clair began to rise, Lyren caught her sleeve. "No, maybe I am. I'm afraid if I go, I'll poison everything." She shifted her gaze away, then said in a rush, "I forgot that no matter how much you know the underpinning of a given event, like a wedding, when it actually happens, emotions come to the surface. I truly was perfectly fine until today. And I might very well wake up tomorrow and think I was being a watering pot."

Now Clair was fairly certain she had the missing pieces of a puzzle she'd only half-recognized, after a couple of months of Aurora's intermittent chatter. She said with care, "What is your foremost emotion? If it's longing for someone, that's different from—"

"No someones to long after." Lyren flickered her fingers as though shaking something off. "It's regret, mainly. Regret for some silly decisions that I thought were for the best. Or rather how I went about it. Not sure I'm wrong, actually. But I definitely have no desire to, ummm, pick up my old life where I left it when I came here. It was fun. I don't regret that, at all. But it's definitely done."

"What does Liere say?" Clair asked.

"She says to follow my heart. Which is, I'm beginning to realize, great advice when you know what your heart wants. Which I don't. Mine keeps beating merrily away, minding its own business, and not interfering in the least with its neighbors points north. And south."

Clair laughed. "If your heart is minding its own business, I'd venture to say you ought to go. If a part of your life is over, might attending Carl's wedding bring you resolution?"

Lyren sighed. "If only life were so easy to divide off, like the end of a paper, or a road. But you're right. Resolution. I'll see you next week, and thank you!" A brilliant smile and Lyren flitted off, quick and light as a butterfly.

Right about the time Lyren burrowed into her bed and dropped immediately to sleep, the sun crested the horizon in Everon, and Carl entered the sunny breakfast room, which Lyren had insisted needed repainting.

Carl stood inside the door, remembering how she had looked about, bewildered; it had seemed all right. Clean, functional, something with which she'd been familiar since babyhood. Now it was a warm peachy white, inviting, somehow, with its lightwood furnishings upholstered in spring green satin. She had picked the green herself, after Lyren brought in several swatches of fabric in complementary colors, saying, "It's you who will sit here every day from now on. What's going to please you most?"

"Laban will sit here, too," Carl had said, hating the way she wondered if there was anything underneath Lyren's words. Despising herself for thinking it. She was determined to dig this nasty instinct for jealousy out of herself. Even if it made her understand her mother better — this was a monster one had to fight, or surrender to. Tahra-Mama had surrendered, a warning of what could happen.

Because there wasn't anything underneath Lyren's words. It was a straightforward question, Carl saw immediately when Lyren said, "True! I'm so used to sitting in here with you seven, with or without Tahra. Why don't you show Laban the swatches? You can tell me what the two of you decide tomorrow. Auntie Merry's weaver friend won't be back until Fourthday..."

Carl blinked away the memory.

With the wedding three days away, and only the last few items still be done, such as Laban sending over his belongings, Carl sometimes wandered from room to room, admiring how elegant things were now. And she thought about how delicately, but definitely, Lyren had withdrawn from making over everything to her own taste. She had consulted everyone, including Cook and the Sandrials, as well as the sibs. There was a message here that Carl was only beginning to see, as she wrestled the monster that she was *not* going to permit to ruin her wedding and coronation.

She knew some of her anxiety was due to the fact that though the evidence of Lyren's brains and talent and diplomacy were everywhere, Lyren herself had yet to return. Carl envied her but missed her far more. And Carl was sure her monster was directly at fault for Lyren's absence.

"Well, at least it's not going to be a harvest-time fools play," Wenwen grumped, tugging her gown impatiently into place.

"Fools play?" FJ asked.

The two yelled across the cubby between their bedrooms. In his room, FJ was busy drawing and flourishing an old sword that had apparently belonged to their grandfather. The baldric Jessan had dug up certainly dated back that far; apparently Grandfather Berthold had worn it when he was a teen, and FJ was the only one it fit.

Wenwen listened to him grunting as he slew imaginary hordes. Had anyone ever called FJ Franklan Jessan? She shrugged that question away, too impatient with the world to consider anything but her own discomfort at even the limited formality demanded of the dreaded wedding, which they were supposed to be rehearsing yet again as soon as the bell rang. "You know. Every ruler we can name, and some we can't, all lined up to inspect us, and watch us trip over our hems or splat food on our fronts."

"*You* can fall on your face," FJ stated with no hint of sympathy. "I won't."

"Huh. You will if you sneak the spiced wine." She went to his door to look in.

FJ only laughed. Of course. Then he paused in the act of waving the sword around and touched the worn carving on the hilt. "Wonder what this means," he muttered. "Odd symbols."

"Isn't that Grandpa Berthold's blade?" Wenwen asked, fingering the lace on her sleeve.

"Yep. Wish I knew the story behind it."

"Maybe you can find out."

"Not here." FJ grimaced.

Tahra-Mama had not really cared much for her father, so somehow there was little trace of him in the palace, besides his accession portrait and a few trophies such as the sword, buried in storage.

They looked at one another. "Mad would know," they said together, and laughed.

Madelon had long ago made it her business to seek the truth behind Tahra-Mama's distorted stories about the Delieth past. She was usually either spelunking in the old archives or writing; Wenwen's early memories featured Mad working with characteristic intensity, her pen stabbing into the inkwell then dashing across her paper in neat lines. Madelon had often fastened her pages into little books, and then, quite suddenly, they'd disappear into the fire and later the other sibs would find ashes or bits of burned paper on the grate. Mad never showed anyone what she wrote. *Not until I'm good enough*, she'd snarl, kick the ashes, and stalk away, if anyone dared to ask.

They'd all stopped asking. It was much safer to ask Mad for stories she could tell out loud.

A distant bell rang. FJ cocked his head. "Almost time."

The twins Sed and Glenn appeared at the door, along with Mad.

"Come on, you two," Glenn exclaimed.

FJ turned to Mad. "This sword—"

"Grandfather Berthold's," Mad said after a glance.

"I know. Who's it from? What's this stuff on it?"

"That one's from Colend."

"Colend! Phew!" FJ whistled.

What could homey old Everon have had to do with Colend, one of the most powerful and long-enduring kingdoms in the world, from which most of the best music and poetry and plays came?

"Grandfather made a progress when he was your age. They did those things then. We can talk about it later," Mad stated, giving him a shove. "We have to go. We can't make Carl late for her own rehearsal."

"Yeah. Tahra-Mama might show up and haul us into the Study for treason," Wenwen put in, and they all laughed.

"A good day," Mad exclaimed in her Pronouncement Voice. "Let's have a *good* day."

"I know, I'm just hoping being queen won't somehow make life harder for Carl. I don't think she wants to do it."

"Sure she does," Mad contradicted with older-sister loftiness. "She just hated being heir, because she had to enforce all Tahra-Mama's stupid laws. She'll enjoy doing her duty now that she gets to decide things."

Wenwen shook her head. "Then why is she so blocked off from us? She's not protecting us from Tahra-Mama anymore. What's missing?"

"You tell us, Princess Dena Yeresbeth," Mad teased. "No one else noses into others' heads."

Wenwen's ears burned as she shrugged. "Something is."

Jessan appeared at the other end of the hall, looking fine in his fine new tunic. "It's time to go."

"We're ready, we're ready."

As they started back down the hall, Jessan remarked, "Mad, I have finally figured out who you take after, more than any of us."

"Who?" Wenwen asked, looking from him to Mad. She often forgot that Jessan knew at least as much about family history as Mad. He just didn't talk about it as much.

"Grandmother Mersedes Carinna."

"She had moods, eh?" Sed asked.

Jessan grinned. "A temper. And a ready sense of fun."

"Not a talent for queening," Mad said, flinging her hair back.

"Few are born with both the desire and the talent," Jessan said. "Haven't you seen that yet? Our grandmother loathed the idea of queenship, and acceded only on our grandfather's account. She couldn't get him any other way."

Mad scowled. "If this is a sneaky way of nagging me about offering to take some boring position with the scribes..."

Jessan stopped in the middle of the second hall, and they all stopped with him. He gave them a sober look. "All I'm saying is, Carl has neither the desire, not really, nor the talent to march out and command all the attention the way monarchs are expected to. She has instead a tremendous sense of duty, shaped by all of us leaving her here with Tahra-Mama while things were getting worse. I blame myself most."

"We thought it would never end," FJ said.

"And we could do nothing to fix it," Mad added. "What do you want us to do?"

"We joined the Knights," Glenn said, turning his thumb between himself and Sed.

"Isn't Laban going to bring some of his own people in? Cousin Carinna says Silvanas is going to replace her," Sed added.

Jessan shrugged., and started walking again. "Everon is still going to be half Delieth as well as Dei. Look for something. You know she won't ask."

The hour bell rang, and they walked faster.

28

Three days later, Carl woke to a world that looked the same but felt wholly different. Today she would be crowned and married. Laban would live here. Her life would become his life—but only in the governmental sense. She must be careful to make no demands that lay outside crown business. She'd promised him that at the outset and she would keep that promise. It was for him to change the conditions.

She bathed in rose-scented water, then walked into her new dressing room where lay the exquisite gown that Lyren had talked her into ordering.

Enna Sandrial, her new wardrobe maid, was waiting to help her into it.

"Not too fancy," Carl said when Lyren first broached the subject. "I don't want to look like a cross-eyed jug in a bride-gown."

"A jug?" Lyren had repeated, her brows contracting in a way that reminded Carl strongly of Laban.

"I have a mirror," Carl had said. "I want it stylish. I still have your taste for style. But it has to be plain."

"You will have what makes you happiest," Lyren had promised.

And so the plain gown first had needed to be made of glossy cotton-silk, not linen, for one doesn't want anyone to think the bride is only wearing an under-robe, does one? Oh, no no no. The shade of white that Lyren brought somehow made Carl's sallow skin look like a warm, dusky gold, and the line of the design made the most of her slender build, and somehow that had emboldened Carl enough to agree to the leeetle additions Lyren suggested, the embroidered green lilies down the neck and sleeves and along the edges of the outer skirt. And once the lilies were on, it was somehow all right to add a few pearls here and there.

Ansa, promoted to chief maid, rushed in, her eyes wide. "Lyren — that is, Honor Lyren," she conscientiously amended, "is here!"

Relief flooded Carl.

"She asks if you have time to greet her, and if not, she'll join the guests."

"Send her in," Carl said urgently.

Lyren appeared, wearing a simple robe of periwinkle blue, her hair tied back with a blue ribbon. To Carl's eyes she was more beautiful than ever, and Carl fought the instinct to look at the cross-eyed jug in her mirror, to force herself to acknowledge the difference that would never be bridged.

She steadied herself: Laban was marrying her, not Lyren.

"How do I look?" Carl asked, glad her voice was steady.

Lyren assessed with narrowed eye, her gaze landing on the half-finished back-of-the-neck bun that Carl had insisted on. That would never do. With a sympathetic smile and a, "Could I be indulged one last time? You remember how much I loved doing up your hair," Carl smiled. Ansa nodded at Enna, who handed Lyren the hair brush, and bowed herself out.

Lyren's strokes in her plain brown hair were even and gentle. At least her hair had a shine to it, after years of assiduous care — another Lyren gift. Carl felt tension she hadn't even been aware of drain away from her forehead and neck.

"How long since I've dressed your hair?" Lyren asked. "You were small, and didn't want to sit still."

"I was eleven. Hundred strokes a day, you said. I made it two hundred, one morning, one night, after you left."

"So I see," Lyren said. "Your hair has all kinds of subtle highlights that your old braid just doesn't do justice to. Promise me you'll try some new styles."

"Yes," Carl said, and nodded at Ansa, who also withdrew.

Carl said quickly, "I finally learned I never could be you. I know I have to be Carl Delieth, but Carl Delieth is good enough for me now. Today is proof."

"No —" Lyren said, then cut herself short.

"Go on."

"Never mind. Your happiness is all that matters."

"Please." And, desperately, "I've taken on an adult job, ruling, and today I'm doing another adult thing. Talk to me as an adult."

"All right," Lyren said, her hand never pausing as she began braiding pearls into Carl's long hair—already Carl's head looked better, rounder. "First of all, 'adult' is defined by everyone differently. For most of us, it is not opening a door and closing another, it happens by degrees. For you, the first step was learning not to judge yourself by the standards of another, moral or aesthetic. Even one you love."

Carl was silent, sorting through Lyren's words. Finally she said, "I am who I am. And I know that you were afraid for me to meet Laban. Are these two things connected?"

Lyren leaned forward and kissed the top of Carl's head. "In your mind only. I didn't want you to meet him while your mother was here because I knew the secret would weigh terribly on your spirit. Is it an insult to say that you are incapable of lying well?"

"But that was before last year. I mean last spring. Last summer. When you and my sisters kept bringing me suitors."

"It was a clumsy way to catch you up with all the social chances you never got to have," Lyren said. "Didn't you like learning how to meet and talk to other men, even if you didn't want anything closer than acquaintanceship?"

"I did." Carl sighed out relief. "That's what Aurora said, at New Year's. I hadn't even thought of that, but I did have years of learning to do in a matter of months."

Lyren dipped her head in a nod, and then with a quick twist, pulled a rope of Carl's hair up over the crown of pearls. Carl watched, fascinated—this high style, nothing she would ever have dared, was giving her horrible narrow face the shape of a heart. It actually looked … almost good. On anyone else, it would be beautiful.

She squared her shoulders, and decided to get it all out. "You said once that you know Laban like a brother. That he tells you everything. Do you have no doubts about my happiness with him?" She had never dared such questions before, and a rapid heartbeat tattooed not just in her cotton-silk covered bosom, but in her ears. "I'm sorry to be so, so demanding, Lyren, but who else can I ask? Mad flirts with different girls, but her passion is books, and Wenwen still finds romance tedious. Aunt Merry tells me to do what I think best, Aunt Theanra thinks that I should just be myself, whatever that means, and I can't talk to a man about this, even Jessan. And my other brothers are all too young."

"Here's something to consider. Laban and I had an easy sort of relationship, one that was fine for a time, but we both are ready for something else. We talked about most everything that siblings talk about, but we have not—except for the day he told me that you proposed—talked about you. So, any advice I offer might not fit *your* relationship, except this one thing: always talk to him. If you're in doubt, if you're afraid, talk to him. Even if you get angry, talk to him. Don't ever shut him out."

"I couldn't."

"Oh, yes, you could. You did to your siblings, to protect them, and before that to Tahra-Mama to protect yourself. You did it to me, but that's perfectly all right because I'm not family. But you're about to make Laban family in the closest way. Whatever the future brings, don't shut him out. He can be hurt, and he goes silent and bitter. Like me, he's got the Dei moodiness. Ride out the moods because they really don't last. Just *don't* shut him out. Even when he gets mad enough to stamp around cursing, he's never hurt anyone, and I know he will never hurt you."

"I promise," Carl said, then whispered, "What about ..." She shut her eyes, and squeaked, "Heirs." She could not bring herself to say the word *sex*.

Urk. Lyren flinched inside, met Carl's huge eyes in the mirror, and though deep down she was aware of a tickle of humor, she knew without reaching for contact that this was desperately important to Carl. Who, unlike her mother, had a well of affection inside her. Those five dogs lying about in the far room were obvious evidence of that.

So, be practical. "If you want experience first, you could practice with the professionals," Lyren said.

"I did. But they always say yes. That's why you go to them. Well, and to learn."

When Carl stiffened under Lyren's hands, Lyren said easily, "Here's the thing to remember. Take your time. No one in the world needs to know what's happening in your bedroom, or not happening, except the two of you. Make your move when you're ready."

"But how do you ... get it started? What if he says no? It

will kill me if he says no," Carl whispered.

Lyren tucked a strand here, and better secured a pearl there. "I'm not sure what to say, because I don't have a lot more experience than you do. I want to say that you mostly go by instinct, but if you're the kind of person who needs to plan out all possible reactions before trying a new thing—whatever that thing is—my advice is, if you're not ready to talk to Laban about it yet, then go to someone with a lot of experience. Like Liere. Or Clair."

"Clair?"

"That's right, you haven't seen her since you were little, but you'll see her today. I'll wager anything she's only had the one partner, and that very recent, but going by the tight way she and Siamis are with each other," Lyren tapped her head, "it's very clear they figured those matters out pret-ty nippily." She grinned as Carl let out a watery chuckle. "There!" Lyren stepped back. "Do you like it?"

Carl turned her head from side to side. "It looks … actually flattering. My horrible ears are hidden. I don't get how hair at either side of my temples makes my eyes look less stuck together over my nose."

"You look lovely. Let's put a touch of your lip rouge on, and it's time! You've a throne room full of people gathered, and if they have to wait too much longer, they'll start eating your flowers."

"But ..." Carl was too distracted to smile at the joke as Lyren skillfully set the old Delieth coronet among the shining loops of pearl-edged brown coils.

"Be happy, Carl." Lyren lifted her hands and stood back. "No doubts. No fears. Liere said one of the toughest lessons she had to learn lately was to forgive herself for mistakes, and not to anticipate trouble, then decide if it came that she deserved it. Take each day as a new start, and allow yourself to be happy."

Carl turned to look up her, eyes misty. "Once Laban said I deserved to be happy merely because I was born. I liked hearing it, but I don't understand it."

"Because you've been good, and kind, and dear, your entire life, to everyone but yourself."

"But I wasn't good and kind. You know that better than anyone."

"You learned better. Isn't that what we all strive to do, when we make mistakes? To acknowledge that yes, I blundered, but I learned something, and I will not repeat that blunder." Lyren's eyes gleamed with unshed tears which she dashed away impatiently. "Oh, Carl, I want you to be happy. Both of you."

She turned, her silken robe rippling with grace, her gold-highlighted dark hair swaying against her narrow waist, and she walked out with the unconscious swing of hip that Carl was aware was utterly absent from her own walk.

Carl followed more slowly, knowing that when she left that room—that wing—there would never be any going back to the safety of childhood. From now on, she would be sharing her life with another.

Jessan awaited her in the hall. In the distance she heard the bells ringing the rare, sweet chords of the Queen's Peal. Soon they'd play, for the first time in decades, the King's Peal.

Jessan looked tall and competent in his white and gold and green. Officially the heir, he was the one to escort her to Laban, symbolizing to the throngs his willingness to be supplanted.

They reached the great tower, where Laban awaited her, dressed mostly in white and gold, with just enough green to satisfy custom, but not to contrast ill with his sapphire-colored eyes. As soon as her fingers felt his strong, warm grip, her fear melted into nothingness.

Laban said softly, "A quick sidestep."

They started down the tower steps on the way to the throne room, but on the first landing he guided her into one of the old guard rooms. There she found, to her surprise, a group of strangers—males all.

"I have no family to offer you," Laban said apologetically.

Carl thought of Charis-Merian Dei—so much like Tahra-Mama—who'd gone back to Geth with Cath of Isolde, in order to find peace.

"No family but the one I made. These, I give you. They will always be there in time of need." And he introduced them one by one, all famous names, once so sinister.

Last of all was Detlev. Carl looked up into gray eyes flecked with green, and saw only warmth, and understanding, and an endless patience. Carl thought: he made Laban what he is. "Welcome," she said, and meant it.

Detlev bowed his head in acknowledgment.

"Come," Laban said, smiling. "We've got a crowd waiting to see us."

They walked out together, he shortening his long stride to her careful steps, and her heartbeat sped up again. Her emotions had intensified to the point of numbness, and she couldn't think at all. Only notice details: the rustle of her skirts on the old stone steps; the aroma of the garden-spiced spring breeze; the steady grip of Laban's hand; his pulse beating subtly in counterpoint to hers. The slanting morning light bathing the steps through the old arrow-slits, striking glints of sunglow in tiny bits of reflective stone.

They entered the throne room. Strings, winds, and voices surrounded them in a beautiful chorus, a traditional song for spring weddings.

Side by side they stepped toward the long aisle to the waiting thrones.

Then they were there, before the silent people. Lyren smiled encouragingly from one side, holding Liere's hand. Clair stood near them, her white hair icy in the mellow light, Siamis close on her other side. Oh, yes, there was a strong bond between them. Would Laban ever stand like that, so close they could feel each other's breathing?

Here were the siblings, in a row, their smiles and grins so characteristic of each.

And here were Rel and Atan, who had offered to stand in for the family elders no longer here. First Rel spoke, then Atan: Carl distantly heard Laban's voice, and her own, making the vows that would bind them to Everon forever. And that would bind her to him forever.

In her mind, she imagined sliding a gold band onto his hand, the circle of eternity. She had not asked that of him, and he had not offered, but secretly, in her own mind, she bound herself to him for as long as she should live.

If this covenant wasn't forever, if something happened to the person who was central to her life, she wouldn't be able to bear it. The inner vow — that if she were left alone she would walk out into the snow, and there would be no Geres — was so deep that she was utterly unaware of the skilled minds — Laban, David, Jessan, Detlev, Siamis, Clair, Liere, and Lyren among them — who heard it.

The moment passed, and all she was aware of was the cheers of the multitudes, and Laban at her side.

She reached for his hands, wherein her happiness lay, and gripped them tight.

29

Elenzeh Fer Eider snuffed in a deep breath near Liere's shoulder, looked around to make certain there were no sentries on the rampart to overhear, then confided to her tall daughter, "I do love the smell of gerda root."

Liere smiled at the young woman patrolling the far tower. The sentry tapped her fist to her chest in salute.

Liere's mother did not notice. She continued, "That was one thing your father and I thoroughly agreed on: wanting a large family. Though he was thinking of future workers in the store who need not be paid, and I wanted smiling faces around the table, and happy children's chatter." She shook her head slowly. "I saw what I wanted to see, I guess. But you, I'm so glad you intend to start a family right away. From everything I hear around me, he still misses his little girl."

"He will always miss her," Liere said. "Which is right."

"Yes, but you will give him others to think about instead of merely memories and an empty room," Grandma Elen replied. Her daughter had always been odd, and this Sartora business had always been incomprehensible, but on the subject of children, Elenzeh was sure of herself.

Liere did not mention the weeks and weeks of hints with all the subtlety of mule kicks dropped by Senrid's well-meaning friends and subjects old enough to feel that they could speak their minds, welcome or no: *Give him an heir and a spare, and maybe a third for assurance. The sooner the better.*

"Be sure to write to me when you know for certain," Grandma Elen went on. "I told you before, I perfectly understand why you said nothing about little Yossi, such a terrible, terrible thing. Terrible. I always thought there was something wrong about that man, king or not, that I couldn't stay when he imposed on you, as if that Brydon palace wasn't big enough to host the entire family, with room left over for the entirety of Belann."

"Macael never said—"

"Never mind what he said or didn't say. I knew I wasn't welcome, and it wasn't from Andri. Dear Andri! I have to admit I think Senrid is a better husband in all possible ways. Andri reminded me so much of the loungers down at the docks, who work for drink and gambling money, then go right back to lounging. But when you talk to them, you can see the little lost child inside. I always thought that Andri must have been a very sweet little boy, just like little Malcolin is." She wiped her eyes.

Liere said, "Mother, you don't have to return to Imar. Senrid means what he says, you'd be welcome to stay as long as you like. You're right that he wants family around him."

Grandma Elen hesitated, trying to choose her words. "I like visiting," she finally said. "But this isn't home. This language, even with the magic spell you gave us, it's difficult. And Milnat needs me, whereas the two of you really don't need my hands in the kitchen, or my feet fetching the fresh eggs. You have an army of people doing those things. I want to be able to visit. I'm so glad you've given me that, though we decided not to say anything to the neighbors about magic, or kings and queens."

"No? Do they not believe you?"

"Oh, they *believe* us, they just think we're putting on a parade. Except about Marga. I think no one believes she does magic, for there's no sign of it. She says she cannot make a worn bit of fabric new again, or summon up a new wagon. Useful things. But everyone loves her so much they don't mind her being a bit of a gadabout. And she does lend a hand in the shop when she turns up, which is important."

Liere strictly hid the laugh that wanted to bubble up from inside at the idea of Marga being expected to prove herself by doing parlor tricks for the neighbors when she was the most powerful mage in the world. But Liere understood: Marga was at last learning how to shield the effect of her presence. Liere had noticed that at her wedding, before Marga vanished again after an apologetic, *There's something I need to be watching.* Few Marlovens had paid her the least heed, whereas in the past, she

was the center of a vortex that drew anyone who was aware of
magic.

"So many people," Elenzeh murmured, glancing in the
other direction, out over the academy, where youngsters shouted in cadence as they performed drills. "But not a tenth of the
waste there was at Brydon, where everyone belowstairs acted
more like a king than your king did. Always arguing and pilfer-
ing. I sometimes thought it was a miracle you and Andri and
the boy got fed at all. But here, there's not a speck of that. Don't
think I haven't looked."

Liere did chuckle at that.

"I'm serious," her mother said, but the corners of her
mouth quirked. "There's excellent management here, is what
I'm saying. No waste."

"The waste, as you called it, went home in pockets and
buckets to families who had been starving. We knew about it."

"A good part," Elenzeh said. "The rest was being sold for
profit. I knew that, too."

At that moment, Liere felt the inner tug that meant Lyren
had returned from Everon at last. "Lyren's back," she said.
"Shall we go downstairs?"

"Certainly. I want to check on the cakes through all the
steps before I return to the shop. I'm teaching the baker how to
make eight-layer lavender cakes, which Lyren loves."

They parted on the landing, Elenzeh toward the kitchen
and Liere continuing on to the residence. Her mother saw the
castle guard as many, but Liere remembered the old days, when
the walls had seemed to be staffed with half a city; now Senrid
only had guards posted on the towers. If necessary, the garrison
would scramble frighteningly fast. Liere had seen them practice. Everyone, even the youngest sentries, still had memories
of the war, and though the Host and their followers were
mostly gone, save some renegades still lurking in various
corners of the world, problems sadly had not ended. Everyone
in Marloven Hess knew that Perideth was in trouble, and like
many kingdoms before, might choose to solve its problems by
blaming another kingdom and going to war.

This old castle, with its blood-drenched history, was part
of Senrid's bones and sinews. Maybe that was why, despite the
circumstances under which Liere had sometimes visited,
coming here had always felt like coming to safety. It was
Senrid's home. Now hers as well.

So—she adapted. Just as the Marlovens had accepted "Sartora" as their gunvaer. She knew the old Sartora myth persisted, but she'd made her peace with it. If that silliness made life easier for Senrid, then at last it had served its purpose.

Liere started down the long hall, her mind drifting back to Carl and Laban's wedding the day before.

As a wedding it had been splendid—so well organized, from the details of the decorations to how the guests were blended at table and in ballroom, and Liere had detected her daughter's unerring skill behind it all.

Sweet, ardent little Carl had walked like a ghost through the entire evening after the vow exchange, clinging to Laban's hand as if she were afraid he would float away. It was Lyren who had circulated with a smile and a word here and there through the guests and staff to make certain that everything progressed with apparent effortlessness. In her wake everyone mixed a little more freely, the laughter more real.

What a gift! I don't have it, Liere thought ruefully. And my mother even less. Must be that mysterious Dei personality, which totally bypassed us and hit the next generation with double force in Marga and Lyren. She was going to have to ask Detlev about the early Deis someday, she decided as she opened the door to her sitting room.

Lyren had flopped into a chair, still wearing that uncharacteristically plain gown of periwinkle blue. Her arms hung over the chair arms, and her slippered feet stuck out in front of her.

"You look tired," Liere said. "Have you been up all this time? It has to be well past noon in Ferdrian."

Lyren hesitated, then gave a quick summary, beginning when Carl retired to sleep just after midnight, looking impossibly tired and tense. Lyren had continued to monitor the flow of food and drink, guests and musicians. An hour before dawn, Laban had joined her in seeing off the last of the wedding guests, so natural as host it was as if he'd lived there all his life. "… and when I said my last farewell to a very drunk ship-captain related somehow to one of the heralds, Laban thanked me, but his face was so closed, his manner so polite, and the last I saw of him was his back as he strode away, calling to his own man to ready his favorite horse so he could take a ride before breakfast and clear his head. It was exactly the way it should be, but it was also so very cold, almost as if I'd done wrong. When I know I hadn't."

"You know you hadn't," Liere said. "I'm sure he did as well. Remember, his own emotions had to be a tempest: not just his wedding, but he's taken on an enormous responsibility with Everon and its problems, and he knows many eyes are on him."

"Yes. All true."

"So, that brings you to dawn their time," Liere said.

Lyren shrugged. "Little more to tell. I oversaw the last of the cleanup so that Carl would waken to everything being in its place. Anyone else would shrug it off, but that would matter to her. Then I took a long walk through the garden, remembering all the time I spent there with Carl and the sibs. I think I was saying my farewell, too. I saw a grassy spot, and suddenly I was so very tired, I sat down under the old chestnut, and before I knew it, I was asleep. I woke when the noon bell rang — I was drooling on my shoulder, with a crick in my neck, and you can see the mud all over me. I quickly transferred here before the gardeners stumbled over me there, asking a million tiresome questions. So awkward!"

Lyren looked up from her muddy dancing slippers to Liere's smiling eyes. "And that's it," she said, and got up, and went to the window to look out. Senrid's impressive castle lay below. The scent from the rain-drenched plains was so familiar from childhood, a scent she'd never before bothered to define. What was it, anyway? Spring sage? Sage, and weeds, and baking rye from the kitchen out beyond the little courtyard below.

"I feel safe here," she exclaimed. "It was my anchor when I was small, and you went to Geth to study magic. But it's not home. I don't think it can be." She turned around. "That was farewell, I'm determined on it. I can't go back to Everon again until Carl figures herself out. They are both dear friends, but Carl made me into some kind of walking icon of all the arts, something to measure herself against unfavorably. Did you hear her, before the wedding? That terrible image of her walking into the snow, to die, if anything happens — "

"I think we all heard it. Everyone who cares about her will be watchful — she's so very like her mother in some ways, but unlike her mother in that she listens and learns. And she is self-aware in a way that Tahra was unable to be. Clair promised me before Senrid and I left that she'd stay in contact. And Laban's got David and Adam at his back."

"It's Carl I worry about. Laban's like a cat. Always lands on his feet." Lyren turned her back to the window. "I have a question."

Liere's eyes crinkled. "An easy one. I can tell."

"You don't have to answer. Though I'll always wonder. Or maybe I won't. But, if I blunder again, and find myself in a similar mess—"

"Ah. Sex with Macael Elsarion," Liere said.

Lyren's eyes were huge. "Does Senrid know?"

"Of course he does. When you truly love someone, in all the ways known to human beings, the boundaries come down."

"Boundaries," Lyren repeated, thinking of that polite wall of Laban's.

"If," Liere said gently, "you love."

"Love," Lyren repeated. "So inadequate a word, at times. Or is it just me, incapable of loving?"

"You're not—"

"I mean, in *that* way."

"And I repeat, you're not incapable—"

"But it's beginning to seem that way, isn't it?"

"Hear your own words. You are just beginning. Give yourself time!"

"Oh, I'm too tired to debate—"

Senrid appeared in the doorway, and Lyren sank back as he came to Liere's side. If he noticed Lyren's rumpled, mud-stained clothes, or the marks under her eyes, he forbore comment. "Nice work yesterday, commander-in-chief," he said to her. "I was impressed."

"It is rather like ordering a battle, isn't it?" Lyren asked, grinning. "The flow of supplies, what to do with the little social, er, tactical disasters. Keeping the troops—excuse me, guests— moving toward the target."

"I expect organizing a wedding is tougher," Senrid said. "You can't flog your guests for insubordination if they refuse to be herded."

Lyren laughed, yawned, then said, "I now plan to sleep for a week. Wake me at your peril."

"If you can stay awake a bit longer, Grandma Elen wants to return to Belann, but I think she'd like a little time with you first."

"I'll change and go find her." Lyren hoisted herself up and slipped out.

Liere glanced at the closed door and said, "What's happening?"

Senrid's smile vanished as if wiped off. "Halmaer Nothalin of Perideth might have had another stroke, or he's just plain gone mad. He's been raving about our attacks."

"What attacks?"

"Exactly. But he's mobilizing his people. I actually pity Valta—unless he uses his father's madness as an excuse to invade Toth or Telyerhas."

"So … what must you do?" Liere had learned that Toth—once Inda's homeland, then known as Choraed Elgaer—was still mostly Iascan and agrarian. They were nominally a country, but had depended on Marloven ties for protection off and on over the years, and since the war those ties had only strengthened.

Senrid said, "I need to contact my uncle in Telyerhas to find out what, if anything, he expects from me. If necessary I can send South Army down through Toth on spring maneuvers. Entirely friendly show of force. Hatch and Marend can be trusted to hold the southern border, but I'm really hoping none of that will be necessary."

He snapped his hand away, dismissing the subject. "No need to ask if you've been talking rough stuff." He grinned briefly.

Liere laughed very softly. "I take it you were bombarded by Lyren's intensity."

"Clear from the other end of the damn castle," Senrid observed. "Meanwhile, all week I've fielded questions. Even Baudan, who I didn't think took much interest in anything outside of his paper and pens, asked if she has any local interests. Maybe we should toss her into one of the pleasure houses, and hammer the door shut for a couple of weeks."

"And end up with a houseful of lovelorn employees? You know that's what would happen. I don't think she can help the instinct to charm them. She's always been the center of focus, ever since she was two, and her natural inclination is to try to make everyone happy."

Senrid said, "The only thing to do is to keep her busy. With what?"

"I overheard Atan inviting her down to Sartor for the annual Flower Day ball. And I know my mother will ask her to come visit in Belann."

"That's a good start. I'm off to write to my uncle."

30

Grandma Elen returned to Belann, Lyren in tow.

From there, Lyren took off for Sartor, looking forward to learning all the new dances, and renewing her entire wardrobe, which was quietly funded by Siamis, as usual, through Arthur. As Siamis said to Liere in a note, he still considered Lyren a ward until she found a life for herself, and he took full blame for her complete lack of awareness of money.

Lyren was never greedy in the sense of spending gold frivolously on carriages or jewels—she owned very few gems, all gifts—and no carriages or horses. She loved clothes. Though she lived as if she'd been born to wealth, she was never profligate; as for stern lessons on the value of money, she'd heard enough of that from Tahra. It never took.

That same week, alone in their bedroom, Liere told Senrid she need no longer drink gerda in her steep.

His face blanched colorless. He said nothing. He was beyond words. The two of them clung tightly to one another for a long time. Then he recovered, and sprang back into action, brisk as ever, but he coruscated in the mental realm as their lives settled into the rhythm of spring.

And there was much to be done. As Malcolin embarked happily on his second season in the academy, Senrid did some traveling in the south in order to monitor the situation in Perideth. So far, the spring maneuvers on land seemed to be keeping Prince Valta's defense force in check, but the situation was not helped by the king ordering the harbor guard to attack any Marloven ship that dared venture into Parayid Harbor—

and then two weeks later sending angry demands through a wooden-faced envoy to Senrid, claiming that Marloven Hess was ignoring the treaty and leaving Perideth open to a line of cruising warships from Toar.

"There's going to be trouble from Damondaen, but I hope they keep it from spreading across the water," Senrid said to Liere one night early in Fifthmonth, while she sat near the open windows, waiting for a breeze, and drinking ginger-leaf. Summer seemed to be coming early, and he paced around the room, drumming his fingers on every surface he passed.

"Damondaen?" she repeated. "Isn't that the biggest kingdom on Toar? At least in the south."

"It is, but they've been grabby for centuries. Right until recently: Damondaen used the retreat of Norsunder to cross the two rivers and move into Vakheinen, which is mostly a coastal country, and it had been devastated by Efael's pirates. It seems that doubling to almost twice its size didn't solve Damondaen's internal problems, which have been notorious. Even worse than us Marlovens, if you can believe that. It's said they are even related to us, though that's usually accompanied by curses."

He gave Liere the old toothy grin, and she laughed.

"I don't know any more than that, except Jilo reports that Damondaen's scouts have been nosing all along various harbors on both sides of the water, clear up to the Rose Sea."

"That's near Mearsies Heili," Liere exclaimed.

"Oh, Puddlenose and Heraford are up there, and not sitting on their hands. And the Chwahir are not far off. Even if they sail back up the strait, now that the winds have changed, I doubt very much that whoever gets on top of the heap in Damondaen is foolish enough to attempt to invade so far away. That's like me sending a fleet to invade Vidanric's Remalna."

Liere shut her eyes, mentally reviewing the map—specifically the jump past Enaeran Adrani, as Macael called the former two kingdoms now—and the little polities on the other side of the mountains, to the eastern edge of the Sartoran Sea. "You could do it, but then you'd have to hold it," she guessed. "With an insanely long supply line to protect as well."

"Right." He snapped his fingers. "Anyway, we're down there cruising off Perideth, which disinclines any passing invaders, but who knows what Halmaer will spew next." He watched her pour more ginger steep and paced back and forth twice, Liere watching him try to contain his emotions.

Including grief.

He stopped, and came to her. "Savarend, if it's a boy, right? Ndand if it's a girl? I don't think she'd care one way or another, but it seems right." He sat down beside Liere, and said so softly she almost didn't hear it, "I hope it's a girl."

Liere slid her arms around his ribs and laid her head on his shoulder. They remained thus for a time, neither having to speak, until she kissed his cheek and went to drink more steeped ginger.

Senrid sat on the edge of his desk, fingers pinched between his brows. "I think I'd scare myself with the intensity of my happiness, except there is always Perideth to steady me."

Liere said slowly, "This might be a senseless question, but why doesn't Perideth's defense just refuse orders from a king they know is mad?"

Senrid's hand dropped. "Not senseless. They have to be thinking that, every one of them. Problem one: he isn't raving all the time. He slips in and out, from what I can gather. When he's sane, he asks sharp questions, and woe to any who do not have the correct answer. Problem two: when you break chain of command, it's broken. Then what? It's far too easy for things to descend to everyone fighting everyone else. And so you keep your mouth shut, your head down, do your duty — including obeying orders — and hope that someone up the chain of command fixes things. That's how the elder Senelacs as well as most others survived in my uncle's day."

"And now?"

"And now I've changed my mind. My Telyerhas uncle begged me to ride down there myself and strut around looking tough. I hate that. For one thing, we become targets. And though I'm confident we'd win any conflict, why lose lives for absolutely no purpose? But I think I'm going to have to. Because the problem is not just the king, it's also Valta."

Liere had been considering the Perideth situation on her own. "What if I go, too?"

Senrid blinked at her. "What? Ride down there in this heat, when you're still getting nauseous?"

"That's fading off," Liere said, waving a hand. "Anyway, I don't see any utility in my riding all the way. I was thinking more along the lines of riding to the border with you, so any convenient spies see the two of us. Then I transfer back here. See to things. And transfer down there when you near Perideth.

If the Sartora nonsense is worth anything, it might get him to at least give me a hearing."

Senrid rapidly reviewed his options, then clapped his hand on his knee. "You're right. Let's do it. But I'm going to want some protective measures in place first."

"Whatever you think best. If it turns out it's necessary to talk to Prince Valta, let me at him first before you confront him, since I know he's always seen you as competition. And alone, so that he doesn't feel he has to perform in front of others."

"I'll issue the orders right now. The sooner we ride — and are seen to be riding — the better."

Liere mentally reviewed her own schedule, and then stifled a groan. "Wait, wait, wait. Did you forget? I almost did. We've got Thad Keperi's wedding."

"We can beg off that," Senrid said. "Damn! Though Thad is an old enough friend it ought to be done in person. Which is another thing crowding in." Senrid charged toward the door.

"Wait," Liere said, her mind working rapidly. "There might be a solution to that, at least."

"What are you thinking?" He paused, fingers drumming on the latch.

"Why not ask Lyren to attend in our place? She's here, and though she talks about going back to Sarendan to be a roamer again, she never actually sets a date."

"I noticed that. But in her defense, the idea of trudging from village to village through Sarendan's countryside in the stunning heat of summer doesn't appeal to many. She said something about autumn, which makes more sense."

"True. But we have this matter before us right now. I don't think ... You know, it's surprising, considering how very much she enjoys the courtly life, but I don't believe she's ever been to Colend. Not since the alliance days. But then she's always gone to friends, and the alliance ceased having its headquarters in Wilderfeld long ago."

"When Karhin Keperi was killed," Senrid agreed. "And Wilderfeld is barely inside of Colend."

"We'll still have to explain to Thad why the substitution, but he can be trusted to be discreet, can't he? If you're worried about random gossip getting to Perideth."

"Definitely better to explain in person." Colend was nearly a half-day's difference in time; Senrid said, "And I'd best get at it now. I can do that while South Army readies to ride south."

Liere said, "Do you want me to go to Thad? Though I don't really know him very well. It was always Karhin I visited."

"No. I have to go. He and I have been writing back and forth for years. You stay here and guard the kingdom." He leaned over to kiss her. "You'll find armor and a choice selection of weaponry in my wardrobe; if you send the entire army over the border to turf out Macael Elsarion, leave Van Stad a wing or two to guard the country."

She laughed, a delightful sound that carried with him as he did the transfer magic to the back of Alsais's palace, where the staff operated. When the reaction faded, he found himself in a small transfer-room overlooking a courtyard with mosaic brickwork and trellises full of blooms.

Three young stewards and pages clustered in what was obviously an antechamber. One came forward, and led him to a waiting room.

In the old days, Senrid had always gone to Thad's home on his sporadic visits. He spent the short wait looking back through memory to see if he'd actually been in Alsais's royal palace before. Just the once, when Thad begged him to visit in order to slip the young Shontande Lirendi, then ribbon-tied by his own regency council, a golden notecase. That had been with Ret Forthan. Ah, Ret. I will always miss you. Grief pulsed, a familiar pain.

Then Thad bounded in, his red braid flopping on his skinny back. "Senrid!" His brow puckered. "Why are you here now? Not a disaster?"

"No. Just Perideth trouble. Which we've had for years. But it seems to have reached a crisis."

Thad waved him into a room fitted with shelves on which multi-colored folders were stored.

Senrid looked around appreciatively. "Looks like three times the amount of what my own trade minister has to cope with. And only one of you for the job?"

"I have a staff," Thad said, buffing his fingers on his fine light gray robe, one brow arching. Then he grinned. "Who would have thought I'd end up here, all those years ago, when we put together the alliance?"

"Another lifetime ago," Senrid said.

The door opened as a very young page came in, carefully bearing a silver tray with a complete coffee service on it that trailed the sublime scent of fresh-ground coffee from the mountainsides in Sarendan.

Thad extended a hand. "I thought you might be wanting some."

"You thought right."

The page left, and while they helped themselves, Senrid said, "Lyren's back with us."

"Lyren!" Thad's grin changed to reminiscence. "I saw her dancing at your wedding."

"Did you say hello?"

"No. I doubted she'd remember me. She saw me last when she was no more than two."

"You should have. It's surprising how much she remembers. If from the knee-high vantage of two. It's Lyren that brought me, in the sense that we were thinking of sending her in place of us. Because both Liere and I are going to have to see to this crisis, I'm afraid."

Thad whistled.

"We really want to avoid war, which is why we have to act now. Meanwhile, Lyren actually likes plays and music concerts and the like."

"I quite understand, Senrid. Please, the invitation isn't like a treaty between nations. It's all right if you have to skip it. We've already got more people coming than Nalisse had bargained for. Shon made it a court occasion."

Senrid opened his hand, then said, "Here's the thing. Lyren is at loose ends. She's living with us, but she's not involved with Marloven affairs. Liere thinks that a day or so in Alsais, attending a wedding and maybe a play or two, might distract her while she decides what to do next."

Thad was remembering the beautiful figure dancing in the circles, drawing all eyes. "Romance problems? Is every one of your hot young lancers vying for her attention?"

Senrid laughed. "They would be if I didn't have them mounting up at the southern border right now, in case Valta does something regrettable."

"I don't know that I can introduce her to court, but I can try."

"She won't expect that. Turn her loose among the players and singers. Or in your kitchens. You remember, Liere's family is pastry makers. Lyren would be comfortable anywhere, actually. But here's why it's me here, and not a message. I wanted to explain, rather than risk talk about Perideth getting about in diplomatic circles, which is as near as I can tell a fancy term for international gossip. Valta has been tied to his father's heels like a prentice for the past fifteen years, and he's always looking for insult. Your court here gets a lot of international visitors, is what I'm saying. What's for them is idle chat might be misconstrued if it gets to the wrong ears."

"Ah! Yes." Thad's fingertips tapped together as he gazed out the window. "Bee is happily organizing everything, but I suspect he'd be delighted to hear Lyren's voice, after all this time. She played with him so happily when they were both small. Sure, send her as your replacement, and we won't mention you or Liere at all. She'll be Lyren from Marloven Hess."

Senrid turned his palm up. "Thanks for understanding."

After Senrid transferred to Colend, Liere went hunting for Lyren, who had retreated to the dining room, where she could spread out her letters. She'd accumulated a pack of them while she was busy socializing in Sartor. Now it was time to write everyone back, and report on what she'd seen and done in Sartor, tailoring each report to its recipient: Aurora would want to hear about the visit to the morvende, to hear the echo music; Grandma Elen would love hearing about the three lively royal children, all so very different; Madelon would love summaries of the currently popular plays. She was just settling in when the door opened, and her half-brother Malcolin walked in.

Sauntered in, rather, and headed straight for the basket of biscuits Lyren had pushed aside to make room for her papers. Lyren was startled to see how strong his resemblance to Andri was. He moved like Andri as well, that swinging saunter, hands loose, yellow hair flapping on his shoulders. He was dressed in his academy summer uniform, a sturdy cotton sashed tunic-shirt over loose trousers tucked into riding boots.

"Hello, brother." Lyren grinned at him.

"Hello, sister." Malcolin grinned back.

"I thought you were supposed to be in the academy another month or two."

"Got liberty today, because the seniors are off to the border as backup for the spring exercises down south."

Lyren leaned her elbows on the table and smiled as he smeared two biscuits from a jar of honey. "Still like that academy of Senrid's?"

"Yup." He flopped onto a chair.

"Do you still feel ties to Enaeran?"

Malcolin's brow furrowed slightly. "I think so? Or maybe, I feel bad that Yossi had to come into the world as a kind of cost for me not getting killed."

That was an odd way to look at it. Not wrong, though.

"You don't feel grieved that he's a prince and you aren't?" Lyren asked, chin in hand.

"I don't know. I don't think so," Malcolin said. "I think … I think I got away easy, because I'm learning in history class that usually when princes get unprinced, it's with…" He drew his finger across his neck and made a horrible noise. "Goes for kings, too. Like my da."

Lyren's nerves prickled. To hide it, she said, "Then tell me about the academy. Is it awful, or fun, or somewhere between?"

Malcolin talked with enthusiasm around his biscuits, spraying crumbs in his enthusiasm, until Liere entered. "There you are," she said, smiling from one to the other.

Malcolin grinned, then eyed her in suspicion. "You're not going to set me to lessons, are you, Ma?"

"If you want me to—"

"No!"

"One of the Senelac boys is down in the stable, looking for you. Apparently there's a hunt-and-chase being organized in the—"

Malcolin grabbed his second biscuit and bolted.

"—city," Liere finished to the empty air. Then turned to Lyren. "I'll tell him the rest later."

"Rest of?"

"It seems that events in Perideth have reached crisis. I need to catch up with Senrid, once I hand off Malcolin to Fenis Senelac. Though I strongly suspect she's down there, about to intercept…" Liere closed her eyes, listened, and brought her chin down. "Got him. That's Malcolin, safely established. And now to you. I need to ask you an enormous favor."

"I know nothing about Perideth!" Lyren waved her hands. "Or minding a pack of boys used to waving swords around."

"That's all being seen to. This favor will be more to your liking, I hope. Remember Thad of the alliance days?"

Lyren began sweeping her letters together. "The tall red-haired boy. He seemed to me to be as tall as Rel, but that's all I remember. He had a couple of sisters and a brother who made a pet of me."

Liere nodded on each point. "Thad is marrying Nalisse Aliad, once a good friend to him and Karhin, and then his best friend after Karhin was murdered. Not surprisingly, Thad's in a position of responsibility, and he's also a personal friend of the king—"

"King? Carlael Lirendi? No. He died, didn't he? Um, Shontande. Laban mentioned him a couple of times, saying he's friends with Jilo of the Chwahir. I thought Colend and the Chwahir hated each other. I'm glad they overcame that." Lyren was ready to like anyone who favored Jilo.

"Shontande Lirendi is hosting the wedding for Thad. We can't just bow out, when so many expect to Marloven Hess represented, as Senrid was a big part of the alliance. If you go in our place, there'll be less talk. Would you go as our representative? There should be some old friends there, which ought to make it more enjoyable. And I think you'll love the plays and the like."

"Of course I'll go," Lyren said. "A wedding for which I have no responsibilities will be fun, and no chore at all. I've always heard that Colend is lovely, but somehow or other I've never been there. No one there I know."

"The capital is beautiful, that much I remember the one time I was there years and years ago. Built near water, all these canals and fountains. I'm told that music and art and plays are a constant. I think you'll enjoy it."

"Done," Lyren said, digging into her breakfast. "Would that all favors could be so easy."

PART TWO

1

The next morning, Lyren transferred, on Liere's instruction, to the Destination at the Gate of the Lily Path, which was the access closest to the royal palace of Alsais, capital city of Colend, and also the proper gate to enter through if one was not making a formal diplomatic parade. Apparently it was expected to arrive at certain times, which Lyren found intriguing.

She halted to take a long look at the canal, stunned. Was this the prettiest spot in the city, or was it merely spring adding extra grace to everything? Liere did say Alsais was pretty. An understatement! She gazed at the buildings across from the water. Not a one was even plain, much less unsightly. Of course, so near the palace, everything would belong to the wealthy, yes?

But she lingered to take in the diamond-paned windows, the tiny gardens before and between charming buildings — and was thrown back in memory to that house in Tannentaun where Liere had stayed before moving to Choreid Dhelerei. The shapes of the windows, the lines, the proportion of building to trees and gardens were familiar. Was this place the origin of that architectural style?

Promising herself to explore later, she turned again and trod up the path, which was bordered by a variety of lilies in subtly different white shades. The path wound to a graceful archway with flowering vines growing over it, trained in eye-pleasing asymmetry. She stepped through to a terrace, and beyond that a commodious anteroom.

Highly stylized green leaves, edged with gold, had been painted around the walls under the ceiling, each with an elongated lily made of some softly iridescent material. Comfortable furnishings in blending shades of green lined the perimeter of the tiled floor. The chairs were low, with outward-curved legs and rolled arms, the wood inlaid with fine arabesques of gold.

An attendant appeared, her livery unobtrusive shades of cream and green and gold. "May I help you?"

What was this language? Oh yes, Kifelian. Lyren liked the sound of it in her head, echoing behind the Universal Language spell.

"I'm Lyren Sartora, from Marloven Hess, here for Thad Keperi's wedding."

As soon as she said her name, there was a subtle indication of recognition in the attendant's face. "Welcome." She gestured invitation. "Please, come this way?"

This attendant escorted Lyren through a palace that seemed to be made of cool marble and light, with flowing water, growing plants, and exquisite carving. The brightness and heat of summer diffused through the fragrant, ferny greenery and the many fountains and shallow pools. The attendant pointed out key intersections— "and here is Violet Serenity Crossing, with the bluebells on the south end of the square to remind one that is the way to Clear Skies Crossing"—which was full of blossoms in shades of blue, except for Fernleaf yarrow indicating the corridor leading off toward another fountain surrounded by marigolds and butter-yellow daylilies.

In a friendly tone, the attendant explained the layout, which followed the rising of the sun to sunset, without any hint that she might have uttered the same exact speech countless times already that day.

Lyren slowed so that she could better observe the flow of line and curve and the stylized lack of symmetry blended with light, greenery, and water, creating an effect quite unlike anything she'd ever seen. Indoor waterfalls? She paused before one, loving the effect of terracing indoors.

"This palace is perfect for summer," she exclaimed. "But this must be frigid in winter, unless they waste a lot of magic."

"This wing is shut in winter," the steward said, smiling.

"The winter palace is on the north side, to make the best of the low sunlight."

Of course, just like in Sartor. Only Atan had no summer residence like *this*. Oh, this place was as pleasing as its language. She heard the Sartoran roots, and decided to learn the language.

Another low, curving flight up, and they walked down a long corridor with doors well-spaced. A suite awaited her, and a maid appeared, offering to arrange her things. Lyren did not have any personal servants; she thanked the woman, and said she was used to seeing after herself. The woman pointed out the traditional summons rope and bade her use it if she needed anything, then departed.

Lyren pulled from her pocket a bespelled key, held it over an empty space and said a spell. Her trunk appeared, with all her latest clothes neatly folded away. She'd decided years ago that she would only ever have one trunk; if something new went in, something old and seldom worn had to come out, and go to someone who would want it. Of course, compared to Liere's habit of only owning two or three things at most, and wearing them to rags, a whole trunk of clothes for one person seemed frivolous. All right, she was frivolous.

She shrugged, and surveyed the room, which contained a bed, chairs and a desk, as well as an empty wardrobe with a cleaning-frame in white wood painted along the edges with stylized flowers. Lyren quickly set about hanging up her clothes and laying her linens in the cedar-scented drawers adjacent.

When she was finished, she turned to the windows. The sun touched the tops of little buildings in the complicated gardens, lighting ponds and canals with sunset colors. In the distance, if she craned her neck, she glimpsed one of the great rivers flowing toward the meet-point, long since tamed by careful guardianship and magic.

She used the key to transfer the trunk back to its beyond-space and then took a closer look at the room, which told its own story. The room was mostly white, accented with pale shades of peach and rose and gold, with flowers here and there. The windows faced west. The palace appeared to be built into a gradual hill that overlooked the rest of the city, where the tops of many trees broke the lines of tiled rooftops in a profusion of summer green.

Lyren smoothed her dark blue over-robe, which was tunic

length, falling just below her knees, to contrast with her flowing light blue trousers beneath. She touched the high collar, making certain the pretty little mois-stone buttons had not come undone. For the first time in recent memory her manner of dress seemed to matter. She had planned to use the interim between now and the wedding to start on those letters, but the urge to explore was irresistible.

She brushed her hair until it crackled, then pulled the front and sides up to be tied with blue ribbon on top of her head, the rest hanging free down her back. Now she was ready to venture forth and start being a Marloven diplomat, a concept she might once have thought an oxymoron.

The attendant had mentioned the times and places of general gatherings. Lyren wondered if personal invitations to events not open to everyone would be spoken privily, as in Sartor, or via notecase. On the surface at least, Atan had explained once, private gatherings were handled privately, so much more smoothly managed. Only when is any great gathering of human beings smooth, pleasant, and accommodating? Well, whatever political or emotional ambitions underlay the life here, she wasn't involved.

As Lyren descended the curving stairway, she slowed her steps. Her efforts at renovation in Fortnyal Roth and then in Ferdrian only aspired to the blend of harmony and aesthetics she found here: already she could see where she'd erred in doing too little, or too much. Eidervaen was too weighted with tradition, too much a living archive of furnishings, arts, and architectural additions from vastly different periods. There, the freight of historical association made it all work together as a historical artifact.

Only Detlev's place displayed a similar skill of harmonic design, but it was more austere, and of course much smaller. Anywhere else?

Nowhere that I've been, Lyren decided. How had she managed to waste so much of her life, when travel was easy, and her time was her own? Feeling again the sting of frivolousness, she made her way to the informal dining area, which was built on several levels, the tables under golden-leafed trees, and further divided by artfully set screens of lattice carved in complicated designs, the marble so thin that light glowed in the stone. Musicians played and sang off to one side.

At the door waited the expected liveried herald, but he did

not ask her name or make an announcement. Oh, good. Informality? What better way to begin? The herald guided her by a gesture to where Thad had gathered with a group of people. He was immediately recognizable. The gawky, skinny fellow with the unkempt nest of red hair whom she'd first met when small had lengthened into a beanpole of a man with vivid light blue eyes, a long red braid, and a wonderfully changeable face.

A thin silk robe fluttered attractively about his long legs as Lyren caught her first glimpse of Colendi summer fashion: the layers of moth-gauze, or fog-gauze, lace, or what they called cloud, over thin, polished cotton-linen tunics and wide-legged, pleated trousers, sashed by beautifully embroidered thin silk, from which suspended fans. Everything ribbon-tied. Not a button in sight, which meant no gapping or unsightly wrinkles. But it was the drape that caused her eye to linger. It molded to body shapes so flatteringly. How was that achieved?

Thad had been fanning himself. His hand swooped down and slid the fan onto the silken cord as he cut himself off mid-speech. "Lyren! Is that you?" He clapped his hands lightly, palm to palm, in the peace. "What joy to meet again!"

"I'm here as two people," she said, smiling, mimicking the peace gesture. "Shall I go out and come in again?"

Thad laughed. "Enter! You know some of the company, I believe—"

"Lyren!" Madelon Delieth rushed over, gleeful, then whispered behind her fan, "Though neither Carl nor I was born yet when that alliance happened, she thought this would be good practice for me."

"Oh?" Lyren asked. "Are you setting up to be a diplomatic representative?"

Madelon lifted a shoulder. "Carl said, if you come with Liere, I'm to learn from you two, and not cause any incidents. I'm told they have a *lot* of customs here."

"I'm being Liere for now. I don't know any more than you do about local customs," Lyren admitted cheerfully. "Except the one you always hear about, not stepping on someone's shadow. Liere warned me that one is actually real. Also, they don't like saying the word no."

Madelon's eyes widened. "Then how do you disagree?"

"I guess you find a way to get around it. However, we won't be here long, so let's not worry too much."

Madelon agreed, and, then wandered off to eye the refreshments.

Thad had moved away to allow them to speak, but returned, leading a round, wren-like woman with a friendly smile and an observant dark-eyed gaze. She was dressed in shades of brown and cream with hints of gold. "Lyren, permit me to introduce my betrothed, Nalisse Aliad."

Lyren and Nalisse exchanged bows. Thad was immediately called away by someone on the other side of the room. Lyren was going to follow Madelon when she was surprised to see a small, capable hand on her sleeve.

Nalisse said, "Let me show you about."

Lyren would never say that the steward had performed that office. Nalisse, it seemed, wanted to talk to her, and didn't want an audience.

Nalisse led her away. As the voices faded behind, Lyren said, "I don't think we met, did we? I was so small when I knew Thad and the other alliance gang."

Nalisse shook her head. "Hard to know. I spent my early life training to be a courier. That's how I met Karhin and Thad. Then I worked for a wine guild for a time, but what I really wanted to be was a pastry-cook. I did a favor for the king right before the war. In turn, he used his prestige to get me into the best training here in Alsais, where I've been ever since."

"Pastry-cook," Lyren repeated, letting her admiration show in her voice. "Now, that's an art."

"Fact known to few," Nalisse stated, a brief smile crinkling her eyes.

"As it happens, my uncle is a pastry-maker in Imar."

"Thad mentioned that."

"My cousin is learning to run the shop, but they don't trust me to do much when I visit. I know how to frost, and to sell. But I know enough to recognize that a pastry chef must be a level higher than my family's shop."

The fact that Lyren introduced her pastry-making relatives before mentioning the various royal figures related to her earned Nalisse's wary approval. "I passed my mastery project five years ago, and ran a very fine restaurant on Blossoms-on-the-Wind Canal, until I was hired here at the palace by the king to oversee all the pastry-work."

"The king. You mean Shontande Lirendi, right?"

"Thad calls him 'Shon' because they've been friends for

ages, but I find it impossible. It's too much like trying to dance in a dinghy, to say 'your majesty' one day, and 'Shon' the next. They manage, but I am always afraid to err." Nalisse paused, her brown eyes searching Lyren's. Then she said, "The truth is, I'd rather have had the wedding in town, and invited our town friends. All these kings and queens—some of our friends will be here, but—" She shrugged.

"But they'll be using their formal court manners," Lyren guessed. "And the rankers will take precedence, even though it is your wedding, because they always do."

Nalisse lifted a shoulder. "Thad says that this court could use some infusion from outside their circles, which is why he agreed to it when the king made what for him was a generous offer."

Lyren sorted rapidly through the implications, and then wondered why she had been chosen for this confidence on five heartbeats' acquaintance? Was it simply because she'd mentioned the Fer Eiders' pastry shop?

Nalisse, it seemed, did not include courtly dissembling among her arts. "Thad thought you might like to see Colend. You could come on our wedding trip with us. Several friends are, so it wouldn't be a dreaded threesome! Thad and Senrid are even older friends than he and the king are."

"Oh," Lyren said, both surprised and delighted. "Of course I accept—"

Nalisse shook her head. "Wait. I believe ..." She frowned at fine inlaid floor. Not an angry frown, but one of perplexity. Then she looked up. "I believe if you're invited to remain in court, you ought to accept that, and not feel obliged to us. You see?"

Lyren's lips parted. She'd been about to refuse any such invitation, for her own standard of manners would not permit her to drop an invite just because another came along from someone who claimed a higher status, but then she saw that Nalisse wanted her to do just that.

"I don't know that any sort of thing like that will happen," Lyren said slowly.

Nalisse looked down again. "Thad would like to see you stay at court, if you do get the chance. The music festival is coming soon. That's the high point of the year for many. The trip down the river is an alternative. You see?"

Something was missing. Nalisse was no courtier; her

accent was a little different from the melodic rise and fall of courtly voices from the gathering behind them. It seemed to Lyren that Nalisse had either left something out, or had changed her mind between her invitation and her not-quite-disinvitation.

Well, who ever discovered the hidden warp and weft of a social fabric within moments of arrival? Lyren was intrigued. "Thank you," she said.

Nalisse gave her a sudden smile. "Come. We'll walk back. I can see that the head steward wants to announce dinner."

They'd done a circuit of the room, around the waterfall in the larger gathering area, and now were back with the group again in the smaller room with a half-circle of windows overlooking a charming canal and more garden.

Thad appeared, his hand twining with Nalisse's. "The dining area is this way."

Lyren began to follow the two, who were approached from both sides by well-wishers wanting to chat. Lyren dropped back, then heard a step beside her. It was Sveneric, dressed in soft shades of contrasting gray. She saw him so seldom that the changes in him startled her.

"Sit there?" He pointed to a table at the extreme end of the bank of windows. It was a charming spot, set under young orange trees still blossoming. Ah, they were all charming spots; in Sartor, the head table was invariably raised, the others surrounding it. Here, the tables were scattered, but the head table—so Lyren reasoned—would be wherever Thad and Nalisse sat. Sure enough, they settled with Rel and Atan. That would automatically become the head table, if Lyren guessed right. Now to see if the local butterflies surrounded them.

She did not want to be obvious about her staring, so she turned to assess her old friend from their mental circle days. He was tall now, most of the childish roundness gone from his face.

Then she surveyed the foods beautifully arranged on porcelain plates edged in blue and silver. "It's been a while. Miraleste, yes? Is Ian here?"

"He had to remain in Sarendan, and as he never knew any of the alliance people except briefly, there was no urgency in attending."

Lyren eyed the pretty silver utensils. Here indeed was the thin-handled fork with tiny tines, almost an eating stick. The artfully arranged foods came in attractive little circles and squares. The Colendi ate in very small bites, talking in between, but not at the same time. She wondered how they consumed soup.

She hazarded another sweep. She was beginning to descry details. There were far fewer people known to her than she'd expected. "I thought I'd see Hibern," she whispered. "Wasn't she a big part of the alliance?"

"She was. And she was here yesterday."

Great matters in the realm of mages? Or merely that Hibern avoided weddings? She hadn't stayed long at Liere's, either. Lyren studied him. "You know something."

Sveneric gazed at a perfect leaf, admiring the shape while his thoughts arrowed to the painful discovery he was fairly certain that Hibern would want to keep hidden. He understood. They were two people in love with the same woman, but while his fixation had begun as teenage crush, and was now mostly admiration, it was fading—he didn't think Hibern's ardent passion was so easily dismissed.

At least Erenlara was unaware. He and Hibern both were spared her regret, because she would never mock, scorn, or dismiss. Her own eyes were fixed beyond the stars, she'd said, her voice rough with conviction.

That poignant, lingering memory shattered when Lyren gave him a poke in the ribs. "*You're* here. You were definitely not part of the alliance."

Lyren gave him a mock glare, wondering where his mind had gone. But it was back, as his eyes crinkled with merriment. "It's more that I was included. I've been coming here to see the music festival for the past few years. I stay with Bee Keperi." He nodded toward Thad's brother sitting next to Thad. Bee's hair had turned to a ruddy gold, which complemented his cerulean blue scribe robe.

"Hoo, he grew up pretty," Lyren observed. "I remember playing with him. He was so full of questions, mostly about what colors tasted like. He always remembered exactly what I'd said."

"He's a scribe," Sveneric said. "He remembers every-thing."

Scribe training for a blind person had to be interesting. Lyren decided to ask him about that, if Bee turned out to be as friendly as he'd been when they were small. "Training," she said. "Liere's tried to talk me into going to Curtas's House. Tell me more about it. Are you really drudging through Ancient Sartoran scrolls?"

"Only if we want. Classes are very informal. We teach each other." Sveneric's thoughtful brow quirked. "They come, all ages. The first thing they have to do is unlearn bad habits, untangle old angers, parse old nightmares, and then the real training begins."

"Not poopsie training, then."

"Yes, poopsie training." He flashed a quick smile. "But without the Norsundrian posturing. Training on all three levels of awareness, separately, then together. Training in assimilating the disirad. Then in using it. And finally one selects, or makes, a dyr, and goes out to learn how to use it, when, if. First insight, then action, then — maybe, one day — wisdom."

"How long does all this take?"

"Depends on the person."

"Method?"

"For that," he said, "you must come and see for yourself."

"Is that a lure or a put-off?"

"Lure. Of course."

"Um, maybe I will, but first a little more time with Liere. After all, I did promise." She glanced at the rest of the head table, the guests unknown to her. Fans fluttered and gestured, catching the eye, like butterflies in a garden. "Which one is Shontande Lirendi?"

"Not here," Sveneric replied. "A guild matter required his personal attendance in the city, so Thad's standing host."

Thad of the small house and obscure family, host in Colend's royal palace. "I'd like to meet him," Lyren said. "Is the artistry of this place inherited, or is it some of his taste?"

"Both." Sveneric glanced at the waterfall in appreciation. "You'll meet him at the wedding eve ball this evening, I suspect. That is, there'll be numerous guests, but he always manages to talk to everyone."

"Good manners, good taste, good attitudes. Is he perfect?"

"Everyone likes him, anyway," Sveneric smiled.

"Even your father?"

"My father admires him without reserve. The feeling is not mutual."

Lyren sucked in a deep breath of pure pleasure. "Good taste, good manners, does not admire Detlev ... Another long-lost brother!"

Sveneric laughed soundlessly. For a moment his usual expression — a combination of sweetness and austerity peculiar, so far in her experience, exclusively to Sveneric — vanished to be replaced by real mirth. "Alas, you'll never get him to say anything rude about Detlev, at least not while I'm here."

"I can try," Lyren retorted, with great cheer.

This was going to be fun!

2

After that early, informal dinner, everyone retired to change from day clothes to more formal clothes for dancing. Lyren had learned long ago that fashion was communication about rank, alliance, mood, and intent. She dressed to complement whatever company she was in. It never did to be careless with details, but it had to feel good as well as please her eye. Any fad that made her uncomfortable, she ignored.

Lyren put on one of new summer robes from Sartor, floating pale blue over a silk under-gown, with gold trim edging the draped neck and down the bodice in a slant. Her arms were bare, her sandals gold weave. Mindful of the warm summer air, she pulled her hair up in a complicated knot, fixing it with a pearl-and-gold band that Carl had given her. And though she seldom wore jewelry, she decided to add the matching pearl drops to her ears; if Mad was still here, and saw, she would be sure to report back to Carl. Lyren knew how much it would mean to her.

A light tap at her door. It was Atan and Seshe, who were housed on the same hallway. As Rel and Jilo were off with Terry Larensar of Erdrael Danara discussing border and shore patrol matters, they'd arranged to meet and go to the ball together.

Seshe was dressed in silvery green over warm brown, and Atan in a midnight blue gown, made in the Sartoran style, fitted from neckline to hips and fastened by tiny gemmed buttons down the front of the bodice, then flaring out to brush the floor.

Lyren gestured them inside. "Question first?"

Seshe turned to Atan, who said, "Is there a problem?"

"Only unfamiliar social layers. From what I saw earlier, Colend has its circles, though they might not call them that the way you do in Sartor."

"More fluid here, I'd say," Seshe murmured, and Atan's brows flicked up. "But there are shoals."

Lyren said, forestalling questions, "I just need to know if they're going to be using honorifics and moving in rank order, and if so, who are you, exactly, Seshe? Rel told me that Jilo is now king in Chwahirsland. Throne and everything."

Seshe's lips quirked. "He is. He refused until he had a censorship established."

"A censorship? You mean, to criticize other nobles?"

"Other ministers, for no one comes to the Chwahir court without clearly defined work. The censor can call out anyone, including the king. He says that good censors are rarer than kings, and more important."

"Huh," Lyren huffed. "Why is it that the good, kind kings are busy finding people to tell them they're wrong, but the tyrants kill anyone who tries? That was entirely rhetorical. Tyrants think themselves perfect, of course, or else are trying to bludgeon everyone into believing they are."

"Jilo has been reading Wan-Edhe's early records," Seshe said. "And rescinding laws, if they contribute nothing to the wellbeing of the Chwahir. The sad part is, when Wan-Edhe was merely Prince Shnit, he wasn't that bad. Witness his loyalty to his elder brother Kwenz."

"I didn't know he had an elder brother."

"Kwenz had no ambition. He liked the study of magic for its own sake. He lived in a tiny outpost, gone now. It was right there in Mearsies Heili. Kwenz was the one who picked Jilo to train in magic," Seshe explained, her eyes serious. These things mattered to her; Lyren suppressed the instinct to be flippant, and bit off a crack as Seshe added, "We need to go, for the carillon is ringing, and it doesn't do to be late. But Jilo says that Shnit wasn't all that bad in his early days. In many respects he meant well. And he did care for his children, until his son—professing loyalty all the while—tried a coup, wanting the throne early."

"Oh, personal betrayal as well as the usual throne-grabbing betrayal?" Lyren asked. "And so he was forever after seeing assassins in shadows?"

"Yes. And so, to summarize, Jilo knows he means well, but he cannot predict that he will mean well in twenty years. Forty. And yet the Chwahir look to a king. It's deeply inbred. Even when he said he wasn't a king, they made a title of it — the-king-who-is-not-a-king — and imbued it with humble awareness of his low background. He said it's too easy to get used to power, when people look to you for decisions, and obey instantly. He's afraid it will twist him."

"Which is not wrong," Atan commented. "There are certain members of my court who irritate the snot out of me, but being around them reminds me I'm just another human being."

"That is sort of like a censor," Seshe said. "He's even got a sort of court ritual now, though as yet there are very few ministers. But that will grow as the kingdom begins to recover what was once lost."

"And so to my question, who are *you*? I mean, how do I address you before these Colendi, so I don't sound rude?"

"I'm a favorite," Seshe said with a slight shrug. "The Colendi understand that much better than the Sartorans, actually."

Atan rolled her eyes — but she didn't disagree.

"What that means is, I'm invisible in political discussions, and I'm with Jilo in social things. In formal address Jilo is 'his visiting majesty,' and I'm just another honor." And, seeing question in Lyren's face, Seshe gave a soft laugh. "It really is what I wanted. The Chwahir are not ready for an outlander catapulted over them, even worse, one with no family and no twi. I'm invisible in legal and court matters, but I'm there at the castle making life easier for people, something Chwahir women of Narad are beginning to trust a little. Jilo finally gave in when I showed him how much easier it is for the Chwahir that way. They can ignore me when they come to him on business. No one has to pay court to me. Or can try to, to get through me to him. My status may change, or not, as things evolve."

"As you pointed out, we ought not to be late." Atan moved toward the door. To Lyren, over her shoulder, "I tried to convince Seshe that it's wisest to begin as you mean to go on, but she would have none of it. It seems disrespectful to me. And a disadvantage, to not have one's possible prerogatives clearly defined."

"And I see it as freedom," Seshe said in her usual calm tone as she followed Atan out, her posture erect. To Lyren's eye, Seshe moved with the unconscious poise of one trained from birth. "It all has to do with how the Chwahir define themselves. And how utterly unused they are to having a foreigner living in their midst. Because alas, I do stand out." She flicked her blonde hair.

Lyren followed her, eyeing that long, straight hair tied every foot or so with silk so it didn't stray all over or get messy. Hair that long went with a quiet, slow-moving life. Lyren knew she herself had pretty hair, but she got it trimmed when it reached the chair behind her. Sitting on it was enough once, and she hated it getting caught under her elbows. But Seshe did not seem the type to flop down. She was so quiet she was easy to overlook—or so it had been in Mearsies Heili, filled with colorful, outsized personalities in every direction.

The ballroom, walled in cool-toned silver-veined marble, featured furnishings accented with pale blue, the glowglobes made of crystal, set against tiny mirrors to throw back the light without creating more heat.

Again the acoustics were perfect, carrying the music to all corners, but without echo. The cool air moved slowly, carrying a faint scent of the herb garden off the terrace onto which framed glass doors opened.

"Who is behind the splendid design here? Is it really Shontande Lirendi? Or is this the usual situation where someone does the work and the king nods, smiles, and takes all the credit?"

Atan smiled. "It's Shontande. He's very particular about details. His people think he has exquisite taste."

"Stars," Lyren exclaimed. "Has he a wife or consort as perfect, I hope? No one would want to live in the shadow of a nonpareil."

"He's not married," Atan said, adding in a neutral voice, "though there's talk of him shortly allying with a local count."

"Causing general heart-burnings?" Lyren asked, wiggling her brows.

Atan looked amused. "I can fairly promise you that just about every romantically inclined man or woman within a radius of three kingdoms vies for his attention. I've watched it happen, and when he does finally choose someone, or as they say here, grant entry to Winter Gate, there will be record numbers of tear-dampened pillows."

"Winter Gate?" Lyren repeated.

"There are numerous gates to the city, with various romantic names that have little to do with their functions, which have evolved to have various meanings. In this case, it has come to mean that one has been chosen as a candidate for the new privy council. He's been slowly rebuilding trusted people, after the disastrous regency council of former years."

"Disastrous?"

"You were too young to hear about it, but they controlled the kingdom until he revolted by coming to visit me, and bringing government to an utter stop. Perfect timing. In fact, it was right about now, just before the music festival." Atan's smile turned sardonic as she stared into the past, then shivered a little. "As it turned out, that council didn't survive the attack a few months later. Anyway, now there is speculation that it might mean choosing a queen."

"Has he given in, then?" Seshe murmured, her expression shuttered.

"Speculation says it's political necessity. But I don't know who is chirping that, as they say here," Atan responded under her breath as she glanced around at the gathering knots of people, fans and robes a-shimmer, voices bright with anticipation.

Atan looked about for Rel, usually instantly recognizable. "Here's what you ought to know. Nothing in Colend is ever simple. Including attending a ball, it seems. Where are Rel and Jilo? Rel promised they'd finish up and meet us here."

As Atan looked about, Lyren did too. She detected subtleties of alertness, of nerves, even. For a ball? "Some kind of crown crisis going on? Ah, besides the prospect of the Perfect Paragon marrying?"

"Not a crisis, but besides the border discussion there was something to do with Princess Gwasan's maid. Rel likes to visit her from time to time," Atan said.

"Wait, not your daughter's maid," Lyren said. Atan did not call her little daughter Princess Gwasan unless in court.

"Rel's mother's maid, before Wan-Edhe had the princess assassinated," Atan said. "She's there in Chwahirsland. Ah. There they are, just coming in with Shon." Atan tipped her fan toward a sizable group of people rapidly coalescing on the other side of the room.

Rel towered over everyone else. He smiled in their direction, his approach generating a ripple of deference and change of position. Lyren glimpsed what had to be Shontande Lirendi: an absolutely perfect profile—as promised—and long beautiful auburn hair above a slim body flattered by a sashed tunic-robe, slit up the sides, and beneath, pleated trousers that hinted at the shape of long legs beneath. Then the crowd closed in again. "He certainly is pretty."

"He spent most of the war disguised as a woman," Atan said.

"Really? I think I heard that." Lyren recalled some of the stories.

"His HQ was a girls' school," Atan went on. "Rel was there briefly—"

"Disguised as a woman?" Lyren asked, delighted with the image of tall, broad-shouldered Rel, with his craggy bones, mincing about in ribbon-tied shoes and lace ruffles.

Atan laughed. "As a stable hand."

"Even Norsunder's soul-bound wouldn't have been fooled by the sight of Rel in a woman's gown," Seshe said, hiding a smile behind her fan.

Regardless of when the carillon had indicated the hour, whenever the king showed up was on time. The music began, not with the usual quick, almost-surreptitious tunings and harmonizings. A single tiranthe had begun to play a slow, contemplative melodic line, presently joined by another stringed instrument, and then a flute added a different melody, harmonizing. The players did not quietly tune their instruments, as happened before the start of balls otherwhere. Each musician joined in, at first playing a note or two, then tweaking if needed, after which he or she added to the building promenade.

Now that the king had arrived, the fanfare that heralded the promenade pealed out, a fall of notes in two chords familiar all over the world, dating back into the early days of Sartor.

The flash and glitter of jewels as the assembled guests wove themselves into line struck more color from the crystal and glass. The effect was as if someone had gathered up a handful of the stars in the summer sky and scattered them about the room. Lyren glimpsed Shontande Lirendi's long auburn hair swaying between two straight shoulders covered in shimmering blue. At his right, Thad's Nalisse, the woman of honor for the evening. They led the line, Thad behind with one of his mothers, this signaling that rank order was deferred for the evening.

Sveneric reappeared at Lyren's side. With a gesture of exaggerated politesse he held out his arm. She smiled, glad to have so easy a partner. Rel and Jilo had appeared to walk with Atan and Seshe, Jilo dressed in black, as usual, but his clothes actually fit. Seshe must have seen to that.

Lyren spotted Bee, Thad's brother, on the arm of a tall, laughing fellow with chestnut hair. Bee's blind gaze focused nowhere, but his head moved incrementally, bringing sounds into focus.

The promenade circled the vast, shining floor of the ballroom, then the flourish of trumpets brought it to its end. The superlative musicians blended the fading sound into the opening strains of a haltas, another age-old favorite dance, with its endless twirls in seductive beats of three.

Lyren watched the dancers form up, with no attention paid to social hierarchy. Since anyone could join at will, Lyren turned in expectation to Sveneric, to discover him deep in conversation with Leander Tlennen-Hess.

Lyren mentally shrugged, and moved away to let them have their talk in peace. She listened in pleasure to the music. Though the beguiling rhythm of the haltas was familiar, it seemed that the style here was to accentuate counterpoint, the wind instruments vying with the strings, chasing one another in and out of the melodic line, turning it inside out, then striking out in another line altogether.

Colendi custom or simply this particular group? She fought the instinct to dance in place, something she would have done without thought anywhere else. Diplomat, she reminded herself as she followed a trio of young women who seemed to be searching for familiar faces among the dancers.

Anyway, she also wanted to get a better glimpse of Shontande Lirendi, whirling away expertly in the center of the ballroom, crowned by glorious light from the chandeliers. His partner was a dainty blonde in a floating robe that seemed to be spun from ice and spider-silk. Her heart-shaped face lifted, her focus confined to her partner as her lips moved in private conversation. He looked about as he danced, the host who never ceases vigilance.

Dancers twirled by, hiding then revealing him. Lyren

studied him covertly. He had long, expressive hands, their touch on his partner butterfly-light, impersonal, whereas her small, tapered fingers had spread over his shoulder. That spread of fingers suggested possession rather than affection—though Lyren couldn't be certain. She'd been trained to watch hands and eyes, but these were Colendi, whose fans expressed another language, and who had been trained since childhood in their melende, which Lyren understood to be social grace. Those gripping fingers might signify affection, or simply a grasp on an old and trusted friend for balance if she'd had a cup too many of the cool wine-punch.

A pair of women twirled expertly past. One of the women laughed as her long ribbons wrapped around her partner. They expertly reversed step, unwinding themselves. As they passed between other dancers, once again there was Colend's king in Lyren's full view.

His vigilant gaze lifted, and dark blue eyes met her golden gaze.

She couldn't breathe.

She gazed for a measureless time into those eyes, deeper than a twilight sky, more dense than diamond, until that gaze was shuttered by heavy lashes, and another couple whirled in front of Lyren, two solid, unconscious curtains in fluttering silks.

Then Shontande was on the opposite side of the room, and Lyren could breathe. Could move.

Lyren turned her back, and made her way toward the seats along the wall, habit making her smile gently at graceful nods and slight bows in passers-by, though she trembled, every nerve alive and burning with heightened awareness.

Huh.

Memory brought Laban's voice, so assured: *Because I don't believe in love at first sight. Lust, yes.*

This much she was certain of. This shock that rendered her entire being lighter than air was far more potent than her idle attraction to Laban. But she didn't trust it for its very strength. She understood now how people could mistake attraction for something more enduring. Believe it life-changing. Even the light in the room seemed altered—brighter—every sound, every scent, a whirl of puzzle pieces interlocking in a new pattern, into which she stumbled, sensitized to an exquisite anguish.

It took all her control not to turn and to seek him. She reminded herself of what Atan had said: attraction for Shontande Lirendi was the fashion. Lyren couldn't even manage to pick someone original.

Thad appeared. "There you are, Lyren. I see your old friends have abandoned you, probably going off to rattle on about magic or abstruse Sartoran word forms. I wanted to introduce you to some of my friends, in case you might like to dance." He made a careless wave in the direction of Sveneric and Leander, head-bent in converse on the other side of the room.

Thad went on to present three smiling young people to her. They made the peace, she made the peace, they uttered politenesses—Lyren heard herself respond in kind, though not what she said—and she put her hand out at random, to find it taken by a tall young woman. And then she was dancing.

She danced, she smiled, and afterward could not remember her partners' names, nor what had been said. She knew she responded, because it was reflex; she'd long been able to say the right sort of social chatter while her mind raced ahead to what must be done next. Now, when her mind wouldn't work at all, at least no one knew. No one knew.

She needed to get away—no, that was silly. Nothing had happened other than her body waking up and singing the spring song of all animals who breathed. She'd be singing it, too, she thought wryly, if the other half of this song had been that short man with the curly light hair who Thad had introduced her to—or dear Bee Keperi, though from the looks of things he was fairly serious about that handsome young man with the chestnut hair. *Anybody* other than Colend's king, the lust object of half the people here, according to Atan. There was no good end to playing favorites with kings, because with kings you couldn't not get politics stuck to the bottom of your shoes. Though Seshe was trying.

Yep. She definitely needed to douse this inconvenient fire with practicality, and anchor flesh to the ground again with the truth: desire was just that, however strong it hit. And when many wanted the one, that one was probably not worth the wanting. Who wouldn't become an arrogant snot under those circumstances?

The prospect of a new form of line-dance broke the ice gripping her brain: she had to observe to mimic the steps. The challenge steadied her until she heard what her new partner said; she heard voices again, she heard the music. Smelled the chilled wine, the fruit drinks, the subtle perfumes worn by other guests. Felt fingers touching hers at intervals in the line dance. She smiled back over her shoulder at her partner, a middle-aged woman with elaborately dressed brown hair, and got a sunny smile back.

The dance ended, and Lyren found herself in the middle of a crowd.

Atan appeared at her shoulder. "Lyren. I promised you an introduction, I believe."

Lyren glanced past Atan's gesturing hand to that pair of dark blue eyes. Control! Every nerve was alive, but she commanded herself from brow to fingertips to heels.

"Shontande, this is Lyren Sartora, standing in for Liere and Senrid, who had unavoidable business at home," Atan's calm voice went on.

"Welcome to Alsais." Shontande's face was perfectly proportioned: high, broad, intelligent brow, the curve of his cheekbones somehow both extravagant and refined, an enticing curl to the shape of his lips above a clean-cut chin, just the right masculine balance to a face otherwise so beautiful it could have been sexless.

Rather than be caught staring, she wrenched her gaze away.

And Shontande could breathe again. His heartbeat drummed in his ears as he said, "I'm not sure that Senrid dances, but I am here to offer you Liere's." He held out his arm.

Someone played a few sprightly notes on a flute. Hoping this dance would be a circle or line, Lyren said, "Will I have to dance with her when I return?"

Her voice was lower than he expected, a little breathy, utterly enchanting.

"Alas," he replied, with a glance up at the musicians. The quiet humor in his voice fired Lyren's nerves and kindled deep in her belly. "Diplomatic necessity. Every step."

And the musicians smoothly transitioned into the triple beat of a haltas.

"Ah, well, then." Lyren laughed. Her laugh, so light and free and absent of well-bred artificiality, flared along his nerves. "Duty calls!"

As a first conversation it could not have been more banal,

yet every word seemed imbued with chambers of hidden meanings, and both longed to hear more, though neither could think ahead enough to speak.

She put her fingers lightly on his sleeve, too lightly to feel the flesh beneath.

He did not claim rank precedence, as she'd noted before, but he didn't have to. Wherever he went, dancers eddied around them. She looked past his shoulder, trying to distract her heightened awareness by the subtle signs the Colendi made — a twitch of a shoulder, a shimmer or flick of a fan, a smile — that deferred, or claimed precedence; one who seemed to circle like a pole star, was that same petite young woman whom Lyren had seen him twirling with. Her heart-shaped face followed Shontande Lirendi, her expression observant, even slightly wary.

Romance? Lyren flicked a glance at Shontande Lirendi, to discover him looking in the other direction as the dancers dipped and turned, changed partners, dipped and turned again. Ah, she could safely leave their private matters to them, and laughed inwardly. *I'm here, and this avalanche of attraction isn't what you'd call an unpleasant sensation. Why not just enjoy it until it burns itself out, probably by morning. Nothing this intense ever lasted, that much she was certain of.*

The music changed without missing a beat. "Double," someone called.

Lyren waited to see if this meant a partner change. It did not. Smiling, right toe pointed, left arm held high and wrist arched at the correct angle, she stepped shoulder to shoulder with Shontande Lirendi, guided by a melodic line she knew she'd remember for the remainder of her days as she breathed in his clean, masculine scent under the drift of astringent herbs. Her heightened senses caught the shift of fabric as he moved, and the light the tap of his heels on the marble floor. Circle, part, bow, step-step-step, hands across to the next person in the square.

His mind had hazed. Far too many disparate matters, carefully worked into order of urgency, had just been smashed into shards still spinning. He did not know how many partners he'd had over the years, but this had never happened before. Oh, the physical effects, yes, but not this sense that he had known her forever, before either of them were born. He glanced back over his shoulder as his hand met that of the woman to his right—and once again he met that amazing honey-colored gaze, and he ached to answer the question in her eyes.

Their hands touched, high, brief, and the fire of her proximity heightened to lightning, so sweet it was painful.

"They make a handsome couple, don't they?" Atan said to Rel as they sat down near the door, where the breeze was cool.

"Trying to recall if they've ever met," Rel said.

"I think," Atan rejoined with amusement, "if that had happened in front of us, we would have remembered."

Standing near the other side of the open doors, Sveneric observed how almost all eyes were drawn to that pair midway down the middle line. It was always that way for Shon, so Sveneric had seen on his yearly visits for the summer festival. Colend's king didn't demand it, or even appear to expect it, but it happened all the same, and he bore it with the skill he brought to every other duty.

Tonight there was a difference. He was not exchanging light comments or smiles with those who looked his way. In fact, he was not smiling at all, but performed the steps of the dance with the deliberation indicative of leashed energy, of total focus. Lyren moved with her customary grace, so practiced it had become effortless. Only this time there was a subtle addition, difficult to define. It was almost impossible to look away; she moved as if outlined in starlight.

Sveneric watched his old playmate in admiration. The way they drew the eye might have been merely the pairing of two remarkably attractive people who were at their best on the ballroom floor. He closed his eyes. In the realm of the spirit they were like eclipsed suns, their thoughts utterly shut away, but the leak of light around those suns radiated with startling intensity.

A profound sense of unease gripped him. He had partnered Lyren in the promenade because they were old friends, and she had seemed grateful for the easy introduction to a new setting. That would be innocent enough in most places, but he was in Colend, where everything symbolized something else, where life was a medium—a metaphor—for art, and metaphor shaped life.

And so he saw his action not from within, but from without: how Detlev's son had partnered the beautiful young daughter of the famous Sartora. He had marked her to all observers as another of Detlev's people.

And there it was. He had marked her to Shon as one of
Detlev's people.

Sveneric drifted behind the dancers to where he could
observe the pair. Neither was readable in their invincible
politesse. Lyren's eyes glittered like polished gold metal,
reflecting the flames in the chandeliers overhead—her chin
lifted, neck at a graceful angle. Shon's gaze had narrowed.

The dance ended. Shon spoke. Lyren spoke. They parted,
going immediately to other dancers. Neither looked back.

Sveneric looked down at the ring on his hand, wondering
if he had made a very great mistake.

3

After that, Lyren made an effort to dance with every guest who hadn't a partner, while staying on the opposite side of the room from Shontande Lirendi. Whom, she noticed, she sensed no matter where he was. She needed some thinking time.

The ball was supposed to end at midnight, but people kept dancing, an atmosphere of expectation gripping them. The musicians kept playing as the punch flowed freely, until the single ring of a carillon broke the exhilarated timelessness, reminding everyone that there was a wedding at dawn. They parted to refresh themselves, change their clothes, and then foregather again.

Sveneric fell in step beside Lyren as they crossed the ballroom. "Need a pointer back to your room?"

"I remember the way," Lyren said. "It's not all that far. Why isn't it that far? This ballroom is different from yesterday's. How big is this place? How many palaces have more than one informal ballroom, and why haven't we had to walk half a day to get here, which such places usually require?"

"This is the summer wing, I'm told. If you look carefully, you'll find that many of the walls are actually large screens, which can be moved about to create bigger or smaller spaces."

Lyren paused. "Around these pools and waterfalls?"

"Some. But take a look. You notice most of these growing things are in pots and boxes. Some of these structures can also be taken apart, and the pool floors either sunk further to create a listening space, or raised to the level of this floor." He pointed at the mosaic under their feet.

Lyren looked up, for the first time noticing that the ceiling was a complication of angles leading the eye upward, with glass insets facing north to let in indirect light. This clever combination of carved marble screens and panels, paired with mirrors and painted screens, embellished with living things, was so very much her favorite kind of decoration that she had to go from pot to pot, sniffing as well as looking. Yep, the pots had been chosen for complementary aromas. *No* one did that. She'd thought such things the height of frivolousness, but surely, once you established the plants and the pots, wouldn't it be cheaper than building, tearing down, and repainting constantly?

She remembered how the music had begun, with no awkward tunings.

She turned to Sveneric, lips parted.

"Music here truly is an art," he said. "And art is life. It's not just the nobles, you'll find if you go into the city. Art is defined in so many ways; even south at the river docks, there are no unsightly piles, no things abandoned, nothing unpainted or untended."

"Me-len-deh." She breathed in sheer pleasure as they walked out of the ballroom, leaving it to be efficiently dismantled by waiting day staff. "Then it's not an accident that their word for honor is so close to the Sartoran 'malend'?" One of the reasons why she'd always loved Sartor was because of such words as malend, which was a verb for the appreciation of grace in dance. "I've been seeing forms of malend since my arrival. Hearing it. Touching it, and breathing it in. Tasting it in those complicated flavors so delicately arranged on those platters."

"All true."

"Now I'm beginning to understand what people meant when they talked about Colend. This place, at least this palace, and what little I saw of the city, is not at *all* fussy over-decoration, or pompous pretense at poetry. Who was it who once complained that you can't simply say it's raining, if you are in Colend, you have to say something like 'the glorious globules of glamour gushed from the gray grottoes of the sky?'"

"It might have been said by someone before the war. The previous regency council, I'm told, was decided in their notions of exclusivity. One couldn't simply say it rained. It had to be expressed freshly, preferably in a quotation from some obscure poet, which of course must be capped. Though I doubt that they talked about rain being globules. Or if they did, I wish I'd heard that." He grinned.

She grinned back, but inwardly she was aware that what she saw here was what she'd always wanted, and never thought to have.

They parted at the hallway leading to her guestroom. She let herself in, looking around the quiet room as the eastern sky began to lighten. She would have to bustle. The wedding was to take place as the sun began to rise, a very Sartoran custom. But it seemed that, like the language, the Colendi had made it their own.

She longed for a cool bath full of rose petals, and a morning to consider what had happened. But all she had time for was a step through the cleaning frame. She picked a floating pink gown with tiny embroidered rosebuds slantwise down the bodice, and ribbons with silk rosebuds binding up her hair; though she'd seen plenty of flowers outside, she had not been invited to pick them.

Then she hurried out, making her way along the designated garden path, where she spotted Atan. Who beckoned to invite her.

The sky stayed clear, but even at dawn the heat was like being slapped with a wet towel. Severely short on sleep, the wedding party and guests assembled on a broad lawn under silvery-leafed poplars.

There was a sense of high expectation that had little to do with the pair about to be joined. Or so it seemed to Atan. The fast, musical, elliptical speech of the Alsais courtiers almost always masked innuendo. And who could follow all the ins and outs of local gossip except the locals?

The rim of the sun crested the rooftops to the east, limning Thad's ruddy hair as he and Nalisse took hands, to become not just married, but lifemates. Nalisse spoke in a low voice, her dark gaze raised to that of her beloved.

"I offer you this ring, which has no beginning and no end. It is a symbol of our love, which has no beginning and no end."

Atan considered Nalisse. She rarely shared whatever it was those round, birdlike eyes saw. Not with queens, anyway. She had been tight-lipped with politeness when they'd been introduced, as if they'd met before, which Atan did not remember. And she trusted her memory. But Atan had watched Nalisse draw away Lyren—who Atan was sure Nalisse had definitely never met—for a very long conversation, directly after Lyren's arrival.

Lyren stood beside Atan, looking like a rose in pink. If she'd spoken ten words since joining her, Atan hadn't heard them.

Thad's clear tenor voice carried on the fragrant summer air. *"I offer you this ring ... "*

Semaphore caught Atan's eye: flickers of fans, slightly raised brows, meaningful wisps of smiles. There, and there, and there, mostly in the circle around that small, fair-haired Honor Talian, Count of Ariath.

"... which has no beginning and no end ..."

Atan wondered if it related to that obvious and instant attraction between Lyren and Shontande. Fans flickered, performed with a turn of wrist or cant of head in oblique communication whose significance Atan was not quick enough to catch. She perceived only that it was propagating through the court's leaders—and through those who wanted very badly to be court leaders.

"...to witness my vow to share with you all that I have, and all that I am..."

Shontande. She'd not met him until the summer before the war, for his father had kept him all through his childhood in a silk-lined prison, and then the regency council had kept a firm grip on governmental powers well past his coming of age. Supposedly it had been a protection-measure against the poisonous fingers of Norsunder, who had for a while made a fad of using magic to play with the minds of various reigning families.

A fad initiated by Detlev.

"...that your sorrow is my sorrow, that your joy is my joy..."

There was Sveneric, standing with Leander, looking pensive.

"...your prosperity is my prosperity, your hardship my hardship..."

Atan strongly suspected that if anyone in the world knew the inside workings of Detlev's mind, it would be Sveneric. She accepted the fact that she would never reach the profoundly cerebral level of observation to which Sveneric had been born. Alas, he was at least as close as was his father.

"... as long as we both shall live."

A soft-voiced acclamation rose as the couple kissed, and then someone brought forward the wedding bread, a country custom often introduced in ring ceremonies. The couple broke the bread, each took a piece to offer the other, then passed the rest from hand to hand, until the entire circle had shared a piece. It was supposed to signify the harmony of the community, but how much harmony existed in this court, beneath the smiling surface?

Rel moved a little away with Sasharia and Jehan of Khanerenth, the latter reminding Atan strongly of a white-haired MV. How long had these two been married? Since before the war. They still seemed like newlyweds, standing there with their fingers intertwined. The Khanerenth rulers were joined moments later by Jilo and Shon. Where was Seshe? Ah, over there talking to Terry Larensar of Erdrael Danara, with little Madelon Delieth at her side, and Atan knew that politics were back. Atan sighed inwardly: duty called.

Then Talian stepped before her and Lyren. The count said, "We're honored to find you among us, your majesty. And ... Honor? Princess? Lyren?"

"I've no title," Lyren said.

"Are you Sartor's guest?" Talian asked, smiling. "Alsais is honored by your presence."

Lyren tried belatedly to adjust her mental view: she had come to stand with Atan and Rel because they were old friends; while Atan had always been queen of Sartor, Lyren hadn't known what that meant, and Rel had been a traveler during most of her life. A friend, not a king.

Atan glanced at Lyren's fixed gaze, then said smoothly, "Lyren is always welcome in Sartor, but she is currently living in Marloven Hess."

Talian's singsong chimed like bells. "If there is anything we can do to enhance your stay among us, please ask. We hope you will take a favorable report back to Marloven Hess."

Lyren was going to curtsey, but remembered to touch her palms together in the peace. "I most certainly shall," she return-ed, wishing she were not so tired. No, she'd danced all night countless times, and functioned adequately the next day. It was this haze in her mind, aftereffects of the lightning bolt.

The count touched her fingers together, the picture of amity, responded to something said behind her, and moved two steps back. It was adroitly done; she smiled, greeted a newcomer, asked a question, and drew her two auditors along with her.

Lyren kept smiling, but softly, so that Atan barely heard, she whispered, "Was I just invited, in the nicest way possible, to go home?"

Atan flicked a glance at her to see that Lyren was trying not to laugh. "Did you hear it that way?"

"Am I wrong? I hope I'm wrong."

"Though come to think of it, it seems odd that she made that offer, but didn't make any suggestions of things to do, much less ask."

"I do need to learn this language," Lyren returned, her eyes on the newlyweds making a last circle to greet everyone. "I think that 'we' was plural informal, but it sounded very much like a royal 'we'. I've been trying to figure out if there's an understood relationship there?"

"Not that I know of, but then I know very little of Shon's private life," Atan said. "Politically, there have been chirps — what they call rumors — that the Count of Ariath and Shontande will make a match of it. She was raised to it, Hradzy Wendis tells me. Ariath is small, but old, and reputed to be wealthy; the count is alone of the family, her mother having been on the regency council."

Lyren remembered having met Hradzy Wendis when she was a teenager, and attended her first grand ball in Eidervaen. He couldn't have been over twenty then, though to Lyren he'd seemed so old. She chiefly remembered him for his kindness. Apparently he'd been posted to Colend as ambassador after the war.

"The regents were assassinated when Colend was invaded, I think I heard?"

"Yes. Hradzy says that Talian fought in the resistance with Shon and certain others of the younger generation of nobles. They had, maybe still have, a special status, what we'd call an inner circle within the first circle. That's about all I know." She glance at Rel, who was still with Jehan and Jilo. "Let's go see what's going under the linden trees."

"Besides shade," Lyren commented.

"... have to remember, if Damondaen tries another cross-ocean attack, they'll hit Geranda first. Unless they've enough stores to make it past," Jehan was saying.

Jilo had been frowning at the ground. He glanced up. "It's just that there are so many rumors going up and down the coast of Halia as well as Toar's east coast. It doesn't make sense to me to have rumors flying off their west coast, too. I mean, not if they intend invasion. No one invades in two directions, am I correct in that assumption? No one who isn't mad," he corrected.

Sasharia said, "I don't know about invasion. All I feel certain in passing on are words from someone I trust, who overheard talk in a harbor among the Westward Isles off Toar. The most consistent rumor is that someone in Damondaen's royal family survived the war after all."

"And so the faction that claimed the throne is running a search to make sure that errant weed stays yanked?" Rel asked.

Sasha turned out her hands. "Elba reported gossip to the effect that some secondary relations to the royal family are also searching. I think another throne faction."

Rel thumbed his jaw. "Seems to be that an earnest search might be cover for scouting for invasion."

"That's certainly what I've heard, Damondaen having made grabs right and left as Norsunder's forces disintegrated." Jehan grimaced. "I'll send an envoy to Gunter in Geranda."

Jilo said, "If you want Silver Fleet for exercises, we'll gladly cooperate. But here's my second concern: someone will have to talk to the envoy from Breis. They still really hate us Chwahir."

"And us," Jehan said wryly. "They haven't forgotten my father."

He and Jilo turned to Rel and Atan. She said, "Yes, I'll talk to the Breis envoy."

"Then let's hold that exercise before the autumnal storms begin brewing," Jehan said, his last words interrupted by a sweetly ringing carillon. "Ah, I believe yon herald is here to summon us to the wedding breakfast."

The group began walking, a few speaking their farewells before separating off, the rest following the herald. Seshe waited for Jilo, who joined her, slouching at her side; they were returning straight to Chwahirsland.

Atan set a slow pace, and Rel matched it as they dropped back, leaving space between them and the others. Presently he said, "What have I missed?"

"I hope I'm not so obvious to everyone."

"And if you are?"

She muffled a laugh. They were last, no one looking their way. "All right. Lyren and Shon. Should I want them to match up or not?"

"I can consider the consequences of prospective tyrants trying to expand across a continent, but when it comes to predicting relationships—especially those two—I can only point upward, like Peddler Antivad in the tale, and ask, *What's that round ball in the sky?*"

"I know I said we should leave right after the wedding, but I want to stay for the breakfast. Everything's quiet at home. Your father is having a great time spoiling our children. The staff is starting to turn everything out to clean before Midsummer. I'd like to spend a little more time here. See what happens."

"Stay it is," Rel said.

Lightning strike, Lyren was thinking as she followed Jehan and Sasha across the garden. As she'd danced the night previous, she'd tried a mental exploration of various Sartoran verbs and their equivalent in Kifelian through the Universal Language Spell. The scribes updated both languages frequently, unlike, say, Chwahir; in reviewing verbs, she'd discovered that Kifelian was entrancingly polysemous, terms winking in and out of fashion like fireflies. Take that lightning strike. There was a very old word for it—zalend—that now connoted a sort of lusty vulgarity, what she understood as the dockside version of *"You! Me! Now! A bed, and lose the clothes along the way!"* Forthright in some cultures, risible in this one, it seemed, for its loss of control. Or lack of grace.

She really needed to learn this fascinating language!

Her awareness snapped outward, encompassing the beautiful garden, and the glimpses of buildings reflected in the still waters of a canal. She could feel Shontande Lirendi's presence in everything she looked at, the scents she breathed, the sounds she heard. The palace was an extension of him—she knew that, and she also recognized that from her first sight, her first breath of the air, she had felt ... familiar. Call it that.

There was one last social demand: the wedding breakfast. She briefly closed her eyes, and sensed Liere focused on ... ah, she was thinking about Perideth. Far more vital than this situation. Anyway, Lyren knew what to do. If she was going to have to think about him all the time until this zalend-thing starved itself away, it would be more entertaining to have memories to look back on than the worthlessness of endless speculation.

Therefore she would go to the breakfast, and see from there.

Sveneric was one of those who left. Between one step and another, he arrived at his father's house where it was still night. He found Detlev on the upper balcony over on the west side of the house, drinking coffee and watching a cascade of starfalls shooting across the sky.

Detlev smiled a welcome. "Something happened?"

"Lyren and Shontande Lirendi met for the first time."

"The sun and the fountain?"

"The sun and the waterfall," Sveneric said, turning his dyr around on his finger.

"Except?"

Sveneric sat down, relieved to be surrendering his dilemma to Detlev. "I'm afraid I didn't foresee any of it, and I partnered her at dinner, and again at the promenade, the first night she was there."

"And kingdoms will collapse," Detlev said, looking amused.

"I've misjudged?" Sveneric wished he could find that amusement.

Detlev's smile was no longer teasing, but it was still there. "Shontande Lirendi would have associated her with us whatever you had done, whether you were there or not. Your gesture of friendship will have been noted by his courtiers, who are not nearly as observant."

Sveneric thought that through, then made a gesture of assent.

"It will be difficult," Detlev said. "And I do not refer to Lyren's putative association with my tarnished name. The two of them might not be able to surmount the complexities that only they can perceive."

"But of course I must stay out."

"Out, but not away. You have been attending the music festival there for some time, and your absence would be misconstrued. Go back. Have fun. Interact, but don't interfere."

"Lyren, and Colend," Sveneric said. "I never before considered it. And I wonder that she hasn't been there before."

"Like a homecoming, I would guess," Detlev said, sipping. "She found Colend, and Colend found her, when each was ready."

"She's still stumbling around sun-blinded. But were there the possibility of her staying there ..." Sveneric lost himself in contemplation.

Detlev saluted the last fiery golds and crimsons and violets of the swarm of shooting stars. "The old glory days of Colend would be no comparison."

Sveneric moved to the balcony to stare out at the vanishing light-path across the water. "Did you foresee this, how we are taking these places?"

"'Foresee,'" Detlev repeated with good-natured irony.

"Shorthand," Sveneric said. "Internal shorthand. I know how you've planned for all possibilities, and when one set of circumstances comes to pass, you set into motion corresponding circumstances."

"If you perceive my actions thus, answer your own question."

"But the obvious answer isn't really an answer. You saw that we all—including Lyren—got the training, and as places opened, some of us took them. Will take them. But I don't see the pattern, the end result."

Detlev saluted him with his empty cup. "You don't see it because you have not yet found your place in it. Go, and live, and observe. Act when it is time to act."

4

Breakfast was held in a shady room built around silver-leafed argan trees. Magic pulled air from high above the clouds down to ruffle over the shallow pool, cooling damp skin. That and chilled coffee and fresh berry-and-citrus juice revived tired guests enough to do justice to shirred eggs, light biscuits, and fresh berries.

Thad and Nalisse and their families sat together in quiet contentment, far too exhausted for polite converse. With family, one needn't be social. Madelon Delieth had been appropriated by a pair of teen nobles new to court who found the princess from Everon delightfully quirky, her accent droll. And she was a princess. Jilo and Seshe had returned to Chwahirsland, for Jilo had his court duties. Terry Larensar, more elusive than ever, had slipped quietly away after the ceremony. Rel and Atan sat down, their presence commanding the eye. Atan beckoned.

Shontande Lirendi was not yet there.

Lyren went to Atan, and found herself at a table with mainly visiting monarchs, nobles, and envoys, all at least nominally known to Thad; as the conversation turned to trade and border matters, then trended toward the war, she began to suspect that that white-haired woman from Breis had not come with weddings on her mind.

The other half-morvende, Jehan Zhavalieshin of Khane-renth, turned to Lyren, his voice slightly raised, "How are things in Marloven Hess? Isn't it time for the summer games soon?"

He doesn't know about Perideth, Lyren thought. "Oh,

indeed it is," she said, though she had no idea when the games actually happened other than some time before the end of harvest season: the last time she'd seen those games she'd been five or six. "It's considered a festival by the city. Everybody turns up who can get away from work. There are even street vendors who make a brisk living selling their wares to the audience."

"I remember," Jehan said. "Our academy students and Senrid's have been sneaking off to watch one another's war games for years now. And they join in when the games are open to all comers."

Lyren smiled. "And then debate who's the toughest?"

"Of course!"

Jehan only partly succeeded in diverting talk from the war. Conversations separated off: weather, schedules, music, travel passed under swift review. But those who were going to reminisce went from academy games to army maneuvers and right back to the war.

"I remember hearing that he ..."

Lyren tried to shut it out.

The white-haired envoy from Breis interrupted, her voice raspy as she rode over the others. "No, what *I* heard was that Detlev himself attacked Efael's stronghold on the Chwahir border that last winter of the war. I was told no one actually saw him, which reduces all this speculation about his supposed heroism to mere rumor."

Jehan gave up, and pointed at Rel with a hilt-roughened hand. "Puts me in mind of a question I've had since then. Was that your plan independent of Siamis and Detlev there at the end, to get us all to attack on the same day, or was it not?"

Rel's deep voice commanded attention even when he didn't lift it. "Siamis was the global link, but we were all under Detlev's command. All I knew was Sartor's strategy, which Atan put together. I just led when Siamis called for the signal to go out."

Vis of Decael on Khanerenth's coast gave a grunt of acknowledgment, and stroked his long beard. "You were out to sea, eh?" he addressed Jehan.

Jehan grinned. "I was. We hit Ellir to prevent reinforcements from being sent. But we obeyed Detlev's signal."

"Willingly?" the Breis envoy asked.

"Willingly and enthusiastically," Jehan said with a wry smile.

Rel put in, "Detlev didn't force anyone along. Falling in was more of an inevitability, like being carried downstream in a flood. You can swim, you can even get out, but you can't alter the course of the river."

The calm, serene Marta, duchas of Locan Jara, observed, "I have heard that Detlev was acting on a plan of very long standing."

Rel said, "It's only true with respect to defense. He didn't loose Norsunder on us."

"Yet their first commander was one of his boy assassins," Leflin of Devrea stated, frowning, as the Breis envoy nodded, eyes narrowed.

"Initially," Atan said. "He left that group. The attack was coming, it's just that the Host initially put Imry Llyenthur in charge of the invasion as a lure to Detlev."

"You defend Detlev, then." The Breis envoy turned her wary gaze from Atan to Rel.

Rel shrugged a massive shoulder. "Just stating what I know. I will say this. I'll fight with him at my back any time he wants me."

Jehan raised a hand in salute, his morvende-white hair glistening in the sunlight. Sasharia smiled with good-natured irony.

"I feel the same way," Atan said. "Despite the past."

The envoy turned to Lyren. "What say you? According to the stories, you, or perhaps it's more precise to say your mother, has been threatened by Detlev for longer than any of us."

Lyren's nerves unsheathed. How did she get into this conversation? She was aware that Shontande Lirendi had joined them. What's more, all the tables were paying attention now.

Lyren had been holding her chilled coffee in her hand, admiring the delicate painting of berries and leaves around the rim. She set the cup down as her mind raced. Memory, Sveneric's voice, so casual: *My father admires him without reserve. The feeling is not mutual* ... Sveneric, her very first dinner partner, her first dance partner. Yes, that envoy had noticed, and in spite of the reference to Liere, she was as much as calling Lyren one of Detlev's minions.

What an irony!

Lyren suppressed the impulse to deny, to toss off an insult. It was one thing to run Detlev down to the likes of Tahra, for it had enabled her to do some good for the children. But impatient as she'd felt at his interference on her behalf, she knew very well that sending Siamis had been because she'd become a brat beyond Liere's ability to handle, and as for the poopsies making her learn self-defense, she knew she'd needed it, she just didn't like being told to do it.

And she refused to curry favor from possible Detlev-haters.

She shrugged. "Oh, he was like a bossy uncle. He and Siamis both. But come another war, I'd follow his lead—complaining all the way, because I do so hate marches, tents, and camp food. Not to mention taking orders, and getting dirty."

On the chuckles following that, the subject ended.

Lyren observed signals among some of the guests as they began to rise and move away. Private talks, eh? Politics, ugh, as well she had no part of them. She sought a familiar face to walk out with, but Leander had vanished, and so had Mad and her girls. Then Lyren spotted Bee not two paces away. "Bee, it's Lyren. Do you remember me?"

"Lyren," Bee said. "There you are! I wanted to greet you..."

As they began catching up with one another, Atan and Rel started out, intending to return to their guestroom to fetch their belongings before transferring back to Eidervaen.

But here was Shontande Lirendi. "Before you leave," he said. "May we speak briefly?"

"Certainly," Atan said, sending a look Rel's way. He interpreted it successfully: he'd pack up their things on his own.

She said, "Anything you need me for?"

Shon's gaze met hers, and then shifted. "Some matters having to do with the Chwahir."

"And Rel knows the people involved," Atan added.

Shontande smiled. "Doesn't he know everyone?"

No, Detlev does, she thought—a heartbeat before Shontande said, "If he doesn't, Detlev does."

She glanced at those dark blue eyes, a deep, dark blue of rare purity—like the night sky just before the stars come out. Her own eyes had been called violet, but that (she believed) was by flatterers, or friends; her own mirror showed her a dark blue slightly muddied by flecks of brown. The shared color was no surprise, as the Lirendis and Landises had intermarried several times, back in the empire days. When she was small, before the brown flecks appeared, her eyes had been close to his color, though the shape had always been what she privately termed Landis gooseberry. Of her three children, her middle one had inherited them — thus the nickname Froggie, which, he being a small boy, he considered a high compliment.

"Is this a conversation about Detlev being an enemy still?" she asked.

"There was a time when you were ambivalent, not to put it stronger," he countered reflectively.

"It's true. Ever since he claimed to have left Norsunder, I made it my business to read about Detlev's actions in whatever records I could find, a project made easier as most magic workers in the world still honor tradition and send our scribe-archivists a copy of whatever official records go into magical or royal archives."

Shontande gestured with his palm in appeal, inviting her to go on.

"I've come in these past couple of years — and not without reluctance — to the conclusion that Detlev had acted to prevent war, not to start it."

"Ah?"

"His manner of doing it was regrettable, to say the least. But Tsauderei was the first to point out to me that Detlev had to carry out his plan right under Norsunder's collective noses."

Shontande murmured, "And so he bound the families where one would expect Dena Yeresbeth to make its first appearance into time-frozen enchantment, ostensibly as entertainment for his superiors."

"Families like your own," Atan said. "And mine. Is that why we're having this conversation?"

"Yes, and yes. But it's begun to appear to me that the intent was to deflect attention from them until the disirad was truly ready. I've been studying as well."

Atan found that she was relieved; she didn't really like to defend Detlev, but now understood that she did not have to. Shontande's purpose was what, Detlev-adjacent? "It seems we are only beginning to comprehend. That, Tsauderei said as well."

Shontande had put his hands in his silken sleeves. "Understood. My qualms, if I may put it that way, are bound up entirely in the personal cost." He said nothing more than that; belatedly she wondered if he meant not just his father, but himself, who had been locked up as a child in case he showed signs of madness. Every utterance evaluated for the good of the kingdom, that regency council using the possibility of Shontande's potential madness as their excuse for holding onto the government.

It seemed he required no response, for his tone lightened. "Jilo says that Mondros has shifted back to his mountain cabin."

"He's with my children now, so that we could come to witness Thad's and Nalisse's wedding. They adore him, possibly because he told them once that he's a pirate."

Shon's laugh was soft. "What did Rel say to that?"

"Nothing. Of course. He knows the children would love having a pirate for a grandfather. Much more interesting than a mere mage."

"And so?"

She never talked about her children unless asked.

"And so Kaelan-Dei was the one to scout the records and burst that bubble, a year or two back."

"What did Mondros do?"

"Offered to get a boat soon's Kay turns twelve, and take him out on the high seas. If he understands what a chart is, and how to read one."

"And so the boy must tend to his studies before being introduced to the delights of piracy?"

Atan nodded. "I learned something then. Parents prate of duty and responsibility, but grandparents can promise the likes of brigandage on the high seas. Or a grandfatherly version thereof." She added, "I do look forward to being a grand-mother."

"I look forward to meeting all three of your children," Shon said. "Before or after they set out to roam the waves."

They passed into the garden, and the departing courtiers who made king-watching their business saw Shontande walk out with the queen of Sartor: international politics, then.

A few pairs of eyes looked for Lyren, who was over there with the king's scribe. And so the last of the guests exited, as Bee caught Lyren up on his scribe studies and offered to introduce her to Ruislan Altan, chief of the palace herald-guards. And also Bee's husband.

"I'd like that," Lyren said, noting the ring on his hand. "I saw you dancing with him last night, and wondered who he was."

"He had to leave for duty midway through the night or I would have introduced you. He loves to dance," Bee said as he led the way out the door, his walking stick barely used, except a light tap here and there. He had to know the space very well, she was thinking, when Bee halted, his head turning.

She looking in the direction he faced, saw only a trellis of climbing impatiens, then realized he had turned his ear toward footfalls. She swiveled, to find herself face to face with Shontande Lirendi. Ah, so Bee wasn't only catching up, this was a deft handoff.

And here was the lightning again.

Zalend! Vulgar or not, it was so very much the right word.

He was finding it difficult to think at all, but years of practice got him over the surface. "Have you had a chance to see our rose garden? Atan once told me it was her favorite in the entire world—perhaps a compliment kindly meant, as Eidervaen has its own magnificent gardens."

She suppressed the words *I haven't even slept yet,* reminding herself conscientiously that she was a diplomat. "I would like to," she said.

He led the way through the trellis to a path full of summer blossoms in an explosion of color and scent. Her steps lagged as she tried to take in the astonishing variety of shapes, shades, and fragrances. Past another trellis, and here was what at first glance appeared to be an ocean of roses, shaded in gradation from pure white to deep burgundy. Around the edges the roses grew on trees roof high.

"It's very old," he said. "Begun by an ancestor, and tended intermittently by other relations since."

Lyren's senses swam. She bent over a cream-colored bud, but did not touch. "It must take an entire staff to tend them."

"The chief gardener has a staff, but there are many who have inherited rights to the petals and hips," he said. "Rose candies—sachets—steeps—apparently this garden is popular for such things."

Tiled roofs rose beyond the rose trees. She had yet to see the whole of the palace.

"This garden is not quite at its best," Shontande continued. "By midsummer everything will be in bloom at once. Our music festival begins on Midsummer Day. If you have the time, you might like to stay, and see them both."

"The time." She stared down at a pale pink rose blossom.

She had the rest of her life free and unscheduled. But one didn't say that. What did one say? For it was an invitation framed as a comment, offering her the graceful out.

She wavered; her headlong rush of senses clamored for her to stay, and stay, and stay, for ever and ever, until the stars burned out. The very strength of her response froze her tongue, until she remembered how adroitly Bee had brought her out for this private meeting, without his courtiers being aware.

She turned to look at him, trying to read him. Impossible. Of course. He'd no doubt been trained from babyhood to assume that polite mask, and — she hazarded the briefest check on the mental plane — his shield was as impervious as Senrid's. Like polished steel.

You won't get a better chance than this, she told herself, and said, "What happened last night. I've been trying to compare a bit of your language with Sartoran. There's this word zalend, which I guess is vulgar." Her fingers brushed over her heart, then extended toward him. "Or was it all in my head?"

Nothing had prepared him for last night. For this moment. This year — this spring — even this week, he had stood poised between doing what the older members of his court, Colend's backbone for generations, felt was most suitable, and his own inclinations. Except he'd had no alternative.

Then suddenly, here she was. Except it was never that simple.

"Zalend is the right word. Or perhaps the essence of zalend," he said. "We have another term, equally old: rafalle. Even more overused, I regret to admit. My new shoes are rafalle. The apple dishes at The Crimson Lily are zalend. My uncle's clever knot design is rafalle."

Rafalle, she repeated: bright fire. "Oh, what a perfect word."

"Too perfect," he conceded. "Until it was perfect for every convenience, many times a day."

"So now you say…?"

"Winter swim."

She gave that free laugh, quick, a little husky, and it warmed him to the core. He wanted to kiss her, right there in the middle of the roses, where once Curtas and he had found their way to friendship.

Regret and ardor tumbled around one another in his mind as she tipped her head, her gaze lighting on his lips. Then flitted away, a pulse ticking in the sweet hollow of her neck. "The shock of ice water?"

"And a reference to Winter Gate, which in its turn connotes going from the howling ice wind to warmth and comfort. I'm afraid our language is full of idiom. We grow up hearing them."

She understood then that he'd accepted her deflection into the meaning of words, embroidering it to give her more time, but his invitation still hung in the air between them. It, too, shimmered. Everything in this moment shimmered.

She met his gaze, and again both of them were drowning in light.

In heat.

"I'm new in this situation," she said in a voice so soft it was difficult to hear.

"And I." He stepped closer, clenching his fists behind his back. "And I."

She bit her lips, then straightened her shoulders. "And you are you. What would your invitation mean? Though I know it's probably too vulgar for words, I'd love to spell out what I want to happen next. But, well, you are you. We are all born naked into the world, but from your first breath you had duty, expectations, status. Whereas I had nothing. Not even a home of my own. Only in the sense of ownership. I've never gone without, ever, I hasten to say. This is no bid for pity. I've had an excellent life. Just … no status, duty, or expectations. If it's a dalliance you want, I'm ready, but what if that's not all? Is it only I who feels that cannot be all?"

How to answer that? He had a hundred poems by heart for every situation that might occur in the Chamber of Cranes, but he refused to use them now. She watched as his face sobered, and she fought the instinct to lean toward him.

"All I know at this moment is that I would like you to stay." His voice roughened. "But I understand if you decide against it. From what little I've seen of you, this…" He swept his hand out to include the garden, the palace, the city. The kingdom. "Is more of a drawback than a draw. This is my life, here, for as long as I live."

She loved that he was talking back to her in plain language, no poetic persiflage, no six layers of innuendo. His gaze was steady, as dense a blue as a twilight sky.

Stay? What did that mean right now? Stay a night? A lifetime? Her mind had hazed impossibly, but it caught on one thing. "You said the music festival," she said.

"Stay as my guest?" he asked. "Until then?"

"Until then," she said. "Then … then we'll see."

He waited, hands still clenched behind his back, for her to make the first move. She was poised to make it, but fear held her still, not even breathing. Not fear of him. It was the opposite. She knew if she touched him now, there would be no returning from that, not without pain that even contemplating in this moment was nearly unbearable. White fire was the right term, trite or not, because fire *burns*.

If only he was just a man! But he wasn't. She *had* to think about what that meant.

And so she made herself turn toward the garden gate.

They walked side by side, until they reached the place where Bee was waiting. "Bee will get you comfortably situateed," Shontande said, and the polite mask was back, but there was a smile in his voice. "Matters await. You will pardon me?"

He made the peace. She made it back, and he walked away as Bee said, "I'm so glad you're staying, Lyren. Here, let's begin with one of the better guest suites…"

5

One of the qualities that made Bee a superlative king's scribe was his instinctive awareness of when to listen to a conversation, and when to remain out of earshot.

Most of the time it was easy: those the king did not trust got listened to. Those he trusted didn't, unless Shon spoke one of their private code words, or tapped Bee twice on the elbow if speaking was not convenient.

With Lyren, Bee wasn't certain, so he'd brought her out of the informal summer breakfast room and waited until two pairs of footfalls returned, both persons with the breathing of suppressed emotion.

It seemed she was going to stay.

Bee gladly led Lyren across the garden to the residential wing, thence to the suites around one of the pools, which everyone professed to find beautiful. The fragrances of running water and growing things flowed into each of the suites through garden doors. He explained that a page would deliver a royal token, and she should feel free to ask for anything she should need.

When he returned to the royal suite, he knew instantly by the sound of Shon's breathing that the king was still awake.

"Thank you, Bee," Shontande said, and papers rustled as he set them aside. "I can read you these reports later. Nothing vital. Most of it is Thad's; I told him to have anything needing a seal sent to me while he's gone. Is Lyren Sartora established?"

"She is."

"You knew her, yes? Before you came to Alsais?"

"When we were small." Bee considered Lyren's warm voice, which resonated with the same warmth on the mental plane. No false warmth and cold thoughts. What's more, she had not turned her head from side to side while they spoke, which he had learned long ago signified someone looking around to see who might be witnessing speech with an underling. This behavior didn't make such individuals evil. Uncertain, perhaps, as well as preoccupied with social hierarchy. But he had learned to reserve trust around those so preoccupied with rank. "She has not changed in essentials."

"Essentials being?"

As a child, Bee had discovered that what he perceived on the mental plane was actually closer to how animals relied less on sight than on other senses. This was not much help in explaining his perceptions in a language that, however rich and expressive, had evolved mostly around sight. "Warm, chiefly," he said.

"Warm," Shon repeated. "I hadn't thought of that. Especially now." His laugh echoed off the window, which was shaded against reflecting the heat of summer. "Warm, but no flattery. Cautious, but not calculating." His tone shifted to musing. "I've been attracted at first glance countless times. Especially when I was young, and could not get through a day without my desires catapulting skyward with the cranes. In those days they just had to be breathing. Though equal enthusiasm did help."

Bee smothered a laugh. He remembered his teen years as well: everything had reminded of sex all the waking day, and then he dreamed about it at night.

"Meeting her gaze was akin to that, but it was more than that."

"Selenbeth?" Bee offered.

"I try to avoid overused Sartoran terms, just because so much of the meaning has been debased. Especially in translations. 'Old soul.' What does that really mean?"

"Except that some do seem far older than their years when met by mind," Bee murmured.

"Yes. Jilo being the chief example. That frighteningly competent, patient child who came through here with the relay, during the war. The Venn princess. She was scarcely twelve, or so she'd said, but she did not seem childish in any sense. Ah! I recollect. Erenlara was her name."

"And there is Marga," Bee offered.

"Yes—but she's even more than that, because her essence is more than human. But Lyren Sartora ... there was this inexplicable sense of *There you are! I have been waiting.*"

"There are many who subscribe to the belief that souls return to be born again," Bee observed. He found the idea that identity persisted beyond death fascinating, some minds so strong they guide themselves from the unknowable back into the stream of the finite.

"I could believe that Jilo is such a one," Shontande said. "He seems to transcend so many of the human demands that the rest of us consider vital. Though he says his memories scarcely reach into childhood. With Lyren it's more a sense of the Sartoran yereselen, our true melende, graceful in intent as well as in behavior? Or is that merely what I want to see? Ah-ye! I think I am beginning to cloud the impression instead of defining it." More rustling of papers, as Shon tried to concentrate. "We're getting closer to establishing agreed-on standards of weights and measures with the Chwahir."

Bee had been listening to his brother's excited talk on the subject. Trade with the Chwahir so far was developing steadily, but each commodity had to be negotiated separately. The weights and measures of the Stringers' Guild, known over the entire Sartoran continent, and in some other places that traded south, had been unknown in Chwahirsland for centuries. They had their own system, just as they had their own coinage, unchanged except in minor details for millennia—until Wan-Edhe had taken that away from his people, so that they were forced to depend entirely on him.

Shon tried to get his tired mind to work as he stared at the two reports handed over that morning. Then gave up. "I'm not making sense of any of these. I'd better try a cold bath. Maybe it will wake up my sodden brain."

"You've been up through two nights," Bee said. "Perhaps a rest?"

"If I can make it until tonight, I ought to be able to sleep," Shon returned with a smile in his voice, and Bee retired.

He had been granted the remainder of the day off, and he had already received status reports from his staff that all was as it should be. A bath was a fine idea, and perhaps a rest until Hour of the Harp, when Ruis would be free.

But all that vanished from thought when he sensed his brother's presence in his outer salon. Why would Thad be *here*?

This house, which went with the responsibilities of the chief of the palace-guard, was secluded, east of the garden, which was the opposite side of Thad's living and working areas.

Bee entered his outer salon. "Thad? I thought you and Nalisse would be gone by now."

Thad's breathing, and the small sounds of his movement, indicated turning his head from side to side. "I was just thinking that I'm never here. You always come to us. But this place is very nice."

Ruisande's uncle Donais Altan had been the previous chief, but he'd died defending the palace during the initial invasion. Because the palace guard had traditionally been a prerogative of the Altan family, the house had stood empty until Ruis — deserving though still young — was recently promoted into his uncle's place. "We changed little," Bee said. "The furnishings are sparse, but comfortable."

"It must be, if Detlev's boy keeps coming to stay with you instead of anywhere else."

"He likes the quiet, I think," Bee said. "But you did not answer. Why are you not on your wedding journey?"

"Did you know that Lyren Sartora has *not* been living with Liere all this time? In fact, I don't think she has lived with her mother since long before the war."

Bee sat in his usual chair as he sifted through the emotions Thad was trying to suppress. "I did not. Why does this matter?"

"Because she seems to have been living with one of *them*."

"Them? Ah-ye, Detlev's 'them.' I overheard that, too, from the Everoneth princess. It seems Lyren spent some time with the Dei descendant. Laban is his name. Is that a problem that must be solved now? Ought I to summon Ruis and the guard?"

It was a very mild joke, meant to steady Thad, because Bee was very certain that Lyren was no threat to either Shontande or to Colend.

"I don't believe she's a threat," Thad hedged. "And I know that Detlev's people are no longer enemies. And yet I have misgivings, mostly about how she showed up here. Now. Just in time, you might even say."

"I thought you were delighted. Relieved."

"Until I overheard Princess Madelon chattering about how Lyren spent years with Laban Dei, and she trained with the rest of them, and she was tutored by Siamis! I began to wonder if Detlev has been maneuvering once again, and helpfully presented us with the solution to our dilemma."

Bee said wryly, "Did Shon express any misgivings?"

"Not to me."

"Not to me either."

Thad remained silent. Bee couldn't see him, of course, but he heard in Thad's breathing, and in the restless shift of cloth, that his brother was struggling with conflict. He knew that Thad resisted grudges. But he also struggled with the circumstances of their sister's murder.

Bee said, "I don't think he's going to consider whoever she might have been living with to be problematical. You must remember that Curtas not only gave his life saving Shon, but he also saved the kingdom. You were in Sartor, and I was the one here. I know it for a fact, as I've maintained for ten years."

Thad's breath hissed out.

"What does Nalisse say?"

Thad sighed again. "We just now had our first married argument." But he finished on a note of humor. "She took a strong liking to Lyren. Says she ought to be regarded as the miracle we hoped for."

Bee said, "It seems that you are troubled on your own behalf. I suggest you take whatever you require of my transfer tokens, and seek the answers you need? You do have this time off, so you needn't account for it to Shon if you don't wish. Delay your journey for a little. No one will know."

Thad thanked him, his relief intense. Though he also had not slept, he knew he would not rest until he obtained some understanding. He remembered that the little Delieth princess lived in Ferdrian, capital of Everon, and soon found its royal palace's Destination.

Bang. Jolt. He staggered out of a Destination alcove into a plain hall that smelled of beeswax polish. From the lack of light in the small window, the sun had come down.

A page appeared to ask his business; Thad blinked as the Universal Language Spell echoed in this flatter form of Sartoran. "I seek an interview with King Laban Dei."

The page scooted off.

"Thad? Thad Keperi of Colend?" Laban sifted immediate memory, and not matching name to any face or correspondent of Everoneth affairs, reached back into the past. "Oho."

He observed the page standing there before his desk and suppressed the urge to laugh. Intrigued, he laid aside his pen.

"Please. Bring him in. He needn't wait."

When the footman was gone, Laban—knowing how long the walk was from the outer reception rooms—opened the windows of his new study, located across from Carl's, to sniff the air and look out over the young trees in the starlit garden.

Here was Thad, never actually met. Only Curtas and Adam had gone to Wilderfeld village to join the young allies—until Noser found his way there, and ended their chance of blending in along with Karhin Keperi's life.

Thad was tall, red-haired, with tiny laugh lines at the corners of his eyes and mouth, his expression both humorous and heedful, though when their eyes met, his changeable face lengthened to somber. Wary.

"Come in. Sit down," Laban said, abandoning protocol as he indicated one of the comfortable chairs. "I don't think you and I have met. Though I take it your reason for coming relates to others of my cohort?"

"In a sense." Thad looked pensive.

Laban said, "We didn't have anything to do with Carlael Lirendi's murder, you know."

"We understand that he was assassinated by Efael of the Host." Thad sighed. "And people I respect have insisted that during the war that most of you were firmly on our side."

"Except for Imry, who left us years before. We had no idea he'd turn up in charge of the invasion until it happened." Laban waved that off. "Congratulations on your marriage."

"And you on yours as well," Thad said, making the peace. "I know you're busy, and I do thank you for seeing me, and without any posturing delays."

Laban looked askance.

Thad's fingers flickered, as if he turned a fan over. "Wrong tone? Your pardon. What I meant to do was resolve some old questions, so that I can get on with my wedding journey."

Laban said, "I'll do my best."

Laban ran his quill feathers through his fingers as he observed Thad's slow assessment. "Did Detlev intend for you to assume Everon's kingship?" Thad asked, after the pause had begun to stretch into a silence.

It was a surprising question, one no Everoneth had asked, though some probably thought about it.

"No," Laban said, noting how Thad's muscles tightened at the blunt negative. He remembered that Colendi avoided that, and tried to soften the effect with an explanation, "He kept me on Geth during our first field runs, and when we came over here he did his best to keep me focused elsewhere. It didn't work. I rebelled. Left the group after we ditched Norsunder, years after Imry left. Came back during the war, but that was my choice. That, and Adam acting as my conscience."

"I remember Adam." Thad could well imagine Adam assuming the role of conscience.

"Detlev didn't say a word, didn't lift a finger. And he could have."

"Could have indeed," Thad repeated, considering what had been said, and what had not been said. "Your ambitions were all yours, then."

Laban sighed. "Ambitions ..." He tossed his pen onto the desk and sat back, regarding his guest gravely.

"How would you characterize your motives, then?"

"The first time I stepped over the border I felt I'd come home. I saw a job being done badly, that needed doing right." Laban's vivid blue gaze tightened at the corners from amused to sardonic. "I suppose that sounds as facile to you as 'ambitions' does to me."

Thad shook his head. "I don't know what to think. That's why I'm here." Then: "Did you know that Lyren has come to Colend? Senrid sent her in his and Liere's place."

Laban hid the impulse to laugh. "Madelon told us she saw Lyren there. Lyren often travels around. She was used to that, when she was small."

"But not to Colend."

Laban said with care, "Liere used to take her to your town, but I believe that ended when Lyren was very small."

"Right," Thad said. "When one of your cohort killed my sister Karhin."

Thad struggled not to accuse, to rant, but Laban sensed the deep scar of grief. And Thad, watching closely, saw the wince of regret in Laban's lowered gaze.

"That was against Detlev's orders. He'd told us to lie low, but Edde—Noser—ah, I won't explain his motivation when I didn't understand it myself. Let's say he was unstable. We were trying to untangle the knots of his mind. We thought we were succeeding. We failed."

"You say much what Adam said." Thad shook his head again. "I've walked through all those shadows again, with the light of hindsight, so to speak. I also know that Curtas died trying to save Shon." He glanced at the window, a sheen of moisture there in his eyes. "Karhin would have liked the world we're making, I think." He pressed his palms together. "I really didn't come here solely to accuse."

You came to interrogate. "You mentioned Lyren. I trust she's having a good time," Laban said, and then helped Thad along by observing, "You know she spent a few years with me, in Wnelder Vee, and she was also here, as royal governess, when my wife and her siblings were small."

And Thad took the bait. "That seems odd. That she wasn't with Liere, I mean."

"Liere got married at the outset of the war," Laban said. "Lyren felt ... displaced. But Tahra needed her skills here." He waved his hand around, then pointed northward toward Wnelder Vee. "She's got a knack for making friends. For smoothing impossible situations. For seeing the best way to make something pleasing out of an unprepossessing environment. Everon needed those gifts of hers, during the bad years after the war. The devastation was fairly grim here, especially on top of years of inept stewardship."

"Ah."

Laban shrugged. "When Carl and I decided to marry, Lyren decided to move on. Last I'd heard she was going to take up life with Senrid and Liere."

Thad bowed, thanked him for his time, and left.

Laban prowled to the window again, turning when Carl glided through the open door. "Ah, you heard we had an unexpected visitor?"

She gave a small nod, her gray eyes full of question, and Laban outlined the conversation.

He finished, "So, what to do? Nothing. This is just another conspiracy theory relating to Detlev. Who actually was the master conspirator, but never the ways they assumed."

Carl had been slowly learning about some of those. Her cheeks reddened at the memory of Tahra-Mama's rants, and how very wrong they'd been.

But Laban made no reference to her. "We've been hearing them for years. Thad doesn't seem to be looking for trouble as much as answers. I expect that Arthur has either already been visited or is next on his list of people to question, and Hibern, and maybe even Senrid." What would they say? Would they counteract Laban's good work?

Carl said, "Mad said Lyren danced with the king! I hope there won't be trouble for her from this Thad person." She then went on to talk about the matter she'd been working on.

He listened with part of his attention, internally shrugging off Thad's quest. With an inward laugh, he thought, look out, Colend. Lyren's here.

6

Liere experienced for the first time the complicated logistics that made the Marloven ride into the south of Halia look smooth and competent.

Once she'd seen Malcolin established with the Senelacs, she'd transferred to Senrid, who pointed out that Perideth's people, "are us. It's just that for various reasons their training has fallen off over the generations, except at the harbor. Whose leaders are descendants of the Noths, a very well-respected family not unlike the Senelacs. There's been rising tension between the harbor people and Perideth's ruling family for the past fifty years. Longer."

Liere had been reading that history. "Perideth split off into its own kingdom during the bad times under the Olavairs, but it wasn't entirely united even then."

"United only in hating us," Senrid commented with a sardonic look. "Not solid ground on which to build your fortress. As for today, they don't seem to be aware that disguising scouts by putting laborers' shirts on warriors wearing riding boots, carrying swords, and going about in pairs, doesn't work. We've been letting them see what we want them to see. Whereas our scouts have been in place ever since it looked like we were going to have trouble. And no one thinks anything of a graying auntie bringing a cart of broken harness gear to be repaired or traded, and chatting at the local inns while the work is done."

The concept of spying, especially effective spying, troubled Liere, but she knew she was not going to change anything by protesting. She accepted that, knowing Senrid's visceral rejection of kingdom expansion. He put spies out to be prepared. Though she and Senrid did dyr work when they could, his resistance to being taken by surprise was so deeply a part of him she doubted she could ever untie that knot.

Over the next few days, she and Senrid both transferred between those riding across the border and the companies he had sent south much earlier in spring, once his uncle in Telyerhas had issued passes. The columns, riding in precisely spaced order, made the groups of Perideth military — who had no passes — evaporate and retreat south. Was not that terrible war enough for you? Liere sent the silent thought after them all: the Perideth riders menacing the Telyerhas people, who had no army, but also the proud Marlovens with their weapons and their beautifully trained war horses and their snapping banners. They were superior warriors, and they knew it. Deep was their pride.

But so far, at least, there was no war.

Liere transferred to Choreid Dhelerei at night to sleep, until the daily transfers began to discomfort her. She had to make the time to learn that transfer-slide, she promised herself once again. The magic was clear at least in theory, it was the ability to step from one place to another that disturbed her. It had to be firmly done, or one could step through to… No one knew.

She rejoined Senrid at a campsite. This was the vanguard, who traveled with their own supplies; she had learned that one of the reasons Marlovens were known for their speed was the lack of supply wagons dragging the pace. The slower force behind brought extra supplies if needed. Senrid's orders had been quite firm: no disturbing so much as a blade of grass owned by the locals, unless the quartermaster and her staff negotiated a mutually satisfactory price.

That meant horse cakes and local forage for the animals, and travelers' loaves and cheese for their riders.

The command tent was larger than the others, to accommodate a gathering of captains around a map. Liere wandered through camp while Senrid spoke to Van Stad. She was amused to discover that among themselves, Marlovens on campaign complained as much as the Enaeraneth ever had: one riding captain cursed everyone in sight when he discovered the greens he'd packed so carefully had gone slimy, and elsewhere a tough old veteran aired his opinion of the sticky fingers (or so he claimed) who pilfered his travel bread. "Everyone knows my brother makes the best travel bread in three jarlates, and this loaf was two fingers thicker when we camped last!"

But the next morning, when they encountered riders from Perideth, everyone snapped to attention, united in their well-practiced maneuvers. "I understand now," she said privately to Senrid. "It seems I'm inside, rather than outside. No one minded speaking about slimy greens before me. I don't remember anything like that when I camped on those summer games with you, when we were young."

"Could be. But I suspect you're more observant than you were back then? You might remember us as silent and formidable, but I can assure you, the squabbling was far worse, ending in duels as often as not."

They waited through the day, the only movement the return of scouts to report that the Perideth force was also camped. They estimated numbers, but couldn't get near enough to hear anything.

The following morning a party was seen carrying a parley flag as well as Perideth's silver-crowned banner, meaning the prince was riding. "Valta," Senrid murmured to Liere. "He really hates me. You'll see. This is probably where I might have to hand things off to you, if he tries to start anything. We'd better ride out to meet him. Jan! Whistle up an honor guard!"

The Perideth company and Senrid's people halted in a field with a clear view all around. Liere scanned mentally for anyone readying with intent, and braced against an intense mix of anger, curiosity, dread, envy. She was surprised, and a little unsettled, to discover that most of the envy emanated from tall, well-made Prince Valta Nothalin of Perideth.

"I have been sent by my royal father to demand your intention," he said to Senrid, as riders from both sides ranged behind, hands to weapons. His emotions spiked bitterly on *sent*.

"And I've been sent by my royal uncle in Telyerhas to demand *your* intentions," Senrid countered, his tone mocking the word *sent*.

Already they were miscommunicating, Liere comprehended; before either could say anything more, she urged her horse forward, and when the furious prince turned her way, she waited until she drew his angry gaze then said, "I have volunteered to interview King Halmaer on King Havlad of Telyerhas's behalf."

Prince Valta twitched his gaze away on meeting hers, but he looked back, scanning her civilian riding clothes. She felt his frustration spike, followed by the bleak realization that an otherwise worthless interval would buy him time.

Valta said peremptorily, his effort to establish ascendance obvious, "And you are?"

"Liere Fer Eider," she said, breathing out thoughts of peace, peace, peace.

"That's Sartora," whispered an aide, as if he could stop sound between his prince and the Marloven party five paces away. Or maybe he wanted to be heard.

At any rate, Valta grunted, his surface thought clear, *So it really is her.* With an exaggerated politeness, he bowed from the saddle, and said, "I am here to accommodate our royal neighbor." Then his eyes narrowed. "But only you. Not him," he said rudely in Senrid's direction, without daring to meet his eyes.

This prince was in such emotional turmoil that Liere had to shield against the maelstrom. Was this one of Detlev's catalyst moments? Oh, if she began thinking like that, then every single decision became a catalyst. She dismissed that path of speculation, said clearly to Senrid, "I'll return once I have a chance to speak with King Halmaer," and urged her horse forward.

"We'll wait," Senrid said, leaning his forearm against his horse's neck. And his thought came to Liere: *I didn't expect that right off. What did you do to get him to let you in? What did I miss?*

She shaped a quick reply: *It was the frustration, and shame, behind that word 'sent.' You didn't hear it?*

: All I heard was his usual whiny anger. Ah, I made it worse, didn't I?

She felt his regret at missing a clue. But his dislike of Valta was too old for her to try to diffuse the tension now.

Prince Valta snapped sullenly in Senrid's direction, "We're not finished."

Senrid prudently remained silent; Liere could feel him mentally surrendering the matter into her hands.

Valta began by abruptly initiating a gallop. Liere kept up easily, having been riding with Senrid most every morning unless there was a blizzard, once she discovered that he relaxed after his morning exercise by taking the fastest horses out and target shooting. She wasn't that good at archery, but she liked riding with him side by side as much as he liked having her there.

Judging by the flutters inside her, the babe within enjoyed the rhythm of the gallop, which made her wonder how much of such things were learned and how much inherited.

There were a few more inconveniences that she suspected were meant to shake her, such as no offer of dinner, but she had some oat cakes in her pocket that sufficed while they changed horses. She listened to the local language, which was an interesting amalgam of Marloven and rather archaic Sartoran. Mostly the latter's word order: Valta was Prince Valta, not Valta-Sierlaef, as in Marloven.

She spoke only once, to ascertain that her horse would be cared for while she was away. She was assured stiffly that the mare would be waiting for her on her return. Liere thanked the person as if the answer had been offered in a friendly spirit instead of one of affront.

It was in that atmosphere that they rode into Fera late that night. Liere sensed how tired her escort was; even if they had sneaked off to eat during the changes of horses (and she knew they had), they still had to ride every bit of the same distance she did. Was the purpose to impress her or discommode her — and was this an example of Perideth's underlying tensions, expressed through covert challenge and competition?

She knew that the ruling family — whose name had Noth as a root — had had to move the capital several times over the past couple of generations, one of those since the war. They passed rings of guards whose patterns reminded her of her Enaeran days, when numbers rather than discipline informed the security plans.

She kept her expression polite, and said nothing until Prince Valta walked off abruptly, and a young page approached her. "Please follow me," she said with a bow. And a quick look, her surface thought clear: Is this truly the famous Sartora? Is she going to blast my mind?

Liere suppressed a laugh, reflecting that such an atmosphere must be miserable to live with. As she ought to know. This reminder of the weeks after Andri's death, when she had to shut out the shock, anger, and betrayal of the Enaeraneth, careful of every word and gesture lest she start off the bloodbath the Adranis were very ready to quash, sobered her, and suddenly she was bone-tired.

The room they gave her was clean, the bed comfortable. A jug of fresh water on the side table. Even the sound of sentries clumping back and forth outside the window did nothing to disturb her. Whether they were there to keep attackers out or herself in didn't matter.

She stretched out, and fought off waves of exhaustion so that she could check all three of her children. Lyren was awake, but intensely focused, so Liere withdrew; dawn was an hour off where she was. Yossi was also asleep. Malcolin was suffused with laughter; from the quick impressions she gained, he and his pack of urchins had been permitted to camp outside under the stars.

She slept until her door opened abruptly when a new page brought a hot muffin, a boiled egg, and some plain coffee along with the news that his highness awaited her in the Interview Chamber.

She reminded herself of her mission, took one sip of the bitter coffee, set the cup down, slipped the muffin into her pocket for later, and cracked and peeled the egg in two practiced moves. "Lead the way."

The page's round eyes took in these movements, then she said, "This way."

No honorifics. Interesting! Liere ate the egg as they walked, keeping her expression calm and polite the way she had learned to do all last year, while living as Macael Elsarion's hostage.

When they reached the interview chamber, the page bowed her in. Prince Valta awaited her, his face tight with tension. His jaw muscles flexed a couple of times, a pronounced bulge that indicated he had been gritting his jaw for a lifetime. She also noted that the sides of his thumbs were red from chewing—a habit she herself had had as a child. "His majesty my father has graciously permitted an interview," Valta said in a flat voice.

Ah, so the early summons had a purpose besides more covert intimidation.

"I am ready," Liere said.

7

Prince Valta led the way into another room, where an older man with silver hair slumped half-sitting on a divan. Attendants hovered about. It was immediately clear that, though someone had done their best to prop the king up, his right side from the shoulder down had ceased to function.

"This woman claims to be the famous Sartora, eh?" the king said to Prince Valta.

The prince flicked a glance her way, lizard-quick. Rude he'd been, but not quite to this extent. "Yes, Royal Father."

Already Liere had a fairly good idea of the relationship between the two. She said, "Would you like me to prove my identity to you?" She used the formal mode of verbs, but no honorific, a reminder that they were equals.

Now Prince Valta flicked a look his father's way, without moving his head so much as a hair.

The king's eyebrows drew down. "Not if you really scrape people's minds out. Oh, I've heard the gossip. I thought that sort of thing was confined to Norsunder."

He was both threatening her *and* begging for a display of power. She said, "I'm capable of it. But I don't actually do such things. Just as everyone in this room is capable of stabbing the defenseless, but I trust controls themselves like civilized beings."

The king worked his jaw, and Liere followed the progression of his thoughts without lifting her shield: dislike of the comeback, but he tolerated it because of the implication that he could wield a knife. He'd fooled her! He looked as strong as ever even to this supposed mind-killer. And he *was* strong! He just had to...

She decided it was time to redirect the subject, if she could: "The King of Telyerhas is concerned about companies riding along the North-South road without due notice and acquisition of pass-through, which is in direct contravention of several treaties, going back to the Treaty of the Rivers."

The king scowled as he brought his thoughts away from himself. "But that stinking Tdanerend doesn't ask for pass-throughs, any more than his damned father did."

The hairs rose on the back of Liere's neck. The king, until now, had been surly, but he'd known who Sartora was at least enough to insult her. Another look from Prince Valta, this one a suppressed look of impotence, even horror, and now Liere began to perceive the whole of their relationship.

"What have you to say to that, eh, girl? I know Tdanerend is talking to that shit Dzydes—don't think he hasn't been around here! But we're not that stupid!" After naming a Norsundrian mage who had been dead for a couple of decades before the war, he turned to Prince Valta, and roared suddenly, "Tell her, Jarid!" His face had crimsoned deeply. "Tell her, tell them, we will never give him the harbor, no Marloven will get the harbor..."

Valta gestured toward the door. Liere followed; by the time they reached it, the king's words had turned to gibberish, mixed with orders to execute every Marloven spy.

For a moment they were alone in the hall outside the door. Before any servants could show up, Liere pitched her voice low, and infused as much sincerity as she could, "I am sorry. This must be so difficult, and so much worse when it's your own family."

Valta's face flooded, his mouth a rictus. Sick with remorse, she was afraid she had misjudged and broken the already bad thread of communication, but then he sighed as he looked around. His hand clawed his dark hair back. He was actually a handsome man when anger and affront did not pinch his face into furrows.

Liere went on, so that he would not have to respond, "He seems to remember the days when Tdanerend Montredaun-An was the regent of Marloven Hess."

"Yes," Valta said on an exhaled sigh. "Mostly he goes back to the days when the old king was a threat. He was a boy, then."

"When all the adults around him were tense?" she guessed. "I remember my own childhood fears, some distorted into terror simply because the adults around me did not seem to know how to keep the world safe." Once again she breathed out peace, peace, peace.

Valta scowled, his gaze on the stone floor. Liere dared a quick contact, bracing for the layers of fear and anger. And there they were, pungent, inexorable, distorting every memory. And veining it all, the creeping sense of shame that he was a grown man still tiptoeing around like a boy, because he was as powerless as a boy.

"He's twice ordered us to ride against Tdanerend," Valta said, then added caustically, "as if I don't know what would happen to us if we tried to attack Senrid. He's rubbed it into my face often enough, every time we meet."

"Your father has periods of sanity, demanding reports? Can you predict them?"

"Yes. And, no."

A door opened, and an armed guard poked his head out. Valta waved the guard off without looking. The door shut; Liere wondered why they didn't move to a more comfortable room, then the obvious occurred: all those listening ears. The king had his adherents, whose livelihoods, if not their lives, depended on carrying out the wishes of the one who still held the power. However mad he might be.

"What do the healers say?" Liere asked, using the dyr to draw away any anger Valta was willing to lose. It was a ticklish procedure—Adam had taught her, but it took practice to remain neutral, and permit the person to act, rather than acting on them.

"They don't dare say anything but what he wants to hear, when he's sane. He had two executed who tried to ask questions that would establish his sanity." Valta looked away, and Liere was bombarded by his memories, days of distrust and threat of execution. The king did not seem to see that Valta—were he actually going to kill his father—would have acted by now. But there was still decency beneath the years of distrust, abuse, and frustration.

Valta turned to her. "About those mighty powers of yours. I suppose you'll tell me they are very mighty when it comes to scraping brains, or whatever you call it, but actually fixing a problem like this is impossible?"

She reached past the sarcasm to the anxiety prompting the question. "We are in the process of translating healing texts, hidden from the ancient days until after the war. I can do a certain amount. I could try when he sleeps, for example, during his dreams. There is less chance of his losing his temper, which is a threat to his health, as you no doubt know."

"It was during one of his rages that he fell down again, and this time, he lost the use of his right arm and leg. For a day or two he couldn't speak, or he did and he sounded drunk, but his speech came back."

"If he loses speech, you could act?"

"I got that much cooperation from the healers," Valta said. "This is … what are you going to tell Senrid?" The suspicion was back.

"Exactly what happened, of course: that you are suspended between moments of the king's sanity, and memories of the past. That you, with the most proximity, are in the most danger."

Valta's expression eased slightly. "You saw that, did you?"

"It's apparent," she said. "I can't promise anything until I try. And," she raised a hand, forestalling him, "if you like I could do the dream examination for you first, so you will understand what I do? Or we could try a waking contact right now."

He recoiled, then looked puzzled. "I don't understand how any of that is possible."

"Then here's the waking test," she offered. "Think any thought at me, as if you were speaking, but don't open your lips, and I will listen." She tapped her forehead. Valta's contact was shout-clear, as she said, "'Turn around three times! What if she's lying. I would never know—"

She had begun to spin on one foot when he said, "Stop, stop, stop."

She stopped spinning—and shielded. "I can't hear you now," she reassured him. "It takes concentration. But you see I can do it."

"I believe it," Valta said hoarsely. "And now I know how that shit Imry Llyenthur always—ah, never mind."

"You needn't tell me what nasty tricks he tried," Liere said, and ventured an equalizer, "I already know. I was his prisoner once. An experience I would rather never repeat."

It seemed to ease that incipient sense of judgment, of

competition that was apparently part of Valta's personality. He led the way to his private suite, where a blond woman Liere's age and size waited with an anxious face. Liere had heard that Valta had been obliged to make a treaty marriage. It seemed there was little trust here.

Valta said stiffly, "See to refreshments, Starliss."

Consort Starliss went off in silence. Valta scowled at the clean-swept floor, then flicked a look at Liere, who had pulled out the muffin from her pocket. Slightly squashed as it was, she devoured it in three bites; she had reached that stage in pregnancy when her appetite roared.

Valta glowered, then he seemed to feel it necessary to say, "I know Starliss spies on me."

Liere wanted to comment that winning her to his side might be the best effort he could make, but decided it was far too soon. She did not know their relationship, or what sort of a person Starliss was.

The refreshments came, several cold dishes. Before Liere could thank Starliss, Valta sent his consort out.

Liere helped herself to pickled cabbage and more boiled egg as Valta began to ramble about how difficult everything was, and how thankless, with an increasing number of less and less oblique cracks about Senrid's posturing and arrogance. Liere kept eating so that she would not have to answer. She hadn't long to wait; apparently the king would fall abruptly asleep at any time.

When an aide came to report, "His majesty is asleep," Valta turned to Liere. "If we go in there, the spies will be making up their own version of what's going on."

"I can check from this room," she said, without explaining that her having met the king enabled her to find him on the mental plane.

Valta scowled, but this scowl reminded her of Malcolin when he'd scraped himself up, and had to permit someone to clean and wrap the scrapes, though he knew it would hurt.

She sat squarely on her chair, put her hands in her lap, composed herself, and reached. And flinched back. It was like trying to make sense of a thousand shards of a mirror, with large gaps of darkness between. Instinctively, she called: *Adam!*

    : I'm here.

    : Here is my situation.

She had become very good at containing and sharing

memories. She gave him the entire morning, and then sensed him reaching past her to King Halmaer. He was back within a few heartbeats: *This is beyond me. May I contact Siamis?*

: Please.

Liere sensed not only Siamis, but Clair's presence, soothing and sane and infinitely generous. Again it was only a few heartbeats before Siamis's thought reached them: *He has not long to live. I cannot predict with any more accuracy than perhaps a few days. The connection between his troubled heart and his mind is disintegrating rapidly, worsened by his craving for spiced wine. If I had to guess, I would venture to say his caretakers are trying to hurry that along, more to pacify him than out of any actual malice. But it's hastening his end, nonetheless.*

: Suggestions? This is a new situation for me.

: The king is not going to survive even if you intervene successfully. His body is losing its struggle to hold onto life. Do what you can for the son.

Adam and Clair echoed their agreement, and Clair assured Liere that she would be there if needed; that same sense of sustaining support wreathed her from the other two, who were more experienced in wordless contact.

Liere kept her eyes shut. What to say? She was nearly overwhelmed by the desire to lie to Valta—to say she didn't know, and to get herself out of there. His trust was so tenuous. But he was in need, and in a sense he had asked for her help, however reluctantly or suspiciously. Therefore she must do what she could.

She opened her eyes, saw his apprehensive, distrustful frown, and said softly, "He has only a few days to live."

And sure enough, came the expected first question, almost eager, "Can you tell me who is loyal to me, and who isn't?"

"No, I can't," she said. "Any more than I would listen to your thoughts without your permission."

"Then you aren't much use, are you," he shot back—but the gnawing new worry beneath dissolved, that she could wield war just with her thoughts.

She did her best to infuse her voice with peace as she murmured, "Will you listen to what I have to say?"

His gaze was unblinking, desperate. "Not if you're going threaten me with Senrid," he muttered sullenly.

"Nothing about Senrid," she responded, peace, peace, peace.

Valta's anxiety bombarded her, with it an awareness that she had been married to Senrid very recently, even less time than he'd had Starliss spying on him, so maybe she hadn't turned Marloven.

Regret suffused her. "I will say nothing about Senrid, but I know a lot about history and its patterns. You will shortly become king, which means they will all look to you now. You can begin by executing all those who now surround your father—many new kings begin that way—but that starts your reign with blood, anger, terror. Or you could commend those persons for their loyalty to your father, give them a pension, and award them with positions on the periphery of the king- dom, where they can do you no harm. No blood, no lost life. Coercion doesn't inspire respect, it only causes a pretense of respect, but mostly fear. And people tend to want to act against the thing that makes them afraid, do they not? That's all I have to say. What do you desire me to carry back to the king of Telyerhas, and to Senrid?"

Valta's gaze shifted, as his right forefinger picked at the rough skin around his thumb. Liere looked away, the memory of that level of anxiety visceral. She breathed it out as Valta said sullenly, "If what you say is true, I cannot be anywhere but here. Nor my trusted aides, so you will have to wait for an escort."

It wasn't quite a threat—nor quite a plea. Somewhere between, perhaps an impulsive grab at any anchor. She could of course transfer out, but her safety was not threatened, and to transfer would startle Valta into defensive reaction.

"I will stay," she said, and decided to begin with Consort Starliss.

8

Lyren's new suite had a tiled bath the size of a small pool, with fresh water carried in from the nearby canal. There was a firestick adapted for heating the water, but she left that untouched. She wanted cold water, which was a delicious shock. She'd filled the bath with some of her aromatic dried blossoms, and scrubbed herself and her scalp until her skin glowed. When she climbed out, her body hummed with an anticipatory languor. Tired as she was, her mind still raced.

She tried lying down. Though her grateful body sank into a bed that was clean, cool, and cloud-soft, she heard every cheep and twitter of the summer birds outside the window. She smelled lilacs and heliotrope and gardenias. She thought about Shontande Lirendi, reviewing every word spoken, relishing each beguiling alteration in timbre. She marveled at the exact shade of ruddy gold on the tips of his eyelashes in the morning sun. And she contemplated how much she'd wanted to step closer, close enough to tease his scent from the surrounding riot of roses.

This was not putting her to sleep.

She gave up and began to dress for outside. She was even more dissatisfied with the tiny buttons she'd once found so elegant. Perfect in winter, but at the height of summer, fabric tended to cling to one's flesh, and buttons gapped. That would have to be amended, now that she'd seen the solution.

Meanwhile, there was an entire palace to be explored! She slipped out, then remembered that royal token, and went back inside to fetch it. In all the palaces she had stayed in so far, she was recognized by the pages and guards, but that was not true here.

She slipped the token into the pocket of her under robe, patted it firmly to make sure it had not leaped out, then turned to leave again—and almost ran down Nalisse. Who was supposed to be sailing down the river on her wedding trip right now.

Nalisse said, "I was just coming to see if you were free."

"And I was about to learn my way about. So far I've only seen those celebration chambers and the rose garden."

Nalisse smiled. "The king took you to the rose garden? He rarely takes anyone there."

"I don't know why not. It's beautiful! Or does he think it'll get trampled?" Lyren asked. "More important, I thought you were departing for your wedding journey?"

"Oh, we'll leave tomorrow, I expect. Thad thought he'd left some trifles undone," Nalisse said as she stared fixedly at the outside pool. "I'm glad they put you here. It's the prettiest set of rooms in the entire guest wing, I think."

"Bee brought me here," Lyren said. "So friendly and kind, Bee. Treating me like a visiting princess, even though I'm not one."

"Enjoy it," Nalisse said with a quick laugh. "How many times in our lives do we get more than we think our due? But first, I came to see if I could show you my part of the city."

Lyren drew in a breath of pleasure. "Oh, please!"

And that was why Nalisse liked her. Not a single thought to who might see them, or whether Nalisse's area of Alsais was suitable for her rank. "What we might do is take a boat around the inner canals. Once you recognize Crown Skya, Lily, and Alassa Canals, you will never get lost, as all the side canals eventually bring you back to one of them. And of course you can always ask directions. Anyone would be glad to point you back to the palace…"

Lyren and Nalisse walked along flower- and tree-lined paths toward the grand canal south of the summer palace, as Nalisse commented tartly on *her* part of the city, *her* part of the palace, and *her* friends, until Lyren finally said, "And yet you had your wedding in the palace, with the court there."

"Not all the court," Nalisse said. "Some had genuine conflicts. Others specious ones. Then there were some who came solely so the king would see them… Ah-ye, you ought to know that I dislike most of Colend's court. The king meant well in offering to host our wedding, and Thad agreed because he thought it honored us, but I would rather have held it at my guild center, which has the prettiest covered garden with ancient latticework overhead, and wisteria growing all along it."

"If it's blooming now, that would be gorgeous," Lyren said.

"And so it is, which is why I'd chosen this time of year. But the king wanted to remind the court that during the war, there were no commons or nobles. We were all effectively hostages in our own kingdom. Our wedding was a part of the many celebrations we've had this year, the ten-year anniversary of the war's end. That's the stated reason."

"And the message to the court thus goes unspoken?"

"That's it. Me, I don't think it's enough, but, ah, I'm merely a pastry chef, so what do I know? Or so would say those who need the message most." Nalisse brushed her sandal over the shadow of an archway, and Lyren recollected that treading on another's shadow was a serious breach of manners in Colend.

Nalisse flicked a look Lyren's way. "You look surprised. I'm sure you held celebrations where you were. Everybody did. With reason!"

"We did, but it was subdued in Everon, because of the queen going missing the previous spring," Lyren said, hesitant to add that she really didn't understand this shadow business, though she'd heard a little. She was apprehensive that even a question might be rude.

"… manage to miss the message," Nalisse was going on. "But the king never forgets the barge and boaters, who were the first resistance. Those of us who know the city, know that the barge guild is the true wind under Alsais's wings —"

"Wind? Under wings?" Lyren repeated, but the Universal Language Spell only offered Sartoran translations word for word.

"Hour of the Bird," Nalisse said as they stepped through a fragrant bower, onto a brick path alongside a canal. "When the chirps, that is, the news, gets spread. You'll see."

When "chirps" got translated as "gossip," Lyren realized there was a message here, though Nalisse didn't quite seem to be getting directly to it. Then she forgot the matter when they crossed a pretty arched bridge, passed a flowering tree, and beheld a wide curve in the canal. All along the edge, workers were busy decorating banana-shaped houseboats with bunting and streamers. "Oh, do people live in those?" she exclaimed. "How fun would that be!"

"Only in summer," Nalisse said. "And in Alsais, only for the music festival. These sweetboats would be impossible to warm in winter, and damp besides, even if the canals didn't freeze." She grinned. "Visitors rent them, but everyone knows the little boats are for lovers."

"That's why they're called sweetboats?"

"Yes. Imagine drifting cozily along, listening to music. In the few days before the end of the festival it can go on all night."

Lyren clasped her hands, admiring the boats' graceful lines. The covered central section was squarish, with long windows, or round windows, or diamond-shaped windows. Some had shutters, others panes of glass, with curtains inside. "I want to peek inside one."

"Right now, the bargers and boaters and the inn guild are busy cleaning and setting them up. But you ought to come back in two days, three, and the owners'll show you over them, especially if they think you've money."

As she spoke, Lyren glanced into the open windows of a sweetboat, glimpsing a bed built into one end, and at the other a tiny table with cupboards around it. It was like looking into a doll house. "How charming!"

"If you like boating, you'll enjoy the barge parties," Nalisse said. "The king brought back the fashion after the war, when everything was so very costly and no one had a tinket extra. It kept this guild alive."

All this insistent praise of the king might have had the opposite effect from what Nalisse intended, except that Lyren could hear a thread of intent beneath it that was less smug than guarded. Having something to do with the king? No, with Thad?

Lyren internally shrugged, and let Nalisse's chatter flow over her as they crossed back over another delightful arched bridge, and then mixed into cheerful foot traffic before a row of intriguing shops. Then the smell of spiced food drew them both.

They bought flamed corn on sticks from street vendors, crispy fish slices grilled with wine and herbs, and followed it with dainty little persimmon tartlets, which were like silky-smooth starbursts of cinnamon and mango with a hint of pepper that complemented the persimmon. Lyren never would have tried them, as she did not care for persimmon ordinarily, but Nalisse recommended these. "Mine are good, but hers are perfect," she said.

She was right. They bought a basket, and ate these while sitting in a long, narrow craft expertly poled by a girl who offered poetry or stories for an extra charge.

"When the festival comes out, these boats will be filled with musicians," Nalisse said. "You'll see."

"All of them?"

"Most."

"Doesn't that turn into a cacophony?"

"No, because the best change their songs and harmonize with passing musicians. No one knows where and when a judge might pass by. They don't simply judge the pieces, but performance as well, and that means making an effort to create harmony, not drown everyone out."

The sun was dropping westward when Nalisse brought them full circle to the palace again. "Remember, *Lily Path Before Summer Palace*, and you'll always know where you are," Nalisse was saying when Thad arrived from an adjacent path, long sleeves swaying.

All three stopped short. Nalisse's chin came up slightly, and Thad's head dropped, a singularly foolish smile aimed down at his toes, his cheeks a dull red that clashed terribly with his hair. Then he made the peace with a full bow to Lyren. As if they'd just met, instead of having shared breakfast that morning. She bowed back, puzzled.

Thad blushed again, but addressed Nalisse. "Our boat is waiting over at Pecan Petals."

"Then we should not keep it waiting." Nalisse turned to Lyren, gave her a quick, hard hug, and started off before Lyren could say anything.

Thad followed, then glanced back to say, "I hope Alsais pleases you, Lyren," in an oddly apologetic tone. Without waiting for an answer, he made the peace once more and hurried after his bride.

Lyren wondered what all that was about. She was not quite certain what had happened there with Nalisse and Thad, but instinct insisted that if there had been some conflict, or question, between the two, it had resolved itself. They had only been married a day, but it was clear that they had been in one another's lives for a long time, building mutual trust.

Attraction. Meeting of minds. Trust. All three so important.

On the adjacent pathways, palace staff began lighting the hanging lamps. The golden glow strengthened as the hues of sunset faded into shadowy shapes. It was so adroitly done, so lovely, that Lyren's eyes stung. Tears, at a pretty scene? She definitely needed sleep.

She fought yawn after yawn as she walked, snuffing in the fragrances of the flowers that only opened at twilight. Everything in Colend so far had taken her by surprise.

She reached her suite to find something waiting on the little table inside the door. This tiny area was too small to be a vestibule. She had assumed that the plate-sized table with its lyre legs had been mere decoration, but now she saw the purpose: for correspondence.

She stared down at her first Colendi invitation, cleverly folded into a lily. She unfolded it, to find a beautifully scripted request for the honor of her presence at a musical gathering the next day. Signed by Hradzy Wendis, Atan's ambassador to Sartor.

She lit a lamp and wandered into the bedroom. The windows were still wide open to the lovely scents. She flopped onto the bed, staring out into the shadowy garden, the trees silhouetted against the golden light from the charming lamps along the far pathway. She lay still, a soft breeze drifting in from the open windows; she was aware of floating in that delicate and delicious state between awareness and dream. When would she see Shontande Lirendi again?

And there it was, wakefulness again.

She sighed, shut her eyes, and reached for Liere ... who was instantly present, as if she'd merely been in the next room: *Lyren?*

: Liere? I hope you weren't asleep. It must be horribly early in Marloven Hess.

: I am in Perideth, and it is early, but I was very nearly awake. I can let myself lie here to rest a bit more if you need me.

Lyren had to concentrate, but she had gotten better over the past year at isolating a memory to share. It still took effort — unlike Liere's sharing. But then Liere had always been good at cutting her thoughts from her physical self. Too good, Liere had cautioned her daughter many times. It was not always beneficial to ignore one's physical self.

But Liere's unspoken assurance buoyed Lyren as she shared with Liere what she was beginning to think of as The Dance, then: *I already know I don't want a night of fun and then I'm away. It feels too much like, like cutting the roots of a growing thing. Sense?*

: Sense to you means it's sense, came the reassuring soothe.

: And so, it seems to me that in addition to that fire — oh, how it burns, I cannot sleep! — there has to be the meeting of minds, which I keep feeling we already have. As if we know each other. We've known each other. But didn't know we were looking until there he was. And finally trust. These three?

: These three are very important between all living creatures. But there is a fourth you will need, if you are to pursue this relationship. At least, so I believe.

: You're going to remind me that he is a king, and a lot of people already want his attention for personal as well as state reasons. I know that. I saw it. And yet Nalisse, now married to his friend Thad, seemed to be hinting at something else. And Lyren shared that conversation.

Liere absorbed that, and at the end came her calm thought: *Being a king means he doesn't get a private life in the way others get one. Private is public for monarchs — it's a part of the workings of monarchy. Everyone speculates about a king's most intimate moments the way they might talk about a sibling, a cousin, or a friend down the street, not simply out of curiosity, but because these things can matter to everyone's life.*

Lyren stirred, her tired, heavy body curling up, arms folded tightly across her chest: *How I hate that.*

: He might hate it, too, but he's caught fast, unless he runs away altogether. You know this. You left Everon for a similar reason.

Laban. Lyren was aware again that the thought of him had ceased to bring up anything but fond memory. Distance really did wither simple lust over time. But would moving to other worlds wither this new ... whatever it was?

Instinct whispered, No.

And silver fire ran through her veins at the rightness of it.

Lyren obediently thought back over her most recent experiences in Everon, and suddenly her perceptive landscape shifted completely, as if she'd been looking through a keyhole into a bedchamber, but found herself gazing out a tower window over the city and the land below.

: The court. The kingdom. If I am to go about this in the best way, she thought slowly, forming and considering each word, *I must not only court a king, but a kingdom.*

: Court. Serve. Protect. Love. Support his vision, if you agree with it. I urge you to seek counsel from others you trust, if you are still troubled. I come up against my own limitations every day! I am here in Perideth, trying to ignite that idea within someone who has been hemmed and boxed and stepped on as his roots tried to find the light. And I'm very much afraid I am failing. But in the hours remaining to me, I feel I must keep trying.

: Who ought I to go to? Clair doesn't have a court. Atan is ... Atan, shaped by Sartoran tradition —

: Erenlara of the Venn, came Liere's thought: *Clair has come to trust her, young as she is. The Venn are equally traditional, and their ritual is far more complex. And yet Erenlara, following what her innovative brother began, has brilliantly both united her court, and spread its power downward, one individual at a time, without most being aware of her intent. It sounds to me, from what Nalisse said, that Shontande Lirendi is attempting something similar, in revitalizing a somewhat reactionary court. And has been meeting resistance.*

Yes. Thank you: Lyren's love and gratitude caused a surge right back to bathe her spirit. And Liere did have another little gift to give: Lyren slid down into sleep.

9

Lyren woke refreshed and brimming with vitality long
before dawn the next morning.

Her first task was to calculate the time difference. Ah!
Bereth Ferian was already at midmorning. And there it was
winter. Lyren used one of her hoard of transfer tokens. She had
to learn transfers, she promised herself yet again. If only it
didn't hurt so much! She could not bear the idea of practice.

When she recovered, she hurried to her favorite dressmaker—who was finishing an order for Midyear celebrations,
Midsummer in the south. "Lyren," she exclaimed. "It's been a
long time!"

"I had these robes made in Sartor. I thought them so very
fine, until I went to Colend. I know so little about sewing! Did
you know they get that flattering drape by turning fabric slantwise?"

The dressmaker laughed. "Of course! This elegant drape
you like so much has been around for centuries. And as you
noted, it is achieved by cutting on the diagonal, which is very
wasteful of the weavers' hard work. They hate it. In some lands,
they even got it outlawed, as there is little to be done with the
oddly-shaped scraps. You only find it in fashions for the
wealthy, and that not everywhere. But the Colendi get around
the waste by favoring layers of thin fabric, the thinner the
better, which bears uneven hemlines."

"I saw that!"

"These Colendi layers and panels and pleats are very costly
because the stitchwork is so fine, before you even get to the

embroidery. With gauze, you cannot make a mistake. Whereas heavier fabrics are more forgiving. Except silk."

"I see. That's fascinating!" Lyren meant what she said, and it showed. Though she'd always been too impatient to learn to sew, she appreciated skill as much as she did art.

The dressmaker said, "Now that you have been enlightened, what can I do for you?"

Lyren had learned that when you wanted instant and smiling service, you paid double. As long as Arthur said her budget was bottomless, she was happy to pay double, though she was aware now that she'd reached adulthood, one of these days Arthur was likely to declare an end to it. He was already more than generous.

With that in mind, Lyren said, "Can you remake these Sartoran robes to at least get rid of the buttons?"

The dressmaker took the robes, hmmmed over the design and stitchwork, then said, "I can. Removing buttons will change the hang, but for the better, as I can take away these inner plaquets that were needed to support the buttons, and... Give me a few days, though."

"I have until Midsummer."

"Midyear," the dressmaker translated, for it was winter in the north. "That will do."

"I'll leave these. But do you have anything ready-made that I can wear to an ambassadorial party this evening?"

"Traveling in high circles, are you? We always knew you would be," the dressmaker replied. "I don't. I've been mostly making orders for Midwinter. But I know who does..."

Lyren's expedition required a thumping sum and two extra transfers, the effects of which made her head pang when she arrived back in Alsais's summer heat, but she returned with three new outfits with interchangeable layers. The one she liked best was a delightful pale yellow robe with floating sleeves and panels, over a thin cotton-silk underrobe. And everything draped on the bias, which made the most of her figure.

She took another cool bath to rid herself of the last of the transfer reaction, and bound her hair up in pale yellow ribbon with silk buds fitted around it.

When she was ready, she used the summons rope. A page turned up very quickly, and not only had directions to the Sartoran ambassador's quarters, but offered to have someone light her path if she wished.

Lyren cheerily turned that offer down, saying she wanted to learn the way on her own, and set out along the enchanting paths until she reached a house among a cluster at the west end of the palace area. It glowed with lanterns out front and along the short walk to the entryway. She noted a table just inside the door, this one with a huge, gorgeous blue bowl. The ambassador got a lot of invitations, did he? Lyren wondered if the Adrani ambassador would be there. And how she ought to act if so.

She'd paused for a moment, which gave Hradzy Wendis a moment to recognize her. He had not seen Lyren since she was a bright, charming if slightly alarming teenager who had required everyone to call her Lyren-Sartora. Atan had explained in a private note the previous morning that the "Sartora" had been quietly moved back to the place of a family name.

Hradzy knew that the most dramatic changes in people tended to occur during those years when fledglings grew their adult feathers and began to fly, but he was not prepared for the adult Lyren, arriving alone out of the soft summer night. She was all shades of yellow and gold, except for the waves of dark hair rippling down her back from a simple headdress of silk buds. No gems whatsoever, and yet there was a sense of shimmer about her as she floated inside, her entrancing mouth smiling with those deep dimples at either side, her dark-fringed golden eyes glittering with the reflections of his candelabra.

"Welcome," he said, meeting her at the door with hands outstretched—knowing that the courtiers inside would note this welcome and adjust their expectations. He lowered his voice, "Atan requested I look out for you, and may I add, never before have I been more elated to say that to hear is to obey?"

Lyren's smile deepened to laughter that didn't quite bubble over. She was certainly no child anymore; the years between them dissipated like smoke as he gestured an invitation inside. He was very ready to flirt, except there was no heat in her friendly golden gaze. No speculation.

Lyren was glad to see that he had not changed. If anything, he looked as if he had somehow done the Child Spell, though she knew that in light magic that was impossible once puberty had set in. It had to be his round face and high forehead, subtly emphasized by his short, curly light brown hair. He was short for a man, barely taller than she, and slight, his voice a pleasing tenor as he said, "I did so want to see Thad Keperi married. We got to know one another while he was Colend's ambassador to

Sartor. But the king and queen were present, and I'd already promised to attend the birthday celebration for the dowager Duchas of Desentis out at Sentis. Have you met any of the Desentises? Such agreeable people."

"Not yet. Sentis?" Lyren asked. "Or Desentis? Which is it?"

"Both. Ah, there is a vexed history there, and I will tell you briefly so that you will not be confused. Their holding is still officially Sentis, and the family name is Desentis—a blurring of Dei-Sentis from a marriage long ago."

"Let me guess, the Deis again," Lyren observed as they crossed a beautifully tiled floor in shades of blue and silver. "Meddling in local history, as they do."

"Just so." Mirth crinkled Hradzy's eyes. "The traditionalists of course do not want the horror of changing their age-old maps—which incidentally have changed twice in the past twenty years, but no one seems to regard the return of Eth Endra and Endralath to Colend as change. Everyone else likes the euphony of Desentis of Desentis. The dowager will be polite whatever you call her, and the present duchas, Nashande, will solve it all by insisting you call him Nash. But the family prefers to be known as Desentis of Desentis."

"And the king?"

"I am no confidante of his, of course, so my surmise is merely that, but I expect he will choose a middle course, which is to wait until his cousin marries, and regularize things on the marriage treaty."

"Marriage treaties being when family names are most often changed," Lyren guessed.

"Precisely. And here is the man himself! My dear duchas," Hradzy said with an airy bow and a wide, graceful gestures that fluttered his lavender sleeves embroidered with dragonflies and poppy blossoms. "May I present Honor Lyren Sartora, representative from Marloven Hess?"

Lyren found herself face to chest with an exceedingly handsome man made in the heroic mold. Not as tall or as broad as Rel, but nearly, with a fine cleft chin, a mobile mouth, and a pair of eyes with faint laughter-lines in the corners, burned there from riding in the sun. "Call me Nash," he said. His voice was appropriately deep for that splendid chest. "And welcome! Here, have you met…"

Nash and Ambassador Wendis between them introduced Lyren to the round of guests—which, to her relief, did not include the Enaeran-Adrani ambassador—before the chime of soft singsong voices carried in from the open doors, and the circle gave way for Shontande Lirendi.

Everything Liere had said was illustrated as the guests rearranged themselves around the king, including the comet tail of courtiers who appeared behind him. King-watching, Lyren translated to herself as Talian of Ariath gracefully made the peace in a swaying of floating pearl-white silk embroidered with lotus buds and hummingbirds on the wing. Lyren looked at her with interest; she was the one who had invited Lyren in the smoothest way to return to Marloven Hess. But if Talian was surprised or disappointed to see Lyren still there, she gave no sign of it.

"And last comes Alarcansa," a familiar voice spoke next to Lyren.

She turned her head. "Sveneric! I thought you left. No, you said you are here for the music festival?"

"I am. Hradzy invited me tonight."

"You seem to know everyone."

Sveneric laughed. "It's actually he who does. We met when Atan was sending him as unofficial envoy to Detlev's house, right after the war. As for the Duchas of Alarcansa, I only know him by sight. He's hard to miss."

Lyren glanced at the newcomer, who paused in the doorway to survey the room through his one eye, the other covered by an eyepatch. Above and below that eyepatch extended a white scar.

"Alarcansa?" Lyren repeated. This man certainly had an air. He alone dressed in dark colors, matching that eyepatch which he did nothing to hide. His dark hair was braided with tiny diamonds, which flashed when he turned his head. In her two days in Alsais, Lyren had glimpsed both at Thad and Nalisse's wedding and here and there about town some disabled people going about their business. A very common sight in Marloven Hess. Here in Colend, a walking stick was carved and decorated with tassels; there a loose sleeve billowed, obscuring the fact that no arm hung within.

"Mathias-Caid Lassiter, Duchas of Alarcansa. He joined the defense of Colend very late in the war," Sveneric said. "His relations kept him locked up until then. He was one of the fiercest defenders when Norsunder was destroying all they could on their way out. Siamis did his best to patch him up, or he might not have made it at all."

This duchas paused there in the doorway, his head turning as he took in the gathering, then he sauntered in the direction of the king to make the peace, the long silken tassels on his knee-length sleeves his only ornament other than the diamonds in his hair and the patterns of vines and long-tailed swallows woven into the midnight blue silk of his over-robe.

Lyren said, "When does the concert start? Most of us are standing, or did more people show up than invited? How do the Colendi handle that?"

"I don't know how many were invited, but this is a musical gathering, not a concert."

"There's a difference?"

"The first is informal. The second isn't. At a gathering, guests entertain one another. A concert is given to hear a performance. But the point of gatherings is actually dancing, I'm told. All very informal, which is something the king has been emphasizing of late."

Ambassador Hradzy strolled out into the center of the room, a wind instrument with a sharp curve in it in one hand. Gradually the talk ceased.

"The company is present. Shall we commence? Honors Khanerenth. Dazci. Would you oblige me by covering my lack of talent with your expertise? I have several instruments over here."

Silent servants in Sartoran livery were just then laying stringed and wind instruments on a side table. Two nobles joined Hradzy in a melody with a decided dance rhythm. A few people had brought instruments of their own, and joined in. A couple of others went to the table, one to pick up percussive beads in gourds, and the other taking up a round-bodied instrument with a bow and three strings.

At first people listened, but gradually they resumed soft conversations, and, when one piece ended and another began, a pair of eager girls of seventeen or so made their way to the center of the room and began to dance together.

The Sartoran servants in livery opened two side doors onto a terrace lined with potted trees — and two joined, then three, then four, pairing off and rejoining in complicated steps. The king was one of those sitting out; as Nash left his royal cousin, Talian Ariath slid into his place as if she had been waiting just for that.

Ah, Lyren thought. Attraction or ambition? Both? Expectation, certainly.

Nash crossed the room to Lyren. "Do you know our dances? I can show you."

"I do, but—please forgive an ignorant question—don't you have to go to those with the highest rank first?"

"Only at formal affairs," Nash said. "When it's spontaneous like this, those rules fly to the trees."

Thoroughly expected spontaneity, heh. Lyren held out her hand, and they found their way into a circle being made up. The floor was soon crowded, but surprisingly, no one elbowed her in the side, or bumped into her back. No, not surprising. There was a pattern here.

At the end of the piece, Lyren fanned herself, miming a drink. Nash bowed, smiled, and reached for another partner as a new musician added himself. A mellow wind instrument brightened the music.

Lyren drank some chilled water, and then drifted along the wall until she reached a grouping of ferny plants. She halted behind some fronds to survey. Her gaze snapped first to Shontande Lirendi, who was of course surrounded. He tapped a knee in counterpoint to the dance's rhythm, and when that dance ended, Talian leaned toward Shontande—a heartbeat late. He'd risen, fingertips together as he threaded his way toward the instrument table, where he picked up a hand drum.

Nash had been watching. He went to Talian, but he was a heartbeat too late as well, for she took the hand of a woman with long pale blond ringlets. They moved out to the center of the floor as another dance began, and the two clapped twice, then began a flurry of steps, flourishes added to an already complicated dance. The room was crowded, but the dancers deftly maneuvered around one another as they performed the intricate steps.

"For someone who likes to be decorative, you are very effective at making yourself invisible," Sveneric murmured, coming up beside her.

Having been part of a circle with him since puppyhood, Lyren did not have to assume polite manners. "I just pick a place between the focuses of attention."

Sveneric said, "Which are?"

"The king. Of course. Talian Ariath. Who's watching him. Nash, who watches her. Alarcansa, who watches them all. And, with less … intent, the dowager duchas and that other elderly person on the other side of the room."

"You're watching instead of dancing because?" he prompted.

"Because the hive is buzzing, not humming." She flicked a quick look his way. "Know what I mean?"

"I've been learning about bee language ever since one of the dyranarya students, who comes from beekeepers, taught Adam how to set up an apiary. We all had to learn how to live with bees because the garden is now alive with them. So I know what you mean. You sense the undercurrents. And?"

"And … something Liere said. But it sounds too arrogant put into words."

"When has that stopped you? Or me," he added with a soft laugh.

No, she was not going to say that she had to court a kingdom, not just a king. Because she was not yet sure she would. Or that she could.

Another dance began, but they were down to four players, as one and another of the wind instruments was laid down so its player could dance or get something to drink. Then a trio of elders picked up instruments, and worked their way into the current song.

The company danced on, talking, laughing, flirting. Fans twirled and flickered, spread and snapped, counterpoint to the fluid voices.

Sveneric waited.

Lyren said presently, "Though trailing ribbons might brush against others, no one bumps, or trips, or jolts. They're so aware of who gets the right of way, and who must defer."

He accepted the deflection. "They're raised to it."

"I'm beginning to see another pattern. I think. It's why there's a buzz, not a hum."

As she spoke, Shontande Lirendi passed the hand drum to someone, and engaged Hradzy in conversation. They laughed, and Shontande turned to the next person.

"Why are you here?" Lyren asked Sveneric. "Arcane orders from the Lord of All?"

Sveneric snorted. "I've been coming here for several years now, to see the music festival. No orders, arcane or otherwise. I suspect were I to even try to interfere, I'd find myself booted right out again. Nicely, of course. And I don't want to miss it."

"I didn't know you were that immersed in music." Lyren turned to study him.

"I'm not. That is, I am. I think, after my early years spent in the arid noise of Norsunder, I will never get enough music. But I'm most interested in proving or disproving my theory."

"Which is?"

"That this music festival—here, in Colend, where life is a constant negotiation with art—is the cauldron of our human society."

Lyren was going to point out that there were surely plenty of places that had their own music. That was too simplistic. Sveneric's reasons for anything were rarely simplistic. He saw the unspoken question and said, "It's not just the music, but the listeners, everyone talking and sharing ideas, and taking the new ideas, and melodies, and books, and arts, back home again, which in turn spread."

"This music festival used to be in Sartor. Wasn't that the cauldron of tradition? We were certainly taught that."

"Tradition, yes. But I didn't say that. I was of course never there, but as far as I can tell from the records, though people came from all over the continent and some from Toar and Drael, everything was aimed at being as Sartoran as possible. Detlev agreed with that much, though he said he spent very little time in Sartor during its years of hosting the music festival."

"And he was too busy being nefarious to keep a journal," Lyren commented, brows aslant.

Sveneric knew she was teasing, but he spared a moment yet again to regret that Detlev saw no reason to leave behind any of his inner thoughts. Or really much of anything—the house belonged to whoever lived there. Curtas's House the same. Though Siamis, Sveneric had discovered, felt much the same as Sveneric did.

That regret remained unspoken, as usual. He said, "In Colend, there is more of a sense of evolution than tradition. Mmm. I'm getting thirsty." He moved away, having noticed before she did that Shontande Lirendi was working his way from person to person toward the door—and Lyren was halfway there. Sveneric liked Lyren the more for having not noticed as quickly as he had. Though he'd sensed her effort to keep her eyes from straying kingward.

Sveneric downed some of the citrus punch, thanked Hradzy, and slipped out. Lyren stilled, debating within herself.

Ought she to stay where she was, or … do what? Every nerve was alive; you don't court a king, you court a kingdom, she reminded herself.

And then here was Nash again, utterly unaware of any of these things. His honest gaze was unselfconscious and appealing as he said, "Ready to dance again?"

Smothering a sharp stab of disappointment, Lyren smiled. "I am."

She gave herself up to the dance, as behind her, Shontande moved along the row of people, thanked his host, and vanished out the door.

The dancers joined into foursomes, turned, changed partners, and changed back, which brought Lyren and Nash together. He said, "Do you like boating?"

"I do."

"I'm putting together a boating party for the festival opening," he said. "Shon will be there, and he always brings Jilo of the Chwahir. Seshe'll come, too. I think you know them both? A couple of other friends as well. It will be merry."

"I'd be honored," Lyren said.

By the end of the dance, the atmosphere had changed. In the center now, three circles: Talian Ariath, Hradzy, and Nash and his friends. Lyren danced continuously after that, as she slowly began to perceive the hidden pattern, the one that kept the atmosphere a buzz, and not a hum: by now she was gaining a sense of hierarchy. Before the king left, those of the upper ranks, particularly around the little blonde count, chose partners below their rank, but managed to keep themselves from being chosen back. And after the king left, they smilingly, deftly, stuck to their own kind.

Lyren danced with everyone she found alone and looking for a partner as she considered this pattern. Now that she'd recognized it, she remembered most of her partners having been among Thad's and Nalisse's friends at the wedding eve ball.

Later, as she walked back to the guestroom in the still, warm night air, she saw at last the unspoken … oh, call it a rope-tug going on: the king, with his current favoring of less formal gatherings, mixing all the ranks, and certain among the court—led by the Count of Ariath—wanting the perquisites of rank preserved.

A buzz, not a hum.

10

A volatile weather front sweeping down from the
northwest over the Sartoran continent did little to
alleviate summer's heat, though the air cleared. During
those four days, the King of Perideth succumbed at last, dying
before dawn's light; in Shiovhan on the other side of the
mountains, in what used to be the capital of Enaeran and now
was becoming the new capital of Enaeran-Adrani, little Prince
Yossi experienced his first real pain while teething. That pain
echoed to his mother.

And in Colend, on the fourth morning, the night of thunder
and lightning and pouring rain refreshed crops and gardens
alike, which freed the army of pages from having to go around
at dawn and dusk with buckets and dippers to revive parched
flowers. The crowded city — with more straggling in on river
boats and along the fine paved roads — found Alsais washed
clean and looking its best.

There were no more invitations. Lyren had decided to use
the intervening time to wander Alsais, sample more delicious
street food, and listen to people. When she had a better sense of
the language, maybe attend a play. She still sensed where
Shontande Lirendi was, and wondered if he sensed her. She
would find out, but not yet. Not until she had a better grasp of
this art-filled, artful, entrancing and elusive setting that had
shaped him, and from which he could not escape.

Because she was young, winsome, and very ready to fall
into conversation, she met a lot of different people, from a
young street vendor caroling her delicately candied haws to an

elderly boater renting three sweetboats. The sun-browned wo-man explained that she and several friends in her guild had bought and rebuilt and decorated the flatboats themselves, in order to earn some extra, their goal to retire to a pretty house there in the city center instead of having to live in the guild dorms. Lyren spoke to a joiner who had a lot of interesting things to say about how buildings were put together so that int-ernal rooms could be changed; the best buildings, he said, had not a single nail in them, except to fit in decorative moldings.

She also counted at least ten different languages or dialects among the visitors crowding in. This close to the start of the festival, most of the inns were full, and had posted signs that only attic bedrolls were available, dormitory-style. But many had gotten creative, camping on or under wagons, parked behind stable yards (also expensive, and locals patrolled regularly to see that no refuse was piled up), and also camping with far more space outside the city. The boaters were busy plying visitors back and forth along the crowded canals; on the third night, Lyren sat at a tiny table outside a restaurant, eating a delicious dinner of wine-braised fish, spiced rice, and a tiny spray of grapes, as she watched the canal traffic. Every type of flatboat imaginable wound its way along, most decorated with bunting, lanterns, garlands, and boughs. The polers and rowers seemed to know when to defer and when to move ahead. There were blue-painted boats of husky barge people and herald guards, with little bells at the front and back of their boats. These regulated traffic, and righted stranded visitors who'd thought it would be easy to navigate the pretty boats.

On opening day of the festival, Lyren put on her yellow butterfly outfit again. In some courts, wearing exactly the same outfit marked one as risible, but she had learned to shrug that off during her teen days in Sartor. The people who mattered to her did not care if they had seen a lovely outfit before; in fact, Atan had commented New Year's Week when Lyren was seventeen that she looked forward to seeing a purple and silver velvet gown that Lyren had worn often. She was interested to find out how wearing the same outfit would be regarded in Colend.

The light slanted golden and mellow through a few wisps of clouds as Lyren made her way to the Canal of the Lilies. Voices echoed over the water as people gathered on either side of the canal as well as on the water. The fiery rim of the sun topped the distant rooftops, ruddy light flooding a natural outside stage, with a sloping lawn on one side, and a terrace on the other. It was shaped around a loop in the canal, with a raised stage at the midpoint. A half-circle wall baffled sound. People gathered on the grass, their brightly colored blankets creating squares of conviviality, picnic baskets of every kind holding down corners. For those who had forgotten to bring food and drink, brightly dressed vendors walked back and forth, crying their wares in singsong.

A line of barges of every type floated alongside the canal. Lyren scanned these, then turned back to the enormous one with the blue and silver banner. And there was Nash, standing with one foot propped on the rail. Little strings of glowglobes gleamed above his head, like frosty stars. "Lyren!"

The barge was fashioned to look like a swan, with swept-back wings extending a little ways out from the rail, and a high, gracefully arched prow. From what Lyren could see, Nash's definition of "a couple of friends" was extraordinarily generous—either that or, equally likely, people had invited themselves, and he was the type to never turn anyone away.

The barge sported a blue canopy at its middle. Beneath it, shaded from the sun, servants tended sumptuous refreshments, with liveried servants standing by. A quintet of musicians had crowded in among them, sitting hip to hip. Two of them played on a tiranthe and a flute as Nash's company chattered over the soft, soothing melody.

Nash smiled in welcome at Lyren as she trod up the ramp. "Delighted to see you! Find a seat anywhere!"

Lyren looked around. No doubt Nash meant to be informal, but that simply meant there was no designated throne-substitute. The back of the barge had fewer people besides the polers. At a guess, people of lower rank? Lyren saw no jewels glittering, and few silks. Unlike those at the front of the barge. Shontande Lirendi sat on the bench behind the prow, surrounded by richly clad courtiers talking and laughing, fans shimmering. Lyren's heart caught when Shontande smiled as he made the peace in welcome; she comprehended in his manner that he was staying in the background, so that his cousin could be host. There was of course nowhere to sit by him. Then she spotted Seshe and Jilo seated by Bee Keperi. Seshe beckoned, pointing to the bench beside her. Lyren sat down as they greeted one another.

A new arrival elicited a glad, "Caid!" from Nash.

The Duchas of Alarcansa sauntered up the ramp, last as usual. His single eye, dark as the eyepatch, swept over her to rest on those gathered at the prow as Seshe held out a cup to Lyren. "Wine?" she asked. She had glasses and a carafe on a little tray, so Lyren accepted some. It was a white wine, cold, and tasted like sunbursts on her tongue.

"Enjoying your stay?" Jilo asked.

"Very much," she said. "But I have some questions about this festival. Bee, might you know?"

Bee said, "You've come to the right source. Ask away."

"Are you part of the organizers, then?"

"I'm the palace liaison between the king and the organizing committee, which oversees the judges' matters, guild relations, and contestants, among other things."

"Do the contestants come out on a stage one at a time over days and days?"

"Some will, having made arrangements with theaters, or with guilds who have outside stages. Others wander. For the next couple of weeks musicians of every sort, singly, in pairs, and in groups, with singers and without, will perform all over the city."

"Here?"

"Here, and in parks, and on barges, and in coffee houses and the two best pleasure houses — both have theaters — and in the four guildhalls and wherever else people can fit in to play, and to listen."

"Then anyone can hear them! That's splendid."

"Anyone who wishes. You'll get some of the best musicians in the world performing on street corners."

"Who pays them?"

"They don't get paid. But they don't pay, either. If they can get here, we provide temporary housing and meal vouchers. That's why the organizing committee is quite large."

"So the crown actually supports the cost of the festival."

"Yes. Though it will get much of that back from the guilds, who will take in a river of gold from visitors. The entire city will be filled with music until the last week, when the wandering judges pick the finalists."

"Who are the judges?"

"Unknown," Jilo said. "Different ones each year. I got to do it once." The brief smile that lit his somber, unprepossessing face made it clear that the mighty King of the Chwahir had considered wandering for days all over summer-parched Alsais, painfully transferring back to Narad every night late, a rare honor.

"The official opening! It's starting!" someone called from the quay. "Let us sit!"

"Official opening?" Lyren asked Bee, and glanced at Shontande, at that moment talking to a pair of just-arrived courtiers. "Does not the king have to preside?"

"If he wants, but all the city knows that the festival begins with a performance from the previous year's winners. They've had all year to prepare something special. It's the equivalent of a master's master work."

Just then a sound like angels' laughter rolled across the water and up the breeze-stirred lawn. Lyren turned, staring entranced at the short, stout young woman standing alone on the stage, with a harpist behind her playing accompaniment. Her voice soared up the scales, lark-song ascending to the sky.

Silence fell over the barge, as both Lyren and Jilo shut their eyes. He listened with all his focus, for he wanted to remember how this singer captured life, and love, and laughter, within the gossamer frame of song.

For Lyren, the dazzle of joy altered subtly. The flesh knows, even when the spirit is exalted; she felt Shontande's gaze before she opened her eyes. He had moved quietly to one of the other benches because his back had been to the stage. Now he sat across from Lyren. She was aware of the sound of his breathing, of the reflected glow of light highlighting the silken sleeve that molded the muscular contours of his arm, which he had stretched along the rail as he gazed across the water at the singer.

Seshe observed him, and Lyren, and smiled inwardly, hoping that these two were going to find one another. Both so complicated, and Shontande, she had sensed for a couple of years at least, was lonely.

Jilo was unaware of any of them.

Even the tower bells had been silenced as, one by one, the world's finest musicians wrought history and glory and anguish and laughter, love and hatred, fear and faith, into sounds that lanced into souls and lit them from inside. What poet had said that music was the knife of light? He'd always thought it awkward, for music was sound, and light was a matter for eyes, and knives cut. But now he understood that it was not flesh being cut, but the mind's rind around emotions.

When the previous year's Silver Feather winners finished, all around them rose whispers, and rustlings, and fifty paces away the fretful wail of a tired child. Most of those on the lawns were city folk, with work awaiting them the next day, or even that night. The stage was now empty, but all along the canal, the other contestants began to perform.

"Cast off," Nash called.

And the barge polers moved them out into the water. The blue banner assured that all the other barges and boats would wait for them to move first, and in their wake a slow jockeying for place began, as the dark waters between the swan barge and the traffic jam slowly widened.

Jilo seemed to be enthralled by the liquid light reflecting in the barge's rippling wake, cast by the lanterns they passed by. Bee sat in silence, chin on his chest; Lyren wondered if that was the pose he adopted around court, or if he was always that reticent.

Talian Ariath was the first to rise, making for the spread of tantalizing foods. She piled a tiny dainty from two or three trays onto a small plate, as people moved around her. Behind that group, Shontande moved again, to the empty spot beside Bee as he leaned out and addressed Lyren, "I trust that discussing so illustrious a name as Sartora will excuse any impertinence, for it's certainly not meant."

Lyren grinned. "Go ahead. I'll answer if I can, though questions about it probably ought to go to Liere."

"Only this: you were introduced as Lyren Sartora, but I believe I've been told that her family name is Fer Eider?"

"Ah," Lyren said. "It is. But when I was born, she was trying to use Sartora as a family name, partly to sidestep the Girl Who Saved the World legend, and partly because she knew Norsunder was familiar with her name, and she did not want to draw any attention to her family if she could avoid it. There were other reasons, but those were the main ones. I could go by Fer Eider—I'm very proud of my relations—but habit is strong."

"Thank you," Shontande said, as Talian passed by, her satellites following. She hesitated a moment at the empty spot to Lyren's right, or maybe it was the movement of the barge, which was navigating ripples from a passing craft, then she sat down again beneath the prow.

"I always thought Liere Sartora sounded well," Seshe said. "Though Liere Fer Eider also has a nice ring to it."

"I like my name," Lyren said. "Though I did play around with it a bit in my teens. I suspect that happens more often than not in one's teens."

"Or even earlier," Bee murmured.

Lyren turned to him. "That's right! I don't remember your given name, but I know I was told. Though I was two at the time. And I loved Bee."

Bee's voice warmed. "It was probably inevitable, as my way of navigating rooms then was by humming or buzzing. My given name is Aural. But no one uses it, not even our mothers."

"Names," Jilo said, his eyes still closed as he tried to hang onto those exalting images. "I used to think the Mearsieans made their names sound all alike as a kind of audial disguise."

Seshe smiled, and patted his hand, but said nothing more about names as she offered wine all around. The barge floated around a sharp bend in the canal, and she glanced back at the other barges. The musicians on the three biggest managed, with surpassing skill, to play together, so the music blended and surrounded them. Past outreaching branches and greenery she glimpsed people on a terrace outside an inn as the merry strains of a vigorous melody drifted over the water.

Nash clapped his hands to mark the rhythm. "Ah-ye, now I'm for dancing!"

"Surely not here," another man exclaimed.

"A dance on a barge?" a young noble with long black curls and cobalt gems in his ears said, fan twirling idly. "I confess I know not whether it's daring or desperate, but this I feel is certain, those who weren't giddy before would share the experience with those who are."

Alarcansa drawled, "That is a threatening prospect."

Talian turned her shoulder, her fan snapping shut as she set her empty plate beside her, taking up a space where someone could sit. None of the returning courtiers dared move that plate as she observed, "Music is never a threat. It is a grace."

"Will you demonstrate?" Nash asked her, coming up to her other side, as her satellites deferred gracefully, like flowers following the sun in their soft, summer-colored silks and linens. He bowed and offered his hand.

"I spoke mere nothing," Talian replied, her fan open again, at an angle that looked as if she were about to ward him off. But then she coyly turned the gesture into a beckon as she said, "A general observation that, perhaps, is better left general, given the circumstances."

"Ah-ye, please tell me not that you are hinting at the heaviness of my feet."

Several of the female courtiers cried out in instant protest, their laughter singsong waterfalls.

Nash bowed again, reached for one of the trays filled by silent servants, and raised a cup. "Here's to you, Caid: threat it is."

The black-haired Caid Alarcansa saluted Nash Desentis back.

"Wit, Nash?" Talian asked, still smiling, but the lift to her chin and the angle of her head were a little too surprised. She tossed her fair hair back.

"Not if you have to ask," he retorted in his good-natured voice. There was no other sign in his face of a reaction, but Lyren sensed that he heard her words not as a joke but a jibe. She also sensed that Shontande Lirendi did not like his cousin being baited.

Talian saw it as well, for she was watching Shontande for a reaction instead of Nash. She rose and tapped Nash's wrist with her fan. "I know I ought not to tease you, but it's such old habit from when we were boy and girl. Next thing to brother and sister, so often we played in the garden while our parents did their duty as regents through those long, long hours."

Nash's smile flashed, guileless and warm. "Those were fun days, weren't they? Seem so very long ago."

The flock of pretty young courtiers who obviously admired him united in to praising his dancing and the barge party, as the musicians played on, unheard. Only Alarcansa turned away, apparently absorbed by a trio of wind instruments on a passing flatboat.

Talian then began a game of "Do you remember," first with Nash, but very soon she turned it toward Shontande, as the others among their inner circle responded eagerly.

Jilo closed his eyes, reaching for the syncopated music drifting from the nearby shore; Bee withdrew again, as Seshe watched dancers twirling on a lantern-lit balcony next to a long, low building. The swan barge was reaching the outer loop of the canal, with intervals of darkness broken only by the tiny lights on the barge, and the stars overhead.

Unnoticed by any, Bee frowned, head bent.

Jilo twisted around, half out of his seat as he strained to hear the last of the unusual rhythm. Lyren was just beginning to say, "I recognize that song from a dawnsinger festival—"

"Now," a musician snapped, and several things happened so rapidly that instinct was faster than thought.

A weirdly glowing vine or rope snaked out from under the canopy, snapping around Seshe, and dragged her off the bench to the deck of the barge. "Seshemerria Jevondyan, heir to Damondaen!"

His voice collided with Bee's, "Ruis! To the king!"

Seshe, struggling violently, recoiled as if she'd been slapped, her face blanched with horror.

"It's her, it *is* her," one musician cried in a strained voice.

Two husky servants in Nash's livery vaulted over the canopy, sending food crashing in all directions. One lunged at the musicians, and Ruisande's Altan upended a serving tray and held it before Shontande—just as Talian Ariath launched herself, arms wide, in front of Shontande, as if to block a weapon with her body.

She collided with Ruis, banging into the tray and dragging them both off-balance. Shontande shot to his feet to help. At that moment, the third musician, startled by Shontande's sudden move, threw a knife straight at Shontande's head.

And Lyren, whose sense of timing had been honed by years of dance, heard David's voice speaking out of the past, *All you have to do is block anything I throw at you and you're done*, and she whirled up and kicked the knife out of the air.

11

"Grab her and let's get out!" one of the false musicians ordered, pulling two knives from his sleeves.

Shontande had already ducked down to snatch up the tray as Ruis thrust Talian off him and launched to attack the musician who had shouted the order. "*Now,* Soraq!" the man added, and moved to block Ruis from reaching Seshe struggleing violently against the weird vine that everyone could see kept tightening.

Jilo muttered. Green fire glowed around his hands; the Colendi, who had regarded Jilo much as they'd regard a hapless street mutt that the king happened to favor — harmless but unprepossessing — scrambled out of the way of that terrifying green glow, as the second musician blocked Alarcansa, who had snatched up a couple of serving utensils and gripped them as weapons.

Barely a heartbeat passed between that *Now!* and the third musician slapping a token to Seshe's shoulder. She vanished just as Jilo's green fire froze him in a stone spell.

The one fighting Ruis looked over, grinned fiercely, and vanished, followed by the second one.

"No," Jilo whispered, staring at the deck where Seshe had lain. "No, no, no!"

Lyren sprang to his side. "Jilo, we'll get her back —"

Jilo didn't even see her. He transferred.

Shontande threw aside the beautifully engraved silver tray, which had bent, and said to Bee, "How did you know?"

"Their music," Bee said, his face moving back and forth,

his expression anguished. "I counted five musicians. Two were very good, but when the others joined in, they were ragged. I was trying to explain it to myself as seasickness, or drunkenness, or the conflict of the different rhythm from over there." He waved a hand toward the terrace that he could not see. "Then one forgot his mind-shield as he did some sort of magic."

The king then turned a severe look to the remaining musicians, who still sat on their bench, frozen in terror and bewilderment.

Nash, seeing his cousin's angry glare, said, "Blame me. I just hired the two, thinking of space, but those three turned up in similar robes. Said they'd never played for a king before, and they could spell my regulars, for free. So I told them if they could fit, they'd be welcome."

"And I did not think to question them, to my shame," Ruis added, head bowed. "I will resign at once—"

Shontande waved his hand in a negating circle. "Nothing like this has ever happened before." And, to Bee, who was even more bewildered, "They made away with Seshe."

"Ah-ye," Bee said. "I ought to have spoken at once."

But they both knew that Bee never spoke first before courtiers—and no one had expected trouble. There hadn't been any trouble like that in all the years since they'd recommenced holding the festival.

Shontande tried to reassure Bee as Lyren reached past him to offer Talian a hand up, to be ignored. The humiliated count picked herself up from the deck, drenched from the pool of wine and punch she and Ruisande Altan had landed in, but at least she and Ruis had both missed the shards of dishes that had shattered.

Caid Lassiter of Alarcansa, who had vaulted over to back up the guards, looked past Talian to Lyren. "Nice kick."

"I saw an instant later it wasn't needed, but." She shrugged. "Old training."

Caid said in his caustic drawl, "You'd think old training would keep stage performers from hammering down the defense."

Talian betrayed not by a flicker of an eyelash that she had heard. Her friends closed around her, praising her for her bravery and lamenting over her ruined gauze as Shontande said, "Are you all right, Talian? Ruis?"

Talian put her hands together with all the dignity she could summon.

"Yes, sire," Chief Altan said woodenly, not looking at the count, and moved off to take charge of the force he saw at once had been far too small; still dripping with spilled wine, he directed the polers to proceed to a certain spot, and got the other two disguised guards to station themselves on either side of the stone-spelled man, as the frightened courtiers all talked at once.

Lyren sat back down, trying to calm her juddering heart. She was not alone. The sophisticated, artful competitors had become a gaggle of startled men and women. Each seemed to have to give voice, asking one another who, and why, which of course no one could answer, even if they heard.

"What is Jilo going to do?" Lyren murmured.

"That's my question as well," Shontande said, his gaze resting on the frozen conspirator. "Let's get this one to the shore before that spell wears off."

One of Ruis's herald-guards was at that moment leaping to the shore from the barge. He took off through the trees to fetch reinforcements.

About the time Lyren tried to help Talian out of the mess, Jilo staggered into his study, still nauseated from the transfer. He picked up a wooden tray of reports from his desk and hurled it to smash against the wall. Papers flurried like frightened bats. Sobbing with rage, he picked up his chair and smashed it against the table, which teetered and slammed to the stone floor — the fine stone whose renovation Seshe had overseen.

"SHIT!" Jilo shouted.

Erol arrived at a run, trailing the aromas of the spiced rice and cabbage he'd been eating. "Jilo?"

"She's gone! Some soul-suckers disguised as musicians … they knew her name! Her real name! And she's gone!" With the words Jilo blasted Erol with the image of Seshe lying on the deck, the cling-vine, the musicians.

Erol got from that a general idea of what had happened. He said, "Gone where?"

"I don't know! Oh, it has to be Damondaen. They knew her name…" Jilo paused, eyes wild. "Opun. Where's my note-case…"

"Jilo, hold rein. You're not about to sic your entire army on

Damondaen, to rescue one person?"

Jilo whirled around, his face ravaged. "If you're about to give me all that Detlev shit about one life against the many, you can get out now. And never come back."

Erol's jaw worked, then he said in a low, steady voice, "Do you really think that one life doesn't matter to me? You know how I still miss Curtas. How we're all still bearing the cost of Noser's murder of Karhin Keperi."

Jilo uttered a sob of anguish, but at least he was listening.

"Whatever Detlev has done, or thought, is difficult, maybe impossible for the rest of us to understand. And he can speak for himself. If you *ask* him. But I can tell you that sending an army to invade another country in order to rescue one person *never* works. You'd be spending countless lives for a plan that *never works.*"

Jilo's breathing was still harsh. He wiped his hair back with shaking hands. "What does?"

"A couple of us going in-country is my first thought. Talk it out with better strategists than me. I'm purely tactical. As you know. Take the time to consider, because one thing for certain, those people didn't mount what has to have been a costly plan, taking months, maybe even years, to track her down and make that grab, in order to kill her. I'll bet you any amount of money you can name that, right now, they're cooing and petting her and knocking their foreheads against the ground in remorse for daring to touch her precious self, because they surely want her for something. Figurehead queen at an easy guess. If so, they won't touch a hair on her head."

Jilo snorted out a breath, his gaze shifting. "I get it," he muttered hoarsely, and uttered a wild, ragged laugh. "For the first time in my life, I see it, what makes a Wan-Edhe." He lifted his face, his gaze painful. "You know what I was thinking first? That I'd kill Kirech if he tried to stop me."

"But you didn't," Erol said.

"I didn't because he wasn't here." Jilo pressed his hands against his face, then flung them away. "One person really should not have this power. It's insane. *I'm* insane." He whirled and went to the wall, raising his fist.

"We're not going to solve the dilemma of human governance today. And Jilo, I have to add, breaking your hand on that stone might give you a heartbeat's ease, but the resulting pain won't negate the pain in your heart. And a double dose of pain doesn't help clear thought. You need to think clearly right now."

The tension in Jilo's arm did not ease, but his hand dropped. His fingers still shook.

Erol said. "Time might actually be on our side. Because if my guess is right, they are going to have to convince Seshe to act for them. And if so, you know as well as I how well that's going to go."

Jilo whirled back. "What if you're not right?"

"Then put me up against a wall," Erol retorted, arms wide. "I might even cut my own throat and save you the effort if I'm wrong and she's harmed. But I'm sure enough that I urge you to take a little time to put together an effective plan. First, I suggest going back to Colend so you're right there as soon as that stone spell lifts. Unless you put time over it?"

Jilo shook his head. "Would have taken too long. I was too slow as it was. *Damn* it." He began pacing around the walls, his gaze blank. "How would they discover her name? Did the Mearsieans let it slip? No. Only Clair knew. She'd never tell." He stopped, rage flaring again. "It has to have been someone among *us*. Who else even knows Seshe? Someone, a Chwahir! Sold her out." Again he covered his face, his fingers stiff with rage. "I want to find who it is and rip them apart myself."

Erol said, "It probably was a Chwahir, but equally probable, not deliberate. Our sailors have been in ports up and down the western seas as defenders for ten years, including along Toar's coast. Seshe's a figure of curiosity to the Chwahir, though she tries so hard to be invisible. It's more likely idle, innocent speculation."

"You really think Damondaen would snatch her to put her on a throne? She's been gone since she was twelve. And I remember Ferret telling us when those scouts from Damondaen first started turning up in foreign ports that the royal family was all dead by the end of the war. Ten years ago!"

Erol was trying to remember Ferret's report. Damondaen's secondary royal family — claiming the Jevondyan name — and the survivors of the royal guard had been fighting over the throne, but the guards won that battle, and invaded their neighboring countries. However, their hold on the kingdom was as stable as ocean sand with the tide coming in. Erol remembered David speculating that Damondaen was probably solving internal problems in the time-honored fashion, by sending their restless military somewhere else to make trouble. *I hope if they do, it's against Senrid. That'll be salutary,* he'd said. *Senrid will smash them. And he needs a win.*

Erol said to Jilo, "If the secondary family is trying to claim that they represent the long-established Jevondyan family, then having an actual member of the primary family in hand might help establish their claim."

Jilo flung away again. "Seshe would rather cut her own throat than do anything for them. She hates them, as much as someone like her can hate. Said they were all wicked."

Erol had been standing against the wall, arms crossed, thinking rapidly. Seshe had never said anything to him about her origins. "The more I think about it, the surer I am that grabbing her took some careful planning. If they heard about her from dockside gossip, they must have someone on hand who knew her back then. And they did their digging. You don't go to all that trouble and expense to make a snatch in another kingdom, on a royal heir who ran as a child, to bring them back for assassination. If they wanted her dead, they would have done it right there in Colend."

Jilo's fists tightened, but he gave a brief nod.

"They found out that you regularly visit Colend. Likely they also figured out that they wouldn't get past us here," Erol said. "It's not a secret that you've gone to that festival before."

"First day," Jilo muttered. "Every year, if I can get away. And it's Colend." He sighed. "Nash would have been talking to all his many friends about the barge. It was supposed to be five or six of us, and there must have been fifteen or sixteen on that thing, not counting Bee and the guards. And the spies, dressed as musicians."

Erol said, "Ask Shontande if I can be there for the interrogation."

Jilo looked up, his mouth tight with decision. "I still want to kill that soul-eater. I don't know how to do interrogation, and you do. I'll send you."

"And you?" Erol asked.

Jilo smiled bleakly. "Talk to a strategist, as you said. I'm going to go to Senrid."

At that moment, Senrid was sitting with Liere, alone. He was appalled when she transferred back to him not an hour earlier, as the main campsite was finishing the midday meal.

Liere used Senrid as a transfer focus. She looked around, her face greenish except for the mottled red from the heat, but it was her expression that caused Senrid to chuck his half-eaten sandwich and spring to her side. "Water?"

"Oh, please."

He poured some, brought moments ago by a runner from the nearby stream. "Bad?"

"It was ... stressful. But that's not what..." She sank down onto a cushion, and let the water she'd just chugged cool her from inside. "It's Yossi," she said. "He's been cutting teeth, I think. The pain was in his head, that much I could get, but what hurts was the day nanny shut his bedroom door and just let him scream."

Senrid pulled her against him. "Anything to be done?"

"I nearly broke my promise and contacted Macael. I don't want to do that for a number of reasons, until Yossi turns one, and Macael expects me to visit. I don't want him knowing how closely I watch over Yossi." She sighed, sagging against Senrid. "But today he figured out that the nanny was leaving him to cry."

"And? Where'd he stash the body?"

Liere huffed a little laugh. "She's washing dishes right now. Lots and lots of dishes, for that palace is huge. She's not a bad person, just lazy. She was fine as long as Yossi was cheerful and liked to play, but she hated his crying, and was starting to leave changing him for the night nanny, now that he's eating food, and diapers are more odorous." She looked up into Senrid's face. "Thank you for letting me talk about him. It hurts so much to know he's in pain and I could do nothing."

His grip tightened on her. "Talk away."

"I'm done. I'm always going to regret the situation, and second-guess all my decisions, always. I have to live with it. Malcolin and Lyren, at least, are doing well."

"What's new with Lyren?"

"It seems she has been given a royal token. Which enables her to go anywhere, and she will be given anything from any store."

Senrid grunted. "Have you explained to her that every stick of cinnamon or pair of embroidered socks she picks up will have to be paid for by the crown—and noted down for anyone to see?"

"She's already figured that out. She's inclined not to use it except for food because it would create a trail of her personal likes, dislikes, and so on."

"Not wrong," Senrid commented, rubbing her back.

Liere leaned into him, then sighed, and said, "Starliss and I got along fine, but she's being kept out of any decision-making. We talked a little about treaty-marriages, which is not unlike being a hostage. I told her a lot about last year. She said she found it helpful. Time will tell. You know I failed with Valta. I couldn't transfer earlier because I had that honor guard of his, and I needed to get my mare back. But once I rode over the border, I found Jan Senelac's riders waiting for me. I was able to turn her over to them. They ought to reach here tomorrow or so."

"First off, I don't think you failed as much as you believe."

"How so? He was invariably rude, alternately complaining and bragging whenever he talked to me."

"That honor guard, for one."

"I assumed that was merely to make sure I left Perideth."

"No, he would have sent scouts to watch from the rear. An honor guard shows respect, and respect is important to him."

"I saw that much."

"Also, he's *always* whiny and braggy. Always. The fact that he kept talking to you, unpleasant as it was, means that he was getting something from what you said. Time will tell how much. Meanwhile, the king's been dead how many days, and no declaration of war has come. So we'll continue as we have— ah, there they go."

Liere heaved herself up. Not that she was all that large yet. It was the heat, and tiredness. She and Senrid went to the front of his tent to look out. A tiny breeze had kicked up, under an unstained sky. Senrid smiled as his lancers formed up for evolutions, which included riding at one another at the gallop, tigging the lances, then passing by. Anyone who missed the tap of the "tig" got hooted at—as Perideth's warriors watched from a distance.

Liere could feel the intensity of their fascination. Here it is again, evidence of the human drive to glorify violence. We have stylized it, hedged it round with rules, and maybe one day can turn the impulse to games, but it's still here. A vivid image of Senrid galloping fast as he shot arrows at a target, and she smiled grimly: she'd be a hypocrite if she did not acknowledge that she adored exhibitions of his physical prowess.

"Huh." Senrid grunted, and slapped at the pocket of his summer uniform.

He pulled out his golden notecase, and whistled when he saw the note. "Jilo. In a sweat, back at Choreid Dhelerei. Want to be part of whatever this is?"

"Maybe I ought," she said.

Senrid opened his hand, then said, "Transfer back. Calm Jilo down, will you? I'll be there as soon as I give some orders; if we haven't heard anything by tomorrow, I think we can safely bring everyone back home. Except my spies," he added, with a sardonic look.

Liere accepted that, and transferred. A second transfer in a day felt exactly as nasty as expected, but at least she'd had a little rest between. As soon as she could walk without her stomach churning, she crossed to Senrid's study, where she found Jilo pacing back and forth, so agitated he was striding instead of shuffling in his usual slouch.

"There you are," he exclaimed. Little as he understood people, he had figured out in the months since Liere had come to live with Senrid that what you told one reached the other. He poured out his story, as Liere sat, more appalled by the moment.

"Seshe," she exclaimed, horrified. "Damondaen. I had no idea."

"No one did," Jilo said. "She never wanted anyone to know. Wanted that part of her life behind her. Forever."

Senrid charged in then; Liere had shared with him on the mental plane as Jilo spoke. "Got it," he said to Jilo, who nodded—as expected.

"Want a suggestion?" Senrid said.

"Yes. Please."

"Send your war party. Lined up on the ocean off-shore. Make it look good."

Jilo's jaw dropped. "But Erol said…"

"Erol's right," Senrid said, with the toothy grin that had gotten him into so much trouble when he was a boy. "They're probably expecting that. In fact, they'd probably longing for an attack, because then they can try to claim they're being invaded, and everybody hang together against the evil Chwahir who were part of Norsunder, blah blah blah. But take your time, see. Bang your shields, look tough. While they're watching you, someone goes in undercover." He snapped his fingers. "Find her, she's out. You go home. And you set up a really nasty ward, so anyone comes near her in future, they're sorry for it."

"Yes. Yes," Jilo said.

Liere held up her hand. While the two had been speaking, she'd steadied herself on her chair and reached for Seshe. "I found her. All I got was a cloud of anger. She's very much alive."

Senrid rubbed his hands. "Jilo, let's go to Colend and get the details."

12

Senrid only knew the general palace transfer Destination in Alsais. Jilo explained the private one Shontande had given him to use, and they each transferred.

When they came out, they were surrounded by herald-guards. Senrid assessed them from long habit; they'd formed a defensive circle with commendable speed, but the way they looked at one another, the nervous gripping of hands on weapons, made it clear this was their first true alert. They had not fought in the war.

One recognized Jilo, but seemed uncertain if this was a bad or good thing: to Senrid that meant the lines of communication between king, commander, and guards were too slow. Well, this was Colend. They did not have a blood-soaked history of war to refine their call to arms. Mentally he saluted them as he helped them along by saying, "We've come to consult with your king. Tell him Jilo of the Chwahir and Senrid Montredaun-An of Marloven Hess are here."

More looks, but the leader of the group dispatched a runner with a wave.

Jilo murmured, in Marloven, "I should be doing something."

"Getting information is doing something."

Jilo flexed his hands. "I ..."

"Jilo, you've got allies. They're going to back you up. In fact, if CJ isn't already on the way down to Damondaen with some mad plan, it'll be only because word hasn't hit Mearsies Heili yet. That reminds me. Is Seshe still wearing that medallion

Clair gave her girls? I remember there was a transfer worked into it."

"No," Jilo said with regret. "She gave it back to Clair when she moved to Narad. Said too much work went into it, and Clair ought to save it for anyone new who found a haven there."

"Typically generous. And regrettable—"

The runner was back. "Please come with me."

The two were conducted over winding, lamplit paths between buildings featuring many doors and windows. Senrid looked about, considering what a logistical nightmare the place would be.

On the other side of the summer palace, herald guards had met the debarking party. It took only a quick glance between Chief Ruis and Shontande to get the prisoner escorted in one direction, and the guests and servants offered escort to their quarters. It was very polite but very firm, so that even those who felt that they ought to be exempted found themselves dispersing. Many still talking; Nash offered to see Talian back to her quarters, but she gave him a stiff bow, and marched away.

Lyren started to disperse with them, but Shontande said, "Lyren. A moment?"

"Certainly." She turned back.

"You've surely known Jilo longer than I have. What do you think he will do? I admit to some concerns."

Lyren had been thinking about that while the barge eased to the shore and the guests were helped to land. "I've known him all my life, but not well. However, my first thought was that he would go to Senrid. He used to visit him a lot. Maybe still does, I just haven't seen it. And if anyone would know what to do in this situation, it would be Senrid."

That was when the dispatched herald-guard was waved through, to say, "Sire, arrivals, Jilo of the Chwahir, and Senrid Montredaun-An of Marloven Hess, to see you."

Shontande shot Lyren a smile, his brows raised.

She grinned. "It was a guess. Sometimes I guess right."

Instinct prompted him to say, "Will you stay?"

"Glad to—if there's anything I can do to help," she said. "Though I cannot imagine what. I've visited Senrid a lot ever since I was a baby, but I've never set foot in his training academy, except to watch their games when I was little, and I spent most of that time admiring the horses."

"I think you've had more training than you admit to," he retorted, smiling.

"And I complained at every step."

Jilo and Senrid appeared then. Senrid glanced her way. "Lyren. Still here," he said, not sounding surprised. "Anything new since Jilo's departure?"

Shontande said, "Other than the arrival of Erol, who said that you had dispatched him, Jilo?" On Jilo's nod, "No sign of any further disturbance. My herald-guards have secured the assailant over whom Jilo dropped the stone spell."

"Which ought to be wearing off now," Jilo murmured, tight-voiced.

"Do you need me?" Lyren asked. "I am really no use in planning rescues and I don't want to be in your way."

Senrid raised a hand to halt her. "With everyone's permission—I don't want to thrust myself into command role here—"

Shontande bowed, his palm up. He recognized Senrid's attempt at diplomacy.

Senrid said, "Lyren, come along to get whatever details this person furnishes. I think, all things considered, you'd be the best one to inform the Mearsieans. They are Seshe's adopted family. You'll know how to handle them."

"Yes," Jilo exclaimed. "Yes, good thought. I don't know what I'd say. Except it'll be wrong."

Lyren made a short bow, and they proceeded from the guarded pavilion where Ruis had brought them to the herald-guards' own area at the northeast of the palace buildings, surrounded by high vine-covered walls.

Erol was there, having been considering the best approach for interrogation. During their time in Norsunder he and Detlev's boys had seen the brute force forms of interrogation. They'd learned from Detlev and Siamis that torture seldom elicited truth.

If they had to question enemies, the threat of torture was usually enough. Or, less dramatic, but far more effective, the dangerous herb kinthus, especially in the white form. *Very little is needed*, Siamis had told the boys, holding up one hand and using the other to measure half of the tip of his little finger. *Much less than you think. Always use as little as you can. If you have to add more, you're able to, but too much not only endangers their life, but it also puts them out more quickly.*

Before transferring from Narad, Erol carefully put a pinch

of the ground herb in a bit of paper, and twisted it into a screw; he kept the stuff on hand for the occasional assassin who came after Jilo. And it had turned out to be useful for other serious crimes, almost all of them among the military, as Jilo slowly demobilized them.

The herald-guards had put the magic-frozen man on the floor of a small, bare room used mostly for rowdy drinkers to sober up. As always, the Colendi placed lanterns at the four corners to banish shadows. "He'll probably be vilely ill when that spell wears off," Erol warned the wide-eyed Colendi herald-guards. "Bring me a jug and water. He'll also be thirsty."

In silence they obeyed, the two designated to guard the room semaphoring relief and uneasiness back and forth with tight mouths and raised brows. This black-clad platterface at least hadn't brought a lot of sinister implements. But maybe he used his hands? Wouldn't that be worse?

They fetched the water and the plainest and oldest of the cups from their mess hall. By the time they returned, the prisoner had begun to stir, groaning. Limbs flopping. So far, he was very much like the drunks who usually graced that cell. One guard thoughtfully brought an ensorcelled bucket, in case the prisoner was unable to manage the Waste Spell.

While they waited for the effects of the stone spell to dissipate, Erol considered the man. He appeared to be somewhere around fifty, with sparse blond hair mixed with silver. Lanky. Bowed shoulders and callused fingers indicating someone who either spent his time at a desk writing, inscribing, illustrating, or etching. The ill-fitting musicians' robe should have been a clue, except Jilo never looked at anyone's clothes, and these Colendi didn't have the experience for that sort of assessment. Social clues, yes. Not an anomaly pointing to danger.

With a final moan, the man pushed himself to a sitting position, and then flinched when he saw Erol. "No! A Chwahir!" he yelped.

The Colendi stared aghast at this rudeness, but Erol did not react.

The noise of approach brought Jilo, Senrid, Lyren, and Shontande. The herald-guards made space for their king and his august visitors, who sat on the only available bench.

Erol dropped half of the pinch of white kinthus into the water as the man blinked, rubbing shaking hands over his face. It wasn't going to take much. He squatted down, and, relying on the Universal Language Spell, said, "Drink. You'll feel much better."

The man took the cup in both hands and slurped down the water, then wrinkled his nose at the taste. Then horror lengthened his face. "Did you poison me?"

"It's kinthus," Erol said. "You'll survive."

The man's bloodshot eyes shifted from Erol to the silent Colendi. "Where are Vali and Aksal?"

"I don't know," Erol said. "They left you behind."

The man licked his lips. Erol poured him more water. After he drained the cup, he said, "Where is the royal princess?"

Erol ignored that. "What is your name?"

"Why do you need to know?" the man countered, his voice high. "We came to find the missing princess! That's all!" He blinked, and looked around as the kinthus began to take effect. "I'm Ivki Soraq," he said. "Second scribe at Tain House."

"What is Tain House?" Erol asked in that same calm voice.

"We make books." Ivki Soraq mimed writing. "We're known all over the kingdom, not just on the mountain. I have a staff of three..." The tension in his voice slowly eased as he blathered on about the process of making books — copy, checking, illustrations, binding.

Erol poured out more water, and when the scribe paused to drink again, Erol said, "Who is the royal princess?"

"Seshemerria Jevondyan," the scribe said.

"What do you want with her?"

"To take her home! Before the Arrows find her."

"Who are the Arrows?"

"Our name for the army. The general made himself king, but everyone hates him. Aksal said we must find the princess first, before they can kill her."

"Why were you chosen to find her?"

"Because I'm the only one who ever saw her. She was only a little girl then, when my sister had charge of her. Thirva used to bring the royal princess to our house sometimes, until that was forbidden. I remember she used to like the figs on our tree..."

It went on in this manner. Erol tried to be as specific as he could, because the generality of people under the influence of kinthus not only helpfully offer every scrap they know about the question, but their incidental thoughts as they occur.

After a time, Erol looked up in question.

Senrid said, "I've heard enough. You?" to Jilo, who shruged, anxious to be doing something.

"There is a more comfortable room nearby, where we may reflect," Shontande invited.

They walked out, each of them aware that there was little enough to reflect on. Ivki Soraq had been brought into the conspiracy after all the plans had been made. The man named Aksal—Soraq had no idea if it was a real name—needed someone to identify her, and it seemed that Ivki Soraq was one of the few left from the old days who had seen the royal family's faces. Heard their voices. He agreed because he believed that they were bringing the royal princess back to the throne that she had rightfully inherited, once they rescued her from the villainous Chwahir, who had fought on the side of Norsunder during the war.

The next room was another cell, this one tastefully appointed; it was for high ranking detainees. As soon as they sat down, Senrid said, "My guess is, they'll never come back for him."

Shontande made the peace. "I concur. I propose we continue to house this man until Seshe is restored, and then turn him loose."

Jilo did not care what happened to him. "We have to find a way to get into that royal palace. That man said he has never been permitted inside it. He's useless."

Senrid said, "If Liere doesn't know Seshe well enough to find her through dreams, Clair will. Lyren, it might be faster to send Liere to Mearsies Heili. She'll know how to break the news, and how to talk about the limits of farsense, which I'm probably never going to understand."

"And then?" Shontande asked. "I speak from ignorance of such situations, but I found that man far more pathetic than sinister. He really seems to believe that they are going to offer Seshe the position she left. If that's all there is, then she will be free to choose?"

Senrid said, "He definitely thinks he's doing the right thing, but we don't know how much of what he was told is fart noise. There are too many questions, such as, if they mean as well as he thinks, then why not send an envoy to Chwahirsland to petition her return? Or here, if they are too frightened of the Chwahir?"

"This is true." Shontande looked disturbed.

Jilo said slowly, "He mentioned being ahead of assassins

sent by the present king."

Senrid lifted a shoulder in a shrug. "But again, all they needed to do is let any of us know about these assassins. Instead, they went to the trouble and expense of this secret mission. I don't trust any of it."

"Then I ought to raise the army, as you suggested before?" Jilo asked.

"Yep. As loud and pompous as you can. Scare the shit out of every one of their spies and scouts along the west ocean coasts by mustering your navy as noisily as possible. If you've got blood hunt flags, put them up on every ship. If you don't, make some. But take your time at it, see? I'll go back to Liere, fill her in, and we'll both go to Mearsies Heili, which is still in daylight right now. How does that sound?"

"Done," Jilo said, and disappeared.

Shontande cherished Jilo, but sometimes regretted his utter unawareness of manners. "Thank you," he murmured to Senrid.

Senrid grinned as he smacked his hands on his knees. "I'd just as soon be a part of this, as it was clear Damondaen was going to be trouble sooner or later."

Lyren said, "Tell Liere that I'm willing to help if there's anything they think I can do."

"I will." Senrid patted her shoulder. "If it turns out we need to send a neutral envoy, I can't think of anyone better than you." He also vanished.

Lyren turned to Shontande, upon whose physical presence she had been trying not to focus this entire time. At least Senrid had plunked down beside him, Jilo on the other side, or she would never have heard a word. She forced a smile, and a breezy, "I will now get myself out of your way."

Shontande said, "Have you dined?"

Of course she hadn't—the barge party's lovely food had ended up splashed all over the deck.

She said, "Not yet."

"Will you join me? I need to consider what to say to court and country, as the chirps will be wild by Hour of the Bird tomorrow. I would welcome your thoughts."

"I'd be honored," she said.

13

Seshe had recovered from the transfer to find that thing wrapped around her tightening as she tried to break free. Soft, quick footfalls approached, barely heard—servants' footfalls. In Damondaen, servants didn't last long who could not learn how to be unobtrusive. Not invisible. There was a difference; anyone who was perceived to be sneaking in and out also didn't last long.

Sensory memories flooded back on a tide of anxiety, and anger. The smell of leddas wax used on furniture and floors, with a hint of verdigris; the muffled rumble of thunder in the distance; even the light was somehow familiar. It was clearer, sharper. Mountain light. She knew, even though she lay on the cool, beautifully tiled floor with her hair spilling over one eye, that she was back in the royal palace at Jevondyan Mountain.

Careful hands reached to right her, as voices, trained to humility, poured over her, *Oh, your royal highness, welcome back — very sorry — what can we bring —*

Someone spoke a blurry magic word, and the merciless cling-vine slackened and dropped away.

At once those hands tried to clear her hair back, and straighten her twisted robes. Furious, she wanted to fling them all off, but she knew these were servants, doing what they were supposed to do. They had not caused her to be here. The cowards who were to blame seemed to be waiting for the servants to take whatever reaction she was going to give.

She slung her long hair behind her, held up a hand, and they all backed away. Sickness burned in her stomach: she recognized the summer sky painted in vivid shades of blue over the vaulted ceiling, and stars represented by carved crystals suspended from thin strings, glittering in the light of glow-globes. Her adult eyes registered the beauty of the room, but memory drowned aesthetic awareness: this was the queen's interview chamber, where Seshe's mother had sat on that throne carved with soaring horses, and toyed with her victims before condemning them or rewarding them according to her whim. This is where her mother had toyed with her children if they got too clever, and punished them for weakness.

Seshe shut her eyes.

Soft-voiced questions fluttered around her like leaves drop-ping. She closed her eyes and remained silent, struggling to bring back a semblance of calm. The happiness she had striven for — always conditional, always — was gone.

Damondaen had found her.

She knew no magic. Because she had never wanted any vestige of power, once she had freed herself from Damondaen. Magic was a form of power. Alas, she had also given her medallion back to Clair, for what had seemed at the time the best of reasons.

When she perceived that the questions were being repea-ted — which meant the servants had orders to elicit a response — she opened her eyes again, and this time was prepared to see the familiar gilt furniture on a grand scale, decorated with stylized begonias and queensblossom, the paneled walls with the twining vines and gilt pictures of past Jevondyan in golden frames. All of whom had slain their way to this throne in this chamber.

"Leave me," she said, and it came out in princess-to-lower rank imperative, not just because it was habit from childhood, but also because it was the only mode to supersede whatever orders had them standing around patiently repeating their questions, *Are you well? How may we serve you?*

If their orders came from someone considered her super-ior, then they would keep asking. And she would know something about who was giving the commands.

But they crossed their arms over their chests and bowed, then shuffled out the servants' narrow door, still bent with chins to chests, in that horrible backwards walk that Nanny Thirva had once told her took hours to practice. You *never* turned your back on the royal family; after her escape, Seshe had thought, how very true.

She was left alone. She sprang up, the idea to leave, but she had scarcely crossed the room toward the inner door when the outer door opened and in came a tall blond man that she recognized from the swan barge on the Canal of Lilies.

"Your royal highness," the man said as he bowed, hands to his sides in liege mode — that is, someone either connected to the family or sworn to some capacity as a chief, rather than born to servitude. "Welcome home."

It took all her control not to spit in his face. *Choose love.* Those were the last words Nanny Thirva said before Seshe's older sister Efridarlian had her put to death on Seshe's twelfth birthday.

He had light blue eyes, curious, steady in the manner of one who knew he'd done right.

"I want to go home," Seshe said, again in princess mode — which she had sworn never again to use.

"Your royal highness is home," the man responded, bowing again.

His straight brows were familiar. Mean, sneaking Cousin Eirdain Gamlasko, that's who he resembled, except this man had lighter hair, a clean-cut jawline, and long earlobes. He couldn't be older than thirty, if that.

He said, "I am Aksalkirek Gamlasko. I would be honored if you would address me as Aksal, for we are distant kin."

The Gamlaskos were considered second family rank. That is, fifth degree or more away from the Jevondyan primary family, on Seshe's mother's side — thus the distant before the word kin.

"I see your royal highness recognizes the Gamlasko name —"

"I want to go home," she said.

"Your royal highness is home," he repeated, gently. "You are safe, and you are needed. Desperately needed. Everything is ready for you. You've only to…"

She shut out the flow of his words, the harsh, icy waters of desolation as strong as they had been when she stared, disbelieving, at Nanny Thirva's lifeless body when she was twelve. But shockingly clear in memory, mercilessly immediate. *Choose love*, Nanny had said, though she knew that her end was nigh. Seshe had not believed Efridarlian would go through with it. But Efridarlian had always relished nasty surprises.

Seshe had not been able to choose love at age twelve. Love had died with Nanny Thirva. So she had chosen escape. Freedom, she had called it, and had exulted in the years after, though always that fear of discovery had never quite gone away. Now she understood, with sick conviction, that what she'd had was merely the illusion of freedom.

She became aware that he had stopped talking.

"This is no longer my home," she said, using neutral verbs — as between strangers, or enemies with whom one must parley. "As you would have found out if you had sent a messenger or a letter."

"Letters so easily go astray, and would a messenger survive Chwahirsland? They fought on the side of Norsunder during the war," Aksal said, with that maddening tone of conviction. "Also, and this was imperative, we had to reach your royal highness before Okren's Arrows did. What can we get for your royal highness to make you comfortable?"

Choose love, choose love, choose love. She tried repeating the words, but they were dead leaves falling around her. Her mind had retreated into the constraints of childhood, first rule of which was, avoid danger. Revealing anything of her inner thoughts was the first rule of avoiding danger. "Okren. I remember the Okrens were part of the military."

"Halrin Okren was the General of the Royal Army when you were small, yes? Styan Okren, his son, claimed to be king at the war's end. His father did not survive Norsunder's attack."

"I'm the prisoner of this new king, then?"

"No, no, you are not a prisoner. You are home again, the only true Jevondyan. No prisoner would grace the queen's own suite, which has been made ready for you this past year. He does not yet know we found you. He's at the head of the army, poised to take Rhengal. And then the islands, which he can use as a staging point to move into Halia."

"Then … you and your companions are part of a rebellion?" She stayed in neutral mode, deliberately leaving herself out of the discussion.

Aksal's brow furrowed. "It is not a *rebellion*. The Arrows rebelled when they took the throne after Norsunder's defeat. We are taking the kingdom *back*. Everyone hates Styan Okren. I refuse to regard him as king."

"Who expects to be ruling through me?"

Aksal blinked. Did he actually expect her to believe that this pretense of assuming her old rank meant she had authority? "You will rule," he said with that same air of assurance. "We know you were a child when you left Damondaen. We will be honored to brief you on the situation today, which is very different from it was then."

She wanted to retort that things looked pretty much the same—treachery and trouble—only the names changed, but she kept that back. Offer no information. Her survival as a child had depended on being docile and dull. Resuming that façade now seemed a good idea until she could assess the situation. Jilo was surely trying to find her—Clair, too, once she found out—except Seshe could not depend on them figuring out where she was. She must try to save herself.

Dull and docile. "I have a terrible headache. I need to be alone."

"Of course, your royal highness. These are your chambers, as I said. Everything has been prepared. If there is anything you lack, we will be honored to furnish it."

Except a transfer token to go home.

He bowed and backtracked the requisite five steps before he turned and walked out. Seshe stared at him, remembering the robe with the uneven hem and the sleeves that were far too short, before that cling-vine had yanked her off the bench. Her first mistake, and it was a serious one, had been in ignoring the servants and musicians on Nash's barge—something she had tried never to do. Regard all people as if they matter, that was what Nanny Thirva had said, and it was the way that Clair lived, as naturally as breathing. If Seshe had noticed how badly that robe fit, would she have understood the threat? Now was not the time to fight that battle within herself. First, escape.

The door shut. She ran to open it and looked out. There stood two burly servants in Jevondyan livery. Both bowed, arms crossed over their chests. "Your royal highness's desire?"

"I desire fresh air," she said. Remembering what she'd just told Aksalkirek Gamlasko, she added, "My head aches. I will walk on the rampart."

"It is raining, your royal highness," one said.

The other added, "These your servants would be honored to inform your royal highness as soon as the rain ceases, and we shall accompany you to the rampart, ensuring your safety and comfort."

In other words, stay put. And when they let her out, they'd stick to her shadow.

She shut the door. As expected, she was a prisoner.

She turned back, rubbing her eyes. The sun had barely gone down in Colend, making it early evening. Damondaen was almost exactly on the opposite side of the world. The gloomy light was early morning. She was alone, but for how long?

She looked at the crystal stars, and the fine gilt-edged panels with the twined lines and stylized larkspur painted cobalt blue. She avoided looking at that throne for all the ugly memory it churned up. There was nothing in this room to make her want to stay. The inner door had once led to the rest of the queen's suite, but she had never been permitted beyond it.

She crossed to that door. When she opened it, a maid leaped from a hard bench, hands crossed, head down. "Your royal highness desires?"

"To be left alone," Seshe replied. And then, remembering how servants had had to stand for hours against walls when in the family's presence, she added, "You need not wait. I want to be solitary." Let the woman be able to sit down, at least; it was not her fault she was commanded by some as yet unknown person to spy and report on whatever Seshe did.

Seshe crossed the short hall. On three sides, wide, carved doors. On the fourth wall, a narrow door painted to look like the paneled wall: the servants' corridor. There would be no escape that way. She'd tried, when small, and learned that those corridors were crowded with the many servants constantly crossing to and fro fetching, carrying, disposing of unwanted things, and bearing the implements of cleaning and repairing. So much repairing. She remembered hearing the sounds of smashing wood and crockery when she was small: her elder brother in one of his rages, throwing things at the servants, usually after some conflict with Efridarlian.

One door led to an enormous wardrobe. The stale air whiffed of bergamot and jasmine, her mother's favorite scent. It drove her out again. Nausea rose, choking her. She thrust her crooked arm over her nose, breathing in the slightly damp, salty smell of her own sweat, and under it, the cedar she stored her clothes in. Cedar, she remembered, was considered common by the royal family. Maybe that was why she liked that scent. It had no terrible associations.

She tried the next door: a vast tiled bath chamber, with a bank of windows, now gray with running rain, and vague dark green beyond: ah, the garden, surrounded by trees. It was a small garden, to fool one into forgetting that they lived enclosed in a huge stone prison. There was an enormous bath, with water and heating wands. A fireplace, with firesticks waiting in it. Summers could be cold on the mountain.

The last room was a grand bedchamber, with a huge canopied bed. Here, everything had a new feel, which surprised her. Tradition was paramount when she was a child. But that rug worked with patterns of pink climbing roses and crowns against a pale blue background looked new. The hangings above the bed also looked new — and then the obvious struck her. This might very well be where her mother had died when Norsunder attacked. No doubt pushing her maids in front to shield her, though none of them would have had weapons.

Seshe looked around carefully for possible means of escape as ancient ancestors gazed into the distance from their gold frames. Though the castle was honeycombed with passages, the servants and guards knew them all. There had been no hiding from her prowling siblings. Her only defense had been to be docile and dull.

Noises broke her reverie: the maid was back, leading a string of servants bearing ornate, silver covered trays of food, and some neatly folded fabric. She looked past the offerings to the silent message: she was not going to be left alone for long, whatever she said.

CJ and Diana and Gwen, who had been street rats, had taught her that if food was offered, you ate it, even when you were a prisoner. Because you never knew when you might break free, and no one runs well hungry.

She waved off the clothing, and sat at the beautifully carved table with ancient raptor legs. As the servants set out enough dishes to feed six people, Seshe gazed through another window, through the slanting rain in the direction of the far wall, which hid the kitchen courtyard from royal eyes. Escape had been a chance thing, a moment's decision while servants were arguing about who was expected to tend her now that Nanny Thirva was gone. Alone and unwatched for the first time — *docile and dull* — Seshe had spotted a wagon full of empty cooking oil barrels standing in the lower court as wagon laborers went back to fetch the last two barrels. No one, in that moment, noticed her.

She'd not hesitated but a heartbeat before leaping into the wagon, making her way among the barrels, and then, trembling all over, lifted the wooden lid and climbed inside and crouched down, working the lid back into place with her fingertips.

She could still taste the sharp, greasy smell of olive and old wood. It had been years before she could tolerate food cooked in pressed olives. There she'd remained, heart thumping in terror against her ribs, until the wagon gave a lurch and began bumping and rumbling in movement. Through the gates, down and down and down, as thirst agonized her, and her skin began to itch from the oily residue.

But that miserable journey had ended when the drivers stopped at an inn for a meal as the oxen munched. She'd slid out and away, and thence had begun her three years of wandering, living hand to mouth as she shed the princess who'd had every physical need instantly tended. And grieved for Nanny Thirva, the single beacon in the night of her life.

Then she met Clair.

14

Icy horror gripped Clair as she stared at Liere and Senrid. "Not Seshe," she said, willing her disbelief to be true.

"Lyren was there," Liere said. "As well as Jilo. And just before we came, we learned that the assailants are from Damondaen."

"Jilo was there?" Clair repeated, and the horror flared into alarm. "What will he—"

Senrid said quickly, "Dealt with. He came to me first. I figured he'd want to hurl all of Chwahirsland against Damondaen, but I talked him into making it a bluff. He's mustering the navy right now. Not saying he won't battle himself every step of the way, then maybe find an excuse to make it real." He flattened his palm. "Idea is to get someone incountry to yank her out before he gets to the islands off the Toaran coast."

Clair said numbly, "Seshe is his person. It's so much more than just a romance." Memories flickered: Seshe suggesting that Jilo wasn't so bad, when they were all just kids; Seshe making sure he ate when he worked on the antidote to the poison ward, at the end of the war; Seshe, a few years ago, after both of them had lifted the Child Spell and had left the changes of adolescence well behind, coming to Clair for advice, *He believes so deeply that he's unworthy that he will never even touch me. I have to initiate everything, what do I do?*; and most heartrending of all, and most recent, *We've figured out sex, but what he desperately needs is tenderness. Sometimes we just lie in bed with our arms wrapped around each other, all night long. I think that's the only time he sleeps undisturbed.*

Senrid glanced around, then said uneasily, "Where's CJ?"

"She's in Wnelder Vee. Sailing with Gwen again. It's Gloriel," Clair said. "Trying to hang onto her humanity. CJ is fascinated by the whole undersea world, and Gloriel responds to her."

"Good," Senrid said bluntly.

No one argued. Everyone knew that CJ would run to the rescue whether she had a good plan or what only she thought was an "okay" plan. Because—in typical CJ reasoning—all plans go flooey anyway, right?

"She'll be mad not to be included," Clair said.

"But mad and alive is something we can deal with," Senrid retorted.

"Leading to the question: what is to be done for Seshe? I'm not good enough at farsense to reach someone who keeps her mental shield so firm."

Liere said, "Firm indeed. I tried as soon as Jilo turned up. It has to have been fairly soon after it happened, and Seshe's mental shield was thin enough that I sensed anger and shock. But nothing since." She turned to Siamis, who emerged from his study, his pen fingers still inky as he slipped his clean hand into Clair's. "Maybe you'd have more success?"

Siamis's gaze diffused, then he said, "Your skills in farsense are probably better than mine now. Certainly as good. And, no, I can't find her."

Clair looked from one face to another. "I never dreamed I would say even this much, but if those kidnappers said her name right out, then the secret is no secret anymore, right?"

"Correct," Siamis murmured.

Clair said slowly, "Seshe has always been the best of us at shielding. Any time there's danger, that was her first reaction, once she learned how. She's been afraid ever since I met her that her family might come after her. But I thought they died in Norsunder's attack."

"Right," Senrid said. "At this point, I'm confident in saying that the more you tell us, the better chance we have at figuring out how to get to her."

"The only time we talked about where she came from, and why, was when she first joined us, so what I know is outdated." Those innocent, easy days seemed epochs ago, beginning that morning in late spring, when Clair was walking in the forest and Seshe emerged from the dappled light as if a thousand pale-yellow bright-moths coalesced out of the shadows and formed into a girl on the young side of fifteen, wearing dirty, ragged clothes. Seshe stared into the churning waters of Dhana's waterfall, entranced as some of the lake beings rose in iridescent, shivering bubbles, dancing in the wind, then sank slowly back to the water.

Clair blinked. "I promised to keep what she said a secret. I even lied to cover that I knew, so that there would be no evidence of a secret. Some of the girls were curious, and lively, and a mystery was like a game to them, especially in the early days, when the worst thing that ever happened was being chased around the forest as Jilo tried to find out where our hideout was. But I did some very, oh, call it covert checking now and then over the years, mostly through my cousin Puddlenose, and everything I heard about Damondaen matched what she said." Clair glanced up. "Senrid, Damondaen sounded like it was even worse than your kingdom back in the bad days."

"No surprise," he said, his expression sardonic. "They were us before we became Marlovans. After a huge and bloody clan feud, some went over to Toar with their horses. Mixed in with the local toughs. Favorite sport seems to have been conquering ever since."

"Seshe said the traditional way of choosing the royal heir was to make it a contest. A feud, really, if all the royal children wanted the throne. Only the strongest could rule." Clair looked away, the shock of the news congealing into worry.

Siamis said, "That meant the last one standing. Sometimes they bustled things along by taking out the older generation after they finished off the younger."

Clair tried to shake off that sick sense. Now was the time for clear thought. "Seshe was the youngest in their family. She had no desire to rule. She was close to her nanny — getting close to servants was considered a weakness — and her older sister had that nanny put to death the day Seshe turned twelve. Seshe ran that day. I don't know the details. She never said."

Senrid made that flat gesture again, as if pushing something away. "I'm familiar with the kind of thinking that keeps that tradition going: there's pride in surviving. Also, the sense that if I had to go through it, you ought to, too. And I'm certain the populace was too intimidated to rise against them too often."

"Until the war," Siamis commented. "According to Ferret's report some years ago, the military took over as Norsunder left. When the kingdom did not settle down, they forced conscription on the populace and invaded the coastal countries to the south. It seems they're expanding again." He tapped his head with the one finger not smudged with ink. "Ferret is willing to go down there to investigate, and act if he finds a way in."

"And I will try tonight to reach Seshe in the dream realm," Liere said. "If Lyren has nothing further to report from the Colendi."

Lyren was still with Shontande Lirendi.

It was quite dark in Colend, music drifting on the breeze that had risen over the river. He had invited Lyren to dine with him, but at every intersection along the winding path to the residence, apologetic heralds or servants waited with urgent reports and questions.

Lyren remained silent as Shontande was told first that the two musicians from the barge did not know the three assailants. They'd been offered a thumping sum to include the three, who had desired all their lives to play once before a king. They'd thought five would be better than two, and to be paid for expanding their number, what an opportunity!

"Their biggest concern, before they were taken by surprise, was that the newcomers' skills were not polished, sire," the herald finished.

"Let them go," Shontande said wearily.

"Will I sound ignorant if I admit that I did not perceive any difference between the two real ones and all five together playing?" Lyren admitted as they began walking again.

Shontande appreciated this attempt at distracting him from the constant barrage of stresses. "If you are ignorant, I'll join you. Perhaps we might have noticed in a concert, without all the other noise, but Bee's hearing is so much better. I'm going to have to alleviate his sense of guilt for not having spoken earlier."

"Who expects that sort of trouble at a music festival?" Lyren said.

Shontande had no time to reply. They stepped through a trellis supporting three shades of starliss to discover another waiting herald, who reported that wild talk of attackers — a new war — was making its way along the entertainment houses on the Chandos.

"Counter it. Tell your chief to request the bargers to spread the word that the troublemakers are gone."

Which was true enough, but the grim facts remained the same: Seshe had been taken on Colendi ground. As the herald sped away, Shontande said, "We did not keep her safe. It is a moral debt I cannot pay. And to Jilo, of all people. Ah-ye, how bitter is my regret!" His profile was distraught.

They started walking again. "What will Nash's guests say to the rest of court?" Lyren asked.

"That's what I'm wondering. I do not want people taking it upon themselves to raise difficulties for visitors to the city. Not at any time, but especially now, when there are probably more visitors between musicians and listeners than there are residents. My concern lies not so much with court. Half of them have gone home to their estates, to return when the festival ends. What concerns me are those who remember the war, and who might endanger visitors if wild rumors fly about abductions."

After another fifty paces of brooding, he stopped, hands at Rue. "I would like nothing better than to sit somewhere on the water and converse on civilized topics, but I'm beginning to suspect it will take all night to compose a suitable report for the heralds to post at Hour of the Bird."

"I understand," Lyren said with a cheery smile. "Restoring calm is important, especially with the city full of us foreigners."

"There is that, but I believe I must send a note to each of Nash's invitees on that barge to enjoin them to silence, while acknowledging that we are entirely at fault for a guest of the King of the Chwahir being taken while among us. And I'll have to meet with Ruis to implement some sort of plan to watch for trouble—*and* to see that no more of Soraq's conspirators are lurking in the city."

"A city full of strangers," Lyren said. "What a nightmare. It seems to me the best way I can help at this moment is to free you, and wait for news from Liere or Senrid. I can send a note if there's anything to report?"

He was so grateful for her quick understanding, and for her lack of panic: there, in mind, was the image of Talian Ariath's totally unnecessary dive to "protect" him that had only served to plow Ruis down. He knew what had driven her to do it, and this, too, added to his weight of guilt.

He bowed, making the peace.

Lyren made the peace back, and sped away down the path.

Until Seshe got down some of that unwanted meal, she had not noticed her awareness shrinking to her immediate surroundings, anchored by constant shocks of memory that she had tried so hard to hard to forget.

But clear thought began reasserting itself. Midway through a flute of creamy hazelnut custard, she remembered that she had not eaten at all that day. Jilo had been so busy trying to get everything done so that they could stay away the entire day and evening that she'd postponed a morning meal three times, then had given up, reflecting that the Colendi were sure to lay out a sumptuous spread.

With clearer thought, needles of worry jabbed her, first of all about Jilo. Last thing she'd heard before the transfer spell yanked her away was him muttering magic spells, his voice harsh and high from stress.

Once again, regret seized her. She had done her best to suppress the nascent Dena Yeresbeth she'd discovered in herself. Unwanted. Even regarded as dangerous, because sending your mind out to others meant that others could find you. And what you hid. She dared not lift her mind-shield, because she would not be able to reach him, but who knew what malevolent mind lurked nearby, waiting to pounce on her.

Oh, Jilo. Her eyes stung. She knew with absolute conviction that he would be feeling torn to pieces. He wouldn't be able to use his considerable magic skills to find her. Even as a child she had heard about the wards protecting the royal castle from outside mages. "Go to Clair," she thought, though she knew that the thought would not reach him. "Go to Clair, if Shontande can't help you."

The king of Colend would be worried as well. She knew how much Shontande liked Jilo. *He's a miracle,* Shontande had said once. *How could someone from such a background emerge with such a clean heart? Like the lotus, rising from muddy waters. It seems fitting that the lotus is so revered among Chwahir, as well as the linden.*

Seshe could not eat another bite. She laid aside the golden spoon, and the waiting servants, who had stood against the far wall while she ate, flowed back again and removed all the dishes one by one.

Alone again, Seshe rose. Rather than brood, she needed to be active in finding a way out. The prospects dimmed with each opened door, which revealed at least one servant waiting outside. More pairs.

A sudden shaft of light lancing in the windows announced the end of the summer storm. And, true to the promise she had regarded as a politeness at best, the burly liveried guard knocked politely and entered the interview chamber to announce that the rain had ceased, and the rampart was rapidly drying.

Very well. She'd go for that walk, and count up how many pairs of eyes would have to be evaded.

Not only the two door guards, but four maids followed her out, one carrying a cloak, another a hat, the third a rain canopy in case rain threatened again, and the fourth for who knew what purpose.

The air was humid, smelling of wet stone. Steam rose off puddles in the strong sunlight. Sights and smells roiled the ugly mud of memory from every side. So much mud; when she reached the far end of the rampart, she glanced down at the steep rooftops of the village in the valley below, between the castle and the city. The bluish haze of humidity obscured the stone houses, slate roofs, and the tall pines and cedar. In that village Nanny Thirva had lived with her family. As a small child, Seshe had been taken to that house, which she had found enchanting in its simplicity and its lack of threat. Everyone had used the verbs of family, and so she had, too—and was overheard. Once she recovered from her mother's beating, she discovered that those excursions were forbidden.

She turned her back on the village, and paced the other way in defeat.

Barely noon. Time weighed on her, invisible chains. Anger stirred as she rounded the main building adjacent the queen's tower. Why should she return to her cage without pushing at her limitations? She remembered the door she had just passed. It led down to the library, then to the king's tower.

She swerved. Skirting a puddle that was already vanishing, she stepped toward the heavy, iron-reinforced door, expecting at every moment to be blocked with some polite excuse.

But one of the guards ducked around and opened the door, bowing her through, and the entourage trailed her, the maids still carrying rain gear, as she trod down the slate stairs to a short hall that opened onto a hexagonal space with a door in each wall.

Library, that one. She recollected a huge room full of dark bindings, and dreary records extolling bloody deeds. But that was a child's view. She might as well take a look—and perhaps shed some of this unwanted train, if she lingered long enough?

That was the plan, but before she reached the library, a couple of servants emerged from the door that led down to the kitchen and bakery.

She glanced at the servants, and was going to turn away, for up until now they kept their heads bowed so that she saw no faces. But one had her head only partly tipped, and eyes met eyes. The woman was tall, lanky, thick dark hair twisted in a servant's knot. Thin nose in a round face, like a bird's beak —

"I remember you," Seshe exclaimed. "Don't I?"

In the light of the glowglobes high on the walls, the woman hesitated, and then swept a deep bow. But that look, the hesitation, those were not in keeping with servant behavior.

For that matter, neither was the rustle and exchange of uncertain looks that Seshe sensed more than saw, among those following her.

"Sewing," Seshe said. "You were a girl doing sewing repair."

The woman bowed again, then said, "Would your royal highness care to step into the library? That's where you were headed, is it not?"

Seshe stepped to the library door, which again one of the guards opened. Seshe walked through, looking back—and saw the woman make a sign to the following maids, keeping them back, as the two guards entered.

Ah. The anomalies began to add up. This woman, who Seshe remembered as a girl, had to be part of whatever plot was going on. She certainly seemed to be giving orders.

"Shall we sit?" the woman said, still in servants' formal mode, but she'd forgotten the honorific. Or was this a test of sorts?

"Yes," Seshe said, and headed toward one of the huge eagle-clawed, wingback chairs that were said to be a thousand years old. Yes. A test. No servant would ever have sat down in the presence of the royal family, much less suggested it. "Are you the one behind the plot, then?"

"Plot?"

"What else would you call it when I'm forced here against my will? You were one of Nanny Thirva's relatives, weren't you?"

"So you remember her?"

"Remember her? She was…" Seshe closed her lips, her jaw locking. Then, "You're one of the Soraqs."

"Brin. Two years younger than you, but you seem to have found someone to do that Child Spell. Which I don't understand anyone wanting," Brin added. "I don't suppose you know what happened to my uncle?"

"Who?"

"All right, I thought not. Aksal said the whole thing was sudden, and they almost lost you as well as Uncle Ivki—"

Here, Seshe interrupted. "Why did those people force me here?"

"We had to rescue you from the Chwahir. Ahead of the false king's Arrows, I might add. You ought to be grateful."

"I'm not," Seshe retorted. "As I told your Gamlasko compatriot, I want to go home."

"This is home," Brin said. "What else would you call home? You were visiting in Colend, you don't live there. Where were you all those years?"

"My home," Seshe stated clearly, "is Chwahirsland."

"That's impossible," Brin said. "Unless you threw in with Norsunder!"

"I most certainly did not." Seshe leaned forward, her gaze steady. "The Chwahir suffered horribly under their mad king."

Here Brin nodded a little.

"—and now, with the new king's guidance, they are coming out of the terrible years at last. They never were on the side of Norsunder. The people, I mean. But they had to obey orders, or die. Surely you understand that much." Seshe swept her hand around.

"Yes. And that's why … go on. Your royal highness."

"You can lay aside the honorifics. I haven't heard them since I left Damondaen. As for the Chwahir, I'll say only that Chwahirsland is recovering every day, under Jilo's guidance."

"So you weren't enchanted into being that new king's toy?"

"Toy!"

"If not a toy," Brin said in a reasonable tone, "what are

you? Even the Chwahir don't seem to know."

Seshe became aware she was trembling. She closed her eyes, and breathed deeply once, twice, three times. Then she opened her eyes to say, "*Everything* I did was to try to make myself as invisible as possible. So that no one from this accursed hole into damnation would ever find me again." Her voice rang with absolute conviction.

Brin sat back. For a long moment, the two women gazed at each other, neither sure if they had crossed the line into enmity.

Brin spoke, for the first time a note of uncertainty in her tone. "We really could use your help."

"Then you ought to have asked." And when Brin's gaze shifted, and Seshe intuited Thirva's niece was going to launch into self-justification, based on her idea of the Evil Chwahir, she added, "The Chwahir are not the world's enemies. If you know anything of events after the war, you should know that the navy has been cooperating with several governments to clean up piracy and leftover Norsundrians. And now —"

'Yes, but —"

"Permit me to finish," Seshe stated, raising her voice. "And now, I would not be surprised if they have become *your* enemy. I hope not. It would grieve me terribly if Jilo sent the entire navy down here to fetch me back. I can't bear the thought of lives lost on my behalf. But I wouldn't be surprised."

Brin's lips thinned to a line. "I think," she said in neutral tone, "I had better tell you everything."

15

"What we really want is to govern ourselves," Brin said finally. "I'll begin there." But then she frowned down at her hands.

Seshe had expected anything but that.

One of the two guards spoke up. "I can fetch Aksal. He's good at explaining."

Maybe to other men, Seshe thought.

"Good idea."

The man took off, as the four maids and a teenage boy entered, standing behind Seshe's chair.

Brin gave Seshe a pained look, not quite apologetic, but unsettled, her gaze anywhere but meeting Seshe's. "I can see that we might have been wrong. About your royal highness. We believed you were merely a favorite, toy of the enemy, with more hair than wit. Or you were enchanted. Our plan was to flatter and pet you. The last Jevondyan. Give you everything a princess expects. So you'd be willing to cooperate."

"I hate those things," Seshe stated. "The flattery and all the bowing as well as the golden utensils. *Hate*. Them." She was going to go on, beginning with being so rudely snatched, but *choose love*, Nanny Thirva whispered a heartbeat before she died. "That is, I love beautiful things. I love beauty. But I don't love the memories the beautiful things here bring up. I ran away to escape this place."

"We thought Bloo—ah, Princess Efridarlian had driven you into the forest and you died," the second guard said earnestly.

Brin added hastily, "We were all young, but we remember-ed you as such a meek mouse."

"Bluh what?" Seshe asked, looking at the big guard, who avoided her eyes. "I hope you had a private name for my horr-ible sister, and that it was sufficiently descriptive."

"Bloodsucker," the teenage boy muttered from behind.

"She would have loved that, I suspect," Seshe said. "Though she would not have loved what she would have consi-dered impertinence."

Brin narrowed her eyes as though trying to bring Seshe into focus. "You really don't care?"

Seshe sighed. "My earliest memory of her is how she'd creep into my bedchamber while I slept and yank me out of bed by my ear, by my hair, and later by slipping one of my ribbons around my neck and dragging me. Then she'd start snarling at how coddled I was. How I'd better start toughening up. But I could have endured if she'd not had Nanny Thirva killed."

"Why? No one ever knew."

"Of course not. When I look back, I realize she was always careful to torture me when I was alone, and even if the servants heard, they knew better than to do anything. Efridarlian was Mother's favorite. No matter what dispute we had, Mother always favored her, then punished me for whining, and then Efridarlian took revenge for my having asked for justice. As for that day…". Seshe's throat tightened. "She had recently started giving me little presents. Things I liked. She was very clever — she knew my favorite foods, and books, and toys…"

Efridarlian's image rose before Seshe's eyes, not a lot different from Seshe: ordinary of features, with blond hair, only hers was a wild mane of curls that she'd been very proud of. Her expression, a wicked smile with deep dimples at either side, could turn threatening as fast as a striking snake. Still the smile. It was her eyes that would suddenly narrow to a glare of anticipation.

Seshe tried to shrug away the memory. "She asked if I was ready to duel for the throne. I told her I didn't want to rule. She knew that. It was no surprise. I really think that's why she and Vihariliot left me alone most of the time. They, she, really, tormented me when she lost to Vihariliot. His anger was spent on the servants."

"We all remember that," Brin said. "It was after the prin-cess lost one of their fights that she had my sister blinded just for looking at her new gown too long. Smirching it with her dirty common eyes, she said. But go on."

"She told me that she would reward me well if I began working for her. As soon as I understood that I was supposed to spy on our brother, and attack him for her, I said no, and she asked why not, and I made the mistake I've regretted ever since of saying that Nanny Thirva said to choose love. And I was trying to choose love. I had just turned twelve, and thought she could be reasoned with. She did not want reason. She wanted obedience."

Tears gathered anyway, but Seshe kept her voice more or less steady. "It happened so fast. I knew she'd had servants put to death, which she'd claimed had been for theft, or disloyalty, or for lack of proper respect, but somehow I thought Nanny Thirva would be fine because she was respectful, obedient, and never hurt anyone. I was wrong. I was in the kitchen court afterwards and saw empty oil barrels, climbed in, and got away."

Brin's sharp nose had pinked along with her eyes. "We all loved Aunt Thirva," she said fiercely, and wiped her eyes on her apron.

Seshe then confessed, "In those early days, when I was filthy and hungry and drank from rain puddles, hiding every time I heard a voice, I'd hoped Efridarlian would get into trouble for my disappearance. But I doubt that she did."

"The king did order out a search. That was how my sister and I got away. Thunderstorm that night, and Horq from the stable returned with one of your shoes that Kilit had fetched from your chamber. Said it was found on a boulder near a cataract, and two of Prince Vihariliot's chamber boys tried to search, slipped and fell—we said they died and were swept out to sea, but they escaped, too. Everyone but those of us who knew about the ruse with the shoe assumed you'd gone into the forest, or been driven there, and died. But there was never any sign of you after, so we thought you were really dead, just that you'd died somewhere else."

Seshe saw no reaction to that, but then there wouldn't be, from people who were so used to sudden death by whim, and by the pervasive sense that their own lives were worthless. "You say you escaped. Where to? I remember that servants who ran got dragged back and executed."

Brin leaned forward. "We'd been hearing about a place called Freedom Village."

A gasp and some whispering caused Brin to look past Seshe to the circle. "Why not? Did we not agree that our plan is all or nothing? Anyway, what matters if she hears the name? I didn't say where it is—"

The door opened, and the guard returned, along with Aksal and a string of other people in livery. Kitchen, stable, upstairs, laundry. They filed in, forming a circle around the two chairs, in a room that hitherto they had been forbidden to enter unless to dust and clean, and Seshe said, wonderingly, "Do you hold the entire castle?"

Whispers and glances all around, then Brin said, "We do."

"But ... where are the Arrows?"

"Styan Okren hates this place," Brin said, looking past Seshe. "Tell her, Ris. I think it's fine."

An older woman, gray and stout, wearing the livery of housemaids, said, "We drove him out. Not by fighting! Everything damp. Especially in winter. Mildew. Cold food. Mouse droppings everywhere. Beds. Shoes."

Another maid added in a squeaky voice, "We told him the royal family was used to it, that it had been that way for centuries. How would he know different?"

Seshe looked around. "Are you saying the entire staff was in on this conspiracy?"

"Not everybody," Aksal said. "It was us from Freedom that brought the plan back, right after the war. We had to convince the others one by one."

"Some just wanted to be rid of the Arrows, once we knew they were going to be worse than the king and queen had been. Styan Okren tried to make the palace over into a garrison," Brin explained.

At that point, the dam broke. The servants, so silent hitherto—when in these chambers—talked over each other, each trying to get their story into Seshe's ears. To explain. To justify. To release pent-up passions that had festered across generations.

On the surface, what had occurred was easy enough to comprehend: on the eve of the invasion, Imry Llyenthur had infiltrated the palace, assassinated the king and queen, and left as a contingent of Norsundrians fought the castle guards who hadn't faced serious trouble for a generation. They then did their best to commandeer the army into switching sides, promising loot and rank. And an appreciable number had shrugged and joined Norsunder, since fighting was what they were train-ed to do.

The servants, terrified, shocked, and angry, had gone wild once they realized the royal guard was fighting down at the palace gates, and thus Efridarlian met her end at servant hands, along with servants known to be spies and toadies. Vihariliot had tried to escape, but was shot by an arrow from the wall, whether by a guard or by a Norsundrian, no one ever knew.

Then the Norsundrians established their main base for Southern Toar right there in Damondaen.

Seshe tried to navigate between the personal stories and opinions in order to find a coherent narrative, learning that Freedom Village had been a refuge for well over a century, and it was not the first haven. Life was tough there, as it was diffi-cult to get any supplies they could not make or grow them-selves, but they governed themselves. They had survived the war by hiding out. And afterward, had emerged with the idea that with the Jevondyans gone at last, the people of Damondaen could rule themselves, just as they'd done at Freedom.

Except they found the remains of the military, now exceed-ingly tough after two years of covert warfare, entrenched. Styan Okren's plan for settling the nation was to unite them to carry war to the neighboring kingdoms for badly needed supplies, as the Norsundrian depredations had been enormous.

"I was one of those conscripted," Aksal said. "My elder brothers had fulfilled the Gamlasko military quota, so I'd taken over my grandfather's glass shop. At first I was willing enough to go. The kingdom was in such terrible case after the war. They gave us a little training, and then said we were going to streng-then Damondaen to its glories of old by invading Vakheinen down south. Why? They had nothing for us, once the wind-runners left."

"Probably," put in one of the guards, "the windrunners knew the war was coming. That's why they vanished, my Da said."

Seshe remembered having heard about the mysterious white, flying horses as a child. And flying horse motifs were common in local art and music. Vakheinen had traditionally given them to the royal families of Damondaen as tribute, but Seshe had never been permitted to see them.

That is, until she joined Clair's gang in Mearsies Heili, and found one living right there below the white palace. "I actually know the history there. Do you want to hear it?" She was testing her status now, as her own mistaken ideas evolved. The castle servants and their allies had been wrong about her, but she was beginning to perceive how she had been wrong about them.

"The royal family had no windrunners in the stable," someone said. "They were kept at the king's summer lodge. And then they all suddenly vanished, right before the war, just as Halfdyan said. Not just the king's, but all of them, including all the ones in Vakheinen. How would you know, when you were not even here?"

"Because I learned to ride on one, after my escape. Hreealdar lived far in the north, where I was staying. And I ended up being taken to their world. The windrunners' world, I mean. Do you remember a night of bright light in the sky, a few years before the war?"

"Yes!"

"Oh, yes! Everyone saw that! The queen said..."

Seshe did not want to hear what the queen had said. "That was the night that Norsunder was expelled from their world. I was there to see all the windrunners come home."

A brief silence fell. Did they believe me, Seshe wondered, then Aksal said, "As for us, after the war, I did not want to be killed by someone defending their kingdom, and for what? I deserted, with some others. Those of us who survived made it to Freedom."

Brin took over. "We met up, and the two of us decided to go over to the Sartoran continent. We wanted to see Sarendan firsthand, because my uncle, who had been smuggling books to Freedom, where there weren't any, had included one that talked about that. It was even translated into our language on one page, and on the other, the original Sartoran. Uncle Ivki wasn't able to say where it came from. Someone else had copied it. But we read that one aloud to everyone, because it was talking about people, like us, who tried to govern ourselves."

Aksal said, "So we two learned Sartoran, and went across the sea..."

The words came faster now, everyone still talking. Seshe concentrated, for she sensed that they were coming to the part that concerned her.

So it was. With the kingdom in increasing turmoil, the harder Styan Okren tried to impose military discipline, the more the conspirators decided to spread out and recruit village chiefs and clan heads to the cause. To discover that they were not hailed with welcome as they had confidently expected: yes, the rulers had been tyrants, but they'd largely stayed in their mountain palace. The military was worse, and who was to say that some newcomer claiming to rule wouldn't be even nastier? With the Jevondyans, everyone knew what to expect. Half the country wanted to sit tight, heads down, and let those at the top kill each other off, as had happened in days of yore.

Others were skeptics, sure that self-rule meant the thieves and thugs would create little kingdoms and there'd be no recourse.

Brin and Aksal had returned with the news that there was still a king in Sarendan, after an extremely bloody revolution that had been worse than the naysayers predicted. He was scarcely more than a boy, and what's more, he granted all kinds of powers locally — and there was recourse when local bullies tried to force people to follow them.

It was just after their return that gossip filtered through the families of conscripts — conveyed through scouts — that the king of the black-haired, pasty-skinned platter-faces had a blond plaything named *Seshemerria*. It was Jilo himself who had been heard speaking her name, when she first moved to Narad: a five-syllable name to the Chwahir had spread fast, so astonishing it was.

Styan Okren had dispatched a team to find and capture or kill her, and the conspirators had assembled a team of an archivist, Uncle Ivki (the only one who had seen the princess when she was small, Brin having kept her gaze lowered on their few encounters) and Aksal to find her first.

That was the gist. When people began repeating themselves, and justifying their assumptions, Seshe finally raised a hand. "This is a lot to think about. I'm very glad you told me these things. I want to cooperate as much as I can, though I do not intend to stay. This is no longer my home, and never will be. In the meantime, what I said before might impose a time constraint."

Brin said, "About the Chwahir? Sailing against Styan Okren? Why should we care about that?"

Seshe considered the variety of expressions around her. More evidence of the lack of value for human life outside of their trusted circle. They were not unlike the Chwahir in that way. She had spent a lot of time listening to Jilo and Shontande talk about the social contract, and about the boundary between military and civilian—the Colendi believing that the "noble warrior" who kept strictly aloof from politics was met more often on stage than in real life. A standing army, Shontande maintained, was a danger at home as well as to possible enemies.

Seshe said, "Do you really want another war over mistaken assumptions? Wouldn't it be better to find a solution that does not include spending the lives of conscripted Damondaen farmers and harness-makers and woodworkers, even if you don't care what happens to their commander?"

A silence fell, and Seshe looked around at the troubled faces. "We've talked a long time, and I hear thunder in the distance. Nothing is going to happen today, yes? My suggestion is that we all take this time to ponder what we've learned, and then talk again. That, by the way, is the essence of the Sarendan government. I know this because I am acquainted with the young king, Darian Selenna, and I know that his system works because everyone participates, from villages with three houses to noble estates and trade towns. Successful government, to Sarendan, and to the Colendi, as the Chwahir are beginning to learn, is based on compromise. And compromise means discussion in safety."

Another brief silence, then the teenage boy swallowed, his skinny neck knuckle bobbing, and said, "How many rulers do you know?"

"Personally? Six … seven, maybe? Let's see. There's Chwahirsland. Colend. Sartor. Erenlara of the Venn. Khanerenth. Marloven Hess."

"You know the king of Marloven Hess?"

"I do. Old friend. And the one I value most as a friend is the queen of Mearsies Heili, at the other end of this continent."

The stout cook rose, shaking her head slowly. "I need to see to my cakes."

That sparked a general exodus, until Aksal and Brin remained.

Seshe stood up, glad to stretch her legs, then took in their expressions. "I'm telling the truth," she said. "I really do know them all. They're all just people. Like you and me. Even Senrid of the Marlovens," she added, knowing that he would appreciate the irony.

Aksal uttered a humorous laugh. "Since I saw you in company with two kings, I believe it."

Brin crossed her arms. "It's just that we sat here and watched you assume authority. Because that's what you did. Did you mean to do that?"

"No," Seshe said, not hiding her surprise. "It's you who brought me here against my will, merely because of my name. It seems the name has the effect you wanted, convenient or not. I can't tell you how much I dislike that. But maybe there's something to be done with it to circumvent any more tragedy. I really need to contemplate everything you said."

Brin uttered in a stifled voice, "Shall I have them bring you dinner?"

"Certainly. Thank you."

The two left; as the big door swung shut, Seshe heard fierce whispering. She looked around the tall bookshelves, and breathed in the distinctive aroma of ancient paper and ink. Still a prisoner? Maybe, but the quality of the relationship had altered. Into what, to be determined. But the sense of threat had considerably diminished.

Seshe thought about demanding, or requesting, a different room, then shook that off. The entire castle held bad memories. As for the queen's chamber, she discovered when she reached it, the sinister atmosphere was gone. It was just a room, full of fine furnishings. That nasty scenario had been her own imagination, coming from a part of herself she disliked, but she had to admit was there. Though Seshe was absolutely certain that her mother would have ordered her servants to use themselves as living shields before her precious self, it had not happened. Imry Llyenthur had probably cut the queen's throat before she was even aware, whether in that room or another altogether; though Seshe had heard plenty to his detriment, and believed it all, she'd never heard that he toyed with his many victims. These new furnishings were a bid to please the figurehead everyone had expected to be a person with more hair than wit.

Seshe had to face the fact that it was her own furious imaginings that had filled this room with its sinister import.

There was work to do, on herself most of all.

But not right now. Exhaustion weighed on her.

She'd brought a couple of books back to read. Nothing of Damondaen's history. She felt no connection to this land where she had been so unhappy, and where she had no remaining familial connection. She did not want to read its history. She'd chosen something about the windrunners of Vakheinen, now back in their own world. The other was a book of travel reminiscences—she hoped there'd be something about Mearsies Heili. She was sure she'd enjoy seeing that beloved place through someone else's eyes.

The servants brought dinner, the youngest maid chatty, her verbs and pronouns mixing with traditional servant-to-princess, neutral-familiar, and back again. Seshe responded to the many questions about what it was like meeting kings, and were the Chwahir really as wicked as everyone said. Seshe answered patiently and kindly, promised to talk to everyone on the morrow, and after she ate, they took away the dishes and left her truly alone. With more clothing offerings.

She read, then took a bath as a summer thunderstorm rattled the windows. She climbed into the big bed where her ancestors had lain, feeling no connection. Some might not have been altogether wicked. She was certain that even Efridarlian might have been different if she hadn't been slapped into fighting back by Vihariliot. And he might have been bearable if both their parents hadn't begun so many punishments with exhortations that they'd endured the same and it had made them stronger—one a prince, the other destined to marry a throne.

She read some more, but the travel memoir was dull after all, more concerned with how many nobles the writer had met and been entertained by. She laid aside the book and fell asleep early, more exhausted than she'd realized.

Though matters were far from settled with respect to the castle conspiracy, as she was beginning to think of Brin and Aksal's ring, she was significantly relieved. So much so that she did not take the time to mentally construct a shield of steel, as she had done when fearful or tense. Efridarlian was truly gone, with her the threat of Jevondyan vengeance, which Seshe had learned when young could burn through generations.

Should she reach for Clair? Instinct fought with inclination. She felt a sense of duty here after all; she would leave things better than she'd found them, if she could. And then she could contact Clair, with the conviction she had done her best.

And, so, she was deep in a dream centered around CJ and the girls, when among the girls there emerged a familiar figure—it was Liere, as Seshe had known her long ago.

"Liere," Seshe exclaimed. "Did Clair send you? Wan-Edhe has been trying to…"

Seshe woke up—but held onto the connection. It was a little like pushing from the soft mud of a forest pool, past water plants, sun shafts, and layers of blue. There she was on the surface, out of the dream as Clair joined Liere in Seshe's mind: *We found you. Can you tell us what happened?*

Seshe had shared memories before. The first time, when Clair returned from Adam's mountain and needed to see what happened in Imar from Seshe's perspective. A few more times, for less harrowing reasons. It was easier, somehow, now. She sensed a whiff of garden rose from Liere, and there Seshe was in memory, on the barge. Everything flickered by in a sensory jumble. Memories from childhood mixed with today, in no order. But Clair's calming whisper was there: *It's fine, it's fine.*

Seshe's thought ended the memory: *I never saw it as clearly, how the shadow of war, of anger shared by all, reaches not only into lives now, but over time. I understood today that if I said, "Of course you grabbed me, it made perfect sense to you, because the consequences to me didn't matter. All your lives, what happened to you did not matter to the royal family. You are so very angry." They would have said, "We're not angry." And would have believed it. I don't know what to do.*

Liere's thought came, clear and clean as a waterfall: *Would you like our help? Though I believe there is already some maneuvering in the background.*

: Maneuvering? Seshe repeated.

: That book they found and shared. If that is not a catalyst … but I'm making assumptions. Rest and sleep, Seshe. Talk to the people tomorrow. We will tell Jilo that you are safe. If you want us, call in mind: Clair is listening.

And Seshe slept.

16

Lyren tried twice to go to sleep, but the rustle of foliage in the warm breeze, and the flutter of night birds on the wing, kept her awake. Her mind dipped to the surface of the lake of dreams, then sprang to wakefulness, until there was Liere: *Seshe is safe.*

Lyren's wordless query elicited a flood of images. A year ago, Lyren would have struggled to comprehend, but she had been refining her Dena Yeresbeth skills as Liere did.

It was a short contact, for Liere was tired. Lyren sent wordless gratitude, and looked around her quiet room, the furnishings barely distinguishable in the moonlight. She struggled against the urge to let Shontande know. When did being helpful tip over into being interfering? She knew quite well that part of that urgency was her own wish to see him, talk to him, and relish the warmth of his attention. As did a good portion of his court.

She wavered, then finally decided to go walking, since she wasn't going to sleep anyway. She breathed in the soft, fragrant summer air, and looked about the moonlit palace at night. Fewer lamps lit the paths. Servants had put out those directly outside windows. Others clustered at intersections, and around night blooms. Night or day, this extensive garden, far larger than the palace, enchanted her. She wished she could see it in winter.

Twice she encountered herald guards on the move—now that she knew what they looked like, they were no longer unobtrusive. She held up her token, and they bowed her past.

She'd decided along the way that if no lights glowed in the king's wing, she'd walk on by. But the entire wing was lit.

She encountered another pair of heralds, and this time, as she held up her token, she said, "If the king is free, I have a report for him."

One herald looked aside. A page in dark clothes, hidden in shadows before, scampered away on noiseless feet, and returned very quickly. She made a quick bow with that airy, open-handed gesture that Lyren now knew was invitation. "The king bids you welcome."

Lyren found Shontande sitting by a window overlooking a canal, a book open before him. The fine skin under his eyes was marked with tiredness. Lyren said abruptly, "Seshe is safe. Liere just contacted me." She brushed her fingertips across her brow.

"Safe with Jilo?"

"She is still in Damondaen, but what that poor book-copier said was true. From their perspective. They really thought they were rescuing her." And at the question in his face, she explained what Liere had shared, ending with, "Siamis and Ferret have transferred down to southern Toar to survey matters. They will act if necessary."

At the end, Shontande said, "Then — no thanks to us — all's well. Or soon will be, I gather?"

"That's the impression I got. If anything does go wrong, Liere and Clair are in contact with Seshe. Between all those people, I believe I can predict that Seshe will be perfectly fine. Also, there is no animus whatsoever toward Colend."

Shontande looked pained. "That is kindly meant, but it does not exonerate us."

"Is it too inquisitive for me to ask why not?"

"Ruis left a short while before you arrived," Shontande said, and Lyren came forward, laying her hands over the back of a chair. His lips twitched in a smile. "Please sit, if you will."

Lyren's charming grin flashed. "I'm trying not to be intrusive here. You look tired. I know I'm tired. And yet I feel it's important to emphasize that I sniffed no blame toward you, or Colend, from Liere, or from Seshe through Liere."

"And I've received the same well-meant reassurance from Jilo." He tapped a note on the table. "Yet it happened here. It was a deliberate plan, by people who have never set foot in Colend, but who confidently expected that we would not be capable of protecting a guest. What does that say about us? Ruis and I have been debating that for the past, oh, three hours."

There was a time when Lyren would have merely repeated herself. As if reassuring Shontande that no one blamed him would end the matter. But all those conversations with Laban, and her experiences in Sarendan, and those nightly contacts with Liere as she navigated her hostage year, had brought a certain awareness of the invisible chains binding rulers.

"Does Ruis think that Colend needs more herald-guards? Better trained, perhaps? So that the occasional kidnapper would find them more threatening?" Lyren asked.

Shontande's gaze snapped to hers, and searched it. "That was one of the matters that we discussed." He ended on a note of question.

Lyren whisked herself around the chair in a flutter of yellow gauze, and perched, light as the butterflies embroidered all over the outer panels of her robe. "I am what the Sartorans call a hereandtherian, a wanderer who has never settled, and so I know that the idea of offering an opinion to a ruler is as preposterous as it is impertinent. And yet, I've listened, oh, so much, to talk among rulers. May I make an observation or two?"

Shontande gestured Deference, a hand touching his heart and opening outward with a graceful gesture. "Please."

"I think one of the primary reasons I looked forward to coming to this kingdom was because I knew there had been no wars. I'm not counting Norsunder." She touched a finger to her lips and snapped it away, Colend's courtly version of spitting — a gesture Lyren liked. "*That* to Norsunder. Further, I think a good part of your visitors dancing till dawn on the Chandos canal at this moment would say the same. It feels safe here."

"Yet, if I may demur, it was not safe for Seshe. Further, if Jilo is not blaming us in his heart, it's only because of his character of forbearance. That does not excuse us."

"I think that Senrid would say it could have happened anywhere." Lyren's smile vanished as she said softly, "Senrid's little daughter was in the middle of his castle, which has more guards, better-trained, than most places in the world. Granted, this was at the worst point in the battle over Marloven Hess, but still, Crystal Ingrid died. Right there. Not far from Senrid. It can happen anywhere."

Shontande's lovely hands opened like flowers in the

gesture Lyren had yet to learn the name for, but she translated it mentally to conditional agreement, and also invitation to go on.

She went on. "Further. I've heard Senrid, and Laban, and Atan, observe that when you train people to become warriors, they are warriors for life. That means violence becomes one of their modes of solving problems. It often is the quickest one. If the training is good, it's the easiest one."

Shontande bowed slightly.

Lyren was not certain she was making sense or blithering, for she knew he'd be polite either way, but she gritted on. "Marloven Hess is at peace, and yet Senrid still sleeps with a knife under his pillow. My impression of Colend is that nobody ever thinks of sleeping with knives under their pillow. Flower petals, yes. Even if a bad thing happens somewhere, they don't take steel to bed. All right, I had my say. I'll go away and leave you in peace."

Shontande held up a hand, and she halted.

"It's rare," he said slowly, "that someone understands that it is not my emotions that matter in state questions."

"Your emotions do matter." Lyren spread her hands. "You're a person! People's feelings matter! But isn't that a separate matter from what you call state questions? Especially the question of standing armies?"

"Thank you for seeing that." He bowed.

She uttered a quick laugh. "I'm just parroting what I've heard. And I just now realized that you're probably going to need to redo whatever it was you were going to have the heralds post in a few hours. Good night!" With a quick swirl of gauze, she flitted away.

He wanted to stop her, but he, too, had realized he must redraft the heralds' announcements, and also rewrite each of the notes he'd put together for Nash's barge guests. He had to let her go.

Seshe woke to clear skies and the familiar scents of the mountain. Unease stirred within her. It was old emotion, never eradicated. Just pushed down.

By the time she'd bathed and dressed, the young maid, Peri, breezed back in with breakfast, chattering the while. Seshe learned that Aksal had ridden out the night before, intending to bring the Gamlasko clan leaders back to the royal castle to talk to Seshe.

Good. The more the better. Seshe had no idea what to do next, except to listen to all the complaints. If they wanted to talk to a princess, that was fine. Centuries of understood hierarchy would not break down overnight. But she, in her turn, was going to make it absolutely clear that she was not going to stay.

She wanted to leave things in somewhat better shape than she found them, but even that might be presumptuous. All she could do was her best.

Her thoughts flitted immediately to Jilo, but she knew that Clair and Liere would have let him know what had happened.

She emerged from the queen's chambers to find that teenage boy waiting. Ought she to learn names when she did not intend to stay? Everyone deserved to be a someone with an identity besides cook or housecleaner.

He spoke as soon as he saw her, letting her know that the lower interview chamber was filling up. Bemused, Seshe walked downstairs to the great room she remembered one or the other of her parents presiding in. Never together. In hindsight, she could see that they'd tolerated one another for purposes of state, and had divided ruling tasks according to some rubric only known to them.

She was not prepared for the fact that the room was packed, the only place to sit being the throne on its dais. Word had clearly flown down the mountain during the night. She stopped in the doorway, considering requesting a chair so that she could avoid that preposterously decorated throne, except that she wouldn't be able to see everyone. The sheer practicality of thrones was not lost on her, though she resented every symbol of power encrusting it and extending upward to an absurd height that had terrified her as a child.

All eyes followed her as she crossed the chamber. The crowd compressed, creating an aisle, then closed in behind her as she mounted to the throne. She pitched her voice to be heard, the way she had a very few times in Chwahirsland, before she'd given up trying to win over the women of Narad. "I am Seshemerria Jevondyan. I left this kingdom years ago. I do not intend to stay. But before I leave, I want to help you to replace what I left all those years ago, with the beginnings of something better. It will only happen if we work together."

A single heartbeat of silence, then everyone began talking. Shouting.

She held up her hands, and waited until the roar quieted to a rumble, then silence. "One at a time, or nobody will be heard. I'll stay here until everyone gets their chance. Please be orderly."

Whispers rustled through the crowd: "'Please' … she said *please* … neutral mode …"

They were trying to push authority onto her. Seshe sighed within, and pointed to a random person. "We'll begin with you."

Three days later, she was still listening. By now the testimonies had begun to fall into patterns: outrage, complaints, accusations, followed by hectoring worded as suggestions. Questions, also. So many questions. She answered them all, aware that her answers, too, were falling into patterns. But what else to say? Humans made patterns. Even in situations where everything was changing.

At night, Clair and Liere contacted her together, first conveying encouragement and admonitions to stay safe from Jilo, and then listening to her summation of her day before they discussed it. Seshe thought hard about those answers.

On the fourth night, she said, "I get the sense that the country is waking to the fact that something new is going to happen. Though no one knows quite what. But right now, those who want to be heard are being heard, whatever their rank in life. I'm glad to do it, even though no one is ready to believe that the change will be real until 'something' is done about Styan Okren. Everything always comes back to Styan Okren."

"Everything," Styan Okren was fond of saying to his captains, "comes back to the old glory days. Once we regain Rhengal, and push up into Teredaln and Edal Haven, we will be at our old strength. From centuries ago. Once they see that, the people will settle down."

No one wanted to point out that he'd said that before they conquered the southern kingdoms, which brought little but the need for garrisoning, stretching their resources further. The skeptics among the captains shrugged at predictions of glory and honor and plenty. As long as they obeyed orders, they got to eat. Which was more than they'd had that bad winter after Norsunder left.

When Okren saw the expected obedience in the faces of his captains, he settled back to review the map once again. Two more position reports, and he could signal the attack. Until then, why hadn't he heard anything from the garrison at the mountain?

He was considering sending a galloper in case the company holding the capital had somehow lost their transfer tray, when a flurry outside the HQ announced the arrival of a messenger having been passed through.

A mud-splashed boy rushed in, his voice cracking on every other word as he said, "Captain Nidiar had to withdraw to the old base. Sent me to report that rebels took over the mountain. Hundreds and hundreds of them. Our people outnumbered by tens and twenties. And leading them is the missing princess!"

"What? Someone found her?"

"Yes! Brought by magic. She's here!" He passed a grimy hand over his face, leaving a sweaty smear, then corrected, "That is, she holds the royal castle."

"She's welcome to sheets smelling like swamp and rat shit on every tray," Okren commented. "Go and get some water. Something to eat. Report back for orders."

What to do now? He'd left barely enough staff to hold the garrisons, mustering the entire army for this push to round out the kingdom. He was so busy considering alternatives that he didn't think much about the short scuffle noises and a couple of clangs coming in the open window. Drills were frequent, especially within the first perimeter.

An unfamiliar man slouched into the office.

Okren looked up impatiently at the interruption. He still hadn't decided what to do about the princess — everything was committed here. If he divided his force, he endangered the primary goal, so...

The inner dialogue died away as he stared at the lugubrious face before him. Sickly pale skin. Black hair tied back. Black long tunic over equally black riding trousers and black-weave boots. Wait, wait, wait, *a Chwahir?*

Disbelief robbed him of wits as the fellow walked up to the desk and glanced down at the map. Okren reacted at last, crushing the map against his chest. "Who are you?"

"Name is Jilo," the man said, his accent heavy. "We need to talk."

He was unarmed. So was Okren—he never kept swords in the office. Okren shouted for his duty sentries, and got no response.

"They're tied up outside the door," Jilo said, as Okren thought, could this be *that* Jilo? King of the Chwahir?

He was no coward, but shock could shake anyone. He half-rose, looking out the window, to where a tall, knife-lean, black-haired man lounged against the wall, cleaning his nails with a two-edged blade. One boot rested on the prone figure of a sentry. The sentry seemed to be alive, but for how long?

Okren's gaze snapped to the other watchpoints. Another tall man, also black-haired and in black—no, that was a woman. She stood beside a sentry bound in rope. She wore some kind of harness. What was that she was carrying behind her? A weapon? Okren saw a little fist waving. A *baby*? A stealth attack carrying a baby? Were these Chwahir? Their skin was normal, not the color of uncooked dough, like this Jilo waiting in front of the desk.

Okren looked in the other direction—and that one definitely had to be a Chwahir, for he was as pasty-faced as Jilo. He seemed to have stopped a sentry and the post runner. And the silence from behind the door indicated at least one more enemy behind him.

Jilo said. "Seshemerria Jevondyan is going to be Queen of the Chwahir as soon as I can talk her into it. Touching her is a direct threat to me. Do you understand that?"

Okren stared, but before he could bluster, Jilo said, "I expect she will be returning home soon. As soon as she finishes matters in your capital. She had better remain unobstructed while she is there. And forever after."

"Or?" Okren managed, his heart thudding in his mouth. Reality had set in: he'd been taken utterly by surprise.

"Or the Chwahir navy, which will be here in two, maybe three weeks, depending on weather and currents, and our allies, the Marlovens, will be landing on these shores. We won't be bothering Rhengal. I spoke to their royal council this morning, and promised we'd pass through without disturbing them, if we had to land. But I cannot promise the same for Damondaen." He pointed at the map still crushed against Okren's chest. "By the way, the two captains you're waiting on,

Hedryan at Lake Falls and Rakir near the Rhengal and Teredaln border? They won't be making reports today. They have troubles of their own."

Okren let the map fall to the desk, the markers spilling unnoticed.

"Consider cooperating with whatever the princess and the people decide. If that happens, then in three weeks, your scouts off the islands will be seeing a joint Chwahir-Marloven naval drill. It should be fun to watch. But if you insist on going ahead with this attack, or you try sending any more assassins, you'll be meeting the Chwahir Gold and Silver armies, and the Marloven West Army, personally."

Jilo went to the window and raised a hand. All three of the visible enemies vanished in transfer magic, one by one. Jilo lifted a hand in salute, and vanished as well.

17

Sveneric knew that his father was not omniscient, or even infallible. He'd never pretended to be. He would discuss his own errors in that instructive, dispassionate tone that masked the internal cost—and in masking it, underscored its presence.

As Sveneric moved along the carved and painted corridors of the Lirendi royal palace, he amended his mental observation. His father had not pretended to be omniscient after the supposed Great Switch. Before that, yes, he had affected omniscience—even when engineering his own defeat—but that had all been part of his persona in Norsunder. There, all one respected, understood, coveted, or obeyed, was power. The pose of omniscience meant that he never had to explain.

How far ought control to reach? No, the question perhaps ought to be posed differently: how does one know when to act and when to stand back?

He suppressed a sigh, wishing he could discuss it with Detlev, but he was gone on one of his mysterious journeys. This time with Lilith and Hibern, so it had something to do with magic.

It was as well. There was far too much to learn.

He turned his attention to his two weeks as a secret judge.

Every day for fourteen days now, he had wandered the pretty streets, and stood on the arched bridges of Alsais. He'd drifted along the canals, and wandered in and out of buildings, always listening. He had been surprised and, at first, gratified when Shontande Lirendi had come to him not long after his arrival and asked if he would function as one of this year's judges. Sveneric had agreed, been told to select one name for each of five categories, and meet with an appointed person whenever he had decided, up until the morning of the last day.

He was on his way to keep that appointment now. Outside, the day was bright and miserably hot. Sveneric had elected to walk the long way rather than cross any of the gardens in the merciless sun, partly to avoid the heat, but partly to appreciate the clever design behind the cool tiled corridors along which garden-scented breezes flowed.

Despite the size of the buildings, very little magic was involved, and Sveneric sensed no imbalance in that realm. The fountains and falls, shockingly cold, sent the cool breezes stirring the air; the hot air swooshed upward and escaped through angled windows through which the sun's rays did not fall in summer.

It was very much the same sort of design that Detlev had employed when building his place: diffuse the summer sun, and permit direct shine in winter, maximizing light and heat. Only there it was harmonious, here artistic, for water, mirror, windows and garden motifs had been employed so that though he was actually surrounded by walls of stone, he was aware only of light, cool air, and greenery.

Shontande Lirendi presided in the State wing, which was thronged with liveried heralds, pages, guild representatives, and stewards. One or two courtiers came and went, obviously on matters of import. This was no place for loitering. Though Colend's kings kept court, the nobles apparently did not see them govern—not unless there was an issue that directly concerned their holdings. Either that or some kind of capital case. The everyday connection between the smooth hum of administration and crown was the privy council, at the outset of the war all killed.

Shontande was in the midst of building a new privy council, slowly, and with care. Yet one could not call this process secret, for it was all quite open—more so than the government of other kingdoms Sveneric had visited.

Sveneric found it all endlessly fascinating, the methods by which the ebb and flow of power was controlled. He looked forward to discussing it with David when he returned to Curtas's House. He wished he could discuss these issues with Shontande Lirendi, but he knew his motive would be suspected because of who he was. That he had been invited to serve as one of this year's music judges was surprising enough. Maybe it was a kind of test.

Sveneric was used to that.

He exerted himself to move unobtrusively until he was intercepted by a steward.

"May I help you?" she asked.

Sveneric smiled. "I have an appointment with Rascande."

"Please. This way." She gestured.

Sveneric followed, noting the strength under that plain livery, the way her gaze covered everyone still in her field of vision. Herald-guards were posted in public places, but wearing crown livery, no uniforms. The illusion of no military presence, age-old, was strictly preserved.

Through a door, which closed out the noise behind them. Down a carpeted hall to a plain chamber overlooking one of the tree and fern-lined canals. The furnishings plain but good, the aspect impersonal; this was a waiting room, not someone's place of labor.

Within very few moments entered a tall, thin man with gray hair tied back. He was dressed anonymously. He gestured to a chair, and they both sat down.

"I am Rascande," he said. "The king asked me to coordinate the judging this year. Have you decided?"

"Yes," Sveneric said, and he named his choices.

Rascande listened, put palms together in the peace, and said, "Have you any observations to offer?"

"I have no criticisms, "Sveneric said, noting that Rascande had not written down his choices, but he knew better than to think they might be forgotten. Or ignored. "Observations, yes."

Rascande gestured, palm up. "I am in no hurry. You are the last, and we are interested in any reflections that the judges might wish to share."

Sveneric said, "At first I was overwhelmed, and I thought it would be impossible to evaluate everyone fairly. It occurred to me that the judgment, however it were decided, particularly as the judges acted separately and not as a body, would be at best arbitrary. The greatest might not be found, only the standouts among the most prominent."

When Sveneric paused to consider his next words, Rascande said, still in that neutral tone, "Did you discover other judges?"

"I did," Sveneric said. "Or at least, I suspect that I did. I spoke to no one, of course, for secrecy had been the only rule that was definite."

Rascande smiled a little. "Go on."

"By the fourth day, I was afraid that I would have to resign my mission. But over the next day or so, I began to perceive a … pattern, an order, shall I say, that lay outside of the question of winners and losers. The musicians were all listening to one another at least as intently as I listened to them. They were not just listening, but learning from one another. One group I revisited, and I heard subtle changes propagating through their work."

Rascande nodded, still smiling.

Sveneric looked out the window at the breeze-ruffled canal. "The cauldron of our culture," he said. "It's an easy phrase, and the notion that fashion begins in Colend is not new. But during these two weeks I became convinced that it was true, and I saw how it was done."

He turned his attention back to Rascande.

"And so?" The man asked.

"And so it's true that it doesn't really matter who wins those silver feathers. Another set of judges might have selected different people than whoever will win this year. But that doesn't mean the contest is irrelevant. The silver feather is the draw that brings the best from all over the world. The real winners are everyone, for none of these musicians will go home complacent. They are all fired with new ideas, and determination to refine their art. They have been, in fact, training and inspiring one another, and inventing new forms, quite separately from the question of the competition. It's a remarkable process. I am honored to have been a part of it."

Rascande stood, and bowed. Sveneric also bowed, and after polite words of mutual goodwill, he left.

That same day, Seshe said her farewells to the people of Damondaen.

A few days earlier, while she was lying half-asleep in that state bed, a memory had emerged from what seemed a lifetime ago. It was a day or two after CJ and the girls had been captured by Kessler Sonscarna, the mad heir to the terrible (and even more insane) Wan-Edhe, king of the Chwahir. While Kessler waited for CJ to join his group of youths being trained to assassinate all rulers, and replace them with Kessler's own followers chosen by merit, the girls had been stuck in a single room and kept on very short rations.

Most had played games, or talked, sang, told jokes, or composed insults for this new set of villains, confident that CJ would find a way out. Diana, the other who had never spoken about her past, had whispered to Seshe, *You can spend your life always hungry, dirty, and scared. But given safety, cleanliness, enough to eat, you get used to it so fast, the moment it's taken away, you resent it!*

Seshe did not want to be Princess Seshemerria. She longed to get back to the life she had chosen. And yet, after a week of steadily asserting that she would make no decisions—the people must find agreement and compromise—when the talkers began talking past her to each other, and then coming back having discussed alternatives and alliances somewhere else at night, she'd discovered in herself a sense that events were leaving her behind.

Human nature. So slippery!

The other, less unsettling surprise was the return of former king Styan Okren, who sent a messenger to Seshe. At first worry had spiked that here, after all, was the threat she'd dreaded when she first was brought back. But when they met and spoke, it turned out under all the rhetoric about only wanting to serve the kingdom and to restore peace he wanted a place in the new government. Since troubling reports were trickling in of youths going wild and breaking into the homes of former governors and the like, Seshe easily convinced the Gamlaskos and the others who seemed to be coalescing into some kind of advisory council, to request the general to disperse the army to its garrisons again to restore order. *Civilian* order.

After that, she bit back on her opinions, and once more became solely a listener. The tide of talk sloshed back and forth like water in a basin, sometimes becoming heated. There was enough of the old authority left that when disputants began raising voices and coming close to hurling threats, they'd turn to Seshe. Who, it was generally assumed, could whistle up General Commander Okren.

She'd keep silent, letting pauses stretch out until tempers calmed.

Talk circled and circled again, as the days blended into one another, until yesterday, a page hurtled in yelling, "An army galloper! Says that Chwahir ships have been spotted on the horizon! And Marlovens!"

Into the ringing silence, Seshe said, "They have come for me. I will depart on the morrow." She added after a very loud thunderbolt rumbled away into the distance, "My last suggestion is to dedicate this castle to the governing body. And name it for Thirva Soraq, who believed in loving one another."

She looked to each of them, from Peri, who was surprisingly tenacious in her determination to be part of things, to Grandmother Gamlasko, who was emerging as a voice of reason. She, having survived the Jevondyan years as well as the war, was stern, but she had a way of seeing past oblique threats and false-premise arguments.

Brin said into the silence, "I never really knew her, but I favor that idea."

"I knew her well," Ivki whispered—the Colendi having sent him back via transfer. "I would like to see her so honored."

Not everyone agreed. Many had been killed for no reason beyond whim. But they were getting into a way of talking out alternatives that gave Seshe hope that maybe something new would emerge—and if it turned out they fell into the old ways (they were also talking about "new" ranks) it might leave the door open for a better balance of power in the future. The name Jevondyan would now belong to aging tapestries and moldering scrolls warning the reader of what could happen if they were not vigilant.

The royal palace still was stiff with wards, but Jilo had arranged to get a golden notecase to Seshe, along with a very short note in his messy handwriting that she sensed had taken him hours to compose. Every line breathed love. And with it, a transfer token.

She decided the best time to use it was after the navy had been sighted. The farewells over, she told Grandmother Gamlasko that she would be welcome to write, if she so desired, and then she used the token—

—and found herself staggering on the heaving deck of a ship. A moment of nausea, swept away by a clean sea wind, and there was Jilo, surrounded by sailors. By him stood Gold Admiral Opun, and the Gold Army First Division General.

Jilo stood there, his hands twitching uncertainly, and with a swoop of tenderness and sorrow and joy, Seshe knew that even at this moment he would not make the first move, because he still was convinced that he was not worthy, that anyone who got close would find him repellant.

She had learned to keep gestures of affection private because of how they made the Chwahir uncomfortable, but this time her step didn't falter. She threw herself into his arms and kissed his face all over, tasting the salt of brine, and maybe tears. Jilo hummed in pleasure before she let go, lest too much embarrass him before his commanders.

To her immense surprise, she found broad smiles in the faces around, and the sailors smacked their chests, an accolade that she attributed solely to Jilo.

It was then that she realized the deck was not only occupied by Chwahir: Siamis was there, and next to him, Clair's pure white hair gleamed like the snow on a mountaintop.

Seshe turned from Jilo to Clair, who hugged her tightly. "Well done," Clair whispered.

"I don't know if anything I said or did will make the least difference," Seshe murmured back.

"Damondaen will do what it is going to do. I meant you, confronting your past. Not easy."

Sailors scrambled overhead, followed by the thud of huge sails. The ship heeled, water feathering down the side below the rail. Seshe looked around again, this time beyond the rails, and discovered what seemed to be a thousand ships sailing in orderly lines, masts aslant, curved sails belling in the wind.

Her eye caught on one different from the rest. It looked like something out of an ancient tapestry, with a great curving prow that ended in a silhouette of a dragon head. "What is that?" Seshe asked.

"Senrid's over there. He invites us aboard once the exercise is finished."

Exercise. Seshe discovered that the two great navies were in the middle of a mock battle that soon included blunted arrows flying back and forth, chases with sails flashing out then disappearing, and finally, as the fiery ball of the sun hovered above the coast of Toar, they finished up with some boarding and mock-fighting, both sides enthusiastic to the point of warriors—not used to ships—falling overboard, to hoots of scorn from sailors on both sides.

Far away over the water, the wink of field glasses testified to many watchers from the craft that had prudently stayed in harbor, or hugged the coast. At sunset, the great drakan sailed close to Jilo's flagship, and the commanders plus Jilo and the visitors all elected to climb down and row over rather than endure a transfer from deck to deck.

From one ship with mostly black-haired, pale-skinned sailors to the drakan, with mostly blond or brown-haired crew with various shades of brown skin. Senrid was among them, Liere at his side, one hand supporting a sizable mound of belly.

They entered a great cabin, and paused to take in the ancient Venn splendor. "That was fun," Senrid said as they all took a seat at the fine table. "Excellent work," he added, opening his callused palm toward the Chwahir admiral and general.

They both deferred to Jilo, who said, "I thought so, too. I trust that will suffice to keep them inside their border." He turned to Seshe. "Okren heeded our hints, then?"

"Hints?" she said.

"He didn't tell you that a few of us paid him a visit?"

"No," Seshe said, round-eyed. "Clair only said that you had communicated with him, and she hoped that I would be receiving a message soon. What happened?"

Senrid grinned. "Siamis scouted. Erol and a few of Detlev's boys sat on Okren's inner perimeter. Okren listened. Not a drop of blood shed," he added, knowing that that was what would mean the most to Seshe.

"I only had the one meeting with him, when he returned to the capital. I did not find him to be a bad person, for a general bent on conquering. He really believed that army discipline was the solution to all the kingdom's ills. If only common folk could be bludgeoned into sense. And he had spent decades cleaning up royal errors. He discovered he liked doing that." Seshe smiled ruefully.

"From there an easy leap to bypassing royal messes entirely, with him as king?" Senrid guessed.

"Pretty much," Seshe said, and could not prevent a glance toward the west, as if she could see the mountain from there.

Clair, Liere, and Jilo noted that inadvertent glance, but said nothing as the conversation became general, with a great deal of mutual compliments on the day's exercise. Once the meal of fresh fish, rye biscuits, and pickled cabbage had been consumed—enjoyed by Chwahir and Marlovens alike—Siamis and Clair bade everyone farewell, and transferred back to Mearsies Heili. Clair first promised privately to be available whenever

Seshe was ready to talk about her experiences.

The Chwahir and Seshe rowed back. When they reached the flagship, Jilo lifted his voice to be heard over the entire ship: "Good work."

No speech. But the two words, for the Chwahir, meant more than any amount of fulsome words.

Then Jilo said softly, with a look Seshe found difficult to interpret, "Ready to go home?"

"I am."

She endured the second wrenching transport of the day, but when the reaction wore off, there she was in Jilo's study, the beloved quiet chamber with its gleaming, clean furnishings, and the scent of stone. "Home," she said on an exhaled breath.

"Still?" Jilo asked, still with that oddly intent expression.

"Always," Seshe said, coming to him and laying her hand on his chest. She could feel his heartbeat drumming beneath her palm. "Is something amiss?"

Jilo said slowly, "The brush-scribe makes art of the poet's words." And then in a mumble, "I tried to find something written by the wise ancients that would express how I feel. Be suitable. But nothing was good enough. Marry me, Seshe. Please. I know that marriage won't suddenly make you safe from threats, much less harm, but I have never been as wretched as I was when you were gone. And since. Even when Wan-Edhe tossed me into his dungeon."

Seshe gazed in alarm at the gleam along his lower eyelids. "Jilo?"

"I thought you would not come back to me," he said, low and fierce. "What would you come back *for?* Once I knew you were safe, that was such a relief, but then I thought, you would be perfect to rule there. You were born there. They seemed to value you, so why shouldn't you?"

"It was never a temptation," she exclaimed. "I've been feeling a bit ambivalent because it seems selfish of me not to be tempted. Maybe I ought to regret it? But I do not. I came to value many of the people there, but that castle, that identity, was never home. I never understood the concept of home, until Clair welcomed me to Mearsies Heili. And then I came to you." She drew an unsteady breath. "I'm no longer afraid of someone finding out who I was. It actually happened. And I survived. And yet the greater problem still remains — I am still a foreigner to the Chwahir."

Jilo blinked, then took her hands. "Didn't you see?" His cheekbones blotched with red. "When you kissed me. How they saluted. Smiled."

Seshe stared at him, and then the obvious hit her. "Oh. I hadn't thought of that. It's the princess title? Ugh! As empty a title as ever was."

"Not to them," Jilo said. "Not to them. Consider how valueless so many of the women still feel, though I, we, are doing everything we can to get rid of Wan-Edhe's poisons. I hadn't seen it either, what a blow it was to them that I didn't look at a Chwahir woman, but brought in a foreigner with what seemed to be no twi, no family, no place as places are valued by us. But then you were taken. And it turned out that a powerful kingdom wanted the single heir to the throne back. You had a name, a royal name. You had a royal rank. But you rejected them in order to come back to us. It makes all the difference. To everybody. That you, who could be queen of a powerful country, chose Chwahirsland. And, um, I gain, too," he mumbled, eyes lowered. "If you say yes. We shall commence the work together."

"Yes, yes, yes," Seshe exclaimed, laughing raggedly. "I do hate finding myself respected for something that has nothing to do with my brains and skills, such as they are. But I know there is no changing human nature overnight. I will happily marry you. With whatever sort of display that will do Chwahirsland proud."

She could see his answer in his face, and this time he kissed her first.

18

Flash! The hunger for touch burned as Lyren walked away from the meadow north of the palace, where horse racing was held. It was Shontande on horseback just now, hair flying, his body lithe, graceful even when exerting strength, as he and his horse raced down the last of a grueling trail and then took flight over a stone fence. Only Caid of Alarcansa was faster, though many had tried, including Lyren: they were all excellent riders, but it seemed the duchas had the fastest animals.

She'd been among the first group, on a horse borrowed from Nash, the consequence not only of Siamis's patient teaching all those years ago, but five years of riding Vana's tricksy, half-trained young horses.

Lyren was beginning to learn, bit by bit, how very lonely the crown prince of Colend had been. First isolated by his father, who trusted no one, then by the regency council whose primary goal had been to hold onto their power. Isolated in the midst of the world's finest palace, every whim served instantly. Except the desire for the kind of friendship that most everyone else found easily. For free.

She didn't always see him at events. Through Nash she was meeting courtiers, many of whom invited her to social occasions. None of the inner circle around Count Talian of Ariath. But Hradzy Wendis, and the Khanerenth ambassador, and of course Thad and Nalisse—back from their wedding trip—included her in boat rides, concerts, gatherings, picnics, and street wanders.

Since the night of Seshe's disappearance it had gradually become a habit to go walking late at night to see if the lights glowed in the king's residence. She did not even have to show her token, not after the third evening. She passed through the shadowy perimeter of watchful guards, into the light and airy room overlooking the waterfall, and they talked. Sometimes until the eastern windows reminded them that the world was still there.

It had become a necessity, those late-night talks, even if she was always short on sleep. They sat on cushions, not even the hems of their garments touching, and let words flow. At first, it was mostly Lyren talking. Chat had always been easy, and interesting, and fun. For him, dangerous, because of the weight others attributed to the most inconsequential, unconsidered word.

She chatted. He could not seem to get enough details of village life in Sarendan. Or of the underground hideout in Mearsies Heili, smelling of old meals, with childish scrawls tacked up on the dirt walls, battered old furniture, and the constant sounds of jabber and laughter and play. Of the weird lights over Bereth Ferian in certain seasons, while she and Mac had romped through the gardens. Of selling pastries in Belann, and sleeping under the attic roof with a cousin who often turned into a bird...

"Are you ignoring me?" Sveneric asked. "Or merely lost in aesthetic contemplation?"

Lyren hadn't even seen him join her. "I'm tired. And sweaty. I stink of horse, and I desperately want a bath in a nice, cool, shady place."

Sveneric's eyes narrowed in sympathetic amusement. "No need to ward me, Lyren."

"What's the use?" She tried for humor as they reached the north garden, and started down a shady path. "You probably know all my thoughts before I think them."

"Sure. I control the entire world as well, and just chose to be here out of mere caprice."

"Don't be difficult," Lyren said. "I just don't want any questions. Or comments at present."

"And I'm incapable of discerning that? From omniscience to density in one step."

"Two," Lyren said primly, pausing to sniff a moon lily. Then she sighed. "I don't want any of your helpful insights.

And don't tell me you've never helpfully advised people despite the fact that they didn't want to hear it. For their own good, always. Because I can remember plenty of examples."

Sveneric's smile was unrepentant. "And you don't?"

"When we were small doesn't count."

"For me, either, then. In the last few years ... since I learned a modicum of discretion ... when have I spoken unless there was some wish, however ambivalent, to hear my perspective?"

"And *always* in the form of a question," Lyren said. "You got that nasty habit from Detlev."

"It works." Sveneric shrugged, giving her that quizzical smile. "In answering, the person perhaps solves the problem, and I don't have to say any more. Adam's better at it."

Lyren sighed. "Your mountain school again." She nerved herself, then stopped in the middle of a wide, tiled court near one of the indoor fountains. The chuckling sound of falling water would muffle their voices — should anyone be about. "All right. Spit it out. What am I doing wrong?"

"I'm not here to interfere," he said. "I'm here for the music. Even if I wanted to interfere, I don't know enough to have any confidence in my actions. But if you want my opinion, inexperienced as it is, you'll have to ask."

"Inexperienced?" she repeated, and was going to ask what all those visits to the beautiful, intense Erenlara Sofar of the Venn had been, if not experience?

She didn't ask, in case there might be hurt beneath his Detlevish exterior, but he saw it anyway.

His smile turned wry. "She little-brothered me before I turned sixteen."

"Little — she's your age!" But she stopped there. Though Lyren was a year older than the other two, she had always felt junior to Erenlara. Frivolously junior. Not that the Venn princess ever said or did anything to cause that. It was just her ferocious self-discipline, and that sense during the war, before she and CJ left for the Land of the Venn, that she would never attain some impossibly high standard that she seemed to have set for herself. Lyren hadn't seen her for a few years, but she got the impression that Erenlara had mitigated that drive somewhat. Arthur had said of her, *It's impossible to believe Eren was ever a child, even when she was young. It's those eyes of hers, so aware. So patient.*

"Nothing wrong," Sveneric said, sidestepping the subject

of Erenlara. "When I say I hope you know what you're doing, what I mean is, I hope the end result will reward your effort. Bah. That sounds equally trite, and fatuous. Never mind. It's too hot to think of anything except the prospect of the last public concert before they announce this year's silver feather winners. It's bound to be the best of the best."

They chatted about concerts and musicales they'd witnessed over the past two weeks, then she asked if he was leaving right away. Sveneric said that Bee and Ruis had invited him to stay as long as he wanted, and as Detlev was apparently gone off somewhere, and the students at Curtas's House were all on field trips, he was on his own. He did not ask if she was leaving.

They parted when they drew near the vine-covered wall that discreetly divided off the herald-guards' area, which included the command residence, and Lyren continued on to her suite, a cold bath in mind.

The bath was large enough for the wand to bring water with the rush of a stream. It was delightfully refreshing, a sense she needed with so much shorted sleep.

Nothing was wrong. But Sveneric had still dropped a clumping hint: he niffed intent, even if he hadn't grasped her plan to court a kingdom before she let herself court its king. Lyren was exerting herself with every nerve not to court Shontande, much less seduce him. Though especially on these warm nights, when the glow of candlelight painted the severe cut of his lower lip, and the entrancing curve of the upper one as it parted, revealing the edges of brilliant white teeth, she fought against desire. How would those lips feel, the graze of those teeth?

Not yet. Not yet.

Every passing day convinced her the more deeply that he needed a friend far more than he needed yet another lover. He had friends, of course. Thad being an excellent example. But who did not need another friend? Not just the Colendi king, but in all his court?

Foolish, or arrogant to assume she could be that friend? One could insult Sveneric with impunity, but dismiss his observations only at your peril. She ducked down again, laughing under water. The bubbles floated up, dazzling spheres of diamond-bright blueness. That was the westering sun shafting in. Time to ready for the end of the festival.

She sloshed out of the bath, knowing the water would dry

fast in this heat—by the time she had rubbed her skin to wakefulness, her hair was more damp than wet. She dressed in soft linen trousers and top with a gossamer robe of blue lace over it, and headed out.

Ochre rays slanted down through the whispering linden trees when she trod the long way through the palace, just so she could pass along the little rocky trail through the grotto near the waterfall. The trail led down through a dense part of the garden alongside one of the residence buildings, then under an arching stone bridge, artful with twining vines and hanging lavender flowers, above which were *his* rooms. She stood poised, relishing the sheer simplicity of their talks—last night, of apples: blossoms, crisp and new, baked, flavored at winter's end, when one looks forward to the flowers of spring.

She couldn't give him the cleverness of courtiers who'd had to copy out books and books of poetry while refining their handwriting, and whose word games thus were formidable to anyone who had not the same upbringing. She couldn't give him much besides simplicity, but she could hear in his voice how much he appreciated it. She knew that because just in these past three days he had begun to talk. Low, slow, mostly of inconsequentials. Last night, after the apples, it had been his evaluation of different companies, before settling on hiring the Vareseh Company for this last concert.

She ran up the trail and over the hill to the broad, sloping sward. Already people had crowded onto the grass around the stage, which was raised above the level of the canal.

She followed the crowds along the pebbled walkway that paralleled the canal, her thoughts in such closely walled turmoil that she did not see Talian Ariath's watchful gaze from the decorated barge in the prime position, noting who among the court walked alone and who not. Nor did she notice the one-eyed gaze of Matthias-Caid Lassiter, Duchas of Alarcansa, which was for once neither lazy nor cold.

Caid watched from his solitary vantage, within the first wall, noticing how glorious Lyren Sartora was, limned in the fiery smolder of sunset, damp curls on her brow and neck, her enticing curves shaping a blue outfit she'd worn several times. Not for her the insistence on something new—or something appearing new—each day. Within those soft blue contours, her easy grace, so easy and so graceful there was no breath of artifice there, no calculation of effect.

It was time, he vowed as she approached the grassy bowl, to exert himself a little.

While back in Alsais, high in the tower that Shontande used when he needed to work without interruption, he was alone with Thad as they worked through the last of a pile of orders that had accumulated while Thad was gone. When they laid aside the last paper, there was no reward or congratulation. The pile would begin again tomorrow.

But for tonight, that tray was empty. Reward enough. "Thad," Shontande said.

"Still here." Thad eyed Shontande, who looked more tired than he ever had, even at the end of the war. And yet he was not distraught. More … puzzled?

"I thought I had a plan. It was not what I wanted, but it was what the court expected. The country? They merely want peace and plenty, and who can argue with that? But comes someone from outside the country, who freely offers me the perfect meeting of minds that I had finally accepted that I would never have. Perfect," he repeated, voiceless as a whisper.

Thad had hoped for that very thing, but hid it. He had truly thought it would be more simple. He ought to have remember- ed that nothing was simple in Colend's court, with its genera- tions of interconnections, the hidden net of obligation that everyone understood. "Are you sure you are not merely dazzled by the flight of the cranes?"

"We have not touched one another except in dance."

"Not?"

"Even a kiss." He paused, and Thad did not need Dena Yeresbeth to know that Shontande was contemplating that not touching. Every sense alive. An astonishing, and perhaps be- guiling, change from instant gratification by very willing, eager partners ever since he reached the age of interest.

Then his fingers flicked airily in Sweet Tension as he said, "Once that happens. If it happens. I don't think there will be any turning back. And I can see it in her eyes, in her breathing, that she knows it, too. Everything is at stake. Everything."

The hand that swept out took in the entire kingdom. The words, wrenched from what had been, until this moment, a per- fectly modulated voice, invested that stake with personal cost.

"Ah-ye! Do not answer. I'm merely tired. We both need to ready for the festival end concert. I know you will like the company, and the piece, that I selected."

Thad left, then slipped through the servants' byways to the perimeter of the palace complex, noting whose servants were where — who watching whom — and then, with relief when he'd made the perimeter unobserved, hired a barge to take him home.

Nalisse was waiting in their pretty little round-walled house, for she would not settle in married life within the palace, though that was a perquisite of both their positions. All the windows were wide to the sound of the plashing canal. She followed him into the bedroom and studied him, lips pursed.

"It's Lyren," he said, stripping off his sweaty clothes and flinging them through the cleaning frame.

Nalisse stooped to pick up his shirt, but he waved her away. "I will do it."

She sat down on their bed, her good robe fluttering like moth wings. She smiled. "You look after me when I'm angry."

"But I'm not angry. Bemused. Perplexed. Astonished." And he told her every word of that private interview. She drew in a breath when he repeated the words 'everything is at stake', giving a fair imitation of Shon's self-mockery, but didn't speak until the end.

"It's the cost of kingship," she said finally.

"There's nothing wrong, at all, with the prospect of Count Talian as queen — she is brave, smart, loyal, and would do a good job. She knows court, and the court knows her."

The corners of Nalisse's mouth tightened. "She would freeze the court in ritual, centered around herself. Already started. I can see it, merely in the pastry orders I get. And when you freeze things, they can shatter." She crossed her arms. "Also, he was forcing himself to it. He ought to be able to have something for himself."

"Besides the entire palace, and every want satisfied?" Thad put his palm up. "I know what you will say to that. It's romantic talk. It's fine, for us, to be romantic. We have more freedom than he does, can't you see?"

Nalisse gave her head one shake. Said in a low but steadfast voice, "I know what I see. Lyren isn't oblivious. She is on a mission. Give her time."

19

As the younger, sporting courtiers walked away from the horseracing field to get ready for the festival's end concert, that cold-blooded reptile Caid Lassiter of Alarcansa appeared behind Talian Ariath. What did he want, compliments on winning? Never.

But no, always on the attack. He said, "You claim to be a connoisseur of art. For two weeks now, I've been observing our guest. As you have."

She said on a sigh, "I watch everyone." As a queen ought.

"Now tell me," he said, his slow voice indolent and insolent at the same time, "is so much natural wit and grace art? Nature," he added, "is never artful, is it? Is that why we profess to admire it?"

"It's the fashion to admire waterfalls, and autumn colors, and verdant meadows, though I do not think of them as art."

"And people?"

"I defer," she said, bowing mockingly, "to the artist." She knew it was weak—that though the adjective *artful* and the noun *artifice* were very close to *artist*, he wasn't either artful or artificial—and that she had not answered his imputation that she was both, because, ah-ye! she was. Wasn't everyone? Was that not part of court training?

She shrugged, fan at Alas, which meant, "Bored." It was perfectly acceptable to be bored. Furious, no. For fury made faces ugly, moreover, fury, rage, wrath—however well justified—implied a lack of control. Boredom meant well-bred endurance, an oblique slight.

"It's too hot to eat, but we've time before the end of the festival," she said to her select, well-born circle following at a discreet distance, though every pair of eyes was avid. She had been taught to regard them as the queen's inner circle, her own court. "Let me summon a boat, and some music, and we'll while the time along the water, where at least there might be a breeze, before we take our places at the barge." Implication: Caid was not invited.

He sauntered away, his laugh floating back on the heavy air.

Talian breathed out her hot ire. He had only become more obnoxious since the war. She refused to acknowledge him.

She glanced toward her maid, who rang for her runner and issued the order, then turned back, knowing that all would be ready when they reached the canal—or the maid and runner both would be unemployed, for she did not keep incompetent servants.

They reached her suite, where they could all get a drink of water and pass through the cleaning frame,

She caught a thoughtful glance from Faria's chocolate-brown eyes and forced a smile before plying her fan languidly, wrist arched. She sighed as she cast a glance about her suite, which she had not even redecorated this season, so certain she had been that by summer's end she would be renovating the queen's chambers. Everyone had expected it—she was not wrong about that. It was proper procedure. She had been raised and trained to it. But then along came this outsider, and Shontande was notorious for his wandering eye. But why would that affect matters of state?

Frustrated, she led the way out.

Faria Dazci, now Count of Eth Param, deferred to the others, walking last so she could observe.

They walked through the cool, breezy gallery to the Lily Canal, where a first-rate boat was being pulled to the dock: the party barge was already at the concert site, where it had been since morning, securing the best vantage. This craft was sufficient to get them there. Faria's mind darted between observations: the slight ruffle of the fringe round the barge canopy, indicating a breeze over the water; the sparkle of the sun on the slow eddies going out, Talian's tight-pressed mouth.

The hired musicians arrived at a run. Talian's friends quite properly appeared not to notice them as they clambered over the low rail at the back, leaving the carpeted ramp for the noble count and her guests. Faria watched, met a distracted gaze, and made a tiny nod of reassurance.

The very young man who was apparently the leader of this quartet did not respond overtly, but relief eased his brow as he motioned his players to their places.

Talian, Faria knew, would not have noticed them, unless they were too late, or clumsy. How strange, that someone so alive to the timbre of voice, who understood rhythm and danced well, would be so impervious to music? But she was. Talian settled at the prow, farthest from the musicians, then surveyed her little party, her eyes passing the musicians and the barge-polers as if they did not exist.

"Cousin," she said to Faria, her hand open.

They were all outside five degrees of kinship, but "Cousin" was a pretty way of inviting Faria to sit next to her, instead of Ladete Bevis, who was the Count of Bevis by marriage-adoption and not by inheritance, and thus could have claimed precedence of Faria.

Not that she would. The tall, dark-haired, infinitely indolent Ladete would never exert herself in any precedence maneuvering. Especially in hot weather.

"I think we might have rain," Faria said as she sat down and disposed the filmy fabric of her robe.

"So?" Talian asked, looking interested.

"Caelad went out riding at dawn, and said he saw thunder atop the mountains over to the northwest."

"Then it should be here by sundown, I trust," said Merenith, Talian's chief follower, wrinkling her little nose. Already her curly red hair clung to her hairline in damp whorls, despite the attempt to draw it all back into an elegant knot.

Talian signaled to the waiting polers, who eased the barge out into the stream. The musicians, taking the launch as their cue, began to play softly, three strings and a tambour, for Talian found the instruments of wind too noisy.

As they glided down the Lily Canal toward the first intersection, Talian lifted her voice slightly. "Avoid Canal Sentis; it seems hotter there, little breeze." The tone of her voice was sharp, and Merenith flushed.

They all felt it, then, the jab at silly Merenith, who had shown a tendency of late to join the admirers of Nashande Desentis?

Talian watched in mordant satisfaction as Merenith smoothed her ribbons in an attempt to show unconcern. How could she chase after a fool? Especially when Talian had made it quite clear that he was not the fashion.

While Talian glared, her head panging from the headache inevitable after too much time in the strong sun, over her head Faria signaled the fifth "cousin" with a glance, and placid, plump Coral pulled from her pocket a pack of cards. "Anyone wish for a game?"

"Oh, it's so hot for cards." Merenith sighed.

"Not even for an enticing stake?" Coral asked, leaning forward.

"Not truth." Merenith wrinkled her nose. "We all know each other's secrets anyway, so what's the use?"

"Ah, innocence," Ladete drawled.

Merenith snapped her fan open, and plied it, coming very close to the aggressive angle of Bumptious.

"What stake?" Ladete asked, some of her indolence — which was only half assumed — vanishing.

"Anything, as long as it's interesting." Coral's fingers rapidly shuffled the cards. It was an expensive set; the backs of each depicted her family shield, hinting at the wealth of detail on the cards' faces. No cheap signs these, it was a full court deck, with all the colors and symbols, meaning one could play the full range of court games.

While the three spoke in well-modulated low tones, Faria pitched her voice under the plash of water down the barge's sides, "My dear, it seems you do not like our guest?"

Talian looked up. No use in asking which guest; though there were many, the king's gaze only followed one. Pretending not to see would cause Faria to look askance. Kind she was, but smart and observant.

Observant. Ah-ye, here was the second person to hint that Talian was too overt. Caid's opinion she despised, excoriated, loathed. But Faria's view was not so easy to dismiss.

Talian leaned over and trailed her fingers in the cool water. A silvery fish darted close, mouth opening and closing, but seemed to see that the enticing fingers were attached to an arm; it shied off, and vanished under the barge.

"I can't say dislike," she responded at last, as always choosing words that she would want repeated through the inner conduits of court gossip. "For as yet I do not know who she is, other than common and foreign; for all her mother married two kings, both barbarians, she was born a shopgirl. We see only the flattering charm of the adventurer."

"You think her here to throw a lily garland, then?"

"Why else?" Talian lifted a shoulder. "Why else?"

"The music? People come from all over the world to hear the festival."

"Pah." Talian dismissed that consideration. "Then she could as easily have stayed in town, and vanished decently at the end. She took one look at our golden lily and joined the throngs who want to pluck his petals."

Faria's fan slanted downward in protest at the uncouth metaphor. "Think you so?"

Talian frowned at her friend. Drat those stupid strings, masking the crucial nuance of voice! But they also kept this conversation from the attention of the gamblers, it seemed.

"I wish he'd crook his finger, vanish with her for two days — two weeks — or however long it takes to get shed of this return to the tastes of early boyhood, when variety was more important than worth."

Faria sighed. The truth was, Talian had been expected by the elder generation to become queen — she'd been raised to cherish tradition, including social hierarchy. There had been far too much mixing during the war, leading to presumption afterward. Bordering on chaos. Talian was an excellent manager of Ariath. Talian disdained wild and indecorous romances. Everyone knew that. Yet it seemed queenship had become a matter of pride, muddying the waters of emotion, desire, ambition.

Faria suspected that Talian had no true confidantes; Merenith was a dedicated follower, but an inveterate gossip. You told Merenith only what you wanted spread about. Ought she to speak? She still remembered with poignant sweetness her own brief dalliance with Shontande, before the war. She had initiated it — and it had not lasted. Their parting had been friendly, for Shontande was as kind as he was disinterested.

It had been a hard enough lesson, to learn that one's passion, no matter how intense, did not guarantee returned passion, but it had afforded her clear vision in learning to differentiate the man from the crown. With it the poignant awareness that her older sister — who had died early on in the war, in trying to rescue Shon after he'd been taken prisoner — had been motivated by passion for man *and* crown.

That grief she'd kept private.

Coral saw it, too, she suspected. What was the right answer?

The barge drifted on its way, the music, ignored by all those in the boat, sounding softly over the water; the musicians, experienced with noble vagaries, understood they were there to create elegant background noise, and to be visible evidence of noble wealth and taste.

As the boat headed toward the Crown Skya Canal leading to the grassy bowl around the outside stage, they passed numerous people, mostly palace staff or from the city, converging toward the grass. The crowd, to the women in the boat, was merely part of the panorama.

Not so to Sveneric, part of the crowd on the walkway alongside the canal. He watched the faces around him as he considered the symbolism of this festival concert: an agreed-on resumption of accepted social usage.

For two weeks, at least in the city, there had been a relaxing of the expectations of rank in all public places. Anyone could listen to the performers. A count would find herself next to a baker's boy. A duchas sat with joiners and wagon drivers. Sveneric, evaluating these interactions as well as the music during his two weeks of wanderings, had made several interesting discoveries.

One he was reminded of as he watched Talian's boat reach the magnificent decorated barge that she had hired, parked alongside the canal's edge near the stage. It was filled with servants making ready for an exclusive party, and fending off the curious until its owner arrived.

Talian's hired boat reached the barge. As Sveneric passed along the walkway in the stream heading for empty spots on the grassy slope, she and her guests debarked from the boat, leaving the hired musicians to scramble out and then onto the big barge from the back, as the count led the way up the ramp to the shaded part of the decorated barge.

Sveneric had become aware over the two weeks that the tiny blond count seemed to be tone deaf. Was she in some wise related to the Sonscarnas of Chwahirsland, through which family tone deafness was common? Or was it merely that her ambitions left no room for art? Sveneric had seen her from time to time, always with her impatience controlled, but her imperfect shield made it plain that she did not listen, but waited for the noise to be over so she could get on with her social campaign.

He niffed a sharp anticipation from her. Of what? Surely not the announcement of the festival winners and the public concert offered by the crown, unless she'd gambled against this or that performer, as he knew some of the wealthier people of whatever degree had.

The nobles appeared on hired barges along the edge of the canal behind Talian's, with a close view of the performance platform. This was where the sound would be best, baffled by the half-circle of the slope with a fence at the top. Loitering along the walkway, paid runners chatted as they waited to carry back announcements to those gathered in more comfort in the city.

The shadows began to blue when the last golden shafts of sun faded. Sveneric found a grassy spot that would afford him good sound, and sat down. Now he could watch the jockeying for position among the ambitious when the king appeared. Liveried servants ran back and forth, bringing refreshment or removing dishes. Some, like him, had already chosen a seat, glancing northward at a dramatic tower of thunderheads.

He also assessed the clouds, calculating when the rain would likely begin, until someone spoke next to him, "Your pardon, Sveneric, for intruding on your solitude."

Sveneric got to his feet, politeness automatic, and sketched a bow. "No intrusion," he said, glancing in mild surprise at Colend's king, standing on the grass before him.

Shontande Lirendi said, "May I join you, then?"

Sveneric hid his surprise. Surely the king had been invited to at least one of those decorated barges along the canal, with the best view and hearing. But then he might not wish to be in a barge again, a reminder of that disastrous first day of the festival.

Sveneric opened his hand, and they sat on the grass. "It was with you in mind that I arranged tonight's performance," Shontande went on, as the inevitable courtiers began to approach, no one too swiftly or too directly, though who was fooled? "It is the Vareseh Company."

"Ah," Sveneric exclaimed, again surprised. "I thank you."

It took that long for nobles of the first rank to use prestige to clear off the city folk scattered nearby. Count Talian arrived with two of her satellites, gowned in filmy things with drifting ribbons, and a pretty sight they were, fans fluttering, curls swaying, gentle laughter soft on the scented summer air. They had left the great hired barge without a thought to the cost.

Talian waited regally; young courtiers and city folk alike deferred, scooting over, or moving away altogether. She settled, as one who had the right, at the side of the king. No one spoke; the grass was free to all, but few were tenacious enough to sit tight while fragrant nobles crowded around them, shoulders turned as they plied fans and chatted in melodious voices.

Shontande's attention remained on Sveneric; if he was aware of this polite maneuvering around him, he gave no sign, but Sveneric intuited he did not like it. And for some reason, he did not interfere. "Where did you say you had seen the Vareseh?"

"In Eidervaen, once, and again in Ellora."

The king made a slight graceful gesture with two fingers. "Ah, way to the north. In Maer Bereth, yes?"

Sveneric indicated agreement, and because the king's inquiring air invited elaboration, he said, "The program is very different there, influenced by the Venn. Whose tastes, especially in winter, incline toward narrative poetry and complicated polyphonic choral music. Lots of local references, and old innuendo about long-dead heroes."

"Old gossip?" Nash asked, dropping down behind them. His voice, easily heard, widened the conversational circle, an oblique invitation to others.

Shontande smiled over his shoulder at his big cousin's open, handsome face.

Sveneric said, "They all know it. Makes for very obscure jokes."

"A taste for poetry is hardly confined to the north," Talian said, marking her entry into the circle.

"Or a taste for obscure court insult," came a familiar drawl.

Everyone looked up, the count quickest of all, as the Duchas of Alarcansa arrived, dressed in layers of green so dark it was nearly black, with iridescent gleam in the weave. He arrived with Lyren at his side, having encountered her at the upper gate.

His attitude, lounging and indolent, was somehow subtly proprietary—though Lyren circumvented it by smiling a greeting at Sveneric, bowing to Shontande and the rest of that elegant circle, then without betraying the least impulse to claim the precedence of a guest, settled with Thad and Nalisse some twenty paces away. They sat with Hradzy and a few of the young, sophisticated diplomats that wiser monarchs, since the war's end, had sent to Alsais in place of older and more portentous figures.

The sun was gone. Shontande Lirendi spoke under his breath and gestured, one of his rare uses of magic in public. The glow-globes sparked into brilliance, bathing faces and fabrics in a soft silvery glow.

That functioned as the signal. The Grand Herald appeared from the temporary tent that housed performers, and stepped up onto the performance platform.

He bowed toward Shontande, struck his staff of office down on the wooden platform four times, and then announced the winners, pausing only long enough for reaction to burst forth and quickly die.

Then swarmed musicians and friends of same to various waiting celebrations or commiserations, for the winners were not expected to perform extemporaneously after two weeks of tiring competition. Their time would come the first night of next year's festival. Everyone else filled in their spots, waiting in expectation for the festival's final performance.

Talian waited patiently, finding the tension unbearable. Now that the festival was over, would the shopkeeper's granddaughter get her quittance? Oh, it was too much to hope for. There were still weeks of danger until the Blue Night Masque, when court broke up to go home for harvest and tax matters.

As the talk came to a natural pause, she addressed Sveneric for the very first time: "Now that the festival is done, I fear that we will lose most of our guests, and we shall be left with only one another again, until the summer season officially ends."

Sveneric understood what she wanted: not his, but Lyren's intentions. The way she worded her comment made it plain that she regarded him and Lyren as part of the same entity, however that entity might be defined. He did not know how many might share that attitude, and regretted it, insofar as it might harm Lyren in their eyes.

He began to frame an answer that would address both matters, but before he could speak, Shontande forestalled him. "I invited Lyren Sartora to remain here until the Rose Garden is at its peak," he said, and Sveneric sensed the *When?* Semaphoring among those courtiers who made it a business to listen to anything their king said. The raised brows and the fans flickering at the angle of Surprise indicated no one had heard that invitation spoken, as Shontande went on, "Why don't you stay as well, Sveneric? It's a sight to be seen, at least once, if the Queen of Sartor is to be believed."

"Her recommendation is to be relied on," Sveneric agreed, swiftly assessing reaction: Talian's parted lips, the glimmer of glowglobes reflected in the Duchas of Alarcansa's single eye. All betraying intense emotion, strictly controlled.

Lyren laughing with a couple of envoys twenty paces out of earshot.

Shontande's shield, as impervious as Detlev's.

"I thank you," Sveneric said.

The opera performers, who had been waiting in the tent with instruments and scenery during the announcements, had finished their setup, and with fearful glances at the sky, struck up their overture.

Silence fell, and the performance began, at perhaps a brisker tempo than rehearsed. The clouds, as if the elements in Colend had taken on the politesse of the kingdom, waited until the last strains had died away before sending down their first fat, warm drops. The crowd began to disperse, some holding their folded sitting blankets overhead as they laughed. Thad and Nalisse arrived with Lyren as Thad thanked Shontande earnestly for choosing his favorite company.

"Did you enjoy the concert, Lyren?" Shontande asked.

Lyren enthused as Thad and Nalisse exchanged glances and melted away.

The moment Lyren finished, Talian spoke up. "We shall not have so dull a summer after all! But we must employ your talents. I propose an old-fashioned Reading in the Reeds, tomorrow sunset. We haven't had one since our grandparents' day, yet if the old folks are to be believed it's the most exquisite form of performance in existence, and a quiet variation after the weeks of musical entertainment. I hope you will favor us with a poem, Lyren."

There. And let anyone mutter about 'observations' now, Talian thought with a narrow glance at Faria. During that interminable singing, Talian had decided that she would smother Lyren with graciousness—the graciousness of a queen. And had directed a few soft-voice requests to those at her side.

"Poetry?" Lyren asked. "I can always bring out 'Riding the Tides of Air,' which I memorized one very wet spring. If you haven't heard it too often." Lyren opened her hands. "But what, please, is a Reading in the Reeds?"

"Oh, it's a very old tradition that goes in and out of fashion at least once a century. We have them still, at home," the cousin of a baras said with studied brightness, then glanced around.

Sveneric sensed a riff of sharp awareness going through the listeners, but he did not catch the meaning as the courtier went on in her smooth and musical court voice, "At sunset the participants are hidden in the reeds or flowers along the chosen canal, each with a candle. The guests ride a barge from light to light, listen to the performer, who then joins behind."

"It sounds very romantic," Lyren said. "Thank you, I would like very much to join." And wondered what the pitfalls were as she met Sveneric's considering gaze.

Talian gloried in her success. As they began walking in a group toward the covered walkway, everyone clamored in well-bred fashion to be chosen as one of the twelve reed readers. Talian smiled in the darkness. Once again she had taken the lead, proving that she ought to hold the guiding rein on court—if not the kingdom. Tomorrow morning she would be directing, and just see if she didn't get everyone harmoniously and smoothly returned to their proper places in the social hierarchy before summer's end.

The rain fell faster. People dispersed in all directions.

Talian was still laughing inwardly at the memory when she reached the walkway nearest her wing of the palace. The day, so ill begun, had ended well, she decided as she brushed raindrops from her face—until she caught a faint whiff of vetiver and amyris. She fought the instinct to snuff it in as she registered Caid a few steps away. She and the Winter Duchas were alone. His dark clothes and hair made it appear in the dim light of the lanterns that he had not managed to get wet. Or had he contrived to escape the operatic squalling?

"Good night," she said in a tone of finality.

Lightning flared across the high windows, silhouetting a knot of courtiers in a distant corridor. In that moment, faces turned their way. She stepped back, resenting the inevitable suppositions, and hating the burn of desire. She *loathed* him, for he was utter poison. "Good night," she said again when he didn't speak, and turned to go, but he touched her shoulder with one finger.

The touch was light, barely there. It was she who stilled as her nerves tingled downward. She gritted her teeth, and he smiled to see her betray that much reaction. "That was quite a performance," he said.

She knew he didn't mean the opera.

"I thought so, too," she said blithely. "Now, I really want to get rid of the headache I've had all day."

But he hadn't lifted his hand. She would not move until he did. Her will would prevail. Not his.

"I wished to congratulate you," he said, with that hateful smile. "You got that so swiftly planned under the singers, right down to that fool Thaellis mouthing out that nonsense about 'how they do it at home.' And that reference to our respected grandparents to remind even the most obtuse that that there hasn't been a queen since before Mad Carlael's day."

Even the most obtuse. Typically arrogant! "Not everyone sees what is not there, as you persist in doing. We merely spoke of traditions," she countered, a hand flat and adamant in Absurdity.

He flicked his fingers, dismissing her words as irrelevant. "Let us review tradition, since we are the experts, then. The Readings have traditionally been the queen's prerogative, is that not true?"

"Not always. And traditions change." She lifted her chin. "It's absurd to let a lovely idea die out merely because of dynastic circumstance."

"But it won't die out if we gain a queen." He smiled down into her eyes, annoying her afresh with the advantage that height gave him. "Or are you worried about the prospect of one who won't know our traditions?"

"Is that why you've been sniffing after her? To start a new tradition?" she retorted, and immediately regretted the vulgarity.

He just laughed, a soft laugh that she barely heard as he moved away. "I trust you'll explain what type of poetry," he said over his shoulder, and vanished out into the night.

"Of course I will," she said in her sweetest voice, her gracious voice, her queen voice, not caring if he heard her.

She would not slight Lyren, or leave her to fumble into reading a poem about birds when the theme must be love. No, she would shower her with precedence, and praise, as surely as the gardens outside were now being showered with long-awaited rain.

20

Late the next morning, Count Drenate of Ymadan emerged from the breeze-cooled privy chambers of Colend's royal palace, walking next to her childhood friend, Caras of the old and prestigious Altan family. Neither had been included in council the generation before; they were cousins of the primary families. Their ambitions had extended no farther than the duties of good stewardship in their home counties, but the war had changed all that.

Having finished a morning with the king in the privy chambers, they were the last counselors to leave. Drenate wanted only a cool room in which to read her morning's letters. Honor Altan wanted to discuss the king, for she misliked his abstraction of late, but her decades of court had long ago taught her to only talk in the open air.

The two friends walked slowly down the tiled steps and stepped onto the pathway. Caras Altan was considering how to frame a question when they spied a round figure in a green gown bustling their way through the privy garden.

The count recognized her daughter. "Liss!"

Lissanre looked up, smiling, but it was a tight smile, and her long, winged brows quirked at the ends.

"Ah, a Thorn Gate morning, I apprehend?"

"Thorn Gate with a blindfold and twelve archers," Liss said in her low voice.

"And the condemned would be?" Caras Altan asked, chuckling.

"All of us. Except Talian. She actually had the spice to chide us into rank order before we even began rehearsing for the reading. I don't know if it's the weather or what, but everyone was in a temper, and my head aches."

"It is thunder weather indeed," Drenate said. "I long for shade. And quiet."

Liss fanned her mother so vigorously the silk flowers in the count's headdress began to flutter, and bits of hair flew about her face.

The count smiled fondly as she touched her daughter's wrist. "I'll survive until I reach our suite, I believe. You sought me, my dear?"

Liss said, "I came to tell you that Caid somehow got snowpunch, and a few of us are going to his rooms to drink it and cool off before tonight's ordeal."

Liss knew that her mother had been no friend to the former Count of Ariath, killed with the old council at the beginning of the war — merely weeks after they had lost their power — and as far as anyone knew, unmourned. Perhaps even by her daughter.

Liss chuckled, her large gray eyes crescents of mirth as she said behind her fan, "Just as Talian galloped through Crown Gate, Caid appeared. Cracking pecans. I nearly died trying to keep my face."

The count gave her a mock frown, then said, "Though snow punch sounds lovely, quiet repose appeals more."

Flipping up her fan in Mirth Hidden mode, Liss bustled down the pathway again.

"Pecans. Oh dear. That was rather overt," Caras murmured behind her fan.

"No doubt," the count replied, pausing to pluck a weed from a bed of starliss. "But apparently it did suffice to keep the rehearsal short. Which is only proper, as a Reading of the Reeds requires merely one stands and reads as the boats go by."

Caras Altan considered that. The privy council had all expected Talian to be the first of the king's generation to reach the council, which would, in her case, probably have led to marriage negotiations after a successful winter session. Count Talian knew her duty — her power-avid mother had seen to that.

Caras Altan mentally shrugged, then, glancing after Liss, "You trust your daughter with the Winter Duchas?"

The count laughed softly. "Liss has been on her own for five years now."

"That young man is worse than mere ice. He is more like cut glass."

"But not to his lovers. If he flies with someone more than once," the count returned, pausing to yank another weed shoot. The gardeners had obviously been overworked of late, what with the festival, and the heat. "When Liss realized that the lily had begun leaving his admirers standing at Silver Willow, she and young Caid had quite an affair."

Caras Altan twirled her fan in So True?

"He is cruel to those he deems, oh, let us call it disingenuous, but Liss maintains that in the dance of dalliance he's gallant. More telling, I have seen myself that they remained good friends after."

"Has he friends?"

"Oh, he has, though he lets no one close."

Caras thought of Liss, barely sixteen at the outset of the war, working through the duration in the kitchens of that girls' school, a thankless, arduous chore. She'd had no spectacular adventures, but she'd shared every bit of the danger, for her job had been to run messages with deliveries in and out. Young Liss had been, but she was no fool.

Caras's fan twirled in Reverie. "This Reading. It appears to be a gesture toward Crown Gate, an assumption that all the court is behind her. For the benefit of the wild rose."

Lyren had become the wild rose; no one knew who'd first spoken the term. Just as "bored" was understood as "angry," "wild" denoted an outsider, not a courtier.

"The wild rose." The count tossed a weed away. "The lily has always favored roses."

"Enough to establish one at Crown Gate? Or is this merely a return to young days, constant migrations in and out of the Chamber of Cranes?"

The count paused, looking down at bees bumbling about the fragrant pink blossoms with vibrant slowness. She could have said many things, some of them very sharp indeed, for she'd once had ambitions for her daughter, who was smart, and kind, and well-liked by everyone.

But Liss did not have ambitions, beyond riding fast horses, and a mild interest in the family's tapestry house. To be a queen—not a mere consort—required dedication as well as skill, if not ambition. The count had made peace with her daughter's choice, still grateful that their family was one of the few to survive the war intact.

Speculation about Lyren Sartora, the wild rose, had been spreading through court. Many maintained it was merely a matter of dalliance, but if so, the king was not following his old pattern, with sumptuous parties centered around his latest favorite, held in his private chambers. Instead, though he was of course invited to every significant court affair, in recent years he had attended fewer and fewer. And now, it seemed, he turned up at events that included this mysterious wild rose, daughter of the Girl Who Saved the World.

The count said, "Summer is not yet over. And youth will be youth."

They reached the end of the Lily Path then, and saw others walking about, so they shifted to matters that could be overheard.

That night the candles along the canal glimmered with ethereal beauty, a peaceful sight in spite of the intermittent lightning flares on the southern horizon. A little harder to ignore were the leashed tempers around Lyren as the chosen readers gathered, but she did ignore them, feeling badly for the ones who had been snubbed at the rehearsal that morning.

Lyren had seen that Talian intended to organize this reading as swiftly and effectively as possible, despite the heat, and the wandering attention of her chosen readers. The problem had been in her striking too imperious a note in directing them, when so many already had assumed their places, knowing what was to come. Talian appeared to be assuming a precedence that conflicted with the easy and egalitarian social interaction that Shontande appeared to prefer.

Lyren kept her lip resolutely buttoned, for she had begun to suspect that imperious attitude was assumed for her benefit. Though she didn't understand some of the murmured innuendo. She knew that the city gates featured in many idioms. She'd seen some of those gates on her musical wanderings during the festival. They were all quite beautiful, a couple only accessible by canal.

She'd even seen one called the Gate of Pecan Blossoms, a graceful archway with vines trained over it in a profusion of charmingly tinted flowers. So why had the mere cracking of pecans in Alarcansa's strong fingers made Talian's face blanch to the shade of old lace?

Nobody had said a word directly, but Lyren knew that something had been said, all right. She just didn't know whom to ask. Certainly not that slack-lidded Alarcansa, who showed far too much interest in her, interest of a direct, unnerving sort.

Lyren did her best to avoid him. Brrr! The way he sniped at Talian Ariath was cruel in its precision. Grace would dictate pretending not to notice. She considered him as she trod along the canal to her position, taper in hand. One of Talian's personal servants was there, sparker in hand, to light her taper.

Lyren smiled her thanks to that unresponsive face, and then moved to her carefully tended flowering shrub to wait for the barges. She had time to think now, unlike earlier, for she'd gone on a ride with Nashande and some of his friends after the rehearsal, hoping that the wind created by a race over the downs north of the palace would cool them off.

It hadn't, or was that only that odd fancy she'd had, that Shontande had chanced to look out of those windows that overlooked the downs, and so her nerves had flared with heat, as if limned by the sun?

Sigh. Speculation was stupid. She'd be better off doing another quick read of her verses. She'd selected a romantic poem about Lasthavais Dei (one of Lyren's ancestors, but no one here needed to know that) and part of Colend's and Sartor's history. An obvious choice, maybe even trite, but diplomatically sound.

Darkness intensified swiftly, as the greater part of the sky to the south was blocked by those clouds. Occasional fireflies winked in and out of view among the straight reeds, and tapers glowed through a lacework of ferns at stations along the curve of the canal. Golden reflections from the tapers rippled in the water, flickers of fire going out in slow rings as silent fish dove to the surface and then plashed down.

The barges appeared. Talian had asked Lyren to be first, with a graciousness that Lyren had thought was well-intended, even if it had sounded a bit forced.

Lyren's poem was not a performance piece. She did not intend to orate with dramatic fervor, though she'd been trained to do so. Training, Siamis had told her all those years ago, did not mean hammering the listeners with ranting, but judging just how best to adapt to one's company, to know how to do one's role with grace and ease.

Timing was a part of all the training she'd had: sword,

singing, dance, speaking. Even writing. And so it seemed natural to begin in a clear voice when the barges neared enough for her to be heard. As they drew nigh, to deepen pitch, softening tone to intimacy, and as the barges passed, she increased her pitch again, fading the last few words.

Silence, complete silence from the two barges as they moved toward the second reader. She extinguished her taper, and slipped toward the edge of the canal, taking care not to thrash her way through the shrubbery.

The third vessel, a low boat, drew up and she stepped aboard, whispering her thanks to the silent polers. She was the first performer, and so she was alone except for those guiding the boat.

The second reader began, her voice stiff, too fast. The third was also too fast, except for falters when her candle flickered: she clearly had not practiced that poem. Four began a shade too soon and finished when the barges were even with him; five was excellent, and so was six. Seven ranted, but ended on a note of self-parody that caused smiles. Eight and nine read well, ten was loud but wooden, at least to Lyren's sensitive ears, eleven too fast, and twelve — Talian — read beautifully.

Lyren comprehended on hearing voices without seeing faces and interactions, that her training surpassed most that these courtiers her age and a little older had received. She was used to thinking of herself as the hapless Liere-Daughter, frivolous and good for little, living in borrowed homes. She had often heard about the formidable courtly training of the Colendi. Perhaps it had been superior in the past, without the interruptions of regicide, war, and the subsequent recovery.

The Colendi courtiers were human under their fabulous clothes. Their spoken codes were still opaque, but so would those be of any group living together for a long time, from stable hands to marble carvers, anywhere in the world. Their recondite customs were learnt from the cradle, their words quick and sometimes witty and full of obscure reference — but underneath all that they suffered the same emotions as she. Recognizing those emotions unlocked the door to her ready empathy.

The other readers stepped on the third barge behind her, until all twelve were there, and she heard their sporadic whispers, some soft laughter, and a couple sighs. Then they reached the debarking site as the tapers were lit again and there was the king leaving the first barge. Talian leaped neatly off the boat before it had been secured and advanced to his side, in expectation of the listeners' courtly applause.

"An exceptional diversion," Shontande said, leading the praise.

Everyone else added their mite. And when that had ended, Shontande said, "I think we should adjourn inside." He indicated the storm, which had during the last half of the readings blotted stars closer and closer overhead. "There is a supper waiting. Please join me."

Bows, murmurs of precedence and deference, as people divided into twos and threes to walk through the lightning-charged summer air toward the distant golden lights of the palace. Some, Lyren saw, were essaying pathways that did not debouch directly onto the palace. Detours for private entertainment, most likely.

She thanked those who complimented her, returned compliments—all of it the sort of pleasant automatic chatter that took no thought—then saw a familiar outline moving with languid deliberation through the people before her. Tall, straight shoulders, long black hair. Oh, not now, she wailed inwardly. Not just now—

And before Alarcansa could reach her, Sveneric appeared adroitly at her side, holding out his arm.

"Oh, there you are," Lyren said with what she hoped sounded like expectation, and not relief.

Caid of Alarcansa stopped a pace short of them, his single eye reflecting the golden points of candle flame. His expression was impassive as he regarded Sveneric, but his countenance somehow expressed menace. Ah. Was that the aroma of wine on the sultry air? Would he actually start trouble? She'd heard furtive whispers of duels, but those were rare. Yet the way the tall duchas contemplated the shorter, slender Sveneric made her uneasy.

Sveneric seemed tranquil enough. He was dressed quietly in blue, white, and gray, his hair simply pulled back, the light on his high forehead revealing no tension or creases, his manner utterly unthreatening.

There was nothing remotely prepossessing about him, but Lyren knew his skills, and she felt a brief, distinct wish that she could precipitate something just so she could watch Sveneric let a little of the Winter Duchas's hot blood.

But that was unworthy.

She greeted the duchas calmly, her air apologetic. He bowed in silence, and ignoring the others who lingered, watching, trod up the pathway without any partner.

Lyren let out a long sigh. As soon as they were out of earshot she said, "Thanks."

"You seemed to need a diversion."

"Obvious, or was it just you?"

"Just me," Sveneric said soothingly. "Are you really afraid of that fellow?"

"Not in the least. I don't like unkindness, and he's unkind. Even when he's unkind to those who are silly or tedious, or—"

"Or arrogant?"

"Sveneric, do you know what cracking pecans means here?"

He laughed soundlessly. "It could be a very nasty score-off. Don't tell me—"

"I won't, if you like—"

"Alarcansa cracked pecans near Talian?"

"Yes. At this morning's rehearsal."

"Oh! But he didn't read."

"No, he refused, last night, when she chose her readers. With at least superficial grace, but in such a mocking way, and then he showed up this morning as we gathered to rehearse. He was riding past with a couple of his friends, and paused to greet everyone, and from his pocket he drew the pecans. Cracked one, then two, in his fingers. Ate them. Every single person stilled as if he'd, oh, stepped on their shadows."

"That's because he did. Symbolically."

"Is it the gates, somehow? Atan told me that they use those city gates in slang. I haven't been able to ask Shontande as I don't know what to say if he asks what I heard and who said it. I don't want to lie, but I also don't want to make trouble."

"The gates have ancient traditions attached. I don't know it all, because I'm only here in summers, and never this extended a visit. Thorn Gate doesn't even exist anymore, but it used to lead to a castle beyond which the military held tribunals and such. Though it's been gone for centuries, its shadow remains in speech."

"Ah. Go on."

"You saw that the Lily Path is where visitors come to the palace, so if you make any kind of reference to lilies or the Lily

Path or Gate, then you are probably making reference to the Lirendis."

"I have heard lilies referred to. I assumed it had something to do with court, from the context. Others are more obscure."

"The Gate of the Silver Willow was the old processional for mourning, but now it mostly means failed love affairs of various sorts, or failed romantic hopes."

"Oh, so that fancy one, Crown Gate, refers to Shontande somehow?" She cast her mind back, trying to make meaning from obscure words.

"Actually not. He's the lily, as I said. Crown Gate is where masters of whatever art go to process with their guild, in effect announcing their new status. But references to Crown Gate usually mean arrogance, or pushing."

"And pecans?"

"The Gate of Pecan Blossoms is where weddings traditionally begin processions."

"Oh. Oh! I think I get it. Atan had said something about Winter Gate, not Pecans, though, when I first came. Referring to Talian."

"Winter Gate is a reference to the private party Shon holds here in winter, when the other nobles go home after Oath Day. The Winter Gate leads to the court's winter quarters. To be invited is to be considered for the privy council. So far, all the members are older. And married. If rumor was right—"

"I see it," Lyren said, as lightning flared over the summer garden. Heavy drops of rain spattered them. "So, cracking pecans was a way of jibing at her expectations? Oh, how *cruel*. Rain! Let's hurry. She hasn't been asked, is that it?"

"Not yet."

Lyren brooded, and Sveneric watched her brood. "I'm still missing something important. And I think it has to do with Alarcansa. No, I'm quite certain," she muttered, and swung her intense golden gaze his way. "He seemed almost ready to call you out, just for walking up to me."

"I suspect he's been drinking too much snow punch all day," Sveneric said. "Resulting in a desire to let out his frustrations by teaching me what's what and who is who. If I were taller and broader, I suspect we'd already have been out behind the stables by now," he finished cheerfully.

"He's testing me, then?"

"Either that or testing the attraction between you and

Shontande. Everyone who can sense such things senses it. But Shon is not whisking you off for dalliance. Instead, there you are, charming the hangers-on, and chatting up the diplomats from other countries. No one can figure out what you're doing."

"I talk to Hradzy because he's kind and comfortable. I know him from Atan's court. And I spend time with those poor people from Melire — how can you call them 'hangers-on'?"

"*I* don't. Castoff royalty, penniless, hangers-on, living on Shontande's generosity, that's how Talian views them. As does her circle. Lyren, what do you want? It isn't like you to toy with people. Why don't you make a move?"

"I cannot be the stake driven into his court, splintering it. Nor do I want his mantle cast over me, to protect me from that court. I despise the very idea. If I haven't the skill to win the friendship of all the court, not just those left at the fringes, then I ought to go away. But I can't go away," she admitted. "Sveneric, laugh if you must, but this is the most important task I've ever faced, and yes, I realize quite well that no one gave it to me."

"Ah."

"It's useless to be logical. I can only feel, and follow my instincts, which clamor for me to stay, and do what I can to befriend them all, while avoiding that Caid, who hardly knows me enough to pursue me with quite that much intensity."

"Um. I would say that you underestimate your effect, but you're right, there's unspoken challenge there, not just aimed at you. I expect it goes back to interactions during the war. Caid of Alarcansa was not part of Shontande's resistance ring. Siamis told me he was imprisoned outright by his aunt, who would not risk the Lassiter line dying out, until he escaped his family near the end, and nearly got himself killed in his first attempt at a campaign."

"You can tell by the scar and his eye that he fought. You'd think that would suffice in proving his honor, if that's what the problem is."

"Siamis told me that his aunt wanted him to be the kingdom's heir, if Shontande, who barely had established himself as king, had fallen. His reputation, fostered by the old regency council, was..."

"... not good. I've already heard about his thousands of lovers. He hasn't said, but I'm wondering if that episode in his life was a way of saving his sanity. As he was effectively a prisoner."

"It's possible. This way, a shortcut," Sveneric said, pointing. "We don't want to arrive sodden."

"Or together," Lyren added, and he laughed.

The shortcut afforded them a clear stretch of grass, and no one around.

Lyren's eyes reflected the lights ahead. "I think I know what to do," she whispered. "That inner ring really ought not to be used as a social weapon. Not only against me, but Talian uses it against Alarcansa."

Voices approached. The rain began to pelt in earnest and people dashed up the last flagged pathway. Sveneric turned down a side path, leaving Lyren to be swallowed by a group of young courtiers who charged through the glass doors held wide by liveried servants and then laughed as they smoothed their expensive clothes and shook drops off their hair.

Lyren followed the others across the tiled foyer, past plants and mirrors and lamps, into a pale pink marble summer room with potted ferns along the walls, growing a profusion of cream-colored blossoms.

"Lyren!" Nashande called, surging forward. "Come join us. I liked that poem of yours. And you read it off so fine."

"Thank you," she said, taking his offered arm.

She didn't look left or right, or calculate where she would sit, or by whom. She greeted everyone with sunny impartiality, as tendrils escaping from her high-piled hair curled about her face, and drops glittered on her long, fringed lashes.

Lyren took a random seat, but as she exchanged greetings and compliments, people gathered around her. The king smiled at their chatter. Alarcansa was watching, and Talian was watching him watch. Her triumph at the success of the Reading was dissolving. She had to reclaim it.

21

The evening had begun so very well for Talian. Everyone had deferred to her, a glorious triumph that had taken little effort. Unlike that miserable morning. But she would do nothing whatsoever to Caid Lassiter until she had a crown on her brow, and unassailable precedence.

The supper room Shontande had chosen was the circle table, so everyone could see one another, which also meant informality. But of course the chosen place was near the king. Though she had walked by his side, leading the way to the palace, in the press to get inside the door and then spread out, somehow he ended up sitting between the Sartoran ambassador and one of the minor Ranflars, newly returned to court after the birth of her baby.

Hradzy Wendis had his latest flirt on his other side, a minor baras's heir. Talian bowed in greeting to Hradzy, and addressed enough questions to him about the reading — how he liked it — did they do such things in Sartor — empty chatter, while she stood her ground until the flirt finally perceived the hint and made an excuse to get up. Whereupon Talian sat down in her empty chair.

There followed food, wine, and the noise and parade of a dinner. Exhaustion and tension closed around Talian's head like a vice. Thunder crashed overhead, and crystal on the table rattled with a high-pitched tinkle, sending a corresponding pang through her forehead. She gulped at her punch, though she must not permit it to fuzz her mind. At least it was cold.

A toast to the readers broke through Talian's mental haze.

Bow, smile, drink. Good, she needed another sip.

"A toast to the organizer!"

Back to the reading? She bowed toward the center of the room, and smiled, hiding her disappointment, for the speaker was just that lackwit Nash. He was watching her, the idiot, for a sign of — something.

Disgust lanced through her. She would never forget how Shon had left them together so blatantly one night, all those years ago. Just because she'd dallied with Nash when they were teens, Nash was presumptuous enough to conceive a tenderness for her, and wouldn't take a hint that it would *never* happen again. He'd been fun to dally with, but so had half the court when they were all young, and the war was over. Shon had actually thought she'd throw herself away on a mere cousin, and one with no brains? Though Nash's doglike devotion did come in useful from time to time. As long as he understood that he must never presume any relationship closer than that of dog and human.

Rain drummed against the windows, and lightning flared, sparking in jewels, in the stemware, and from a trick of light in Lyren Sartora's eyes. She was speaking. Who had gotten her to speak? Talian had worked for two weeks to make certain that the interloper stayed out of the inner ring, and here she was, all eyes on her. All, not just the hangers-on and the foreigners.

"... practice with a most exacting master," she was saying. "But I'm certain all of you remember tutors of the very same kind. I know you have musical gatherings. I've enjoyed several. Tell me, did you also have amateur theatricals in order to train voice?"

A clamor of response.

Talian winced against her headache. It was a transitional question, that she recognized. Lyren had seized the talk, but she'd turned it outward; it was the same technique Talian used, except she always turned it inward, toward herself, toward her chosen friends, for was that not the way that power flowed?

Why would Lyren seize the conversation and then scatter the focus out again? Yes, they were all listening to that fool from Eth Endra, who spent all her time blithering about ancient art. Why even ask the opinion of such a nonentity? What could it possibly be worth?

Ah, how she missed the war days, when talks alone with Shon had occurred almost every day. Always to plan, and far too brief, but of course their lives had been in danger. It would almost be worth it, if Norsunder were to...

No, don't think like that.

A burst of laughter brought her out of her haze. She reached for the punch, then pulled her hand back. She'd had too much without having eaten all day. She couldn't think, and thought was necessary. She *was* at war, though the weapons were not swords anymore.

She forced herself to pick up a flaky little butter biscuit and scanned the smiling faces to find the source of wit. Lyren again! She really was astonishingly beautiful though her features were ordinary enough when examined one by one, even those so-called golden eyes which were merely light brown, like her own. It's just that Talian's eyelashes were also light brown, whereas Lyren's were dark and lush. It was the dramatic contrast, and how Talian wished she would go away!

"Is that a threat or a challenge?" Shontande asked, his voice slightly rough with suppressed laughter.

"A challenge, of course," Lyren retorted in a joking tone.

"Then I take your challenge. The stakes?"

What was the subject? What was the subject? Talian's inner voice cried against her having fogged at so important a moment. Lyren had never spoken out like this before, and what had caused it? She'll ask for a personal stake! I would! How to prevent it?

Lyren opened her hands. "I think universal mirth is enough of a stake, don't you?"

She didn't address Shon. She looked round the room, pretty hands open in appeal. There she was again, throwing the question back.

And nonentities spoke, some actually funny, most repeating what they heard, and looking sidewise for approval, as nonentities always do. Talian frowned, control surging back. General chatter was just noise; Lyren had destroyed the proper boundaries. Wits, Talian's chosen wits, ought to be the only ones to speak, and the others to listen. That was order. Hierarchy. A smooth, refined flow.

"It's a risk," Shon said, after the last fool had spoken.

And Talian smiled. "As if anyone would laugh at you." Time to draw the reins again, though carefully, carefully, until she found the subject.

Lyren turned Talian's way. "Do you think him safe, then?"

It was an opening for Talian to speak, to take control, but she didn't have the subject!

Caid sent one of his lazy looks her way and drawled, "Laughter at royal foibles tends to be confined to private memoirs."

"Silent, but enduring," Shontande said with imperturbable irony.

Nashande lifted up his head. "Nobody's likely to laugh at you, Shon, in person or by proxy, because you can sing."

Sing! A court performance using music? Talian's heart contracted. She had to take charge, or who knows what disaster would occur, but oh, music, how to control that, it was like that rain out there, impossible to catch and to hold!

Nash was still blathering. "... used to be pretty good at singing, but after my voice broke it stayed broke. I bray like a donkey now. All I have to do is start warbling, and we'll be hearing the laughter for two generations."

"Then you can spare yourself," Talian said, careful to pitch for joke, "and your audience. Organize the scenery instead. Lyren Sartora, your taste is so universally admired, surely nothing but general approbation would accrue if you were to honor us by taking charge of the costumes. The rest of us can divide the risk equally among ourselves by assigning out the singing roles to those we know have had some experience." There. That put Talian squarely in charge.

Shon tented his fingers, elbows propped on the table. He looked across at Lyren. "But then you will be ducking your own challenge," he said. "If I sing, you have to sing."

And instead of seizing control, Lyren again turned her golden gaze toward Talian, and handed it right back. "What should I do, then?"

Talian tried to hide her triumph.

Be gracious, be gracious, though the last thing she wanted to deal with was opera. "What do you wish to do?" Complimentary tone! "For you are a guest in our kingdom. We defer to visitors' wishes whenever we can." There! Underscore the temporary nature of her presence.

"What I wish to know," Lyren said, smiling around the circle again, "is who likes to do what?" She turned to Nash. "If you don't sing. How about taking charge of the staging, as Talian suggested?" She waggled a finger as if sword fighting. "I know you're good at that."

Talian glared down into the dark red of her crystal flute, feeling control slipping again. Not opera! Had she done it on purpose?

"Noria?" the hated voice went on. "I know you sing delightfully. I've heard you. Will you help?"

Noria! Of course the stupid little twit turned bright pink. Talian had never once acknowledged that fool, barely seventeen, from a minor family on the eastern border, who compounded her drawbacks by having the bad taste to moon after Nash. *She* could sing?

One after another Lyren called on people around the table, too swiftly for Talian to easily grip control again. And everyone she asked said yes!

"What work have you in mind?" Faria asked.

"Something Sartoran?" Baras Arbias asked, exchanging glances with Nash.

Interpreting that look correctly, Lyren said, "No singing in Sartoran, I promise." Another quick look Talian's way disclosed the same tight brow of irritation. Her attempt at a compliment toward Talian, who had organized the Reading in the Reeds, had clearly tumbled off the cliff of Good Intentions. How to shift gracefully? Ah!

She glanced around the table, noting the chilled punch passing freely. "Colend has so many wonderful plays and operas, I've discovered. Sadly, I am ignorant of most. Perhaps this can happen later, once I've found the right piece. How about another type of fun altogether? It's a dance that I learned from Wnelder Vee's dawnsingers."

"A dance?"

"Are the steps a quick study?" Liss asked.

"One of the best aspects of the apple dance is that no one has to learn new steps," Lyren said. "You'll be able to dance right away, or as soon as you get used to the rhythm, which might be a new thing here. At least, I have not heard it used anywhere these past two weeks."

"Rhythm?" Nash exclaimed. "What is there besides one, two, three, four, and one, two, three, one, two, three, in the haltas and the taltan?"

Lyren knew that Talian liked to dance. She'd seen her at it. Music appeared to leave her indifferent, but rhythm?

"This is a five count."

"Five?"

"That's new. How does it go?"

Lyren tapped on the table, "ONE two three FOUR five, ONE two three FOUR five."

A few hesitant hands tried tapping along with her.

"It's a shift-rhythm," Noria said. "My music teacher taught me that. She said it came from the morvende, who used it in their cave echo music."

"True," Hradzy spoke up. "Played fast, it sounds like a gallop."

"The Marlovens use it," Lyren said. "They add more drummers, who in turn bring more syncopation. I'll give you a quick demonstration, if you'll keep the five count going."

She shifted on her seat as she smacked her hand down on the first and fourth beats. When the company had the rhythm going, she began snapping her fingers in a counterpoint, ONE, Two, three, four, FIVE. Pause, TWO-THREE, pause FOUR-FIVE. Then she traded between finger-snaps and tapping on her glass with a silver spoon, for a different sound.

In the background, the musicians who had been providing melodic background music finished that familiar summer ballad, and, tentatively, the two with percussive instruments picked up the basic rhythm, *thrrrump*, two, three, *four*, five. Lyren rose, casting a glance at the rest of the hexagonal room. Ah!

"Wonderful—thank you," she said to the musicians, then flitted to the space between them and the round table. As the musicians got a feel for the beat, Lyren began tapping the rhythm out with her feet, coming down with a clap on the first and fourth beats. The tiranthe player began tapping on the back of his instrument, which made a mellow thok. Another rustled a hand drum from behind her chair, and began working up a counter-rhythm.

"Oh, that's it," Lyren said, still tapping and clapping.

"But where's the apple?" Nash cried.

Lyren laughed and began to twirl between claps, first one way then the other. Twirl sway, clap-clap. Twirl, sway, clap, tap!

"The dawnsingers bring this one out in autumn. They dance in pairs, balancing an apple between their foreheads."

Eyes rounded. Fans snapped and arced. Even Talian was intrigued; she noticed Caid sitting, arms crossed, as usual, but he was listening.

"You cannot touch your partner otherwise. It's a trust dance. You can do any steps you like, but you have to figure out how to do them with your partner. Who wants to try it with me? We haven't any apples, but the variation is to look into your partner's eyes. You cannot look away for the entirety of the dance. The game is to maintain the rhythm, and get as close to one another as you can, without ever touching."

Liss, one of court's most sporting courtiers, leaped up. She shook out her rippling ribbons, and stepped up to Lyren, who tapped and danced in place. ONE, two, three, FOUR, five… the urgency of the beat, with the drumming counterpoint, deepened as two more musicians began experimenting with a familiar minor key melody, but adapted to this new rhythm, it became slightly sinister, and utterly compelling.

Liss moved close to Lyren, the two gazing into one another's eyes. Liss uttered an uneasy laugh, then, gallant and reckless, threw herself into the dance. She began clapping and snapping her fingers in counterpoint as Lyren added a hop and a dip of her hip, which Liss picked up on the FOUR beat. Thump! Lyren's foot came down. Dip, sway, sway — the swaying became more sinuous as one then the other echoed it, hips swinging.

"Wait, I think I just got it," Nash called, sauntering over. "Autumn. Spring is when the dawnsingers want their babies born. This is a courting dance?"

"It's whatever you want it to be," Lyren called. "Children do it, usually to challenge each other with tricks, but it also gets the shy dancing, because you can mimic another's moves in a shadow dance."

Hradzy and his friend joined. They started out with a hand's breadth between them, but within a few short beats, they edged closer, loosely adapting some simple steps, one backward, one forward. The circle dance they adapted was for everyone of all ages, but executed to that rhythm, it became something altogether different. With hierarchy utterly banished.

"Arbias! I dare you," Nash called.

The baras laughed as he joined Nash. After a knock of knees, and an elbow smacking a hand, they found the rhythm. Used to the demands of hard sport, they began a vigorous shadow dance, one's right mirroring the other's left.

Exhilarated with the strong punch, one by one the others

joined — the last few not to be left out, especially when Nash turned away from Arbias with a, "This is fun!" and pulled the king up from his chair.

"Change partners!" Lyren called.

Liss whirled away from Lyren and confronted Arbias. Nash came to Lyren, stamping in a counterpoint as he swayed back and forth, hips one way, shoulders the other.

The musicians dared more syncopations, and ventured into experiments with melody. Even if the melody faltered, the strong beat pulled it all together again, with different emphasis.

"Change," Lyren called out. "To your right!"

Everyone turned to their right. Even Talian, who though indifferent to music, responded to rhythm. She twirled and clapped, blond hair flying.

This became the pattern then, with dancers finding themselves with new partners when someone or other called the change.

Then, "Change!" Nash shouted —

And Lyren and Shontande found themselves eye to eye. Shoulders rolled counterpoint to hips, one shifting left to right, the other out and in, then stomp! Clap! Their bodies cinched closer, tassels dancing, ribbons rippling. Blood afire, nerves alive to each other's quickened breath. Heartbeat. Scent. The tip of Lyren's tongue touched her lips, longing for taste; Shontande could not have looked away for his life. He clapped. Lyren swayed close. Closer, so that their breath mingled, hot and spicy from punch. Taut muscles, sinuous swaying, *thrrrump!*

He stamped. She swayed. Hips and lips moved in perfect synch, as around them heads turned, one by one, caught in the thrall of that dance.

"Change!" Talian shrilled.

Lyren turned. Shontande turned, and the spell was broken.

They continued to dance until Coral dropped into a chair, plying her fan, and the others joined her, reaching for the chilled water, wine, and punch. Laughter and chatter finished the evening, but every person there was still seeing the afterimage of those two moving in counterpoint, gazes locked, bodies poised in perfect tension.

The company parted, most to untroubled sleep, or to more intimate enjoyments; Shontande, who had the shortest distance, slipped through a discreet door and across a small herb garden to a garden arch. Through that and up a little hill made by steps of fine rock, to the top, where he dived past the waterfall, still clothed, into the shocking cold water fed by an underground stream.

Lyren slipped along the pathway she knew well by now, and when she reached her room, her distracted gaze noted new invitations in the basket, made with smooth, colored rice paper. Some folded into pretty shapes.

Before Hradzy left, he'd said, "Don't forget the opera. They'll be expecting it."

Her status was changing, slowly. She would care later, but right now the most urgent task was to fill that bath with un-warmed water, throw off her clothes, and sink in over her head, staying underwater as long as she could hold her breath. When she popped up, hair streaming, she laughed, half-expecting the water to be boiling around her.

But cold water works its magic on even the most heated bodies. When she finally felt a chill, she climbed out, toweled off, slung her wet hair into a loose braid, and when she had pulled on a fresh outfit, she gazed at the window. Yes? No?

Yes. Always yes.

She thrust her feet into her sandals, and set out to take that nightly walk.

This time, every window in the royal wing glowed.

She'd forgotten her token. But the shadowy guards let her pass, and she walked through the open glass door to discover Shontande with his wet hair combed back, robed soberly in green. He bowed a welcome, the silken tassels sliding over the contours of an arm, folds hinting at the slim line of a hip.

Their gazes blended. The intensity between them crackled.

"Lyren," he said, low, hand open in appeal.

Oh, that voice! The heat was back, hot as fire, but she raised her own hand. "We both know what will happen the instant we touch each other. And I want that, oh, do I. Like nothing else in life," she said, her gaze honest and steady. "But I also know what will happen, beginning with me talking myself out of the goal I set for myself. It might be frivolous. It might be arrogant. Impossible. But I have to try."

She stood, poised as a butterfly.

"As you wish," he said, though it took all his strength.

Thunder charged the air; she sank onto her cushion cross-legged, gauze fluttering around her in folds, but for once he did not imagine what she hid behind that gauze. He was taken by a sudden fancy: hair, silvered in age, her face full of laugh lines, and he knew with inner conviction that however old they became, he would always find her entrancing.

"Your turn for a topic," she said, fists on her knees, eyes bright with laughing challenge.

He had not neared any subject related to kingship since that first troubled night after Seshe's abduction. But now he sat across from her, and said, "Political—moral—accountability. Should it be to the law, or to the people as a whole?"

Lyren blinked. Where was *this* coming from? "Are you expecting something clever? A quotation, perhaps?"

"What," he countered, "did Detlev teach you?"

"Nothing," she rejoined tartly. "He knew better! Instead, he sicced Siamis onto Mac and me. I told you that. Mac was a diligent study, but I ignored tedious books, and books about politics are the most tedious. At least, politics as ossified by state archivists assuming a neutrality that I am beginning to think doesn't exist."

"The winner, so to speak, deciding what the truth is," Shontande said. "And so, accountability?"

"First, how do you define that? While I was living in Wnelder Vee, I had to hear a lot about the effect of bad laws, and the tension between a government that must heed them, or alter them—and what happens if you change laws rapidly. Senrid also used to talk about those things with Liere, when I was small. I saw it in action in Sarendan, so when Liere talked to me about what was going on with the Adranis…"

22

Summer weather was fretful this year, causing farm folk to poise for early harvest. Everyone felt that the storm season would arrive early. In Everon, Laban and Carl worked in tandem until the inevitable strife between three of the great landholders of Imar boiled up in its own threatening storm. All three were maneuvering to claim the Eid, the Dei holding blasted by Norsunder, now fully recovered from its years under water, and wonderfully soil-rich.

Laban and Carl met in her study that morning, which was slightly cooler than his, and when he proposed going into Imar in person, she had to agree.

"I'd better go myself," Laban said. "I'm going to re-establish ownership of that land. Everyone knows it's Dei land. Everyone also knows I'm a Dei. And that puts me among them as a landholder of Imar, which enables me to propose we re-negotiate the terms of sovereignty there."

Carl agreed soberly, hiding how anxious she was at the prospect of him leaving. "If they're going to benefit from our trade, and the protection by the Knights, then they can contribute themselves, rather than leaving their guilds to bear the burden."

Laban flashed a sardonic smile. "And incidentally, find something else to do with those private armies that keep getting bigger. How about a private army tax? Though we won't call it that. Something pompous. Flattering, even."

Carl's eyes were crescents of mirth. "But it will be stiff enough that they might rethink paying both the taxes *and* housing and feeding people who sit around all day sharpening weapons, and practicing how to use them."

Laban grinned back. When their minds ran in tandem like this, he was discovering, marriage was no mere duty. She was an excellent partner, far better than he'd let himself hope.

He departed in a good mood, as she hid her hurt at his casual, "I'll be back as soon as I can."

There was no use in mourning what was not there, she told herself yet again. Be grateful for what you've got.

As Carl returned to her desk, not far to the north, in Dtheldevor's underground hideout on Dthel Rendm, CJ backed away from the wall, crossed her arms, and let her gaze travel over the big map that she had just finished. Maps were almost like a mural. She'd discovered long ago that she loved making murals. It was like making a story with images, not words. Since she'd given up writing, the urge to paint had gotten stronger. The girls had enjoyed her murals, back in the old days. They'd left them up on the walls in the Junky until the paper was mildewing and damp from the humidity of an underground hideout.

Julian Landis stepped up beside her. "Oh, that's perfect."

"All color-coded," CJ couldn't help saying, though she knew she was pointing out the obvious. "Bad wander houses red, good ones green. Watch-out ones yellow. Ones with particular requirements, blue. And each color gets a tray." She pointed to the trays below, the corresponding colors painted along the rims.

Julian took in the countries carefully labeled, each with cities that had hostels for youth on the wander to stay. "They won't even have to change the pins. I'll do that. All they need to do is write up the wander-houses they stayed at, bad and good."

The general rule had always been that youth on the wander worked for shelter and food. In most lands along the great trade roads, guilds, or groups of shop owners and innkeepers maintained some sort of dormitory housing, and oversaw the meals, in turn for youths providing free labor—message running, sheep tending, and similar tasks that required little or no training. The tradition was centuries old, though the war had interrupted it.

"Dtheldevor must have kept it all in her head," Julian said.

"Gwen says she has charts aplenty on the *Berdrer*," CJ said.

"My guess is, she had no interest in maps, because she didn't like traveling on land unless she had to. Anyway, the important thing is, kids won't have to paw through that old basket that nobody ever emptied, with all those grimy bits of paper, written in a zillion different languages, to find out the places to avoid. Not if everyone gets in the habit of using this system."

"I'll see to it," Julian said. "When I first tackled that mess in the basket, there were five different warnings about the same two places, where they grabbed husky youths to stick in their military. And three about that one on the Goerael coast where they were selling the wanderers' labor, and not giving the workers so much as a tinket."

The sound of quick footsteps in the tunnel caused the two to turn. A pair of kids of about ten scampered in, one saying, "CJ, the mermaid is back!" Having delivered the message, the girl turned away, without a glance at all CJ's hard work.

CJ was getting used to that, finally. There was no changing the fact that, like it or not, kids had no interest in grownups. They looked at her and saw grownup, no matter what funny songs she made up, or how much she enjoyed talking to kids. It was a kick in the heart. Almost as much as it'd been way back when Atan organized the refurbishing of the Everon royal palace, and CJ discovered that no one but her—and Clair's gang—liked her art. That still rankled, though she tried to hide it.

She charged up the tunnel, as barefoot as the kids. Nobody could make her wear shoes if it wasn't winter.

She found Gwen down by the pier, where the *Berdrer*'s hull below the waterline was getting careened of barnacles and seaweed. Gwen had turned into a short, stout young woman who was fast getting sun-seams around her eyes, her ear-length blonde hair bleached a yellowish white.

She looked up from talking to a circle of teens taller than she was, most carrying buckets and scraping tools. For the tenth time, CJ promised herself to research some kind of ward that would protect the wooden hull from that stuff attaching itself, but so far in her sporadic searches she'd had zero luck.

"CJ!" Gwen called. "Gloriel is over there. Wants to talk to you." Gwen pointed to the water on the other side of the pier.

CJ scrambled down to the little boat they kept tied to a piling, hopped in, and rowed around to the other side, away from the ship. She glanced back once; it seemed Gwen had pretty much lost interest in Gloriel after it became clear that Gloriel was not really equipped to do hull scraping.

CJ glanced around the choppy waters without seeing any-one. She merely had to wait. Gloriel would see her from below and pop up.

She sat back, staring at the *Berdrer*'s masts and yards with their sails brailed up tight. There'd been a lot of storms lately. It was the season for them.

Splash! There was Gloriel, silvery gray as a dolphin, except for her long, trailing hair that looked more and more like seaweed without leaves attached.

"Welcome back," CJ called. "Glad to see you!"

She'd been afraid that Gloriel was gone for good after Falinneh's shapechanging experiment had gone flooey — Falinneh looked like a mermaid, but the gills were mere flaps on her neck, and her eyes stung horribly when she opened them underwater. And her hair had stayed hair. Proof, as if anyone had needed it, that Falinneh's shapechanging was confined to human shapes, and Gloriel was no longer human. Human-*ish*, at best. They probably ought to have figured that out when Falinneh had never been able to shapechange to animals.

Gloriel squeaked a breathy, "Happening." She pointed below, her fingers webbed.

"Is there danger coming?" CJ asked, leaning on the gunwale.

She and Gloriel had been trying to figure out a kind of sign language adapted from the mer sign language. They were frustrated largely by the fact that so much of undersea life had no land equivalents in any language. Their conversations were always short, and days apart. Sometimes a week or more. But that was okay. CJ didn't mind transferring back and forth. Or, staying here for longer, if she had something to do, like copy that world map from one Senrid had given Puddlenose.

Gloriel whirled her hands around in the air as her powerful tail kicked below the surface, keeping her upper half out of the water.

"Many?" CJ guessed.

"Don't know."

"Is it another kraken attack?"

Krakens were a big deal in the ocean world, CJ had learned. Some got along okay with the merfolk, but some hated them. And they weren't the only undersea dangers. Huge sharks liked mammalian creatures for their tasty hot blood, but the even bigger squids thought shark a delicacy, whereas mammals were the undersea equivalent of eating insects. But some squids found merfolk a nuisance, and had summary ways of getting rid of them. There seemed to be plenty of borders to undersea life, even more—ha ha—fluid than land borders.

Gloriel threw her arms wide.

"Bigger attack, or a bigger creature?" And when Gloriel shook her head, "Bigger problem?"

"Maybe," Gloriel said, her voice thin and reedy, air whistling through her gills. "Didn't understand it all. New. No one knows. So much talk."

She tapped her head, whirled her hand around, then pointed, which they'd established meant a different pod of mers. Some, CJ had learned, lived in fantastic undersea cities. Clair had spotted one once, when she, Julian, and June the offworlder had gone underwater during the war. Others migrated with currents and seasons.

Clair! CJ had thought a few million times about asking to borrow one of those underwater armbands from the other world, but the problem was, using them meant you lost track of land time. It might be fun to go wandering undersea, but CJ had always put it off, just in case something important was happening on the surface that she might miss.

"Danger to us on land?" CJ asked. She didn't think it likely. Except for occasional trouble for ships, the undersea world and the land world pretty much kept separate.

But CJ's nerves chilled when Gloriel nodded slowly, and said, "Maybe. Don't understand. Guessing." She winced, which CJ had learned meant her throat was drying out from the effort to speak, and she ducked down.

Well, that didn't sound good.

When Gloriel popped up again, CJ gritted her teeth, then said, "Norsunder?"

Gloriel looked aside, then said, "Bigger."

Okay, that was *definitely* creepy. "What should I do?" CJ asked.

Gloriel had no answer to that. CJ straightened up and looked from sea to sky. Then she snapped her fingers. "Should I come underwater, if I can get Clair's armbands? Can you show me what's going on? Or take me to someone where we might find out?"

Gloriel shrugged. "Try?" Part of her motivation was the sheer loneliness. Even after all this time she still missed her siblings, and Dtheldevor, and sailing. She could never have any of those again, but having a friend might help.

An adventure? CJ shivered at the prospect. She'd been trying to tell herself that adventures were over, now that Norsunder was gone. Not that she wanted war and death and misery, no, no, no, ugh. But outwitting bad guys—winning—having people respect you when you did something good, oh, she did miss that terribly.

She looked around again, aware that the color of the water seemed to have changed to a weird greenish shade. The sky had begun to fill with a slow-moving mat of little clouds, which meant a thunderstorm on the way.

What to do?

She had nearly talked herself into taking Sveneric up on his offer to introduce her to a drawing school, though CJ didn't like the idea of setting foot among those Adranis. Except that the school was in a tiny town alongside a river, in which the creepy king had never set foot, Sveneric had insisted. It would be fun to learn how to draw well, since it seemed she was unable to figure it out on her own.

But what if there was an adventure beckoning…

CJ turned back to Gloriel. "Gunna ask Clair. I'll be back."

Gloriel nodded, and vanished below the surface.

CJ spun the little boat about and rowed to the pier to tie it up, then ducked her head and ran for cover as the daylight glared weird blue—lightning, out over the water. That stomach-clenching sense of danger eased only when she reached the tunnel to Dtheldevor's caves.

CJ still hated thunderstorms, though they didn't make her sick with terror anymore. That had worn off while living with Clair's gang. She still didn't know why she'd only felt safe with the girls around her, but it had made all the difference.

Julian and Gwen sat in the kitchen alcove as the sounds of a fast game of Cards'n'shards echoed from the main room. "Does Gloriel want something?" Julian asked.

CJ told them. Gwen looked uneasy. "Trouble undersea? Have anything to do with ships?"

"I'll find out. I'm going to bucket back to MH," CJ said.

While CJ had been talking to Gloriel Warren, Clair gazed down from one of the spires into the terrace garden outside the kitchen of the white castle, at the two slim figures chatting by the low fence. Aurora's posture was utterly unfamiliar to Clair. Usually Aurora flopped into chairs, head on one armrest, legs over the other, or lounged, but now she stood with her feet together, arms crossed, her long white hair a contrast to the short black curls of the boy—no, the young man just out of adolescence—talking to her, his attention solely on her face.

A step beside Clair, and Siamis slid his arm around her. She leaned into him, saying, "Dirk Sonscarna?"

"Detlev brought him back before he left for Songre Silde. I don't know for how long. He might not know, either. Adam sent him to me."

As yet, no one knew where Detlev had taken Dirk not long after the war ended, and it had become apparent that Dirk was having a bad reaction after killing Wan-Edhe.

Detlev had said privately to Siamis, *He did not comprehend until after that event that that was the purpose for which he had been born. And trained.*

But Kessler cared for him. As much as he was capable of caring for anyone. We saw that, Siamis had protested.

Nevertheless. I believe he will need a different environment for a time, one that will not bring up memories. Or inspire him to emulate his father.

"Does Sveneric know he's back? Does Darian Selenna?" Clair asked softly, as if the two young people below could hear them. Which they wouldn't. It was very evident that their attention was solely on one another.

"I don't believe so. Ordinarily I'd expect Sveneric to niff him on the mental plane, except Dirk is extremely adept at hiding himself when he wants to."

Clair sympathized with the boy who had had such a strange upbringing. But she was startled to see her daughter showing interest in him—the first time that Clair had ever seen Aurora showing that quality of interest in anyone. That stance of hers, muscles taut, toes and heels together, that was physical awareness, as well as mental focus. "You are more adept at boy body language than I. Is he interested back?"

Siamis understood her trepidation. He murmured with an air of sympathy, "It might be the best thing for him right now. That someone would find him appealing. And not threatening."

Clair bit her lip. Dirk Sonscarna!

She was not ready for this sense that the ground had crumbled beneath her and she had fallen into a fast-moving river. She had no experience with what everyone else went through in adolescence. For her, there had been Before, when she was oblivious to the world of physical attraction. Then came the war, and Ilerian trapped her in a never-ending nightmare centered first around her own family, distorting her childish memories with horror: her mother merely a drunken lush, one aunt a selfish playabout who abandoned her son to be tended by someone else, their brother a sniveling worm crawling at Wan-Edhe's feet.

But Siamis had brought his own memories of them, gained when he had slipped into his old home from time to time, and through his eyes, Clair had seen bewildered, heart-starved younglings easy prey to Wan-Edhe in his campaign to get control of the magic in that palace one way or another. The attempt to destroy her connection to her family failed, evoking only Clair's endless well of compassion.

Ilerian had retaliated by dragging her into Siamis's memories of Efael, and Efael's of Siamis. There had been utterly no physicality to it. Ilerian could not damage her through dreams—forcing her to witness a stab in the eye still left both her eyes intact—but Ilerian mired her in Siamis's violation, and its attendant sorrow, pain, anguish and anger, but for every sordid memory Siamis gave her one of beauty, of joy, of shared companionship and laughter, love and trust, as their memories bonded ineradicably.

Siamis had been her safety net. She knew at the deepest level that he'd seen her as another child to be rescued, the way he'd seen them all, even Imry, when Siamis was a teen himself. For him, rescuing children was his way of healing those long-ago, terrible scars.

When Ilerian was at last extirpated from the world, the bond between Clair's and Siamis's minds and spirits remained fused. His memories were hers, and hers, his. But he'd left her with Adam, and then went to help Detlev with war detritus.

That had not troubled her once she understood that he'd return after she healed. It was only after she had decided to permit her body to resume its natural march toward maturity that she began to perceive why he kept his distance in the material world, though he was always there in the realm of the spirit.

Healed, she had begun to learn new magic, one that would enable her to heal others. She already knew that the teacher, in teaching, is also taught. And when at last she was ready to live again in the material world, she accepted that there would never be anyone else for her, ever. If Siamis did not return, or could not see her in the same way, then she would remain solitary in the physical sense—but there would always be that sustaining bond between their spirits. Which was why, when Seshe had come to her a few years ago, saying that she needed to get some sexual experience, for Jilo seemed to be too shy even for touch, Clair had sympathized, but sent her to Erenlara of the Venn—at their same level in maturing, and exploring the same new sensations and questions.

And now, here was Clair's daughter, fixing this young man with the attention of her entire body.

"She'll figure it out," Siamis said softly.

With Dirk Sonscarna? Clair wanted to protest. But that was unfair. She could not live Aurora's life for her; she'd made her peace with that long ago, when Aurora kept taking off with Puddlenose for yet another cruise.

Maybe it was time for Aurora to get the experience that was normal for everyone else. For not everyone could have a Siamis, who had walked back into Clair's life at the exact moment she was ready to meet him on equal terms. He was patient, and kind, and had not opened the door to the flames hotter than the sun until she battered down that door to find him.

"Clair?"

A familiar voice, high and bell-clear, brought Clair's head up. "CJ?"

She flew down the stairs, Siamis behind her. CJ had been mostly gone since spring, Clair suspected as CJ's way of coming to terms with the Junky, the girls' underground home, passing to Aurora's generation. Dtheldevor's caves were over there on the other side of the world, full of kids and talk of travel and fun, but without the poignant weight of memory.

Clair found her in the library.

"Clair! Siamis! Any news here?"

"Not here. The only news was Seshe's—"

"Seshe's? Isn't she with Pilo?"

Clair tried to remember who knew about Seshe's misadventure in Damondaen and who didn't. "Were you aware that

Seshe was abducted out of Colend?" Clair asked.

CJ's eyes rounded. "No! Who? Why? Let me pack—"

"She's back in Chwahirsland, safe, as of a few days ago. Everything is fine. Better, actually, in that she no longer feels she has to hide her origins."

"Whee-yew!" CJ wiped her brow in a dramatic movement, then grinned. "I was ju-u-u-st about to snark at you for not coming to get me, but it sounds like all's good. I want to hear the entire story. Or will it upset her if I bomb over to Jilo's castle and corner her?" She grimaced. "Though maybe not yet. I came to ask if I can borrow that armband, the undersea one Kyale gave you. I want to go undersea with Gloriel, because she says there's something weird going on in the ocean world. I figure, if she can handle it, so can I."

"Of course you can have it. Puddlenose hasn't mentioned any sea mysteries of late."

"That's because it's not on the surface, according to Gloriel. And maybe if I go underwater, I might learn to understand them better. They do have sign language of a kind, but so far, Gloriel finds it too hard to teach it to me."

"That's what Falinneh said, when she came back from Wnelder Vee. Just remember the armband will make you invisible to sea life."

"Including to Gloriel?"

"Not if you touch her."

"Okay. Maybe that's even better," CJ said. "Hey, if Aurora is around, and not hanging out with Mad, maybe she would want to come."

"You can ask. She's out on the kitchen terrace," Clair said. "I'll get the armband." She ran down the hall to her room.

Siamis said, "I can fill you in on Seshe's inadvertent adventure, if you like."

"Sure thing," CJ said, as they started down the stairs.

Siamis gave her a succinct summary, hugely entertained by the variety of her reactions—*Ugh! Ick! Gnarg!*—until they reached the glass doors leading to the terrace. Siamis had just reached the gathering on Fox's drakan when CJ stopped short, her face blanching.

Then her color was back, bright red. "That guy is Dirk, *not* Kessler," she muttered. "Dirk grown up. But he looks exactly like..."

The two on the terrace noticed they had company, and each

stepped away instinctively, though there had already been at least an arm's length between them. Both looked a little uncertain, having stumbled into new and intriguing terrain.

"Hi," CJ greeted them. "I'm recruiting for an underwater adventure. *Maybe* adventure."

Siamis was secretly amused by how oblivious CJ was to the atmosphere between the pair as she launched into a description of her conversation with Gloriel Warren.

By the end of her explanation—mysteries bigger than the giant squids of the deep, underwater cities—Aurora was thrilled. She loved everything about the sea.

She sidled a quick glance at Dirk, whom she'd remembered from the war, but who was totally different now. He looked back, his thoughts parallel: during the war, Aurora had been merely another urchin romping about in the garden with the Delieth brats. But now she had turned into someone altogether interesting, and he had nowhere to go, and no claims on him. He did have his old friends, but one was neck-deep in ruling, and the other apparently somewhere in Colend, involved in that musical competition they made so much of...

"Why not?" he said.

Aurora bounced on her toes; Clair, who had just appeared with the single armband, looked from one to the other, then to Siamis's smile, and said, "I guess I'll get the other two bands."

23

In Alsais's court circles over the days that followed the Reading in the Reeds, Talian Ariath noticed with increasing frustration how one simply could not get away from musical parties, musical gatherings, and impromptu balls, centered around that apple dance. Everyone who played an instrument seemed to have to explore this new rhythm, and everyone else was entranced by a dance that had no choreography whatsoever.

It was beguiling, but in a purely physical way, that had nothing to do with years of tradition as experienced through the complex steps of Colendi court dances. These dances were admired precisely because they were difficult to master. Well danced, they looked elegant in their ever-changing patterns of two, four, and eight. That apple dance made most look like they ought to be in the Chamber of Cranes — which was, when you thought about it, odd, as no one touched, and of course one was fully clothed.

There simply was no melende in it.

Talian's most reliable source of gossip was Merenith, she of the curly red hair and short nose. After a card party one morning (*no* music!), Talian walked out beside Merenith, who gabbled away about the opera Lyren Sartora had chosen, apparently to everyone's approbation.

Talian regarded Merenith as a lackwit, but reliable because she never stopped talking. Merenith was more interested in people than in things, especially who was doing what with whom. Talian found her invaluable as a conduit as well as a follower. After all, wasn't 'friendship' a romantic term for those who knew how to find their natural position in the proper hierarchy?

"... but a tedious lot of talk about opera, now that one has been chosen," Merenith finished, with a quick sideways glance. And she yawned behind her fan.

"I suppose it's fine if one likes it," Talian said, in case Merenith was repeating her words to others; she never forgot that conduits ran both ways.

"Or professes to," Merenith replied, tossing her ribboned curls. "Why do we have to *perform* opera? It's all very well if one can sing, but not everyone can. When did that come into fashion?"

"It will soon go out again," Talian promised. "Precisely because not everyone can sing. At least it's better than the old king's day. My mother told me back then it was all gambling, or games of wit. With ruinous stakes."

"Ah." Merenith's hand gestured Rue as she wrinkled her pretty little nose. Merenith had been very tiresome about her little nose in those early days, after Alandaer of Kharenth had written a poem about its cuteness that had been witty enough to gain popularity. But Alandaer was five years married now, to someone else, and what was cute at sixteen was not at near thirty. Talian suppressed the urge to make a comment about pig snouts.

"For me, music has a single purpose: dancing," Merenith went on. Not the apple dance *again!*

"The rose seems to think differently, or she wouldn't have actually forced an opera on us." There. Let's get to the gossip that ought to go out by morning.

"But she didn't," Merenith countered. "Did you not hear? You were so quiet last night." She shot Talian a speculative glance.

"I was listening to Honor Drenate, who was talking about that book on the origins of silk. Why would anyone claim that the Chwahir had invented it? Diplomatic persiflage! Acquit me of deliberate inattention, as I had the count talking in one ear and Liss in the other. You know how they are about weaving." Talian had done her best to shift the subject from the opera, but had only succeeded in starting an even more tedious one.

Merenith's fan tapped her cheek in Alas! "Alarcansa issued the challenge, insisting that the perfect piece would be

Jandrilas's *Sun and Star*, and she could play the main role, for was not Lasthavais the Wanderer her foremother? And Lyren said she was foremother to most everyone there, as far as she could tell, and if you go back far enough, everyone is related to everyone else."

"Ah-ye! The Winter Duke actually uttered flattery, and she didn't accept it?"

"She didn't seem to comprehend that it was flattery. She went right on to say that she preferred something lighter, such as *Love's Favor's Cost*, which she'd found in the archive. And he said there was a company still in Alsais who had that in their repertoire and he would hire them to perform for her, and *she* took it up, but suggested they make a party of it. Surprised me, for I didn't think he cared for music. Or much of anything, except the cut of steel or word."

"It might be a wager," Talian murmured, fan twirling in Alas.

Merenith wrinkled her nose again, her head tilted to one side as she contemplated Caid Lassiter of Alarcansa. "There's a taste I could have, if his tongue weren't so horridly sharp."

As if Caid would ever look twice at her, Talian was thinking.

Caid. Truth was, she did find him attractive, and their one night of dalliance, after a party with too much wine, had been hot as fire. But she had refused another lest he develop expectations. She admired him *distantly*. As one might admire a fine sword. Shontande was so mild. Talian was confident that she'd be able to order court as she liked. Were Caid king, there'd be no gainsaying him.

Think! To the purpose!

Talian said in a speculative voice, "I'm surprised Lyren encourages Caid." And at Merenith's interested look, she added, "But it could be that where she comes from, it's appropriate to collect hearts indiscriminately."

"You said that once before," Merenith observed. "About Lyren and the Winter Duchas. Last week, when he tried the apple dance, and then wouldn't dance with anyone else. Do you really think she has dalliance in mind? Or the Alarcansa coronet?"

Talian had said it twice, the first time in Shon's hearing as well as in Merenith's, and firmly subdued her impatience. She'd taken care to suggest it a few days after that disastrous first apple dance, when someone brought apples to the Ranflar party. At least that idea had dropped fast. Apples were far too awkward to deal with.

"People have mentioned it to me," Talian stated, making certain that the gossip would only include her name as corroboration, and not as origin. "I don't know that I agree, but it does match what I see in her conduct." She shrugged. "But, to be fair-minded, perhaps that's the customary behavior in barbarian Marloven Hess. Here, where manners are finer, many observe that her behavior is clumsy. Too familiar."

"Familiar, true," Merenith said, her eyes narrowing. "The king seems to like it. You know he has been endeavoring to relax strict adherence to rank."

There was a wide divide between vulgar familiarity and a polite acknowledgment of those below one's rank. How to indicate Merenith wasn't subtle enough to perceive the difference?

"Our elders would have pointed that out as an error in correct behavior," Talian observed. "She dances with everyone, which shows a complete lack of discrimination. It might be only her method of flirting."

"As for flirts," Merenith said, "the Winter Duchas flirts with *her*, if you want to know what I think."

I don't. I want you to think what I think. Talian tried another tack. "They do make a handsome couple, don't they?" Go ahead and repeat that in front of Shontande!

"They would if she gave him the smallest vestige of encouragement," Merenith said, sticking like a terrier to her trivial point. "The one she seems closest to is Detlev's son. But that's not surprising, I guess."

"You mean, as a couple?" Talian asked in surprise.

"Them? Ah-ye! You never had a brother," Merenith added with a note of—was that really condescension? "They are like brother and sister."

Talian gritted her teeth.

"I wouldn't mind a try with him myself." Merenith yawned again behind her fan. "If he showed the slightest interest. Contemplate." Her fan swirled in Speculation. "Detlev's son. How very strange!"

"Except the omniscient and all-powerful defeated villain seems to have retired without a kingdom, or a title, or any influence anywhere," Talian said more sharply than she'd intended.

Merenith was irritating, Lyren was impossible, Shon so ... so unaccountably reserved, these days, and as for Detlev's son, he was attractive—very—but his eyes made a person very uncomfortable. "And so the son will inherit nothing."

"Ah." Merenith touched her fingertips together in the peace as they paused at the foot of the staircase. "There's nothing and there's potential. But you are first through Lily Gate there." She made a good-evening peace and sashayed up the stairs, three pairs of ribbons dancing about her heels.

More days passed.

The long summer drought to the south of Everon ended at last. In Alsais talk of the festival had long since died away in favor of measuring how low the canals had gone, the oldsters comparing levels to those of former years.

No one worried unduly about drought, for it was not a serious threat there. Hundreds of years of careful compromise between land and mage had produced the extensive canal system that joined rivers, with long-maintained spells that brought water from the lakes, and the water table below the land, to the fields when spring gave way to summer and all the rain went north or south. The pattern was old enough and expected enough that it was a part of the rhythm of life.

But the storms had finally arrived, rolling through almost daily, many crashing spectacularly toward Chwahirsland with lightning and thunder.

More thunder rumbled in the distance of a humid, gray day when Nashande slipped up into the herald-guards' watchtower where his cousin hid out when he wanted to work alone and try to catch whatever breeze might exist.

He was working when Nash topped the stairs and peeked in the open door. Nash, in excellent shape, still paused for breath when he reached the landing. The heavy air, saturated with the mixed scents of sodden garden, made one sweat after the slightest effort.

Nash hated this weather. Everyone hated this weather. Tempers were thin; he'd ducked several gatherings and had gone riding in a fruitless effort to cool off, but at least he'd avoided sparks. Except for one gathering: he never skipped Lyren's rehearsals in the palace's private theatre.

"Shon? You want to be alone?"

"I'm nearly finished." Shontande laid aside his pen. "How

was today's practice?"

Nash grinned. His finicky cousin wore only a loose under robe, and the robe wasn't even laced. No one elsewhere would ever see him thus.

Taking Shon's dishabille as an invitation, he pulled off his outer robe and slung it over the back of his chair. He'd forgotten his fan—again—so he picked up a diplomatic dispatch with which to fan himself. "Fun," he said, pausing to scan the dispatch. Something about shipping in nearby Breis. "This important?"

"Feel free to sweat all over it."

"Now, don't you get snappy, too. I've had four people Thorn Gating me today, and all over nothing."

"Not Lyren?" Shon's brows went up.

"Not her. Everyone arrived in moods. You can imagine who, and what tempers were like, but she teased us out of it. At least for a time." Nash looked out at the brooding thunderclouds. A bluish flicker on the horizon was followed by another long, low rumble. "I wish the curst rain would stop playing hide and find, and settle already."

"By and bye. Tell me more. Lyren smoothed the mood?"

"All except Caid. And Talian—who now comes to the rehearsals. She smiled, but—" Nash thought of Talian's bird-light body, her lovely face, sweet back in the war days, sweet only when she was around the king, he'd recognized long ago. Of late she was brittle and sniffy, though never as grasping as her mother had been, back when Nash was a boy and the regency council ran the country.

Regret suffused Nash. "Talian smiled," he said to the clouds. "But not willingly." He turned around. "I know it's not right, but I sometimes miss the war days. She was a good companion then. Matched me ride for ride. Quick. So quick! She was brave as anyone when we found ourselves in a tight spot. Nowadays her smile—"

"I know Talian's social smile. Never mind."

"Ah-ye! I do think she almost laughed, once or twice. When Lyren plays the fool. She does it in a way that ... In a way that ..." Nash faltered, thinking back, struggling for the right words. "Why won't my tongue ever get the words for the picture in my head?" Despair washed through him. In truth he was beginning to believe Talian's gibes: maybe he was stupid. He hadn't been, ten years ago. Did one get stupid over time?

"Because you are a man of action," Shon said, leaning back in his chair. "Always have been. You were too quick to bother with words when we were small. Why do you think I relied on you so heavily during the war? Too many of us thinkers second-guessing ourselves, and Norsunder would have had a far easier time with us than they did have."

Nash sighed. "I wish—I wish she wouldn't look at me like I'm nothing." The words wrung out of him. He realized then that the topic had been Lyren, and not everyone was always thinking of Talian the way he seemed to, but as usual Shon knew what he meant.

"Talian has her own shadows to fight, Nash," he said. "Be patient. I'm hoping she'll win her battle, and see your worth, as a friend again even if nothing closer. But it's going to take time."

"How much time?" Nash asked, feeling his way, for the question did not just concern himself. But Shon never talked about his own affairs.

"That I cannot tell you."

Outside lightning flashed, much nearer, and the thunder echoed from the stone walls. But still no rain.

"Going to hold the Blue Night Masque, or postpone it?" Nash asked.

"We'll hold it," Shon promised. "Despite the weather. I'm afraid a postponement would only prolong the heat."

The heat. Shon was talking double again, a sure sign there were some stakes that Nash wasn't seeing in what he thought of as the state gambling game. But Shon wouldn't spell it out until he'd resolved whatever it was.

Nash shrugged it away. "As to the opera, they're ready for you whenever you want to join the rehearsals."

"Already?" Shon had his pen in his hands again, and was running the feathered part through his fingers. "That's rapid progress."

"I started to tell you. Lyren teases us, but then it's to work, with the teasing still there, if you get my drift. With her as the target. She doesn't sting anyone, not even the young ones. Huh! That pretty little one, Noria, with the pansy eyes. Lyren put her in the main role, though she could've sung it. But Noria, what a voice. As good as a real player."

"Lyren sings well?"

"Yes, though she says it's training, and not talent. I can't hear any difference, but Caid said it's a fair assessment. Good but not great. She doesn't posture. He likes that. At least, he's there every day, sitting like this." Nash mined a lounging pose, arms crossed. "And I never saw him take any interest in opera before, but you never know."

"She's been very well trained."

"That's what she said! She said Siamis taught her how to listen, and some tutor up there in Bereth Ferian drummed the singing into her head. Think of that! I always thought Siamis would only know war drill. Remember him at that ambush at the old guildhall? Caid was there, too, as I recall." Nash smiled at the memory. "Hot fight, that one was. Siamis saved us."

"Yes," Shon said. "But why are you surprised? You've observed Sveneric. Does he exhibit martial skills to the exclusion of all else?"

Nash grinned. "He never brags. Not even a whiff." He tapped his palm to his chest, chin lifted, miming the fan gesture called Deplore, which signified arrogance. "But I'd be willing to bet he knows his stuff. Ever seen how he scans a room when he comes in? Or how fast he is if there's no competition going on? He just watches the contests."

"I've noticed." Shon's voice was wry.

Nash kicked the leg of the desk without realizing it, and frowned in puzzlement. Lightning and thunder struck almost simultaneously, so bright and loud neither could speak to be heard.

When it died away, he said, "Now that's one fellow I'll never make out. But I'll say this. He never stings people, and I think he could."

"He could."

"So why's he here, Shon? Music's over."

"He's here," Shontande said, "to see the rose garden."

"But it's all over petals. Smashed in that storm last before one!" Nashande looked up in honest surprise, then smiled in relief as, with a steady, hissing roar, the rain struck at last. Almost immediately the air cooled. "Think he's, ah, got an interest in Lyren?"

Shontande laughed without making any sound. "As a kind of sibling," he said.

Nashande got to his feet and walked to the door, but with the lagging step of a man with something on his mind. He half-turned, then said with shy difficulty, "Now, don't you bite at me, but I wouldn't mind if Lyren stayed around. For as long as the two of you liked."

The awkward implication was kindly meant, and Shontande knew it. He also knew that his cousin would not willingly betray any private conversation. On the other hand, his face, his attitudes, his moods, were so very transparent!

"Lyren Sartora will never be a favorite," he said at last, in his most gentle voice.

And Nash sighed, looking really grieved. "Ah, it's not my affair, of course. But I wish —"

Shontande forestalled him. Quickly. "Would you choose a thousand-year-old cup of carved jade to bail a leaky barge? Lyren has been training her entire life, with the world's most influential people. Our leaky barge of a court is only beginning to see that. Some things take time."

What things? Leaky barge? Even more puzzled than he had been at the outset, Nash muttered his farewell, nipped up his robe, and flung himself out the door.

24

The Masque of the Blue Night was the last official, formal affair of Alsais's summer season, as the King's Regatta was the first official, formal affair. Social events might extend either way a month before or past these events. Other years, at least by the Blue Night Masque, both palace servants under the direction of the Head Steward and personal liveried retainers were busy organizing in the background for departure after the Blue Night Masque ball. This year, most of the court was lingering until the opera that many of them were performing in, *Love's Favor's Cost*, which would be presented in the royal theater. Everyone seemed to agree that that would be the last event of a surprising season.

It seemed quite fitting that the surprise would be presenting the opera.

Traditionally, the invitations for the king's winter private party were issued up until Blue Night Masque. Everyone knew that. But things could change, couldn't they?

Would they?

"Blue Night," Lyren said at the end of that day's opera rehearsal. "What's the name from?"

"Full moon." Nash jerked his thumb toward the window.

"Hard to believe, but the night has actually had frost on enough occasions in the past for the name to stick," said the Count of Ymadan, who had come to rehearsal to hear her daughter sing the part of the cook disguised as a princess.

Her daughter Liss, she of the happy smile, added, "Grand ballroom, white-gold marble. Everyone wears blue."

"So that's why I was told to wear blue. I wondered if it was a delicate hint about my butterfly robe having appeared once too often," Lyren exclaimed.

"Some things are worth seeing more than once," Arbias said, with a gallant flourish of his fan. "Like roses."

Lyren bowed in thanks, then turned to Liss. "And masque as in masquerade? I have some lovely masks from winters in Sartor, where masquerades are frequent."

"Masquerades are for masks," Faria spoke up. "A masque these days means only that rank is relaxed, as of course it is when we go masked. But we don't wear masks at the Blue Night Masque."

Lyren held up fingers. "Blue Night Masque, no masks. Masquerades, yes masks. That's actually very straightforward for Colend. What happened?"

Most chuckled as they parted to ready for the evening.

You will shine them down whatever you wear, thought Matthias-Caid Lassiter, Duchas of Alarcansa, but he didn't speak it aloud.

For the Winter Duchas, the event had always signaled the end of an amusing season of diversion. A summer of observing the vagaries of one's fellow nobles was about as long as Caid's interest endured—and that, customarily, with frequent trips home, was there any sign of trouble with the wine crop, or word of roaming troublemakers leftover from the war.

There had been fewer of all three in recent years. Other than the calculated incursion by an alliance of former Norsundrian hirelings into his northeastern mountains—an attempt to carve out a little kingdom for the lawless rejects of the coastal countries, plus a few of Wan-Edhe Sonscarna's renegades—two years ago, Alarcansa, and the areas along the great river Elarca, had been relatively quiet.

Caid had given up hoping to pit himself against a truly worthy foe. The utter unfairness in this regard made him bitter, and he knew he was bitter, and why: he had been raised to consider himself a worthy replacement for the long-reigning Lirendis. Too long, his great-aunt had insisted, in various ways all his life, as he strove to be better.

He knew history. He knew laws. His family had held the eastern pass against the Chwahir for generations. And so he had been trained in the martial skills to defend a holding—and a kingdom. But when war came, he'd been confined, forced to watch from a hiding place in the mountains as Alarcansa fell to a vicious company of Aldan's Norsundrians, with the Chwahir Green Army coming in for the occupation. And when Caid finally escaped his elders, it was to discover that the weak, decadent Shontande Lirendi was running a resistance — with covert Chwahir allies.

Caid never lied to himself. Shontande had worked as hard as he had, and as long. He could have used his looks and skills to make himself a hero, as Mathias the Emperor had, but he hadn't. That added to Caid's bitterness, and to the mordant humor inspired by years of watching this soft-spoken, reclusive, Chwahir-loving king his own age sidestep the ardent crown-hunters among the women. Even Talian of Ariath, who represented the old hierarchy, everyone in their proper place. Shontande had come very close to acquiescence — but now he seemed to believe it was time for change.

Caid's mind ranged over his plans as he dressed for the masque. Every detail was overseen with his usual care, and then he gave the last orders for the emptying of his room and the preparation for his departure directly from the ball.

He smiled in anticipation, paused to make certain the midnight blue tassels at sleeves and waist hung free, and started at a leisurely pace through the mostly-empty Alarcansa mansion on the canal, his servants bowing low as he passed, for they recognized his mood.

He didn't see them. His thoughts had arrowed straight to Lyren again. How fast she was! Every bit as fast as he: to see the hidden barb, the implication beneath a pretty metaphor, the innuendo. But she almost never answered in kind.

Her motivation? Her wants, desires? As elusive as a butterfly in the wind. What was her game?

Time to find out.

On the other side of the Grand Skya Canal, Lyren stood at her window on the palace's guest suite, hugging her elbows close. It was frivolous, even arrogant, to see symbolism for human actions in the patterns of weather and season! As if human passions were important enough to move vast currents of air and water. She knew it was absurd. Why, wasn't the first spring of the war one of the prettiest she'd ever seen? And the winter after the peace one of the sloggiest, and most bitter?

It was only the poets who patterned storm and balmy

breezes with the emotions of their heroes. And yet, and yet, it was so overwhelmingly tempting to ascribe poetic portent after poor Nash took her for that walk in the rose garden, just to find it had been mostly blasted by hail.

"Ah-ye, it's usually so very fine," he'd said, hands on his hips, staring in dismay at the carpet of petals that gardeners labored to sweep up. "But this here is Thorn Gate come again."

"The fragrance is lovely," she'd said to soothe him, but he hadn't stayed soothed, poor soul. She already knew this was why Shontande had not brought her out to this garden, the unspoken question between them: next year?

She still had not said yes, and gazed with hungry eagerness at the familiar roof-scape that had become so dear. How she loved this city, with its extravagant gates, and all those pretty buildings along the canals, vines trained up round stained-glass windows, and the unexpected little gardens that could only be seen from bridges. She had made it her business to walk every street of Alsais during free moments, and boat along every canal, under every bridge. Nothing was ugly anywhere, to the trees planted so assiduously before old warehouses along the big shipping canals, part of the city-wide conspiracy to create an urban work of art. The music everywhere, the processions, the dancing under lamp-hung trees in the little streets!

How she wished to see Alsais in every season. She wanted to see all of Colend! She wanted to see Lissanre's tapestries, and to find out whether Nashande would ever discover Noria's steady heart, despite her young age. So like Carl Delieth, she was. Would Hradzy, the Sartoran ambassador, ever find a love, or was he destined to be a poet's dream—successes in diplomacy, and tragedies of the heart? And all the others she'd come to know, to laugh with, and ride with, and dance with, would they forget her within a week if she had to leave? Probably, though she'd remember them all, for the rest of her days.

And worst, by far, was the prospect of groping her way through the rest of her life without ever seeing Shontande Lirendi again.

She would finish the opera, and if she had not succeeded in winning over all this court, she must consider leaving Colend, because she would not let her failure create yet another burden for Shontande.

Not two buildings away, where the former council had claimed lodgings in the palace, tears dripped down the face of Anrel, Talian's ex-personal maid, but she made no noise. Only kept her head bent, her hand stitching with swift precision, her body leaned slightly back so the tears would fall on the bodice of her livery, and not on the delicate lace in her hands.

Talian sat on a hassock, in her lace-edged under-gown, while her hairdresser brushed a lock of her heavy honey-blond hair with sure, gentle strokes, wound it expertly with a string of pearls and sapphires, then pinned it up in a complicated, glittering coronet that suggested a royal crown.

No one spoke. The only sound was drapes belling in the wind that swept the last of the rain clouds from the sky.

Talian kept her back straight, and her hands folded. But she saw the closed faces of her maids, and knew that they resented Anrel's demotion. But nothing must go wrong tonight.

"Anrel." Talian kept her voice even.

Anrel slid to her feet and bowed over her palms. Talian studied Anrel's folded hands, the lowered face. "You think me unkind, but you must understand the justice of my decree. You had one single command during the past two weeks. One, and only one."

Silence.

"It can hardly be a state secret, what shade of blue the king intended to wear this evening. You are friends with Enraq." Referring to Shontande's chief valet.

Silence.

"And if Enraq, for some reason, could not impart the information, there were the Residence stewards, the royal tailors, the royal fabric suppliers. Even the keeper of the gems."

Silence.

"I realize there was a great deal of work to do here, and it was hot. But you could have delegated some of your work to Kheriate, or to Peras, or even to Onla, who is young but trustworthy, or I would not have brought her to Alsais. And it may seem whim, but there is great importance in just that kind of detail."

Anrel kept her head bowed, but nothing could prevent the awareness that if the king had wanted Talian to know what shades of blue he wore, then all Anrel would have had to do was ask.

But she knew better than to speak. She liked her position, the castoff gowns, the handfuls of money and extra time in the city when the count was in a good mood, and of course she'd had high hopes of being chief wardrobe mistress to a queen. Though that one seemed less likely by the day, if rumors all around the kitchen, the under-stewards and minor heralds and scribes, even in the stable, were to be believed.

"We shall be leaving by the week's end, for it's nearly harvest time," Talian said, hating the necessity. But best to hide her hopes that her plans would materially change. "You will please me greatly by ordering everything for either swift departure, or—" She hadn't meant to say that. "Or alternate plans."

Anrel bowed and knelt by Kheriate, to see that only the one ribbon she'd been working on remained. With a few swift stitches she finished it, and then the two carefully lifted the gown made of the finest snowflake lace, edged with tiny pearls and diamonds. It floated over the count's head, both maids making certain not to touch the elaborate headdress.

The gown settled beautifully, the only color those pale silk ribbons drifting down from the arms, and peeping at the hem. It was matchless, a gown for the most formal of state occasions. And it was so costly, so very costly, it would easily befit a queen: Talian had had it made months ago, relying on the correct shade of blue for the finishing ribbons to match Shontande's color scheme.

Balked of that knowledge, she'd used the most neutral blue ribbon she could find. The gown was exquisite, and it fit her with flattering grace, but Talian could not be pleased. Symbolism was all-important, and now the subtlest part of her plan for this night had been ruined.

Talian glanced down her length and gestured for her diamond necklace. Still angry, she ignored Anrel, picked up her fan, and said, "Kheriate. Peris. Come along."

She intended to be a trifle forward of the time, for she had plans for her entry, but she was not there before Caid.

The early arrivals were the usual foreigners busy intriguing, sycophants waiting for patrons among the great, and hangers-on of various degrees. Perhaps fifty in all gathered in little groups along the perimeter of the great ballroom.

Up in the gallery beyond the new-polished crystal chandeliers, the king's own musicians played softly, just loud enough to mask the hush of this vast white marble room with its silver-leafed argan trees along the walls, the ice sculpture on the great damask-covered refreshment table, the tiny blue lamps winking coolly in the trees out on the terrace. A spectacular fall of water down one wall, lit by hidden blue-painted glowglobes so the water sparkled and gleamed in shades of blue, sent cool air ruffling across the floor.

Caid strolled inside, looking around appreciatively. He ignored the herald at the great door but the herald, who knew his job well, was familiar with the duchas's attitude. Alarcansa did not even listen for the announcement of his names and title, though all was as it should be, for Shontande did not have inept servants.

No one he favored or found interesting had yet arrived. The hour struck before he was ten paces into the ballroom. He listened to the echoes go out through the city as he strolled not toward the terrace, or the refreshments, and lounged at an unhurried pace to one of the side arches, and he went out again.

He had a private wager with himself. Was he right?

Ah, he was always right, at least about Talian. How she would squirm to know how amusingly predictable she was! There she stood, chattering with one or two of her sycophants, obviously just arrived, and a maid on her knees. They were lingering with artificial nonchalance in the far alcove off the main archway.

As Caid strolled nearer he saw the maid in Ariath livery sewing some kind of gem to the count's gown, which was otherwise quite spectacular. All conversation stopped, and the women made graceful little curtseys. He bowed. And, ignoring the maid — and the pretense of something amiss with Talian's gown, so that she did not have to enter the ballroom yet — with a smile he offered his arm.

She flushed. Yes, he'd been right.

Her lips parted as she saw comprehension in his eyes. And a sardonic smile that was an oblique threat. Her friends did not, so far, see through her innocent little stratagem, but Caid — damn him — was quite capable of calling attention to it.

As if to underscore that comprehension, he glanced toward the far doors, adjacent the outside entrance, and the partly concealed maid standing there with a tray, as if to serve someone. But the silly young twit was wearing Ariath livery: her job, obviously, was to watch for Shontande's entrance, so Talian could appear at the same moment, and his innate courtesy would require him to offer his arm so they could enter together.

She placed her hand on Caid's sleeve, but her cheeks

glowed with annoyance.

He liked her angry. She was real then. "An impressive gown," he said.

She flushed. It really was a degree too formal for this occasion, but during spring, when she'd ordered it, she had expected to be making a formal announcement at this gathering.

She snapped her fingers at the maid, who bit off her thread and backed away. Talian faced the grand entrance, but he guided her back to the far archway. "I've already been announced," he said. "No one needs to be made a present of my name twice." And, in a lower voice, "Astonish the multitudes with a subtle entrance for once."

The color in her cheeks gave her a delightful glow. So too did the wide angry eyes. If only she wasn't so predictable! Amusing, but, when compared to Lyren, tedious in her single-minded obsession. He had given that throne up. Why couldn't she?

They stepped through the arch, and were alone for a long stretch.

"I suppose," she said in a low voice, husky with suppressed passion, "you think being hateful is entertaining."

"Observing the truth is hateful?" he countered. "Have you yet to see that it's only forbearance that prevents him from speaking the truth?"

"Truth—" she began.

"Did I misstate? Then permit me to rephrase. Speaking the obvious."

Her fan snapped to the angle of boredom.

He smiled. "You really don't know how obvious you are? It would be a shame to find out that that splendid aura of arrogant unconcern is born of mere—I hesitate to say it, but ... ignorance." And when her chin came up in challenge, "Join me," he asked, though he hadn't meant to, "in the promenade?"

"Why?" she whispered. "You can't find another partner?"

"I didn't ask another," he went on, watching those restlessly scanning light brown eyes. "And no one asked you."

Even now she was waiting for Shon! His amusement cooled, leaving him annoyed. "I usually prefer to come and go alone, and I seldom give countenance to thrusters," he said. "Why I make an exception now shall probably require meditation."

That got her attention.

He went on, staring straight down into her eyes, "Did you think to force him through the doors tonight, and stand against all comers at his side?"

"Why ask me?" Her voice thinned at the end. "You seem to know everything I think!"

"I do," he agreed. "You saw yourself at his side all night? For the promenade, just to cut Lyren out, without considering that he probably asked some married woman weeks ago?"

"You want me to dance with *you* instead?" she rejoined, her tone precise as ice chips. "Why? To make Lyren jealous?"

"Of course," he said, laughing.

"It might work if she had the slightest interest in you." She snapped her fan up as a pair of courtiers strolled near them, nodding greetings. Still furious, she struggled to find a shaft that would sink into his heart as his did in hers.

He watched her rally. Then she uttered a strange laugh, looking off toward that far alcove.

He turned his head. There was Lyren, framed in the doorway.

"Honor Lyren Sartora, envoy of Marloven Hess," stated the steward. Crack! His staff struck the marble floor.

Lyren wasn't alone for long. People drifted toward her from all sides until she stood in the center of a crowd, slender in a layered gown of ice blue mothwing gauze. She wore no jewels, as usual, only silken flowers with which she had pinned up half of her hair, from which two wide ribbons rippled down to her hem.

Nashande gave her a flourishing bow and she took his arm, smiling up into his face with the unconscious and friendly ease of the generous heart. Then she turned her head and raised her other hand in a salute.

Caid had to look: there was Sveneric, also silently arrived, sitting with diplomats from Sarendan and Sartor. He nodded at Lyren and then turned his head, and for a moment Caid met his gaze across the width of the ballroom floor. Damn, how did he do that? That gaze of his like an arrow shooting the width of the room, past eyes and skull to scrape the back of one's head.

Caid's fingers tightened on his ornamental fan, then he forced himself to relax. To laugh inwardly at himself.

He was as tense as Talian, but then he, too, had a personal stake.

Only no one perceived his.

25

The royal fanfare pealed, chord on shimmering chord. Shontande stepped through the double doors with tall, exuberant Sasharia of Khanerenth on his arm. When had she arrived?

No matter. Talian stiffened beside Caid as the Crown Herald struck his staff four times and announced their majesties. Caid could feel how her every nerve strained to be instantly at the king's side, fending off all rivals. "Let him come to you for once," he said, soft enough for only her to hear. "Or are you finally aware that he never will?"

The gems in her hair glittered like the waterfall just beyond. He did not want to see grief. Anger, yes; comprehension, acknowledging that he was right, so that she would revert to the gallant count he'd glimpsed at the end of the war.

The Crown Herald knocked his staff on the ground again, four loud claps, and announced the Promenade. And, above, the first horns sounded as the guests glided to partners and formed a line.

"Come along," he said.

"I would rather," she whispered, "promenade with the cook's boy."

Ah, there was the spirit he'd seen during the war!

"Let's find you another partner, then," he said, guiding her to the crowd around Lyren.

"I can do that for myself," she retorted, but he gripped her arm so that she could not get away without drawing attention. Mass, unfortunately, wins over temper: she was too light to plant her feet and yank without drawing every eye, which would not befit the dignity of a count, much less Colend's future queen. And so she had to follow, dignity intact, as he led her to Nashande's side, and murmured in his ear, "Do you know, Talian is tired, possibly of me. Would you refresh her spirits?"

Nash smiled sweetly at her. He was not whom she would have chosen, but at least he was infinitely preferable to that poisonous Caid!

Caid then shouldered his way through the crowd around Lyren, using his rank to achieve deference. Count Drenate of Ymadan, who had offered her arm to Lyren, deferred with a graceful if slightly mocking snap and twirl of her fan. He then held out his arm with so proprietary an air that he sparked a sardonic smile from Lyren. It really was a sardonic smile; the corners of her mouth deepened, and he fought a sudden, almost overwhelming urge to kiss her right there on the ballroom floor; careful. He probably should not have been drinking earlier, though it had seemed an excellent idea at the time.

The echoing horns died away, and they stepped into line.

"I'd like," Lyren said in an undertone, "to believe that you did that out of kindness." Her low, slightly husky voice — her charming Sartoran accent, after Talian's lofty fastidiousness — was sweeter than the flutes above, as restful as a real waterfall, as shaded with oblique meaning as light through a cut diamond.

"It was kind."

"Oh?"

He looked down at her as they paced around half the room. She returned his gaze fearlessly, her eyes a dense gold, the dark-fringed lids curved in smiling humor. Her hair curled up from a perfect hairline, redolent of summer herbs, threaded with a ribbon and a couple of sprays of silken flowers. He found the simplicity more elegant than any of the elaborate, expensive headdresses around them, especially Talian's coronet fashioned to resemble a crown, complete to diamonds scattering light every time she moved.

When the Promenade circle was complete, he shot a glance at Talian, who struck an elegant little figure. With Nash she didn't posture or preen, which rendered her far more captivating than she was at that moment aware.

His attention snapped back to Lyren, who'd been watching

with interest, and he smiled with anticipation. "You don't believe it?" he asked. "Or you won't?"

The musicians transitioned perfectly to the ancient, staid complication of the ball's first line dance, as complicated as a military exercise; the pairs fell into the pattern of four couples.

"Leaving aside the question of motivation," Lyren responded as she tripped lightly around him, "you will admit that it seldom answers to maneuver people for their own good." As she should know; she smiled ruefully.

Caid turned, bowed, stepped twice to the right, and bowed to the baras there without even bothering to look at his face. His mind was entirely on Lyren, now four steps to his left. He heard her exchange a low, laughing comment with her new partner, then she danced on and the fellow turned to watch in appreciation as she danced back to Caid's side, long ribbons fluttering.

"But I don't want to do good," Caid said.

"I do," she countered, turned, hand high, and stepped across to curtsey to the Altan cousin at his right. Dip. Twirl. Change.

When she whirled back he said, "Dilemma."

"Contradiction," she retorted, smiling over her shoulder in challenge, and then gave her hand to the next person in the line.

Caid spotted Shontande dancing with Baras Albias, both conversing with obvious amicability; across from them Talian watched, the little jerks of her head betrayed by the sparkling jewels in her hair. Caid decided to provoke Lyren the way Talian so easily was provoked. "But doing good *is* maneuvering people for what you perceive as their good," he said. "Will they see it as good?"

She dipped, smiled, and gave a slight shrug and a brow-lifted glance over her shoulder.

He tried again. "They will see it as interference, which is commonly condemned as evil."

Step, dip, turn, bow.

"Do you really want an answer to that?" she asked at last.

Bow, step, step, turn.

"Humor me," he drawled.

"Why? Isn't that doing good, and therefore evil?"

"Then convince me," he said. They were together again at last, and the figure dance all but finished. He bowed, holding onto her hand, and she curtseyed, and somehow her fingers slid from his grip.

"You must convince me first that you wish to hear my reasons," she said. "I will not discuss questions of ethics merely for you to entertain yourself by arguing. It is not entertaining to me." And she made a gracefully formal peace, to the same precise degree as his first bow, with exactly the same degree of irony. "Thank you. I must return to my original partner, who generously asked me. I still owe her a dance." She started away, but he matched her step with one long stride. "And after her, Nash."

"I invite you to reconsider. If he's with Talian he's happy, the poor mutt."

"My sympathies are always," she murmured, "with the mutts. For they deserve love, too. As for Talian, if she stays with him long enough, I'll gift her with the chance to cut me out. I suspect she's had little enough pleasure so far this evening."

She smiled, stepped expertly around a talking couple, and out of his reach.

For now.

Lyren did not see the smiling anticipation on his face, for her back was turned squarely to him. She found Drenate, who turned at once to Lyren, and they joined in another of the more complicated figure dances.

By the end of that one, she hoped that Caid would leave her alone. As she and the Count went to get something to drink, she dared a glance back, to see Caid sauntering toward the other end of the refreshment tables where servants poured wine into fine crystal. Lyren stepped behind the taller count so that Caid wouldn't see her, and swept the rest of the ballroom, trying to spot Nash and Talian.

Ah. There were Nash's broad shoulders in a lake-blue brocade robe. But Talian's distinctive headdress was not near him.

Lyren turned her steps toward Nash, for she had promised him a dance, but slowed when she saw that Noria got to him first; he smiled kindly and held out his hand. And as the musicians spun out the airy prelude to a haltas, Lyren looked up to find one of the western border counts before her, saying, "Come now, you did promise to dance with me if I sang that blasted duet."

"I did indeed," she responded, smiling.

He liked to dance fast, and so did she. Music, the whirling

lights, the flash and glitter of fine fabric sparkling with tiny gems, how she loved this sort of life!

Three more dances followed, one after another, for as soon as one ended there was always another partner, and the unspoken custom was, you did not monopolize someone unless you were lovers. And so she bowed for the fourth time, and then looked up into Shontande Lirendi's face.

The wonder, the rush of white-fire pleasure, were at least familiar by now, and the effect controllable except for the racing of heart and blood.

"Are you free?" he asked—as the triple beat of the haltas brought couples together.

"I am," she replied, wondering how many questions underlay those three words. Then she laughed at herself aware that every hopeful partner had to think the same of any question he asked.

The enchanting rhythm of haltas intensified his bedazzling proximity. Though his clasp was so light she could have easily whirled out of his touch, while the music lasted, the world and time suspended.

For him, dancing with Lyren obliterated the room, the noise, and the predictability of most human interaction. But even a king cannot command a haltas to go on forever. And so when the music ended, there was his marble ballroom, refashioned a generation ago, and his guests, some watching overtly and some covertly.

Lyren made the peace as she backed a step away, leaving air between them. The body, obedient to the will, had disengaged, but the mind clamored for joining. Through Lyren's mind a thousand trivial questions and comments streamed, to be consciously dismissed.

Ah. He was speaking. "I meant to ask last night: Nash believes my absence at the rehearsals of your opera have slowed progress. Is it true?"

"You'll be welcome whenever you can spare the time. Really, everyone has been so swift in learning their roles, and they all perform charmingly."

"I have held you up, then. I apologize."

"But you've matters to tend to, and we've had fun. I think some will even be reluctant to quit when we do come to perform."

She meant it as a joke, though some of her performers

really did have a taste for the stage. (But then wasn't being a courtier a kind of living performance?) His smile was more polite than humorous as he said, "You have the remedy to that."

"To do another?" she asked, the implications dizzying. Want conflicted with *too soon*. "But what if they tire of me as director? Ought not by right one of their number be chosen?"

"Do you desire to be quit of your role, then?"

There are two conversations here, and this was not yet the time; she could feel Talian's angry gaze. But it was only Talian now. Her followers had become steadily more respectful, and Lyren sensed that if their leader could choose neutrality, at least, they would follow it. Even so, she tested, saying, "They could desire to be quit of me."

"From what I see," he said as they walked slowly down the room, "the welcome has only strengthened."

"Ah, but would they tell you if it had not?" she retorted, fanning herself, though she knew the warmth she felt was more from within than without, and she did not wish to be shed of it.

"Is that a challenge?" he asked, smiling.

"Come to the next rehearsal, and witness for yourself," she invited. "If you need the time, the palace lights need not shine when the moon rises."

"They will always shine when the moon rises," he promised. "I value our discussions too much to deny myself a one. But you are evading my question."

"I am not evading it," she said. "I'm … postponing it."

His gaze diffused, two steps, three. Always at that slow pace, taking no notice of the glances their way. He was inured to the constant attention, and Lyren sympathized. Could she live her life in public? Ah, but things would change if they —

"What," he asked presently, "would you do in my place?"

The implications! Her fan never faltered, but her mind sped from one path of possibility to another, until she realized that the pause might become a silence, with its own message, and so she resorted to one of Sveneric's old and unloved tricks: "Hold up a verbal mirror?"

He laughed, a real laugh. "I should have expected that anyone trained as you have been trained would be adept at evasion by question."

She sighed. "To mix an old but serviceable pair of metaphors, 'I scent the shadow of Detlev, do I not?'"

"If it's there, it's benevolent. I learned that at our northern border."

He had returned a serious answer to her flippant one, for he had, at last, disclosed the story of Curtas's heroic rescue, while they sat on either side of a single candle, fireflies dancing outside. Grief still there.

"Let us make a pact," she suggested, and switched to Sartoran, for this conversation had become too important, too fraught, for what might be still-hidden shoals of Kifelian. It was a heady thing to know with utter conviction that each of them wanted to give a gift to the other; he did not need her to prove herself to him. But she needed to prove herself to herself first. "Each of us must answer one question before posing one of our own, or we'll begin hooting queries at one another like a pair of owls."

He said, "As you wish. My question stands."

They had reached the vast waterfall.

Trusting to the muting effects of the falling water, she said, "Come to the rehearsal tomorrow, and sing, and you will also see what they think of my tastes in Colendi opera." Her tone was playful, and she smiled, a smile of surpassing sweetness.

"I shall," he said. "But since you did not answer, I demand a chance to put another question."

"Which is?"

"I will ask during our next dance," he said, "And expect to hear yours."

Next dance—she knew that would be the midnight dance. Which, at a formal affair like this, was as much a declaration as words could speak. Perhaps it really was time for her to compromise. She bowed and moved away one, two steps, out of the royal presence, to find any number of eager and interest partners awaiting her.

She smiled, took the first hand held out to her, and moved instantly to the next dance, but not without scanning the room once.

She saw, with pain, Talian's tight grip on her fan before she turned a shoulder, and sustained a swoop of warning at Caid's slack-hidden, watchful gaze.

She did not see Sveneric's reflective countenance as he watched them all.

26

The spectacle of Shon deep in conversation with Lyren for an unprecedented time — a slow stroll the entire length of the ballroom — caused a ripple of fan gestures and exchanges ringing outward through the guests. The moment the two parted, Talian fluttered toward Shontande, the moth ever drawn to the flame as Caid watched in disappointment. He also noticed that Lyren never glanced back.

A glass of wine later, Shon and Talian were treading the figures of a line dance, and Caid began calculating how long before he could be gone.

Talian kept her head high, though she watched for Lyren. How had she managed to monopolize Shontande for so long? Was it really that regrettable opera, as some whispered?

The dance ended far too soon, and Shontande thanked her with a grave air, bowing with palms together. And then he was gone off with the envoy from Breis, but at least Lyren was on the other side of the room. She walked away, affecting unconcern as all those jewels pressed on her head. Her scalp ached. Her eyes ached.

"... the taltan?" Here was Faria.

The music was familiar, and her feet knew the dance.

Adroit as always, Faria seemed to pick up her mood, and said nothing. Good. Talian's only responsibility was to convince Faria of her indifference to the spectacle of the two biggest catches — the two most powerful men in court — dangling after that foreign, rankless interloper.

Rankless. She'd tried to make it true, but knew that it

wasn't. Lyren's mother a queen, and there were too many references to Lasthavais Dei, so many that Talian had gone when no one was aware to see the portrait in the old gallery. Lasthavais had been nearly forty when the king fell in love with her. Her features were not completely like Lyren's, but there was a strong resemblance in their dark manes of hair, the mirthful gazes, the air of melende that was so much a part of them. Lyren could have gone anywhere in the world. Why did she have to come here?

The truth was Lyren did not pursue Shon, or Caid. They did the pursuing.

Sick to the heart, Talian wished this nightmare would end.

At last, at last, the chords signaled bows, and curtseys, and she performed her part, though her head had begun to throb, and had she forgotten to eat again this day?

Another haltas began. She felt the touch of a hand on her wrist, and looked up, uncomprehending, into gray-green eyes.

She couldn't seem to speak, but he didn't wait for her to. He slid his hand over hers, and somehow she stepped into the light clasp of Detlev's son, of all people.

Sveneric. Vague alarm sang through her nerves, but she dismissed it. He had no power here, so if he was rude, or horrid...

But he did not speak. They simply danced. Presently she became aware that the slow circles he made, the easy rhythm, were curiously soothing. A ring on his little finger winked and glimmered like water, no, like silver, only silver seen in a fog, or a dream. The ring was carved in a pattern of vines and leaves. She turned her head to watch the gleaming ring on his raised hand that clasped hers in such a cool, steadying grip.

That gleam. Her eyes ached less, somehow, as she contemplated how it first winked blue, then it reflected a pure light, rather like the fountain in the west garden if you observed it when the sun was just right. That fountain never failed to arrest Shon's attention, and she'd noticed, but she couldn't comprehend why.

Ah, don't think about Shon. Just the ring, and its never-ending circle of silver leaves and vines. She watched it as they whirled slowly down the room, and only became aware of the abatement of her headache after it was completely gone. The physical pain faded, leaving the mental anguish.

"Do you like the rhythm of haltas?" Sveneric asked.

"Yes, I do," she said, grateful that he hadn't spoken until now.

"It's probably the most enduring of dance forms," he said. "Most of the others go in and out of fashion, but this one, with its beguiling triplets, has persisted throughout history."

"So I learned when I was small," she said. "Was your father around when it originated?"

"Ah, that is a mystery. Dancing was part of ritual in his day, altogether different, and afterward, he was seldom in places where people dance. But he thinks that this dance came through a worldgate. Others insist that we invented it, and took it to other worlds." He paused, guiding her with skill between two couples in danger of colliding.

"Perhaps it is a form inevitable for humans," she said. "Two people, the turns, the rhythm evocative of cantering horses."

"A good point," he answered. "I wonder how many things we've reinvented for ourselves on every world we spread to?"

This was an odd conversation, and with one of the oddest persons to come to court. "Interesting question that probably no one can answer," she said. "One question we could answer: in what countries on our world do they not dance, and why? For example, until the war I heard any Chwahir woman who danced with a man would have been killed."

"The image of Wan-Edhe Sonscarna dancing will not form in my brain." Sveneric breathed a soft laugh. "Though from what I understood men did not dance, either. Instead, they marched in unison. It was a requirement of Wan-Edhe, who wanted to see thousands in those perfect squares, moving exactly alike, an extension of his will."

"Ah-ye! I never saw him, of course, but the stories about him when I was a child used to give us nightmares. Some have told me that their nannies threatened to send them to Wan-Edhe if they misbehaved. Horrid threat!"

"There was remarkably little that could be attested in his favor."

"Did you ever see him?"

"Yes," Sveneric said. "Not an experience I enjoyed."

Another reminder of who he was—and what that really meant. Raised among the worst villains the world had ever known, far worse ones that the likes of Wan-Edhe of the Chwahir. Involved his entire life in world politics, and not just the jostling for rank in a single court.

She asked abruptly, "If even a small portion of the stories are true, your father could have done anything. Had anything, at the end of the war. He could have taken over Colend. I don't think Shon could have stopped him. I remember Shon even said as much. I was there."

Sveneric shrugged. "May be true, or may not. It's irrelevant."

"How so?" He was so easy to talk to. No innuendo, no veiled threat, no sarcasm, no wit at another's expense. No shock, or pretended shock.

"Because Detlev only wanted one thing, his freedom. Nothing else matters, though he does like comfort if he can get it. His house is very comfortable."

"But ... to be that powerful, and to give it all up?"

"Give what up?"

Talian's mind wheeled. "Rank. Fortune. Influence."

"He never had rank, or not in the world that we recognize. Never wanted it. As for fortune, his requirements were comfort, as I said, and also the wherewithal to carry out plans. Once he judged he had enough for that, the acquisition ceased to be of interest. Influence..." Sveneric smiled. "He still has that."

"He does? But one never hears of it."

"I believe that is so," he said, still smiling, and once again steered them away from possible collision.

"If you will honor me with explanation, how can he possibly have influence?"

Sveneric paused for a fast-whirling pair of men to pass. His eyes were shuttered by his lashes, unexpectedly long, then they lifted and he looked at her and said, "If a hand smites the calm pond, ripples ring out, yes?"

"Yes." Obviously.

"The ripples can be so strong they overturn the floating lotus, and the leaves drifting on the surface can drown the small insects feeding unaware. If the hand dips and stirs very slowly, the current still rings out, but nothing is disturbed on the surface."

She frowned, sensing the proximity of meaning, then gave a mental head shake. How could anyone have influence without a position of power? And what could one possibly get out of it, if one hasn't the privilege of rank? Colendi loved metaphor, but this was one she did not hear used.

"Does he get any kind of reward?" she persisted.

"Yes," Sveneric said. "Success."

She considered. "You can't mean personal success."

"How do you define that?" he asked. "If you mean gifts, adulation, praise, titles, you are right, he acquires none of that. He's careful to effect changes without making himself a recognized agent of change. That 'hand through the water.'"

"That means he assumes false names or guises? Or does he use magic to turn invisible? Though I'm told that magic cannot really make one invisible."

"True about magic, at least as it is practiced on Sartoriasdeles. Long ago he used the semblance of disguise, but that was to ward Norsunder. Now he appears and interacts as another person. His name is known, but so few have really seen him, you see."

"Yes, that's true. I have no idea what he looks like." She peered into his face. "Do you resemble him?"

Sveneric smiled. "In some ways."

"He doesn't use his name, and that's a disguise? But who would listen?"

Sveneric's laugh was soft, and not at all superior. "They listen."

"Ah?" There were two issues here, both of which required separate thought.

The issue of personal reward could wait for the leisure of contemplation once she had been crowned by Shontande and reigned over court and Colend. Then, the subject of personal reward would be sweet, for she would be the grantor, not the beggar.

The second concerned the true meaning of power. Rank conferred power. That was the accepted definition, the universally acknowledged hierarchy. How, then, could anyone influence anyone else without either rank, an army at one's back, or at least the aura of menace of a famous name?

Obviously, first one needed to be near those in power, in the right place, at the right moment, and say the right words to net any effect. An impossible situation! Or had Detlev somehow perfected it over his zillions of centuries?

She frowned, feeling that the real answer eluded her.

"Thank you," Sveneric said, and only then did she notice that the dance had ended.

She made the peace to him, a gesture he returned gravely,

the little ring glinting on his finger. She watched him drift into the crowd, talking to this person and that, her feelings a strange amalgam of gratitude, intrigue, and confusion.

Intense reaction, but short. At least she had lost her headache. And he was interesting, in a mild way. She could not remember ever having had a conversation quite like that one.

For a moment she wavered between pursuit of this strange path, and habit.

Habit, and ambition, won. Where was Shon? Ah, over there talking to three different ambassadors. What could they be talking about but trade or border issues? She suppressed the urge to take her place by his side, to insinuate that his business could, and should, become her business. He had never discussed foreign affairs with her; she did not have all the facts. Court kept her occupied enough. She would take an interest in border matters as soon as she had the power to make an effect—

For a heartbeat her certainty wavered when she recalled what Sveneric had said about Detlev, but she dismissed it. Detlev wasn't like normal people. Useless to even consider what he did and why, really. And foolish to think she could penetrate his motives when she couldn't even parse Caid, blast his soul to Thorn Gate.

Caid—where was *he?* Watching her from somewhere, that detestable knowing smile on his lips? She turned, to catch a glimpse of Caid and Lyren at the far door. The corrosive stream of jealousy flooded back, stilling to surprise when she saw Lyren jerk her hand from Caid's fingers.

Then he laid a proprietary hand on her arm, smiling down at her in a way that Caid had once smiled at Talian. Fury boiled in Talian, then stilled. Lyren's manner was not that of someone slipping away to an assignation. Talian wished she could see Lyren's face, but she and Caid vanished through the alcove that led to the garden, and were gone.

Was Caid, by any chance—any justice—benefiting Lyren with an excoriating examination of her conduct, as she herself had been so benefited?

Ah! Talian wished her joy of it.

Smiling, she decided to favor Nash with a dance. At least he would keep her well within Shon's proximity, and there was always the midnight haltas to look forward to.

Caid of Alarcansa had noticed years before that the patterns of movement in a ballroom resembled the ebb and flow of sea tides, a curiosity of nature he'd once witnessed while traveling away from land-locked Colend.

After a decent interval, many of the older people retired from what, to them, was yet another end-of-season ball, on a night when summer persisted well past its welcome. It remained for the young and passionate, those whose lives were still unsettled and alive with promise, to dance the night through, whatever the weather.

When the crowds thinned, people generally drifted to one end or the other, not noticing how they stayed in a group. Couples might peel away for a stroll on the terrace, or even venture into the garden, if the weather was nice. It wasn't nice tonight, it was dripping from the earlier rain, though Caid had planned for any eventuality.

He waited until Shon was busy at the far end, talking diplomacy. Talian was with Detlev's boy, and wasn't that an odd combination! Everyone else focused down toward that end, leaving the waterfall to plash and thunder unseen, the alcoves unused. Caid strolled out to make his move, using rank's privilege to drive off the young sparks round Lyren. "Come. Take a stroll, where it's a trifle less noisy," he said loud enough to be overheard.

Lyren looked up at Caid with a slightly puzzled frown, and he said again, "A stroll. Fresh air."

"The air is not overly warm in this room," Lyren countered. "The magic sees to that. Nor is it stuffy."

What had they talked of for so long, she and Shon? Annoyance tightened his grip, an instinctive reaction he didn't quite control; again, he regretted that extra glass of wine. "Ah, but it will be sweeter outside. The gardens, after a rain, raise quite a scent."

"They will in the morning, too," she responded, smiling a little, but there lingered that questioning quirk to her eyelids.

"But it's at its freshest now," he said, taking her arm. "You will see."

Four, three steps to go.

"It can wait," she stated, drawing her hand away.

He understood that he'd been too urgent. "The truth is, I wanted to talk to you about the war, where it's not quite so noisy," he said. "This way, a few steps, it's quieter."

He took her arm to show her. She allowed it, but said, "I

was not quite in my teens. Nothing of my experience would be the least use to you."

"But you know all the important figures, I'm very sure. As for experience, you hardly could have less than I had. I spent most of it locked up, until I managed to escape my own family. My great-aunt never forgave me for that," he said as they walked through the open doors into one of the great public gardens. The scents of woodbine and jasmine and queens-blossom did perfume the air, as he had promised, and moths danced near the doorway, their wings golden-lit in the crystal-enhanced light.

Lyren's eyes, still dazzled by the brightness within, made out only unfamiliar shadows. Caid went on talking about blundering toward Alsais with a band of agemates, alternately hiding and trying to find the enemy to fight, as below his voice, she noticed footsteps on the gravel, and the soft snort of a horse.

A *horse?* Here in the palace garden?

She turned her head, her eyes adjusting rapidly, and made out the silhouette of a saddled charger, and a man beside it, waiting in the concealing shrubs. Not just one saddled horse — two!

She pulled away. "What," she demanded, cutting into his flow of words, "are you doing?"

His fingers had been a mere touch, guiding her on the path. But his grip tightened instantly. She shifted her stance, yanked her arm out of his grip, and spun away, almost out of his reach. Taller, faster, and stronger, he closed the distance, and seized her more firmly.

It was a quick, desperate fight, for she was very well trained indeed, and knew subtle movements that did not rely on strength or size, but she hadn't the speed of recent practice, and her long fluttering sleeves and ribbons were easy to wind around her.

Prevail he did, though carefully, so as not to hurt her. Aided by her long ribbons, he held her gripped against him, one hand round her prisoned wrists, the other covering her mouth. He felt her trembling against the length of his body, and nearly laughed out loud for pleasure, and anticipation.

Then came the least pleasant aspect of his plan. He bound her himself. He did not permit his waiting lackey to do it, for he trusted only himself to find that balance between security and comfort, and he would not have any hands but his own touching her.

Silken bonds only, wrists, ankles, mouth. Then he snapped his fingers, and his waiting liveried man silently brought forward his fastest and heaviest cross-country mount.

He carried her himself.

The lackey rode behind as they trotted along the tiled garden path to the outskirts, between the wide-spaced peacetime guards who watched for trouble from without, not within. He knew where all the herald-guards were, and their patterns of movement, for he had made it his business this past week to master them. They wound through the gardens, across a bridge, and another bridge, to where the paths linked up with one of the main city roads. A turn to the north, away from the few buildings, to the yard of the last inn on the north end of Alsais.

There the remainder of his servants waited with a four-horse carriage. Still mounted he glanced inside, saw by the single lit candle that all his commands had been carried out with exacting precision.

He dismounted, lifted Lyren down, and set her unresisting body on the coach seat against the silk-covered pillows, and he paused in the doorway, watching her angry eyes above the black sash, gleaming in the light of the candle now held by a lackey.

"We are going to Alarcansa," he said.

She didn't blink, just stared coldly at him. No sign of fear, of pleading, of tears. Even when he removed the gag, she said nothing at all.

He shut the door, and motioned the lackeys to take their places as he remounted his horse. He waved for the driver to loosen the reins and roll out.

All night he rode beside the carriage, smiling in anticipation.

27

Dawn in Marloven Hess.

A long, low-flying line of geese honked across the grassy plains, white against the peach-pale sky. Wind whispered through the browning grasses, heard by the horses, whose ears twitched back and forth. The ears, in turn, were marked by the riders.

Senrid watched the young animals and humans, satisfied with the voiceless communication each to each. Riding was an essential part of Marloven life. The summer games tested physical skills as well as cooperation.

As he watched the riding classes, the academy watched him more covertly. It was a compliment when the king came, for he didn't always, but it was also unnerving because you didn't want to bungle before those steel-colored eyes. Whispers had been that marriage, after so long a wait, would make him mellow on the field, if not as soft as a civ on a picnic.

Wrong.

They were watching when his chin jerked up, that all-seeing gaze going distant, far distant, as a day's long ride behind them Liere woke from troubled dreams to reach — found the bed empty and cold beside her, and remembered that Senrid was still out in the western plains with the academy.

Chilled, she sat up, comforting herself by the sight of their bedroom with the beautiful drawings of Lasva's garden on the walls. She looked around at his things mingled with hers, and knew that her dream-self had objected to an empty bed, and her body remembered late pregnancy with Yossi, and the gnawing worries about the infant she knew she would have to leave behind.

Her arms cradled her stomach as she reached on the mental plane for Yossi. She found him concentrating on the all-absorbing intricacies of standing to take steps without holding on. Satisfied, she withdrew, just as Senrid's wordless contact became a question. She reassured him equally wordlessly. The academy, still watching, saw a faint but tender smile curve their king's lips before he blinked, and lifted a hand to the senior commander. The horns blew, and the signal flags rose on their lances, placketing in the wind. The company broke into a gallop as the sun crested the distant hills.

Back in Choreid Dhelerei, Liere slid her hands over her eyes and listened on the mental plane for the greatest dream-walker she knew — and sure enough, there was an answer.

: Liere?

: Adam. Please don't tell me you listened in on my dream.

Exasperation without any heat or hurt whatsoever infused Adam's thought: *You sent it to me. In the middle of a training session with the young ones, I might add. Very disconcerting.*

She chuckled, aware that he heard everything, sometimes whether he wanted to or not, from exceedingly strong far-senders. She was one of the strongest.

Liere decided to reassure herself by checking on the other two.

Malcolin and his class were on their own field excursion, which involved a lot of swimming and diving on a river. Lyren was still in Colend, her contacts infrequent — she pleaded very late nights. Lyren was shielded, which did not disturb Liere unduly. Lyren was a grown woman. She deserved her privacy.

Liere dressed and sat down to breakfast with its single place setting, looking through the windows at the jumble of rooftops already throwing back sun glints from what would be a warm day.

She inhaled her breakfast, as the life within her wriggled and squirmed. There wasn't much room left inside. *I expect you'll be joining us soon, little one.*

Her golden notecase flicked her inner awareness. She pulled it from her pocket and took out a tiny folded square, with her name written on the outside. Since this was her golden notecase, it seemed someone wanted to make extra certain only she read it.

> *Liere: I would like to consult you on some questions.*
> *Carl*

Just as well Liere had planned little for the day. She heaved herself to her feet.

When her transfer vertigo had passed, she made her way from the destination chamber into a hall that smelled of paint and fresh-cut wood.

All the windows were open. She glanced through, and heard the sounds of labor, and, nearer, the scolding of birds who found the unaccountable actions of the humans quite annoying. Ought she to take her dyr out?

She decided against it. The effect was the same whether or not it was seen.

A little page appeared, her cheeks dusted with sugar. Eyes watering, the child swallowed down the last of the pastry she'd stuffed in her mouth, gasped, and bowed. "Pardon, honor —"

Liere waved a hand. "I can see that you're busy, and everything is all turned upside down. Just let the queen know that Liere is here."

"Liere," the child repeated, executing a creditable bow. "Please wait here." She started away, then turned around, almost bumping into a cover-shrouded table. "Liere — uh — are you *that* Liere —"

Liere tried not to laugh, an effort that made her ears pop. "She's expecting me."

The child ran off, but had not gotten ten steps when Carl herself appeared. "Liere!"

Liere looked at the wraith-slender young woman in the exquisite gown. Delicate color glowed in her cheeks. Liere enfolded Carl's fragile warmth in her arms, felt the compression of fine bones in their thin casing of flesh, then looked down into Carl's misty eyes. "Are you all right?"

"Oh yes. Happy. So happy. Forgive us — the rebuilding —" Carl's frail fingers fluttered round in a circle.

"It looks extensive. You must show me around."

"Oh yes! Laban can explain how we're restoring the old queen's garden, and rebuilding the… but would you like some refreshment?"

"Just had breakfast."

Carl led the way to a pretty study, shut the door, and stood against it, her brown cheeks reddening as she pleated her skirt.

"I think—I ought—you see, I really thought to have you come because—well, because—"

Liere tried to spare her. "Because you wanted to talk to someone who is married?"

Carl looked startled. "Is it so obvious, then? Oh, please sit down! Would you like a cushion?"

She eyed Liere, who, like most women with slim builds, projected forward when pregnant. Marlovens, who were not the least shy with personal questions, especially concerning their possible future ruler, often asked if she was having twins. If not triplets. But there was only one little mind inside.

Carl would carry the same way, if … and if. Yes.

Liere said, "I'm fine," and dropped into the chair. "'It'?" she repeated, and smiled. "A guess only, that you might like to chat about some of the difficulties of newlyweds the world over."

Carl sighed with relief as she pulled her chair from behind the desk, and settled close to Liere, almost knee to knee. "Is it really difficult for most? Did you have, oh, questions, when you were first married?"

"At the very first the war was on, and we'd had so little time together," Liere said, her mind winging back to her early days with Andri. Grief panged her heart. Complicated as their lives had been, they had shared nearly ten years, and made a child together. "What you and I possess in common as newlyweds, I suspect," she said, "is a lack of experience as well as a lack of information. You and I each had a mother, but the life I saw my mother leading had not been acceptable to me, and yours had an antipathy to the idea of marriage."

Carl's fingers laced together in a white grip. Liere resisted the impulse to touch her dyr; its effect, passively benign, would be felt whether it was seen or not. This effect was somewhat like entering a warm room after walking in a bitter wind. It created an atmosphere in which one could choose to look past anger and anxiety—or not. Using the dyr was a different matter, and required showing it to the person, before offering contact, either sharing a memory or receiving one.

"You can't discuss it with Laban?" Liere prompted.

"Lyren—before my wedding—warned me never to shut him out. To talk to him. And so I have, except for—" Her face heated, and she whispered, "Things. About himself."

Liere sat back as the baby decided it was swimming time.

"I think Lyren tried to tell me, but in hints. She was being very delicate," Carl went on quickly, her gaze sliding away.

"All right, let's begin with the basics. Are we talking about sex?"

Carl nodded violently, staring down at those pleated fingers.

"How much do you know?"

Carl sighed. "Oh, I have known the fundamentals for a very long time. You can't have a brother your exact age and not learn that much." She smiled a little, despite the twisting fingers. "But sex is altogether different. When—it seemed—that Laban might possibly court me, I thought the best thing would be to get rid of ignorance. And Jessan had said that the best pleasure house for first timers is Aunt Hollis's, over on the other side of Ferdrian, and so, um, Merry and I went together."

Good choice, Liere thought, an image of Merry Dei's kindly face before her eyes.

"I was able to learn what must be learned, but it took so very long for me to feel any, well, pleasure, or desire, anything at all, really, that I was afraid I would always be passionless, but at least I knew what to do. But then Laban treated me with such courtesy that passion never seemed to be a possibility."

"Ah."

"And so when we married, it's stayed that way." Carl looked up and away. "He's as kind as can be, ever so. But we part every night and he sleeps in his room. I was relieved at first, for I was so afraid he would offer to come to me out of *duty*. I know what I look like, and I know he's dallied with beautiful people. Lyren told me that in the days when we were young and it was a matter of teenage curiosity. But now that we've been married, how can I tell him how much I want him? I cannot *make* him want me back. So I avoid the subject." She looked up wistfully. "Is that wrong?"

Liere said, "It's ... where your mind has been. It seems your mind is changing. Which is perfectly fine! Go on."

"Well, I want more. But nothing ever happens, and he must think me too ugly to want anything to happen." She spoke the last in a rush.

"Wait. Wait. Slow down." Liere reached to take hold of the tense, twisting hands. "What has he said? Done?"

"Nothing. Nothing! He's always so courteous, and kind. Always. I've seen him get impatient with other people, and he can say some very cutting things to Vana, who only laughs. Even with Mad, when she'd in one of her moods. But never, ever with me. Not once."

"All right, then, that's another good sign. He obviously cares about your feelings. But you never tried anything while you were alone with him?"

"At first I was too frightened by my own feelings. What if he said no? I sense no passion from him, so what if he feels *obligated*?" Carl's forehead puckered. "I think Laban might have tried to talk about it, right before our wedding, but I sensed he was doing his duty and I just couldn't bear it. He hasn't mentioned it again. At first I was relieved, but now … I'm not."

Liere envisioned Laban's vivid blue eyes, his expressive, sardonic brows, the mobile mouth. Passionless? Not likely. But he had obviously learned to control it.

Carl pleated her fingers. "Do you sleep in the same bed with King Senrid?" She had not completely outgrown her childhood habit of using titles.

"Yes."

"Did you with King Andri?"

"Yes. Most of the time."

"And did — *it* — happen right away with them?"

"You have to realize that with Andri the spark had come before we were married. And with Senrid, it was the opposite, at least for me. He felt it first, and I didn't realize it until later."

Carl frowned. "So it's really not instant and, and equal in intensity?"

"No, not always. Why do you think there's so much poetry and drama about love?"

"But love is … love. I mean, I know there are different kinds of love," Carl said. "For siblings, for friends, for family. For one's kingdom, and the people therein. I thought couple love was one thing — united together — but I cannot seem to find my way to …" Her thin fingers gripped tightly.

"The physical spark is unpredictable," Liere said. "As far as I've observed. It doesn't always conveniently hit both partners at once, and with the same degree of passion. And when it does, it's not necessarily anything but that, the spark of physical desire. Which can be a part of the enduring love that makes a match mind for mind, spirit for spirit, for a lifetime. Or not. So many different types of love."

"You had it twice, then?"

"My heart really belonged to Senrid, but I first felt the spark of physical desire with Andri. I did my best to call it heart-love, forever love. He cared for me, as he cared for others. It was never heart-love. Yet we had a fine life together. He understood about Senrid long before I did, but kept it to himself, because his caring was generous."

Carl whispered, "If he hadn't been killed?"

"We probably would have gone on so, for I had walled away my real feelings, the deepest ones, I mean. As long as I never saw Senrid again, or heard his voice, I would have worked hard to be content." Liere was aware that her explanation was simplistic, but if Carl was to live a life with a one-sided passion, she needed to know it was possible to make it work.

Carl drew a deep breath. "How do you know when the other person has the spark?"

"If there is a question, then it's probably not there. That doesn't mean it might not come in its own time. But that might not happen if one person in the couple perceives a greater necessity."

"'A greater necessity,'" Carl repeated slowly, as if tasting the words.

"More persistent, or urgent. Example. If Laban feels he has to protect you, to shield you, that he must treat you like fragile glass that easily breaks, he might be too apprehensive to progress beyond newlyweds."

"But I love him so desperately!"

"Sounds more like emotional need. Which is perfectly fine if it doesn't become obsession. You had to learn that with your twin, remember?"

Carl's eyes widened. "Our tenth birthday. When Jessan left."

"Isn't that why Lyren first came to you as a companion, after I had to waken you from the long sleep?"

Carl wrung her hands. "Are you saying that it was I who drove Jessan away, and not Tahra-Mama?"

"No, no, no. He had to escape her. Your part was to learn to let him go."

Carl nodded quickly, relieved. "That's right. I had to see our boundaries as individuals. That we were not the same person, though we shared our thoughts. You're right. Still, am I so much like Tahra-Mama? I use love to bind people, instead of hate?"

"I don't believe you intend to. But being aware that the instinct is there might require some reflection. What do you think?"

"It's true." Carl's breath shuddered, but Liere sensed her rallying, for these were surmountable problems. "And they all protect me. Even the younger sibs." She gave a tremulous smile. "Is poetry all a lie, then? Love at first sight is—a myth, say, if not a lie?"

Liere smiled back. "I don't know. All I can tell you about is *lust* at first sight. It was fun while it lasted, until I tried to make it out to be more than it was."

Carl laughed a little.

"All right again?" Liere rose.

"Yes. Thank you. As you say, I need to reflect. Oh, what you said is such a relief. I really do have Tahra-Mama's instincts, but when I *see* it, then I can learn to *control* it. And I do *not* want to be a fragile piece of shattering glass that cuts *everybody!*"

Liere hugged her, but when she reached the Destination chamber, she paused, her fingers running absently along the dyr below her collarbones. Ought she to talk to Laban, to make certain he understood Carl's problem? Or would that be officious?

She needed a male point of view, one who knew Laban.

The time, so far south, was probably a little earlier, but Liere remembered that David was an early riser.

And so she did the transfer, appearing in the entranceway of Detlev's academy on the mountaintop. The atmosphere was profoundly peaceful; she heard the soughing of firs through the open windows, and birdsong rising in chromatic efflorescence. In the distance, the chatter of students' voices.

She walked in. The fall of light through the windows high and low, the complex blend of pine and mountain herbs, filled her with sensory beauty and wrenching memory.

She stopped by the stairway, breathing in the pine-tangy air, and fighting memories of Macael Elsarion, whose company she had so recently left the last time she was here. But they weren't so easy to banish. The disirad on the higher plateau intensified memory, emotion, motivation, intention. Macael's tight-leashed silences that had shielded so much pain and isolation.

Leaving Yossi in her thoughts. She sent a tendril mind-questing. Yossi was asleep after a tough morning of trying to walk. He dreamed, but he knew her presence immediately, and within dream-forms he delighted in finding her there.

She projected an acceptable dream-form for him, and for a time they cavorted as mama cat and kitten, until he sank into deep sleep again, profoundly comforted by the image of her wrapped around him warmly, purring.

When she opened her eyes, she fought the brief vertigo, and found herself looking up into David's face as he lounged on the stairway, waiting. Despite the mountain chill he wore only threadbare shirt, unlaced and unsashed, and long trousers — no shoes.

"Adam said you were here." He smiled a greeting. "He's with students. I'm free. Will I do?"

"I was hoping you were free. I need advice."

"Easiest thing in the world to dispense. Hungry?"

"Just ate."

He waved Liere up to his room, which was as plain and impersonal as ever. She stood at his open window, looking out at the mountainside, and beyond, the blue-gray line of the sea, finding balance with the heightened awareness.

She watched David drop into the window seat, observing his version of the Montredaun-An economy of movement and strength.

Why had she never been attracted to him? Lyren had been, and in truth the Montredaun-Ans were a handsome family. Even the evil brother was attractive in a kind of oblique way, though the notion of languishing after green-eyed Imry was about as appealing as the idea of collecting handsomely patterned poisonous snakes. Would probably feel about the same, too.

David sat back, the early morning light outlining the bone-structure of cheek and jaw — so subtly familiar — and striking highlights in his waving blond hair. Again, so much like Senrid's, both in color and wave, and also the fact that both of them wore their hair square-cut at the collar in back and no longer than eyebrows in front, combed straight back though it didn't always stay; only when Senrid's hair tumbled over his forehead, the sight of a single lock in disarray could strike her weak-kneed with desire.

David's wide-set brown eyes were unlike either Senrid's or his brother's. "Speak," he said. "Or have I altered in some alarming way? You're staring."

Liere smiled. "Blame the distraction on time, and transfer, and your mountain plateau. This is not a great catalyst matter— I still don't know if I detected Detlev's hand in Damondaen, or imagined it—but a personal dyr question. I want to know if a talk with Laban would be helpful or meddlesome." And she showed him her memories of her conversation with Carl.

He'd gotten even better at contact. She was scarcely aware of his mental presence, and niffed no hint of reaction. It was probably a reassuringly neutral effect for his students or others he encountered, but for her it was a daunting indication of his growing expertise.

He said, "And so?"

"And so to approach Laban to reinforce what I said might be a mistake? Or do you disagree with what I said?"

He shrugged slightly. "Why do you feel the impulse to reinforce your words with Laban?"

Liere thought that over. "Am I implying condemnation? I hadn't intended any."

"And yet?" David prompted. His chair creaked as he tipped back, propping his crossed feet on a chair back. He closed his eyes as the autumnal breeze streamed in, ruffling through his hair.

Liere felt the bite of impending winter in that breeze, and sat in the corner. "Perhaps I was afraid that his regard for her was ambition after all, despite his unerring care. And as such, the care might not last."

"Ambition is too simple a word," David said. "So simple it connotes judgment. But you're not settling for that or you wouldn't be here."

"Tell me, then," Liere said, leaning forward. "Laban's and my experiences of one another have been quite brief. And we are such very different people."

"I'm beginning to believe that land ties are innate. When we were small, Detlev took great care to keep us confined to Geth for our first forays into the field."

"I remember," Liere said.

"When we finally came here, we'd formed some experiential ties to Geth. For MV it definitely worked. He had no interest in Geranda. For me it also worked, more or less. Other than a burning desire to find Senrid and match wits against him, I didn't feel any particular ties to Marloven Hess. Interest, by all means. It was somewhat the same for Imry, whose vision was a lot broader, though he returned to Marloven Hess from time to time."

"Alas." Liere winced.

"For Laban, Detlev may as well not have bothered. When he first stepped onto the coast of Everon, he felt he'd come home. From then on he was almost impossible to control, especially as he could see how badly governed all three kingdoms were. Every plan he made had to do with that area in some wise, no matter how ridiculous or how reckless. Remember when Siamis made his break? We got ourselves into big trouble with the head snakes in Norsunder because Laban staked out a corner of Wnelder Vee and got MV to ward it against adults, just so we could begin to carve out a little kingdom — and Efael noticed us."

"I have not forgotten that episode."

"Spring from the past to the present, within the context of your conversation with Carl. I'd sum Laban up by saying that he's in love with the land, and might not ever have room in him for the kind of relationship Carl wants. Or, he might come to love her. This I'm sure of, he'll try to make sure she's happy, as happy as he can contrive."

"Bringing me back to my question. Do you think I ought to talk to him?"

David looked at Liere there on her chair, earnest, very pregnant, and somehow, despite two marriages and between that, one of the strangest affairs that he'd ever witnessed, she retained some quality of guilelessness that seemed essential to her nature.

He shrugged again. "Relationships can change. Friendship becomes heat. Heat cools to friendship. And so on, infinite variety. But there can be reasons to work at relationships. We're not all helpless in the grip of pure instinct. Which is the long version of: if it were me on that chair, I'd leave them alone. You gave Carl something to work on. Laban's going to see that. He'll reflect, and compromise, and she'll compromise, and because they both have good will, they'll find their particular balance."

That did not promise Carl happiness. But then whatever Liere would say, or do, wouldn't guarantee happiness either. And — perhaps most important — Carl had not asked her to speak to Laban, nor had he requested interference in his life. "And so," she said slowly, "I must learn to step back. Got it."

28

Transferring back hurt even worse. Someday she was *going* to take courage in hands and learn the slide, but not when she was two people. But oh, it was so very good to find herself home.

Home. A wonderful, delightful, enduringly delicious concept.

Why had Liere never realized that the sense of belonging, the safety, the welcome she'd taken so for granted whenever she came to Choreid Dhelerei meant home? How that smell of sage and horse and stone had worked its way into her bones and brain and heart, probably when she was ten?

Joy rippled through her when she sensed Senrid in his study, and saw his face when she dashed through the door straight into his arms. His kiss melted her body and sent her spirit reeling. Then silent laughter shook him, and she disengaged enough to realize they had company. She looked over Senrid's shoulder into Sveneric's appreciative gray-green gaze.

"Sorry," she said, for form's sake, though she didn't feel sorry—nor did he look the least discommoded. She turned to Senrid. "You're back early..."

"... to the news that your daughter has either been abducted, or has eloped," Senrid said. "In the middle of one of Colend's fancy balls."

Alarm zinged through her, to fade when she saw that neither Senrid nor Sveneric seemed particularly incensed. She sat down by Senrid. "Enlighten me," she said. "Or I ought I to say, entertain me? Who is the villain—or swain?"

Sveneric's lips curled. "The Duchas of Alarcansa. Know him?"

Liere thought rapidly. "Isn't there a river with a similar name, somewhere in Colend?"

"Northeast," said Senrid the mapmaker. "Elorca River. Not the same."

"I know little about Colend," Liere admitted. "I take it she's in no danger?"

Sveneric and Senrid exchanged brief glances, and Liere knew that this question had been thoroughly explored before her arrival.

She looked down, working to steady her splintering focus, then sensed a tendril of question from Senrid. She gave him a private sign that her errand was nothing dire as Sveneric said, "There's no danger, as in physical threat. I wouldn't be here if there were—"

"Lyren wouldn't be," Senrid pointed out. "Laying aside the question of self-defense, and her training therein, she could contact any of us for the transfer spell, if she hasn't a token with her."

"No danger, then, but a fraught situation. According to the gossip that ran through court earlier today, she ran off with him, but—though I did not witness the deed done—I don't believe she was a willing participant. At least at first."

"Ah," Liere said. "If this event occurred at court, did this duchas have implicit cooperation from Shontande Lirendi? Lyren is, after all, his guest, or such was my understanding."

"He has not reacted at all. The prevalent rumor, as I said, is that she eloped with Alarcansa."

"Eloped! Why would she need to do that?"

"I don't believe she would," Sveneric said. "I did some investigating to prove it, and I have two pieces of evidence. The duchas's servants appear to have been a trifle surprised at their orders; one of Alarcansa's stable hands let fall to a palace steward that the next time they came back, the duchas would be bringing a duchas, though she didn't seem to know it yet. And outside the ballroom, where a side door gives onto the great garden to which the public have entrance, I found signs of a scuffle."

"What's Shontande Lirendi say to that?" Liere asked.

"Nothing at all. And I don't know whether he has investigated parallel to me; his herald-guards are very discreet."

"So he's not going to send a galloping horde to the rescue, then?"

"And risk civil war?" Senrid put in, smiling sardonically.

"Oh. I hadn't thought of that," Liere said.

Senrid pointed a finger upward. "You don't know the half of it. Apparently your daughter has charmed most of his court." The 'your daughter' was a private joke between them, since Senrid had been a sort of guardian from Lyren's birth. "Including its monarch."

"Oh dear."

"Not charmed." Sveneric used the reproving tone of the scholar, but his eyes, like Senrid's, betrayed inward enjoyment. "That would imply machination on her part. Not true."

"She's befriended them, then," Senrid said, shrugging. "Why quibble about terms? What it comes down to is, if her stay here during winter is anything to go by, half of 'em want to sleep with her, and the other half want to tell her all their problems."

"I want to hear more about Shontande Lirendi and being charmed," Liere said, though she suspected she now had a name for the joy she'd sensed below the increasingly infrequent contacts of late.

Sveneric said, "What I have to offer is observation only, as I have discussed this business with no one there. I am a guest on sufferance, you have to remember. There remains the matter of my background."

"Granted," Liere said, leaning forward. "Is she courting him publicly, or privately?"

"I suspect you won't believe me, but their courtship is done. It was done the moment they first saw one another."

Liere blinked. "Oh?"

"Detlev," Sveneric added with wry portentousness, "was not surprised."

Senrid lifted his hands and gazed skyward. "Oh, well, then, there's nothing more to be said."

Liere smothered a laugh. "Go on."

"She has not actually said," Sveneric put in with scrupulous care, "but I believe Lyren has been courting Shontande's court."

Senrid added wryly, "Perhaps the most sophisticated, if not the most influential, on the continent, besides Sartor. And she's hypothetically doing this because?"

"Because she has to marry a kingdom, not merely a king; if she takes the one without taking the other, she believes her action would doom them to stress and discord."

Senrid rubbed his chin. "That's strategic thinking."

"Here's what I find worth contemplating," Sveneric said. "She doesn't need to strategize, or not in the sense that most understand it. She was doing it by nature, because that's what she does best. That's what she's always done, ever since I first saw her, even when she blundered, it was always with good intent. Only now she does it so well that no one really quite knows what she's doing—except Shontande saw it from the outset. And—I think—at first he couldn't believe it. Couldn't permit himself, is what I suspect, but again, it's me observing. He doesn't talk to anyone about it, near as I can tell. Not even Thad, or Bee. Not about that."

"What's he like?" Liere asked. "Shontande, I mean, not this duchas. If he grew up even half as handsome as he was when I saw him last, years ago—"

"Better," Sveneric said. "Nearly every heart-free human being in sight range meets him and wants him. It, too, is innate. He can't control it, and probably would if he could. His nature is actually solitary, or as much as one can be when living in the theatre that is Alsais."

"Remember how he spent the war dressed as a girl?" Senrid observed to Liere.

"So I heard." She blinked, recalling Enaeraneth history—and whom Macael admired the most. "It sounds like he's a throwback to Emperor Mathias the Conqueror. The one the Colendi call the 'Magnificent.' Yossi is named after him, in part." Liere grimaced. "Not sure whether I ought to be glad or sorry if Lyren is going to get herself tangled up with those Lirendis."

Senrid waved a hand. "Never mind the Lirendis, past and present. He'll either act, or he won't. Main thing is, we know Lyren. If she hasn't already skipped out on this duchas, then there's a reason."

"Has she shifted her attraction, then?" Liere asked Sveneric. "You said something about gossip and elopement, which implies that she wanted to go. Yet you say that she was taken."

"I don't think she wants this duchas, not for marriage, any-way," Sveneric said.

Liere rubbed her eyes. "It's so hard not to think like a parent. Does she need rescuing, or not? In other words, is she going to want us to interfere, or not? But she hasn't contacted me..."

"I was there. I saw them all," Sveneric said. "My feeling is that she's determined to handle it on her own. But I felt that you ought to know."

Now it was Senrid's and Liere's turn to exchange looks. His raised brows left the decision to her.

Carl—Lyren—Macael. Liere tried to focus, then finally shook her head, remembering what David had said just before her arrival here.

"Leave her be," Liere said. "As Senrid said, she knows where we are. We shall wait."

Lyren had seen three opportunities to escape the night of the Masque, but each of them would have been drastic and probably painful. Leaping from a galloping horse in the darkness is seldom comfortable, even when your hands aren't tied. Next morning, she spotted four opportunities.

Each of those four would have involved hurting someone, which—as yet—she was unwilling to do. She did not believe she was in any danger. She was angry, mostly because she had missed the midnight dance with Shontande. She was also thoroughly disgusted with Caid Lassiter of Alarcansa.

She'd thought it all through as the beautifully sprung carriage rocked and rattled northward, pulled by four fast horses. Shon's roads were very good, she observed. So too were Caid's horses, carriage, and his servants. She decided to enjoy her first view of Colend's countryside in the moonlight.

The pauses to change the horses were accomplished swiftly and smoothly. At one point a liveried man poked his head in, scrupulously respectful of demeanor, and offered Lyren a steaming, fragrant cup of hot chocolate.

"No thank you," she said.

The man seemed nonplussed. He hesitated, bowed, and withdrew. Before his bony face vanished Lyren saw telltale red along his cheeks. Lyren felt some regret, for the air was chilly for the first time in several weeks, and the chocolate would probably have tasted as good as it smelled, but she'd determined on passive resistance for the nonce. Caid — curse his twisty little brain — had enjoyed her fighting to get free. She'd not give him that pleasure again.

The coach began rolling, and no one came near her again until well on into the next day.

Noon came and went. For a time she was uncomfortably warm. Her blue mothwing ball gown felt grimy and the skirts looked draggled. She gazed out the window at the changing scenery, farmland, and well-tended canals giving way slowly to hills, with mountains nearing. She leaned out once, to see farther, but her eyes unexpectedly met Caid's black gaze as he rode next to the carriage.

She sat back, and refused to look again.

On the second stop, the door opened once more, and this time it was Caid himself. He reached to untie the sashes round her wrists and ankles. Glad as she was to be free at last, she would give him no sign of reaction.

"Are you hungry or thirsty?" he asked.

She didn't answer.

"Will you have something? Bread? Coffee?"

"No," she said — well aware of the extreme rudeness of that word to the Colendi.

He shut the door.

They rolled on very soon.

Presently the carriage began winding its way up increasingly steep inclines. They stopped more frequently, through a day and another night. She slept once, and woke to find water and biscuits inside the door. The water, she drank, and after a time ate the biscuits, since no one was there to witness her resistance. No one came to the door, and she did not open it, or try to run, for she sensed alert minds waiting nervously outside.

She would not involve servants, if she could help it. This duel was a matter between her and their master.

She dozed off and on as the light disappeared, and finally dropped into sleep again, to jerk abruptly awake when the carriage stopped again. The changes of horses had been swift all along, but for some time now, there had been no negotiation for post horses. That had to mean they had reached his lands. This time, there was no more hitching once the horses were unhitched. They must have reached his citadel.

She registered excited voices, and saw the orange flares of

torches outside the window. From the light it must be near dawn. People hailed one another with the lilting intonations of those happy to be home.

The voices abruptly stilled. Lyren could envision Caid making a gesture of dismissal. The coach door opened. In the reddish, uneven torchlight from beyond, Lyren recognized Caid's silhouette.

"Will you step out, Lyren?" He held out his hand.

There would be no profit in suffering the indignity of being dragged forth and lugged inside like a sack of onions. She stepped down, avoiding his hand, and shook out her rumpled skirts.

"Please, this way," he said.

She paced beside him without speaking. Caid, looking down at his prisoner, saw only stony control, and that innate grace that informed every movement even when she stalked, disheveled, in her wrinkled ball dress.

Lyren ignored him. A surreptitious glance around the outer court revealed a formidable castle, which was not surprising for a border duchas. Built for defense, and to ward fierce mountain winds, weather, and warriors.

Inside, she found civilization, and the well-maintained tastes of former generations. The outmoded furnishings amused her in their homeliness, all those heavy carved chair arms and legs carved with dragons around them. Chwahir influence, surely, right here in the border. Caid led her down a carpeted hall to a room whose chill was in the process of being banished by a two-firestick fire in a great fireplace. Autumn came early to the mountains.

Two great wingchairs sat angled toward the fire, with a table between them. Caid indicated one, then he bent to augment the firelight by touching candles to the flames.

One he set in a waiting brass holder on the table; another he used to light candelabra on either wall.

In the golden light he looked at least as disheveled as she felt, and a great deal more tired, for he'd ridden that entire distance on horseback. On the internal score sheet she mentally awarded him points for his straight back and alert (though narrow-eyed) gaze: he probably had at least as great a headache as did she. But she permitted no sign of hers in her demeanor. And certainly no sympathy.

He sat in the other chair, and a sigh escaped him.

She remained standing, a relief after that long, stuffy ride.

"Shall I summon refreshment?" he asked as he drew off his riding gloves and laid them on the table.

"Not for me," she said.

His lip curled. "You intend to starve to death?"

"I have not yet decided what to do," she stated in as cold a voice as she could contrive. "Until I do, I've no wish to touch anything of yours."

He leaned back, hands idle on the chair arms. A ruby on his little finger winked with rich burgundy light, the steady beat ticking with his heart. Her tired eyes were drawn to that warm glow, so she forced her gaze away.

"What are your choices?" he asked, in the voice of power humoring the powerless.

"Whether to leave or to stay, of course," she said, her tone one of surprise.

"Meaning?" he prompted.

"Meaning either I cut my way through your people—something I contemplate with distaste—or I remain and dwindle to death, another unpleasant choice."

"I'd rather you do neither," he said, still humoring her. "Though I confess I'd like to see you try the first."

"I know you would," she retorted. "The prospect of killing your servants for your entertainment does nothing to enhance my diminishing respect for you."

"Will it bolster my declining prestige if I admit that I don't think you capable of killing any of my people?"

"You would be wrong." Her steady gaze reflected the candlelight, gold within a ring of black, within a ring of gold. As enchanting a pair of eyes as ever art or magic could conceive.

His brows lifted slightly. "I'm inclined," he said at last, "to give some credence to your claims, judging from how close you came to grassing me in the great garden."

She remained silent.

"Who trained you?" he asked.

She did not answer that, either.

His fingers drummed on the arm of his chair, but only for a few moments. He became aware of the movement, and ceased.

"Will you consider a third choice?" he asked presently.

"That depends."

"I want to marry you," Caid said.

"Then you should have asked."

"And you would have said?"

"I would have refused. And this situation we are in now is not likely to change my decision."

"Maybe," he admitted, smiling a little. "But I was bored with court, and with waiting on the fools who surrounded Shontande Lirendi, and so I decided that someone needed to take action, and why not I?"

Her lips parted, but she closed them.

He was bemused by her lack of reaction, as she had hoped. She knew that anything else—tears, fury, haughty resentment—would have entertained him. Begging would have disgusted him, but it would have disgusted her more.

"Will you tell me what criteria will affect your decision?" he asked.

"Yes. If you offer me violence, I'll use it right back if I can."

"I will not use violence," he stated flatly.

"Then whatever I do, your people will take no harm of me," she promised.

His brows lifted again. He was too tired to mask his reactions, so she saw that he was beginning to believe that she could do what she claimed.

"And me?" he asked next, lips curling.

"You deserve whatever you get."

"So I cannot touch you without leave, but you are bound by no such constraint?"

"I am here against my will," she said. "I see it as a way of restoring a semblance of balance."

"May I defend myself?" The amusement was back.

"Yes," she said tranquilly.

He steepled his fingers. "So you've been trained to strike once, have you? Ah, I'd forgotten the scholarly Sveneric. Or rather, his antecedents, around whom you presumably must have spent some of your formative years, eh?"

She did not answer.

"Interesting. So the personal risk is mine. It seems fair enough. Ah-ye, I accept your rules." He paused. When she remained silent, he said, "Does that mean you'll take food and drink?"

He spoke in a plaintive tone a shade too obvious to be serious, yet she sensed the concern behind it.

"Yes."

"I'm relieved." His court drawl was back. "Would you like anything now?"

Her stomach squeezed, but she decided her point was best made if she steeled herself and did not share a meal with him, or pretend a semblance of normality. "No." And watched his muscles tighten at the blunt word that Colendi never used.

"Then I'll show you where you'll stay."

He rose, and in silence she followed him out.

Of course it was a tower room. She took a good look at access and egress, not caring if he saw her doing it. When he had seen her inside, he said, "I wish you a good rest."

She did not respond, for she'd decided that the circumstances obviated politeness. She would not say please to, or thank, an abductor. What they had was a truce, not a relationship.

When he realized she would not speak, he shut the door. She heard a lock engage on the outside.

She looked around. There was a fireplace. Someone had raced up here to ready the room, and a clear, warm fire burned. Pleasant if heavy furnishings evoked traditional taste. She wondered as she looked at the bookcases and the fine linens on the bed if this had been where Caid was locked up by his relations during most of the war.

She stepped through the cleaning frame beside the empty wardrobe, took off her gown, and laid it aside with care, then climbed into the bed. A water pitcher and glass rested on the bedside table. She helped herself, drank deeply, then burrowed down into the pillows and dropped into sleep.

29

Talian lay back in bed, stretching luxuriantly.

Lyren still had to be missing. Talian's servants had strict orders to report any court news, and that would certainly top any list, especially after Talian's inspired hint to Merenith the day after the ball.

She glanced at the window, and laughed. How often had she ever woken this early? Not often. The morning after the Blue Night Masque had begun as a good day, with Merenith bustling in at the barely-civilized Hour of the Deer, gabbling breathlessly, "Did you hear? Lyren is gone, and so is the Winter Duchas!"

Talian remembered then what she'd seen the night before, and had promptly forgotten for more important matters such as the midnight dance—which had gone to the queen from Khanerenth after all.

Talian had seen at once how to destroy Lyren forever as a threat, but still not harm a hair of her pretty, barbarian head. "You don't mean that Lyren eloped with him at last?" Talian had asked, yawning behind her hand.

Merenith's face! She'd never forget the sight of those pop eyes, the round mouth, the pig nose twitching. "You knew? You knew, and you didn't say anything?"

"And trespass against melende?" Talian gestured shadow-ward, imagining Merenith's busy chatter up and down the halls of the palace's guest wing, then over the bridges into the great houses along the canal.

"Ah-ye, and you said nothing! What did you know?"

Merenith looked askance. "If you say that Lyren told you her plans I say you dreamed it."

Talian bit back a hot rejoinder, and once again offered a carefully worded retort, one that would be less likely for Merenith to misstate: "Melende required I say nothing last night, when they so obviously wanted privacy, but yes, I saw them go out together, directly from the ball."

All strictly true.

Merenith scarcely stayed long enough to be polite, leaving Talian laughing as she threw off her morning wrapper and raced into fevered preparation, so that Shon, in coming to corroborate what she had witnessed, might find her appropriately employed. She could then commiserate, and suggest they put their heads together, to decide what to say to court. Because Talian always thought of the kingdom first, and not merely of her own pleasure, as Lyren had done.

She'd whiled the long day doing artistic things, twice having her maids bring in fresh flowers and throw out the old, while the minstrel she had her maid hire plunked away in the alcove. But no one showed up at all, so she ordered dinner delivered, and dressed for evening.

Nothing.

No visitors at all.

Talian rolled over, looking across her empty bed. How long since anyone had slept beside her in her beautifully embroidered cotton-silk sheets? An internal image, strong but unwanted: Lyren and Caid wrestling in bed. Caid's hands, his long black hair, unbound, drifting across one's flesh, so soft, the scent of it. Did Lyren twine her fingers through it?

Talian flung herself out of bed. How weak! One drunken night with Caid, so very long ago, and while it had been good — *very* — he was not a king.

As the Hour of the River carillon played pleasantly outside the palace walls, she sat down to her breakfast.

A knock at the outer door, and her maid came in to say, "His grace the Duchas of Sentis requests a private interview, my lady."

Nash? He'd certainly know what was going on. And he'd be a fair gauge of the atmosphere of court.

"Bid him enter," Talian said.

She had scarcely finished buttering her second little roll when Nash strode in, dressed in riding clothes.

"Talian," he said, without any vestige of the niceties.

"Sentis." She nodded regally. "I am just finishing breakfast. Would you care to join me?"

He ignored her gesture at the other chair, and her question. He looked perplexed, compressed his lips, then burst out, "That gabbler Merenith has spread it all over court that you saw Lyren fly off with Caid."

He hadn't even waited until the servant was gone.

She set her pastry down with delicate care. "Is that still the subject? I am just as glad I had a headache until today. What of it if she chose to go away with Caid?"

"Did you really see them?"

She did not like his tone of voice at all. How dare he, who had known her since childhood, imply she had lied! But now was not the time to put him in his place, or what would be his place, when her rank exceeded his. "Ah, Nashande," she said with a soft sigh, her hands at Rue. "The business is too painful to discuss. Why does it matter what I saw?"

He blinked, the dolt. "I'm sorry to upset you," he said finally, tapping his fan against the back of the empty chair before him, thump, thump. Before she could request him not to damage her furniture, he said abruptly, "I'll leave." And he stalked out.

In Alarcansa, Lyren faced Caid's wardrobe steward, who had come herself rather than send one of her underlings, and said, "I appreciate your effort, and I shall make certain that his grace knows that you tried. However, I will not wear anything but my gown." Lyren indicated her blue moth-gauze, which of course looked bizarre in daylight. But her wearing it would underscore the fact that she had not consented to be here.

The poor woman glanced up, then down, her mouth working as she tried to find better words to plead her case.

Lyren smiled in sympathy, and spoke again, to make it clear that the steward was absolved of any possible blame. "These robes you brought are very fine, and under ordinary circumstances I would have liked them very much."

The woman bowed over her crossed hands, then slowly folded the outfits she'd brought. She glanced once more at Lyren, as if mentally begging her to change her mind, then quietly withdrew.

The door shut. And locked.

Lyren closed her eyes, checked—and sensed the huge armed guard posted directly outside the door. She suppressed a sigh and combed out her hair, then hunted fruitlessly for the pins and silk flowers that had no doubt fallen out of her hair during her garden struggle. Even her ribbon was gone. She swiftly fingered her hair into a plain braid down her back, and finished at a knock outside the door.

"His grace invites you to breakfast, honored one," came a voice.

"Very well," she said.

Outside stood not just the guard in mail and fighting livery, but a sizable herald. Both looked at her with eyes slightly distended, and she controlled the impulse to snicker. Were they really expecting her to take them on in a wrestling match? What had Caid said?

Oh, she'd ask him. Why not? The situation could hardly be more absurd.

She was still smiling when she walked into that same room with the big chairs, which she was to come to recognize as Caid's favorite—and probably the most comfortable room in the castle. Downstairs were the great state rooms, for this was the main residence of the family, but those were vast and this time of year unpleasantly cold.

"You are amused?" Caid asked, rising. "Good morning," he added.

She did not respond to his courtesy, but sat down. "What did you tell those enormous guards? They looked at me as if I'd bite them in half."

"Ask them yourself," he retorted. "I recommend the cheese-pasty. My cook is better than Shon's, at least with breakfast."

"That I can't believe," she said, selecting flaky-crusted pasty, fresh fruit, and bread that must have come straight from the oven, for it still steamed. A cup of fresh butter stood at the side; she helped herself.

"Have you thought about what you would like to do to occupy your time?" he asked, with some irony.

She matched his tone exactly. "I really thought that that was in part up to you."

"Ah. You can stay here and read, or talk to my head

steward. She'd like nothing more than to discuss the intricacies of housekeeping. Or you can ride along with me, for I've a number of pressing matters to see to, not surprising since I've been away since before Midsummer."

"I'll ride. I need the exercise," Lyren said.

"Shall I arrange for riding clothes?"

"No."

His eyes tightened at the word. How many times had he ever heard it in his life? Not enough.

Then he rubbed a thumb across his brow.

She grinned, and addressed the unspoken question. "I might make a spectacle of myself riding about in a ballgown, but I won't entertain the countryside with heroic escape attempts. Since we have this much of an understanding, I don't intend to go anywhere until you escort me back to Alsais, everything proper and in daylight."

"Ah," he said, speculatively.

She knew he misconstrued, but that was all right.

He'd find out.

And while Lyren spent a day as the Duchas of Alarcansa's silent shadow, watching, listening, but not interacting as he went about his business, back in Alsais, Talian Ariath emerged from her rooms to discover that the social season really did seem to be ended.

Ended, except the palace was curiously full of people. So far, it seemed, the only departures were Lyren and Caid. And indeed, all up and down the guest wing of the palace, doors were still closed, which indicated occupancy. When people left for home the rooms were opened, aired, and cleaned.

So people were around, still, but nowhere in sight. Further, no one appeared to have scrambled together delightful parties, or outings, or even concerts or readings in order to pass the time.

After a strange, strained afternoon wandering about the rain-sodden gardens, and through the great antechambers, she passed on. Where was Shon? Oh, probably in the Privy Chambers. The reminder irked her with frustration. The winter's invitation would have given her passage to those rooms by now. She *knew* he'd meant to give it to her, then Lyren came, and destroyed everything. Now that Lyren'd ruined herself, Shon surely must intend to come forward again?

Talian returned to her rooms and summoned the maid.
Anrel bowed, eyes lowered.

"Have there been any invitations?"

"There has been nothing, honored one."

Odd. If nothing else, there was always the weekly gathering at the Sartoran ambassador's. Mostly foreigners there, usually, but now?

She dressed more formally in dark green silk, and crossed to the state wing, where the foreign delegations were housed above the state chambers. Wendis's apartments were reputed to be as grand as the royal ones. As befitted the representative of the queen who was first in precedence all over the southern world.

Talian arrived late, so as not to appear too eager, or that she'd had little else to do. So unsettled was she that the familiar faces of Faria, and Coral, and even Liss of Ymadan, were a relief.

The Sartoran ambassador, Hradzy Wendis, rose at Talian's announcement, as a good host should, and came forward to greet her. He came forward for all his guests. Even the minor ones did not just get a rise and the peace, but the greeting at the door. That was exactly why she avoided these general invitation affairs. She shrugged internally. She was here to find facts, and here were familiar faces playing cards. Games and gossip often went together.

Coral had brought her court deck. Faria made space for Talian at their table. They were playing Foray, one of the longer court games. And from the look of it, wagering small stakes.

As she watched the snap and flick of cards going back and forth from hand to piles and then to other hands, Talian determined that she would not play for high stakes. It had taken hard work, but she had managed to hide the fact that Ariath was not all that wealthy since the war years, when she'd had to begin paying taxes. Careful guardianship provided her with enough income to dress well at court, but all her jewels were inherited from her mother, who as part of the regency council, had exempted themselves from taxes.

Talian no longer heard the snapping of the fire, or the drum of rain against the windows, and the tiny noises made with the cards.

"... the garden?" Dorete Jherad was saying.

"Ah! I haff read this one, this poem," spoke up the exprincess from Melire. "Tis very good, yes?"

"It is very well written indeed." Faria gestured amity with two fingers, her pleasant voice soothing to jangled nerves. "But, if you will honor me with a moment of rebuttal for the sake of discussion—"

A gracious opening of the hand in Pardon-My-Shadow. Talian fought impatience.

"—I find more beauty than wisdom in his sentiments."

Dorete Jherad reached to discard, casting a questioning glance across the table. "Then you favor the garden over the gardener?"

"I do," Faria stated, but in a humorous voice. "Now, see if you don't agree. The garden is free to grow, to flourish, to attract the eyes of all. The gardener has no such freedom."

"But the gardener selected the garden, and thus gives it its beauty, is that not so?" Coral sighed, as the Meliran princess looked from one to the other.

"The gardener has chosen the land, the flowers, and how they are tended," Faria said, laying down four cards on her ally's pile. "But that does not mean the garden is solely for one's own pleasure."

Talian recalled the poem from her youth. Putting that together with the court metaphor, she translated it into a discussion of whether it was better to be the lover or the beloved.

"No, the garden's purpose must be to please." Dorete smiled. "Its nature, merely to be itself."

"To please whom? Either my gardener relinquishes the garden to others, or walls it all up and guards day and night against trespass," Faria stated.

"Except we come back to the beginning: your gardener had the power of selection. One must not overlook the fact that it was this gardener who chose the soil, and the seeds, and tended them ..." Coral laid down a card on each point.

Talian's attention drifted. It was a general discussion, speculation only. No one knew anything. Philosophical discussions were occasionally amusing, but not when she needed actual news. Yet the topic wouldn't entirely go away. Was it better to be lover, or beloved?

Her thoughts reached first for Sveneric and his mild voice as they'd twirled around the marble ballroom, but she shrugged that off, and mentally picked at the sore that was Caid and Lyren. Ah, useless to think of them. Which left Shontande

Lirendi, and the contrast between his neutral, benign manner toward her and his preoccupation with Lyren since her arrival.

Love? It couldn't possibly be love. They did not even know each other. Lust, certainly. They all had it. Dramatic as it was, her mother had stated times out of mind any form of romance had very little to do with royal matters.

Talian looked down at her empty hands. She knew that she had come very close to gaining the crown this spring. And she'd confidently assumed that with it came Shon's very appealing person, but ... for the first time, she wondered: would it have?

"Crown, crown, crown. Crown," Coral stated in satisfaction, laying down four court cards.

"Ah-ye, another loss," Faria sighed. "Who has the score? Is it as bad as I think?"

"It is," Dorete said with mild triumph.

The usual exchange of wins and losses took place, and Coral said, "I must bow out of another game, if you permit."

Everyone touched fingertips or murmured suitable words. They all looked tired, in truth, even the foreigners over by the fire, who had been talking in low voices, probably to cover their lack of good manners in using their home tongues. Talian rose as well, for she wouldn't stay without friends, and all her friends wanted to leave.

Faria leaned over and whispered as they started out, "If you have nothing better, tomorrow night a few of us are going into town in mask, for a little diversion."

She moved away, talking with one of the foreigners, before Talian could refuse, as she had for the past five years.

Annoyance surged through her at Faria's question, which suggested that Faria had not even noticed that Talian had held aloof from those excursions, because the king did.

Talian returned to her rooms less satisfied with the world, and with herself, than when she'd gone out, and her mood was no better the next day. Another early rising meant a long morning of nothing stretching out before her, with only harvest accounts from Ariath to occupy her. She would read them—duty—but she knew they would be correct. Ariath was only a means to wealth to her, not a home, for her mother had taken very good care to raise her right here in Alsais, a queen in the making.

Instead, Talian occupied her time having the maids take

out her summer clothes, choosing among them which to keep and what to discard, and giving orders for more fabric and ribbons. She may as well have a few autumn robes made up while she was here. As she watched her maid carry away those she'd rejected, she was tempted to recall them, to have them unstitched and the fabric—perfectly good, not the least bit worn—reused, but Merenith's sharp eyes might recognize formerly worn robes, unsuccessfully disguised, and give rise to gossip. Oh for the blithe confidence of a barbarian wild rose, who wore the same three robes to every event!

After the noon bells, Talian went out on another walk, and once again blinked away images of that carved ring, and that odd conversation with Detlev's son. Why think about it? There was nothing to be gained. And yet, it had been a relief, possibly *because* there was nothing to be gained. She frowned out the at the gray sky, and rounded a corner, then staggered as a figure almost ran her down.

"Oh! Your honor! I am sorry!"

It was that twit Noria. The girl picked up the pink rose that she had stuck behind her ear, and bowed in a formal peace, her manner so humble and contrite Talian nodded more graciously than she'd first intended and said only, "I trust there is no emergency—no fire?"

"Alas, I overslept so horridly, and now I'm late. Are you coming, too? Someone said you were ill."

"Coming?"

Noria looked as blank as that lackwit Nash she admired so much. "Of course," she said then. "You remember: *Love's Favor's Cost.* Rehearsing. The king has taken over himself."

Lightning blinded Talian. She barely had time to recognize that it was from within, not without, that the rain beating against the windows was the steady rain of a cool storm, before she heard her own voice say, "Ah, of course."

And her feet followed along down to the king's theatre, where they were all gathered, including Shontande. As she and Noria entered the rise and fall of a man's and woman's voice reached them, along with the strains of a full orchestra—the entire staff of the king's own musicians.

People looked their way; Talian took in colors, decorative touches in fans and embroidery, and always, the color of ribbons. A great deal of … rose. And roses.

"Ah, there you are," exclaimed one of the Altans, coming

forward to claim Noria.

Nashande was right behind his cousin, his expression difficult to interpret; it was a face she'd never seen before. He made
a semi-formal peace, then turned back to the matters on stage.
Shontande also made the peace as he asked if she was recovered? Both so polite, so ... *not* intimate.

"Yes, sire," she said, returning the same semi-formal peace.

"Thank you for joining us. Your act is just finished, but
we'll return to it again," he said, and turned his attention back
to the stage.

Somehow she made it through the rest of that day, standing on the periphery of that crowd and watching that absurd
opera being put together, as if it had any importance, as if it
mattered. She sang her one song, remembering her training.
Somehow she made compliments when they were due, and
accepted same, and then retreated to her rooms, where Faria's
runner awaited her.

In mask. There were no actual masks, of course—hadn't
been for a couple hundred years. Nobles donned ordinary
clothing, as worn by the wealthier citizens of Alsais. That
meant, like the Masques, no claims of rank or precedence.
Though one might be recognized, no one spoke of it, but one
couldn't use one's rank, either. And so a duchas might sit next
to a seamstress's apprentice at an inn, but if the dinner was
good, and the talk engaging, there was a kind of freedom in it,
an escape from the fraught consequences of court.

And though she had refused for five years, she was unsettled enough to snap her fingers for her maids, and send them
running for her mask clothes, packed at the bottom of a trunk
somewhere.

Through the evening she followed Faria's group from
place to place, ignoring the noise, the music, the laughter,
smiling and smiling as the tedium wore on. Some went upstairs
at the Amaryllis Sprig for pleasures of another sort, carefree
and anonymous; ordinarily Talian would have followed to
obliterate her worries, but they wouldn't stay obliterated. And
her head ached so, and all she could think about was Shontande
Lirendi directing that opera as if he had nothing else to do. And
that look in Nashande's eyes, the steady and distanced stare of
hurt, of sadness, of disillusionment.

Success, Sveneric had said. That implied taking action.

Why not? She gained nothing waiting around here.

She returned with the others, who were tipsy, singing a ballad in round as a long-suffering barge poler returned them to the Grand Chandos. Talian shut out the warbling; by the time they were helped out of the barge by waiting servants, she had gained enough clarity to make a plan.

And by the time Faria and her friends had sunk into slumber, Talian was dressed and down in the stables, readying to ride.

30

"In fact I was supposed to spend the winter in Sartor that year, but war prevented my foray into worldly polish," Caid said wryly as he and Lyren sat over breakfast. "Afterward there was too much to do for protracted absences, so I have that pleasure yet to experience."

"Perhaps we might have met," Lyren said. "What an odd thing, to look back and wonder about such possibilities of encounter! Liere and I were in Eidervaen earlier that same summer, before we went to Enaeran. I first met Hradzy Wendis there. His sister has the title, you see, and he was new at court, and though he was there as a real grownup, and I was just a child pretending to be grown up, he was so kind to me."

"Wendis is a smart man," Caid said. "He's close — very close."

"He'd have to be, I would think," Lyren said sunnily, and he wondered if Lyren had any idea how many couriers, diplomatic agents and outright spies drifted in and out of Wendis's hospitable chambers. "I know Atan thinks highly of him and his family."

"Tell me about Enaeran." Caid reached to pour more freshscalded coffee into his cup.

Lyren cradled her steep in her fingers. "What is there to tell? Everything I was used to is gone, and Trevor Macael Elsarion rules now."

"Yes, that's what I want to hear about. The present ambassador has been effectively shadow-warded; we're told a new one will be sent at the turn of the year. Not that that will make much difference. Why the look of regret? You cannot possibly sympathize with the Adrani king? People liken me to winter, and similar hum—eh, foolery, but I would never threaten someone's life in order to get an heir."

"I do not sympathize with him," Lyren stated. "Not the least bit. Though Liere manages to empathize, for reasons she would have to explain herself. However I know Marten Eldias, who I was told would be sent here as ambassador at the turn of the year, and he is one of the most good-hearted persons I've ever met. And he's not Adrani, but Enaeraneth."

"Ah," Caid said, his expression difficult to interpret. "Of course you know him."

"Yes. Also one of the kindest."

"And so, after a year, when the heat has died down, Macael Elsarion sends someone like that? Shunning him would be like kicking a bunny. Is that how the Adranis will win back melende?"

Lyren tipped her head, considering. "Difficult question. I expect Marten deplored Macael's action as much as the rest of us. But he'll be scrupulous about all other matters."

"Interesting."

"As for Macael..." Lyren considered what Liere had told her about Macael. She would never share a word of any of that! Not that Caid wanted to hear it. His interest was in policy.

"I think," she said, "he can do almost anything, and the Adranis will support him. Which is also interesting, because he, too, is Enaeraneth. But they both have relations on either side of the border, which Macael is determined to erase. That border, I have to admit, has caused generations of discord."

"He really did knife his own cousin? And the kingdom put up with it?"

"He had people in all the key places, you see. He'd planned it down to the last detail."

Caid whistled. "And people call *me* cold."

"I was young when Liere married Andri. That was our first visit, at the end of their latest civil war. Laban told me that civil war was like a climate cycle in Enaeran, coming back around every twenty-five or thirty years. They were so busy fighting themselves they left their neighbors pretty much alone, but when Macael gets them built up again, who knows?"

Caid leaned forward. "There's been a lot of talk between the Sartorans and Shontande about these places west of us, up against the Wern River, south of the Redmonds—"

"I know. I've been through there, at the start of the war," Lyren said, waving a hand. "Senrid said no natural defenses, I remember that much, though I didn't really comprehend what it meant."

Senrid. Caid considered the ease with which Lyren named these rulers. Laban. Atan. Even Macael—she knew them personally. But she didn't seem to be aware of the effect, because it was her natural state. "Some of them are turning to Sartor for protection, but my understanding is that the queen does not want an empire. Others are turning to us. I don't know what Shontande is contemplating. His first priority always seems to be protected trade, but defense is under discussion because, as he says, this country is really not defensible. Not without allies."

"And defense is still extremely expensive," Lyren said.

"So we've got couriers riding back and forth, hither and yon, and the shrewder younger brothers and sisters and cousins of interested monarchs coming for sightseeing tours," Caid said, smiling. "You noticed how many of 'em Wendis hosts in that mansion of his?"

"I noticed," Lyren said. "I did wonder, once or twice, how many were friends, and how many had nowhere else to go—like poor Nellas from Melire. And how many are really spying for someone else, underneath those smiling exteriors."

"Adding to the absurd, the Adrani king is in some wise related to the Lirendis. Did you know that?"

"Oh, everyone at that level is related," Lyren countered, laughing. "I nearly fell off my chair when Atan told me once that the Landises were kin, way back, to the Sonscarnas of Chwahirsland!"

He laughed with her, but was struck again by her easy reference to "Atan"—as though the world-renowned queen of Sartor, descendant of the longest line in the world, was equivalent to the aunt she'd mentioned earlier, who ran a pastry shop. Maybe to Lyren they were.

"I wouldn't put anything past that Macael," Lyren finished. "He's ... very strange."

"Something I trust Shontande is aware of," Caid said. Bells ringing outside made him set his coffee aside. "Alas. Much as I would like to continue this discussion, I've judicial duties awaiting my attention."

Lyren waved a hand. "Go on. It seems a good day to sit by the fire and read."

"You do not wish to accompany me, and add your wisdom to my attempts at justice?"

"Not the least," Lyren said with cheer.

He'd seen that indefatigable cheer when he'd mentioned social obligations. His being back from court meant that he now belonged to the local gentry, with whom he had to maintain good relations. And that meant smiling his way through interminable dinners, concerts, and dances, when he would rather have stayed there with Lyren.

Lyren refused to go to any of these. Riding about the countryside overseeing trade she seemed to find acceptable; social engagements weren't.

Ah, the rules governing the civilized abduction!

He rose and excused himself, seeing no reason to abandon good manners because she had given up the spoken forms of politesse. It was part of the delicate balance between them. He was far from regretting his stratagem. Each day he found more interesting than the last, and he would not permit himself to think beyond that.

As for Lyren, she would not admit by the slightest change in voice or manner, but she found Caid the governor, in his plain but well-made riding gear, far more prepossessing than she had Caid the drawling courtier in elegant silks.

They had not discussed Shontande at all. Though his name came up from time to time, the subject of Shontande as person was tacitly forbidden, as was Caid's motivation for doing what he'd done. She knew that it was not simply a matter of unbounded lust. There was in some wise a challenge to his royal relation, one that Shontande had not responded to, though he could have.

They both knew he could have. From brief references, and from the subtle signs of guard and watch round Caid's castle, Lyren gathered that Shon could, and had in the past, suddenly exerted his kingly powers, and that he was all the more effective for the rarity and the expert quietness with which he acted when he chose to.

But no guards in royal livery galloped up to the gates demanding surrender of Lyren's person. Nor did any well-trained spy-type slip in and appear at her window, which was the possibility she'd dreaded. She expected Sveneric to have the wit to leave her alone, and she was determined not to contact Liere until she had good news to report. (Or defeat, if it came to that.) But it seemed that Shontande was trusting her to solve her dilemma, which made her love him all the more.

And so another day passed, and its evening, which she spent prowling among Caid's books. His servants — obviously resigned to the strange vagaries of nobles — kept a respectful distance.

Lyren retired early, waking only when torchlight flickering in her high window, and the sounds of voices from below, indicated that Caid and his escort had returned from their outing.

It had been a late hour, but he was there at breakfast when she came down, as usual in her blue moth-gauze ballgown, her hair in a plain braid. The warm, silvery glow of dawn struck muted color in the splendid fabric. She was thoroughly tired of that gown by then, but he found the spectacle quite agreeable. He also knew better than to say anything.

He rose to greet her, as had become customary, then sat down again, frowning over what was obviously a letter.

"I have to ride up to the high-level vineyards today," he said as she helped herself to fresh-baked oatcakes and berries-and-cream. "It's a long ride, but you might find the area of interest. It's one of the oldest in the kingdom."

"I'd enjoy that." She was pleased at the prospect of getting outside again.

"Do you know anything about the wine-making process?" he asked, after studying his letter again.

"Very little indeed."

"But you know something about human interaction. Will you give me the benefit of your observations after witnessing the dispute? This is not an official judicial matter. It touches on personal concerns, and so my judgment might be at fault. I won't say more, lest it prejudice you either way."

"If you like," she said. "As long as I remain an anonymous bystander to these individuals." She was not going to countenance his insinuating her into the lives of his people, under the present circumstances.

The bells rang the start of the day through the valleys when they galloped out of the Lassiter castle on fast cross-country racers, eight armed outriders behind them. The air was chill in the shadows, but the sun shone brightly, making south-facing cliffsides pleasantly warm as people worked to bring in the last of the grape harvest. Caid tried not to be obvious in how many times he glanced appreciatively at the spectacle of Lyren riding like the wind, that absurd ballgown floating out behind her, making her appear a figure in a romance.

They changed horses once, for it was a considerable climb up. The wayside inn was full of people in Alarcansa livery, who regarded Lyren with passive faces and slanting glances of muted curiosity. But all were scrupulously polite, taking their cue from their duchas.

The ride was necessarily slower as they reached the steep paths of the heights. There, Lyren could look across at the rows of gnarled vines, some of them very old, as Caid talked about the history of the place, and gave her a quick, rather wry lesson in the process of making wine.

The local winemakers had gambled on the recent hot weather for a last spurt of ripening sun; as soon as it broke they'd gone into a frenzy of harvesting, for the timing of grape harvest was a tricky matter. They were nearing the end of what had promised to be a harvest of rare vintage—but in this particular vineyard the press and storage had come to an abrupt halt due to an unforeseen event.

At noon they reached their destination, the central meeting house of the vineyards along the southwest slope of a great mountain, below the eastern pass into Chwahirsland and tucked against the border of Breis to the east.

The principals in the dispute were obviously waiting, the tension high in the whitewashed room that smelled of wine and wood smoke. A peat fire smoldered on the old, blackened hearth as the company rose and bowed, then sat again at a gesture from Caid.

More glances slanted Lyren's way, but the clusters of people on either side of the room were too agitated by their own problem to pay much heed to a slim young woman in a courtier's summer ballgown.

Both sides began to talk at once, until Caid raised a hand.

"Mov, begin."

A short, thick-chested man around Caid's age stepped forward. His skin was sun-browned, his curly brown hair streaked with yellow. Two blue eyes dominated a long face.

"It's Malla," he said, in an unexpectedly deep voice. He flushed. "I don't marry any woman as has changed her mind.

Not even though we've been promised these past five years, both families sealed on't. Nor has any Uleg ever since we come into these mountains, no matter how much trade is offered."

He paused to wipe his face with a handkerchief. Behind him, an older couple nodded, their faces closed and angry, and what appeared to be a younger brother shuffled his feet, eyes down. The brother and the father were as short, thick-chested, and thatch-haired as Mov Uleg.

Mov continued. "So let her go off and marry yon string-tinkler, if she wants. But fair's fair, and there ain't no Uleg barrels no more, unless they be paid for, fair price. And for the past five years." Here he smacked a muscular hand on a clay wine barrel, sitting alone, as if it was a piece of evidence in a justice dispute.

Gasps from the other side of the room. Lyren, who had faded back by degrees, surveyed the opponents. A thin blond of about her own age, or a year or two older, stood, her face pale and mutinous, her eyes puffy from long weeping. She clung tightly to a tall, handsome young man in harper's green. Behind them stood a pair of older people, the woman looking very much like a faded version of the daughter. They were the ones who had gasped. Next to them stood what had to be a brother, blond and sturdy, his expression bemused.

"We charged nothing for the barrels, five years," Uleg said. "Good faith. But business is business."

"And you got your wine," Malla's mother said.

"Said I'd pay for it," Uleg began. "But you can't—"

"We'll pay starting this year—"

Each side began trying to shout the others down.

"Peace." Caid didn't shout, but he pitched his voice to be heard.

Silence.

"Malla?" Caid turned her way.

"I want to marry Thalek," she stated, chin lifting. "I love him."

Uleg stuck a finger out. "He appeared scarce a month ago, courtin' her like he come a-purpose to do it. She don't know anything about down-mountain strangers—" He stopped and shook his head.

"I know love," Malla said in a trembling voice. "He loves me."

Caid turned to her parents. "And what say you?"

The man gestured for his wife to speak. She said, in a higher voice than her daughter's, but just as trembly, "Thalek says he will join the family. Share heir's responsibility with Malla. We think it fair to pay for the barrels starting this year. But the past—we gave them wine in trade—"

"Worth half! And you still have our barrels!"

"That's right," said the older Uleg, in a voice so deep it sounded like it came from under the mountain.

"You were ready enough last spring to marry this harvest-season," Mov Uleg added.

"That's right," his father rumbled.

"We can't pay for those barrels." Malla's mother's eyes filled with tears. "We'd barely recovered from the war when those renegades came through and set us back two years—" Her voice suspended.

Caid turned to the minstrel. "You are willing to give up your calling?"

The man's voice was mellow, as you'd expect from a singer. He gave Malla a smile, then said, "It's as she wishes."

Malla smacked her hands together in the peace and bowed over them.

Caid asked a few more questions, and Lyren stood in the background next to the fireplace, listening and watching. The tension did not ease; Uleg veered between angry accusation and misery. Malla remained tragic. Both sets of parents were ill-at-ease. Only the minstrel continued to smile.

Finally Caid said, "Enough, you're going around in circles with these denunciations and counter-charges. Permit me to retire to reflect." He walked out, leaving them there.

Lyren remained where she was, watching. Of all those waiting, only the minstrel seemed to be aware of her; she caught one or two speculative looks from him—heels to curls—and when she didn't respond to his slow smile, he turned and nuzzled Malla's ear.

Lyren eased away from the fireplace and stepped outside onto the tiny porch, beyond which the eight liveried riders waited, one holding the reins of Caid's and Lyren's mounts. The sun was advancing, the shadows extravagant, as they often are in the mountains. In the distance towering clouds blanketed the higher peaks.

Lyren pulled the aged wooden door shut behind her.

Caid leaned on the stone porch railing, both hands apart.

"Ah-ye, what a morass." He flicked a glance over his shoulder, unsmiling. "Have you any observations?"

"My suggestion is to offer some sort of trade that cuts Malla off from inheriting."

Caid's lip curled. "So you don't believe in a month's courtship either?"

Was there extra meaning in that? Probably. And it was fair. "A month, a moment, ten years, it's all relative," Lyren said, her voice steady. "But I do not trust that minstrel. I think he's a fortune hunter."

Caid grunted. "So do I. Let's try it out."

"I'll wait out here," she said. "In truth, I feel for Uleg."

"Oh, they grew up together, and she liked him fine, until this spring. Just as he said. And she's usually a sharp bargainer, but here was this harper, something new, probably singing romantic foolery into her ears. Mov Uleg sings like a bullfrog in a well. I expect they'll make it up if she ditches the harper."

On that last word, he returned to the disputants and Lyren gazed out through the late afternoon haze over Colend spread below. Though of course she could not see the capital, her eyes followed the slow, winding river and her imagination took her to Alsais, where it was still warm, and to the rooms overlooking the waterfall…

Caid reappeared, smiling faintly.

"All settled?"

"Not yet. But it will be. Soon's Uleg caught on, he started in with all kinds of trade proposals, only constant being Malla rescinding heirship to her brother. The harper smiled and smiled but began shifting on his feet. I swear he was calculating how fast he could be gone. I suspect Uleg will see to it that the negotiations will last until he vanishes down the mountain."

"Poor Malla," Lyren said, but softly. For a marriage with that fellow who'd given her those speculative looks would be no joy, she suspected.

"Poor Malla indeed." Caid was going to say something more, but shook his head. "Honor me with your company? We've a long ride, and I believe we're going to make most of it wet."

He was right.

Before they had ridden half an hour, the clouds overtook them. "Want my cloak?" Caid called to Lyren. He lifted an arm, indicating his black riding tunic. "My clothes are stout enough without it."

"No," she said.

He said nothing more, but gave her a skeptical glance, then faced forward. The rain started soon after, a drenching, chill rain that promised snow on those mountains before too long. The rain lasted until they changed horses again, as the afternoon light faded and the unseen sun vanished beyond the western peaks.

Lyren had not had to exert such strong, sustained physical control for a very long time. She managed, forcing inner warmth to kindle, and took no harm, knowing the cost would be a tremendous lassitude and a voracious appetite. If she ate well, and slept well, she would be fine on the morrow.

Still, never had she been so glad to see lights and civilization as she was when Caid's castle appeared at last. Round, down, and into the stable they rode, the animals glad to be home, the stable hands rushing to care for them.

Lyren found that her control could not be relinquished yet; she had to dismount, and she would not fall, despite watery knees and trembling fingers. Her face had gone numb. As she followed Caid upstairs to the little drawing room they customarily met in, it seemed her brain had gone numb as well.

There was the fire. Its heat drew her, and she stretched out her hands. Slowly she began to thaw.

"Permit me to assure you," Caid said, unsmiling, "that your point has long been made, and you needn't take such risks."

Lyren glanced back. His manner was one of cool reserve, but she sensed the concern that lay beneath it. She forced herself to say cheerily, "Oh, I had a kind of wager with myself. I still don't know if I won or lost, but I promise this: no more chilly mountain rides until I recover my wardrobe."

She turned back to the fire, breathing slowly, for the lassitude had hit her, but she would not give in to that, either. Gradually she became aware of a wonderful summery scent: Sartoran steep.

She hesitated, not wanting to remove herself from the fire, for her gown was still rain-drenched, unpleasantly clingy and cold. But a little sound—the clink of porcelain on wood— behind her caused her to turn her head. Caid was within arm's reach, his head bent, face hidden as he poured out the steep into a porcelain cup. Then he stepped back, pulled off his soggy tunic, and slung it carelessly over a table by the door.

Lyren picked up the cup and held it gratefully in her hands, then lifted it slowly and sipped, eyes shut, savoring the taste of summery fields full of wildflowers, utterly unaware of the striking picture she made, the still-damp gown molding every subtle curve of her splendid body, her profile outlined against the fire.

Warmth worked its way down to her toes in their dancing slippers, and stayed. She opened her eyes, and began to set the empty cup on the tray, her gaze going to Caid. Then she stilled, staring blankly at that unblinking black eye.

Warmth. The numbness was gone, all right, leaving her senses sharp with an extraordinary clarity. Each sound, each snap of the fire, the patter of rain against the glass of the windows, Caid's breathing, all seemed to take on meaning beyond comprehension. Scents: the summery steep, her wet hair and gown, the faint burning-wood scent given off by magical firesticks ablaze.

She could not look away from Caid. Hazy observations worked their way into her consciousness: that she had never before seen him as attractive as he was now, sitting there in damp shirt and riding breeches, the fine fabric of which outlined his lean, strong body, his sharply-etched cheekbones flushed with returning color, his long black hair, usually tied in a neat queue, hanging in wet strands across his brow and down over his shoulders onto his chest, which rose and fell with each breath.

He did not speak, or drop his gaze.

The thaw had warmed to a tingle. Not that painful needle-stab of chilled flesh, but the inward, glittering prickle of anticipation, for whatever the masks the mind chooses to wear while gambling with emotions, the body's needs are plain — and direct.

The focus of his eye shifted, and it struck her that her ballgown of fragile gauze had to be plastered over her form as revealingly as was his clothing. The realization, the caress of his long, deliberate gaze, made the tingle flare into the heat of desire.

And despite the leap and crackle of the fire, and the rise and fall of Caid's breast beneath his shirt, the world stilled.

In Alsais, light gleamed in the garrison tower, visible through cold sheets of rain.

Sveneric stood in a window alcove, looking up at that tower. It was located over the herald-guards' dormitories, adjacent to the stable. If the courtiers ever thought about that tower at all, they probably assumed it was solely a lookout over the city, for it was on the opposite side of the residence and state wings.

Sveneric, used to perceiving patterns of movement, had pieced together the places of retreat used by those he was observing.

Shontande Lirendi was perhaps the most oblique subject for observation as yet encountered, if not the most difficult. One could only surmise what he did when not in public view, what he thought even when he was right there before you. But the light in that tower, or its opened window during the day, matched the king's absences too often to ignore.

Sveneric was certain that Shontande Lirendi sat up there in that tower right now, on watch by farsense, while below his courtiers amused themselves in various ways, and his kingdom set about ending another day. He'd been there since sunset, having sent some sort of graceful excuse to Nashande, who'd proposed an evening of music and maybe impromptu dance.

The impulse to let Shontande know that he did not watch alone strengthened as time slipped along its remorseless stream. Yet Sveneric felt that a contact would be a mistake.

Instead he stood at a window across a courtyard from the base of Shontande's tower. He knew the light framed his silhouette; he lifted his mental shield. Doing that always carried its own risks as well as fascinations. One heard across the unending mental plane the emotion-charged whisperings of countless minds.

Detlev had first shared this experience with him years ago, explaining what it meant, showing how to sift and sort, and protecting him when a sudden, corrosively fierce intent seared one's focus, like a thousand tortured voices shrieking in one's ear without the relative limitations of vocal projection, air as conduit, and one's own physical boundaries.

At least Talian was gone, riding swiftly northeast, taking with her that imperfect mental shield. Sveneric pitied her, but her presence grated in the way that a very fine musical instrument could when played continually a half-tone out of tune. He'd done what he could for her, but she had not asked for his help, so all he could offer was distraction, and the neutral peace of the dyr.

He listened on the mental plane. The palace life murmured around him. At least four small parties gathered into focal points, like bright hives swarming with glowing bees. He resisted the impulse to probe, and stood, passive.

When a discreet page appeared with a spoken invitation, he followed, and soon found himself in that tower, standing before a high window, looking through rain-streaked glass over the gold-windowed palace, beautiful at night as it was during the day.

Shontande Lirendi sat beside a plain wooden desk. He still wore the dark green outer robe in which he'd presided over state business, but the robe lay open, the sash beneath gone, his shirt loosened. These were mere signs of human weariness. More surprising was the half-empty bottle of very fine whiskey sitting before him. No glass.

Sveneric took these things in, then met Shontande's dark blue, ironic gaze.

"You do have a lot in common with Senrid Montredaun-An during the war," Sveneric said appreciatively.

Amusement banished the self-mockery in that beautiful face. Or almost did.

"The choice in family or in anesthetic?"

"I think his preferred anesthetic was bluewine, if I remember right," Sveneric said, and added, "I visited there a few days ago. As Lyren's nearest relations, I felt they had a right to know what had happened."

"Yet they don't interfere." The voice was uninflected.

"Of course not," Sveneric said. "Lyren might not have gone up there of her own free will—I don't think she did—"

"It was you, then, whose prints added to those we found in the garden?"

"Yes."

"I rather thought so. Your pardon. Go on."

"The fact that she hasn't escaped means she's on some kind of crusade."

Shontande said nothing for rather too long; he was listening by farsense, and something was happening. A crisis of some kind. Taking place at that very moment.

A pause to appreciate the magnitude of Shontande's farsense—either that or the profound depth of his bond.

Presently Colend's king reached, drank from the bottle, and set it down with a frowning precision that testified to quantity he'd already consumed.

Then he lifted his gaze. His eyes were remarkably clear, but his face no longer masked his emotions, nor did he seem to care. What was he listening for? Sveneric fought the urge to compose himself for farsense. His job was here, and his aspect must remain neutral.

What he did not know, yet, was whether Shontande had brought him up for distraction or for challenge.

"You recognized her crusade?" Shontande said, after another swig.

"Yes," Sveneric said. "She'll be tempted to reform your maverick, if she can."

"I know." *It's how.* Shontande's fine mouth curled in self-mockery, and for a heartbeat there was a striking resemblance to Caid Lassiter. Kinsmen, then? Probably. That did not matter. What did? Sveneric saw that Shontande's distrust did not extend to Lyren so much as to himself.

Silence fell as rain drummed at the window.

Lyren stared for that measureless eternity at Caid, every nerve singing. She knew that though Caid had contrived her presence here, alone with him in his castle, the choice to act was entirely hers. She had only to reach out her hand, and they could embark on an interlude of sensory pleasure that would last as long as she desired.

So ... why shouldn't she? There was no fault in shared joy, was there, when no vows had been spoken? Most likely everyone back in Alsais assumed that they'd been in bed for the past four days.

Everyone? She would not think about Shon, she would not, and yet even now, with her senses simmering with anticipation, she remembered the sweet anguish of the very first touch of his fingers to hers, and the promise in his gaze.

Be true to yourself.

And the truth was that this fire she was feeling was mere lust. Not love. Even limb-tangled, she would still be thinking of Shontande. And though many would shrug and accept that as a part of life, to her it constituted a betrayal of both that as-yet-unspoken bond with Shontande, and the bond of friendship she was striving to establish here.

And so she breathed deeply, set down her empty cup, and walked out.

Sveneric felt the atmosphere intensify — and then, quite suddenly, the tension was gone.

Some resolution had been made, some crisis had passed. Shontande Lirendi looked around as if he did not understand where he was, or how he had arrived there.

Sveneric watched comprehension return, and wondered if Shontande, in remembering his presence, was going to regret having revealed himself as much as he had. Now was the time, Sveneric thought with humorous resignation, for Shontande to ram Detlev into Sveneric's teeth as a method of dismissal.

Instead — unexpectedly — there was that self-mockery again, but with it real humor. "I think I've finally solved the mystery of your presence," he said. "Tacit approval from the formidable guardian?"

"Detlev knows I'm here, but not why," Sveneric replied. Then he laughed, realizing that Shontande had, in fact, meant himself.

"So you do live in his shadow," Shontande observed.

"Say rather in the light of his sun," Sveneric said, and watched Shontande sort rapidly through the implications.

"My father used to be likened to the moon," Shontande said at last, hefting his bottle, and turning it in his hands so that the fire reflected through the liquid, gold, amber, honey. "Appeared infrequently, shed little light, and no warmth." He smiled, got to his feet, and with a sudden violent gesture flung the bottle into the fireplace, where it smashed and sent up a shoot of blue flame.

They watched the blaze flare and subsided.

Shontande turned his head. "Are you sitting on good advice that you simply must impart?" he asked.

"I am not," said Sveneric.

31

Though the annoyance of steady rain after weeks of clear skies chilled Talian, her spirits stayed high.

She'd ridden through rain before. During the war days she'd ridden through all kinds of weather, and the first gift Shontande had given her—true, he'd given them all—was a rainproof cloak that she'd treasured ever since, and wore now. It was a relief to be riding to action again, without threat of Norsundrians, while warmly embraced by Shon's gift.

As she rode that last distance, she thought about Sveneric's words at the Blue Night Masque. The kind of influence he meant had to be this rescue she planned, and had dreamed out in detail over the long, lonely ride.

The pleasure of that image had obliterated the, ah, uncomfortable reaction, call it, that she'd sustained when remembering the disillusionment she'd seen in Nash's face. Strange, that. She'd never cared a whit for his years of devotion, but as soon as it was gone she felt the lack. Of course rationality was not far to seek. Adulation from a hummer—that is, a fool, no one was supposed to say hummer anymore—was better than scorn from a fool. And, more telling, it was the possibility of scorn from those who were not fools that was galling.

But she could take action, just as she had twelve years ago, and have influence thereby.

The inner vision never diminished as she urged her flagging post horse to the next posting inn. She would rescue Lyren in Caid's teeth. Lyren, of course, would be grateful. If, that is, she really didn't want to stay with Caid—and if she did,

Talian would have a different message to take back, and she'd say to Shon ...

She'd say to Shon ...

That part was more difficult to figure out. But at least Shon would see her selfless act in riding to the rescue, just as she'd rescued prisoners from Norsunder during the war, earning adulation from everyone who mattered. And this time she would be rescuing a rival. Surely that would recover her prestige in all eyes!

She changed horses, using her maid's name, as she'd done the previous day. She rode on until she reached the outskirts of Alarcansa, spending the night in a roadside inn as a substantial rainstorm battered the countryside.

She set out before dawn into a clean, rain-washed day. The sky was clear, the air cold. As she rode, she looked about with the eyes of a count, and what she saw impressed her. Villages, lands, everything well-tended.

Well-tended, and extensive. She hadn't realized just how extensive Alarcansa was — for his primary residence was located, she knew, at the southwest corner of his lands, and yet she had a very long ride ahead. Mute evidence of the difference between a duchy and a county. Alarcansa seemed a little kingdom. In fact, it was probably the size of some of the smaller kingdoms.

When she stopped for the midday meal and to rest the horse, she listened to gossip at the inn, again like the old days. She didn't want the war back, but oh, the companionship of those days, the private planning sessions of the inner ring...

Ride on.

When she came within sight of the castle, she stabled the mount at a village inn and set out on foot to make a leisurely approach under cover of falling darkness, trusting to her old skills so that she could evade question. She would slip in, noiseless and unnoticed.

And then!

While Talian smiled with anticipation, Lyren was summoned from the library, in which she'd sequestered herself all day, to supper.

She braced herself. Inclination was very much against a

meeting, but she knew that was cowardice. The day had passed without any communication between Caid and her. Now it was time to talk.

The amused awareness in that black eye when they met in the drawing room made it clear he felt the same way. While the servants were there, laying dishes and food on the table between the two great wingchairs, they spoke little. As soon as they were alone Caid sat back with his wineglass in his hands.

Lyren looked at that familiar sardonic expression and recognized that she had the courtier again. She said, "If you're anticipating being entertained by recriminations or protests, you'll have a long wait."

He lifted his glass in a salute. "Recriminations have become a habit."

"I think you thoroughly enjoy your reputation," Lyren rejoined.

He smiled a little. "It has its benefits, mostly at warding the bores and fools. You have no observations to make, then, about last night?"

"I do, if you really wish to hear them."

"Please."

She touched her fingertips in the peace. "Denying the intensity of attraction would be as injudicious as acting on it."

His brow lifted in surprise.

"It won't happen again," she said. "Now that I know the possibility is there."

"Then it remains ... an unresolved issue," he said mildly. "Where's the wisdom in that? Certainly no pleasure."

"I make no claims to wisdom at any time," she said, "but my pleasures, or lack of them, lie outside the boundaries of your interests." And when he continued to look skeptical, she gave up trying to be oblique, and went for the blunt. "I once overheard a Sartoran talk cheerfully about how she imagined her favorite faces over those of her lovers, but I am not one who can superimpose another's face over the one on the pillow next—"

A wince and a lifted finger stopped her. She had guessed right. He was secretly a romantic. He could have easily laughed. Vana would have.

And finally, insight: the romantic in him had not looked past getting her away from the king's dazzle, so that he could court her on his own.

She tented her fingers over her cup. "I grew up with kings around me," she said, her head tipped. "I learned before I ever had any interest in such matters that kings have two relationships, and the one with their kingdom had better come before any relationship of the heart. I never wanted any part of that life."

Silence reigned, except the crackle of fire. She watched him work his way through the several meanings: that she stayed in Colend in spite of Shon's title. That she was in love with the man.

That she was not going to fall in love with him, even if she felt the spark of desire.

She shook her head. "I cannot speak for you, obviously, but for me it is resolved. It's an attraction of the senses only, for we don't really know one another, and though I can see that you are brave, intelligent, a good governor—"

"Please! Spare me," he cut in, bowing over his touching palms, "the consolatory encomiums."

She grinned. "But they're true. You're also selfish, enjoy verbal cruelty just because you can do it, and you are able to do something like this—" Her gesture took in her presence there, in his castle. "Caring nothing for the consequences."

"I don't think you can prevent it happening again." He did not refer to abduction—he never repeated himself—but to the spark of desire.

Lyren said, "Do you speak generally or specifically?"

He looked wry. "Since my selfish nature is established, I'll claim only that which pertains to myself."

"I—" Lyren's gaze diffused, and for a short time all the humor vanished from her face. "I dare not say 'never', for who can predict what circumstance will bring? I'd thought, once, that I had suffered the worst temptation of a lifetime, until last night. And yet I think I can sustain this one again, intense as it was at the time, and the outcome will remain the same."

"Your original temptation does not sound recent," he ventured, watching her closely.

Her gaze was still distant as she said, "Oh, it wasn't. During the war." Suddenly she was present again, instead of caught in the past. There was that in the shape of her smile, and the cant of her head, that betokened remembered anguish as she added, "War stories are a bore, so I won't burden you with the details. Suffice it to say that I won, and it was good that I did, for the consequences far outdistanced my little concerns. Far, far, *far*," she added under her breath.

Knowing whom she had lived with, and a little of whom she had spent the war with, he suspected that what she referred to was very likely larger and more important than she admitted.

She drank some wine, then said, "This particular temptation won't occur again because I know the possibility is there, which makes it easy enough to avoid. Because I know that passion without companionship of the mind cannot last. We could become friends, if we work at it. We could be enemies, though I'd rather not be. But we will never be lovers." She smiled at last, a bewitching smile full of fun and challenge. "You need someone who will fight back."

He laughed, hand up acknowledging a hit. And then said, "You realize it might be to no purpose. Not," he added slowly, "because the wish is wanting, but the exigencies of circumstance."

"I know," she acknowledged, and because she was kind, she did not point out the obvious: that Malla was not the only one suddenly smitten with the new, while waiting on the old love.

He reached to pour more wine for them both, then sat back again. "It's not your worthiness. I'm beginning to believe that what I'd thought impossible has indeed occurred: that you are, in fact, not merely equal to the exacting requirements of Colend's court and country, but surpass—" A discreet knock interrupted him.

Caid frowned, got to his feet, and went to the door in two strides.

A whispered conversation took place with a servant, then Caid said, "You'll pardon me?" The courtier was back, behind his mask of cold amusement.

She raised her glass, and he went out.

She was still staring down into her glass when the door opened again, and to Lyren's surprise, in slipped Talian, dressed for riding. As Lyren smothered a sudden, intense impulse to laugh, Talian tossed back a lock of draggled blond hair, glanced out the doorway, then eased it shut.

Then she turned around, and her smile of triumph sagged into surprise when she registered the blue ballgown. Why was Lyren still wearing that?

Not that it mattered. She reclaimed her moment of triumph and said, "I'm here to rescue you."

In all her imaginings, she thought she'd covered every possible reaction. Lyren would either storm in helpless anger, or weep in relief, or maybe even act haughty. Disappointment, perchance, that Talian came to her rescue, and not Shontande.

But she never pictured what she got: cool amusement.

"Who said—" Lyren's eyes widened. "—I needed rescuing?"

Talian stared. "You mean you did come willingly after all?"

"Of course not. Glass of wine? You must be cold."

Talian gave her head a shake. "I don't—"

"Think, Talian." Lyren rose and came around to face her. "Think. Would you jumble off in the middle of the night, taking no belongings, not even warning your maid much less sending a note to your host, by choice?"

"Ah-ye, I would not," Talian said, furious with her shock-numbed mind. She breathed deeply, then repeated, "I wouldn't."

Lyren nodded once. "As anyone who cares enough to consider the circumstances would realize."

Talian bit her lip. "Such as Shontande," she said, feeling brave indeed as she broached the barrier that lay between them. "He probably does know. But then why isn't he here instead of me?"

"I will not discuss Shontande Lirendi with you, Talian," Lyren said. "You would not accept me as an acquaintance, much less give me the chance to offer myself as a friend, so until we can change that—and I hope we can—to share my thoughts with you would enable you to use them against me as weapons."

Talian flushed, knowing it was true. Lyren didn't even sound angry, merely resigned.

"Ah-ye! Shon's response—or lack of it—will remain a mystery. But to return to you here, if you don't need rescuing, then why did you stay? I see no guards or weapons about."

"Oh, we made a truce, Caid and I." Lyren saw what she'd sought through these long days, and the possibility made her fizzy with hilarity. But she must step carefully indeed, for both Caid and Talian were quick, smart, and horrifically sensitive. "Caid would make a formidable enemy or ally," she said at last.

"I have been doing my best to work for the second prospect."

And he listens to you? Talian wanted to ask, but she knew the answer: he did. Lyren betrayed, even after several days, none of the anguish that Talian always felt after a brief encounter with Caid.

In short, he respected Lyren.

Talian backed up a step, her throat tight, her eyes aching. There was nothing to do but leave, then, and concoct some sort of story on the long ride back to court. To pack up, and retreat to Ariath with as much grace as she could muster.

She owed Lyren Sartora nothing. And so she turned her back, and slipped out the door again, and Lyren did not attempt to stop her.

Outside the room, Talian peered about the hallway. No one in sight.

Rapidly reviewing her internal map, she slipped past the servants' stairway, finding that full of traffic, unlike the tiled stairway that unknown generations of Lassiters had used. She must not be distracted by the details of his house!

She eased down to the next landing, softly lit by glow-globes. Paused, listening, her senses alert. To? Something, something ...

She reached a foot to descend the last stairway, and jumped violently as a hard hand closed on her arm above the elbow. A strong, familiar hand.

Her head jerked around, and she stared up into Caid's face. He looked down at her with no evidence of surprise, his most hateful smile instantly kindling her slumbering rage as he drew her a few steps into a room off the landing, then shut the door and lounged against it, still with her arm in his grip.

"Let me go." She tried to wrench free.

"Would you prefer to conduct this interview down in the main hall?" He was now on the verge of laughter.

"I don't want any interview," she retorted, yanking harder against his grip.

"Did you really imagine you could steal into my land, much less my home, without my knowing?"

She stared, then managed, "Did Lyren know?"

"She did not. I was curious. Did you really ride all this way just to rescue her?"

"Yes." He had let her go. She crossed her arms. "*Somebody* had to."

"What precipitated this act of altruism?" He smiled again, that hateful smile that never failed to enrage her. "Not, surely, a sudden loss of prestige?"

Heat flooded from her neck right up to her hairline, and he laughed. "Ah-ye, Talian, you are so predictable."

Predictable! Never. No one, ever, had accused her of that, in so contemptuous a tone. Reliable, yes, expert, yes, for once upon a time she'd sailed into action with sword in hand. Oh, true, those fights had numbered fewer than half a dozen, and always with the soul-bound ones who had little volition, but ah, it had been so good to fight and know that she was right to do so.

The enemy then had been clear, and was clear now, so clear that the impulse to action seized her with inescapable grip. Too long she'd suppressed every passion, every emotion, toward attaining the long goal, which was gone now, forever out of reach, leaving only Caid's lounging, laughing amusement.

And so she gave in to reckless, glorious rage, and flung herself at him, swinging a fist with all her strength.

He put up a hand to block her, and a wild struggle ensued. Her one desire was to claw the sneer from that face. And so she fought, and kicked, and writhed, until he managed to catch hold of her wrists and twist them up behind her, holding her immoveable against him, chest to chest, until all the rage died away, leaving her puffing for breath.

Sanity trickled back into her mind, and with it the awareness of proximity, of the rise and fall of her breasts within their sturdy tunic against his velvet-covered ribs. She threw back her head to see his gleaming eye, and a curious smile on his lips.

"Done?" he asked, tossing his head slightly to shift the fine hair that had drifted into his face.

She nodded once, not trusting herself to speak, and he released her wrists.

She leaned against a massive table and crossed her arms again, aware of tingling warmth on her wrists where he had gripped them.

"'You need someone who will fight back'," he said as he righted an overturned chair and dropped down onto it. "That was fun. I wish ..." He paused, grinning. A twisted grin, not that hateful cold, superior smile. "I wish you remembered as fondly as I have a certain spring night, not so long ago."

"I was drunk," she stated, and sniffed. "Why did you drag

Lyren up here?"

He laughed. It was so unexpected a sound it caught her by surprise. "To see who would come up here after her," he said. "Fancy that! Count Talian to the rescue."

His voice was unsteady, pitched to provoke, but not to flay. And so it was not with the intention of doing damage, this time, when she uncrossed her arms and took an open-handed swing at his face.

The next morning, the two met Lyren in the dining room, their faces a study in conflicting emotions. She smiled as she saw the tentative détente she'd hoped to see, and indicated the loaded table. "I took the liberty of ordering breakfast. I have an idea," she said.

Two days later, Sveneric eased through the gathering crowd with the expertise of old habit. He had to witness for himself the arrival of the three everyone had been talking about for over a week.

Word had zapped ahead, somehow, as if borne upon lightning, testifying to the interest all three possessed. Not that the most prominent courtiers were as rude as the younger court arrivals who crowded the palace's stable yard. Oh, no. But a remarkable number of personal runners had business in the vicinity, so it seemed. And that drew the curious and the idlers who happened to be strolling at that end of the canal, and whisper ignited whisper, the words *a queen at last* most often heard.

Sveneric made his way politely among them, stopping under the eave of the feed-storage building.

From this vantage he saw the three ride slowly through the Gate of Silver Reeds, Caid's entourage following out of earshot behind. There existed, it seemed, a shared hilarity between all three. Caid rode in the middle, impeccably turned out in riding clothes of black. At one side was Talian Ariath, also in riding clothes, her sun-bright hair bound up in a simple coronet. On the other Lyren rode in a ball gown that looked much the worse for wear, though her straight back and her smile transformed the oddity into the glamour of adventure.

As Sveneric watched, unnoticed, Talian leaned across her horse's neck to address a remark to the other two. Caid smiled. Lyren laughed.

They rode slowly into the courtyard, pausing only when Nash Desentis of Sentis, who was too honest to even think of pretense, rushed up.

"Damme, we worried! What's toward?" he addressed all three with unaffected pleasure.

Lyren said in her clear, sunny voice, "Oh, it was a matter of a wager between the three of us."

Nash whistled. "A wager, you say?" And laughed heartily. "Ah-ye, that explains everything!"

It explained nothing whatsoever, except perhaps to the sport-mad among them, whose bets often got more bizarre with every bottle. But Nashande Desentis was popular, moreover the king was also there at the top of the path, also smiling, and whatever the king smiled on meant all was well.

"Can you turn down a challenge?" Lyren added, miming disbelief. "I admit it. I can't!"

Sveneric watched her words rustle back through the crowd and laughter after it. A wager, a challenge, ah-ye! To be young and gallant again!

The three dismounted and were surrounded by those with rank enough, or courage enough, to demand the stakes, and who won? But when it became clear that all three would give the same answer—expressed through characteristics typical of each: Caid's faint smile, sardonic at the edges, Talian's ceaseless gauging of others' gazes, Lyren's easy grace—the atmosphere dissolved into general hilarity.

Sveneric allowed the press of people to surge beyond him, stepping back and back until he was free again, still unnoticed. Even by Lyren, who tried to navigate the press around her, everyone wanting to be heard. She—as did Caid and Talian— noted that many, if not most of the court, wore shades of rose in ribbons and fans, and roses numbered among the embroil- deries, along with butterflies and hummingbirds.

It was as much a declaration as words ever could accom- plish, and Talian blinked hard, but kept her chin up. Caid gripped her hand, whispering for her ears only, "You will have far more fun as a duchas."

She did not argue, as short, slight Hradzy Wendis eeled his

way to Lyren's side. "Have you read Lasthavais Dei's memoir?" he murmured, as others laughed and teased, and Noria pressed up on the other side, the word *opera* the only one Lyren made out.

"Oh, years ago. I think," Lyren said.

"You might revisit her again." Hradzy smiled. "She speaks directly to her descendants."

Lyren turned to gaze at him in question.

He laughed a little. "How many years have I walked down the gallery in Rive Dien? You are remarkably like, all except the color of your eyes." And in Sartoran, "Don't make him wait any longer."

"I won't," she said, and the press carried Hradzy away. From somewhere the sweet sound of wind instruments and little tinkling brass cymbals caused the crowd to part, as several local children danced in a circle.

Old and old and old, these dances were, metamorphosing slowly over the centuries, all over the world. But one constant remained: dance was a celebration. Courtiers and citizens alike clapped and laughed, and Lyren found herself next to old Dowager Duchas Sentis with her graying hair and wise, lined eyes. The woman smiled on her with compassion, though Lyren had scarcely exchanged ten words with her. "Don't make him wait," the dowager whispered, and moved on.

Lyren excused herself left and right, until at last she reached the edge of the crowd, and here was Shontande, with a respectful moat of air around him, though all watched from the sides of their eyes.

"Who won?" he asked, for her ears alone.

"All of us." And tipped her head toward Talian, standing next to Caid, her eyes flitting over the crowd.

He took her hand. "They are expecting you to lead the opera," he began. "Rehearsals every day."

"And so we shall," Lyren promised, as herald-guards closed in behind, keeping others from following them up a shady path.

He knew all the palace byways, of course. This one, not far from the stable, had to belong to the herald-guards, for the walls were plain, with only flowering vines on one side. They entered a narrow door that disclosed narrow stairs. She climbed up, her eyes and mind busy with impressions. This was the first day of her new life, and in her bliss she resolved that she must remember everything: the worn ovals in the stone steps; the smell of old smoke; the sound of her slippers on stone.

The open door, and now they were alone, the mellow light highlighting his splendid bones with warm color, and spilling milky gold along the high collar of his fine linen shirt, fading into shadow along the folds of his robe.

How to say what is in the heart? Obliqueness didn't work, not for her. He was far more adept at that than she — up there in Siamis and Detlev's level, conversational fog-makers.

But he spoke first. And it was not through some poet's polished words.

"You have the freedom of the entire world." he said, hands wide. "There is nowhere I can go. What you see is what you can have or leave, as you will. I—" He shook his head. "I don't know how to express it. I *had* to leave you the freedom, lest there be any vestige of constraint."

She had not talked through all those nights, circling through every subject under the sun until he finally ventured near the personal, without learning that he was reticent. Surprisingly so, perhaps, given his reputation.

"I know," she said, and took a step nearer. "You trusted me. I cannot tell you how *fiercely* I loved you for that."

He blushed like a boy whose first crush had just handed him a rosebud.

She went on, "Though you can command the illusion of privacy — such as this moment — there really isn't any, is there? Though we are alone, I expect half of those avid eyes out there are wagering how fast we go horizontal. But in an odd way, I've always lived a public life, bouncing from palace to palace by way of the Fer Eider pastry shop. So I understand the cost of living in a court that speculates about everything from the scent on your wrists to your conversations with Jilo about the Chwahir border."

"Can you make my sorry, fractured, gossip-ridden Alsais your home?"

"*Everybody* gossips," she responded, and he laughed a little. She added, "Fractured? I don't see that. Personalities will clash. That's human nature. But it seems to be all your symbols, the fans, the ribbons, even where one stands in a room, are ways to speak without speaking. And while I came to understand that some of that is covert challenge, it's the sort of challenge that leaves room for negotiation and compromise. Much better than steel."

"So my ancestors believed," Shontande said, holding out his hand. As she laid hers in his, and their fingers twined, he said, "But the steel is there. Absolutely against the law. And I am not inclined toward generosity. My usual reaction is a long visit home to cool tempers when I find out there have been duels. But dueling does happen. I blame the war; there are those who discovered a taste for resolving matters with steel. They hide it. But mostly, I find out."

She could see how much he hated it. Hated admitting it, as if the fact that some of his courtiers had discovered a taste for violence was somehow his fault. But she knew the blame belonged to Norsunder.

And she knew what he was really asking. "We'll show them a better way," she said, and rejoiced when the tension around his eyes relaxed.

He concentrated, initiating a transfer so quick and so subtle that she almost felt it was the shift of one dream to another. So he had the slide!

They stepped onto a high terrace above a deep lake. Behind them, a tower access. He murmured a word and a glowglobe lit a stairwell.

"This is Skya," he said. "I was prisoned here for a part of the year when I was a child. Partly for protection, and mostly for convenience. It was not in any way arduous physically, but I learned about appearances and powerlessness here, and then I learned how to release my mind to attain an illusion of freedom. Right now we have a different illusion of freedom, a place away from those avid eyes. But only until dawn, when duty draws me back—"

She reached up to touch his lips with her fingertip. "Then let us use the time we have," she said, and to make herself absolutely clear, "I choose you. I choose *you*," she said again, replaced her finger with her lips, and the fire of all the stars consumed them both.

32

Laban Dei stood on a second story balcony and looked out over the palace. The brief snow squall softened the contours of the stone fortress that had been destroyed and rebuilt so many times during a long, turbulent history, and was in the process of being expanded — and restored — now.

He clasped his hands, exerting enough control to keep his fingers from going numb. His gaze ranged beyond the castle walls and towers to Ferdrian beyond, clean and prosperous, and attractive under the dusting of snow. To the north the haze hid Wnelder Vee; to the south lay Imar, loosely joined to Everon once again.

In the distance he heard voices, people out celebrating First Snow, though real winter was likely a month or even two off. He felt no sense of celebration at the changing of the seasons. If called upon to join he'd go through the motions, but to him First Snow meant winter was nigh, and he ought to be thinking ahead to its demands.

The apprehension of the sacred — the celebratory impulse — kindled in him when he stood, thus, and looked over what he fashioned with mind and hands. He was here, at last, where he belonged. He had regained his name, and his place, and he and Carl Delieth governed well.

He closed his eyes, remembering the very first time Detlev had permitted him to come here, how that smell — oak and lichen and moss, cedar and stone — had seized him, almost paralyzed him, and he'd known he was home.

Home.

He turned to look inside.

The welcome golden glow beckoned. He knew that Carl would be in the dining room, waiting.

Not long after they met, Laban had considered the possibility of rejoining the kingdoms through marriage. So much better than war, was it not? He had gone to the archives and traced, in secret, the thoughts of kings and queens through the centuries who had made that same decision, to find that there were as many variations in consequence as there had been in motivation.

Ironic, how Tahra—obsessed with hatred—had almost seemed to know his plans before he'd formed them. How assiduously she'd labored to guard her children from the taint of his presence. And how those very acts had cast a glamour over him that was utterly irresistible, that he never could have contrived on his own. In marrying Carl, he'd gained a partner of surpassing sweetness, honesty, kindness, dedication, and terrible need.

Or, so it had been at first. Since the harvest celebrations, just when so much undiluted need could have become overpowering, she'd somehow found balance. And a sense of humor.

At first he'd metaphorically held his breath, lest he be imagining it. But with each day the impression strengthened. No more haunted eyes, pathetically grateful for every smile, hungry for every moment of his time that he could spare, yet ever needing more. When one observation turned to two, then more, he began by degrees to relax. He even ventured a joke or two. And watched her shake with mirth.

He enjoyed watching her banter with Wenwen's gang of roistering wanderers. He appreciated her joy when Jessan turned up, and how tranquilly she accepted his vanishing again to Curtas's House. He observed with pride the intelligent sensitivity she brought to court interviews, her innate goodness teamed with honesty gaining, more often than not, true respect from those who arrived angry, or grasping.

He relished small things, the way her graceful fingers neatened things. The tiny gulp that was her laugh, like a kitten's mew. The fresh scent she always wore; he'd found himself breathing in her nearness as she passed by.

The light around Laban had gradually blued. The day was gone.

Carl waited inside.

He found himself anticipating dinner, and was grateful. Those early days it had taken all his resolution to maintain an even, benevolent countenance, which meant a hard rein on his moods, and his tendency to sarcastic hyperbole. That was the duty he'd accepted, and he'd trusted time to harden that rein to habit, only to discover of late that he felt less constrained, for his occasional lapses had not brought shock or sorrow, but a raised brow, or a shrug, and once a poker-faced retort that so took him by surprise he'd almost choked on his wine.

He went inside and ran down to the warm dining room, which smelled of savory sauce. Carl stood at the table, peeking under silver covers. She was robed tastefully in rose with hints of blue, the neck and sleeves edged with lace. A crimson sash encircled her waist, and was she looking less frail?

She shifted to lift another cover, and he realized that — somehow — that her skinny, childish form was no longer so childish. The soft fall of her silken blouse hinted at charming curves, and when she moved to the next cover, for a moment he saw, with surprise and a spike of pleasure, the rounded flare of hip. When had *that* happened?

"It's just the two of us. Everyone else is doing other things." She smiled a welcome over her shoulder. "I couldn't wait to see what Cook decided on."

"Whatever it is," he said, "I'll eat it."

They sat down, and she said, "News from Vana?"

Laban helped himself to rice, sauce, vegetables. "Nothing new — the same posturing."

Carl's straight brows puckered a little, then she gave a single nod. "They're not going to trust that we mean what we say, are they?"

Laban nodded. "Not without some sort of gesture." He watched her over the rim of his wineglass, enjoying the dainty way she ate. Not finicky, or pretentious, but with an artful grace that she'd learned from Lyren and then somehow made her own. Her glossy hair neatly framed her long face.

He studied that face as she poured out wine. Feature by feature it was unprepossessing. He remembered well his first glimpse of her. Poor, homely little mite! He would have steeled himself to marry a monster in order to get where he was now, though he would have contrived to live his life on his own terms.

Instead he'd found this plain little person of transcendent goodness. To her he would never admit that ambition had brought them together. Never. Everything else between them, therefore, had to be truth, or he'd be living a lie. Keeping silent on that one thing made it his burden, and not hers.

As he watched her neat little hands setting down the wine decanter, he realized that her plain features had come to be more dear, somehow, than mere beauty.

Was this love? There was no wildfire or sunburst or flood—all the tried and trite expressions for what down in Colend they used to call *zalend*. Thunderstrike seemed an appropriate turn for the witlessness of those who got ambushed by attraction, love, whatever you wanted to call it. Maybe he was too aware all the time to be swept away. As well. He knew only that within the last week or two he'd found himself wanting to run his fingers through that soft hair of Carl's that she brushed so assiduously each night until the brown shone with muted highlights of red and gold. There were moments, especially when she smothered that tiny laugh of hers—like him, she was so controlled—he was surprised by the impulse to take her by the shoulders and kiss her silly.

Of course he forbore pestering her. She seemed to have found some delicate balance inside, and he dared not disturb that hard-won equilibrium. He had never sensed the least passion in her, just that yawning emotional need. Had that, too, changed?

He couldn't test it now, not with a very difficult task ahead. So far he'd contrived to tie his daily schedule to nightly proximity, after one single absence early on that had thrown her into panic and despair. Since then he made certain to transfer home each evening. But events were making that increasingly difficult.

He looked down, realizing that he had eaten mechanically, that he hadn't tasted any of the delicious food. Carl sat waiting, a quizzical smile on her lips.

"Done?" she asked, when he set aside his fork.

They walked into the little salon adjoining, where the coffee service awaited, the steam of fresh brew enticing.

Carl poured out coffee for each, adding cream and honey to hers, and then they sat down next to the fire as rain fell outside.

"Anything to report?" he asked.

"A quiet day," Carl replied. "I expect because of the early snow making things slippery. Several petitioners on personal business, easily accommodated. In truth, most of my afternoon I spent with my magic books."

"General reading?"

"More of a long-term project," she said. "I'll describe it if you like, but I'd rather not be boring without direct invitation."

He smiled at the gentle joke, then said with care, "About that gesture."

Carl looked over, her dark eyes considering, then she smiled. "You're going to have to take command of them in person, and not by proxy, and ride down to Imar to be truly effective, is my guess. If the weather eases off, and I think it will—it's too early for any earnest snow—why not now?"

It took him by surprise.

"A real demonstration will take a few weeks, maybe a month," he ventured. "Slow and deliberate."

Carl said soberly, "Isn't it true that Jilo taking his fleet along the strait and down to Halia a few weeks back was just as effective as having to wade in with sword and knife?"

"Absolutely true. None of those blowhards in Imar want any fighting on their own ground."

"Of course," she said lightly. "If you're to be away longer than a couple of weeks, shall we use notecases?"

In other words, she was not expecting him to transfer back each night?

"I can carry one," he said slowly. "But wouldn't it be as easy if I report myself?"

"Only if you want to," she replied. "I've been thinking. Transfers every night are so wrenching. Why not stay with the Knights, and just write if you have anything to report?"

He looked at her thin fingers gripping her cup, and sorted through the tones in her quiet, pleasing voice. Then he dashed the contents of his cup into the fireplace, set the cup down, and knelt at her side.

"Are you certain?" he asked.

"Of course I am, or I wouldn't have suggested it," she said, her gaze, as always, honest and true.

He took hold of her fine-boned, warm hands, and felt a tremor in her fingers.

"Carl," he said, and laced their fingers together.

Her gaze lifted from their twined hands to his face. He met

that gaze, so sweet, slightly worried, but without that terrible despair he'd always had to brace against. Full of love that she never hid. Love, and — instead of the yawning emotional need, was there a trace of desire?

Then she leaned down and kissed him.

This first kiss landed more on his jaw than his lips, and their noses bumped. But she came in again more firmly, and when he opened his lips to her, she embarked on an eager and thorough exploration that kindled the passions he'd thought banked behind a wall of brick and stone and steel.

They broke, both short of breath.

"Carl?" his voice roughened.

She hummed with laughter, and freed her fingers to run one hand up the back of his neck, under his hair. Her other caressed his face, and then locked with the other to pull him close for another kiss.

Desire. Pleasure. The prospect had wakened. They kissed, and kissed again, until she smiled up into his eyes. "We can be more comfortable elsewhere," she breathed. "For example, on a bed?"

He laughed. "This is a conspiracy to keep me here?" — then winced, wishing he could cut out his tongue. It would be his fault if she retreated to that hurting need again.

Her eyes widened, searched his, and then crinkled. "Is it working?" she ventured, blushing deep red. And, bravely, "If it doesn't, think what you will come back to!"

They laughed, Laban heady with surprise and joy. They were so intent on each other that they missed Jenel Sandrial, approaching from another hall to discuss a domestic issue. She stopped short, took in those flushed faces, and the intertwined arms, and backed up a hasty step or two.

She was on her way to give orders to the rest of the household when Silvanas and Sed passed by, clearly on their way to Laban's office to finalize the details of the Knights' departure for Imar.

She grabbed the long, flapping back panels of their riding coats and they halted, turning in surprise. "Leave them be," she said.

"Huh?" Sed asked, then, his eyes round, "Did something happen?"

Silvanas regarded Jenel Sandrial's blank expression, and registered the "them" in *Leave them be*. He grinned, and Jenel

Sandrial's lips tightened further, confirming his guess. He was about to crack *It's about time!* but prudently held that back. While he owed nothing to the Sandrials, he knew quite well that Jenel Sandrial ruled the palace more strictly than the actual king and queen. She could make life miserable for him.

Considering Sed's bewildered expression, and the chief steward's severe one, he ventured, "All's as it should be."

Jenel Sandrial's mouth relaxed by a hair: conditional approval.

"We'll come by later. In the morning. Late morning," he corrected, and that time, received a single, sharp nod.

Drawing the still-protesting prince after him, he effaced himself, and returned to Knights of Dei territory, where he smothered questions and speculation by ordering a surprise inspection.

33

Adam watched Leander's dark head bend over the equally dark fur of his dog companion Rori. Leander's fingers gentled over the dog's graying muzzle, scratching under his jaw and behind his ears as Rori's eyes slitted in pleasure.

Rori, soon to be a grandfather, was getting a bit stiff now; he had not been young when he and Leander found one another twelve years ago. Rori no longer ranged as far as he had over the mountain, preferring to lie in the sun on the disirad plateau as his two offspring, plus various adoptees, took over sniff-patrol on the mountain.

"It's not that I don't want to marry you," Leander said finally. "I don't see a need. Neither of us has children, much less anything to inherit. And after so many years of being tied to duty, I am still relishing utter freedom. Not that marriage to you would be an obligation. I think it's the necessity for ceremony and implied legalities that I'm resisting."

"Legalities… Ah. Registering in Sartor."

"As Sartorans," Leander said. "It's a fiction that Detlev adheres to for the sake of peace. I know he pays estate taxes, though we're so far beyond the western border of Sartor that there is absolutely no benefit to it. I have nothing against Atan and Rel—like them very much. But I'm not a Sartoran. I resist being numbered in their records. And if you and I do chance to have a family, such things will matter to them."

"It's as you wish. I'm content either way," Adam said cheerfully—as Leander had expected him to. "I think our household here wants to hold a wedding, there being so much talk of them this year. And you and I are the only pair within reach, except for MV and Mildred — and no one dares to put any sort of question about their relationship to those two."

"Nope." Leander grinned. "It is the year of the weddings, is it not?" He gave Rori one last, lingering caress, then went to check that the bedding they'd laid down for the soon-to-be mother was still clean, with fresh water nearby. Adam smiled as all the dogs leaped to their feet to trot after Leander. When they were outside, they had their own hierarchy, but indoors, they followed Leander from room to room.

Adam tipped his head, eyes closed as he listened both aurally and on the mental plane. The brief drifts of early snow had ceased.

And Imry was back, up on the plateau.

Six months ago, after half a year of Imry turning up, fencing verbally, reading in Siamis's archive (and refusing to discuss what he read), camping on the plateau, then vanishing when it got too cold for a tent, Adam had gone to Detlev to report failure.

"I can't seem to reach him," Adam had admitted. "He barely accepts me as a peer. I ought to hand him back to you, but he hates authority as much as he did when he was small."

"He was betrayed by authority," Detlev corrected gently. "It was not merely his father. The guise I had to assume created a sense of falsity that he intuited, but could not explain, except in his own terms, and I was not quite able to bridge it. And so I lost him. But his days among us were not without effect, I believe. Give him time."

Adam considered that. There were moments — always unex-pectedly — Imry would demonstrate signs of humanity. But if anyone so much as hinted at an awareness of these, he'd snap back, at his most obnoxious, and vanish again.

"He needs peer guidance," Detlev said. "The lightest rein possible. I suspect he won't be able to tolerate me again until he convinces himself he's my equal. That definition is probably going to change over time, but that's not your concern. You've a single task: to get him to coinhere with the disirad. Single, seemingly simple, but vitally important."

"It's not simple at all," Adam had admitted. "And yet the youngest of our students come up here and coinhere with the disirad in a day or so. Some in hours. Liere..."

"Liere's coinherence was at the far end of the spectrum of possibility," Detlev said, smiling. "There were only two like her in my day as well. Imry is at the other end of the spectrum. And it's not merely a matter of temperament, though you are bearing the brunt of that. Well, I ought to add."

Adam blushed, warding off the compliment. "It's not well if I don't succeed."

"But these are two different matters. His surliness was always a defense. You know that. It's no different now. As for the coinherence…" Detlev closed his eyes, and after a time said, "Coinherence is not a single thing. As you are aware." And when Adam signed agreement, Detlev said, "Think of Imry's situation as a broken mirror. His perception of the world is in shards. I'm one. David is another. Senrid is a shard. Marloven Hess is one. Norsunder was one, fitted together in pieces corresponding to the different personalities. His talent for healing is also a shard, one he's never been able to fit among any of the others."

"His perception is like a warren of walls, you mean?" Adam understood compartmentalization. Kessler Sonscarna had been the most disturbingly compartmentalized person he'd ever met, and Dirk had learned that way of viewing the world, but his friendship with Sveneric, Darian, Jessan Delieth, and a few others had enabled him to dissolve the walls when needed.

"I think the broken mirror is a better metaphor because Kessler Sonscarna could, sometimes, remove a wall. He did with Jilo. No reaction—done is done. Imry, up there on the plateau, reluctantly sees how to fit his shards back together, but in doing so cuts his fingers and they bleed. Then he has to go away until they heal. Or, to jettison the metaphor, until he can come to terms with each alteration in perspective. A perspective, I should add, that is ever closer to what he would have been like had his father not smashed and scorned and tortured him into the Imry we lived with."

Half a year later, Adam still prickled with chill when he comprehended what that meant: as Imry slowly began to perceive the world from a saner perspective, it was inevitable that he would also perceive what he had done. And what it meant. To individuals, to kingdoms, and to the world.

In other words, his "reward" for all that painful work would be the birth of remorse.

So he was up there on the plateau again? Adam shrugged into a coat and warm shoes. The one drawback of living on the mountaintop was that winter came early. He slipped down the back stairs, noting that everyone was busy with projects or gathered near the kitchen in expectation of the tantalizing fragrances issuing forth. If anyone followed him, Imry would vanish.

Adam bent into the wind and topped the steps to the plateau, making out the silhouette sitting on the table under the gazebo as a cold rain started up again. Imry sat on the table, feet on the stone bench, forearms on his knees, hands empty. His profile was grim.

Adam hunched further into his coat as he slogged across the sodden brown grasses. Imry had to know he was there — he'd hear the chuff, chuff, chuff of his steps if nothing else — but he neither moved nor spoke as Adam approached and ducked under the twelve-sided roof.

"You're back," Adam said as a conversation-opener.

Imry did not look at him, but said to the slushy, muddy ground, "Best definition is that I'm seeing through the eyes of another man."

Yes, Imry had coinhered at last.

Imry looked sideways, his lips twisted in a not-quite-smile. "What? No moralizing?"

Adam had tucked his hands more securely into his sleeves. He pointed his chin at the silver bowl full of glistening dyra. "You have done what I asked. The only other suggestion I have for you is to choose a dyr. Get used to it. It will enable you t—"

"Yeah, we're done." Imry got up, and vanished in the slide.

"—to learn," Adam finished to the empty air. With a small sigh, he mentally relinquished this most difficult of … what to call Imry? Not a student, and still less a candidate for dyranarya. Seeker. That would do.

He sloshed back down to the house, as Imry stood outside the white palace in Mearsies Heili, squinting up at the pearlescent spires. What era did this place belong to?

Siamis appeared in the wide doorway, which suggested some sort of magical watch.

"I wondered," Imry said, "why Ilerian was obsessed with this place."

"And you didn't think to check?"

"I remembered the records," Imry said. "Written by Detlev

himself: old castle, built of white granite. Set on a mountain in a capital smaller than some estates, in a rural kingdom with no defense. Why bother with it? I was just glad it kept Ilerian busy. I see Detlev lied about the old granite castle, even if everything else was true."

"Come see for yourself."

"I can smell it from here. The distinctive stench of disirad," Imry said, hands propped on his skinny hips.

Siamis regarded him for a heartbeat or two. That was no more than standard Imry sarcasm. No sign of bracing, or incipient headache. So he'd finally integrated with the disirad?

: Adam?

: Coinhered. Over to you.

Siamis could feel Imry's prickles like needles, daring anyone to approach with sympathy, or worse, approval. "If you can ignore the stench," Siamis retorted, "you will soon be able to mend the occasional bone without puking, if that's still your intent."

It was, or he wouldn't be here, and they both knew it.

Siamis headed back inside, leaving Imry to follow or not.

Not five steps inside, Imry scanning defensively as always, he comprehended that this place was *old.* "How did you keep the head snakes out all this time?" he asked Siamis's retreating back.

"Didn't. Someone—no idea who—warded it for roughly four millennia. It reappeared about eight centuries ago, but there was so little human habitation around the area that when Detlev discovered the palace was back again, he laid a perception ward over it. Wrote it up as an outpost. Mearsiean refugees trying to escape a Chwahir expansion effort found it shortly after."

"I take it this place predates your lot?"

"Yes. My family inherited it, but it seems to always have been a healing center."

They headed toward the stairway when Clair, hearing voices, came out of the kitchen to see who had arrived, Liere at her shoulder.

Clair did not know Imry by sight, except in Siamis's memories. Liere, who did know him, stopped short, one hand crossing her belly in a defensive block that was entirely instinctive. Then sense caught up with her: it was exceedingly unlikely that Imry Llyenthur was here to kill Senrid's second child. But she did not regret the defensive movement, because the fact remained that he had murdered the first.

Imry saw it all. It was going to be like this, probably for the rest of his life. Unless of course the next encounter was with Senrid, or someone else who wanted to see him dead, and he didn't win the fight. (That was still the rest of his life, but a short one.)

Liere turned away, and passed through the kitchen to the terrace.

Clair's gaze met Siamis's. They understood immediately that Liere had just been presented with an unwanted dilemma: the implied safety of the white palace as a center of learning and healing was in direct conflict with the knowledge that if Senrid knew Imry Llyenthur was there, he might find the temptation irresistible to turn up and visit Marloven justice on his daughter's murderer.

Clair followed Liere.

Imry recognized that white hair. Wasn't she Ilerian's target? He remembered seeing her that day in Imar, when Norsunder ended.

Siamis said, "The translation library is upstairs."

Imry paused at the top for another fast scan, then followed Siamis to a room, stepping around boxes and furnishings. "We're in the process of expanding the library," Siamis said, threading his way through.

This had once been a fine salon, from the looks of the furnishings being moved out. Inside, shelves for scrolls as well as for books had been moved in.

"This is the translations room." Siamis opened his hand.

Imry glanced around, but his attention was elsewhere — distant. "Seems Detlev lied twice in those reports," he said presently.

"Twice?"

"This place is not granite, and it's not a rural backwater. Rural, yes, but there's magic here. Quite powerful."

"You sense it, do you?" Siamis asked.

"A Selenseh Redian, next to civilization? I thought they were all in remote mountains. There's more."

Siamis said, "There's more, though little of access to humans. We're very much the newcomers in this corner of the continent. Over here are the scrolls you might want to look at. Some are copies that I think you've already seen."

Imry glanced around at ten years of careful translation and recopying. "How much more to go?"

"We will not finish in our lifetimes," Siamis said.

"Then Detlev didn't destroy everything back then. More lies."

"He burned everything that Svir wanted him to burn. But it all had copies," Siamis said. "Even he did not know the extent of it, as he'd cut himself off from the rest of the dyranarya, by mutual agreement. That library was hidden beyond time. Here are your texts on the arts of healing human bodies from the mental realm. I think you already read this one, on how to scan within another without the, oh, call it the echo effect, until you get familiar with the ancient vocabulary. It repays rereads, I've found."

Imry stood in the middle of the room, his gaze distracted.

Siamis knew what was happening: Imry was trying to assimilate standing there in a building made entirely of disirad. He said, "For most, the disirad has a calming effect, perhaps a sense of detachment for some. For a few of us, the longer we are around it, the more merciless is clarity of vision. For me, that includes the inescapably sharp memories of a lifetime of endeavor, including those feats I'd give anything to undo."

"But you can't," Imry said, his green gaze sharp.

"I can't," Siamis agreed. "The dead still remain dead. All I can do is put my current work between now and then. The more I accomplish, the more distant those early actions become in my own mind. At least most of those memories lie in the past, a stain on history; I was gone from the world for centuries before I reentered it. That much Detlev could do for me, which incidentally helped me to fog my subsequent actions when we prepared to take down Norsunder."

And yet the dead still remain dead.

Imry lifted a shoulder. "I made my own copy of that text. It's still fresh in mind."

"All right, then. I learn faster while working. If you are inclined likewise, I have a project you could take over up in the Chwahir mountains. There is a community that includes people undergoing complete physical gender alteration."

"That's got to hurt."

"Which is why it takes so long. Everything has to be done in increments, and then the wait for it to heal." And, seeing Imry's interest, Siamis said, "I'll give you the text to study first, and my notes on each case…"

Clair and Liere had retreated to the terrace, where Clair said, "I'm sorry. If I'd known he'd turn up, I could have made sure that you didn't see him."

"The fact that we didn't speak renders him merely another dyranarya case in my mind. Which means he will not become a secret between Senrid and me. Senrid knows that dyranarya don't discuss others' healing matters." Though as she spoke there was a hint of question.

Clair, interpreting it successfully, said, "He's going to need a lot of work, I suspect." She gazed down at the tossing trees far below, their autumnal colors fading as leaves swirled on the wind. "Siamis will know what to say. The two share similar experiences."

Similar experiences. A bland way of saying that they both at a young age had been in the hands of evil people who had caused them to put their considerable skills to evil use.

Liere said, "If he's going to be one of your cases, then I'd better stay away for the duration."

Clair smiled. "We can communicate other ways. Which we'll be doing outside of magic studies. Seshe says that she and Jilo will marry at New Year's. I know she'd like to have you there. I can furnish details as they appear."

"I actually know some already. Lyren and Shontande Lirendi have been consulting Jilo because it's important to Jilo and Shontande to attend the other's weddings."

"Have you met Shontande Lirendi?" Clair asked.

"Yes. He and Lyren came to Choreid Dhelerei a few days ago. Apparently the Colendi court has all gone home to see to harvest and tax matters, which gives them a little time together." Liere smiled tenderly. "I have never seen Lyren this happy. It's as if she sheds light."

"And Shontande?"

"He's very quiet. Not at all the way I'd come to expect, considering his reputation. Though you'd think I'd know better than to listen to such tales by now. I don't have a sense of him yet, he's so very polished and polite. But Senrid likes him very much." She smiled across at Clair. "Have the two of you thought about a wedding?"

"Already happened," Clair said, taking Liere completely by surprise. "It was spontaneous, when we chanced to have

Aurora and Puddlenose here at the same time. When both my Aunt Murial and Detlev were able to turn up, we went down to the waterfall..."

She obligingly shared the memory with Liere: a cold day near the end of winter. Clair asking CJ to sing one of her favorite songs, and as CJ's clear soprano, accompanied by the roar of the waterfall, surrounded them, he dipped a silver cup into the fresh water, gave it to her to sip, then she offered him the cup to sip, after which everyone there also drank.

"It's the way people did it back when Siamis was small. He says there was an entire ritual, but no one knows those rituals now, and the important moment was the sharing of the water with each other and family. It was simple, over before CJ reached the second verse, but it felt very right. And so this place once again becomes the Reverael House of Healing. For I've added his name to mine: it was a good name once, a respected one. It seems right to give it life again."

Liere listened, sensing how right it had been for them both. "Congratulations." She leaned back, suppressing a grunt as her cramped tenant shifted around, probably as uncomfortable as she was. It was not going to be long now; the small muscle spasms down low had already begun.

"Are you all right? Should we find a chair for you?"

"I'm fine. I like the cool breeze out here." Liere shifted again. "Speaking of dyr work. Though Senrid says frequently that he's found the happiness he never thought to have, the habits of a lifetime do not change easily."

"Trust," Clair said. "With Senrid, his trust was the most difficult of the intangibles to earn."

"And the easiest to lose. He'll go out and risk his own life without much thought to the consequences, but when it comes to me and this child, he balked. He would not have any midwife he hadn't met. And he didn't know any midwives," Liere said.

Clair pursed her lips. "Ordinarily I'd give him at least a mental stink-eye for interfering when you're doing all the hard work, but with Senrid..."

"With Senrid, it's different. I could see panic not far below his jaw-locked control. This is a very long fear of his, I think it's fair to tell you, since you've been friends with him nearly as long as I."

"That's true. And in fact I remember how he used to say he kept the Child Spell as a way of hiding in plain sight, and that he was afraid that if he ever had an heir that heir's life would be hostaged against his kingdom, forcing him to an agonizing choice. Though as far as I know, Marloven history doesn't include that particular twist on throne-snatching."

"Exactly. The thing he feared the most, all his life, *happened*. Not the way he imagined it—there was no choice involved—but it still happened. Anyway, I gave in when I saw how disturbed he was. And really, I could birth this baby by myself. I'd feel more comfortable with someone to catch the baby."

"Senrid won't?"

"He's even more tense at the idea. He's so sure he'll do something wrong. Fenis Senelac said she would do it for me. Though she's never midwifed, she certainly knows plenty about babies."

Liere shifted her weight again, making a slight grimace. "How about we discuss these texts you gave me, right now. I'm beginning to suspect that baby-catching is going to be sooner than later. Here. I wrote down a list of words I could not figure out from context." Liere pulled a folded paper from her pocket.

Clair took the list. "Oh, yes. I've got most of these on my own list. The words none of us have definitions for. Detlev did warn us that there are layers of knowledge that were lost, whether because of Norsunder, or because they belong to earlier history. Perhaps we'll find out as the translation project progresses. Keep your list!"

Liere pocketed the list again, then made a fist and shoved her knuckles into her lower back as she said, "Might some of these mystery words have to do with why Hibern is at Songre Silde?"

"Don't yet know," Clair said, and smiled. "But I'm sure she'll share what she learns when she gets back."

"Is Detlev there too?"

"Siamis says he's at Five," Clair said—using the old nickname for the fifth world. "He's looking very carefully at their records, though he has not said why. He promised to be back in time for New Year's Week."

They discussed the rest of the text on disirad and magic, which Liere was still trying to process. She was not venturesome with the ancient magic. Witness her reluctance to make the slide.

Well, everyone has their weak points, she thought later as she braced for what she had determined would be her last transfer until this baby was out in the world.

In Marloven Hess, as usual after a transfer, the sun leaped ahead a short distance. Liere decided to walk off the transfer reaction. The baby had not liked transfer. Maybe she — or he — reacted to her whole-body wince. At any rate, she longed to walk, especially as the baby seemed to like the rhythm of a walk.

She took the long way through the warren of courtyards, stopped by the kitchen to pinch a berry tart, then trudged upstairs to Senrid's study, to find it empty. Walk, she told herself, and pushed on toward the Harskialdna tower, where Senrid always said he felt Keriam's presence, probably just because the desk was where it always had been. And on the walls, the board Keriam had made depicting the layout of the academy, with neat strips of paper denoting each youth's bunk, as well as instructors, and opposite, the schedule. Keriam's presence was strong due to memory, Senrid insisted; Liere knew that he did not believe in ghosts.

She found Senrid busy with his academy leaders, so she lifted a hand and started down the stairs again. She was half-way down when her knees began to shake. Oh, yes. It was almost time.

Malcolin had wanted out fast, once those muscles down there contracted sufficiently. Yossi had been very well-mannered in his birth. This baby — would she be Ndand Elenzeh Lesra? Liere had not permitted herself to say the name out loud once she and Senrid had decided to name a girl after their mothers as well as his cousin — seemed to be taking her time.

It wasn't until midway through the last watch of the night when Liere reached over to touch Senrid. As always, he was awake in a moment, one hand going under his pillow.

"Let's send for Fenis," she said.

He withdrew his hand from the knife he always kept there, ripped into some clothes, and summoned the night runner, who yelped, "At once!" on a high note that sent a tremor of laughter through Liere.

Fenis Senelac had been sleeping in her clothes for over a week now. Finally, was her thought when the runner banged on her door loud enough to cause lamps to be lit along the alleyway off the stables.

When her neighbors poked heads out, someone called, "Is

it the king's baby?"

"It's time," Fenis said, in unconscious echo of Liere.

And it was. Fenis barely made to the royal bedroom before Liere said, "Here she comes!" in a strangled voice. Senrid stood at her shoulder, his entire body as tense as Liere's.

Fenis saw that the house servants had readied everything. She grabbed up a clean, warm towel to catch the little princess—ah, no, not a princess after all, though Liere had been saying "she" for months, because she knew Senrid wanted a daughter.

Once Fenis had toweled the baby off, saying, "You've got a prince," Liere caught a surge of emotion from Senrid. The foremost emotion she detected was a kind of relief, and she began to suspect that maybe it was just as well that this was Savarend. Perhaps a small boy would not snag quite so mercilessly on Senrid's memories of that determined little dog-loving daughter.

"Savarend Retren Montredaun-An," Senrid said slowly, his eyes gleaming with unshed tears.

"If that's for my Ret," Fenis began.

"It is," Senrid said.

"Thank you."

"It's a good name."

"Though it looks like he's going to have your yellow hair. Never met a Retren who wasn't dark." Fenis chuckled.

As they chattered, admiring the newcomer's every feature, Liere lay back, contented to gaze at the dawning wonder and joy in Senrid's face. I am a woman with three sons and one daughter, Liere said to herself. All three of my sons by different fathers.

Life was so strange. But as she looked through misting eyes at Senrid's tender smile, his brow gleaming with sweat as if he'd endured labor, too, she thought, strange but very, very good.

34

I t was the eve of New Year's Week — the last day of the year 4770.

Today Colend would gain a queen.

The city of Alsais, practiced at decorating every summer for the music festival, had turned the entire city into something from a tale of years. Shops competed in decorating their fronts, so that everywhere one saw, and smelled, pine boughs decorated with pink dogwood, viola, and snowdrops. When real flowers could not be found, silken blossoms and butterflies added color to archways and sleighs, doorways and windows. Not even the Queen of Sartor (so the Colendi assured each other) could have had so splendid a wedding, their self-satisfaction scarcely disturbed by the intelligence, known to one or two, that that selfsame queen had had the simplest of weddings in a forest, during the war.

Earlier, Lyren had joined Shontande in ringing the city — traversing all the canals in a sleigh, but this year they not only handed out gold, they also admired all the fine decorations.

Then it was time to return to dress for the wedding. Lyren sat patiently in her new dressing room, keeping very still, as her new chambermaid deftly wove orchids into her hair.

She smiled. The past weeks had flown by, every day with lists of tasks, though she and Shontande still made time for a talk every evening, sitting beside a warm fire. She'd seen that Shontande really enjoyed overseeing every detail of what would be a brilliant day, from the fantastical ice sculptures on the bridges to the illusory stars glittering round every canal and street glowglobe to the glories inside the palace, all white and gold and green.

The maid stepped back and Lyren glanced at the mirror, approving the deceptively simple line of her gown; the exquisite fit was something that Colend's tailors were best at. The over-robe was silk-lace, the most difficult to make, embroidered with delicate threads of gold, the under-gown green silk. She carefully touched the gorgeous gold-centered white orchids that no one on Sartorias-deles had seen, for Mildred had brought them back from Geth as a gift.

A knock at the door.

"Enter!" Lyren called, before the little duty page—goggling as the last touches were added—could dash across the shining tile floor. Lyren gave a glad cry when, in the mirror's reflection, Carl slipped inside.

Lyren took in Carl's smiling face, the filled-out cheeks, the glow of color there. No need to ask: Carl had found what she sought, and of all the people in the world, Lyren rejoiced silently, Carl would appreciate it longest.

"I had to see you beforehand," Carl said. "You don't mind?"

Lyren smiled back. "I'm all done, and have only to wait for the armies below to get in place. Sit down!"

Carl dropped on a hassock at Lyren's feet. "I can see for myself that you are happy, and that's really why I came," she said. "It seemed like a romance from the old ballads, you and the king of Colend. I've heard about him," she added earnestly.

"Nothing terrible, I trust," Lyren said, laughing.

"Never," Carl averred in haste. "But sophisticated. Terribly so. Well, so are you. Mad said he's ever so handsome, but remote."

"Ah, not to me. Not now," Lyren said.

Carl smiled, the glow of color still in her cheeks. "You helped me so, so, so much, you and Liere. Is there anything I can do for you? From my great store of knowledge?"

Lyren held out her hand, and when the delicate fingers touched her palm, she gripped them gently. "I think we've found our way. But you and I have something to share. We can be queens together, and parents, I trust. Let's not lose our friendship."

"Never," Carl promised. "I—" She stopped.

The door opened, and Liere looked in. "Interrupting?"

"No," Lyren and Carl said together.

Liere's gold eyes were intense with an expression that Lyren could not interpret. From the bemused quirk to her brows it was plain that Carl couldn't either. Neither would understand it for many years, until they became parents, and saw a child leave the last of childhood behind in entering a new life.

For now Lyren smiled a welcome. "You look gorgeous," she said, for it was true. Liere was also gowned in green and gold and white, the colors of weddings most of the world over, but it was forest green, the white only touches of lace, the gold tiny knots along cuffs and neck, and in her eyes. "Has Senrid broken away at last?"

"Convocation doesn't start until tomorrow. He's downstairs gabbing military stuff with Jehan of Khanerenth, Malcolin listening avidly. Laban and Rel are there, too. I'm sorry we couldn't get here yesterday. Senrid needed to clear our way so that we can be in Chwahirsland tomorrow. The king not being there for Convocation Firstday is a first."

Lyren nodded, glad she would never have to deal with Marlovens—or their more recalcitrant, less-controlled neighbors.

Carl glanced from one to the other, then rose and went to the door, her gown rustling. "See you anon!" she said, and whisked herself out before either could speak, leaving mother and daughter together.

"How do you feel?" Liere asked.

"Amazement and joy still," Lyren said. "In spring we'll make a tour of the kingdom, but already I can see that there is work to be done."

"I hope the future will be everything you wish," Liere said, and hugged her.

The quality of her voice, her expression, imbued the words with a fervency that shot a pang through Lyren's cocoon of happiness.

"I was afraid to ask. Yossi's first birthday. Were you able to see him?"

Liere turned her head, her profile sad. "For an hour or two. It was a very stiff meeting. Yossi was bewildered. He knows me in spirit, but of course he did not recognize me, and Macael was very on guard. However." Her shoulders relaxed as she sighed. "No doubt he was dreading this first meeting as much as I was, and now it's over. With Macael I learned that the first is always the worst. I'm hoping that as Yossi grows, it will get easier. For all our sakes." She smiled at Lyren. "And so, we are watchful, but we also appreciate every single day of happiness."

They embraced again, wordlessly.

Another tap on the door.

Lyren could sense absolutely no hint of identity outside the door. "Enter."

The door opened. Sveneric walked in, followed by Detlev.

Lyren looked from one to the other. "No wonder I sensed mind-shields of steel."

Detlev was dressed simply in gray and brown linen, his long gray-streaked brown hair pulled neatly back. To someone who didn't know who he was, he looked like a scribe assistant, freed for the festival day.

"Don't tell me something horrible has gone wrong," Lyren said quickly.

"Nothing horrible has gone wrong," Detlev said, and Sveneric gave her an eyebrow quirk: *Really?*

But she was going to make absolutely certain. "A dire warning, then?"

"No dire warnings."

She wondered why her emotions whipsawed like a storm wind, and tried for humor. "I feel a lot more comfortable when you stay on your side of the world — vigilant from a distance."

"I'm sure you do," Detlev said. And, "Our conversations have been rare, but you remember them."

"Yes."

"Some time in the future, when the euphoria of being newlywed has settled into the tranquility of a happy life, I want you to consider your position."

"You mean as queen?"

"I mean as a world leader."

"I'm flattered! Or perhaps I should say that I ought to feel flattered, but shouldn't you be addressing Shon?"

"I hope you will share our conversation."

"Ah."

"It's a good habit, considering the future," he said. "One of the ways we can choose one of the better possible patterns is for you to maintain your childhood contacts."

"What ... no, never mind. If you were going to be more specific, you would have. Go ahead and be mysterious. It's not like this is the first time," Lyren said, arms crossed. "But may I point out, you *just said* you didn't bring any dire warnings."

"If I knew what tomorrow will bring, I would say so. Also, I'm not warning you, but merely encouraging you to continue doing what you do best."

"You want the alliance to happen again?"

"It never truly ended. Which is an excellent thing. Ah. I believe the ceremony is about to begin, so I will leave you with my best wishes."

"Very polite!" Lyren retorted, laughing from an excess of nerves. "I thank you." She curtseyed, as if to a king.

He waved that off and left noiselessly, and she turned on Sveneric. "I have never thought about this before, but does he have *any* kind of a personal life?" She saw Sveneric's lips part, and forestalled him with a raised hand. "Never mind, I know what's coming: 'ask him.' 'The very idea makes me feel the age of my two youngest brothers. And isn't *that* an odd feeling," she added.

"What's a mere twenty-five years?" Sveneric retorted good-naturedly. "I will never know my own siblings."

Lyren drew in a breath. "Adamas Dei."

"That's the one I regret not meeting. The rest … from what records remain, we probably would not have had much to say to one another."

Liere had remained silent. Though she had read the *Conversations of Adamas Dei* the previous year, for the first time, she wondered how that must have felt for Detlev to deliberately leave his beloved son behind in order to protect him from drawing Norsunder's cruel eye. But then he had already lost so much. Did it ever get easier?

A ghost-voice whispered, *Never.*

Liere deliberately shook off the mood. So inappropriate today! At least she would get to see Yossi again — and hopefully more frequently as he got older.

Lyren was laughing. "The idea of Detlev and courtship, it's like, oh, a kraken wooing a bunny."

Sveneric rocked back and forth from heel to toe, his face absolutely blank. "I'm going to tell him you likened him to a kraken."

Lyren surged to her feet, glistening lace swirling. "Don't you dare!"

Shontande entered then, his brows going up as he glanced

from one to the next. "Ah-ye, am I inopportune?"

Shontande was dressed like Lyren in white and green and gold, as always elegant, now formidably so, the long stylized white lilies on the gold silk panels of his over-robe drawing the eye. She held out her hand to him, saying, "If you'll kindly boot Sveneric out..."

"I can take a hint!" Sveneric exited on a breathy laugh.

"Go get married," Liere said. She kissed her daughter, then followed Sveneric out.

Shontande held out his hands to Lyren. "It's time."

Everyone has their cherished ideas of what constitutes beauty. For many, it's gems and jewels set in richly worked gold, everything throwing back glittering light.

Shontande had learned that for Lyren, beauty was found in living and natural things: the light before sunset, even in winter, illuminating every ice sculpture. Pots and pots of living flowers breathing their scents—painstakingly transferred down from the northern half of the world, and before morning would be transferred back before the cold could harm them.

Four choirs had been installed in the corner galleries above the throne room, each beyond a huge crystal glowglobe, for there must be no shadows on this day.

When Shontande and Lyren appeared in the great doors, sound poured from above, cascades of chords in polyphonic weaving. Sartoran triplets echoed brass horns in the king's fanfare, then the descant began, children's voices singing not the usual puffery about the greatness of Colend and the glory of this happy day. Shontande had tossed out most of the traditional anthems sung at such times, asking his chief director to adapt a poem that Mathias the Magnificent had written for Lasva the Wanderer.

Below the descant, also adapted, men's voices sang a piece attributed to Martande Lirendi as a promise to Colend's future. The two melodies, sung antiphonally, caused more than one listener to tear up, hearts full, throats aching.

When the voices faded to an expectant hush, the wedding pair reached the dais and stepped up.

Shontande had also changed the order of events. Traditionally, if Colendi monarchs married, that would come first—to whatever degree the marriage treaty entailed—and following that, the monarch would grant a title and a suitable coronet or crown, anything from the modest silver band of a consort to the very rare crown to match his, implying shared power.

But Shontande refused to bestow a title on Lyren, implying superiority of rank. He insisted on her coronation first, as had happened to every Lirendi since the first Martande declared the Kifelian province a kingdom, a gift from the reigning Sartoran king.

As the beautiful fanfare to the queen echoed through the winter throne room, used only once a year, at New Year's, Lyren Sartora Fer Eider became a queen of Colend in her own right, and following that, Atan and Rel—Sartoran monarchs— stepped up, not as political figures, but as a married couple administering the wedding vows.

The words, the trappings, were all traditional, but the reversal made them new again, and more than one among the Colendi court wondered what changes would be wrought in future. Whispers had already gone round that Lyren hated dueling as much as Shontande did—that secret shame still left from the war, officially against law and custom. But there were still those who felt that steel had been needed to be rid of Norsunder, so why not again, if the cause was just, even if it was personal?

"With my vow I offer you this ring, which has no beginning and no end..."

Atan led Lyren through each line of the ring ceremony, and Rel led Shontande as they each gave the other the outward symbol that their marriage was exclusive.

Then they faced the gathering, "I call upon my family, my peers, and my subjects, to witness my vow!" And to one another, eyes smiling into eyes, "To share with you all that I have, and all that I am."

Lyren's voice trembled once, when she swore to make his sorrow her sorrow, and his joy her joy. But she rallied when— aware that she had come to this country owning six gowns, and little else—she promised to make his prosperity her prosperity, and his hardship hers.

An answering mirth gleamed in his countenance, but his voice rang with absolute sincerity when he finished, "As long as we both shall live."

And it was over, except for the congratulations, and the dinner, and the magnificent ball. Carillons rang the Triumph mode, last heard at the end of the war as young bellringers vigorously competed with each other all over the city to see who could be heard farthest. Which was fine, but the city thoroughly appreciated the crown hosting a splendid meal in every guild house—and if the bargers had an extra wagonload of famed Ellir Gold from Khanerenth, who was to know?

The ball was a masque, which included the king's personal staff. Thad and Nalisse were there, the two radiating pride, Thad—after perhaps one too many toasts—telling anyone who would listen that it was he and Nalisse who had invited Lyren to stay. As if everyone hadn't heard that the king had decided at first glance.

Bee was also present, mostly for the music, though he enjoyed being guided around the floor by his husband, who was never quite off-duty, even when out of livery.

Talian Ariath had begun the day wishing it was she up there on the dais, except she knew by now that her mother had been wrong about Shontande Lirendi, who though soft-spoken, was not weak and easily led. When she acknowledged to herself that Shon would never have crowned her first—at best she would have been a consort—she mentally turned her ambitions toward Alarcansa. They had decided that they would ask Shontande to grant Ariath to them to hold for a future second child, that is, if a first child didn't match with a royal heir...

As the two danced, Talian kept looking around.

"What is it now?" Caid asked, highly amused. Talian's mind was always running, but she was beginning to be less predictable now.

"Someone said Detlev is here. Which one is he? I don't see any armor or swords."

"Pretty sure he's the one over there with Sveneric. The man who looks just like him."

"Ah-ye, *that* one? I thought he was a servant, or an uncle or something. Isn't a sinister war leader supposed to look like a sinister war leader?"

Shontande, glancing over the ballroom, saw Caid laughing, and whispered in Lyren's ear, "You still have not told me what you said to get those two to make their peace at last."

"Ah," Lyren murmured into his shoulder. "I don't think it was words that did it."

By that time most of the visiting monarchs who had come primarily for political reasons had transferred home again.

Remaining were personal friends, such as the pair from Khanerenth, Atan and Rel, Vidanric and Meliara from Remalna, and of course the closer friends from Marloven Hess, Everon, Mearsies Heili, and Chwahirsland.

It was near midnight when most of these gathered around CJ, listening to her enthusiastic, rambling description of amazing undersea sights. "... and you should have *seen* the cities underwater. They looked like they were made out of pearl, but they felt like the stuff our white palace is made of. Disirad, isn't that what Detsie calls it? And they had spires as well, just as tall. No. Taller. And for the first time, I wondered why we had so many balconies so high up, and those bridges between them that you can't walk on, kind of as if they were parking spots for balloons—oh, never *mind* what those are—my point is, they make more sense underwater, because you can float at any level. As for disirad, I still don't really understand what it is. Kind of stone, but kind of not. Is it a property of these worlds only?"

She then turned to tall, black-eyed Hibern, there with Erai-Yanya. "You ought to know. Do they have disirad on the fog-world?"

Hibern said, "The Norss do not permit us to travel anywhere on Songre Silde but the one place they keep specifically for communication for off-worlders, so I cannot say for certain. But I sense something like, if it is not exactly the same."

"What did you learn in this latest journey?" Liere asked. "It seems to me it was quite protracted. Worth it?"

"Everything takes time with them. And I sensed a great deal of interest in what we had to report, though their reactions, as usual, were vague."

"Frustratingly vague?" Senrid asked. "From everything I've heard about Songre Silde so far, their communication seems as foggy as their world."

"Not disagreeing," Hibern said. "You have to remember, though we won the war against Norsunder, and they are very grateful for that, the fact is, we fought a war that began among us. Wars happen here. Whereas they haven't seen war in thousands of years. So though they readily help in many ways, and are grateful for whatever we bring to enable peace, they still regard us much the way we regard small children getting used to fire. We'll let them hold a candle, but we don't let them start fires, or leave them alone with one."

CJ scowled. "But *you* went there, Dets—Detlev. I thought they'd tell *you* all the secret stuff."

Detlev said, "They told me less than Hibern has learned. One of the reasons I've stayed away as much as I can, since what anywhere else would be called a trial."

"A trial," Atan repeated, brows up.

'Yes," Detlev said. "My visits there included questions about the past, some of which a few beings there recollect—perhaps inherited memory, perhaps not—though of course from the distance of their world to ours. After they considered what I said, they took into consideration our work with the ward against Ilerian's kind."

CJ's eyes rounded, and being CJ, she blurted out the question most were thinking, but hesitated to ask: "What would have happened if they didn't believe you?"

"I don't think that was in question," Detlev responded, a hint of a smile narrowing his eyes. "So much as whether or not they deemed me still a danger."

"And?" Senrid asked. "Execution by some other name, flattering themselves it was clean and necessary?"

"Not execution in our sense. They don't take lives," Hibern said.

"But I expect I might have found myself in another place, another time, perhaps another form," Detlev said. "To live out what remains of my life without constituting a danger to others."

Lyren perceived by the brief silence after these mild words that there were some among the company who had not only expected something of the sort, but might even have wanted it to happen. To her surprise, indignation was her first reaction, and a sneaky impulse to partisanship. It had been perfectly fine to revile against Detlev when she thought she was the only one not falling in with his orders.

CJ, however, was not one of the silent judges. "Whatever those fog-world people say, there's something funky going on here. I know that much from Gloriel, though she can barely speak anymore. There's something weird happening, on *our* world, and those Songre Silde groanboils know, and won't tell us for our own good?"

Hibern grinned at her. "Calm down, CJ. I got the impression that they expect us to have learned whatever it is we need to know by the time it happens. Which could be in centuries. I don't think even they know when, even if they know what."

Detlev gave a nod. "I gathered much the same from what little was disclosed to me."

Erai-Yanya spoke up. "One thing I do understand about the Songre Silde Norss is that they take a very, very long time to come to decisions."

The conversation broke up soon after, everyone remembering that this was a celebration after Jilo mumbled to his palms that they had to return to get ready for their own wedding on the morrow, New Year's Week's Firstday.

Lyren made it a point to dance at least once with anyone who showed an inclination. She laughed, chatted, and introduced her Fer Eider cousins to friendly courtiers, as grandmother Elenzeh conversed with the dowager duchases of Gaszin and Sentis, looking on with a sort of smiling bemusement at what had become of the granddaughter she had chided most for not settling down to a practical apprenticeship.

35

The next day, many of those same people transferred to Narad, capital of Chwahirsland, for the wedding of Jilo Ijo—King of the Chwahir—to Seshemerria Jevondyan, last Queen of Damondaen.

The stone city had flowered into color.

CJ, who had never liked coming to Chwahirsland, muttered to Falinneh and Dhana, "Did I get whapped over the head and now I'm dreaming? Where are the black walls? Not that granite is much to look at in the ordinary sense, but a million time better than grimy black."

"Looks as if the Chwahir have been scrubbing every stone in the city," Clair replied, smiling.

"Probably yet another law by Wan-Edhe broken," CJ cracked. "Of course cleaning the city would be forbidden because the people weren't serving him, or fighting for him, or being targets for his torture chambers."

"He's gone now," Clair murmured as they looked around the main courtyard. "And every time I'm here there are fewer signs of him left."

"How he would have hated this," CJ gloated.

The grand gates stood open, affording a view of the main street outside those gates, with a glimpse of a grand square off to the right.

The Mearsieans looked around at the hundreds and hundreds of banners with long streamers billowing in the cold wind. Most of the banners depicted the eight-sided circle of heart-shaped linden leaves in a variety of colors, but mostly red: whereas in most of the Sartoran continent, and places influenced by the Sartoran culture, the chief colors for weddings were spring green and white, in Chwahirsland it had once been red, and was red again, with gold added for kingship. It was a splendid sight.

Having recovered from the transfers, the Mearsieans proceeded into the castle itself. Everywhere they saw touches that they attributed to Seshe—glassed windows. A garden, bedded down for winter, except for pink-blooming plum trees. It was still a fortress, but someone in the far past had known how to lead the eye upward.

A steward came out to meet them, imposing in purple livery that matched the purple and green of the linden leaves banner.

The Chwahir, veterans of organizing huge numbers of people into sharply efficient units, used that skill effectively now, with no threat of annihilation to drive them. The streets were lined, many carrying small banners, and CJ spotted things that looked like lanterns made out of paper. Most seemed to be painted. What were those for?

Clair smiled, eyes half shut as she sensed the pride around her.

The Mearsieans were conducted to the front of the vast throne room, and to one side, where eight wood-carved chairs sat in a line below the throne dais. In the main hall, guests of the king and queen had been given pride of place at the front of the throng, and behind them, Jilo's court, wearing their robes of state, in rank order: these reflected the army colors, a mustard for gold, light gray for silver, violet, green, and a deep red. The lines of these robes were invariably vertical, in panels; the foreign guests stood out in their layers and mixes of bright colors.

Clair spotted Liere in the very front, standing with Senrid, and lifted a hand. On one side stood Mondros and Terry Larensar—the reclusive king of neighboring Erdrael Danara— both beaming with pride. On Senrid's other side, David was almost unfamiliar with his hair combed neatly, and wearing his Marloven uniform, since he had no other fine clothes.

CJ scrunched her toes in the new dancing slippers Clair had suggested she get, which were as comfortable as shoes could be. She noted that even irrepressible Falinneh was quiet, her freckled face solemn—almost unrecognizable without her perpetual grin. Dhana looked around, eyes nearly closed. Sherry stared, whispering to Gwen. Puddlenose and Christoph completed the count of eight, these last three sporting new green independent captains' coats. Siamis stood at Clair's left; her chair was the closest to the throne. Aurora stood behind her mother's chair, mother and daughter's white hair drawing puzzled glances from the dark-haired Chwahir.

Across from the Mearsieans sat Jilo's relatives, the elders in chairs, the younger generation standing beside or behind those chairs, depending on a ranking that made sense to the Chwahir, even if it didn't to CJ.

"Nerves?" Clair turned her head.

"Not nerves," CJ muttered. "It's not that I'm *frightened*, though I can't help but think back to some bad times when Wan-Edhe was stinking up the place. Who would have thought! I just don't want to mess up, and embarrass Seshe."

"Just remember two hands, and the rest is simple," Clair said.

"It was a lot easier when you and Siamis got hitched," CJ muttered back. "Just us — over in seconds — and then on with the good eats!" She sighed. "I can't help but think how much Irenne would have loved all of this."

"And how much Diana would have hated it," Falinneh chirped from the other side of Clair.

"There's that. Though she would have done it for Seshe. Hsssh! It's starting!"

A lone voice rose in a minor key, melodic progression that had nothing to do with Sartoran triplets. No words; as the voice sang up and then hung there, repeating what sounded a bit like a bugle, but very stylized. One by one other voices joined. High. Low. Each making different sounds, as gradually, almost subliminally, deep men's voices rumbled a steady thrum, thrum, suggesting the heartbeat of the world.

The Mearsieans understood then that they were hearing a Great Hum.

Seshe and Jilo entered through the great doors. For once Jilo did not shuffle awkwardly in his purple and green robe — the linden colors, but with red edging. Seshe walked by his side, resplendent in mostly red, with green and violet accents, her ash-blond hair bright against the rich colors.

They passed the packed throne room, and drew abreast of their foreign guests. Jilo sent a shy smile their way.

Senrid lifted a hand in salute, Retren Ndarga next to David breaking into a brilliant smile. Jilo smiled his way, as Senrid reflected that he had not been back to Chwahirsland for years. He was amazed at the difference. Then, the royal castle had been gripped by Wan-Edhe's time-distortion ward, which made moving, even breathing a matter of concentration. But there had not been enough distortion to mask the sour reek of the place, or the mold and grime of decades, maybe even centuries.

All that was gone. The building smelled of clean stone, much like home. That much was expected, for it was stone, built for defense, as was his castle, but the lines were different. Somehow the eye was drawn upward, here.

He remembered the guards as furtive, silent, gazes always lowered except when they threatened you. Now every Chwahir hummed or sang wordlessly, a powerful song as Jilo and Seshe halted before the thrones.

A line of liveried servants brought out carts decorated with linden leaf circles, golden items on them that looked like pots for steep. They were even steaming slightly. Servants set out porcelain cups, and Seshe and Jilo both began pouring a stream of greenish liquid into each cup. The scent wafted close on a current of cold air: it was a slightly sweet, herbal scent. Different from the smell of Sartoran steep leaves.

Then Jilo and Seshe parted to either side and carried a cup in both hands, bringing it to the seated people—Seshe to Clair, and Jilo going to his grizzled uncle Shiam.

"Thank you for my life," Seshe whispered to Clair, with such sincerity that Clair's eyes stung. "I've already celebrated Diana and Irenne," she added.

Clair nodded in understanding as she took the cup with both hands. They had once been a group of nine. If Clair took herself out of the group, as she'd often had to because of her responsibilities, the girls had made a perfect twi in Chwahir eyes. Puddlenose and Christoph made ten whenever they turned up in Mearsies Heili. They'd shared adventures, terrible times, and good, so it was right that they filled Irenne and Diana's chairs.

Seshe brought a cup to CJ. "Thank you for your loyalty and your friendship," she whispered, equally sincere.

CJ's throat hurt. Though this was a joyous occasion, it was sad, too, because this ceremony cemented the fact that yet another of them was gone for good. Seshe had already moved out, but this day made it permanent: when she returned to Mearsies Heili, it would be as a visitor.

CJ took the cup with both hands, and slurped cautiously. It was bracingly warm, but not burning hot. Felt good going down. She handed back the empty cup, which Seshe took with a smile, and went to get another.

So it went on both sides of the dais, Jilo moving down the line of relatives, as Seshe served the remainder of her twi. One side only a twi, with no relatives, and on the other side, only a handful of relations with no twi. Seshe had explained: the Chwahir understood the gaps as a rightness, a representation of their own experience, because so many of them had lost both to Wan-Edhe's madness and tyranny.

When the last cup had been restored to its cart, and the servants vanished, Jilo and Seshe mounted the dais and bowed to the west.

Shontande whispered softly to Lyren, "Saluting those gone before."

They bowed to the east, and Lyren whispered back, "Let me guess: a bow acknowledging their responsibility to those to come?"

"Yes. Now the marriage part."

The waiting servants then held out trays, on which lay … scissors?

As the guests watched, Jilo took up the golden scissor, and carefully, gently cut a long lock of Seshe's hair. He soberly looped it up as she took the scissor and cut a lock of black hair from him. They slid the hair into a waiting bag netted of silk, and then, together, they laid the bag on a brazier that had been brought out.

The silk bag and the air flared brightly, lighting their faces.

"That's it?" Lyren whispered. "No vows?"

"Not in public, is my understanding," Shontande answered.

"That music, it didn't have words, either. Is it that they don't trust words?"

"It's … different. Wait. There will be words. We are not done yet."

And on Lyren's other side, Liere murmured almost voicelessly to Lyren, "It symbolizes their binding together, until death. Triumph or sorrow."

Her whisper hoarsened, her thoughts winging over the past year. Life with Senrid was so good, so very good, though at times it seemed she had fallen into a rushing river. Such as the two dates that five different people in the capital had warned her about. Six people, if she counted David. Two dates, heartbreakingly close together: the day Crystal Ingrid was killed, and what would have been her fifth birthday not long after. *He'll disappear, and drink himself sick,* Fenis had said bluntly.

Except if Liere was there, holding him. Though not a single word was spoken. Until morning, when he said only, "Thank you." And transferred back, and went about his day as if nothing had happened—

She shook that off, and saw that she had missed something: Jilo and Seshe each were given golden cups. A hint of the rich fragrance of wine drifted on the air as the two twined their arms, and then drank, without spilling a drop.

This time it was Senrid whose mind leaped back to the day after Savarend was born, when a message arrived from Siamis, *Fox is awake. But I don't know how long.*

Siamis came immediately, and took the infant by slide, leaving the other two to transfer the regular way. Fox was awake, and aware, his green eyes narrowing in a smile when Senrid held out the infant, and said, "Meet Savarend-Sierlaef Montredaun-An."

Fox lifted those knowing green eyes. Green eyes—a jolt, and a move toward wrist knives. It was less than a heartbeat's impulse, quickly hidden as Senrid recognized that Fox's eyes were the same green as Imry's—

"Senrid?" Liere's murmur was a cool wash, dousing the atavistic flare. Imry had *not* been at Darchelde that day. He was not here in Narad. Liere and David were both guardians over this infant son. Senrid was no longer alone. But the scar of Crystal-Ingrid's murder was not completely healed.

Is that why he grieved so hard for Fox, who had slipped away in his sleep that night? He'd only been in Senrid's life a few years, and those were rare appearances. He shut his eyes and steadied his breathing as Seshe and Jilo stepped down from the dais and started for the doors, which opened slowly.

The Great Hum gained in power: there were hundreds, thousands outside, also singing.

Uncle Shiam and his family rose, and in rank order began

to follow Jilo. Clair rose, and taking Siamis's and Aurora's hands, started out, the rest falling in behind.

CJ looked around, relishing all the changes from the first time she had seen this hall as Wan-Edhe's prisoner after his foiled attempt to take Colend. How much had changed! Wan-Edhe gone — *finally*. The mage geezer CJ had seen in Alsais so many years ago had turned out to be Tsauderei, who she still kind of missed. This city with its banners and actual trees growing was a zillion times better than the Narad of Doom she remembered. Even music — in Chwahirsland! It was strange music, not at all what she was used to, but it was really a lift to the heart.

CJ looked around at her familiar family. Twi was just another name for adopted family, right? They were all together again, like Clair's wedding. How *good* that felt!

She grinned at the way Dhana drifted along, a shoulder moving, an arm swinging a little. Almost-dancing to the amazing swell of sound, as they filed out of the throne room and into the great court, heading for the giant doors.

Hold on, was that Jilo, saying something?

"... my wings skim the pepper trees as I bugle my song!"

And all around the foreigners, the hum dropped to a thrumming hush, as voices whispered, "The swan year ... the swan year..."

"What does that mean, swan year?" Falinneh asked, looking around.

"Lion, Dragon, Dolphin, Eagle, Dog, Swan, Horse, and Otter." It was Dirk Sonscarna, emerging from the crowd of black-haired people lining the street and humming. He had refused to stand with them, and Clair and Siamis had insisted they let him do what he wanted. "Eight-year cycle."

"Lion! Do they even *have* lions here? I thought they were all way up north, in the Helandrias."

"Lions are more common than dragons," Gwen cracked. "Which is fine by me. I don't want to meet anything at sea bigger than a kraken."

Jilo's voice rose again.

"The dew dries early on magnolia leaves at midsummer.
Midwinter the plum begins to blush.
I watch olive blossoms float to the sky.
The spirits eternal surround us in sleep.
I rejoice as I gather lotus petals,

And weave the lithe green vines of ivy…"

It sounded like blither to CJ, but to her amazement, people along the street—still humming, low and soft—were painting some of these lines on their door frames.

But before she could ask why, the Great Hum rose again, an upwelling of sound as golden winks of light flickered to life all around them. The people were lighting little candles, and putting them in those flimsy lantern things.

Once the candle went in, the lanterns glowed with color, and then, one by one, were loosed to the sky.

Let him go, Senrid thought of Fox, his heart aching as he watched the lanterns rise. You had two father substitutes in Keriam and Fox. You no longer need a father. You are a father, once again, and you are not alone in your vigilance. Let him go.

One more child, Liere promised herself, eyes raised to the sky. I'll have my five after all. One more, Ivandred or Elenzeh, and then I am done.

Lyren, on Liere's other side, tipped her head back, assimilating the fact that Shontande, with the most beautiful court in the world, came here year after year to hear the humming and to watch this very different way of greeting the change of the year. Every new thing she learned about Shontande made her fall in love with him all over again.

Dirk Sonscarna took in the hundreds—thousands?—of lanterns, the upturned faces, the hum gradually dying away, voice by voice, and tested the thought: It could all be mine. Then he caught a side-glance from Aurora, her white hair limned in light. "You all right?"

He could take it. But he'd never hold it, and there would be blood and agony all over again. "I'm fine."

The lanterns drifted skyward, their shimmer dwindling until they were lost against the stars.

CODA

E ven in winter the characteristic scent of pine and blossoms bathed the air surrounding Curtas's House, high on a mountain west of Sartor's border.

Erenlara Sofar of the Venn breathed in a lungful of the cool air, fighting against the intense emotional echo of the unseen disirad in the mountain plateau above. It was not easy: scent evoked memory, all those years she'd tried to match this distinctive blend of fragrances by ordering and reordering her indoor garden, after her single tour. Finally, realizing at last what she was doing, she'd reordered that garden yet again, risking rumors of growing madness in the queen on the part of exasperated groundskeepers.

But oh, how she remembered this scent, and the emotions she'd felt the day she first breathed it in!

He had not been present that day, but everything here was so much a part of him, from the ground he had chosen to the house designed by those he had taught, that his presence had every moment been in her awareness. She recalled Sveneric's tour, and now followed on her own ghost-heels, her gaze again searching half-lit corridors and archways, as she recalled how Sveneric had said in mild puzzlement, "He seems to have left." Then his gentle smile. "But that is his way. He comes and goes without warning."

Whenever she came near.

That had been years and experiences ago.

Tonight was a combination celebration of New Year's

Week and a late celebration of Sveneric's twenty-fifth birthday, hosted by Jessan Delieth. She paused outside the doors to the gathering room, sorting through familiar laughs, tones, and languages, until she caught the quiet murmur barely discernable among the high-spirited voices of his group: Detlev.

He was there, talking to two people she did not know. One moment he stood, profile contrasted against a dark window. His head was a little bent, his focus on the speaker, a young man with short, black curly hair and a sensitive profile. Was he the one she had seen with Jilo, during the war? Yes, Retren Ndarga. Now quite grown.

He was speaking a language she recognized as Marloven, "... and I did not think Marend cared one way or another, but when I'd told her I was invited to attend Jilo's wedding at New Year's Week, Marend said that they would not marry at Convocation after all, but in spring, before the academy ride. They already live together..."

Erenlara's attention shifted back to Detlev. His brown hair, a few silver strands highlighted by the candlelight, was tied back, and he wore his customary subdued colors, a dark gray-blue robe, slit high on the sides for riding, linen shirt beneath, over dark trousers. At first glance a man of ordinary height and build, features reflecting the agelessness of those with Dena Yeresbeth; his carriage incorporated the ease and strength of one for whom self-discipline had long since been as natural as breathing.

His head turned, and their gazes met across the width of the room.

She permitted her glance to linger a single heartbeat, long enough to signal recognition. Now he could not leave without at least a brief greeting.

She turned her gaze away to seek the guest of honor. Sveneric stood in an alcove, talking with David, and some of Detlev's people. Sveneric was tall, nearly as tall as David, and even more slight in build. His brown hair waved softly down from a high brow, and long sweeping lashes framed eyes like windows to his ardent spirit. His mouth, curved in an affectionate smile, widened to delight when he spotted her.

Remorse tightened her heart. Nothing had ever been said between them, because words would have been painful: his, a first, teen-age love, and hers, an acknowledgement that she was soulbonded forever, that rare and sometimes inescapably heart-breaking truth. They had not seen one another since the previous New Year. Ah! So much had changed, except their old friendship which had preceded the shoals of adolescence.

"I'm so glad you're here," he said, holding out both hand s—and asking no questions about why she had first returned a negative to Jessan's invitation. "Come, say hello to everyone."

He led her around the room, introducing those she did not know. She smiled her way through introductions and music-punctuated scraps of catch-up conversations, always aware of Detlev's position in the room, though the sustained proximity after so many years of unaccountable silence made her stomach cramp and her legs tremble.

At last they drew nigh, and he had not moved away. Her nerves sang.

Sveneric said, "And here's Detlev, and Tcherys, who is one of our dyranarya."

Their conversation broke, and both looked up.

"Welcome, Erenlara," Detlev said, gaze steady and utterly unreadable.

Sveneric introduced Tcherys, a tall, weedy young woman with a friendly countenance. "Land of the Venn!" Tcherys exclaimed. "I've always wanted to go up there, but I hear the weather is tough on travelers."

"We have one or two nice days a year," Erenlara admitted.

"Ha! You've an interesting history." Tcherys' eyes narrowed with fun, and Erenlara laughed.

"'Interesting'. Very diplomatic!"

Tcherys glanced from one to the other, then, acute as dyranarya usually were, she said, "Sveneric, I noticed we ran out of the cranberry-lime punch. Is there more?"

"Let's go find out." They ran down to the kitchen.

Eren said to Detlev, "You have never come to visit Venn. I will take it as a compliment, if it is true you mostly go where you see a need. But I would like, someday, for you to see what I have done." She said it, though she had for a time suspected that he had indeed been in her kingdom, as part of his ceaseless guardianship.

He responded with politeness, and so the evening spun away in pleasantries. She moved through it, pantomiming the visiting monarch, and smiling at everyone.

At the end of the evening Detlev bade her farewell, but there was no invitation, no promise of a future visit.

All right, then. She raised her hands to perform the transfer magic. She had finished her reconnaissance. She had honed her weapons. The time had come to storm the citadel.

She transferred not home, but to the upper plateau, and sat on the stone bench under the twelve-sided roof, to wait. Twelve, so important a number all throughout the world.

The air was keen and cold, so she summoned a warm cloak from her own closet on the far side of the northern continent; it appeared with a chuff of displaced air and a glimmer of scintillation as the magic dispersed. Then she sat and watched the moon flood the mountain with silver light. Deep beneath her stone bench, the disirad resonated in spirit. Her finite senses perceived the effect as vision and voice, adding subtle color to the silver light, and the echo of a great chord sung by a mighty choir all across the centuries of the world. She knew that, had she not inherited responsibilities that had shaped her life, she would have found a place here.

Time no longer mattered. She watched the golden lights in the windows of the academy building below the plateau as she bathed her spirit in the ineffable harmonics of the disirad. Her awareness expanded and sharpened. Though lights winked out one by one, she knew when it was that Detlev left the Academy and transferred home.

She glanced up once at the brilliant stars, and the moon, which had traveled this way across half the sky, and stood up.

Here is my moment; and she sensed more than heard Clair's endless compassion, understanding, and support.

Erenlara raised her hands, and transferred to that house above the Sartoran shore.

She had also been there once, again on a tour led by Sveneric, not long after the Host War when they were both young teens. She remembered each room as if she had lived in the house, so many times she'd visited it mentally since that day years before.

Detlev's study was on the upper floor. In a moment's glance she saw that the windows were wide, letting in air that was cold on the mountain, but merely cool here, cool and distinctively scented with herbs and pine and the sea.

The door was open.

Lamps cast light on his face from above as he worked at his desk; she saw the shadows of his lashes on his cheeks, and more shadows below his eyes and at the corners of his mouth. He looked pensive, and tired.

She saw that he'd removed the fine outer robe and sat there in his shirt, the sleeves rolled, the high collar loosened. Ever neat in public, he'd expected — wanted — to be alone.

Though she was absolutely still, not even breathing, she only had the one moment before he looked up.

"Eren," he said, still pleasantly, but with question in his gaze.

She entered unbidden, the cloak billowing in the breeze from the windows.

He neither moved nor spoke, made no gesture of invitation or of warding.

All the uncounted years and experiences she'd spent in seeking wisdom afforded her an insight: that in this confrontation Detlev's risk was at least as great as hers.

She stopped before the desk.

She said, "On that day in the war when I was twelve, I met you. Since that day you have taken great care to see that we did not meet again."

He dropped his pen and stood. "You must not think it caused by fault in you."

"I did at first," she said. "The assumptions of childhood. The stigma of childhood —"

He made a movement to protest the word, but understood that even then she had sensed the inexorability of time. And she had comprehended, as few children did, that her own experience had barely begun.

She said, "For years not counted on this world, I traveled to others, and while only a night would pass here, because I had duties to draw me back. I spent months and longer ranging far and then farther on a quest for wisdom, for expertise — and I left behind me good work. How many worlds have stories about Eren Beyond-Stars? But fame across worlds availed me nothing."

She saw the impact of her words in his narrowed eyes. "Erenlara —" he began.

She raised a hand. "I stopped the night travels this year, when at last I realized I did not need further training. That my goal of attaining Old Sartoran sagacity receded as fast as I lunged for it."

He waited now; if she wished to accuse, to rant in anger and despair, he would listen.

She said, "I was my own worst judge, putting my own words and thoughts into the image of you that I carried, ever and ever, in my mind. In my heart. At first I thought you did not come because I was weak, because I was inexperienced, because I was ignorant and young, until I saw that you sent encouraging messages through visitors I valued—CJ. Atan. And especially Sveneric. I saw in them your guiding hand, all sent to bring friendship and care, and offers of help in some skill I might be needing, whether statecraft or laughter."

He sat slowly onto the edge of his desk and folded his hands on one knee, his gaze unwavering.

She said, "I saw that mastering statecraft was not enough, that handing power back to my Venn, through ritual and our notion of honor, was not enough. Nor was expertise in the arts of war, including seeing through to the end a battle against evil intent and suffering, including dealing death by my own hand." She touched the scar at her hairline, and brushed her hand over the cloak that covered her ribs, and a third on the inside of her left arm—not all of them, by any means. But those were the ones that had come closest to killing her. "I have done all that, and when I returned, the same circumstances faced me: you remained here, and I was at my end of the world, ostensibly protected by innocence, my age still against me."

He was silent.

"When Sveneric came last I realized I had still more to learn about the infinite variations of love, and of the risks and rewards of cleaving to another. And so I left yet again, always at night, embarking on a quest to shed ignorance, and at last I saw that I was my own harshest judge, but there was a standard, set that day in Mearsies Heili, when I was twelve years old. It has always been before my eyes ever since, waking and sleeping, always. And forever."

His hand lifted, then dropped, but she felt the impact of her words in how he shielded himself.

She said, "I know now that blame and regret and remorse were your own nightmares, that in keeping silence you thought you granted me freedom to forget, to make my life as I willed, and to be happy. You did not want to get tangled up in my life as arbiter, or authority, or teacher. You wanted," she said, fighting to keep her voice steady, "in case we ever met again, that we should meet as equals. Believing this conclusion, I saw your silence as a gift, one made in hope, and in faith."

She clasped her hands, and waited.

When he spoke, it was to those clasped hands, in a slow, reflective voice. "No one exists," he said, "including my own son, who would not have condemned me for claiming that I'd seen my soul's match looking back at me through the eyes of a child on that summer's day in Mearsies Heili."

Cold seized her, an icy, burning cold that ran through veins, and numbed her mind. "I know you could not have spoken then," she whispered, though it was difficult to speak. "For at twelve. One can scarcely know aught of soulbonding. But you must have known that when I discovered that I had a heart to give, it belonged to you?"

"I knew that I owed you every possible opportunity to grow, to change, to challenge what must seem to anyone else a cruel miscarriage of justice. Of balance. For there remains the matter of my past," he said.

"In all other aspects of my life," she said, "I make others' concerns my own. But in this I cannot."

"Erenlara." He met her gaze at last, and the cold was gone, and with it the protection of distance. "I cannot promise any kind of future." He spoke softly, without moving either hands or eyes.

"I know."

"I did not expect to survive the war."

"I know that, too. I have discerned it in Siamis's writings — oh yes, he has permitted me to see them, at Clair's behest."

"I will never see that." He made a motion, less one of warding than rueful acknowledgment of my presence as listener, alongside Clair. For I had never been able to hide from him. "There are some who wonder that my life, at very long last, has not drawn to a close. And sometimes I've felt the end nigh in the sunsets, in the winter wind, in the turning of the seasons."

"I perceived in those pages that that life, so early betrayed, has been given over all these centuries to others," she said steadily. "Even if our union is only granted for a short time, that is my sole desire."

He drew in a long breath. "I would have been willing to carry this secret to my death."

"Then I would die too, incomplete, for I have experienced all the range of human emotions except for joy. And fulfillment. That is the cost of the soulbond."

For a short time, the only sound was the wind.

When she knew her voice was steady, she said, "Even if I have you only for a week, and I have to live another hundred years, they will not be barren if I have memories of you."

He moved at last, stepping around the desk to stand before her. He lifted a hand, briefly touching her scarred cheek with his fingers. That one day, so many years ago, had been spirit meeting spirit; there had been no spark on the physical plane, for she had not been of an age to know such things, and he had seen her form as unfinished. Now, at last, the spirit cleaving to spirit opened mind to mind. Eyes to eyes, ears to ears. Scent: his masculine, with an overlay of the pine blowing through the open windows, hers the subtle perfumes that delight the Venn in their underground city.

Touch. He stroked her hair with slow, pensive tenderness, and she shivered from scalp to heels. He made no further move, and she knew that to beatify the promise held in the moment, it was for her to close the last distance: taste.

And so she lifted both her hands, and framed his face with her palms as she reveled in the subtle drum of his pulse under her fingers.

His own hands cupped hers. His fingers pulled her hands away, and he pressed kisses onto one palm, and then the other.

She turned her head and where the fabric of his shirt parted on his breast she kissed him, and then laughed when she heard the catch in his breath.

His fingers closed on her shoulders, and he set her a little away. "Shall we allow ourselves a little time for a courtship?" he asked, smiling. And, to me: *You have a suitable ending. Let be.*

"I'll grant you an hour. So long as the outcome is assured," she answered with deliberate ambiguousness, and was enchanted to see his cheeks flush as he laughed.

And then they were alone.

But there is, after all, one necessary addition before I have done.

THE BORDER OF CHWAHIRSLAND

Departing storm clouds left a world of white, the rough mountain peak landscape softened to dips and mounds. In the distance a few conifers glittered in the low northern sunlight, and closer, the lone trail of footprints that Imry Llyenthur had left, skirting a suspicious dip that might hide a treacherous drop.

He'd found a wind-smoothed boulder to sit on as he considered what, if anything, he ought to do. Or even to say, and to whom.

Siamis would be the obvious choice. As a mentor, he wasn't nearly as irritating as expected. So much of Imry's memories of Siamis was of a towering figure always effortlessly stronger, faster, more skilled. His very patience had been irritating. As a boy—a scrawny, undersized boy—Imry had discovered that reducing rivals to tears or incoherent fury not only was funny, but enabled him to win more often than not. Except against MV, most of the time. Siamis, never.

From his adult perspective, Siamis also understood that yawning divide between the Then-Brain and a possible Now-Brain. Siamis had been a teenager when Efael sent him out to commit every possible crime, until he met Isa Cassadas, a few years older, and the turning point in Siamis's life.

That white palace made of disirad wasn't bad either. Took getting used to, but Imry had discovered he could actually sleep through the night, as long as he was in one of the highest spires, all accesses warded.

His gaze traveled along the diminishing footprints to that village out of sight as he considered what he'd overheard, completely by accident after coming down out of the tower in Mearsies Heili. It was one of Clair's followers, the one with the high, clear, singer's voice. It was a carrying voice. Imry, paused on the stairway inside a spire entrance, had listened to an almost incoherent account of what seemed to be a long undersea journey. No explanation of how that was possible, but it didn't seem to be lies. The details were too specific, especially about some vast undersea city that seemed to be made of disirad, and the mers riding the currents south and away from a vast section of deep ocean because of some unspecified threat.

Imry had no interest in undersea life. He listened, intrigued, to her account of something so large it sent krakens migrating, along with the reappearance of disirad, not only in the oceans, but in the Sartoran mountains, and here in the Chwahir range. And now ...

This discovery. Today.

He flexed his hands as he scanned the utterly silent, uniformly white terrain. What was gripping the back of his neck? Cold didn't usually bother him, except at extremes. While working, his tunic had sufficed, but the joints in his hands throbbed, and he thrust his fingers into his armpits.

Not two heartbeats later the ground beneath his boots vibrated, causing him to stiffen warily — then a shower of snow in his face presaged clods of dirt spinning upward, as something shot into the air.

Blinking away the snow from his eyelashes, he caught sight of a strange shape, a hooded eye, then the dirt and snow fell harmlessly to the ground as the shape transformed into —

"*Marga?*"

She floated down to the dirt-dappled snow, smiling. "I thought I heard you here. Weren't you in the village?" She pointed away toward the east, the direction the footprints had come from.

"I was," he said. And because it was Marga, bound by absolutely no rules, he said, "Needed to consider."

"Oh?" She came to his side and sat next to him; though he knew most would consider him dressed lightly for this altitude and weather, Marga wore a summer shirt, cotton riding pants, and her feet were bare. But she appeared to be untroubled by the snow. "Tell me," she invited, her gaze warm and steady.

He hadn't seen her for years; she was the same, yet not the same.

"I take it you know about the Chwahir shells, as they call themselves," Imry said.

"Yes. I found them this land."

Imry looked away from that steady searching blue gaze, down toward the slopes where the rows and rows of small shrubs slumbered, winter-bare. With the first spring rain they would bud, then spout leaves in a haze of deep green that, once picked and dried, would become one of the rarest and most expensive types of steep.

"Of course you did," Imry said. "I don't know how else they would have discovered that area, just below the tree line, with what I'm assuming is the right soil."

"It was so hundreds of years ago," she said. "The soil is good now, but what makes Dragonspring steep so excellent is that the trees' roots reach the hot spring running under us now."

She had put her hands on her knees, and ducked her head so that her short curly hair swung forward, hiding her face. To Imry it looked as if she stared at her toes, or at the snow beneath them, but it was probably more likely she saw far below the surface.

She glanced sideways at him, smiling. "Do you know, before Wan-Edhe nearly killed every living thing, the people had names for each of these mountains? Because each has its individual characteristics."

He waved that off. "One has hot springs, another doesn't. Individual characteristics is just a pompous way of saying that the makeup of the landscape varies."

She propped an elbow on her knee, and regarded him with frank disappointment.

"What?"

"How does it serve you to diminish and dismiss?"

"I'm not. Just stating the facts."

"Facts that demonstrate your typical human ignorance," she retorted with not a whit less of her good nature. "You completely forget or overlook, the living things on and in the mountains, that contribute to those characteristics. Making a whole."

"All right. I'm ignorant. Anyone would assume no one lives up here," Imry said, then hiked a thumb over his shoulder. "Except for this new community. But it seems they made contact with another community, over that way." He pointed back in the direction he'd come. "The two communities have begun trade, not just in goods but in information."

"It is so," Marga said.

"Which included my presence," he went on. "Siamis handed off certain tasks —"

"Healing tasks," Marga interrupted.

"Yes."

"I want to hear you say it."

His mouth twisted, brows raised in skepticism. "Are you going to start expounding on the Good of the World and such morally superior horseshit?"

"I," Marga murmured, her voice soft and smooth as a stone warmed in the summer sun, "want. To hear you. Say it."

Imry sighed, eyes rolling upward. "Healing tasks."

"Good! Go on," she invited cheerfully.

"This village in that valley no one can see from here is so isolated I don't think Jilo even knows about them. They certainly don't appear to have any of the benefits he's bringing to the Chwahir elsewhere. Though I suppose that might change, now, with trade going on with the self-named shells. Either that or they'll up and vanish overnight. I got the impress-ion they have been nomadic in these mountains for generations."

Marga gave a slow nod.

"In some ways, similar to the flyers of the upper reaches of the Ghildraith Mountains."

"In some ways," Marga repeated, agreeing. "I realize you know little of the flyers of Ghildraith."

He sighed, and said it before she could come on with more moral superiority, "Who, by my command, we were shooting out of the sky during the war. Orders I issued because those flyers were carrying boulders and dropping them on our heads! They'd glide so you could not hear them coming at night and — but yes, many were shooting them for sport." Tension furrowed his brow — was she about to start lecturing him?

Marga had provoked him precisely to see that tension; in the past, he'd shrugged off the random cruelty of his followers. But it seemed that now he was beginning to see the conse-quences. No, to feel them.

Change was not going to be easy.

She said, "You could not have learned much about them as they were hiding. They still hide. They have nothing to do with the lowlanders. But in a way, they are connected to these folk you met today, way, way, way back, uncounted generations ago."

He eyed her. "I take it you know what I found?"

"Tell me."

He lifted a shoulder. "I'm trying to figure out how, or if, I ought to describe them to Siamis. I don't know that there is a problem. The villagers don't seem to think so. In fact, they acted as if nothing was amiss. But the shells noticed what appeared to be hunched backs among some of the smaller villagers."

Marga said, "And?"

"And so I found an excuse to test what I saw when one was stumbling as he played about. I picked him up as he slipped on a patch of ice, and…"

How to express it? He was still learning to lay his hand on the outer flesh, and send his awareness inside bone, muscle, and nerve within.

He opened his eyes. "What I found was a huge bulge of

what could be mistaken for muscle, or even a blister of enormous size, over each shoulder blade. But inside that swell of flesh is folded bone. Membrane."

Marga grinned, dimples flashing. "Go ahead and say it. Wings."

"So these Chwahir are part of the Ghildraith flyers?"

"They were, I believe, thousands of years ago," Marga said. "They don't write records, and their tales of years are highly symbolic. In the oldest forms of language of those in Ghildraith, they are called the Ones Left Behind."

"Very poetic," he said caustically. "What does it mean? Why are you even here? To drive me off?"

"No, not at all," she said. "I wanted to see you again. What you've done for the shells is splendid. I admire the fact that you came to this village, on the shells' recommendation, because they were concerned about these people who seemed to be afflicted with what, to today's Chwahir, would appear to be a severe problem. The shells are very sensitive to such things."

Imry grimaced. "I know their history. What I don't understand is, ah, what's going on. If anything is. If these anomalies are connected."

Marga chuckled softly. "Very unsettling, is it not, when one is confronted by the evidence that humans are not, in fact, the primary life forms of this world? Nor even secondary. We are visitors, on sufferance, for those who think in epochs."

"Oh?" He stilled. "Is this some kind of threat?"

"Threat?" She clasped her hands around a knee, rocking back and forth in silent laughter. "No, no *threat* at all! Must you always think in terms of violence—ah, I ought not to tax you with the terrible ways you were shaped when small, through no fault of your own. No, no threat, but change is coming. I cannot say when. It might be within the next generation, if those wings actually sprout." She waved behind her in the direction of the village. "It might be in ten generations. But all these anomalies you mention, I see as a world righting itself again."

"For?"

"What else?" She touched his hand, her fingertip warm. "The dragons are coming home."

AUTHOR'S NOTE

Telling the story of another world is a lot like growing a tree from seeds. The images I got in childhood were about children. It wasn't until 1966, when I turned fifteen halfway through the year, that I began to glimpse the roots ramifying outward, and binding into an interconnected tale.

More years passed, and I had to learn to prune (never enough) and to shape … and there I should probably drop the metaphor, before saying that when I first read JRR Tolkien's *Leaf by Niggle*, when I was in high school, I wept, because he understood was not just the glory, but that what came out was often anything but glorious, in spite of all one's efforts. In retrospect I wish I'd told him that in the fan letter I wrote him in 1972, when I was a college student studying overseas; perhaps it might have netted a meeting, however brief, instead of a polite turndown. Or maybe not, for he did not live long beyond that, and meeting my callow self probably would have been tedious for a great mind in the twilight of his days.

Because I was only beginning to learn that talking about one's passion is tedious unless it is shared—and unless one has charisma. I had, and have, zero charisma, and my early life contributed to my keeping my passion confined to my bookshelves until I reached middle age, and began the long, slow, painful process of learning to rewrite. Still at it.

So I will keep this short.

The long arc is done. If I'm granted more time, there are all kinds of tendrils and offshoots that I can't resist. (The tree again.)

I hope something of my passion sparked for you. Thank you for reading.

Sherwood Smith
June 2023

ABOUT THE AUTHOR

Sherwood Smith studied in Europe before earning a Master's degree in history. She worked as a governess, a bartender, an electrical supply verifier, and wore various hats in the film industry before turning to teaching for twenty years. To date she's published over fifty books, one of which was an Anne Lindbergh Honor Book; she's twice been a finalist for the Mythopoeic Fantasy Award and once a Nebula finalist. Her YA fantasy novel *Crown Duel* has been in print for over thirty years.

She is married with two kids and a lot of rescue dogs. She reviews books at Goodreads and blogs intermittently at Dreamwidth.

Find her at Patreon at https://www.patreon.com/user?u=6632848

Visit her website at https://www. and sign up for her newsletter at https://www to learn about new books.

ABOUT BOOK VIEW CAFE

Book View Café is a professional authors' publishing cooperative offering DRM-free ebooks in multiple formats to readers around the world. With authors in a variety of genres including mystery, romance, fantasy, and science fiction, Book View Café has something for everyone.

Book View Café is good for readers because you can enjoy high-quality DRM-free ebooks from your favorite authors at a reasonable price.

Book View Café is good for writers because 90% of the proceeds goes directly to the book's author.

Book View Café authors include New York Times and USA Today bestsellers, Nebula, Hugo, Lambda, Chanticleer, National Reader's Choice, and Philip K. Dick Award winners, World Fantasy, Kirkus, and Rita Award nominees, and winners and nominees of many other publishing awards.

www.bookviewcafe.com